Juliet E. McKenna has been interested in fantasy stories since childhood, from *Winnie the Pooh* to the *Iliad*. An abiding fascination with other worlds and their peoples played its part in her subsequently reading Classics at St Hilda's College, Oxford. While working in recruitment and personnel, she continued to read across all genres, and started to write herself. After combining bookselling and motherhood for a couple of years, she now fits in her writing around her family and vice versa. She lives with her husband and children in West Oxfordshire.

To find out more about Juliet E. McKenna visit her official website at www.julietemckenna.com

Find out more about other Orbit authors by registering for the free monthly newsletter at www.orbitbooks.net

By Juliet E. McKenna

The Tales of Einarinn
THE THIEF'S GAMBLE
THE SWORDSMAN'S OATH
THE GAMBLER'S FORTUNE
THE WARRIOR'S BOND
THE ASSASSIN'S EDGE

The Aldabreshin Compass
SOUTHERN FIRE
NORTHERN STORM
WESTERN SHORE
EASTERN TIDE

EASTERN TIDE

Juliet E. McKenna

www.orbitbooks.net

ORBIT

First published in Great Britain in 2006 by Orbit
Reprinted 2007

Copyright © Julia E. McKenna 2006

The moral right of the author has been asserted.

A CIP catalogue record for this book
is available from the British Library.

ISBN 978-1-84149-377-0

Papers used by Orbit are natural, recyclable products made from
wood grown in sustainable forests and certified in accordance with
the rules of the Forest Stewardship Council.

Typeset in Ehrhardt by
Palimpsest Book Production Limited, Polmont, Stirlingshire

Printed and bound in Great Britain by
Mackays of Chatham plc, Chatham, Kent
Paper supplied by Hellefoss AS, Norway

Orbit
An imprint of
Little, Brown Book Group
100 Victoria Embankment
London EC4Y 0DY

An Hachette Livre UK Company

www.orbitbooks.net

For my godson Leo

ACKNOWLEDGEMENTS

As always, my beloved husband Steve has supported me through the planning, writing and revising, a task that becomes ever more complex with each successive book, and especially at the end of a second series. Mike and Sue, best of friends, who cannot have known what they were getting into when we started this, have done nearly as much. Any expression of gratitude here is simply inadequate.

My sister Rachel's travels continue to supply me with fascinating material to draw on while my keen readers keep me alert with their questions and curiosity, notably Matt and Toby. This time round, Michèle has helped out above and beyond the call of duty with the final draft.

I couldn't tackle all the multifarious tasks of the writer's life without the cheerful and unstinting assistance of so many around me. Gill and Mike, Ernie and Betty have proved indispensable yet again, not just for me but in supporting Steve, Keith and Ian. The usual suspects have also helped keep me from losing sight of the wood for the trees, with sympathetic listening and offerings of brisk common-sense, coffee, red wine, beer etc., as and when required. My gratitude to you all.

On the publishing side, my thanks to Tim, Gabby, George, Darren and the Orbit sales force. I remain most grateful to Lisa both for her professional contribution and for being such a pal. My sincere thanks also go to my agent Maggie, and all her team, not merely for their efficiency in tackling the business angles but for so much more support.

The broad camaraderie of writers remains a source of inspiration and consolation. In particular, I'd like to acknowledge my associates in The Write Fantastic: Sarah Ash, Chaz Brenchley, Mark Chadbourn, Stan Nicholls and Jessica Rydill, along with James Barclay. Thanks chaps, for everything.

CHAPTER ONE

'*If you tell yourself beforehand how hard the task ahead is going to be, when you actually set your hand to it, it generally turns out to be far easier than you imagined.*'

I suspect some aged and respected philosopher first said that while sitting comfortably on a cushion under a shady tree. I wouldn't mind having him here now, to make him eat his words and choke on them.

The white light surrounding Kheda dissolved piecemeal, drifting away like pale smoke. He felt solid ground under his feet and breathed warm, dry air redolent of slowly rotting leaves overlaid with hints of spice, familiar and unfamiliar.

It smells like home. Only it isn't home. Still, it's closer than I've been since the last dark of the Lesser Moon. But where exactly are we? And where is the dragon?

Opening his eyes, he found himself standing in the shade of tall ironwood trees, logen vines draped thickly over their lower branches. The vines were desiccated, their leaves withered. Moss covering the buttress roots of the ironwoods was dry, crumbling away around the edges where it had retreated and finally died. The sparse undergrowth was parched and dusty.

Will another cycle of the Pearl see me home again? What kind of reception can I expect, returning in rags and wielding a hunter's blade fit for hacking paths through forests instead of a warlord's fine swords? Will anyone care about such things if I have rid another domain of a dragon? Will that success outweigh my lies and evasions?

Kheda shook his head to banish a strange lassitude that seemed to linger after the spell. 'Can you see the beast?' He looked up at a chittering noise in the branches, gripping the long handle of his broad, blunt-ended blade. It was only a loal. 'Risala?'

'No.' A slim girl was circling slowly around. 'There's no sign of it.' She wore a grey cotton tunic and trousers as faded as his own garments. Letting the strap of a leather bag slung over one shoulder slip down her arm, she lowered her burden silently to the dull, dead leaves. 'I can't hear any birds. Can you? And that loal is terrified.' Her wrist heavily bandaged, she brushed a stray lock of fine black hair out of vivid blue eyes as she looked up.

Kheda realised a tense silence held the forest breathless in all directions. He studied the small furred creature clinging to the branch of the ironwood, its pelt as grey as the bark. The manlike hands had longer fingers than those he was used to seeing on such beasts, while its snout was longer and sharper, as were its ears. Tufted with white, those ears were flattened like a startled jungle cat's, and the animal's black lips drew back from a sharp-toothed silent snarl.

'I wonder where the rest of its clan is.' He couldn't recall when he'd last seen a solitary loal.

A hot, dry breeze stirred the withered vines, brushing across Kheda's forehead and tousling Risala's hair.

'Velindre?' Risala looked around urgently.

As the magewoman appeared, the loose fabric of her worn tunic hung motionless in midair, as if she had turned in sudden haste and been frozen in that moment. Then she gasped and the unbleached cotton fell loose around her long-boned frame, the wind ruffling her short-cropped blonde hair. 'It hasn't felt us,' she breathed with relief.

'Velindre! Where is it?' Kheda wasn't sure she had heard him. 'The dragon?'

'I don't know precisely.' Velindre shook her head, more to rid herself of the magic's after-effects than to answer Kheda's question. 'I can't search for it with magic.' Her finality brooked no argument. 'I brought us here using as stealthy a working as I could devise. If I look for it now, it'll sense my affinity and be on us before we know it.'

Kheda nodded grudging acknowledgement. 'We have precious few advantages; let's not squander the element of surprise.'

'We're not here to attack it,' Velindre said sharply.

'It's not as if we could, not if you're not willing.' Ambivalence clouded Risala's words.

'Are you certain you can drive it off or lure it away, all on your own?' Kheda asked Velindre bluntly. 'With some stratagem that won't leave chaos and death in its wake?'

Because the last time you tried this, even with another wizard to help you, the upheaval sent the beast flying away from its distant home where we might have hoped to ignore it. Now it's come to plague these islands.

'Get rid of it one way or another and we can all go home,' Risala said softly.

'That's what we're here to do.' Velindre's attempt at optimism was unconvincing, given the strain shadowing her hazel eyes. Her angular face was as grim as Kheda had ever seen it.

'But where is here, precisely?' He looked up to try to find the sun, to get his bearings. 'How far are we from Chazen?'

My home domain. Where my lady wife Itrac thinks I have spent these past few turns of the moons secluded in peaceful meditation, contemplating the omens that should show me how best to raise our newborn daughters. How to meet the demands laid upon me as warlord of the Chazen domain with wisdom and justice.

When in truth I've been travelling to an unknown western island and back again with a magewoman from the barbarian north. When one law that all the countless warlords of this vast Archipelago agree on is that suborning sorcery deserves death. Itrac would never deny that the crime of magic warrants agonising death for any wizard caught in an Aldabreshin domain. And more often than not, the same fate awaits anyone taken in the offender's company.

Such dangers didn't appear to be bothering Velindre. She scuffed aside the leaves with one bare and callused foot before hunkering down and picking up a stick. 'This is the Archipelago.' Scowling, she scratched harder to score a broad curling outline in the dry earth. 'And here's the unbroken lands, the mainland.' She sketched in a coastline thrusting down to nearly touch the northernmost domains. 'So Chazen is all the way down here.' Reaching out, she found a scrap of bark and set it at the southernmost end of the faint scraping. 'We're in the western domains, though I'm not sure exactly which one.' She arranged more fragments about halfway down the outer edge of the sweeping curve. The cluster was somewhat separated from the rest of the outline.

'I don't think I'll ever get used to your northerner mapmaking.' Kheda calculated the distances according to what he knew of the mariners' route records customarily compiled by the galley captains who plied the sea lanes the length and breadth of the Archipelago.

Supposing we're somewhere in the middle of those western domains, it would take twenty-five days' hard rowing for the fastest trireme to reach Chazen. And probably as long for the same ship to reach the mainland. We're both as far from home as each other.

'These domains are the most westerly islands in the whole Archipelago.' Risala was gazing thoughtfully at the rough sketch in the dust. 'So how far have we come?

Where's that great isle in the western ocean where the dragons were living?'

Velindre had to sweep more leaves away. 'It would be about here, as close as I can judge.'

'That far?' Kheda was astonished.

Velindre nodded. 'It's about a thousand leagues away, near enough.'

Kheda shook his head, bemused. 'And it was no more than a step, with your magic.'

And the barbarians wonder why we hate magic. All other considerations aside, how could any warlord allow any other to have such advantages over the rest?

Risala frowned. 'That land is quite some way further south, nowhere near due west of here. Why did the dragon fly here, instead of going to Chazen or some other southern domain?'

'Like last time,' Kheda agreed. 'That's what the wild men did, when they invaded us.'

What would these western warlords have done if they had been the first ones with these challenges landing on their beaches?

'Even with their wizards' magic, the wild men were still largely at the mercy of the ocean currents.' As Velindre stood up and looked around, avid interest brightened her hazel eyes. 'A dragon can fly where it wants. There must be something around here that attracted it.'

Kheda drew a deep breath. 'Whatever it's interested in, we're here to deter it.'

'You said it's a dragon born of water, more specifically of the sea,' Risala commented. 'Let's make our way to the shore and start searching the beaches.'

'That sounds sensible,' Velindre agreed, sweeping away her rough map.

Kheda licked a forefinger to test the breeze, peering upwards to find the sun through the dark-green canopy of ironwood leaves. The light was yellowing but there was no hint of dusk as yet. 'The wind will still be coming off the sea. Let's try this way.'

He led the way cautiously, pausing from time to time to slice carefully through stubborn tangles of undergrowth that couldn't be skirted or pushed aside. His thoughts kept turning southwards.

What will Itrac say when I tell her I sailed to an unknown island in the far western ocean? That I found the homeland of those wild men who came out of the night on rafts of logs to murder and maim the people of the Chazen domain? Her warriors fought bravely but they couldn't fight the savage magic that the wild wizards wielded. Will she understand, when I tell her their magic depends on dragons? That the beasts have grown accustomed to dining on the dead slaughtered in the savages' wars, on that distant brutal isle stained with long ages of blood and sorcery? When I explain that's why those invaders were followed by the first dragon to set foot on Aldabreshin soil within time of memory?

Will she forgive my deceptions, when I tell her we broke the hold those wild wizards had on their people? That they no longer live like animals in thrall to the magic drawn from the presence of dragons in that land? Can I honestly assure her no such slaughter as Chazen suffered will ever be visited on an Archipelagan domain again? I can't, not while there's a dragon in any Aldabreshin domain. This won't be finished until we're rid of this beast.

He brushed aside an inconvenient branch and fragments of crumbling leaves stuck to the sweat coating his face.

Will Itrac understand if I tell her we didn't exact vengeance on those distant wild men for the sufferings of her people? What will she say if I explain that the only way we could free them was by ridding their island of dragons? That we achieved that through alliance with wizards from the barbarian north? Because only magic can fight magic. Will she forgive me, because that magic was suborned outside Aldabreshin waters? Do I want to rely on such a fine point of law to save my head and my hide?

He glanced over his shoulder to see Risala following close, her intent gaze searching the forest on either side. The magewoman was bringing up the rear, her head half-turned, alert for anything that might be following their trail. Kheda looked ahead once more.

My lady Itrac's young but she's no fool. She'll realise this alliance must go back further than this voyage. She'll guess northern magic facilitated my victories when I reclaimed Chazen from the wild men and the first dragon. Will she call in the captain of my own guard to behead me there and then? Would anyone say I didn't deserve such a death? Not if they learn that driving away the dragons to free the wild men set the beasts free to fly here, to bring new misery and destruction to innocent Archipelagans.

Clarity in the sunlight ahead warned Kheda that they were approaching the edge of the trees. He could hear soft surf on a shelving beach. He ran an apprehensive hand over his tightly curled brown hair, finding it uncomfortably gritty. His eyes felt dry and the parched skin of his lips threatened to crack. 'How good is a dragon's hearing?'

'I've no idea,' Velindre said tightly. 'I've generally been more concerned with assessing their magical senses.'

Risala looked up into the gently swaying nut palms. 'There are still no birds.'

Kheda nodded as he slowly edged forward through the trees fringing the shore.

Before I involved myself with magic I would have been searching for the omen in such silence. I would have been ransacking my recollection of endless portents carefully recorded by warlords who ruled before me. How can I ever tell Itrac that I no longer have any faith in such things? That my doubts had been growing long before I sailed for that unknown western shore?

Philosophers would say that my association with magic is to blame. Just as they say the wielding of magic anywhere within the Archipelago twists and distorts the omens that would otherwise show us our wisest courses of action. I cannot believe that. Not now. Too much has happened to convince me that any man's destiny is shaped by his own hands, not by the uncaring stars of the heavenly compass or the random chances of earthly occurrences.

I married Itrac because the death of her lord Chazen Saril and all his other wives left her and the Chazen domain so vulnerable. Before that, I married Janne and Rekha and Sain for reasons of trade and diplomacy. Of all the women I have ever taken to my bed, Risala is the one whom I have most truly adored. And Risala still trusts in omen and portent. I dare not tell her frankly I no longer believe. I dissemble and demur, for fear of losing her with an outright denial of prophecy.

Will I ever be free of the deceits that have mired me since I first contemplated involving myself in magic? Because I convinced myself that the omens sanctioned such actions.

Kheda halted as he got a clear sight of open water lying before them to the south. 'East or west?' He glanced back over his shoulder.

'Let's head round to the west.' Velindre drew her words out slowly.

'You have some sense of the dragon?' Risala asked apprehensively.

'I can sense the elements without stirring them and letting it know I'm here.' The magewoman's thin lips narrowed almost to invisibility. 'There's a current curving around that headland that's sweeping in from the deep ocean. It's mingling with waters that have circulated in and around this domain since the last rainy season. The dragon will find that fascinating.' She sounded certain of that.

'Then we go west.' As they picked their way through the scattered nut palms, Kheda slid covert glances at Velindre. He noted Risala keeping the same watch on the wizard woman.

Just to be sure she doesn't succumb to the thrall of the dragon's magical aura if we come upon the beast unawares. That could be the death of us all, if she's intoxicated by the power, if she loses control of her own magic. But she has seen such dangers at first hand, just like us. She will be on her guard.

Velindre certainly looked utterly determined.

What must it be like to be mageborn? What manner of sense could reveal the elemental shifts of the air, the unseen currents within the waters of river or ocean, or the consummation of flame? What is it like to know that the very rocks in the earth beneath your feet are as malleable as clay if you summon your magic to work them?

A new sound filtered through the thirst-stricken trees and Kheda abandoned such speculation. Something was splashing slowly and rhythmically. Risala drew up beside him, Velindre arriving on his other hand. They moved forward together, step by agonising step. The noise stopped and they all halted.

Kheda heard Velindre's breath coming faster, rasping in her throat. 'Can you feel its magic?'

She nodded tightly. 'But it's a water beast. I feel it but it doesn't overwhelm me.' She managed a smile like a death's head. 'You might have cause to worry if it were an air-born dragon.'

Risala pressed herself to a nut palm's ridged trunk. 'It's there,' she whispered.

Kheda crouched down behind a bank of earth crowned

with tangles of silvery midar stems, brittle and leafless until the rains should come.

The dragon had found a deep inlet thrusting into the rocky side of the island. The creature floated amid the silken blue ripples lapping out and then returning from the shore. It was resting on one side in the ocean's embrace, its muscular limbs drawn up like a sleeping hound's. Only no hound in the Archipelago or any land beyond boasted murderous talons as green as jade and longer than any sword a warrior might carry.

'What now?' Kheda's gaze stayed fixed on the creature lolling all unawares in the water.

Its sinuous neck was extended, long muzzle stretched out. The crest of turquoise spines crowning its narrow head lay flat and the white pinpoints of fire at the centre of its emerald eyes were hidden by half-closed lids. Its green belly lay towards them, the fine scales in the creases of its lithe limbs as pale as new leaves. Heavier scales darkened to a hue vivid as wet seaweed on its muscular flanks. It might have seemed asleep, but for the vicious spike at the tip of its long tail beginning once again to rhythmically flick idle foam from the water.

So that's the noise we heard.

'There's no malice in it.' Velindre's whisper was harsh with defiance. 'It's an animal, no more, no less.'

'Its magic makes it considerably more.' Risala shot the magewoman a sharp rebuke.

'We've already seen it devastate a trading beach.' Kheda reluctantly looked away from the creature to capture Velindre's gaze with his own. 'Can you be certain it didn't kill anyone? Malice or accident leave people just as dead, children just as orphaned.'

'There will be villages close by.' Risala gestured minutely out towards the sea where the smudges of nearby islands were plain to see. 'Fishermen will be sailing out as soon as the heat of the day is done, or dragging crab pots up from the rocks.'

'I don't believe it will attack boats,' Velindre protested, with the stubbornness of someone returning to an old argument. 'We've seen no sign of this beast hunting for human flesh.'

'We've all been aboard ships smashed to kindling by the creatures. It'll be tempted by such easy meat sooner or later.' Kheda swallowed revulsion at the memories of the dragon born of scarlet fire that had blithely eaten its fill of living and dead in Chazen. 'We have to drive it off before it gets a taste for Archipelagan flesh.'

'Otherwise we'll never be rid of it.' Risala pressed closer still to the nut palm's trunk.

'Unless whichever warlord rules these isles can spare enough men to entangle it in nets and ropes. To hack it to bloody pieces no matter how many of his warriors it kills in the process,' Kheda said ruthlessly.

I led countless men of Chazen to their deaths as we fought a dragon that was already dying in such a fashion. Could such a fit and powerful beast be killed that way?

The magewoman drew a deep breath. 'Then let's see if it's hungry for something more substantial than a few fishermen.'

'Be careful,' Kheda warned before he could stop himself.

The magewoman's sniff spoke volumes of derision. She rubbed her long hands together, nail-bitten fingers spread wide, and the faintest glimmer of blue-green light kindled between her fingertips.

The dragon instantly rolled over to crouch impossibly on the surface of the inlet, foam seething around its forefeet. Turquoise spines running the length of its back snapped erect to scatter diamond drops of water that vanished in the air. The dragon's head whipped around, a white blaze kindling in its emerald eyes. It bared jade teeth, long aquamarine tongue tasting the air. Rearing up, it half-spread its wings in the stiff breeze, rattling leathery membranes that were the blue-green of a storm-tossed ocean.

Velindre swore on her life and her element that she could hide her magic from this beast when she wove the deception she had planned. Are all our lives forfeit because I believed her?

His heart pounding, Kheda swallowed to find his throat as dry as dust.

At the mouth of the inlet, a sea serpent broached the surface in a flurry of slime-laced foam. Where the dragon was scaled, this creature's coarse hide was akin to sharkskin and mottled like a stone-strewn shore. It had no limbs, no neck, just a single pale golden fin running the length of its thick body. Thrashing frantically, it opened its cruel mouth in a soundless gasp to reveal rows of dirty yellow teeth and its gill slits fluttered. Black eyes set deep in its blunt head glinted like jet.

'We know you eat serpents,' Velindre breathed.

The serpent knew the same. It coiled around itself, diving desperately for the depths.

The dragon plunged after it with a splash that echoed all around the rocky inlet.

Kheda swallowed again, the breath easier in his chest. 'Where's it going?'

'I'm sending the serpent far out to sea, keeping it just out of the dragon's reach,' Velindre said tightly. 'I'll tie it to the fast current that sweeps out to the west from here. Then the lure of the deep water currents and the serpents that follow them will take the dragon back to the open ocean.'

'No, they won't.' Risala pointed with a trembling finger.

Out to sea, the dragon sprang up from the water to

glide on half-spread wings trailing chains of silver droplets. Landing on the surface with astonishing delicacy for such a massive beast, it folded its wings neatly against its glossy green flanks to make a shallow dive. They watched it swim back into the inlet, undulating through the limpid water, graceful as a fisher-bird.

Why did I allow myself to hope that this could be so easy?

Kheda did his best to hide his disappointment. 'It can't be hungry.'

'We're to wait till it gets an appetite?' Risala wondered dubiously.

'I doubt that would be wise,' Velindre said grimly. 'It's already suspecting there's a strange magic close by.'

The dragon emerged in the middle of the inlet, crouching on the surface of the water once again. As it looked this way and that, the white fire in its eyes burned brighter and it hissed menacingly. Windblown ripples travelling across the water towards it reversed and fled in fear.

'If it doesn't want to eat, let's hope it wants to fight,' Velindre said resolutely.

'You'd challenge it?' Risala took a step backwards away from her tree. 'After you nearly died the last time? And you didn't even win!'

Kheda reached up for Risala's unbandaged hand and pulled her down to kneel beside him. 'Remember what she said about luring the beast away with distant magic.'

It's difficult to remember that these are beasts in so many ways. Loals and jungle cats and hook-toothed hogs think of little besides eating and fighting rivals for mates and terri- tory and food. Dragons see anything wielding magic as a rival, be it a mage or another of their own kind. And Velindre's proved that she can work her magic at a remove before. Otherwise we'd already be dead.

He looked apprehensively at the magewoman. A

dangerous smile curled her thin lips as she narrowed her hazel eyes, deepening the creases of age and weariness in her face. Thin scars marked her cheeks, barely healed.

She didn't look so worn before we sailed west. What changes will people see in my face if and when I get home?

The dragon whirled around, barbed tail sending spray flying in a tumbling white arc. It roared with a penetrating fury that finally prompted the island's bird life to show itself. Finches and crookbeaks and glory-birds erupted from the trees to flee in all directions, squawking with frantic terror. The dragon ignored them, all its attention now focused out to sea.

White clouds were spinning themselves out of the clear blue sky. The pale threads thickened and tightened into a coil, growing darker and darker. A talon of whirling cloud reached down towards the sea and a waterspout rose up to meet it. The twin spirals danced on the dimpled sea and became one writhing column of braided cloud and water, tantalisingly threaded with aquamarine lightning. The dragon stalked towards it, massive feet treading lightly on the haphazard waves helplessly crisscrossing the sea.

Draw it away. Take it far out to sea till those winds and currents you're so certain of lure it somewhere else.

As Kheda silently willed her on, the magewoman thrust her hands out before her. The waterspout began dancing away towards the emptiness of the western ocean.

Stormy green wings flaring wide, the dragon shot across the sea. It flew beyond the waterspout rather than attacking, the fury of its passing carving a furrow in the water. Circling around, the dragon spat a vivid mist of cold green fury that crackled up and down the interwoven cloud and water. Undone, the plaited clouds unravelled to evaporate in the hot, dry air. A vortex momentarily opened a hollow deep into the sea as the waterspout collapsed. The dragon roared with satisfaction before gliding back towards the inlet with leisurely grace.

'What happened?' Kheda saw a blush darken beneath the tan on Velindre's cheekbones.

'I lured this beast away with a waterspout once before.' Velindre rubbed at the joints of her fingers as if they pained her. 'It remembered.'

'Does it know where you are?' Risala asked with alarm.

'No.' Velindre flexed her long fingers and her knuckles cracked loudly. 'It's looking for a rival trying to use the water against it. It doesn't realise my affinity is with the air.'

'What happens when it does?' Kheda demanded.

'Let's deal with one thing at a time.' Velindre was still intent on the dragon. 'We still have to fool this beast into leaving here.'

The dragon landed deftly on its belly, forelegs and hind feet drawn up as it sank just below the surface of the water to lie relaxed, its chin pillowed on a drift of foam. The spines along its back broached the slow swell and the spiked tip of its tail flicked up and down once again.

It may look as if it's idling but I'd wager half the Chazen domain that it's ready to spring.

'If we can't lure it away with food or some supposed rival to fight, how do we persuade it to go?' Kheda asked slowly.

'Poets have spent lifetimes weaving stories around animals.' Beside him Risala tensed. 'Beyond eating and claiming a territory, they must find a mate to raise more of their kind.'

'But dragons don't mate.' Kheda found himself uncertain and turned to Velindre. 'Do they?'

'Not that we've seen,' she said dryly. 'Not as long as they can gather the jewels that they crave to create an egg and kindle a spark of life within it from their own magic.'

'Dragons born of water crave emeralds, isn't that what

you said?' Risala reached inside her grubby tunic to pull out a sweat-darkened leather thong. It bore a heavy silver ring set with a polished, uncut emerald.

'I have one, too.' Kheda tugged at the thong around his own neck and produced a ring that was twin to Risala's. 'Can you use these stones to lure the beast away?'

'That red dragon had to gather all the rubies ever treasured in the Chazen domain before it could weld them into an egg.' Velindre hesitated, then reached for the rings.

As her fingers brushed the emeralds, the dragon erupted from the water with a shattering bellow. It ran straight across the inlet towards the fragile line of nut palms sheltering them. Fronds thrashed above their heads, lashed by its fury.

'Velindre!' Kheda gripped the handle of his hacking blade with futile defiance and reached for Risala.

The world vanished in a blinding white light, only this time he could still hear the dragon's furious roaring getting louder. He strained to see something, anything, in the featureless whiteness. An emerald glow spread ahead of him, like lamplight seen through fog. It grew brighter and he saw twin sparks of white fire at its centre. The dragon's roar sank to a throbbing growl of ominous concentration.

The emerald radiance blinked out, the white light vanished and Kheda fell to his hands and knees. He coughed. His lungs felt as seared as if he'd been caught in a sandstorm. 'What—'

'I'm sorry,' Velindre rasped. She lay collapsed on the ground like a heap of discarded clothes. 'I had to wring every hint of water out of the translocation magic.'

'Where are we?' Kneeling upright, Risala pressed her bandaged wrist close to her chest, wincing as she used her other hand to rub at her throat.

'I'm not sure.' Velindre caught her breath and pushed

herself into a sitting position. 'The dragon ripped into my spell.'

'Where is it?' Kheda looked frantically around. They had tumbled into a thicket of spinefruit trees. A few banded finches hidden in the dusty leaves called cheerfully to each other. The russet-striped tail of a foraging matia was disappearing beneath a berry bush.

'I don't know.' Velindre's ire was directed at herself. 'It's gone.'

'Gone from this domain?' Kheda wondered with hollow hope.

'When did we last have such good fortune?' Risala said darkly.

Velindre heaved an incautious sigh that prompted a painful bout of coughing. 'I'll scry for it,' she offered when she was able to speak.

'Why not summon some aid from your fellow wizards?' Kheda said sternly.

'I'm the only mage alive who's had significant dealings with dragons—' Velindre began obstinately.

'Apart from Naldeth,' Risala interjected.

'Apart from Naldeth,' Velindre agreed tersely. 'Whom we left a thousand leagues or more behind us on that western isle. And apart from Azazir, who is utterly insane and horribly dangerous.'

'Then what do you suggest?' Kheda rubbed a hand over his beard.

Naldeth chose to stay behind on that desolate isle. Because he believes all wizards have a duty to see that none of their kind misuse their powers. He's there, all alone, watchful lest any children of those wild men mature to find these magical senses born in their blood. He won't allow any of them to re-establish the tyranny that blighted that place for so long.

And he wants to be certain that no mage of his own kind

is drawn there, seduced by the elemental power underpinning the island. What did they call it? A confluence, which first drew the dragons there? Naldeth doesn't trust his fellow wizards. Not all of them, anyway.

Am I really asking Velindre to bring more of these mages to the Archipelago? What among all the omens recorded since my birth could ever have predicted I would propose such a thing? No matter. I have been taught all my life that a warlord must do whatever is necessary to resolve the situations laid before him, regardless of personal cost. If I am to be condemned for bringing magic into the Archipelago to fight against magic, I'll spend my life by bringing as many wizards as necessary for them to be equal to this task.

'Well?' he prompted more forcefully. 'What else do you suggest we do?'

Velindre was gazing unseeing into the depths of the forest. Small black flies hovered around her head but she didn't seem to notice. More fluting birdsong joined the happy chirps of the finches and the matia rustled through the undergrowth to poke its long, inquisitive face out at them, rounded ears cocked forward, its flexible nose twitching and black eyes bright.

'Let me scry, find out where the dragon has gone.' Velindre turned to Kheda, one hand raised to forestall his objections. 'I will take the time to work the subtlest of magics against it. But I'm not translocating us on the basis of a scrying again,' she said with some chagrin. 'That's a horribly dangerous practice and I dare not risk it if there's any chance that dragon can twist my magic again.'

Now it was Kheda's turn to hesitate before answering. 'Very well,' he said at length.

Because I have no means to compel Velindre to do as I wish. Which is merely one of the frustrations of having wizards as allies.

'I don't know about anyone else but I'm hungry and thirsty.' Risala stood up and brushed dust from her knees. 'And we need to find out exactly where we are. Let's see what we can do about that at very least.'

CHAPTER TWO

Well, the dragon certainly isn't here. There wouldn't be man, woman or child left on this island if it were. How are we even going to find a patch of dry sand to sleep on amid all this commotion?

The light galley beneath Kheda lurched and he took a step to steady himself in the absence of anything to hold on to. Up on the ship's raised stern platform, the helmsman hauled on his hefty steering oars and shouted abuse at the angle-sailed skiff that had forced him into the sudden swerve. Rowers sweating three to each bench set in lines on either side of the open deck hurled their own insults at the youths crewing it. The lookout on the low, questing prow let fly his opinion that their helmsman should have let the galley crush the skiff. Smaller boats made haste to get away, leaf-bladed oars raising sallow smudges of foam.

Shipmasters say the waters in these western reaches are more perilous than in any other region of the Archipelago. They're certainly more hectic than any I've known.

The vessel they had managed to beg passage on had been following this coast since before dawn. The far shore of the long, tapering bay had only come into view on the horizon around mid-morning. At first, headlands had come and gone in the distance, then the land had coalesced into a solid tree-clad line. There had been ships wherever he'd looked.

'Was this harbour as busy the last time you were here?' Kheda asked, his voice neutral.

Velindre was standing close by his sword-hand in the

throng crowded between the ranks of rowers. 'No,' she said curtly, glowering at a stout traveller who had stumbled into her, losing his balance as the galley lurched. The light galley slowed still further and the press of boats grew thicker as they approached the shore. Most were single-masted light galleys. A few were the broad-beamed, triple-decked and triple-masted great galleys that risked the more hazardous open seas between one domain and another.

Tucked on Kheda's other side, Risala spoke up with misgiving. 'Are all the islands under Matul Saib's rule so heavily fortified?'

He shared her apprehension as he gazed across the crowded waters. In the arrow-shaped head of the inlet, lofty walls of white-plastered brick stood between the golden sandy beaches and whatever lay beyond. The walls ran for as far as he could see. The midday sun struck silver flashes from the armour of swordsmen and archers patrolling the out-thrust bastions that left no stretch of beach unsurveyed.

'The foundations were being laid for this work when I was last here,' Velindre said reluctantly. 'I had no idea they could build so fast.'

'They say Matul Saib has more slaves than there are pebbles on his beaches,' the stout man declared, stroking his luxurious black beard with unconscious satisfaction.

'They say he's going to throw a wall around this entire island.' A second man standing behind Kheda invited himself into their conversation, sounding less than pleased at the prospect.

'Who says?' Risala looked around with a friendly smile. 'Poets? Or scholars?' She nodded towards Velindre.

'Both.' The stout bearded man shrugged.

Because poets and scholars both trade news and rumour in return for answers to their endless questions. Risala travelled far and wide as a poet, using her eyes and ears in service of her own domain's warlord long before she ever met me, while Velindre sailed the length and breadth of the Archipelago as an itinerant scholar. Which is fortunate now that we have to account for our presence in these islands without arousing suspicion. But how do we ask if anyone's seen a dragon without drawing unwelcome attention? This would be so much easier if we had our own vessel. But Velindre's boat lies wrecked on that western shore. While I'm a warlord without armour, swords or retinue to assert my authority. We don't even have trade goods between us.

'There doesn't seem to be much of a market on the beach.' Velindre gestured at sand entirely empty of the usual vivid awnings shading hopeful merchants and their chests and casks of wares.

'All trade is concluded under Matul Saib's protection inside his walls,' the bearded man said proudly.

Kheda noted the dense crowds on the shore gathered around the towering gates set at regular intervals along that mighty wall.

I had no notion these reaches were so busy with trade. Those waiting crowds aren't getting any bigger, even with all the people being landed from so many galleys and rowing boats. The guards must be letting just about everyone through. So is this warlord shrewd and fair-minded, or just greedy for his portion? Does it matter? The important thing is we can lose ourselves among all these travellers as we try to get close to the dragon once again.

'You're hoping to visit Matul Saib's libraries?' The unseen man behind Kheda turned his attention to Risala. 'You've proved yourself a talented poet on this voyage, my dear.'

'His gates are always open to anyone ready to compose a paean to the splendours of his residence or to spread the word of his wisdom and insight.' The lushly bearded man smirked at Risala too familiarly for Kheda's peace of mind.

But we couldn't have got passage on this galley without

her talents. I've no skill I can trade without people wondering just how a slave came by such expertise.

'Just make sure you're waiting at the gates well before dusk,' another man advised somewhat sourly, 'otherwise you'll be locked out and sleeping on the sands.'

'You could trade this slave of yours to some advantage if he's handy with that blade,' the man behind Kheda mused. 'Brawn for heaving bricks and mortar is easy enough to come by but a man with the wit as well as the strength to wield the whip of an overseer is a rarer find.'

Turning as far as was possible on the crowded deck, Kheda caught a glimpse of a lean man with a hawk's pale eyes above a beak of a nose and a long, stringy beard. Kheda managed to keep his face expressionless as the stout man broke in.

'You'd get a handsome weight of silks or lustre-glazed ceramics for him. Matul is a richer domain than Essa or Zelin.' He stroked his paunch, swathed in an orange silk robe that overlapped across his belly, secured with a broad sash of green silk a shade lighter than his heavier trousers. 'Take such trade goods as we western men excel in back to the southern Archipelago and I'll wager you could secure yourself three more like him. I could make some introductions for you, for some small consideration.'

'But who will carry my bags in the meantime?' Risala smiled with sweet apology and raised her bandaged wrist.

'Galcan is the wealthiest domain in the whole of the western reaches.' The lean man shook out the turquoise sleeves of his own overlapping robe, belted with purple and fuller in cut, as were his silken trousers. 'You would get a wider choice of goods, and in greater quantity.'

Velindre shook her head firmly. 'Thank you, gentlemen, but I have no plans to trade my slave away.'

As long as everyone thinks I am a slave, no one can suspect

I am a warlord. So I must endure being talked about as if I'm not even here.

Kheda kept his face expressionless as the light galley edged between narrow rowing boats crowded with men and women, baskets and caskets and nameless bales sewn tight in oiled sailcloth.

The lookout on their galley's prow platform produced a coiled brass horn and began blowing short, raucous blasts. As a vessel pulled away from the shelving beach, a gap opened up and the helmsman yelled ferociously at his oarsmen. The rowers shouted triumphantly as they hauled on their oars, stealing the anchorage from a slower boat. The defeated helmsman could only spit his disgust. Sand rasped beneath the shallow hull. The passengers were ready for the jolt but Kheda still found himself inadvertently shoved into the closest rower's shoulder by the hawk-faced man. He was more concerned to see that Risala hadn't suffered any jarring to her splinted wrist.

'Sorry.' The stout man grimaced a second apology to Velindre.

'We beach boats stern-first in the southern reaches,' Kheda observed as the rower looked up at him.

'You're in the western reaches now, friend.' The oarsman grinned, not unfriendly. 'Watch your step.'

'I shall.' As Kheda spoke, he was reminded just how different his accent was from all those around him.

Risala and even Velindre sound more like these locals than I do. And these people dress quite differently. We're the only ones wearing tunics rather than these double-fronted robes. What else is going to catch us unawares? Honest error causing unintended offence could still bring us trouble.

Stout ladders were lowered from the prow platform and the first passengers clambered down to splash through the shallow waters to the shore. Kheda gathered up the three battered leather bags that were all the luggage they boasted between them and followed close behind Velindre.

'When were you last in these waters?' he asked quietly.

'In the middle of last year's rains.' Velindre halted to let the bearded man go first, inclining her cropped blonde head to acknowledge his thanks.

'I won't be sorry to see the rains come,' Risala muttered behind Kheda. 'How long do you think they will be?'

'At home? Twenty days or so, maybe a little less, maybe a little more.' Kheda glanced involuntarily southwards, but all he could see was the sparsely forested swell of the island beyond a surprising expanse of roofs. 'Depending on the winds, I suppose we'll see the first storm clouds hereabouts a handful of days after that.'

'We get our first rains at about the same time as the far south. The storms come in from the east with the highest tides.' The lean man favoured Risala with a more friendly tone. 'Will you have your business here concluded by then?'

'I hope so,' she said fervently.

'You're travelling light.' He nodded at Kheda's paltry burdens.

With a slave who doesn't know as much as he thinks he does about the local seasons. No one's going to recognise Chazen Kheda, who led his warriors to slay a dragon. Has that story even reached these waters?

'We were caught in a riptide between Kaive waters and the Essa domain. Our ship was wrecked on an outlying reef.' There was an edge of challenge in Risala's voice as she smiled. 'But we all survived, and poets and scholars both carry their most valued goods in their heads, so on we go.'

'Indeed.' Her words prompted a shadow of concern on the lean man's face and he turned away to busy himself with his own sturdily wrapped bundles rather than say anything further.

Velindre managed to take a few more paces towards the prow, face composed as she ignored the stout man's dubious glance.

A wreck could be a sign that our trip is ill-omened. Had we better think up some other lie to explain our presence here with such a conspicuous lack of trading goods or possessions?

Kheda tried a smile on Risala. 'It's not as humid as it gets at home before the rains.'

'I'd trade some humidity in exchange for all this grit in the air.' She ran a hand through her dulled black hair. 'Where does it come from?'

'The unbroken lands to the north, I suppose.' Kheda looked up at the sky where the sun floated hazy as a lamp seen through a chiffon curtain. The pale blue of the sky was tinged with the ochre dust that had begun to fall in the past few days, unseen yet leaving a fine coating on every surface, no matter how often it was swept clean.

Perhaps it's blown all the way from that far western isle. That land was all dry rock and dusty sand and vicious plants with spiteful leaves hoarding whatever water deep roots might find in such hard-baked soil.

'Let's get ashore.' Up on the bow platform, Velindre reached the ladder with a couple of long-legged strides.

Kheda shivered as the shock of the sea struck like iced water on his sun-warmed thighs. He took a deep breath as the water slid higher until his bare feet found the sandy bottom. Risala slid down the ladder and pushed past him, splashing through water that reached to her waist.

Kheda was struck by the disparity between her and Velindre, and between the two of them and everyone else on the shore. Risala was a head shorter than the mage-woman, fine-boned, her hair true Aldabreshin black while blue eyes and a complexion somewhere between copper and gold spoke of mainlander blood blended in her ancestry. Everyone else close at hand had plainly been

born and bred in these western reaches. Their faces varied
from deepest brown to virtual ebony. Even Kheda's weathered bronze skin looked light in comparison to some. At
least there were other travellers with paler complexions
and light eyes further down the beach. He caught a glimpse
of one man with eyes as green as his own, a rare sight in
any reach of the Archipelago.

He tried to assess Velindre's appearance with a
stranger's eye. She could look Kheda in the eye, easily as
tall as him. A rapid survey of the beach suggested such
height was nowhere near as unusual hereabouts as it was
in the far south. The unforgiving Aldabreshin sun had
darkened her pale northern skin to a deep tan like finely
cured deer hide. Her eyes were brown enough to pass for
Archipelagan, though her cropped blonde hair could only
betoken mainland blood. Most crucially, with her sturdy
garments of unbleached cotton loose about her spare frame
there was no hint of curve to breast or hip.

Is anyone going to see through your guise of zamorin
scholar?

'Do you know how common *zamorin* are in these
reaches?' Kheda glanced around the beach but couldn't
see any other man who looked to have been left beardless
by the castration knife. 'That man on the galley mentioned
a substantial slave trade here.'

'I heard mention of it but I've no idea what the market
for eunuchs might be.' Velindre looked circumspectly at
the nearest gate. 'All such trade's presumably conducted
inside the walls.'

'We had better not idle here.' Risala snapped slender
fingers at Kheda like any mistress recalling her slave to
his duties.

He hefted their leather bags onto one shoulder. 'Our
dress is attracting some attention.' Kheda looked down at
his faded grey trousers, darkened by the water.

Risala was the only one of them wearing any silk. Her polished recitations of the galley helmsman's favourite cycle of poems had won her a long tasselled scarf of deep-red twill as well as passage off the island where Velindre's magic had inadvertently dumped them. The better to play the poet, she had dug a faded gown of soft yellow cotton embroidered with vivid scarlet seashells out of her bag. She wore the scarf wound around her slender waist and cross-tied behind her neck, accentuating both her modest bosom and the curve of her hips. Now the wet dress clung to her legs, revealing, alluring.

You're more confident with every passing day now we're back in the Archipelago, your fears and uncertainty on that distant island now a distant memory. You flirt and charm these men to ease our passage through these islands, yet you won't let me take you in my arms and feel you all woman beneath my hands. Have I brought you home only to lose you?

Kheda relieved his feelings by glaring at a curious youth who hastily found something else to interest him.

'We need privacy to make sure of our quarry. We need to know where we're seeking passage to next.' With Risala's femininity thus enhanced, Velindre looked wholly androgynous in her loose-fitting garb. The harsh lines of her face were made still more forbidding by the thin new scars. 'If the same warren of markets and dwellings that I found last time is still through there, we can probably find a discreet corner.'

'As long as there isn't some two-legged rat lurking just around it, ready to be startled by what you're getting up to.' Risala looked at the closest gate through which the most recent arrivals were trying to inveigle themselves.

'You and I will have to stand guard.' Kheda looked both ways along the shore. 'We certainly won't find any solitude on this beach.'

'Then there's nothing to be gained by delay.' Velindre strode confidently towards the stark white walls. Risala walked beside her with equal poise and Kheda followed two paces behind, as obedient as any good slave.

It will have to be magic, I suppose. We've heard no word of this dragon being sighted anywhere. Has it fled without Velindre's prompting or tempting? We have to be certain. We cannot leave these people to face such a catastrophe without our help, even if they would recoil from the very notion of accepting our assistance. We started this, so we must finish it, whatever the disadvantages we're labouring under.

They joined the throng at the gate and Kheda found himself sweating profusely. Slowly the tangle of new arrivals was drawn out into a single thread. Each individual was given a cursory inspection by a pair of guards before being ushered through the broad pointed arch allowing access through the thickness of the wall. Kheda glanced up to see solid wooden gates hanging in wide slots at either end of the arched passage, ready to drop and seal off the tunnel and any enemy still in it. Faint yellowish smudges trailed from holes at the top of the lime-washed walls.

Sand to pour down and fill this hollow, smothering the attackers.

'Does Matul Saib have reason to fear any attack?' he asked Velindre.

'Not that I know of.' Apprehension was tightening her voice.

'There's been peace in these waters since Matul Rala's day.' A local man in faded brown silk was walking at Kheda's shoulder, a tightly woven saller-straw basket slung on his back. 'But northerners cause trouble now and then. Matul Saib makes sure their merchants know we're not to be trifled with.' He clearly approved.

'I didn't see any boats from the unbroken lands in the bay.' Risala turned her head.

'Precious few come at this season.' A thin-faced woman with wiry black hair braided close to her ebony scalp spoke up. 'But they'll swarm thick as red-arsed kintris flies after the rains, ready to beg for the best of the silks we've been weaving.' Her short smoky jade robe was wrapped tight over a long leaf-green gown. She was carrying a voluminous sack that rustled as she walked, its contents light enough not to burden her.

'Only with their faces scalded red by the sun instead of their backsides.' The man with the basket chuckled, tight black curls dotting his skull like peppercorns. 'And they'll go home with the worst of the fabrics and think themselves so wonderfully clever for winning that much.'

'Is that a fair exchange for the metals your craftsmen need to make their lustre glazes?' Velindre asked mildly. 'Matul ceramics wouldn't be much without the tin and copper that northern barbarians bring you.'

'A fair exchange is one both sides are content with.' The man turned away as they emerged into the sunshine, his pace quickening.

'Good trading.' The woman in green waved a perfunctory farewell before calling out a greeting to an acquaintance and walking off.

Kheda would have liked to stand still to get the measure of this new place, but the steady stream of people coming through the gate forced the three of them onwards. Open ground just inside the lofty wall offered the widest thoroughfare and the crowds hurried along it. There was no point trying to fight the flow.

The warlord's swordsmen doubtless use this route for ready access to the defences in time of trouble. Or to encircle the people within these walls if Matul Saib wishes to enforce his will. I wish I knew what manner of man he is.

'There are so many people,' Risala marvelled.

'I calculated that these western reaches are more densely populated than anywhere else in the Archipelago.' Velindre's words were as dryly analytical as any true scholar's.

'Where are we going to find shelter for the night?' Kheda looked at the narrow alleys opening onto this impromptu dusty road. Each one soon ended in a confusion of single-storey flat-roofed buildings. 'And privacy, for your purposes.'

'Not here.' Risala slowed to look uncertainly at closely shuttered houses separated by blank white walls. Some of the paths beaten into the dry earth between them by countless feet were broad enough for two or three people to walk abreast. Most were only wide enough for a single man to pass. Few ran straight for more than a handful of paces before they jinked around blind corners.

'We had better go on,' Velindre said grimly.

They followed the broad track running along the inner face of the wall. Some dwellings had wide double doors and broad window shutters thrown open to cast light on the activities within. Men and women sat at looms weaving every weight and grade of silk cloth from finest gossamer to sturdy twill, all in gleaming white. Some looms were simple affairs, others more complex and worked with hands and feet. Some were so intricate that four or five people were involved in their management. Here and there, gaggles of children deftly wound great hanks of pale thread onto shuttles and bobbins for the weavers. Older women twisted barely visible filaments of raw silk into various thicknesses of thread. One in a faded turquoise gown looked up and smiled amiably, flicking greying braids back over her shoulder.

'They're not worried that visitors will see their craft secrets,' Kheda observed.

'Weaving is weaving.' Risala still looked keenly into

each workshop as they passed. 'It's the secrets of rearing silkworms they won't let slip. Just knowing how to coax the eggs into hatching would be a start.'

Velindre wasn't interested. 'There's something we need to address. Once we know where we're going, we'll need a boat and we have nothing of sufficient value to trade for one.'

'We have those rubies,' Risala said bluntly.

'We're not trading those.' Velindre frowned, forbidding.

'We need to know where we're sailing first.' Kheda looked around to be sure none of these sociable islanders were within earshot. 'Let's try down here.'

He took an abrupt turn into the mass of buildings. Matul islanders crowded around them, in their double-wrapped robes of coarse silks in shades of purple, brown and green. The women mostly wore silk scarves wrapped around their heads while the men went bare-headed, some even shaven-headed despite the punishing sun. Beards were worn close-trimmed, often little more than a line of bristle along the jaw or around the mouth and chin. Pairs of youths shouldered heavy bolts of cloth sewn tight inside protective cotton covers. Older men and boys pushed handcarts burdened with casks and baskets. The woven saller-straw lid of one had slipped awry and Kheda saw it was full of raw-silk cocoons, still fluffy with their outer layer of floss.

'Where are we going?' Risala asked curiously.

'I don't know. Let's follow them. They look like merchants.' Kheda nodded discreetly towards a man and a woman, neither carrying anything more onerous than bulging belt-pouches. Protective hands hovered by daggers sheathed on their hips. 'Do you know which style of dagger belongs to which domain in these reaches?' he asked Velindre.

If I jostle someone by accident and they pull a knife on

me, it could be crucial to know if they're of Matul or else-where.

The northern woman frowned again, this time in thought. 'Those will be from Zelin.'

'So nothing's disrupting trade in neighbouring domains just yet.' Kheda studied the daggers.

Thinner blades than we use in the south, and appreciably longer. Something to remember if I find myself in a knife fight.

He noted the bright-blue wraparound robes the pair wore. The woman's was embroidered with yellow flowers over a full-skirted white gown. The man preferred plain blue silk above green trousers. 'Do dyers favour different colours from domain to domain?'

'Purer colour tends to go with status and merchants can claim higher standing than most silk farmers and weavers,' Risala replied before Velindre. 'The warlord and his household will wear the brightest blues and yellows, reds and whites. The lowest of the islanders will be in muddy browns and the dullest purples.' She lengthened her stride to make sure they did not lose sight of the two visitors in the jostling crowd.

Western ships will have visited the central domains where you were raised. Where you learned to use your eyes and ears so effectively for your warlord. You're used to landing on strange shores, watching carefully all the while as you learn what you must. Whereas all my boyhood training was in the fine degrees of acknowledging a resident warlord's hospitality with suitable gratitude. No one's going to be welcoming us here with scented baths and exotic delicacies. Still, I managed well enough when I had to travel north in secret to seek out some means to fight magic with magic. When I met your lord and he sent you to help me and we became so close. Where's that closeness now?

There was little shade on the street and the all-pervasive

dust dried Kheda's throat painfully. With so many people pressing close, the scents of fresh sweat and stale perfumes mingled unappetisingly. People intent on some business pushed silently past men and women who were walking more slowly, deep in conversation. Voices rang out from the windows and doors of the workshops and dwellings, prompting answers from passers-by. Heads appeared unexpectedly from behind shutters to shout, all in the unfamiliar accents of these islands.

Kheda's ears were soon ringing and a headache lurked behind his eyes. When an unexpected note of burning charcoal teased his nose, he looked up to see a woman cooking over a brazier set beneath an awning rigged on one of the flat roofs. The heavy cloth stirred sluggishly in the feeble breeze. Down at ground level there wasn't so much as a breath of air moving.

'Where have all these people come from?' He was walking so close behind Risala and Velindre that he risked treading on the heels of their bare feet.

'The western reaches have always traded mostly among themselves,' Risala said breathlessly, 'given the perils of crossing the Dawa Sea.'

'I imagine that's a project prompting plenty of new trade.' Astonished, Velindre stopped dead and this time Kheda did stub his toes on Risala's heel.

'I'm sorry.' He held her shoulders between his hands and looked over her head. She didn't answer. Like Velindre, she was gazing awestruck at the prospect ahead.

A great expanse of the close-packed dwellings had been razed to the ground. No wall stood more than knee-high. Rubble choked the empty remnants of the rooms and there was no trace of those who might have lived there or any of their belongings. Beyond, a massive wall of new brick bristled with scaffolding poles and planks where workmen scrambled, busy as ants. All along the base, mortar was being mixed in great troughs while new consignments of brick and lime were delivered without pause by lines of toiling slaves.

'That's easily going to be as big as the fortifications on the beach,' Kheda commented. 'What do you suppose it is?'

A local with a ragged mossy robe flapping open over skinny ribs obligingly supplied the answer. 'That's Matul Saib's new palace, my friend.' He didn't wait to say more, dodging past them and hurrying away.

'Why is he building such an edifice?' Still astounded, Kheda observed that the wall reached for as far as he could see on either hand, with no suggestion of a turn or a corner.

'Because he can,' Velindre said tersely. 'Or rather, because his slaves can.'

'That's where they're heading.' Risala hadn't forgotten the two visiting merchants in their bright-blue robes.

Kheda saw that a sizeable area amid the emptied dwellings had been given over to a slave market. The walls of the houses and workshops had been crudely rebuilt into waist-high pens and then awnings had been rigged on tall poles to cast some shade over the huddled merchandise. Dealers sat comfortably on cross-framed stools of padded velvet under their own more elegant canopies.

'Shall we see what there is to see?' Kheda suggested.

Velindre nodded reluctantly. 'Perhaps there's somewhere beyond all this dereliction where we can find some privacy.'

Because we didn't come here to trade for slaves. We must know where that dragon is.

'Just look as if they don't have what you want,' Risala advised quietly.

Several of the slave-traders looked up hopefully as the

three of them walked closer. Kheda kept his face impassive. He couldn't see Velindre's expression, but judging by the rapidity with which the slave-traders looked away, it wasn't encouraging.

The man and woman wearing the Zelin domain daggers had stopped to talk to a trader. At the dealer's nod, a swordsman in a nail-studded leather jerkin hauled forward some unfortunate under discussion. The slave wore a dirty clout around his hips and his naked back was scarred with whip marks. His ribs stood out and his eyes were sunken from the effects of long hunger and thirst. A single shackle trailing a length of heavy chain was welded around one ankle, the skin beneath it rubbed red raw.

'This isn't how we do things in the south.' Kheda tried to stifle his outrage.

Do these people care nothing for a man's duty to slaves under his protection?

'He's a barbarian,' Risala murmured, 'from the unbroken lands.'

With a shock, Kheda realised the darkness of the man's skin came from filth and exposure to the sun, not natural colour. The pallor beneath his armpits could only belong to a mainlander.

But he's been worked half to death by the look of him. Why would you want a slave like that, whose condition would be such dishonour?

'I'm afraid we have more pressing concerns than the fate of one man.'

To Kheda's surprise, Velindre spoke in her native tongue, the Tormalin of the mainland that he had learned so laboriously. She also spoke more loudly than was strictly necessary.

The beaten slave didn't look up but the slave-trader did. He stared at Velindre, more curious than perturbed. Seeing her looking away beyond the slave market, he turned his attention back to the Zelin couple, who were surveying the rest of his collection of unfortunates.

For some reason they were only interested in mainlander slaves, as far as Kheda could tell. He also noted several other slave-traders or their swordsmen looking in their direction, their curiosity prompted by Velindre's carrying words. 'We can't rely on no one understanding us if we talk in Tormalin here,' he commented quietly to Risala. 'And I don't have a sword to my name if it comes to a fight.'

He rested one hand idly on the long handle of the broad-ended hacking blade protruding from his own bag of possessions and turned a bland face to the closest swordsman. A faint sneer lifted the corner of the warrior's mouth but he looked away nevertheless.

Risala nodded. 'Plenty of merchants learn something of the barbarian tongue from their dealings with traders who venture into the Archipelago from the unbroken lands.'

'I'll wager there are northern merchants who wouldn't relish anyone knowing all the details of their dealings in these waters.' There was a caustic edge to Velindre's tone as she spoke the southern Aldabreshin dialect again, colouring her words with inflections Kheda had grown up with. 'But unmasking illegal slave-trading will have to wait for another day.' She bit off her words with exasperation.

'So where do newcomers find a meal and a place to sleep hereabouts? And some modicum of privacy?' Kheda tried to curb his own frustration as he looked around to see far too many Matul islanders, visitors and slavers.

'Shall we try over there?' Risala pointed beyond the slave market to a stretch of buildings not yet fully demolished. The valuable wood of windows, shutters and doors had been stripped away but the walls and roofs still looked largely undamaged.

As they walked over, Kheda saw that the larger buildings had already been claimed by sizeable groups sharing similarities of dress and dagger styles subtly at variance with the garb of the Matul islanders. These visitors were all just as tall and dark-skinned, however, often showing the stamp of common blood in their features as well. Men and boys were stowing rope-bound crates and bulging hemp sacks securely within the ravaged buildings, while their women kindled charcoal cooking fires and unpacked brass water jars and crocks of preserved foodstuffs.

'So this is where merchants without a ship of their own come.' Velindre looked around. 'How do you suppose these accommodations are allocated?'

Kheda couldn't see anyone who seemed to be in charge. 'It looks as if it's first come, first served.'

He watched as two men with a couple of boys in tow entered a single-roomed house. In the next breath, they were retreating, their hands raised to show they held no weapons and offered no threat. Three grown men and two youths emerged from the shabby building, bearded jaws jutting belligerently, their gestures dismissive. Four women, two maidens and two matrons, appeared up on the flat roof to add their own shrill rebuttal.

'We'd better look for some hovel suitable to our station,' Risala said wryly.

'With no nosy neighbours,' added Velindre.

They continued walking, leaving the busiest area around the fringes of the slave market behind them. Soon another broad expanse of utterly demolished buildings stretched out ahead. Beyond that, more scaffolding rose up to bar their way, filling the gap between the untouched dwellings of the Matul islanders and a long shimmering expanse of whitewashed wall that could still only be some part of this unknown warlord's incredible residence.

Kheda studied the broken-down buildings before the utter destruction ahead. 'How about that?' He pointed to a small lopsided house still standing in the midst of a maze of broken walls.

'Where everyone else comes to dump their piss and shit.' Risala wrinkled her nose at the scent of ordure as they picked their way through drifts of broken brick.

'You'd think they'd be more concerned about disease.' Kheda frowned, finding fragments of mortar sharp underfoot. 'Especially when the rains come.'

'Presumably slaves will be sent to clear this place before any building work begins.' Velindre scowled. 'Believe me, no one's too concerned about *them* dying off.'

Kheda opened his mouth to protest, then closed it again.

It doesn't look as if the customs we have in the south concerning slaves apply here. I'm as much a stranger in these reaches as Velindre. More so, in fact. She's been here before.

'This looks as if it was built in a gap between two other houses.' Risala was walking around the awkwardly shaped building.

'It outlasted them,' Velindre said wryly.

'That could be an omen.' Risala halted, not looking at Kheda, tension in the line of her back. She fingered a silver necklace she wore, set with tiny shark's teeth. One was caught on the leather thong that held the emerald ring.

Why have you taken to wearing that shark's tooth necklace now we're returned? Because a poet should show a certain amount of ornamentation? Or because I gave it to you as proof that I loved you? Or because it was supposed to keep you safe? But I don't believe in omens any more.

He coughed. 'At least this area isn't too badly fouled.'

Neither woman heard him. Risala had gone inside the little house. Velindre squatted down to examine a blackened scrape where a corner of crumbling wall offered shelter from the breezes.

She held up a scrap of charcoal. 'This fire's been out for days. I don't think we're trespassing on anyone else's territory.'

Risala appeared in the doorway, mindful of ragged brickwork that might snag her silken scarf. 'There's nothing inside.'

'Then let's see what there is to see.' Velindre was suddenly all purpose. 'Kheda, my bag.'

He handed it over, keeping an eye out for anyone approaching or looking in their direction. Few of the strangers hurrying past spared them a glance as they searched for some shelter for themselves or headed for the bustling houses of the islanders. 'Be careful.'

'You're telling me I shouldn't summon up magic in front of Matul Saib's main gate?' Velindre asked sarcastically. 'Believe me, I have no intention of being caught at it.'

'Just get on with it.' Kheda's heart was pounding even though no one was coming close. 'I'll wager the penalties for suborning magic are just as severe here as they are in the south.'

'More so, probably.' There was an edge to Risala's tone. 'These people live so much closer to the unbroken lands. Everyone knows how barbarian lives are horribly blighted by the whims of the wizards who infest the north.'

'I don't know what could be a more severe penalty than being skinned alive to see your hide nailed to the warlord's gateposts.' Quite calm, Velindre unlaced her bag and pulled out a dented and dulled silver bowl. 'I don't particularly wish to find out.'

As the magewoman crouched, wedging the bowl into the remains of the dead fire, Risala unslung a battered brass water flask from her shoulder. Velindre reached up to take it with a nod of thanks. Uncapping it, the blonde wizard poured a scant cupful into the bowl and passed one bony, nail-bitten hand over the water. A faint green glow flared and died, too faint to be seen beyond the confines of the bowl in the bright sunlight.

Blood pulsed in Kheda's throat.

Why is this so much worse? I've seen Velindre work this scrying of hers time and again these past couple of years, and Dev doing the same before her. But now we're in the midst of an unknown domain, where I have absolutely no rank to armour me against accusation. Claiming ignorance as her slave wouldn't save me, not against accusation of voluntarily associating with magic. I could only save myself and Risala by denouncing Velindre before anyone else does it. Could I do that, if it came to it?

Risala had other fears. 'Are you sure you have tight hold of the spell? We don't want it looking back through the magic and seeing where we are.'

'I've no intention of allowing that again,' Velindre said through gritted teeth. 'And there it is.'

Kheda spared an instant from his vigil to glance down into the swirling circle of emerald magelight. 'It doesn't look as if it knows we're searching for it.'

The dragon lolled on its side in crystal shallows where a broad expanse of coral reef kept the surging ocean from disturbing pristine yellow sands. The great creature was close enough to the shore that the ruffles of surf barely reached halfway up the pale-green scales of its belly. As the dragon snapped idly at a swirl of foam, its forked aquamarine tongue flickered around its long jade teeth.

Then the creature rolled over to crouch on all fours, talons green as verdigris clawing the sand. It unfurled its vast wings, and with the sun behind them, the membranes shone brilliant blue-green like the shallows around the coral reef. As it looked from side to side, the turquoise crest of spines snapped up around the back of its long-jawed head. The white fire in its emerald eyes burned with new vigour.

'Has it felt the spell?' Risala couldn't hide her alarm.

Kheda forced himself to look up from the image in the dented bowl to be certain no one was approaching them.

Will it follow the scent of her wizardry here, despite all her assurances? To fall on all these unsuspecting people to gorge itself as it mindlessly destroys their homes and livelihoods?

'It's just hungry,' the magewoman whispered, as if the distant dragon might hear them. 'There's a shoal of blue sheertails on the other side of the reef.'

Satisfied that no one was showing the slightest interest in the three of them lurking by the ramshackle house, Kheda looked back at the spell.

They watched the dragon crouch low in the water, powerful muscles bunching in its hindquarters. Springing into the air, it half-spread its wings to glide over the coral and furled them tight to dive into the sea. Its long spiked tail ripped a white gash into the water as it disappeared.

Kheda stifled a sigh of relief. 'Can you tell exactly where it is?'

'Risala, can you find my route record, please?' murmured Velindre.

Risala brushed hair out of her eyes as she delved in the magewoman's bag to find a thin book bound in creased yellowish leather. She handed it over, sinking down gracefully to sit cross-legged on the ground. She looked up at Kheda. 'Sit down. You'll attract more attention standing on guard like that.'

Kheda took a seat on a broken stretch of wall by way of compromise. 'Where is it?' he asked again.

The magewoman passed one hand over the dented bowl and the vision vanished. Sitting back, she untied the straps that secured the leather flaps protecting the reed paper

pages within. 'Give me a moment.' She began flicking
through annotated sketches of coastlines and sea lanes.

Risala looked at Kheda. 'How can these people not
know there's a dragon in the western reaches?'

'Presumably no one's reading the right omens.' He
regretted the sarcastic remark as soon as he'd spoken.
He surveyed the purposeful comings and goings around
the islanders' distant houses, around the slave-traders and,
closer at hand, among the makeshift accommodations of
travellers and traders. 'Or perhaps Matul Saib has stopped
such news spreading, which makes me wonder just what
manner of ruler he might be.'

Is he a tyrant who keeps everyone in line with an iron hand,
or is he just trying to stop his people fleeing headlong in panic
and spreading chaos throughout these reaches? Has he heard
how unexpected attack threw the southern domains into confu-
sion that's barely subsided? How two warlords lost their hold on
power – myself when I was lord of Daish, and Chazen Saril.

'Don't you think the local soothsayers will know that
much?' There was a challenging glint in Risala's vivid
blue eyes. 'What manner of man Matul Saib is. Perhaps
they've seen portents of the dragon but haven't yet read
them aright.'

'I don't recommend asking any such questions,'
Velindre interjected, still leafing through her book. 'If
Matul Saib is deliberately suppressing news of the dragon's
presence, I imagine he'll be very interested to know how
a travelling poet and an itinerant *zamorin* scholar learned
such news.'

'Word will soon get back to him,' Kheda agreed. 'We
don't want to find ourselves pressed to answer his questions.'

Risala looked away toward the slave pens. 'Perhaps
Matul Saib has seen something to reassure him that this
dragon doesn't mean disaster for his people.'

Kheda studied her obstinate expression, disquiet like a cold draught of water weighing heavy in his stomach.

How can you still believe there's guidance in the flight of birds or the vagaries of smoke, or in the shifting patterns of the stars and jewels of the heavenly compass?

Velindre looked up from her book. 'I think I know where it is.'

'Where?' Kheda moved to look at her open page. Scrawled outlines of islands were obscured by curving arrows, some with solid lines, some dashed or dotted. Compass bearings and other notations confused him further. 'Where are we?'

The magewoman ran her finger around the central portion of the crude map. 'This is the western reaches, all nine domains. Here's the Dawa Sea.' She tapped a blankness to the east signifying the sizeable stretch of open water that divided the western domains from the rest of the Archipelago. Sliding her finger northwards and then around to the south-west, she indicated the two domains that bridged that gap. 'Here's Essa, and Tabril.'

Kheda noted a flurry of lines and the notes marking the comparative risks of the various crossings at both ends of the perilous sea. 'Where are we?' he repeated.

Velindre indicated a domain in the north-east quarter of the cluster: three sizeable chunks of land surrounded by countless smaller islands and reefs. 'This is the Matul domain and we are here.' She tapped the central isle before her finger slid westwards to the next domain. A long, wide island with a broad tongue of land thrusting north lay beneath two lesser isles. 'This is Zelin.' She indicated an islet barely visible beneath the dashed line marking Matul waters from those claimed by Zelin Raes and his fore-bears. 'The dragon is here.'

'So it has crossed almost the whole width of this domain from the island where we first found it.' Frowning, Kheda rubbed a hand over his gritty beard. 'It's travelling west. Why?'

'These are interesting seas. It will be drawn to the blended waters.' Velindre drew her finger along curving arrows that flowed in from the open ocean to the west to strike the barrier of the Archipelago. The currents divided to flow along the northern and western edges of the outermost islands, and beyond them to pierce the Archipelago. 'Currents split and eddy all around these domains before ultimately heading back into the western ocean. I've no idea which one has caught its fancy at the moment.'

'If it's already heading west without us driving it, won't it eventually follow these currents back out into the ocean?' Risala wondered with scant hope.

'I doubt it,' Velindre said reluctantly. 'Not while it has food to eat and the quirks of these currents threaded among the islands to amuse it. It could just as easily decide to set up home in the Dawa Sea.'

'Where it would soon sink more ships than the murderous currents that divide these reaches from the rest of the Archipelago. We have to drive it away for good,' Kheda said firmly. 'Or kill it, if that's what it takes.'

'I've told you, I won't stand for that.' Velindre scowled. 'But we have to get closer if I'm to frighten it off. That's no trading isle, according to my records, so I don't know how we'd get passage there. Because we have to go by boat – I've never been there and I'm not translocating on the strength of a vision again. Not when that dragon will surely sense my magic and warp it.'

Risala looked at Kheda, challenge in her eyes. 'A seer could find someone to take him, if he offered good omens for their own future trade. He could say finding a dragon made sense of the portents that had led him there in the first place.'

'No,' Kheda said curtly. 'I'm done with telling such lies.'

'We need a ship of our own.' Velindre looked weary, the fine lines around her eyes darkened with grime in contrast to the pallor of the thin scars cutting through her tan. She scooped up a handful of water from the silver bowl and splashed it across her face. 'But we're not trading those rubies for one,' she said firmly, before anyone could suggest it.

'I can sing for our supper and some trivial trade goods.' Risala looked dispirited. 'But it'll take me from now until the end of the rains to earn us a half-share in a rowing boat.'

Kheda reassured himself yet again that there was no one within earshot. 'Velindre, you've spoken of contacting Hadrumal—' He hesitated over the unfamiliar name. 'Is there a mage you could trust, like Naldeth? Someone who could help us?'

I would once have cut off my sword-hand rather than suborn sorcery. I would have shunned Velindre and all her kind as the worst defilement. But that was before the savages brought their wild magic and their dragons to devastate Chazen. A warlord's duty is to do whatever's necessary to meet the challenge before him.

'What sort of help do we want?' The magewoman lifted up the silver bowl and tipped the last of the water into her hand, laving her face a second time to equally little effect. 'I don't imagine the Council of Wizards will translocate a ship to us, or send us a warlord's ransom in trade goods by return spell. I could find myself tied up trying to explain myself to Hadrumal's worthies for hours. If the wrong mage gets wind of what's going on and tries to bespeak me to satisfy his curiosity when we're in the midst of these crowds, we could all end up accused of sorcery.' She looked at the ceaseless activity of the Matul islanders with misgiving.

'Isn't there anyone whose advice you can ask, at very least?' Kheda persisted. 'You have said all wizards share an interest in seeing this dragon driven out of the Archipelago. If the beasts go north to plague the unbroken lands, Naldeth said mages will find themselves as unwelcome there as they are in Aldabreshin waters.'

Velindre looked at him for a long moment before breaking the tense silence by standing up. 'I'm not working a fire magic out in the open.' Catching up a half-burned stick, she strode inside the lopsided house, the silver bowl in her other hand.

Risala followed, Kheda close behind her. The shade was welcome, even if it offered no real relief from the all-encompassing heat. He looked out of the doorway, to be sure no one was approaching.

A flare of unnatural red fire caught the corner of Kheda's eye, bright in the windowless gloom. Velindre said something in the barbarian Tormalin tongue and a voice answered her, a distant metallic echo. Velindre interrupted, her words too fast and too colloquial for him to follow.

Kheda glanced at Risala. 'What's she saying?' The magical fire drew his eye irresistibly, a brilliant ring etched into the surface of the upturned silver bowl.

'I can't make it out.' Risala sounded pensive as she too kept watch. 'Do you think these wizards will be more help or hindrance?'

'What other choices do we have?' Kheda sighed. 'We have no trade goods, no status. Even if I admitted to my rank, I have no means of proving it. Neither the Chazen domain nor Daish have any direct trading links with these local warlords and their ladies. We're closer to this isle of Hadrumal where these wizards hide themselves than we are to the southern reaches—' He realised Risala wasn't really listening.

'We're not so very far from Shek waters,' she said absently. The mass of houses and workshops separating this dereliction from the shoreline fortifications blocked her gaze to the east.

Kheda studied her, trying to mask the turmoil of his emotions with a calm expression.

The Shek domain. Your home. You thought you were doing Shek Kul's will when you helped me bring wizardry to drive the savages and their magic out of the southern reaches. You thought the omens sanctioned your transferring your allegiance to me, approved your loving me. Have I lost you by rejecting all such portents? How can I make things right between us?

Velindre's voice broke into his painful thoughts. 'I've spoken to a friend who I think I can trust to be discreet,' the magewoman said slowly. 'He thinks he can send someone to help us.'

'Who?' demanded Kheda.

'How soon?' Risala wanted to know.

'He wouldn't say.' Velindre shrugged. 'In case we're somehow discovered and betray the man before he arrives. My friend was at pains to stress what a dangerous place the Archipelago is for wizards,' she said sardonically.

CHAPTER THREE

The bead-trader looked up from his seat on a pile of cushions beneath the shady branches of a spinefruit tree. A burly man, he was swathed in a voluminous purple robe that might deceive some into thinking him fat and thus foolish. He smiled at the gangling youth who was shifting from foot to foot on the sandy ground before him, one hand playing nervously with his sparse beard. The bead-trader's beard was long and luxuriant, combed out to mingle with glossy black hair that fell unbound to his shoulders.

Passers-by with their tightly cropped curls and close-trimmed whiskers would certainly notice this vain visitor from the central domains of the Archipelago's compass. Only the alert would note that his keen dark eyes were seldom still as he surveyed the morning's visitors to the beach. But most were taking their time to see exactly what wares were on offer before deciding where to propose their own trades.

'Well done, Duna.' His dark-brown fingers, heavy with rings of gold and silver studded with a rainbow of gems, hovered over the goods set out before him.

Crystal bowls held glass beads of all sizes, some as big as a thumbnail, others fine as poppy seed. There were single colours, bright as all shades of corundum. Others were miniature masterpieces of the glass-blender's art, banded and striped. Some were darker mysteries, shifting from black to blue or green at the whim of the clouds and sun above. Spread on a field of black silk, necklaces, earrings, bracelets and anklets showed what could be wrought with such marvels. Some pieces were as fine as a dew-jewelled spider's web, the morning light glittering among the strands. Others lay like coloured drops of rain.

The trader plucked up a single-stranded necklace of opalescent glass beads and tossed it to the boy. 'Be sure and tell me if you learn anything more about those people, anything at all.'

'You can count on me, Ari.' Grinning with delight, the lad studied his prize.

'You won't hear anything more standing here, will you?' Ari raised bushy though precisely shaped brows quizzically.

'I'll be back,' Duna promised, walking away and tucking the necklace inside the breast of his threadbare robe.

Ari twisted around to see another youth leaning against a spinefruit tree and embracing a lissom girl. Her legs straddled his thighs, his broad hands spanning her slim waist. Face upturned and eyes closed in voluptuous pleasure, her fingers caressed the back of his head as he nuzzled her neck.

The trader snapped his fingers. 'Hasu!'

'Yes?' The youth looked up and extricated himself from the girl's embrace before Ari answered. He flapped a careless hand at her indignant protests as he walked away.

'We've news,' Ari said without preamble. 'And just so you know,' he added pointedly, 'I don't want to see any of my wares around that pretty neck later.'

The outraged girl was standing staring after Hasu with her hands on her hips and her luscious mouth half-open in disbelief. The fronts of her scarlet robe overlapped some way below the swell of her enticing breasts and the white silk of her skirt was fine enough to reveal every line of her shapely legs.

'I'm the one who risks blindness making up these pieces.' Unperturbed, Hasu sat cross-legged beside the wide sweep of dull black silk where the dazzling array tempted passing eyes. He frowned and leaned forward to brush the incessant wind-borne dust from the cloth. 'Besides, when did I last take anything I wasn't entitled to?'

'From me? Never.' Ari smiled briefly. 'A few girls might say different.'

'What's the news?' Hasu sat up straighter as a tall woman draped in ruby silk paused to examine the jewellery. She spared him a passing glance – broad-shouldered and elegant in his turquoise robe and green trousers. His curly black hair was braided tight to his scalp and his black beard framed a sensuous mouth. A suggestion of scented oil gleamed on his rich, dark skin.

Ari waited until the woman had moved away. 'Duna, the Galcan mirror-seller's boy, tells me he saw a blonde *zamorin* scholar in the company of a slightly built, blue-eyed poet girl on one of the lesser isles in Matul waters.'

'Is he certain?' Hasu lost all interest in the tall woman's well-rounded rear view.

'He is quite certain, and he said the *zamorin* let slip a barbarian accent now and again.' Ari paused to scowl at a thin-faced man with scabs underlying his sparse beard who looked inclined to approach.

'It certainly sounds like them.' Hasu added his own dark-eyed glower to deter the man. 'Were they alone?'

'Apart from some nameless slave.' As the scabbed man retreated, the bead-trader continued, 'Duna didn't know where they had come from, and that's a puzzle in its own right. He asked around all the newly anchored ships and none of those had carried them there.'

'Did he think to ask if any of the traders had seen them arrive?' Hasu asked quickly.

Ari nodded briefly. 'He did, but no one had. They just walked out of the forest as far as anyone knew.'

Hasu clicked his tongue with irritation. 'Did he know where they were sailing to next?'

'They took ship for Matul Saib's dry-season residence,' Ari said with satisfaction.

'Do you think he's thrown that wall of his round the entire island yet?' Hasu quipped. 'What do you suppose that means?' He frowned.

'For them? I have no idea.' Ari shrugged. 'For us, it could mean extremely favourable trade terms in some choice domains. As well as discreetly valuable gifts from some particularly grateful clients.'

'Do you want to let the doves fly before we know what these two want in Matul Saib's domain?' Hasu sounded doubtful. 'The rains could be here before our more distant clients can send birds to replace them.'

'I think our clients will send us new doves by their fastest triremes, given how often we've been asked for any sighting of that pair.' Ari's eyes drifted to several ships lying just offshore. 'In the meantime, you find someone we know on a galley that's planning to sail for Matul Saib's residence.' He rose to his feet.

'And then?' Hasu looked up expectantly.

'Then we address ourselves to our other clients' interests. I want to find out when Essa Mol and his household plan to move from their dry-season accommodations to the rainy-season residence,' Ari said decisively. 'I've been cultivating some sharp ears among his household.'

Hasu's lips curved in a lascivious smile. 'Are there any fertile spots where I could usefully wield my hoe?'

'Why else do you think I keep you? For your mother's sake? Watch the stock till I get back.' Chuckling, Ari withdrew to a wide, round tent of heavy black cloth pitched in a choice spot within the spinefruit thicket. Anyone not preoccupied with the trade goods on the beach might have noticed he was remarkably light on his feet for a man of his size.

Despite the heat and humidity, the atmosphere within the tent wasn't as stuffy as might have been expected. Vents in the conical roof were tied open to maintain a flow of cooler air. Ari carefully checked a rack of sturdily built cages, all the while marking every shadow passing by the front opening.

'It's time for a few of you pretty things to fly home,' he said softly. Courier doves looked at him, bright-eyed and incomprehending, softly shuffling on their perches or preening their grey-banded wings.

Ari sat down where the sunlight fell through the front panel. Producing a long, thin-bladed knife from some fold in his robe, he unsheathed it and tucked it unobtrusively beside his knee. He pulled a polished walnut box from beneath a casual heap of coverlets and took out an inkpot, a long pen with a steel nib pointed like a needle and a roll of the finest reed paper, thin as onion skin. Writing swiftly in agonisingly small script, he glanced up after every word to be sure he was unobserved. As he finished each brief message, he sliced it from the roll with his startlingly sharp knife. Then he stripped a ring from his nimble fingers and laid it in the open lid of the box, the slip of paper curled within it.

Once five messages were written and coiled within rings, he reached into the box and found a silken pouch holding fine silver tubes adorned with delicate fixings. Rolling each message tight and slipping it into a tube, he returned his rings to his fingers and resheathed his dagger with a grunt of satisfaction. The messages in hand, he rose to his feet and checked there was no one lurking outside the tent before making a careful selection of doves from the cages.

As he fastened each tiny shackle around a bird's leg, he went straight to the open front of the tent and threw the grey-banded bird up high. As he released the fifth he stepped out of the tent and scanned the morning haze still clouding the vivid bowl of the sky. The last bird skirted the shady canopy of the spinefruit trees and soared to dwindle into a mere speck.

His task complete, Ari paused, his gaze momentarily distant. Going back into the tent with a suddenness that set all the softly bickering doves fluttering, he returned to his walnut box and hastily wrote a final message, his fleshy lips pressed tight together. The dove he chose for this message was leaner than the rest, blotches of darker feathers marring its breast. He threw it up into the sky and stood motionless until it vanished from sight. Finally letting out a long-held breath, he returned to Hasu and resumed his place beside the jewellery.

'I couldn't see any sign of any hawks, tame or wild.' Hasu got up, brushing dust from his fine attire.

'Nor me.' Ari's smile widened as he watched a few younger men looking at him. One raised a questioning voice before his companions hushed him. 'Hasu, go and introduce yourself over there. I believe Duna has been telling some newcomers to this trading beach just how widely my brothers and I fly our courier doves.'

'I'll be pestered with all the most tedious news and laughably ciphered trade secrets that we've known about for half a year,' Hasu complained.

'Doubtless,' Ari agreed, 'but you can find the finest pearl in the most rotten oyster. One of them might have some more information about this *zamorin* scholar with the barbarian blood or the blue-eyed poet girl.'

CHAPTER FOUR

How much longer do we wait for this unknown man that Velindre's friend has supposedly sent to us? Is he going to be another mage?

Kheda's first waking thought was the same as the last he'd had before falling asleep the night before, and the night before that. He opened his eyes and looked up at the wooden planks of the flat roof of the lopsided shack. His view was obscured by cotton trousers slung over a rope he had rigged. The trousers were reasonably clean, though he noted how frayed the hems had become.

Not so very long ago I wouldn't have allowed the least of my slaves to be seen in such clothing.

Pressed close beside him, Risala stirred and yawned. 'You had better get moving if you want to be anywhere near the front of the queue for the well.'

Kheda sat up, careful not to disturb Velindre who was sleeping on his other side. The magewoman murmured but didn't wake. He eased himself out from between the two women, passing his thin cotton coverlet to Risala.

She pulled it across her own, savouring the warmth. 'Which traders are expecting you to carry their water jars?'

'Quatyn and Cholai said they can work me all day if I want it.' Kheda stretched to ease the stiffness in his back. He shivered, though the dawn chill at this season was mild enough.

'I should win us all some breakfast with another rousing recitation of *The Owls and the Crows*.' Risala burrowed her chin into the faded blue cotton. 'But don't count on anything to eat this evening if that troupe of Galcan dancers are performing again.'

Velindre rolled onto her back and yawned inelegantly. There looked to be barely enough room for the two women on the straw-stuffed palliasse, never mind all three of them. 'I can see if someone's willing to trade something for lore about the southern domains.'

'We can't eat scrolls or books and that's all any scholar will offer you.' Kheda quickly checked over his shoulder to be certain no one was peering in though the doorway. They'd woken to inquisitive gazes before. 'Besides, you're the only one who will hear if this friend we're expecting calls out to you.'

'I made it quite clear that no one should bespeak me.' Velindre's words were muffled as she rubbed her eyes. 'No one will want my blood on their hands because they've made me the focus of their spell in the middle of a crowd of Aldabreshi.'

Risala reluctantly threw off her covers and sat up. 'You should scry over that island again. We want to know exactly where the beast is every moment of the day.'

'Indeed.' Velindre rose, tugging at her crumpled clothes. She wrinkled her nose as she sniffed at one armpit.

Risala stripped off the creased tunic she had been sleeping in and tossed it down onto the bed. As she reached for her yellow dress, Kheda felt his flesh stir at her lithe nakedness, adorned only by the shark's tooth necklace and the leather thong bearing the heavy silver ring with its uncut polished emerald. She looked at him, her face unreadable. 'You can bring some water back here, once you're done with the slave-traders.'

'As you command, mistress.' He bowed low, not quite mocking her. Stripping off the torn trousers he'd been sleeping in, he pulled the pair with the frayed hems from the rope along with his least-worn tunic. As he dressed, he made sure to tuck his own silver and emerald ring securely inside the neck.

'I'll come back as soon as I have some food to show for my performance.' Risala caught up the bag she'd been resting her head on and brushed past Kheda without a backward look. A solid weight swung against him – the scroll case protecting her precious copies of famous poems, resin sealing leather tight and waterproof over closely joined wood.

Hardly the most comfortable pillow, but that's a secondary consideration to being sure no one can steal it in the night. These things are second nature to you. I've never had to worry about such matters before. I had residences full of treasures and plenty of swordsmen to guard them. I was a law-maker, a healer, a judge.

Kheda looked at the bag containing his own paltry belongings. It was lumpy with the few jars and vials he had been able to salvage from the ebony physic chest he had once carried. The handle of the hacking blade stuck out of the top.

Any warrior would laugh if I proposed fighting him with that. No matter. I can't risk making or facing any challenge, so the only blade I can carry is a simple dagger and that's one in the style of Chazen. I have nothing of the Daish domain that I was born to.

'Do you want me to scry for the beast before you go?' Velindre looked at him, puzzled.

'No.' Kheda gathered his wits. 'I'll see you later.'

He went out into the early morning. Damp swept in by the winds from the ocean hung all around and the unrelenting dust drew a musty veil over the rising sun. A youth was piling firewood beside a circle of blackened broken brick outside one of the larger houses and two women were talking idly in an alley that had wound

through the now-demolished dwellings. The air was sour
with the scent of quenched ashes mingled with filth. Kheda
walked on, mindful of shards and splinters underfoot.
Heaviness of spirit hovered around him.

*I went seeking a wizard because I thought that was the
only answer to the assault of magic on the southern reaches.
And it was an answer – I should at least be grateful for
that. But I have paid a heavy price. I'm driven further
from my home and the life I thought I knew with every
turn of the heavens. I thought I had found a companion in
Risala, a true lover to sustain me. Was I mistaken there as
well?*

As he drew closer to the slave pens he found swordsmen
already awake and making the rounds of their masters'
property. The traders themselves were still snugly asleep
in round tents pitched among the ruins. Brown and grey
canvas was pegged tight to the ground with front flaps
laced firmly shut. Only panels of bright embroidery distinguished each conical roof.

Kheda headed for a ruddy brown tent topped with
broad roundels of grubby white canthira leaves framing
pairs of black cranes, their necks entwined in courtship.
A burly warrior was unlocking a heavy chain attached to
a stake driven firmly into the ground. It ran away to snake
through loops in the shackles around each slave's ankle
before reaching another stake where it was just as firmly
locked. The captives, asleep on the bare earth without a
length of cloth to cover them, hardly stirred.

'Don't they ever try to escape?' Kheda asked unguardedly.

The warrior looked up with a disparaging grunt. 'If
they're fool enough to think there's somewhere to run to.'

The first of the slaves sat up, rubbing at cruel calluses
around his shackled ankle as he pulled himself free from
the long chain that had held him captive through the

night. He shared his glare of hatred impartially between the warrior and Kheda.

'Get busy, southerner.' The warrior stood upright, one massive fist pressed into the small of his back. 'Quatyn won't be impressed if these are all too stricken with thirst to interest the traders.' He scowled to encourage the second slave on the chain to work a little faster as he tugged the heavy links through the loop in his shackles.

'That's why I'm here.' Kheda headed for a stack of leather buckets, took one in each hand and headed for the nearby wellhead. The hopeless loathing in the first captive's eyes still galled him.

Slaves. Nameless and homeless. A fate that befalls those who cannot read the omens of heaven and earth aright and thus find a path to peace and prosperity for themselves. Thus they become reliant on someone else to guide their lives and repay that person with their labour. But what is a slave if I no longer believe in omens?

Nameless and homeless. No one's asked me my name or what domain I was born to. Quatyn and his men are content for me to carry water for them without knowing anything about me. I'm no one to them, no more than these unfortunates waiting to be traded like bales of cloth or sacks of saller grain.

There was already a line of men waiting their turn at the well where a burly Matul islander stood beside the plank-lined shaft. He reached up to haul on the rope that lowered a beam with a rope and wide bucket attached to one end. As he let go of the rope, giggling children in brief breech-clouts jumped on the counter-weight at the other end of the beam, out beyond the pivot post. Water sloshed wildly as the bucket sprang upwards.

'You stop that or I'll throw you in,' the islander growled.

'Then I'll piss in your drinking water,' the liveliest of the lads crowed.

'Then we'll stand around to see if you can climb out

again before you drown.' There was no heat in the well-master's threat.

Kheda took his place in the line. Some of those ahead of him were traders' men. Others were slaves trusted to fetch water for their fellows, the chains on their shackles trailing in the dust. Some of them had raw, angry wounds around their ankles, some did not. Most were working on building the massive new wall, judging by the splashes of mortar and smears of brick dust on their shabby clothing. All looked exhausted before they had even begun their day's work.

Troubled, Kheda edged forward as the line shuffled closer to the wellhead. A hand tapped him briskly on the shoulder. He whirled around, one hand flying instinctively to his dagger.

'I'm sorry, my friend. I didn't mean to startle you.' A stout man half a head shorter than Kheda took a pace backwards, his hands raised placatingly. 'But I believe you're travelling with a friend of mine? Vel—' He cleared his throat. 'Yes, Vel, that's it, isn't it?'

Unsmiling, Kheda studied this newcomer. The man's clothes were of the western reaches: an open-fronted robe of black satin wrapped tight over his generous belly and secured with a wide green sash over loose-cut trousers of a nubby grey silk. He wore neither sword nor dagger but carried a large square bag, its broad strap slung crossways over his chest. The faded black leather was painted with a cracked and worn scene of a trireme at anchor in a wooded bay.

But he was no Archipelagan. Though his face was deeply tanned, the undersides of his forearms were pale where his wide sleeves fell back from his raised hands. Those forearms were well muscled for the man's age; he was at least ten years older than Kheda, probably more. His eyes were somewhere between blue and grey, and what remained of his hair was pale grey, a mere swathe of stubble surrounding a shiny bald pate. There was more colour in his eyebrows and in his beard, cut close around his mouth in the style of these western reaches. In his youth he had been black-haired.

Kheda hesitated as the line shifted and he realised it would soon be his turn at the wellhead. 'Wait a moment, please.'

The children shrieked with glee again as the beam sprang up and water splashed both the well-master and the man ahead of Kheda. Cursing half-heartedly under his breath, the well-master tipped what remained into the buckets the man proffered. Kheda stepped forward onto the muddy patch and braced himself for the inevitable.

'I suppose that's one way of doing your laundry.' The newcomer stood back a prudent distance and chuckled as gouts of water leapt up to darken the front of Kheda's tunic. 'Crisk, help our friend.'

As Kheda looked up from filling his buckets, he realised the newcomer wasn't alone. A second man cowered behind him, shorter and skinnier, wearing a dull ochre robe and trousers originally made for a much larger man. Sleeves and trousers had been rolled up several times, the cuffs sewn into place with clumsy stitches. This man's pale skin was overlaid with countless freckles blurring together in unsightly blotches. Beardless, his hair was a vivid russet, bright as leaves at the end of the driest season. Kheda had never seen such a shade before.

Another barbarian and a strange one at that.

The man retreated from the warlord's curious stare, face anxious as he clutched at a tarnished copper amulet strung on a grubby ribbon around his scrawny neck.

'Crisk,' the newcomer said gently, 'help our friend with his buckets.' He spoke the Aldabreshin tongue fluently though with a strong barbarian accent. 'Trimon would take that for a blessing.'

The red-headed man took a tentative step and stretched out a shaking hand, the other clutching his amulet. 'Trimon's blessings,' he murmured.

'Shift, can't you?' the well-master growled impatiently.

'It's better if I carry both buckets.' Kheda moved away from the shaft, trying for a reassuring smile as he saw the red-headed man look fearfully at the islander. 'Then I'm balanced.'

'As you please,' the black-robed northerner said easily. 'Don't worry, Crisk.'

Thumbs hooked in his sash, he strolled beside Kheda as they headed away from the well. He was looking around, apparently idly.

Only you're as alert as any swordsman expecting a challenge.

'Who's Trimon? Are we anticipating someone else?' Kheda glanced over his shoulder and saw the red-headed Crisk was following close behind. He was shying away from any curious glance from passers-by, hunching his shoulders as if he expected a blow. Plainly well-enough fed at present, earlier privation had left him with hollow eyes and sunken cheeks. Kheda realised with a faint shock that the man's eerily pale eyes were green like his own. 'Is he your slave?'

The northerner hesitated before answering. 'He's my companion. Trimon is a god worshipped in the unbroken lands, where Crisk originally hails from. And you are . . .?' He left the question hanging in the air.

'Kheda. Just Kheda.'

'Kheda.' The northerner nodded, apparently satisfied.

Kheda waited, but this stranger didn't volunteer his own name.

How did you know me, among all these countless traders and islanders?

They walked on in silence until they reached Quatyn's slave pens. Kheda set the buckets of water down carefully and snapped his fingers at the man who'd been unlocking the slaves' chains. 'Tell Quatyn I can't work for him today,' he said without apology. 'Something's come up.'

The swordsman scowled. 'There's plenty more flotsam on the beach who'll fetch and carry. Don't think you've earned anything with just two buckets of water,' he called out spitefully.

Kheda was already walking away. He noticed Crisk's freckled face was twisted with wretched apprehension. Kheda glanced down, but the dragging hems of the frightened man's trousers hid any shackle scars.

'You're a friend of Vel's?' he asked the older man bluntly.

'A good friend,' the newcomer said serenely.

Do you know Velindre's passing herself off as zamorin?

'Did you know Dev?' Kheda looked keenly for any reaction to that name.

'I knew him.' The stranger pursed his lips with unmistakable distaste. 'I couldn't claim we were friends.'

What does that tell me? Dev was certainly a scoundrel and I don't think I would have trusted him, even if he hadn't been a wizard. But he was the wizard who risked his life driving the wild men out of Chazen and he died fighting that first dragon that came to devastate the southern reaches. He died a hero of sorts.

He looked around to make sure there was no one within earshot but still opted for circumlocution. 'You share Vel's abilities?'

'In broad terms,' the man replied easily. 'My interests are in stones and soils.'

Which presumably means you're a wizard with an affinity for the elemental earth. Do I have to fear you wreaking the

*same destruction on Aldabreshin islands that Velindre and
Naldeth visited on the wild men's shore?*

They walked on in silence, the newcomer blandly
observing the growing bustle around the impromptu
dwellings of the boatless merchants. A tang of charcoal
and grilling meat cut the air as braziers were lit and break-
fasts cooked. Kheda's stomach rumbled.

*How soon will Risala be back? Will she have enough for
us all to eat? What will this wizard make of a warlord who
cannot even offer his visitors saller bread and salt?*

He led the two strangers through the maze of broken
walls. 'Vel!'

'Did you bring some water?' Velindre appeared in the
doorway as she heard Kheda's shout. 'Oh.' She looked
utterly nonplussed when she saw his companions.

'He tells me he's a friend of yours.' Kheda turned to
the newcomer, his expression none too friendly. 'But as
yet he has not shared his name or his business in these
islands.'

The black-clad newcomer was unperturbed. 'My name
is Sirince, Sirince Mar.' He smiled amiably. 'For the
present, my business is giving you passage wherever you
need to go.'

'Rafrid bespoke you.' Chagrin coloured Velindre's
words as a faint flush darkened her tanned cheekbones.

'You have a boat of your own?' Kheda asked.

'I do,' Sirince confirmed.

Velindre frowned. 'You couldn't have sailed all the way
here from Hadrumal since—'

'No,' Sirince agreed. 'I was in Penik waters.'

'What are you doing in these reaches?' Now Velindre
was simply puzzled.

This time Sirince took a moment to look around warily.
'I'm buying slaves.'

'What?'

Sirince held up a hand to stem the magewoman's outrage. 'Hear me out.'

'Risala?' Kheda saw the pale flame of her dress hurrying towards their meagre shelter and strode quickly to meet her.

'The word's out,' she said breathlessly.

Kheda rubbed a hand across his beard. 'We have a boat.'

They made haste back to the waiting wizards.

'No one's interested in listening to pretty poems about forest birds this morning.' Risala's gaze fixed on Sirince. 'Who's this?'

'Sirince,' the magewoman said briefly.

'And Crisk,' Kheda added.

'A slave of yours?' Velindre asked, severe.

The red-headed man was sitting loose-limbed on the ground, happy to hunch unnoticed behind a fragment of wall. Hearing his name, he looked up, freckled face crumpling with fear like a child's.

'No,' Sirince said gently.

'You're from the same home isle?' Risala asked the magewoman pointedly.

'We are.' Velindre brushed away the irrelevance. 'What were you saying?'

'News came in with the boats on the first tide.' Risala let her heavy bag slip from her shoulder and rest on the ground. 'A leaf-green dragon has been seen in the waters that divide Zelin and Matul. It's attacked several ships and devastated a trading beach on a treaty isle.' She spared Velindre an accusing glare before thrusting a hand through her hair to brush it back off her face. 'At the moment, people are most concerned with whether it's in Matul waters or Zelin territory. The portents read into its arrival will depend on that.' Now her look challenged Kheda.

He shook his head. 'People will read into it what they want to see, depending on how fond they are of their warlord.'

'Winged snake, winged beast, it's all one.' Crisk spoke up unexpectedly. 'It travels to learn but it meets the Diamond. Diamond for warlord and Opal for truth and Diamond for truth along with it. Warlords must face the truth.' His diction was clear and his Aldabreshin pure, accentless. 'The Pearl is dark, lost with the Sailfish that's all astray on the ocean's currents, ringed around with fears and foes.' He shook his head, brow faintly wrinkled. 'Amethyst says look for friends but be watchful as the Yora Hawk. Ruby says think of hearth and home and parents. The Bowl says don't spill anything.'

'What?' Kheda stared at the red-headed barbarian, bemused.

'Crisk is apt to prophesy.' Sirince brushed the matter aside. 'Zelin Raes is very popular among his people. He's a fair law-giver and his people profit under his dominion. He's made some particularly judicious marital alliances.'

Crisk is apt to prophesy?

Though he'd set his face against all prediction, it took Kheda barely a moment to picture how the heavenly compass would stand at present. The habits of a lifetime died hard.

He knows exactly where all the jewels and constellations are. What manner of barbarian is he? No. We have no time for such irrelevances.

'And Matul Saib?' Kheda tried to recall anything he'd ever heard of the warlord in the days when such knowledge had passed naturally through his hands.

'His people flourish under his rule.' Sirince considered his words before continuing. 'So much trade has to pass through this domain to reach Essa waters and go on through the safer crossings to the wider Archipelago. But he is a remote ruler. He has a slew of stewards who proclaim his decrees and tour the islands taking petitions back to him.'

Risala was still looking at Crisk. 'What do the stars say for Matul Saib?'

The strange barbarian gazed vacantly at her for a moment before his face broke into a wide smile. 'A poet's dress. Trimon loves poets and travel and Halcarion. Halcarion loves the moonlight. Greater Moon for promise and Lesser Moon for mystery.' He shrugged. 'Lesser Moon is dark. All is mystery.'

Risala frowned and turned to Sirince. 'What is he talking about?'

'Trimon and Halcarion are mainland gods.' Sirince looked at Crisk with some exasperation. 'He weaves myth from our own ancient races into every interpretation of the Aldabreshin stars or earthly portents that he's ever heard and glosses it all with whatever songs or poems he currently has stuck in his head. Don't concern yourself trying to unravel it.' He paused to look around the devastation between the tightly packed dwellings and the scaffolded wall. 'I suspect any omens that these people claim for Matul Saib will concern all this.'

Kheda asked the question for all of them. 'What is he building here?'

'A residence that will outstrip anything built in any other domain within the lifetime of anyone born during its construction.' Sirince was clearly quoting someone. 'There will be palaces within palaces, pleasure gardens and orchards and waterfalls. Some apparently extraordinary omens led him to this ambition.'

'And no one's going to gainsay him,' Velindre said sarcastically.

'No.' Sirince paused. 'But there are . . . murmurings. He's spending the wealth of the domain like water to bring in marble and hardwoods that cannot be found in these reaches. And he's buying up all these barbarian slaves to do the building. There are concerns—' He looked at Kheda. 'Have you any notion what will happen when word of this dragon spreads?'

'It depends on exactly where the beast is,' Kheda said grimly. 'Anyone touched by its shadow will be fleeing, whatever the seers make of the omens. Plenty more will flee simply out of fear that it might land somewhere near them.'

'Then let's be on our way,' Velindre said briskly.

'To do what, precisely?' Sirince was curious.

Velindre couldn't hide her momentary hesitation. 'Whatever seems most likely to drive it away, once we've had a chance to assess the situation.'

'I see,' the grey-haired wizard said, a trifle obliquely.

Kheda didn't bother trying to hide his dissatisfaction with that answer. 'Where's your ship?'

'On the beach.' Sirince shrugged. 'Watered and provisioned. What happened to your own ship?' he asked Velindre as an afterthought. 'The *Zaise*, wasn't it?'

Velindre didn't reply, ducking back inside the lopsided dwelling to retrieve their baggage.

'It was wrecked.' Kheda strove to sound offhand.

It was attacked by two dragons, one of fire and one of earth, both intent on our death. Velindre and Naldeth only saved us by throwing the savages' whole island into chaos and nearly killed themselves doing so. And they wrecked the boat.

'Then let's go back to my ship.' Sirince offered his hand to Crisk and smiled encouragingly as he raised the wretch to his feet.

'Trimon always brings me to the ship.' Crisk's sudden smile was pathetically eager. 'Arrimelin blesses the waters,' he assured Risala solemnly.

Sirince peered past Velindre as the magewoman exited

the hovel. 'I can offer you more comfortable beds than a second-hand palliasse.'

'That'll be welcome.' Unsmiling, Velindre swung Kheda's bag towards him.

He caught it and slung it over one shoulder, falling in behind the two women as Sirince led the way back towards the houses and workshops. Crisk pressed close behind the balding wizard, apparently striving to keep his steps in Sirince's shadow and muttering something in a language Kheda had never heard before, repeating the same words over and over again.

Velindre and Naldeth blended their magics to split the very earth and sea beneath the Zaise. Dev's arrogance was the death of him, in part at least. What manner of mage are you, Sirince? Has age taught you wisdom or merely confirmed you in a mage's lethal conceits?

He looked at Risala, hurrying to keep pace with Velindre's long-legged stride. The two women were deep in conversation, their expressions intent. Looking past them, he realised there was unusual activity among the slave-traders. Sirince slowed, his attention also turning that way. Harsh shouts rang out and the hubbub around the pens and tents faded into a tense silence.

'What's going on?' Velindre frowned.

'Quatyn's in trouble.' Risala didn't sound sorry.

'He's not the only one.' Kheda fixed his attention on the situation, one hand going to the handle of his hacking blade.

Quatyn and another slave-trader were besieged by Matul men and women all shouting incoherent demands. More islanders were appearing from the houses and work-shops beyond the demolished area, adding their voices to the cacophony.

'We don't want to get mixed up in that.' Kheda looked for a route to the gates in the coastal defences that would skirt the possibility. He couldn't see one. Any lanes cutting through the clusters of buildings were packed with people streaming towards them. The crowds were heading for the open expanse in front of Matul Saib's mighty new wall. Visitors who'd set up temporary residence in the derelict buildings were joining them. Questioning voices rose in distress.

'Kheda!' Risala's alarm instantly got his attention.

The ring around Quatyn suddenly broke as the decorated panels of the top of his tent bellied and buckled. The embroidered cranes flapped in vain, unable to fly away before they tumbled to the ground. As ripples of confusion further disrupted the circle of yelling islanders, Kheda saw the slave-trader's swordsmen standing their ground in front of one of their pens. Men and women confronted them, shouting and gesturing. He saw the flash of steel and a terrified scream was lost beneath a roar of anger from the Matul islanders. More blades rose up on both sides, bloodied now.

No one paid any heed to a few Aldabreshin slaves seizing their chance and running as far and as fast as they could. Kheda vaulted over a crumbling wall, drawing his dagger. A slave dodged sideways, his hands raised in futile appeal. Kheda lunged after him with a long stride that ripped at a muscle inside his thigh. It was worth the pain. He planted his foot solidly on the chain trailing from the slave's ankle and the unfortunate stumbled and fell to his knees.

'I'm Aldabreshin blood, black hair, brown eyes,' the slave gasped, eyes wide with fear. Tearing open his tattered robe, he bared a rich brown chest. 'No pale skin, see.'

'We have to get out of here.' Sirince had Crisk's wrist in a grip that whitened the wizard's knuckles. The red-headed northerner whimpered pitifully, clutching at the amulet around his neck with his free hand.

The kneeling slave startled them all by spitting copiously at the pair. 'Barbarians. Kill them and see if their blood can cleanse the land. Leave them to face their fate,' he urged Kheda and Risala with sudden sincerity. 'All barbarians are tainted with magic.'

'What has magic to do with anything?' Catching the kneeling man under the chin, Kheda held his dagger ready as if to cut his throat.

'There's a dragon been seen.' The kneeling slave swallowed as best he could in Kheda's merciless grip. 'All the barbarian slaves must die or it'll be drawn to them.'

Screams of terror cut sickeningly short rose above the furious mêlée around the slave pens. A passing breeze was tainted with the rankness of blood, urine and voided bowels.

The dragon might be drawn to Sirince, if his magic is to its taste. What could he know of hiding from such a creature?

'Lose yourself before I kill you.' Kheda threw the slave backwards, releasing the chain pinned under his cramping foot. The man scrambled away, hands and knees sliding in the dust.

'Let's get away from this slaughter.' Risala flinched at a shrill screech.

'We may have to defend ourselves.' Kheda let his bag slide down from his shoulder and pulled the hacking blade free, the dagger transferred to his off hand.

The crowd flowed past on either side of the broken stretch of wall that Kheda had jumped. It was the only thing stopping them all being swept away into the disorder.

'I'm not much good in a knife-fight, Kheda.' Nevertheless, Velindre drew her dagger and glowered as a woman paused to stare open-mouthed at this supposed *zamorin* with such bright golden hair.

'We cannot have you use any other means to defend yourselves,' Kheda said sharply.

'Not if we're to escape this frenzy intact.' Risala had drawn her own belt knife and was looking warily from side to side. 'Stay close to me.'

'We want no part of this.' With menace in his tone Kheda warned off the staring woman and a man who had joined her. 'We deserve no part in it. Sirince, carry our bags.' He used a foot to shove his baggage towards the northern wizard, who caught it up awkwardly, one-handed, still hampered by his need to keep hold of Crisk's wrist.

Velindre also proffered her own bag to the other mage, looking grimly at the uproar around the slave pens. 'Can we take a long way round?'

Sirince took her leather bag and ducked his head through the strap. The body of the bag slapped against his side and he gasped. 'What—' He choked and his eyes rolled upwards, his lips blue, bloodless.

Kheda tried to catch him as he fell but Crisk got in his way.

'No!' Raining ineffectual blows, Crisk attacked Kheda, cursing in his unknown barbarian tongue.

Taken unawares and tripped by something underfoot, Kheda fell backwards. He barely managed to avoid crushing Sirince beneath the two of them or skewering Crisk with a blade.

'You don't hurt him!' Crisk's pungent breath warmed Kheda's cheek, the spray of spittle making his skin crawl. 'You don't hurt him!' Where his pale-green eyes had been vacant, now they were glazed with unseeing hatred.

Letting go of his weapons, Kheda caught the man's bony wrists in both hands and held them in a crushing grip. As pain and perplexity penetrated the smaller man's frenzy, Kheda forced his hips up, using one foot to push against the ground. Twisting beneath his assailant, he had their positions reversed in an instant. Sitting astride his thighs, Kheda pinned Crisk's hands to the ground. Then

he realised their struggle had attracted far too much unwelcome attention.

'Cut his cursed throat,' a shrill woman advised, her
headscarf dragged askew.

'Let me.' The man beside her stepped forward, his
knife ready.

'No.' Kheda glowered, Crisk still writhing ineffectually
beneath him. 'I traded a good weight of metal for this one.'

Risala was helping Sirince to his feet. He thrust
Velindre's bag at her, his hands shaking.

'We'll be gone soon enough,' the balding wizard rasped.

'Taking any ill fortune with us.' Velindre moved to
stand at his shoulder. 'Isn't that better than having it soak
into your soil along with our blood?'

Her fluent mastery of the Aldabreshin tongue gave
those gathering around pause for thought.

'What's that?' Risala's hands flew to her face as she looked
past the crowd, her mouth wide with feigned astonishment.

They surely won't fall for that old trick?

But heads turned, and they stayed turned. Women
raised themselves up on tiptoe to see past taller men or
hurried to insinuate themselves into any space.

'What's going on?' Kheda demanded, frustrated. He
wasn't about to let go of Crisk until the barbarian stopped
struggling.

'Never mind.' Risala had Sirince's arm over one
shoulder, Kheda's bag slung over the other, her eyes dark
with concern.

The mainlander mage was still horribly pale beneath
his tan. 'You carry your own bag,' he spat at Velindre.

'I'm sorry—' She looked aghast as she took it back
from Risala.

*What just happened? Does Sirince have a weak heart?
What use is he to us if he does?*

Kheda set all such questions aside as he got to his feet,

keeping firm hold on both of Crisk's bony wrists with one broad, muscular hand. He found his dagger and sheathed it. Picking up his hacking blade, he gripped the long handle. 'Let's get away from here and take our bearings.'

He forced a way through the crowd, certain at least that they were heading away from the slave pens. Offering the flat of his broad blade to men and women alike convinced them not to block his way. As the islanders yielded, he realised they looked more askance at Crisk than they did at the gleaming steel. All the fight had gone out of the smaller man now and he trailed mutely behind Kheda.

'Try to bear more to your sword-hand,' Risala called out from the rear. 'At least that'll take us some way towards the shore.'

A great cheer of excitement erupted behind them. Kheda felt Crisk flinch. The noise of hatred and slaughter behind them rapidly abated to be replaced with an expectant hum.

A few hoarse shouts lifted above the murmurs.

'Help us!'

'Tell us!'

'Show us!'

'What's happening?' Kheda scowled as a shouting man's breath struck him, redolent of spiced vegetables. He concentrated on picking a path through the crowds as they finally reached the workshops and houses.

'Matul Saib!'

More voices picked up this appeal and repeated it.

'Matul Saib!'

'Matul Saib!'

The chant settled into a full-throated rhythm that shook the air. Men and women took it up, pressed painfully close together whether they wished it or not. The vast crowd spun around and Kheda could no longer force his way towards the shore. Close-packed bodies on all sides made the cool of dawn a distant memory. Everyone was sweating, and by the smell of them, some travellers hadn't bothered with ablutions for several days.

Kheda saw Risala still had Sirince's arm over her shoulders and Velindre was now bringing up the rear, hugging her bag to her flat chest. Crisk whimpered and strained towards Sirince.

'Let him come to me.' The wizard had to shout to be heard over the steady pulse of the chant.

If he does run, he won't get far in this mob. Even if he did, would he be such a loss?

Kheda let go of Crisk's wrists. The red-headed man pulled Risala roughly away to take her place supporting the mage. She hunched her shoulders, cradling her bandaged wrist between her modest breasts. As a youth tried to elbow a way past, Kheda stretched out one muscular arm and Risala accepted its shelter with a faint look of gratitude.

'I'm more likely to stab one of us with this.' Kheda sheathed his blade with some difficulty and slung his bag over one shoulder. Sweat was beading his forehead and trickling down his back, from apprehension as much as the stifling crush.

'Matul Saib!'

All attention turned inland, towards the great wall bristling with scaffolding.

'Matul Saib!'

The swelling chant faltered, broken by cheering. Kheda saw a flurry of activity as eager hands thrust a white-clad figure up onto a scaffold of planks and logs. The man shouted out to the crowd, the skirts of his long robe swirling around his bare bony knees as he turned this way and that. He had the long unkempt beard and uncut hair of a soothsayer.

'What does our lord say of this omen?' The man's voice cracked with emotion.

In the next breath, great bronze horns sounded out over everyone's heads. Consternation rippled through the crowd. Voices took up the chant again, the warlord's name resonating with an undercurrent of anger. The crowd surged closer to the great wall.

'Those horns signal that the gates to the shoreline are shutting.' Sirince was standing solidly once again, though Crisk refused to relinquish his place under the wizard's arm.

'We'll just have to wait it out.' Kheda was relieved to see the wizard was a healthier colour. 'There must be a way open to the beach, sooner or later.'

'No, I don't think so.' Sirince shook his head and said something to Velindre in the Tormalin tongue of the northern lands.

She looked startled and then nodded, her face apprehensive. 'Kheda, everyone's heading towards the inner wall. Take us that way.'

Kheda would have objected but the realities of their situation couldn't be gainsaid.

We can't force a path against this many people and what would be the point if the gates to the shore are shut? But what happens when we reach the inner wall?

More horns rang out atop the wall that was to bound Matul Saib's fabulous residence. Their notes were sharper and lighter than those from the shoreline, their calls more complicated. Kheda looked up to see the hazy sun brushing across burnished steel and bright chain mail amid the bristling scaffolding timbers.

'Kheda, move!' Velindre shouted desperately as the press of the crowd threatened to knock her off her feet.

Kheda summoned up the most ominous scowl he'd ever had to use as the erstwhile lord of a southern domain.

He let his bag slip down his arm and wielded it with one
fist to lend weight to his advance. He kept his other arm
out-thrust to protect Risala, shoving unwary backs and
heedless arms away. Fast as the crowd was now moving
inland, he was moving faster, Sirince and Crisk hard on
his heels, Velindre close behind. If outraged islanders and
traders looked around to see who was pushing them so
rudely aside, they rapidly capitulated.

'Matul Saib!'

All at once the speed of the crowd increased. A scream
was abruptly cut short to be replaced with a rising wail.
Kheda had to break into a run to avoid being knocked off
his feet. He saw a woman stumble to be trampled underfoot. Harsh sounds of alarm cut through the incessant
chanting.

'Stay close!' Sirince shouted behind him.

The mass of the vast inner wall loomed over them,
black against the hazy sunlight. Kheda looked up to see
swordsmen and archers silhouetted against sky the colour
of parchment, their swords and bows like inky pen strokes.
The crowd seethed beneath the massive barrier like water
striking a rocky shore. Men stumbled over logs not yet
used in the scaffolding. Opportunists snatched up tools
and coils of rope tossed aside as the labourers had fled.
The press ahead of Kheda broke to flow around either
side of a waist-high wooden box. Knocked hard against
it, the rough wooden edges of the planking dug cruelly
into his side. He realised it was full of crushed clay brick,
coarse gravels and white dust. He smelled the sharp peril
of quicklime.

The crowd were halting before the shadows cast by the
scaffold, looking up and shouting at the warriors.

'There's a dragon been seen!'

'What does it mean?'

'Come on.' Sirince caught Kheda's sleeve and pulled

him forward into the gloom beneath the lowest layer of planks.

As Kheda followed, Risala still within the protective curve of his arm, a surge in the crowd behind them crushed people against the massive timbers of the uprights. Someone shrieked in pain. The shouts grew angrier.

As Kheda's eyes became accustomed to the shade beneath the scaffolding he saw the wall was being built with huge bricks being made in the wooden boxes. Once water was poured into the mix to work its alchemy, the lime would bind everything together.

Sirince ran his fingers thoughtfully over one of the great blocks making up the lowest courses of the great wall. 'Velindre, you had better bring up the rear.' He rolled up his sleeves with brisk, deft movements. 'Kheda, hold on to Crisk and then take Risala's hand.'

As Kheda caught Crisk's forearm, the gloom of the shadows all around them shivered and for a moment the deafening noise dimmed. Blurred as if he were an image in a tarnished mirror, Sirince reached for Crisk's hand and laced their fingers together. 'Link hands and don't let go.' His words were muffled and indistinct.

Risala reached for Kheda with her bandaged arm. He wrapped his fingers around hers, desperately trying not to pull too hard.

I splinted that broken wrist eight days into this cycle of the Lesser Moon. The bones should be very nearly knitted now. But the break mustn't take any great strain, at least not until this Greater Moon has waned and waxed again to the full. Otherwise the bones may come apart and she'll be worse off than she was in the first place.

The shadows thickened unnaturally, clouding the air like a squid's ink in water.

Magic. He had better get us out of here, because we're

definitely all dead if anyone accuses us of sorcery, especially now they know a dragon is nigh.

Sirince moved towards the wall, Crisk following obediently. Kheda couldn't hold back without hurting Risala. He couldn't see where Sirince was going. As he opened his mouth to say something, sand blew into his mouth.

How can there be wind and sand here in this enclosed space?

He spat it out but the air was full of it. He shut his eyes; he couldn't see anyway as the darkness had become so complete. The wind flung grit against his face, sharp and abrasive. Gravel stung his cheekbones. He had to keep moving, Crisk pulling him inexorably forward. Kheda dared not let go. Behind him, Risala's grip was crushing the blood from his fingers. The wind blew stronger, always from the same direction, unwavering. He ducked his head against it, forcing himself forwards. The wind pressed against his head, his chest, and his thighs. The sand piled up around his feet, up to his ankles. It was becoming difficult to breathe, his chest aching. He wanted to cough but dared not.

If I cough, I'll stop walking. I'm hurting Risala, there's no question of that. If she lets go of my hand, she'll be lost. What happens if we're lost inside a wizard's magic?

He struggled onwards. There was nothing else to do.

Then it was all over. The wind vanished and bright light stung his eyes, prompting tears beneath his eyelids. As he stumbled forwards, he lost hold of Crisk. He still had Risala. Wiping frantically at the sand crusting his lashes, he blinked painfully. 'Where are we?'

'On the shore.' She extricated her fingers from his and cradled her splinted wrist, tears trickling down her cheeks.

Crisk patted her shoulder, awkward yet gentle. 'Trimon blesses travellers,' he assured her, his face all concern.

Velindre fell to her hands and knees, vomiting mucus and bile.

Kheda took an incautious breath to try to clear his wits. Inhaling the dust in his throat convulsed him with coughs until he was retching alongside the magewoman. Finally he managed to recover himself, chest aching. 'What did you do?' he rasped.

'Made a path through the substance of the wall.' Sirince brushed dust from his palms.

Crisk smiled happily at Kheda. 'Diamond is for warlords and nothing is harder. It cuts the path we all must travel.'

Why are you so little affected by this? Because you haven't the wit to fear it?

Kheda saw they were indeed on a beach, some considerable distance away from the shore where the visiting galleys were beached before the gates in Matul Saib's defences. A line of ragged nut palms divided the barren strip of stone-strewn soil where they stood from the foreshore. Massive lime-washed fortifications loomed up behind them, every crevice where the great bricks had been mortared together sealed with paint.

'We walked through that? What if someone saw us?' Kheda looked around hurriedly for anyone gawping at the sight of five people emerging from a solid wall. To his intense relief, there were no figures closer than the distant boats anchored in the shallows. He rubbed his eyes. The distant figures shimmered with something akin to heat haze rippling around them.

'No one saw us. I could wrap an invisibility around us at very least.' Velindre wiped her mouth and got shakily to her feet. She waved her hand and the haze vanished.

'I knew the new wall they've been building was running to join to this outer rampart, so our best way out was simply to walk through it.' Sirince shook his head regretfully. 'I realise the antipathy of earth to air. If there had been any other way—'

'Never mind.' The lines in Velindre's face were more deeply graven than ever, skin drawn tight over her cheekbones and jaw.

Risala wiped tears from her face. 'Where's your boat?' she asked resolutely.

'Beached well away from the gates.' Sirince pointed along the coast where the inlet ran back towards the open ocean.

'You, Crisk.' Kheda snapped his fingers to get the strange red-headed man's attention. 'Carry these.' He took Risala's bag from her unresisting hand and caught up Velindre's from where it had fallen to the sand.

'Kindly do Crisk the courtesy of asking him to do things, rather than ordering him,' Sirince interjected unexpectedly.

Kheda felt rebuked. He shared a suggestion of a bow between the two barbarians. 'Crisk, please would you carry these bags for us?'

The strange man nodded, venturing a sunny smile.

'Let's get on board the boat.' Sirince offered Velindre his arm. 'You'll feel better once we're out on the water.'

'I hate being caught up in earth magic,' the magewoman said with feeling. She still accepted the offer of his support.

'Let me look at your wrist as soon as we're away from here.' Kheda wrapped one arm around Risala's shoulder. 'I have some poppy syrup left, to take the ache out of it, if you want.'

She didn't pull away. 'That will be welcome,' she said tightly.

They followed the two wizards as Crisk ran on ahead. *Well, I don't suppose he's going to desert us just at present.*

'If you're so wary of earth magic, why are you carrying . . . whatever is it you're carrying in that bag of yours?' Sirince's curiosity was coloured with anger.

'Rubies,' Velindre said shortly. 'Tainted rubies.'

'How do you mean, tainted?' Sirince demanded.

'We worked a nexus magic, binding all four elements together.' Velindre drew a careful breath and continued in rapid Tormalin, too quick for Kheda to follow.

Are you telling him the rubies were first offered up to the dragon that was devastating Chazen, as we sought to buy safety for our villages and people with caches of gems of all colours? Our ignorance is our only excuse. We didn't know the beast was collecting rubies to work its own life-giving magic and create an egg. Only Dev's magic stifled the spark at its heart that would have become a new dragon, and he died in the doing of it. Then Velindre and Naldeth used their magic on the great cursed gem that was left. They were trying to defend us as the dragons of that distant western isle attacked us. But the gem shattered and the earth and sea beneath us broke apart, nearly killing us all.

Sirince halted, his eyes widened. 'Naldeth?'

'What about Naldeth?' Kheda interrupted. 'Do you know him?'

'I know of him.' Sirince reverted to his heavily accented Aldabreshin. 'I knew he was working on developing his skills with earth magic, though his affinity is to fire.' He looked suddenly concerned. 'Where is he?'

'How much did Rafrid tell you?' There was a tart note in the magewoman's voice.

Sirince lowered his voice even though there was no one within the possibility of earshot. 'That you had found a vast island out in the western ocean where powerful confluences of elemental energies had lured a sizeable population of dragons.'

'Where those who could do so kept everyone else in thrall with their wizardry.' Risala couldn't keep the revulsion out of her words. 'Savages, all of them, ground down into the dirt, living no better than animals.'

'Surely not?' Sirince was horrified.

'I'm afraid it's quite true.' Velindre sighed heavily. 'With the dragons' auras enhancing their powers, these mageborn were surprisingly effective, for all their magic was little more than instinct.'

'They were tyrants of the worst kind,' Kheda said firmly.

'The natural adjustments of the elements necessary for equilibrium were being prevented by the dragons' presence.' Velindre shook her head. 'The constraints maintaining the confluence were already beginning to break down. Outlying islands had blown themselves apart. Which is what sent those first waves of wild men fleeing across the ocean to attack the southern reaches of the Archipelago.' She sounded quite matter-of-fact.

'They had their magic to counter the currents and winds that should have drowned them.' Kheda grimaced at memories of those first terrifying assaults, still vivid in his mind's eye. 'Then their dragon came after them.'

'But why did you go to find this western isle yourselves?' Sirince was puzzled. 'Didn't you think of the dangers?'

I simply sought to learn all I could about the Archipelago's enemies. My father Daish Reik always said you have to know an enemy to know how to defeat him.

Kheda looked straight ahead to be certain he wouldn't catch Risala's eye.

You believed there were portents guiding us. You thought that I would see the same, that this would bring me back to my senses, to trusting in such omens. Only I didn't. I didn't even look for any such guidance. I let wizards lead us into catastrophe. Is that why you are so angry with me?

'We were only supposed to be reconnoitring,' Velindre said ruefully. 'Things got out of hand.'

'Because Naldeth was as outraged as you seem to be by the notion of wizards as tyrants.' Kheda cleared his throat, determined to keep his tone level. 'He nearly got us all killed by setting out to rescue the savages. What he didn't realise was it is far easier to start a fight than it is to finish it.'

'The only way to finish it was to have Velindre and Naldeth's magic set the fire mountains on the main island erupting.' Risala scowled darkly at Kheda's side. 'Which brought a whole new catastrophe down on the savages.'

'At least they were freed from magical domination and the threat of the dragons.' Velindre was unapologetic. 'The savages' mages would feed whoever grew too old or troublesome to the beasts,' she explained to Sirince with distaste.

'That's vile.' He was appalled still further.

'So now all the dragons have flown away.' Risala's voice was stiff with reproof. 'And at least one has flown here, to bring more death and destruction—'

'It's an animal—' Velindre began heatedly until a paroxysm of coughing silenced her.

'But what about Naldeth?' Sirince paused to let the magewoman catch her breath. 'What happened to the lad?'

'He lives, as far as I know,' Kheda said slowly. 'He stayed there, on that island. He felt obliged to help the people there however he could, because his magic had done them so much harm, no matter how good his intentions.'

'He was determined to show the wretches that magic need not only be used for tyranny,' Risala admitted grudgingly.

'He wanted to be on hand lest any curious mages appear, those with rather fewer scruples than we might like.' Recovering, Velindre looked sternly at Sirince. 'Should the halls of Hadrumal learn of the island's existence.'

'They won't learn it from me,' the older mage assured her. 'I assume you've told Planir at least?' Now it was his turn to look penetratingly at Velindre.

She looked away. 'Rafrid can tell our esteemed Archmage whatever he needs to know.'

Sirince didn't pursue that. 'Naldeth felt obligated, you say.' He pursed his lips. 'The lad's not wrong. I take it we're agreed we're duty-bound to rid these reaches of this dragon that's come here?'

'Absolutely,' Kheda said firmly.

'We have to drive it off,' Velindre agreed, 'for the beast's own sake as much as anything else. Before it's killed.'

'Before it gets a taste for easy killing.' At Kheda's side, Risala couldn't suppress a shudder.

'This will be an interesting challenge,' mused Sirince. He raised his free hand to shade his eyes. 'There, can you see? Crisk has already reached our ship.'

'Who is he?' Kheda asked. 'Crisk – where does he hail from?'

But Sirince was striding on ahead and didn't appear to hear the question.

CHAPTER FIVE

For a barbarian with addled wits, Crisk is a useful hand when it comes to sailing a ship.

Kheda watched the scrawny redhead climbing deftly up the ladder of ropes that ran from the deck to the top of the vessel's swaying mast. Crisk showed no hesitation as he swung into the barrel-like perch for a lookout that crowned it.

Does he believe his barbarian gods will save him if he falls? Or whatever it is he thinks he sees in the earthly and heavenly compasses?

Kheda applied himself to adjusting the cables that governed the cant of the vast triangular sail. The creamy canvas hung from an angled spar deftly made from two long, overlapping timbers and centred on the top of the mast. Laid on the deck, it would have been longer than the whole ship. He looked up again to see Crisk leaning forward at a perilous angle, his unkempt hair tousled by the wind.

Or is he just too stupid to fear the drop?

'You don't like heights?' Sirince was standing a few paces behind Kheda, beside the wooden tiller that governed the ship's steering oar via a complicated series of ropes and pulleys.

'No,' Kheda said tersely. He glanced up at the stern platform atop the rear of the deck. It jutted out over the ship's stern, reached by a couple of steps. The space beneath was too cramped and confined to be used as a cabin as was the custom on larger ships. Here there were merely storage lockers tucked beneath it. Nor were there any separate quarters below decks, just a single long hold that ran from the ship's prow to its stern.

'This is the edge of the outermost group of islands claimed by Matul Saib.' Velindre was up on the stern platform, intent on some page of her mariners' route book. 'We have open water to the north and rocky reefs to the south.' Beside her, a slim flagstaff fluttered with the pennants identifying those domains where Sirince had leave to sail.

Which I cannot identify, since I know less of these reaches than anyone else on this ship, with the possible exception of a halfwit. And Crisk knows more than me about sailing this ship, since it's so different from the ones we build in southern waters. I've never seen anything like that tiller contrivance.

'You don't mind giving over mastery of your ship to Velindre?' he asked the older wizard.

'She has better records of these reaches than me. Besides, a ship is just a ship.' Sirince shrugged his broad shoulders. 'It's a means to an end, a way to get from place to place.' He surprised Kheda with a grin that lifted years from his lined face. 'If she wanted to ride my favourite horse, or hunt with my stag hounds, that would be a very different matter.'

'I know nothing of horses.' Kheda shrugged. 'But we have fine hounds in the southern domains, longer in the leg than the ones hereabouts, and broader in the chest. We hunt hook-toothed hogs with them, and forest deer.'

'On foot?' Sirince looked interested. 'I'm more used to chasing beasts down on horseback over the open plains.'

He would have continued but Risala emerged from the jutting hatch that protruded from the deck. She ducked her head to avoid the edge of the housing that sheltered the fixed ladder leading down below decks. Taking in

Kheda and Sirince, and seeing Velindre up on the stern platform, she looked around for Crisk:

'He's aloft.' Kheda gestured towards the top of the mast.

Risala squinted upwards, the sunlight barely softened by the persistent high-level haze. The air was far clearer than it had been ashore. 'Who is Crisk, Sirince?'

'Over to windward, if you please,' Velindre called down sharply from the stern deck. 'There's a great galley bearing down on us.'

How fortunate for you, Sirince. Once again you can avoid the question you've been so assiduously refusing to answer these past three days.

Kheda moved to the rail so he could see past the shallow forecastle built out over the ship's blunt prow. A sizeable number of ships were crowded into this stretch of safe water between the hazards of the rocks and the open ocean where the sheering winds from the north could make a plaything of the biggest ships. Most vessels were open galleys with a single tier of oars, or single-masters like Sirince's. A few were the great galleys favoured by the most prosperous merchants. Every ship Kheda could see was coming towards them.

'Are these vessels fleeing Zelin waters on the dragon's account?' Risala came to stand beside him. On board ship she had packed her poet's gown away in favour of faded black trousers and a tunic once bold red, now faded to a soft rose.

'Perhaps we'll find out when we get to this outlying Matul trading isle that Sirince talks of.' Kheda rubbed a hand over his beard. 'Hopefully then we'll learn exactly where the beast is.'

'Crisk says we'll find it when the Lesser Moon has passed through its conjunction with the Ruby and the Greater Moon has reached the arc of foes.' Risala looked up to the masthead. 'Sirince, what can you tell us about him?'

To Kheda's surprise, the older wizard finally obliged Risala with an answer.

'I don't really know that much.' He adjusted the ship's course a fraction as the great galley that Velindre had indicated plunged through the rolling swell towards them. 'I came across him just after the turn of the year – our year, not yours. He wasn't speaking, he barely ate or drank.' The mage shook his head reflectively. 'He would stay quiet for days at a time and then turn on someone, hurting himself more than he hurt them. That's what they said, anyway.'

'Who?' asked Kheda.

'The slavers who had him.' Sirince shrugged. 'He was recovering from a beating he'd taken for disturbing some potential customers with one of his prophecies. I bought him, to save him from having his throat cut so they didn't have to feed him any more.'

'He was willing to come with you?' Kheda found that surprising.

'Have you had a close look at that amulet of his?' Sirince smiled as Kheda and Risala both shook their heads. 'No, well, he doesn't let many people see it. There's an owl on it.' He waved a hand around the deck. 'And this ship is the *Tacsille*—'

'The great banded owl that hunts in the cloud forests.' Kheda nodded his understanding.

'That's a plain enough omen.' Risala went to sit on the edge of the stern platform. She drew up her feet and hugged her knees. 'Crisk talks to you now, when he's not talking to those strange gods of his.'

'He still doesn't make much sense.' Sirince grinned, not unkindly. 'His accent tells me he was born somewhere in Ensaimin. That's a broad land far to the north of here.

I've no idea how he came to be chained in an Aldabreshin slave market. Or what abuses left him such a hollow mockery of a man,' he added soberly. 'But something convinced him Trimon saved him. That brings him some comfort.'

Kheda cleared his throat. 'Just what is your business in the slave markets?'

'I buy slaves.' There was an edge to Sirince's voice. 'Specifically, I buy men, women and children who've been seized from the coasts of Ensaimin and Caladhria by the corsairs who trade them on to the warlords of these western reaches for such handsome profit.'

'Corsairs?' Risala was puzzled.

'They've always preyed on the coastal villages.' Sirince sighed and his years seemed to weigh heavily on him. 'They have shallow galleys that they row close inshore and far up into the river mouths. They used simply to attack the villages, to steal anything of value and burn the houses to the ground. They'd carry off anyone too slow to flee, to be sold as slaves. Only now they don't burn the houses and they're careful not to steal too much. They've learned if they don't destroy the villages, people will always return to be plundered anew the next season.' He grimaced. 'There are times when optimism is an over-rated virtue. They take more people every year to feed the insatiable demand for slaves in the northern and western domains.'

'Your barbarian lords aren't doing anything to stop them?' Kheda challenged.

'By the time some baron receives word of a raid, the corsairs are long gone.' Sirince turned a sardonic eye on Kheda. 'Sailing back to the comfortable and ferociously well-defended lairs they have built themselves in the outlying islands of the Nahik domain, or so my inform-ants tell me.'

'Nahik Jarir permits this?' Risala was plainly troubled.

'Why shouldn't he?' Sirince's expression softened as he looked at her. 'Apart from anything else, they scour his islands and the other northerly domains for fugitive slaves. Otherwise runaways would lair up in the mountains and hidden valleys, striking out to raid and to rape his innocent islanders.'

'The trade has gone on for more years than anyone can count,' Velindre said caustically from her vantage point. 'You Aldabreshin don't use coin as we do on the mainland, so we must trade by supplying something that you want and we have. Surplus bodies have long been supplied by captives from the Lescari civil wars or unfortunates taken into debt-bondage, a charming custom held over from the days of the Old Tormalin Empire.'

Sirince nodded. 'But now the Lescari wars are at an impasse and Tormalin sensibilities have decided to be outraged at the idea that even the least of their people should be made subject to barbarians. So the slaves have to come from somewhere else.'

Risala was looking uncertain.

Kheda pressed his lips together.

Can you say mainlanders enslaved in such a fashion are thus proven unable to read the omens that would have saved them from such a fate?

Sirince continued robustly. 'Besides, the corsairs pay Nahik Jarir a handsome tribute and their fighting galleys defend his ships as well as their own.'

'There are plenty of mainland pirates who sally forth from hidden coves between Claithe, Attar and Markyate,' Velindre explained. 'They plunder Archipelagan galleys plying the sea lanes to Relshaz or up to the ports in the Gulf of Peorle.'

I've no idea where any of these places are, never mind what manner of people might live in them.

Kheda fixed on a more immediate question. 'You talk of this Archipelagan demand for barbarian slaves being insatiable. Why is that?'

'Matul Saib wants all the labourers he can get his hands on to build that mighty folly of a residence.' Sirince's eyes hardened. 'Given that his overseers see no need to treat contemptible barbarians with anything but brutality and starvation rations, they die all too fast.'

'One man's obsession is hardly the whole story,' Velindre objected. 'Cultivating silkworms demands countless hands.' She waved an arm towards the green blur that was the Matul islands far to the south. 'Gathering the cocoons, steaming them, unrolling them, twisting the thread – every task takes deft fingers or strong backs, and that's before you've even begun weaving or dyeing. Then there are all the other crafts of these reaches, the glass-making and ceramics. If slaves do all the tedious tasks, the Aldabreshin islanders are free to concentrate on more skilled work.'

Kheda was troubled. 'We have none of this in the southern domains.'

His words were lost in the rushing of waves and winds as the great galley swept past them. Its broad, square sails were furled on its three towering masts in these contrary breezes. No matter; triple ranks of long oars drove it speedily through the water, heedless of the weight of goods stowed in its deep holds. Faintly, Kheda could just hear the regular piping guiding the strokes of the oarsmen hidden in the wide middle deck.

When I came north the first time as an anonymous rower on such a ship, I never learned half the strange customs of these reaches.

The *Tacsille* rocked violently as the galley's wide wake spread choppy white foam around them. Risala set her feet down on the deck and gripped the edge of the stern platform where she sat. Sirince held tight to the tiller, shifting his stance to keep his balance. Kheda grasped a cable firmly belayed to the ship's rail and saw Velindre bracing herself with one hand on the pennant staff.

A noise like coral gulls made him look up. It was Crisk, one hand barely resting on the rim of the lookout post, his other hand waving wildly at the departing galley. The breeze snatched away his gleeful crowing.

'Sirince, just what do you do with these slaves that you buy?' Velindre enquired distantly.

'I take them home,' the wizard said simply.

'To Hadrumal?' Kheda wondered where this piece of the puzzle might lead. 'At the behest of this Archmage to whom you all defer?'

Not that Dev seemed to owe him much fealty, and Velindre largely calculates her obedience to suit her own interests.

'Planir has little interest in such matters.' Sirince chuckled. 'There are lords on the mainland who feel sufficient obligation to their tenants and liegemen to ransom relatives they've had stolen away. Though I'll do my best to rescue any unfortunates who truly deserve my compassion.' He slid a sideways look to Kheda. 'There are some who warrant all the punishment an overseer can dish out for whatever crimes landed them in chains in Relshaz's slave market.'

Risala looked up to the top of the mast again. 'Will you take Crisk home?'

'I've no idea where his home might be,' Sirince reminded her. 'I've called in several mainland ports since I took him on and he won't even set foot ashore. He just sits and weeps and clings to his amulet.'

'It might be preferable that his people think him dead rather than have him restored to them in such a pitiful state.' Kheda voiced the thought aloud.

'It may be that Artifice can bring him back to himself,' mused Sirince.

Kheda frowned. 'I don't understand.'

'The magic of mind and memory,' Sirince elaborated, 'rather than that of the elements.'

'They don't know what you're talking about,' Velindre said up on the stern platform. 'I didn't feel the need to confuse them with such things.'

'Perhaps you would be good enough to explain,' Kheda said, somewhat curtly.

'The magic that I use, that Velindre uses, focuses on the manipulation of air, earth, fire and water – you understand that much?' Sirince didn't wait for an answer before continuing. 'There is another magic used on the mainland, a magic of mind speaking to mind, be it willing or unwilling. Its most advanced practitioners can also affect the physical world all around and keep themselves unaffected by such things. It's known as Artifice.'

'You didn't think to tell us about this?' Kheda glanced up at Velindre.

'Tell me an occasion when you would have benefited from knowing about it,' she invited, unrepentant.

A grin spread across Sirince's face to deepen the wrinkles around his eyes. 'There are those on the mainland who speculate that Aldabreshin auguries are a manifestation of some kind of magic, though you would never call it such. There's debate among scholars as to whether such portents partake of elemental magic, or Artifice, or sorcery of some third nature as yet unguessed at.'

'That's ridiculous.' Risala was outraged.

'Which is what other scholars say,' agreed Sirince. 'They have the highest regard for Aldabreshin skills with mathematics and stargazing and navigation and much else besides. They lament that we mainlanders are still shackled by the superstitions of magic, old and new.' He shrugged. 'Of course, they'd prefer it if Archipelagans would also give up superstitions about omens and truly embrace the clear-sightedness of true rationalism.'

Kheda stared at the mage. 'I have no idea what you're talking about.'

Every day something makes my ignorance seem as boundless as the ocean.

'Forgive me, I'm indulging myself.' Sirince looked mildly apologetic. 'I'm a long way from home and I'm on a boat, which never does much for my mood.'

But you sail these waters for the sake of innocents who have no one else to save them. And you feel obliged to make good the transgressions of all other wizards, as Naldeth did. But Dev didn't. It seems wizards vary as much as any other men or women.

'Show Kheda how to steer this tub and you can get some rest.' The magewoman was leafing through her leather-bound route record again. There was colour in her cheeks and her eyes were bright. 'You can leave the rest to me.'

'Because you are in your element, aren't you, with the winds all around you?' Sirince made no move to offer the *Tacsille*'s tiller to Kheda.

'I'll be happy to take a turn at whatever tasks you care to give me,' he assured the mage.

'As will I,' Risala added.

'We should reach that trading beach well before dusk.' Velindre shut her book with a decisive snap. 'You'll feel better with your feet on solid ground again.'

'Do you suppose we'll get any news of the dragon ashore?' Kheda wondered.

Frustration hardened Velindre's gaunt face. 'I wish I dared scry for the beast.'

'You said we were too close,' Kheda reminded her sharply.

'I wouldn't mind seeing just how it can look back at

us through a magic not of its own making,' Sirince said thoughtfully.

'That's how Dev had his ship sunk beneath us.' Kheda shivered at the recollection of a fire dragon's feral intelligence staring back at him through ensorcelled steel.

'I won't risk this vessel, not when it's the only one we've got,' Velindre assured him. She sighed. 'I daren't even keep these perverse winds in the right quarter with a little judicious magic, just in case the dragon sniffs something on the breeze. We'd have made far better time if we still had the *Zaise*. It was built for these waters—'

'Sirince!' Crisk shrieked from the top of the mast.

'What is it?' Sirince's gaze snapped upwards.

Crisk was scrambling over the rim of the lookout post with a recklessness that made Kheda catch his breath. He slid down the rope ladder and somehow made it to the deck without breaking his neck. 'There's a ship. It's hunting us.' He clung to Sirince's forearm.

'There are a lot of ships in these waters.' Sirince held the tiller one-handed as he patted Crisk's shoulder reassuringly. 'Velindre, can you see what he's talking about?'

She drew herself up to her full height on the stern platform. 'There's a fast trireme following those last few trading ships. It's flying a Zelin pennant.' She paused, mouth half-open. 'It is heading this way. He's right about that much.'

Crisk sank to the deck, pressing himself into the angle between the planks and the stern platform. 'The Horned Fish is sailing with death,' he muttered ominously. 'Poldrion sculls his ferryboat.'

Kheda watched the last of the lesser ships curl away southward, heading for the more sheltered channels that divided these outlying islands of the Matul domain. The trireme continued cutting a straight course in their direction.

'I can hardly use magic to drive it off.' Velindre surprised him with a mirthless laugh. 'Not without running the risk of attracting the dragon.'

'It's probably just escorting those ships that are leaving Zelin waters.' Sirince smiled reassurance at Crisk. 'They must have decided to ask us our business, since we're the only ship they can see heading west.'

'What exactly is our business hereabouts?' Risala was on her feet by the side rail, trying to see past the fore-castle.

'You three are scholar, poet and slave trader.' Kheda then indicated himself and Crisk, a wry twist to his mouth. 'While we two are slaves, of no account as we have no business having any business.'

His attempt at light-heartedness was drowned out by a brazen clamour from the trireme.

'That's our signal to stop,' Velindre said with resignation. 'Spill the wind.'

Risala was already moving to the pulleys to alter the angle of the vast sail. Kheda pulled on the ropes that ran the length of the vessel to govern the long spar's tip, angled down to reach out beyond the prow. The creamy expanse of canvas flapped disconsolately and the *Tacsille* wallowed in the swell, ungainly as an owl waddling along the ground.

Lithe and sleek, the trireme bore down on them, oar strokes flashing in the water, at twice the speed of the great galley. The single mast had been stowed so nothing interrupted the smooth sweep of the unrailed upper decks that served both to shade the rowers on either side and offer a fighting platform for the archers and swordsmen standing ready.

'They're just showing us their seamanship.' Kheda took the steps up to the stern platform two at a time. 'To intim-idate us.'

Risala followed close beside him. 'Can we signal to tell them it's working?'

The trireme's stern timbers curled up behind the high seat where shipmaster and helmsman sat, their view ahead unobstructed by the single slim pillar at the prow. Beneath that the brass-sheathed ram nosed forward. Cross-timbers jutted out to either side to protect the foremost oars whenever that ram ripped into the planking of some enemy ship, to cripple or to sink it. As they watched, the trireme accelerated rather than slowing, the murderous ram cutting through the water with a ruffle of white foam.

Running with a bone in its teeth. That's what my ship-master Jatta called it.

Kheda's heart pounded in his chest as the trireme bore down on them.

The penetrating note of the piper down on the oar deck was lost beneath the rising chant of rowers adding their own menace to the attack. Then a single shout rang out and the oars bit deep into the green sea. The trireme shuddered from stem to stern and the oars lifted high, only to plunge down once more as the rowers set the trireme precisely beside the *Tacsille*. Kheda found he was virtually on eye level with the topmost rank of oarsmen, unsmiling in the shade beneath the side-deck.

'Who is your shipmaster and what is the name of this vessel?' An armoured man strode forward from the trireme's stern platform, one hand in a gauntlet of leather and steel resting on the hilt of the sword thrust through his double-looped leather belt. Bronze links patterning the chain mail of his hauberk gleamed in the sun. He wore a close-fitting helm with a veil of polished chain mail hanging from the brass brow band but had not yet lowered the face plate that slid down the nasal bar. He was tall, a pure-blooded man of the western isles with ebony skin and broad features, his beard little more than a shadow. His dark eyes were keenly intelligent.

'My name is Sirince and I trade in barbarian slaves. My word is good throughout the many domains that have granted me leave to sail their sea lanes, as you see from the pennants we fly. My ship is the *Tacsille*.' Sirince bowed as best he could, wrestling with the tiller. The steering oar was being pulled this way and that by the unhelpful swell and the gap between the two vessels was narrowing.

It would certainly be best if we didn't inadvertently smash any of the trireme's oars.

Kheda noticed that the armoured captain of the trireme's warriors was looking at Velindre, who was still holding her route record in one hand. The trireme's steersman and shipmaster had their heads close together, discussing something, their eyes similarly fixed on Velindre.

'Who are the rest of you?' the sword-captain shouted peremptorily.

Velindre cleared her throat. 'My name is Vel. I am a scholar.'

'I am Risala, a poet once apprenticed to Haytar the Blind.' She spread her arms wide and bowed with a graceful flourish of her hands.

Kheda eyed the swordsmen looking down on them. All were armed with single blades and wearing tunics of studded leather. One of the archers in the trireme's prow nocked an arrow on his bowstring, unsmiling.

'And these others?' The captain spared Kheda little more than a cursory glance before fixing his gaze on Crisk. The red-headed mainlander was still cowering on the deck, hiding his face in his shoulder and muttering in his unknown tongue.

'Slaves.' Sirince murmured something to calm Crisk that Kheda didn't hear.

'The barbarian is a simpleton.' Velindre spoke up with

a nice blend of disdain and sympathy. 'I am travelling to discover what seers and soothsayers make of the omens to be read in his ravings.'

'We are heading for the trading beach on the treaty isle beyond Naia.' Sirince gestured towards the flagstaff up on the stern. 'I have the pennant that permits me passage.'

'That beach has been cleared of all ships and merchants.' The sword-captain's hand flexed in its gauntlet. 'By order of Zelin Raes.'

'But we are still in Matul waters,' Velindre protested sharply. 'And a treaty isle is open to all.'

A swell abruptly drove them an arm's length closer to the trireme's vulnerable oars.

The sword-captain scowled at her. 'Zelin Raes's writ reaches this far just at present.'

Sirince tried a mollifying smile on the warrior. 'Then we will take ourselves to other waters if your lord's are closed to us.'

The captain snapped his head around towards the trireme's prow. 'Take them!'

A handful of warriors jumped across the narrow stretch of water now separating the two boats. Landing in a crouch, they immediately sprang upright, their swords already drawn. One grinned at them with horrible triumph.

So you were only keeping us talking long enough to get close enough.

Kheda kept his face impassive, nevertheless moving to put himself between the swordsmen and Risala. He noticed Velindre slip her hand beneath her tunic to slide her precious route record into the wide pocket sewn inside the waistband of her trousers.

'We can turn about and go back the way we came,' Sirince protested, raising a hand in surrender. Crisk was still cowering on the deck, clutching at his tarnished amulet. The wizard backed away from the tiller as one of the swordsmen approached. 'You can have no reason to—'

'You have a yellow-headed *zamorin* scholar on your ship, together with a poet girl who claims to have been apprenticed to Haytar the Blind.' There was an ominous note in the sword-captain's voice. 'That's reason enough. Search below decks,' he shouted to his men.

The warrior standing by the tiller jerked his head at Sirince. 'Up on the stern with you, you and the halfwit.' He looked up at the rest of them. 'Make no trouble and you won't get hurt.'

Risala jumped down to help Sirince, doing her best to soothe Crisk with soft words. The scrawny barbarian was grizzling like a child terrified beyond bearing. Two swordsmen went below, leaving one taking command of the tiller and another addressing himself to the flapping sail.

'You've got a bold eye for a slave.' The remaining swordsman fixed Kheda with a stern look. 'Don't try anything foolish.'

'I won't, believe me.' Kheda held his hands wide, well away from the dagger on his belt as he took the steps up onto the stern platform.

Is there anything incriminating down below? Risala has her scrolls and her dress; that's only to be expected of a poet. Velindre has nothing to identify her as a mage and she holds enough lore in her head to prove her claim to be a scholar. But there are precious few slaves who would be carrying the array of salves and tinctures that I have in my bag. Will they believe me if I tell them we do things differently in the south?

Everyone stood still, for a seemingly interminable time. The wind teased Kheda's tunic and dried the sweat on his brow. The only sound was the lapping of the sea and the soft splashing as the trireme's oarsmen kept the two ships precisely aligned. That and Crisk's keening as he sat huddled between Risala and Sirince.

'Can't you shut him up?' the swordsman down on the deck asked, more pitying than irritated.

'Pray to Trimon for us, Crisk,' Sirince suggested, 'to safeguard us on this voyage.'

The red-headed man fell silent and fixed the Zelin warrior with a baleful eye. 'Raeponin rewards the just and chastises the unjust.'

'What did he say?' The swordsman frowned.

'Nothing,' Kheda said hastily. 'Just mainlander nonsense.'

To his relief, Crisk said no more before beginning his repetitive, unintelligible muttering under his breath.

The two Zelin warriors who had gone below emerged from the hatch. 'There's nothing down there but pallets and foodstuffs,' one reported, shrugging.

'A few barrels of broken shackles and chains,' the other added.

'There's always a smith on any trading beach,' Sirince began equably, 'willing to trade for old iron, what with ores being so rare in the Archipelago—'

'I found these, though.' The first warrior reached into the folds of his open-fronted tunic and pulled out a wash-leather bag. 'Rubies. At least, I think they are,' he qualified doubtfully, unknotting the drawstring.

'I told you, I trade for slaves. I wouldn't get far trading old iron for them.'

Kheda hoped the Zelin men would mistake the strain in Sirince's voice for outrage rather than fear.

'We are not thieves, master slaver.' Up on the trireme's deck the sword-captain glowered at the warrior, who hastily retied the drawstring. The warrior handed the bag to the swordsman who had been keeping watch on them.

'Your passengers are of interest to my master. Perhaps they are thieves. What do you know of them?'

'We met on the beaches outside Matul Saib's residence.' Sirince licked his lips, his eyes flickering to the bag of gems in the warrior's hand. 'They wanted passage—'

'You must have heard word that there was a dragon in these waters.' The sword-captain looked down scathingly. 'What persuaded you to sail west with that news in the wind?'

'Rubies.' Sirince looked sideways at Velindre with a nice blend of chagrin and accusation. 'I was only going to take them as far as the trading beach. Not into Zelin waters.'

'Since he's failed in that, I'll ask you to return those rubies to us,' Risala broke in with a defiant toss of her head.

The sword-captain ignored her. 'Abari, you sail on ahead. We'll follow.'

The swordsman who seemed to be in charge acknowledged his order with a brief nod. 'My captain.'

'Where are you taking us?' Sirince protested.

But the trireme was already pulling away, the sword-captain striding easily along the unrailed deck to rejoin the shipmaster and helmsman in the stern.

'To my lord Zelin Raes's dry-season residence.' The warrior, Abari, was still holding the rubies. 'Which is further west than you were intending on taking your passengers, so I reckon you've earned these.' He tossed the bag of gems up to Sirince in the stern.

Risala intercepted them with a swift snatch. 'I don't believe so.'

'You'd cheat him?' Angered, Abari took a step forward.

'We can settle this later.' Kheda hoped the swordsman's irritation with Risala had prevented him from noticing that Sirince hadn't raised a hand to catch the bag himself. Or his look of relief and gratitude when she had plucked the rubies out of the air.

Abari shot Kheda a curious look before turning to his companion at the tiller. 'Insefi, get your course straight before the *Reef Shark* comes snapping at our heels.' He gestured towards the trireme, which was swiftly turning itself around, barely taking more than its own length to do so.

'What do we do now?' Velindre murmured to Kheda in mainlander Tormalin.

'You sit quietly and you make no trouble,' Abari told her in the same tongue. 'And you can show me that book you were holding.'

Velindre hesitated before reluctantly reaching inside the waistband of her loose trousers. 'It's my route record.'

Kheda breathed a little more easily.

You don't want to be searched and have these men discover your zamorin *clothes are deception. We're in enough trouble already.*

Abari leafed through the pages before glancing at Sirince. 'You said you were this ship's master.'

'He is.' Velindre's voice was taut. 'I used to have my own ship. We were wrecked.'

'You're not having much luck reading the omens in the halfwit's ravings, then.' Abari closed the leather-bound book and handed it back.

Crisk looked up suddenly. 'Sharks are treacherous and tricksters.'

'I am a scholar, not a soothsayer.' Velindre spoke over him.

'So you say.' Abari didn't hide his scepticism. 'You can go below now if you wish. Make any trouble and I'll have Insefi find something in that barrel of broken shackles to chain you all up with.' He glanced at Crisk but said nothing more.

'We'll go below.' Sirince and Risala got Crisk to his feet between them and led the hollow-eyed man to the deck and then down the ladder into the long hold. Risala was still clutching the bag of rubies.

Velindre didn't move so neither did Kheda.

'What is it about those gems that affects Sirince so?' he asked under his breath.

'We're not entirely sure—' She broke off as one of the as-yet-unnamed swordsmen joined them on the stern platform.

'I'm Gedai,' he announced briskly. 'We're not to kill you, but we are allowed to knock you senseless.'

'Then we'll cooperate and you'll have no reason to do so.' Kheda shared a glance with Velindre and they both sat down on the polished planks.

Abari and his men proved as skilled at sailing the *Tacsille* as the *Reef Shark*'s rowers were at keeping a constant distance behind them. As the sun slowly marked the tedious passage of the day, Kheda surveyed the sea as unobtrusively as he could. From time to time a distant sail skimmed the white-capped swell but no vessel came anywhere close to them.

As noon slid past, Risala emerged from the hold with bowls of spiced finger-fish preserved in oil and the pickled shoots of some vegetable Kheda had yet to identify. There was the last handful of the wilted green leaves of a plant akin to reckal, though the leaves were sweetly peppery rather than bitter. Quite docile now, Crisk followed with a bowl piled high with the leathery saller-flour flatbreads prevalent in these reaches. Together they served the four men on the main deck. Kheda watched keenly but none of the warriors seemed to be regarding Risala with any particular interest, let alone lust.

Kheda took care not to look at Velindre as Risala and Crisk stood at the steps and offered food up to Gedai.

The bowl holding the flatbreads was the magewoman's scrying vessel.

Once the warrior had served himself, Velindre didn't wait to be invited. 'Forgive our paltry hospitality,' she said sardonically as she picked up a flatbread and wrapped it around a glistening fillet of fish.

'Eat while you can.' Gedai grinned around his own mouthful. 'If my lord Zelin Raes doesn't like what you have to tell him, you'll be going hungry till you find some better answers.'

Velindre licked at spiced oil trickling from a tear in the flatbread. 'How long until we can present ourselves before him, and be on our way?'

'Soon enough.' Gedai studied Kheda as he came up to claim a share of the food. 'You look well fed, for a slave.'

'Slaves are treated differently in the southern reaches.' Kheda kept his gaze lowered, looking out at the ocean as he ate.

They were moving well beyond the outlying isles of the Matul domain, out into the open seas. Winds and currents ran contrary, demanding all the attention of Abari and his men if the *Tacsille* were not to be wrenched off course. The *Reef Shark* followed on behind, her rowers scorning such difficulties.

'Make yourself useful.' Abari looked up from wrestling with the tiller. 'Both of you.'

Kheda and Velindre obediently rose at the jerk of Gedai's head. Kheda was perversely amused to see the magewoman meekly following orders from Insefi and the other warriors. There was little time to spare for such diversion as they sailed on, as Abari was plainly determined to wring every scrap of speed out of the *Tacsille*. As the seas rose and the winds settled on their northern flank, Risala and Sirince were called up from below and pressed into service. Crisk just followed the mage around, largely ignored by the Zelin mariners.

'The recommended crossings between Zelin and Matul are either considerably to the south of here, or quite some distance to the north,' Velindre observed as her path crossed Kheda's.

Insefi overheard her. 'My lord will want you and that poet girl brought before him as soon as possible.'

What happens then? What can I do, a mere slave?

By the time dusk softened the light and the sun slid down to gild the western sky, Kheda was exhausted. As Abari barked yet another set of rapid orders from his station by the tiller, Risala fumbled with a pulley and the vast sail snapped angrily.

'You're not much of a sailor,' Gedai observed tartly as he hurried to recover the situation.

'She has an injured wrist.' Kheda recollected himself as he saw his sharp tone surprise the warrior. He tried to sound more humble. 'We have different ships in the south. We're none of us used to this rigging. And I was a rower, not a sailor.' He held up one hand, callus scars from his temporary sojourn at a galley's oar still just about visible.

'Were you now?' Gedai frowned at him and went to say something to Abari, hiding his words behind a raised hand.

Abari stared at Kheda for a long moment before turning his attention back to the tiller.

'What was that about?' Risala came over to Kheda.

'I have no idea,' he said with disquiet. 'It will be night soon. Do you think we should try—'

'What?' she asked, her wry glance around the deck taking in all five of their sword-carrying guards.

'I have no idea,' he admitted. 'Does your wrist hurt?'

'It aches,' she admitted tightly.

Rather than heave to as dark fell, the warriors kept the

Tacsille sailing on. The *Reef Shark* accelerated for a short stretch to draw ahead of the sailing vessel, a massive lantern hauled high on her stern timbers for them to follow. Soon Kheda heard the sound of surf on unseen beaches out in the blackness. There was no sign of any village's cookfires or lamps ashore.

Has everyone fled, just like the people of Chazen when the wild men first fell upon them? Or have they doused their lights for fear the dragon will see them if it flies overhead? Where is the beast? But we cannot ask any of these men without betraying our interest in it, and I cannot see how that could possibly help us.

Belatedly Abari announced it was time to eat and his men helped themselves from the *Tacsille*'s stores, hauled haphazard from the storage space beneath the stern platform. Kheda chewed on a leathery flatbread wrapped around morsels of smoked duck and highly spiced pickled chola stems as he looked up to see where the moons might be. He found the night wasn't even half over.

They must truly believe Zelin Raes wants to see us as soon as possible if they're prepared to risk sailing with the Lesser Moon only at its first glimmer and the Greater fading fast. What omens might have shown us this turn of events?

'Looking for some hopeful sign in the heavenly compass, are you?' Insefi appeared out of the shadows. 'Best of luck. You can go below.' He gestured towards the hatch housing. 'Sleep, if you can. You'll want all your wits about you when you're brought before my lord.'

'Thank you,' Kheda said curtly.

Down in the hold, a single lantern swayed on a central hook. Slatted shutters on all its faces muted its light. Crisk was already asleep, curled up in a nest of quilts. Sirince was stretched out beside him, lying on his back, his hands behind his head. Velindre and Risala were still settling themselves.

Kheda shook out a thick quilt to save his bones from the bare boards. 'Try not to snore,' he asked the mage-woman with a faint smile.

Sirince spoke up from the shadows. 'Didn't Otrick ever say anything about that, Velindre?' His face drawn, once again he was looking every year of his age.

The magewoman said something in rapid Tormalin that Kheda did not catch before dropping down to wrap herself in a quilt. She turned her back on Sirince, stiff with affront.

What was that all about?

Risala looked at Kheda and he saw the same question in her eyes.

'Do you want some poppy syrup?' he asked quietly. 'For your wrist?'

She sighed and shook her head. 'I think I'd better keep all my wits about me tonight.'

They settled themselves slowly, lying close though not quite touching. Kheda drew a deep breath and tried to put the myriad questions tormenting him out of his mind. Some while later, as he sank towards sleep, he felt Risala's hand steal into his own. He held her fingers tight.

Never mind what the moons might have to say for them-selves. We have to face whatever tomorrow brings.

CHAPTER SIX

Ari was sound asleep when the front panel of his tent was ripped open. In the next instant he was on his feet, wide awake, the long knives in both his hands as naked as he was. The mingled light of the two quarter moons silvered his muscular torso before he stepped back into the shadows. Invisible, his bare feet were inaudible on the thick carpets.

'It's me,' Hasu hissed with suppressed irritation.

'Then why charge in like a thief in the night?' Ari hastily pulled on his purple robe as he passed through the moonlight once more. 'Do you want the birds to break their flight feathers in a frenzy?' As harsh as his words were, his voice was a soothing caress as he reassured the sleepily fluttering doves.

Hasu yawned. 'You'll want them ready to fly at first light.'

'Which ones?' Ari kept his voice low as he looked warily outside. 'Who saw you rushing back here like a goose with its tailfeathers on fire?'

'All anyone saw was me strolling back with my robe over my shoulder.' Hasu tossed the crumpled garment into the shadows. 'If anyone has been watching me, all they'll have to tell is I left that Zelin galley captain's daughter with a smile on her face after pleasuring her in ways few other men will ever equal.' Satisfaction hung around him along with the odour of cooling sweat and recent sex.

'So what did she trade for that?' Ari asked with a grin.

Now it was Hasu who glanced out of the open tent panel to be sure there were no curious ears in the darkness beneath the nut palms that fringed this traders' camping ground. He drew close to Ari, his lips almost brushing the older man's long tousled hair. 'She told me there's a dragon in Zelin waters.'

'What?' Ari had been looking down to tie his robe closed. He looked up, astonished, the forgotten silk hanging loose around his powerful thighs.

Hasu nodded just once. 'They were visiting Matul Saib's dry-season residence when the word spread. There was a riot. A mob went to kill any barbarian slaves they could lay hand on – seers were saying any taint of magic from the unbroken lands might draw the beast. The islanders besieged the new walls of that residence their lord's building. They were demanding he explain such a portent, begging him come and read the omens for them.'

Ari drew on a pair of trousers, tying his robe with a swift knot in his sash. 'Did he oblige?'

'No.' Hasu moved unerringly to a chest in the darkness on the far side of the tent. 'Do you want a lamp?'

'Yes.' Ari was searching in the confusion of quilts where he had been sleeping to retrieve his writing box. 'He didn't show himself at all, not even to deny such news?'

'No one saw a hair of his curly head.' Hasu opened the chest and carefully lifted out a sturdy glass globe. Green-gold oil sloshed in the bottom. 'But as soon as his swordsmen had beaten everyone back, word went out that all Zelin ships were to quit the anchorage, by his order. The next day he decreed all Zelin ships were to leave Matul waters completely.'

'That decree hasn't reached this anchorage yet,' mused Ari, curious.

'Word will come on the next trireme,' Hasu assured

him. 'That Zelin galley's oarsmen have rowed themselves near to collapse to get here ahead of the news. The girl's father is desperate to trade their cargo for as much food and water as he can. That's all he wants.'

'Which means no one will be interested in our beads and trinkets.' Ari scowled as he combed his beard into some semblance of order with deft fingers. 'So you had better let the spokesmen of all the villages around here know this news, before they hear it from someone else. We need something to our credit on the positive side of the ledger. Where are they heading, this galley master and his obliging daughter? Is there anything in their plans to add value to the news I send our esteemed clients?'

'They're heading for Penik waters.' Taking a spark-maker from the chest, Hasu flicked the toothed steel wheel against a scrap of flint to light a bent and broken taper. 'If they're not welcome there, they'll go south to Dawa.' Using the tip of his dagger, he lifted the length of wick anchored to a loop of thicker glass in the very bottom of the globe. Lighting it carefully, he let the flame fall back to float on the puddle of oil.

'And after that?' Ari's brow wrinkled as he contemplated the unknown galley's options. 'What's this ship's name?'

'The *Lightning Fly*.' Hasu shook his head, half-disbelieving. 'If Dawa Trin declares them unwelcome for fear of the dragon, she says her father will sail east across the Dawa Sea in hopes of reaching safety in Senana or Vadnil.'

'That's madness.' Ari sat cross-legged on the floor, setting out his writing materials in the golden glow of the glass globe.

'She said her father had put it to the whole crew.' Hasu's handsome face was uncharacteristically solemn. 'They're all agreed that if a dragon is devastating Zelin and they can find no anchorage in the western reaches for fear of its taint following them, they must risk themselves against the currents. If they live, they'll throw themselves on Senana Iresh's mercy, or Vadnil Yesk's. Because if they can make the crossing, that must surely mean they're fated to live rather than die beneath the dragon's shadow.' Hasu shivered as if a sudden draught had chilled him, but the night air was still and humid.

'That's a bold wager to make against the future.' Ari swatted viciously at a gnat drawn to the lamp. 'Keep watch. There may be people awake enough to be curious as to why we're showing a light.'

Hasu caught up a sword from the darkness and moved to stand hidden in the shadows by the tent's opening. 'What does it mean?'

'That Matul Saib didn't deny the news?' Ari wrote swiftly, squinting in the dim light. 'It means that it's true, my lad.'

'I know that much,' Hasu retorted with some irritation. 'No. What does it mean that a dragon has come to these reaches?'

'It means we must have these birds ready to fly by false dawn, if we can persuade them to oblige us that early.' Ari was swapping one slip of paper for another, wet ink gleaming in the lamplight. 'Our most prized clients will reward us handsomely for this night's work.' He paused to remove two rings from one finger to enable him to slip off the third, a battered circle of silver set with a polished, unfaceted emerald. Frowning, he held it close to the lamp and peered inside it. Satisfied, he returned to his writing.

'If Matul Saib is closing these waters, I think we'll head for Penik, too, and Galcan after that. Any word of what's going on in Zelin's isles, or anywhere else come to that, will come to Galcan as quickly as it'll reach anywhere.'

He curled the completed message inside the emerald-set ring and laid it in the lid of the box with the others. 'Our clients will want all the news we can send from there, so we'd better let my brothers know to send cages of fresh doves to await us.'

'Ari, a dragon has come to these reaches,' Hasu said with barely restrained exasperation. 'What does that mean? What manner of omen is that? For Zelin? For any of us?' He gripped his sword's hilt and peered out into the night as if daring some enemy to show itself.

'I don't know.' Ari's pen faltered for the first time. He cursed under his breath and obliterated the blotted message with vicious strokes of his pen. 'I don't know,' he repeated. 'I haven't had two tales about what happened in the southern reaches pass through my hands that don't contradict each other. Some say there was one dragon, some say there were two—'

'There are none there now, we can be certain of that much,' Hasu interrupted.

'Indeed.' Ari sounded dubious nevertheless. 'But can you tell me if the southern reaches have been left cursed by its presence? Every traveller tells a different tale about that.' He broke off, looking out into the darkness, eyes fixed and unseeing. Moving with sudden decision, he wrote three more messages in rapid succession, with no need to refer to any of his rings.

'What do you want from your brothers?' Hasu asked with keen interest.

'Whatever news they can send us about exactly what happened in the southern reaches.' Ari began writing again with renewed vigour. 'Which will be something we can trade to fullest advantage hereabouts. And we'll make it our business to learn exactly what happens to the *Lightning Fly*. Make sure all our usual contacts know that any word of its fate has value.'

'If they do survive the crossing of the strait, that will be an omen to lay before a soothsayer to see what he makes of it. And if they don't,' Hasu concluded bleakly.

'Get some sleep.' Ari slid the tightly furled message slips into narrow silver tubes. 'I'll wake you at dawn to take word to the local village spokesmen.'

Hasu nodded, yawning. 'I want to see that girl again before the *Lightning Fly* sails. I want to give her something to remember me by.' The thrust of his jaw challenged Ari.

The older man forwent any ribald retort. 'Choose any necklace from the top roll in the sandalwood chest.'

'Thank you.' Hasu set the sword down by Ari and dropped onto the crumpled quilts, pulling one up over his naked shoulder.

Ari flipped back a corner of carpet to reveal the sandy earth below. Retrieving the spoiled message slip from the lid of his walnut box, he lit it at the lamp. The fine paper flared to a fragile flame and he dropped it. Words and paper had been consumed by the time it reached the ground. Ari crushed the ashes beneath the heel of his hand and flipped the carpet back over the burned smudge.

Standing up, he watched Hasu for a moment before catching up the sword and going out into the night. He made a slow circuit of the heavy outer skin of the tent, bending every few paces to check the panels were securely pegged down to foil any thief, whether they might be seeking his wares or something else. Straightening up, Ari gazed at the night sky, dark as velvet strewn with his finest crystal beads. His eyes slid round to the north and west, towards the distant waters of Zelin, his face as still and contemplative as carved marble.

CHAPTER SEVEN

We've anchored.

As Kheda woke to that realisation, Risala's voice interrupted Crisk's muttered prayers in the gloom. 'Have we arrived?'

Sirince answered her from the far side of the *Tacsille*'s hold. 'I believe so.'

'Arrived where?' Velindre sat up on Kheda's other side with a rustle of quilts.

'The dry-season residence of my lord Zelin Raes,' a gruff voice informed them all.

Kheda sat up as Risala rolled out of his embrace. A Zelin swordsman was standing in the pool of light where the hatch to the deck had been cast open.

'Who are you? You're not—' Kheda coughed as he realised his tone was inappropriately commanding.

Velindre smoothly picked up the question. 'You're not one of the men foisted upon us yesterday.'

'We changed crews in the middle of the night.' There was a suggestion of contempt in the man's voice. 'While you were all sleeping.'

'We must congratulate Zelin mariners on such deft seamanship.' Sirince rose to his feet and untied his robe in a vain effort to shake out the creases. 'Are we to be presented to my lord of Zelin? I would appreciate an opportunity to bathe and to dress in fresh clothes.'

Their new guard shrugged. 'That's not for me to say.'

'Are we to be allowed breakfast?' Velindre asked rather less courteously.

'Breakfast?' Crisk echoed hopefully.

'I'll ask.' The warrior began climbing up the ladder. 'Wait here till you're called,' he warned as his head disappeared through the hatch.

Velindre instantly pulled her route record from the pocket inside her trousers. She flipped rapidly through the pages and pointed with a nail-bitten forefinger. 'We should be here.'

Kheda and Risala bent close to see in the dim light, their heads nearly clashing. Kheda saw the magewoman indicating a dot inked on the southern shore of the largest island in the north-west quarter of the domain.

'Where's the rainy-season residence?' he wondered.

'Here.' Velindre tapped another dot in the heart of the wide island to the south, reaching as far to east and west as the whole spread of islands to the north. 'That high ground to the west protects them from the storms coming in off the ocean.'

'The rains will arrive in twenty days or so.' Kheda lowered his voice to the barest whisper. 'What will the dragon do?'

'I've no idea.' Velindre tucked her route record back in her pocket. 'The storms will certainly excite it,' she murmured ominously.

Risala moved towards the ladder as the new warrior's feet reappeared. 'Are we to be fed?' she asked with a smile.

'You are.' The swordsman looked her up and down critically. 'You may make yourselves presentable before you come before my lord.'

Kheda saw Velindre made no move to change her clothes. *Where will we find ourselves if your secret is revealed? Better not make you conspicuous as the only one without a fresh tunic and trousers.*

He stayed standing where he was.

'I would rather be taken for a poet than a beggar.' Risala knelt to search in her bag. She stripped off her faded red tunic and went to pull her yellow dress over her head.

Sirince coloured and turned his back, forcing Crisk around as the halfwit gaped openly, slack hand falling from his amulet.

'What's that? Stand up,' the swordsman ordered. He wasn't interested in her nakedness, focusing instead on the emerald and silver ring on the leather thong around her neck. 'Where did you get that?'

'It was a gift from a patron of my master Haytar,' Risala said amiably as she donned her dress and discarded her black trousers.

'Was it, indeed?' The swordsman fixed her with a hard look before glancing around at the rest of them. 'Get up on deck. Empty-handed.' He rapped Kheda across the knuckles with his scabbarded sword when the warlord bent to catch up the leather bag of his possessions.

'Are we to be robbed of what little we possess?' His hand stinging, Kheda spoke without thinking.

'That's for my lord Zelin Raes to decide.' The warrior shoved him towards the ladder with a scowl.

'All we wish is to assure your lord we meant no insult by visiting his waters.' Velindre smiled obsequiously at the warrior.

'Then we'll be on our way.' Sirince dragged Crisk forward.

The swordsman replied with a non-committal grunt, still glowering at Kheda. The magewoman drew in a long breath and climbed the ladder.

'Trimon travels in disguise to test the hospitality of highest and lowest,' Crisk solemnly assured the warrior.

'I'm sure he does,' Sirince muttered, shoving the skinny barbarian up the ladder.

Risala began tying the red silk scarf around her waist. The swordsman reached for her shoulder and pulled her forward. 'You can do that up on deck.'

'I want to look my best for your lord.' All the same, Risala moved obediently to the ladder.

Kheda followed, forcing himself to unclench his fists.

If I raise a hand to any of these men, I'll lose it. That would be the best I could hope for. I cannot throw my life away like that.

He took a deep breath of salt-scented air as he stepped out onto the deck. He blinked after the gloom of the hold though the day was not as bright as he had expected. The sun had not yet risen over the thick stands of shade trees that fringed the broad arc of the shallow bay where they were anchored. Low ruffles of white surf trimmed wide expanses of sandbanks to west and south.

A safe anchorage in fine weather but too risky for the storms of the rainy season. Any ship dragging its anchor would founder on those shallows before a sail could be raised.

He looked inshore and saw a very different settlement from the one surrounding Matul Saib's residence. Hills ringed the bay, thickly forested, and the sharply pitched roofs of pale houses showed through the dense foliage on the lower slopes. Higher up, regular lines and green voids suggested orchards or gardens, more roofs scattered among them. Faint birdsong floated over the water before a fugitive breeze snatched it away.

Where is my lord's residence? Surely that can't be it?

Alone on the beach, four long buildings of whitewashed brick stood above the high-water line. Each had wide double doors closed tight between small, high and closely shuttered windows. A broad hearth in the middle of the square formed by the buildings was a dead scar of black ash.

'Zelin Raes does not open this beach to any and all

traders,' Abari remarked from his vantage point up on the stern platform. He gestured towards a single great galley and a couple of open boats resting at anchor on either side of the *Tacsille*. 'Only those specifically invited may unload their goods into those warehouses to await my lord's wives' pleasure.' His was the only face aboard Sirince's ship that Kheda recognised from the day before.

Sirince looked up to the stern platform, his smile ingratiating. 'How do we get ashore?'

Abari simply pointed to a shallow open boat heading towards them from the shore, continuing to eat a flatbread wrapped around something staining it blood red.

Which I will not see as any kind of omen. Let's just meet our fate on a full stomach.

Kheda didn't speak either thought aloud in case one of the watchful warriors read some portent into his words. Silent, he followed Sirince and Risala to the storage space beneath the stern platform. The Zelin warriors had broached a small cask of scarlet velvet berries preserved in honey-cane sap and mixed with tarit seed. When his turn came, he spooned some into the middle of a flatbread and choked it down as best he could, his throat dry and tight.

'Try some water with that.' Sirince dipped a horn cup in the cask of fresh water and offered it with a wry twist to his mouth.

Kheda nodded wordlessly, taking a tepid mouthful to ease his swallowing. His eyes met the northern wizard's.

Can you carry yourself away with magic if you find yourself facing death? Will you take us with you? If you leave us, our lives will be forfeit. What will Velindre do? If she takes us and you and Crisk are left behind, you'll be dead before the light of her spells has faded.

Seeing the same apprehension that was knotting his gut in Sirince's eyes, he turned to watch the oval rowing boat coming towards them from the shore. It was the only thing moving on the water. The men at the oars were the only people of Zelin that he could see, apart from those aboard the *Tacsille*. He still hadn't managed to finish his perfunctory breakfast by the time the ferryboat arrived.

'In you get,' Abari ordered briskly. 'All of you.'

Kheda dropped the remains of his flatbread into the water before lowering himself down the ship's rope ladder into the ferryboat.

'Looking for omens?' Abari quipped.

As Kheda reached up to help Risala negotiate the ladder in her dress, she looked to see what fish or other sea creatures might rise to the unexpected largesse.

What could you possibly see that would give any clue to this lord of Zelin's mood?

'Quickly, if you please,' Abari prompted.

Sirince followed without Kheda's assistance, Velindre coming after. Crisk startled them all by jumping from the *Tacsille*'s rail to land with a thud that sent the whole ferryboat rocking.

'Fool!' The leader of the rowing team raised an angry shout and a threatening hand to go with it.

Crisk scurried to hide behind Sirince, his frantic movement setting the boat rocking even more violently.

'He is a fool, a natural,' Sirince apologised.

'Then keep tight hold of him,' the rower growled. 'I won't turn back for him if he falls in the water.'

'Where's our ship going?' Crisk whimpered as he groped for his amulet. 'Why did Trimon bring us here?'

Kheda watched the *Tacsille* slip away from them as Abari's new crew raised a shallow reef of sail and coaxed the ship towards the eastern arm of the bay.

'Kheda,' Risala said quietly. As he turned to her, she nodded towards the shore.

A troop of mail-clad men had emerged from behind

the square of warehouses. They drew up in a double column and waited for the ferry. The rowers leaned into their oars and carried them inexorably across the waters, still calm in the windless half-light. The keel touched the unseen sands with a faint grating sound. Kheda squared his shoulders and looked at the others, who seemed equally reluctant to make any move to disembark.

'You can get out and wade or they'll come and drag you ashore,' the lead rower advised.

We must concentrate on being nothing remarkable. We're just traders and travellers, so Zelin Raes can let us go about our business. But doesn't he already know there's something more to Velindre and Risala? Why would he have circulated their descriptions among the triremes standing guard over his sea lanes if he didn't?

Kheda took the lead and swung himself over the rowing boat's rail. He strode through the knee-deep sea. The others followed, Crisk splashing loudly. Risala caught up her skirts to keep the dress as dry as possible, prompting a coarse remark from one of the rowers. Kheda forced himself to keep looking ahead, assessing the warriors waiting for them.

As they reached the beach, the captain stepped forward to address himself impartially to Sirince and Velindre. 'You are welcome to my lord Zelin Raes's residence.'

Such courtesy was somewhat incongruous. These warriors were no mere honour guard, regarding them instead with the wary alertness of men escorting prisoners. Their mail was as fine as any Kheda had ever seen, latticed with bronze links. Even the most junior swordsmen boasted twin blades with pommels of polished agate and chalcedony. The captain led the way and tiny silver mirror-bird feathers hanging from the chain-mail veil of his helm glittered as the sun rose above the eastern treetops.

Kheda forced himself to wait so everyone else could precede him, even Crisk who was clutching his amulet tight, apprehension furrowing his freckled brow.

'The Opal looks for friendship and the Yora Hawk is watchful,' he muttered ominously.

Kheda noted a couple of the swordsmen keeping a particular eye on the halfwit. No one seemed to be watching him.

Because I am a slave, and thus of no account. There was no mention of me among the people Zelin Raes told his men he wanted found. What does he want with Velindre and Risala?

As they passed beneath the shade trees fringing the beach, Kheda saw there were more houses along the shore than he had first imagined. The clay tiles of their roofs ranged from palest cream to dull browns and greys that hid most effectively among the shadows cast by the foliage. All were still closely shuttered.

Their captors led them around a shoulder of land concealing a small valley from the shore. More buildings clustered along its sides and for the first time, he saw Zelin islanders looking curiously out of the wide-silled windows. These dwellings were taller than he expected, raised on brick pillars to leave space underneath where a half-grown child could have stood without stooping. These spaces were empty, though, not used for storage. Kheda soon realised why.

If there's this much water here at the very end of the dry season, this whole slope must be a foaming torrent at the height of the rains.

The land rose steeply before them with streams running down wide steps of rock to fill a succession of pools linked by short, shallow cataracts. Children were watering blue-grey goats at the lowest ponds, where red and gold ducks dabbled and squabbled beneath the spray from the splashing falls. More houses raised on pillars of smoothly plastered brick were scattered between the rivulets.

Their path was marked by broad pale stones. A few women out early to wash themselves or their clothes looked at them, incurious. Girls filling brass water jars at the highest pools didn't even bother to look, intent on their chores.

You seem confident that your lord's warriors will protect you from any threat. Presumably you haven't yet heard there's a dragon making itself at home in his domain.

Once they had passed the last house, everyone ahead stopped. Kheda saw they faced a modest precipice where braided streams tumbled in a confusion of white foam. Steps were cut into the sandy rock on one side, too narrow for more than a single climber. The first swordsmen were already running up them, unhampered by the weight of their armour.

A useful defence against attackers.

As Kheda waited meekly for his turn, movement among the trees clustered thick on the hillside caught his eye. Men in lichen-stained trousers, their ragged robes hanging open, were cutting sprays of dark glossy green leaves from neatly trimmed bushes. Each was intent on filling a basket strapped to the back of a patiently waiting lad.

'Silkworm fodder,' Velindre explained over her shoulder.

'Is that so?' Further away in the forest, he could see long, low buildings with solid doors yet with wide louvres in their windowless walls.

The closest swordsman scowled. 'You mind your own business and we'll mind ours.'

We'll get no chance to agree our story. What if we get separated?

Frustrated, Kheda gnawed the inside of his lip.

When they had all climbed the steep stair, Kheda saw

a broad terrace opening out ahead. Trees grew in ordered profusion between ditches cut deep into the rock. The outermost marked out a sizeable enclosure, broad and the water within still deep, despite the season. The warriors led them across a narrow wooden bridge, interspersing themselves with their lord's reluctant guests.

How are we going to get out of this? What can I do as a nameless slave?

As he racked his brains for some stratagem, Kheda noted archers among the trees on the far side of the channel. There were no rails to stop a man falling from the bridge if he were pierced by a barbed shaft. Moreover, sharp stakes bristled along the steep sides of the ditch. Any man who survived arrow or fall would be trapped for the archers to kill at their leisure.

So Zelin Raes chooses not to rely on walls for his defence like Matul Saib. What other differences might there be between them?

The captain of the guards led them onwards. Now angled channels wove between stands of feather-tipped afital grasses, still full of water, their sides steep with rail-less wooden bridges crossing them.

Easily removed in time of peril.

A handful of children playing around a thicket of red canes plainly felt in no danger. As they saw the swordsmen approaching, they stopped their game to stand looking with avid curiosity. Kheda judged the eldest was nearing the age of discretion.

Unless the greater heights common to people in these reaches make me miss my guess.

The lad stood straight-backed, his shoulders square, as he assessed these newcomers. He wore a robe of golden silk extravagantly decorated with tiny black beads sewn in intricate patterns. A heavy gold chain gleamed around his neck and a gesture rattled jet bracelets at his wrist.

The other children drew close to him, all boys. The tallest one's head topped the eldest's shoulder, the youngest's barely reaching the sash at his waist. All shared the features of common blood.

My lord Zelin Raes's sons? All of them?

Unthinking, Kheda slowed to a halt.

'Move,' the warrior behind him growled.

He hurried to close the gap that had opened between him and Sirince before they crossed another narrow bridge. They passed through a dense screen of shaped and trained trees that Kheda didn't recognise and he had to fight an impulse to gape as openly as Crisk.

'Larasion's touch has truly blessed this place,' the barbarian murmured, awestruck.

Ironwood trees pruned with artful grace were planted in twos and threes around Zelin Raes's dry-season residence. It was a complex of broad, single-storeyed pavilions roofed with green clay tiles. Where the islanders finished their pillared dwellings with smooth white plaster, their lord's solidly planted houses seemed made of shimmering glass. As they drew nearer, Kheda saw the pavilions were indeed decorated with translucent mosaics. The breeze toyed with the tree branches overhead and the strengthening sun struck interstices among the subtle arcs and curves of the stylised decorations. Refracted light glittered and vanished, only to reappear elsewhere. The richly armoured swordsmen urged them onwards, unmoved by grandeur familiar to them.

They passed between two broad buildings, each with long wings reaching back towards compounds of lesser houses. On one hand, the main pavilion was distinguished by flowers and vines of radiant glass built into its walls, all on a ground of softly blushing pink. On the other, the walls were adorned with shrubs and blossoms set against dusky blue and dancing butterflies shone like tiny jewels.

All Kheda's attention was fixed on the third complex straight ahead, bigger than either to the sides. A stepped roof rose above the central section to mark what must surely be the warlord's audience hall. The walls were silver-grey and patterned with trees. Spinefruits and iron-woods with tangles of logen vine around their buttressed roots rose above thickets of sard-berry bushes and other shrubs that Kheda did not know but which looked remarkably like those he had seen the diligent islanders harvesting. The craftsmen who had built this place had worked an exquisite illusion of depth by detailing trees of different sizes seemingly marching away into gradually darkening distance. It was like looking into a forest.

As they walked up the steps and Velindre and Risala entered ahead of him, Kheda saw animals looking back at him. Hook-toothed hogs lurked amid the undergrowth, their black eyes glittering. Jungle cats with menacing agate gaze stretched like mottled shadows along convenient low boughs. Caped loals climbed for higher branches, long-fingered hands holding tight, their fringed tails dangling. Deer stood frozen, ready for flight, their dappled hides mimicking the play of light and shade woven around the motionless trees. Brilliant colours promised birds amid the leaves or scratching in the underbrush, while sinuous shapes suggested snakes poised to catch them.

'Does Talagrin walk these woods?' Curious, Crisk would have broken away to wander around the outside of the building if Sirince hadn't caught firm hold of his arm and pulled him through the wide-open doorway.

Kheda followed and the silent warriors coming after him closed the heavy portal behind them with a solid thud. Smaller doors pierced the white walls, each one closed and guarded by an unsmiling swordsman. The unrelieved gold of the frosted glass panelling within was startling after the intricate decoration outside. A clerestory lifted the roof of the hall a man's height above the rest of the building and sunlight flooded through the transparent panes, falling to tiles the colour of palest sand.

'Good morning.' Zelin Raes sat on a wide bench with a high back and scrolled arms raised up on a dais at the far end of the hall. The ivory brocade of the sumptuously padded upholstery set off the bright gold of his silken raiment. His robe was decorated with canthira leaves sewn from beads of cobalt glass and a belt of wide golden plaques served him in place of a sash. He wore rings and bracelets of silver set with massive rugged diamonds that struck infinite colours from the sunlight. His skin was as dark as any Kheda had seen in these reaches, his features broad. Just touched with grey, his beard was confined to a neat outline around his mouth while his head was clean-shaven. His eyes were so dark as to look black, keen and inquisitive. He might have been Kheda's age, or older; it was impossible to tell.

Two women who could only be his wives sat on either side of him, the seat more than wide enough to accommodate all three of them. Both wore simple shifts of blue silk, one the colour of the morning sky, the other midnight blue. Each woman's dress was overlaid with a lattice of shining beads threaded onto the meshes of a silken net.

The woman on Zelin Raes's dagger hand shifted as she made some quiet observation and Kheda realised the gown of beads was an entirely separate garment. Against the sky-blue fabric, the long beads making the sides of each shifting lozenge were indigo shot with silver, while round silver beads stood in place of every knot. She was a stunningly beautiful woman. Her skin and eyes were as dark as her lord's, her finely chiselled features speaking of blood in her line from more central domains within the Archipelago. A fragile cloud of wiry black curls was held off her face by a silver circlet and silver rings set with sapphires adorned her elegant fingers. Chased silver bracelets reached up her slender arms almost to her elbows and beneath the hem of her underdress, silver chains were looped around her slim ankles.

Her companion wore a net of straw-coloured beads knotted with golden ones, bright against the dark-blue silken dress beneath. All wrought of gold, her jewellery was the palest yellow Kheda had ever seen, set with lapis lazuli of striking purity. With a rich brown complexion rather than ebony skin, her broad features and voluptuous figure nevertheless indicated bloodlines predominantly of these western reaches. Her hair was short, dotting her scalp with tight curls, each one distinct and separate. She studied the newcomers calmly, unblinking, her striking eyes a deep amber. Neither woman wore the intricate face paints that were customary elsewhere in the Archipelago. As with Zelin Raes, Kheda found it impossible to guess their years beyond estimating them to be much the same age as himself.

Three swordsmen stood behind the dais, all armoured with a magnificence that left the splendid armour of the guards and their captain looking commonplace. Each wore two swords and a profusion of daggers, their hilts studded with jade and moonstones. The trio were the tallest men Kheda had yet seen in these reaches.

Bodyguards and personal slaves to my lord Zelin Raes and his ladies. Not that they will have to soil their blades to kill us with all these other warriors ready, willing and able to serve.

The warlord's lady with the amber eyes leaned across her husband and said something softly to her fellow wife. The ebony beauty lifted one fine-boned hand to hide her white-toothed smile.

None of my wives have ever had direct trading links stretching this far north and west. Western silks and glass

*wares pass through many hands before they reach us. Whose
hands? Such matters were never my concern.*

Kheda realised Zelin Raes was allowing the five of them
as much time as they wanted to be thoroughly cowed by
their surroundings. He set his jaw and shifted his feet to
stand balanced, apparently at his ease though tension
knotted his stomach ever tighter.

'Good morning.' Zelin Raes repeated his greeting as
his wives broke apart to sit straight-backed either side of
him once more.

Velindre cleared her throat as the warlord raised expectant brows at her. 'Good morning, my lord of Zelin.'

Zelin Raes smiled briefly as if some unasked question
had nevertheless been answered. 'You are a scholar who
goes by the name of Vel.'

'I am, my lord,' Velindre confirmed steadily, though
there had been no real query in the warlord's words.

'A scholar who has travelled extensively in the
Archipelago, and most notably in the southern reaches.'
Zelin Raes tilted his head quizzically to one side. 'Despite
the remarkably ill omens seen in both heavenly and earthly
compasses thereabouts these past few years.'

'Indeed, my lord.' Velindre made no further response,
merely squaring her shoulders and folding her arms.

Silence filled the broad hall.

'And you –' Zelin Raes inclined his head toward Risala
'– are a poet called Risala, once apprenticed to Haytar the
Blind. I believe you claim Shek Kul as your patron?' That
was definitely a question, with a distinct edge to it besides.

Risala sank in a graceful obeisance, the saffron skirts
of her dress spreading on the pale tiles. She looked
unutterably shabby before the warlord's exquisite ladies.
'My lord of Shek was my master Haytar's patron.'

'You carry Shek's token.' Zelin Raes snapped his fingers
abruptly.

The captain of the guard who had brought them there strode forward from his post by the door. As he brushed past Kheda, ignoring him utterly, he drew his dagger with a steely *snick*. Catching Risala by the elbow, he lifted her to her feet. He slid a finger beneath the thong around her neck to pull the heavy silver ring set with its polished emerald out from beneath the dress. His thin blade cut the leather through with a single stroke.

Who recognised the ring for Shek Kul's? Who told my lord of Zelin so promptly?

Kheda took an involuntary pace forward.

All eyes turned to him and he heard the shifting rattle of chain mail as every warrior stiffened. Kheda halted but did not retreat, fixing his gaze on the guard–captain. The man looked back at him, dark eyes shadowed beneath the brow band of his helm, mirror–bird feathers engraved in the steel. Sheathing his dagger with slow deliberation, the guard–captain closed his fist on the cut thong.

What can I do as a nameless slave? Besides die for impertinence, and whatever restitution this warlord feels inclined to make to my supposed owner?

Kheda fought to stand still as the warrior took the ring to Zelin Raes. The warlord wound the leather thong around one hand and looked past Risala and Velindre at the three men for the first time. 'Who are these?'

'My name is Sirince—' the bald wizard began, the accents of the unbroken lands harsh in his words.

'He's a slaver.' The guard–captain spoke over him as he walked away from the dais. 'A barbarian trading in other barbarians.'

Sirince tried again with a respectful bow. 'I return my fellow countrymen to their families—'

'This one is a simpleton.' Disdainful, the guard–captain nodded towards Crisk, who stood motionless, openly apprehensive. 'The other one belongs to the women.'

Pausing to look at Kheda with some suspicion, he returned to stand beside the three men. 'He carries their bags and warms the poet girl's quilts.'

Abari's men must have told you that. Why is your lord so interested in us?

'Take them away.' Zelin Raes waved a dismissive hand before addressing himself to Velindre and Risala with acid sarcasm. 'Honoured scholar and praiseworthy poet, you will explain why you are sailing deliberately into waters where a dragon has been seen. Don't pretend any ignorance,' he warned harshly. 'I know that this news is now spreading faster than pestilence along all the trading beaches and sea lanes.' Bitterness soured his voice still further. 'You will explain what has brought you from distant reaches so recently plagued by dragons and murderous strangers to my domain, when a dragon just happens to have arrived.'

The guard-captain and two warriors stepped between the two women and Kheda, Sirince and Crisk. One of the swordsmen extended an arm to usher Sirince sideways.

Crisk's face suddenly twisted with anger. 'The sea serpent waits in the darkness for all who abuse their responsibilities.'

'Please.' The wizard raised his hands in surrender as the guard-captain scowled. 'Don't mind him.'

When everyone knows to mark any apparent wisdom in chance-heard words? Crisk is going to prompt far too many questions with his ravings. Or get us all killed if he attacks someone like he attacked me when Sirince fell ill.

Kheda readied himself to subdue the halfwit at the first sign of violence.

'What domain were you born to and who made you *zamorin*?' Zelin Raes was paying no attention, intent on Velindre. 'Guided by what omens? What was your parentage? I hear something of the unbroken lands in your voice. How did you rise from slave to free scholar? The last word I had of you was that you had your own ship and patrons to supply your needs. What reduced you to begging passage with some barbarian slaver?'

'Saedrin is the only judge of men,' Crisk muttered under his breath, outrage burning in his green eyes.

As Kheda grabbed the barbarian's hand, forcing down his clenched fist, he saw Zelin Raes lean forward and fix Risala with a penetrating look.

'Why are you –' the warlord stabbed the air with a blunt finger '– carrying a cipher ring? Is this a code of Shek Kul's? Does he know you carry it? Or are you some southern warlord's spy?'

'Move.' The guard-captain pushed at Kheda's shoulder to turn him around towards the door. 'Keep him under control.'

Crisk spat at the man's mailed chest. The guard-captain looked at him, more bemused than angry, and raised his fist. 'You try that again and see what you get.'

No. This deception of mine no longer serves any purpose. We cannot be separated. I cannot leave Risala and Velindre to face Zelin Raes without any protection of rank or alliance.

'Sirince, get him in hand.' Kheda knocked the guard-captain's plated gauntlet aside with an open hand while warning Crisk off with a glare. He stepped sideways so he could be clearly seen from the dais and called out, 'My lord Zelin Raes!'

'I do not hold a slave responsible for his owner's misdeeds.' The warlord's gaze didn't shift from Risala. 'By that same token, I do not listen to slaves eager to betray an owner's secrets. Leave and count yourself fortunate I am not Essa Mol.' He waved curt dismissal.

'We may not torture unruly slaves but we do flog them,' the guard-captain growled. He reached for Kheda's upper arm.

'My lord, I am no slave!' Kheda tried to step out of the captain's reach but another warrior was standing behind him and seized him just above the elbows. A second held Sirince in the same restraint while a third unceremoniously forced Crisk to his hands and knees with a ferocious grip on the back of his scrawny neck.

'Then who are you?' Zelin Raes demanded.

'I am Kheda, born of Daish and latterly lord of Chazen.' Kheda put all the authority of his erstwhile rank into his words. 'As a consequence of those twists of strange fate that you have evidently heard have afflicted the southern reaches.'

The ebony beauty beside Zelin Raes laughed from sheer surprise, a silvery echo in the jingle of her bracelets as she raised her hand to her mouth.

'Such lies will win you a whipping to flay the skin from your back,' the warlord warned with soft menace. He leaned forward, his dagger hand gripping one knee.

'Do I look like a fool who would tell such a lie?' Kheda retorted. He stood straight, speaking as to an equal, refusing to acknowledge the agonisingly fierce hold the warrior behind him had on his arms.

'Prove yourself,' Zelin Raes demanded curtly.

'I imagine you have already sent for our baggage from our ship, my lord.' Kheda took a deep breath as the pain of the warrior's grip on his arms threatened to distract him. 'You will find salves and tinctures of the finest quality among my possessions—'

'Such things can be traded for.' Zelin Raes shook his head. 'Or stolen.'

'But the lore of making them belongs to warlords and those sworn to them,' Kheda countered. 'Show me your physic garden and I'll show you remedies unknown in these reaches.'

'I teach my village healers and they teach their

underlings. All that would prove is you have learned your skills at some warlord's side.' Zelin Raes sat back, tension in his broad shoulders and muscular arms. 'But let us consider for a moment that you might truly be who you say you are. If it's a mystery what this scholar and this poet seek in my dragon-shadowed waters, then that puzzle's doubled and redoubled.'

Kheda felt the warrior's grip on his arms slacken just a fraction in response. He pulled himself free and took a pace forward. Every warrior in the room stiffened.

Kheda bowed low with practised courtesy. 'Forgive me, my lord, for coming into your domain in such secrecy. I will explain myself once I have satisfied you that I am indeed who I claim to be.' He glanced at the guard-captain, who had one hand on a sword hilt and the other on the dagger at his belt. 'I also carry a cipher ring crafted for Shek Kul around my neck. May I show it to you?'

'You may.' Zelin Raes's tone was non-committal.

Kheda reached inside the neck of his tunic, the guard-captain's dark eyes on him all the time. He pulled the ring on its thong over his head and offered it to the warrior with lordly poise. The swordsman's boots scuffed on the tiled floor as he wheeled around and strode to the dais, the leather thong dangling from his fingers.

Zelin Raes compared the two rings, examining them inside and out and paying close attention to the uncut, polished emeralds that adorned each one. 'Well?'

'Your lady wives must surely have trading links with the domains of the central compass, if not with the ladies Mahli Shek or Laio Shek themselves.' Kheda managed a half-smile, refusing to acknowledge the nervousness curdling his stomach. 'A courier dove could take a message to my lord Shek Kul. He will verify that he gave us those rings, and describe us, so you can be sure we have not stolen them.'

Zelin Raes looked up, his face stern. 'Sending such a message and receiving a reply will take some days. Even if Shek Kul can satisfy me that you are who you claim to be, that still does not explain your presence here, in sweat-stained cottons with a dagger barely more use than an eating knife your only weapon.' He looked Kheda up and down, his lip curled with something perilously close to disdain.

'I am willing to explain myself, if you are willing to listen before you can be certain of my name.' Kheda bowed again, composed.

'Please do so.' Zelin Raes folded his beringed hands in his lap. He glanced at each of his wives in turn, a dangerous glint in his eye. 'This should be interesting.'

'I aim to be of more use than interest to you and yours, my lord.' Kheda dared to walk forward. As no one stopped him, he risked a brief glimpse to the rear to see Sirince had also been released, hastening to take firm hold of Crisk's arm as the warrior reluctantly acceded to a nod ordering him to let the barbarian stand up. Kheda was relieved to hear no sound from the halfwit and returned all his attention to the dais. Velindre and Risala moved apart to allow Kheda to stand between them. Both gazed levelly back at Zelin Raes's wives.

'You have a dragon in your domain,' Kheda stated bluntly. 'As you say, the southern reaches were visited by two such beasts last year. Believe me, my lord, I know every uncertainty, every fear that has kept you wakeful since it arrived. I have plumbed the depths of your frustration and impotence.'

'Do not presume to know my lord's mind,' the guard-captain returning from the dais snapped, anger kindling in his eyes.

Kheda kept his gaze fixed on Zelin Raes. 'This is not the first time I have left my domain and travelled to northern waters without owning to my name. I did so the year before last, when wild men led by savage mages came out of the empty western ocean to devastate the defenceless islands of Chazen. I sought lore to counter their evil and omens led me to believe that was best done in utmost secrecy, in case the corruption of magic somehow ensnared me as I searched.'

What I believed then and what I believe now is a question we won't pursue here.

Kheda saw Zelin Raes's brow crease, plainly disinclined to credit such a tale, though reluctantly too intrigued to call Kheda a liar to his face. Kheda cleared his throat.

'My searches took me to Shek Kul's domain. You must know that he and his household were threatened by one of their own who was seduced into suborning sorcery by a northern mage who promised her a child. Thereafter my lord of Shek sought lore on any defence that might be built against wizardry.'

The amber-eyed woman beside Zelin Raes shifted with a soft rattle of beads. 'I am acquainted with the sorry tale of Kaeska who was born Danak before she married my lord of Shek.'

You grant her ties to both domains by linking her name with theirs and there's pity in your voice. Does this mean you're hostile to Shek Kul? He had Kaeska executed for her crimes. Oh well, I can't go back now.

Kheda acknowledged the amber-eyed wife with a courteous bow. 'Shek Kul was determined that no magic should again bring such grief to his people. He learned many of the ways that warlords of old had kept their domains free from barbarians backed by wizards from the unbroken lands. He generously shared such lore with me. With that knowledge, I led the domains of the south against the wild men and drove them back into the sea.'

It was a little more complicated than that, given I was forced to compel Dev to help me, but you won't want to know anything about that, my lord Zelin.

The warlord's other wife looked at Risala, her head gracefully tilted to one side. 'This link with Shek Kul explains your presence, I take it?'

Risala sank in a graceful curtsey. 'I have not lied, my lady.' Her eyes humbly lowered, her voice was calmly assured. 'Shek Kul was indeed patron to my master Haytar, which is how I came to be one of the least of my lord's eyes and ears. He would not let lore on such a perilous thing as magic loose without sending someone to be certain my lord Kheda would not misuse it.' She slid an unfathomable glance sideways at Kheda. Everyone in the room noted it.

'You say you rid the southern reaches of these wild men and their wizards.' Zelin Raes betrayed a hint of impatience. 'But dragons came to plague your islands the very next year—'

'Drawn by the magic of the wild men still staining our lands,' Kheda answered with resignation. 'Yet the most unpromising oyster may have a pearl within it. One dragon slew the other, and in slaying the remaining beast, the men of Chazen, all unknowing, made their land safe for the future. I have made it my business to pursue all scholarship concerning the beasts –' he jerked his head towards Velindre '– and barbarian lore claims no dragon will come where one of its kind has been slain.'

'Then how do we slay it?' Zelin Raes sat upright and every warrior in the room stirred with him, hands straying to sword hilts.

The amber-eyed woman raised a commanding hand and everyone stilled. 'This does not yet explain why you are come to our islands, my lord Kheda, if that is truly who you are.'

'Of Chazen, or Daish,' her fellow wife added delicately. 'Which is it?'

'I am husband to Itrac Chazen who was the sole survivor of the ruling family of the domain.' Kheda addressed himself to both women as best he could. 'I was born to Daish and ruled as Daish Kheda before I yielded to my son's accession, after events and omens I do not propose to discuss in an open forum such as this.'

After I was nearly killed by Ulla Safar, a tyrant who blights the southern reaches more thoroughly than any dragon could. After I judged it best everyone think he had succeeded and I was in fact dead so I could go in search of magic to use in the fight against magic without anyone being the wiser. After my lady wives decided I was too polluted by what they merely suspected I had done ever to come near the domain of my birth or my children again. After my first wife encompassed the death of Chazen Saril, leaving me with scant choice but to take dominion over his islands, to save Itrac and her people from Ulla Safar or worse.

Kheda smiled serenely, thrusting the guilt, frustration and anger threaded through these recollections to the back of his mind.

'Then, my lord Kheda, whether of Chazen or Daish, may I make known my wives?' There was a hint of sarcasm in his voice as Zelin Raes bowed from the waist to the ebony beauty. 'I present Mian Zelin, born Mian Galcan.' Turning, he bowed to the amber-eyed woman. 'And Kauris Zelin, born Kauris Tabril.'

'My ladies, I am honoured.' Kheda bowed his deepest obeisance so far. Risala sank down in another curtsey while Velindre bowed as smoothly as if she had never worn skirts in her life.

Kheda looked at Kauris Zelin as he stood straight once again. 'I believe the wives of Redigal Coron have trading links that reach as far as the Tabril domain, through ties of blood and marriage traced through Yava and Calece. If you can send word through trusted couriers by that or some similar route, there are southern lords who will confirm what I say.'

'I shall send to ask them, never fear.' She regarded him, amber eyes shadowed with reservation. 'But can they tell me why you are currently in our waters, at the very same time as a dragon has come?'

'Because Zelin's warlord and people plainly have need of the lore and the skills that I have used to save Chazen,' Kheda said boldly.

He hoped the stir of astonishment throughout the hall hid Risala's frisson of surprise, matched by Velindre's on his other hand. He couldn't see what Sirince or Crisk were showing by way of reaction.

Hopefully no one's paying some barbarian slaver and his halfwit too much attention.

But he saw Mian Zelin's gaze shift over his shoulder.

'You have accounted for the presence of the poet and this *zamorin* with this tale,' she said with smooth curiosity, 'but you still haven't explained why you come pretending such lowly status in the company of a slave-trader from the unbroken lands to the north.'

Can I find some explanation that won't condemn us all?

'Barbarians live in lands where magic touches them, if not daily, certainly time and again through the course of a year. Dragons are creatures of natural magic. I would rather take these men and their ship beneath the creature's shadow than expose innocent Aldabreshi to such ill omen.' Kheda shook his head. 'My own life has already been touched by magic, though I never wished it to be.' There was a challenge in his frankness.

I only hope the philosophers of the western reaches agree that innocents touched by magic need not be executed to remove its taint. There are those elsewhere who say such unfortunates

*are nevertheless condemned as readily as anyone deliberately
suborning sorcery.*

'What prompts you to offer us such aid?' Zelin Raes
was openly incredulous.

Kheda shrugged as if this were obvious. 'The wealth
of the western reaches is well known throughout the
Archipelago. Chazen has suffered and must rebuild
through trade and alliance.'

'Such approaches and negotiations should be the
province of your lady wife,' Kauris Zelin said instantly,
her expression severe.

'My lady Itrac Chazen is occupied with twin daughters born not half a year since.' Kheda smiled proudly.
He glanced around the room and was satisfied to see the
assembled warriors looking at him with rising hope. 'And
this is hardly a normal issue of trade.'

*This was the right course to take. I just have to keep this
conversation moving down the paths I wish to follow, avoiding
the questions I don't want to answer—*

'Tell us how to rid ourselves of this dragon and you
can ask us for all the trade goods and terms you might
wish for.' Zelin Raes rose incautiously to his feet, his fists
clenched.

His wives looked up at him with faint outrage but
offered no contradiction.

'Forgive me, my lord, but I cannot do that.' Kheda
spoke calmly. 'Such lore is of inordinate value. I will no
more give it blithely away than you would hand me the
secrets of rearing silkworms.'

For a tense moment, Zelin Raes looked at him, mouth
half-open, before pressing his lips together with suppressed emotion. 'I suppose I cannot argue with that.' He
drew a rasping breath through his flared nostrils. 'What
are you proposing?'

'We will rid you of this dragon,' Kheda said simply.

'Once it is gone from your domain, we can discuss recompense.'

The silence in the room was one of stunned astonishment.

Mian Zelin spoke first, smiling sweetly. 'If you are to present us with such a noble gift, we must at least offer you more fitting hospitality. You will wish to bathe and to refresh yourselves.'

Kauris Zelin rose gracefully to stand beside her husband. 'Akir, show the barbarian slaver and his companion to our servants' quarters. Make sure they are well looked after.' Her body slave obediently stepped around the dais, unsmiling as he gestured towards a door, his gaze fixed on Sirince. Kauris offered a hand to Risala. 'My women will see to your comfort, my dear.'

'Lec will see you have privacy among our own *zamorin*, master scholar.' Inclining her head gracefully to Velindre, Mian Zelin snapped her fingers to summon her own slave.

'You can walk with me, my lord Kheda, of Daish or of Chazen.' Zelin Raes fixed him with a darkly penetrating look. 'Let us talk a little longer while your bath and some fitting clothes are prepared for you.' The warlord turned his back, his slave opening a door behind the dais.

'I am honoured, my lord.' Kheda nodded courteously as one of the swordsmen close at hand bowed low and hurried away through a different door, presumably to relay those orders.

Thus we are all separated, doubtless to be questioned tact-fully yet thoroughly. Our stories should agree, if everyone was keeping their ears open.

Kheda steeled himself to walk after Zelin Raes. Risala was already halfway to a different exit while Mian Zelin's slave led Velindre to another. Swordsmen surrounded Sirince and Crisk muttered something, clutching his amulet nervously, as the two of them were ushered towards the double door through which they had first entered.

Risala will have all her wits about her and Velindre knows any slip means her death as well as likely condemnation for us all. Sirince is no fool and must surely know the same. But what about Crisk?

CHAPTER EIGHT

They emerged from the audience hall into a yellow-walled garden of diligently tended beds. A few bees foraged among scant blooms. Most of the plants still held their buds tight closed, awaiting the rains that would prompt a profusion of colour and scent. A long pool ran down the centre of the garden, the water dark and mysterious beneath wide floating leaves anchored on tortuous pale stems. Vivid as turquoise, a fan-fly perched on a lotus shoot, doubled wings momentarily at rest.

'Your collection of physic herbs is most impressive, my lord.' Kheda identified the plants as Zelin Raes led him along paths paved with slabs of golden stone. 'Blue casque and pella vine, barosoil and fever-feathers. Bee balm and nepethia.' He frowned. 'I don't see leatherspear, my lord. What do you use for burns in these reaches?'

'Leatherspear rots from the root in these climes.' Zelin Raes didn't slow. 'We use the sap of a vine we know as golden serpent.'

'Perhaps you might let me have a cutting.' Kheda could see no climbers clinging to the trees trained in flat arcs against the garden's stone walls. 'We can see how it fares in southern air.'

'Perhaps.' Zelin Raes paused as his body slave hurried to open a double gate at the far end of the garden. 'If you earn it.'

Opting not to respond to that, Kheda followed Zelin Raes through the gate into a broad orchard. The warlord's personal attendant waited for Kheda to precede him, taking the customary place a few paces behind his lord and this unexpected, unkempt guest.

They walked through stands of lilla trees planted to mimic natural groves. Leaves furled by the dryness of the season shivered in the breeze, their silver undersides dulled with wind-borne dust.

'Where is your body slave?' Zelin asked curtly.

'I have none at present,' Kheda replied, equally terse. 'As your enquiries in the south will no doubt tell you, my last slave was killed when we attempted to drive off the dragon that was setting Chazen lands ablaze with its fires.'

The Zelin warlord halted and stared unblinking at Kheda. 'How did you escape with your life?'

'By hiding in a cave like a terrified matia,' Kheda admitted, 'while my slave gave his life to distract the beast.'

You won't learn such unflattering details from whatever news your couriers bring you from the south. Will such honesty convince you that I am telling you the truth? It is true, as far as it goes. Dev was masquerading as my slave to save his own skin. Neither Sirince nor Crisk can betray that particular secret. Only Velindre, Risala and I know Dev used his magic to kill the fire dragon's ruby egg. No one knew he would be lured to an ecstatic death by the seductive sweetness of its nascent power blending with his own.

Kheda cleared his throat, speaking louder than was necessary to foil any tremor in his words. 'His death did more than save my life. While the fire-wielding dragon was intent on him, a second beast came upon it unawares and slew it. That second dragon was left sorely wounded by the battle, which is how the men of Chazen were able to slay it.'

That and because it was dying anyway, a mere empty simulacrum wrought by Velindre's magic. Another secret no one else needs to know.

'So you propose to wound this beast plaguing our domain? How?' Zelin Raes's body slave could no longer restrain himself. 'How many of us will it take to kill it? We will gladly spend our lives—'

'Silence, Felash.' Zelin Raes's rebuke was a mild one.

Kheda took a step, prompting Zelin Raes to walk with him. 'I have vowed not to take another body slave until I am certain I will not lead him into an undeserved death. While I am in Chazen, the captain of my household guard serves as my personal servant.'

'Indeed.' Zelin Raes looked back to exchange a glance with the warrior Felash.

You trust your body slave, my lord, which makes me think well of you. At the same time, it should put me on my guard. Your man will doubtless seek to confirm all that I've told you. All warlords' attendants and their ladies' slaves have their own discreet channels of communication and gossip.

Movement among the lilla trees caught Kheda's eye. Children were stealthily shadowing Zelin Raes, his slave and this intriguing stranger. Kheda swallowed unexpected pain at the thought of his own children, so far away.

Itrac's daughters, little Olkai and Sekni, they will be so changed when I finally see them again. Babies grow so fast. What of my sons and daughters, born to Daish and now lost to me? How are they faring?

As he blinked away treacherous tears prompted by emotion and exhaustion, he realised Zelin Raes was watching him dispassionately.

'My sons, as I suspect you have guessed,' the warlord said calmly. 'Tell me, Kheda, once of Daish, what happened to your brothers?'

Kheda lifted his chin before answering. 'They were made *zamorin* and traded away as slaves, to fulfil our father's deathbed decree.'

'I had heard of such customs in the far south.' Zelin

Raes nodded as if something he suspected had been confirmed. 'We do things differently.' He continued walking and now it was Kheda's turn to follow his lead. 'I was the only one of my father's sons taught to read and write.' He smiled thinly. 'It's difficult to cherish ambitions of ruling if you lack such basic skills. No warriors would follow a leader who couldn't read a ciphered dispatch or consult a book of omens.' He looked at the younger boys hiding rather more ineptly than their elders, affection in his eyes. 'Few are tempted to learn in secret, when they know the first word they write might as well be the signature on their own death warrant.'

'Then where are your brothers, my lord?' Kheda asked boldly.

'Here and there.' Zelin slid a contemplative glance at him as they walked on. 'Married to daughters of Zelin's most favoured village spokesmen, or to girls born to such lesser sons of other domains. They are permitted to own slaves and to trade within their own domains and anywhere they have a blood tie. Their wives keep their ledgers, submitting all such records to my own wives' scrutiny.' Zelin Raes looked up. 'You know, of all the things you have said so far, your interest in my sons' fates has done the most to convince me that you are truly who you claim to be.'

Kheda realised the stands of buttress-rooted ironwoods ahead formed a ring around a tall, slender tower virtually the same height and thickness as one of the trees. At its top was a room walled with glass faceted like a diamond.

Many healers could have identified those plants in your physic garden. Only the rulers of a domain are charged with reading the portents written among the patterns of stars and jewels in the heavens or signs glimpsed among the vagaries of nature all around the earthly compass. No impostor could feign sufficient knowledge.

'Forgive me, my lord.' Kheda shook his head regretfully. 'Do not ask me to take the omens from your observatory with you.'

Zelin Raes frowned ominously. 'Why not?'

'Because I have lost all confidence in my ability to read such guidance,' Kheda said sombrely.

'You led the warriors of the southern reaches to victory over savages coming out of the empty ocean.' Zelin Raes searched Kheda's face. 'The men of Chazen followed you to slay a dragon.'

'Many wise men, my father among them, have long said ill consequences will inevitably follow deceit, however well intentioned.' Kheda didn't try to hide the tremor in his voice. 'I let everyone believe Ulla Safar had truly murdered me, in turn believing such a sham was sanctioned by portent. When I returned, I won my victory but I had to surrender dominion over Daish or take up arms against my beloved son. He had begun to rule in all good faith as my heir, trusting in his own reading of the portents. When I believed the omens bound me to Chazen, I was forced to surrender any claim to the children I had fathered to my wives of Daish, to my grief, and theirs. I must bear the responsibility for all their sorrows.'

How better to convince this honest lord than by showing him the true depths of my heartache? I am still exploiting that misbegotten tangle of lies for my own benefit.

'Your wife of Chazen has borne you twin daughters,' Zelin Raes said cautiously. 'That is surely an omen of surpassing affirmation.'

'For the domain, and for Itrac Chazen.' Swallowing sourness in his throat, Kheda nodded. 'I am not so bold as to believe it extends to me. There are many deaths to be laid to my account.'

'Your actions surely saved just as many lives,' Zelin Raes countered.

Kheda shook his head. 'I wonder if there might not have been some better path. One that would have cost fewer lives and spared some measure of the pain visited upon innocents. This uncertainty has left me unable to trust my reading of the omens that should guide me as ruler of Chazen.'

Will you accept that? I cannot confess that I no longer believe there's guidance to be read in the night skies or the vagaries of candle flames, or the shapes of molten metal or from wax dripping into water. No more than I can admit to consorting with wizards.

'Yet you came here,' Zelin Raes challenged him.

'Because I can rid your domain of this dragon and that beast is an evil no domain should be subject to.' Kheda looked steadily back. 'Or I will die in the attempt.'

Because it's my fault the accursed creature is here, at least in part.

'That's a powerful wager made against your future,' Zelin Raes said softly.

Kheda simply shrugged.

No omen warned me of the consequences that would flow from my decision to sail west, did it?

Zelin Raes looked up at the bright morning sun faintly veiled with skeins of dust. 'The heavenly Diamond that is talisman for all warlords shines with the stars of the Winged Snake, where we should look for omens concerning travel. You don't think this is a favourable omen for your arrival here, at this time? The soothsayers all agree the dragon and the winged snake are akin.'

'This is your domain, my lord,' Kheda said stolidly. 'Such things are for you to say.'

'The Pearl pauses opposite, just for these two days as the heavenly compass turns, in the arc where signs for siblings show themselves. Are not all warlords in some sense brothers? Pearls are the wealth of Chazen, are they not? Even here, we have heard that domain's past two pearl harvests have been richer than any in living memory.' Zelin Raes pursed his lips as he gazed up into the distant empty blue. 'And the Mirror Bird's stars are there. Its tailfeathers are reputed to turn aside magic. The symbol has long been a favoured talisman in these reaches, especially for any who have dealings with the barbarians from the mainland.' He glanced at Kheda, his face questioning. 'As a warlord, you will know the more obscure significances wound around the moons.'

Kheda met this test with a level reply. 'The Pearl is called a talisman against dragons in ancient poems. And the heavenly arc opposite either moon is known as the dragon's tail in certain ancient and obscure books of lore.'

Zelin Raes smiled his secretly satisfied smile again. 'What lies unseen behind the dragon threatens it, does it not? While Amethyst, for new ideas and humility in contemplating them, rides with the Yora Hawk, which is a symbol of strength and vigilance. These can be seen in the arc of friendship. Do you truly come here as a friend, my lord Kheda?'

'I do.' Kheda was glad he didn't have to lie about that.

'I'm pleased to hear it.' Zelin Raes's face was unreadable. 'So Ruby for courage rests in the stars of the Bowl that can represent valuable knowledge gained. I must be bold if I am to accept you and this lore you bring to defeat the dragon.'

'Indeed, my lord.' Kheda inclined his head to hide the ambiguity of his response.

I could argue a very different picture drawn among the stars; one far less reassuring.

'But what of the fainter jewels in the sky?' Kheda looked up to see Zelin Raes staring intently at him, unsmiling. 'Since the new year's stars aligned themselves, the Emerald has passed from the southern half of the compass to the northern, while the Topaz has made the opposite journey. That warns us all to be sure we examine every aspect of the guidance we construe from the stars. With Emerald and Topaz facing each other across a conjunction fixed until the turn of the year, we are in days of great uncertainty.'

Kheda opted for silence as the Zelin warlord studied him.

'I will consult every arc of the heavenly compass before I make my decision, my lord Kheda,' Zelin Raes said with firm decision. 'In the meantime, you must be weary and hungry and – forgive me, my lord – but you reek of stale sweat and a slave-trading ship's filthy holds. Felash will take you to quarters where you may bathe and eat. I will summon you when I have made my decision.'

He walked straight-backed towards the grove of iron-wood trees surrounding the observatory.

'This way.' Unsmiling, the warlord's body slave headed back the way they had come. Kheda followed meekly.

No 'my lord' from you. You're not convinced. Just how much does your master value your counsel?

The slave took an abrupt turn as they passed through the physic garden to lead Kheda through a previously unnoticed gate. It opened into a shaded walk between two long pavilions whose walls were covered with little tiles of pale-grey glass. Kheda thought they were quite plain until a shaft of sunlight reached through the awnings of heavy silk slung between the buildings. He saw pale canthira leaves in the mosaic, woven into the fabric of the wall like the patterns in figured damask.

Felash flung open a door that seemed no different from several they had already passed. 'You will wait in here, if you please.' Despite the man's ostensible politeness, this was plainly an order.

Kheda nodded calmly as he went obediently inside. 'Your lord is most gracious to offer me such hospitality.'

I'm hardly about to start a fight with you, my friend, or with the armoured swordsmen who will doubtless be guarding any other door to these quarters.

The room within was decorated with the sumptuousness reserved for honoured guests in the southern Archipelago, even if the style was markedly different. The floor was tiled with eight-pointed stars tied together by plain crosses. No two star-tiles were alike, different flowers and leaves engraved on each one. Yet the overall effect was one of striking harmony, as every star-tile had a coppery ground of red, while the crosswise ones glowed gold. The silk hangings stirring gently against the walls were ochre shot with faintest yellow and the coverlets heaped generously on the broad bed set against the far wall were purest white.

Kheda walked over to a tall vase of shimmering white ceramic, intrigued. Its pierced outer surface was as intricate as lace, delicately patterned with leaves and birds to echo the decorations on the floor tiles. Within it, he saw there was a second, solid-walled vessel. As he was wondering how one picked up such a thing without breaking it, he heard footsteps behind him.

'My lord.' A slightly built man in a russet satin robe wrapped over black trousers bowed low. Slave or servant? Kheda had no way of knowing. 'You must wish to bathe.'

Kheda saw the man had entered through one of the hangings, drawing it aside to catch on a peg and reveal a smaller room tiled from floor to ceiling. Kheda could see a gleaming brass ewer steaming beside a broad, shallow bath. 'So if that is the bathroom, and this is the bedchamber—'

'You have a sitting room through here.' The servant

went over to the far wall and pulled another hanging aside to show Kheda a second open arch.

'Thank you.' Kheda inclined his head. 'I certainly wish to bathe and I will be inordinately grateful if you could provide me with some clean clothes.'

'It will be our honour, my lord.' The servant bowed. 'If you want anything in the meantime, call for a slave and send them for me, for Dagil.' He opened a solid door concealed behind yet another length of woven silk.

Kheda watched as the man exchanged a few quiet words with an armoured swordsman outside in the corridor. As soon as the door was firmly closed, Kheda made a rapid circuit of the room, checking behind every hanging silk panel. There turned out to be just one entrance in each wall, as he had already seen. There were also slots cut high up in the plain plaster walls, dark against the white.

For better ventilation? Or for the greater ease of eaves-dropping servants?

He also noted that the white glass tiles of the ceiling had patterns of transparent leaves and flowers in each corner.

Could someone be lurking up here to look down on me?

He let the silk hanging fall closed behind him as he went into the bathroom. Stripping off his stained and musty clothes was a pleasure only equalled by the sensation of pouring warm water down his gritty, sticky chest. Kneeling in the bath, he dipped a washcloth in the shallow water and scooped aromatic liquid soap from an array of bowls on a convenient shelf. Once he had lathered and rinsed himself clean, he addressed himself to washing his hair and beard thoroughly for the first time since he had left Chazen waters. Emptying the last of the ewers over his head, he gasped, finding it unexpectedly cold. Once he had recovered from the shock, he found it had driven away much of his tiredness. Stepping cautiously out of the bath, he wrapped a sturdy cotton towel around himself.

At least these people can't use silk for everything.

Wiping water from his beard, he walked into the bedchamber, wondering if Dagil had returned with clean clothes for him. He halted when he saw who was seated demurely on the edge of the wide bed.

'My lord Kheda.' Mian Zelin smiled demurely.

'My lord.' Kauris Zelin was close beside her, her smile less welcoming.

'My ladies.' Kheda bowed as elegantly as he could swathed in a length of cotton cloth.

Mian's smile took on something of the private satisfaction that characterised her husband's. 'Your people are fortunate to have you as a healer.'

'Judging by the salves and tinctures you carry.' Kauris half-turned to look at the contents of Kheda's travelling bag strewn across the white coverlets.

He noted that the back of her overdress of yellow beads only fastened at the neck, falling open below that.

So that's how you manage to sit down without risking glass splinters in your elegant rear ends.

'I hope you resealed anything you opened, my ladies.' Kheda took a few paces to satisfy himself that none of the little clay pots or tightly stoppered vials was leaking. 'Otherwise you'll never get the stains out of that quilt.'

He was saved from trying to find something else to say by Dagil's return. The servant bowed low to his mistresses before offering Kheda dark-blue trousers in heavy silk and one of the open-fronted robes, slightly lighter in both fabric and colour. Both garments were quite undecorated.

'Thank you.' Kheda took the clothes and handed the towel to Dagil. The servant bowed again and left. Kheda noticed that both women's body slaves had joined the swordsman waiting outside the door to the corridor.

Mian watched frankly as he drew on the trousers and knotted their drawstring tight. 'Travelling with barbarians hasn't infected you with their curious fear of nakedness.'

'No, my lady,' Kheda said briefly.

Kauris was looking him up and down as he shrugged on the open-fronted robe. 'Your wife of Chazen is a lucky woman, my lord.'

'You flatter me.' He spared her a glance before concentrating on the ties on either hip that turned out to secure the crossed fronts.

'And your wives of Daish,' Mian remarked. 'Those marriages proved fertile, I believe?'

You two haven't wasted any time searching your memories and ledgers for whatever news you have ever heard from the southernmost domains.

Kheda decided to keep his responses as short as was politely possible. 'Indeed.' He covered his curtness by returning to his discarded clothes and retrieving his leather belt. He settled his sheathed dagger on his hip as he left the bath chamber a second time, smiling blandly at Zelin Raes's wives.

Mian walked towards him, the silver and indigo beads of her overdress shifting over the fine silk of her shift and outlining the lithe grace of her body. 'Do the women of the southern reaches do their duty in bringing new blood into their domains?'

Kauris leaned back, propping herself on her hands, a pose that artlessly emphasised her splendid bosom. 'We have rather fewer opportunities, with all but the crossings through Tabril and Essa waters cut off by the Dawa Sea's currents.'

Mian walked softly around behind Kheda, so close that

he could smell her fragile, intoxicating perfume. 'How weary are you, my lord?' she whispered seductively.

'Not so weary that I would make such a mistake.' He took a step away from her. 'I've travelled too long under strange stars to risk leaving the shadow of my own misfortunes on any domain kind enough to shelter me.'

'You are all consideration.' Mian walked back towards the bed, her shapely hips swaying teasingly.

You're not serious about this. Marriage to three wives back in Daish and latterly to Itrac in Chazen has taught me that much about women. Do you still think I am some impostor who would leap at the chance to bed a warlord's woman? It might almost be worth slipping an arm around your waist, just to see how you react. If I didn't think I'd lose that arm to your body slave's sword. Cut off at the neck, probably.

'We would welcome an introduction to your lady Itrac Chazen.' Mian swept the beads of her overdress gracefully aside as she sat down beside Kauris. 'We have courier doves that can take a letter in your cipher as far south as Calece or Kithir, if you can call on either of those lords to send it on to your lady wife.'

Kheda thought swiftly. 'I believe my lord of Calece would forward a message to Redigal Coron, who is a valued ally of Chazen.'

But have his cleverest counsellors found the key to Chazen's ciphers yet? What news of my travels dare I let loose in those waters?

'We will be mightily in your debt if you can rid Zelin of this dragon.' Kauris sat straight-backed, all business now, her eyes as hard as the amber they so resembled. 'Such debts will be repaid.'

Mian waved a slender hand at the tall vase of pierced white ceramic. 'We can offer our double-shelled wares.'

'Our silk weavers' speciality is two-coloured brocade,' Kauris continued in the same breath.

'My lord's sisters have married into Matul and into Juduc.' Mian folded her beringed hands in her lap. 'We will seek their goodwill on your wife's behalf for favourable terms regarding Matul lustre wares.'

'And their white silks.' Kauris brushed her hand against the coverlet she was sitting on. 'Juduc brocades are many-coloured, and highly prized.'

'While their crystal glass is second to none,' Mian concluded for her.

Kheda bowed courteously. 'I'm sure my lady Itrac will be pleased to offer you the pick of Chazen's pearls.'

'Won't she be surprised to learn you've made such a promise?' Mian asked casually. 'Where does she think you are?'

Kheda stiffened before he could help himself. He could only hope it wasn't too noticeable.

What have you already learned from Risala or Velindre? What will happen if you catch a lie dividing us? Better stick to the truth as far as possible and hope that they have done the same.

'My lady wife believes I am in seclusion on a remote isle of our domain,' he said bluntly, 'meditating on the nature of omens and portent.'

'In seclusion.' Kauris shook her head slightly, a faint frown creasing her broad brow. 'Yet someone brought you word there that a dragon had been seen here, so far distant, so far beyond any of your ties of blood or obligation.'

'The fastest courier dove can fly the length of the Archipelago in a handful of days.' Kheda tried a smile to detract from the evasion.

'You learned of it before word had even spread through these reaches.' Kauris looked at him, questioning.

'Who would possess such a dove, brought all this way, on the unlikely chance of having news to send to Chazen?' Mian shook her head and her cloud of fine curls shivered.

Kauris left Kheda no time to reply. 'While the finest crew of the lightest trireme would be hard-pressed to retrace its flight in anything less than twenty-five or thirty days.'

'News of a trireme making such a journey would fly this way and that along the sea lanes,' added Mian.

'As fast as the courier doves of the message-brokers.' Kauris nodded.

'But we heard no such word.' Mian cocked her head on one side.

'And you were found sailing in some barbarian trader's ship, not a trireme.' Now Kauris stared at him with open challenge.

The only sound in the room was the soft rustle of the silken hangings shifting in the breeze.

'You will have to forgive me, my ladies.' Kheda met the women's eyes with a level gaze of his own. 'I cannot explain myself to you before I have explained myself to my own wife.'

'I wonder what she might have to forgive,' Kauris murmured speculatively.

'We will forgo any explanations –' Mian's bracelets jingled as she waved a deprecating hand '– if you rid Zelin of this dragon.'

'Do so and you will have earned our boundless gratitude,' Kauris assured him. 'Of course, if you are lying to our lord, you will have earned our endless enmity.' Her voice hardened.

Mian's eyes glittered, cold as jet. 'Then your lady Itràc Chazen will find the threads of her trading networks snapping just as fast as we can contrive it.'

'I expect nothing less, my ladies.' Kheda bowed briskly to interrupt whatever threat Kauris was about to make. 'I will either rid Zelin of this dragon, and earn your most valued friendship, or I will die in the attempt.'

*I've been menaced by the likes of Ulla Safar. I've looked
a dragon in the eye and lived to tell the tale. Don't think you
can frighten me.*

This time the silence was broken by a soft knock on
the door to the corridor.

'That's quite a wager to make with your future.' Mian
smiled sweetly as she rose from the bed. 'We are happy
to accept it.'

'If you fail in such a task –' Kauris got to her feet as
well '– it will certainly be best if you die.'

'Oh.' Mian feigned sudden recollection and slid a
slender hand into a pocket hidden in the seam of her
underdress. 'This is yours.' She held out Shek Kul's ring.

'My thanks, my lady.' Kheda slipped the emerald–set
silver onto the middle finger of his sword-hand.

*Were you planning on keeping that, if I said the wrong
thing?*

The door opened to reveal the body slave whom
Kheda thought belonged to Mian Zelin. He bowed. 'My
lady, the lord's poet wishes to enter.'

Risala?

'Indeed?' Kauris glanced over her shoulder as she made
her way from the room. 'It will be interesting to see what
my lord Shek Kul has to say about her.'

'We have sent courier doves to enquire, as you
suggested,' Mian explained sweetly.

Kheda managed a serene smile. 'I assure you he holds
her in the very highest esteem.'

The slaves in the corridor retreated to let their
mistresses leave the room. As the two women strode away,
their bodyguards two paces behind, the swordsman still
guarding Kheda's door ushered Risala inside.

She hurried over to him as the heavy wood closed
behind her with a solid clunk. He took her in his arms.
She was wearing a gossamer robe of palest blue silk woven

with jessamine flowers wrapped over a long sleeveless sapphire shift. She wore her necklace of silver-mounted shark's teeth and a pair of silver earrings wrought from delicate silver twists and spirals. Like him, she'd had Shek Kul's ring returned to her, and was now wearing it openly on the same finger as he did.

Kheda noted she'd discarded the grubby bandage around her wrist. 'How is your arm? Does it ache at all?'

She shook her head briefly. 'No. I think it's all quite healed.'

'That's a blessing.' He wrapped her in a careful embrace and breathed in spicy sweet perfume newly brushed through her hair. 'There may be ears hidden behind these walls,' he whispered.

'I know.' Her reply tickled his own ear.

'Have you seen the others?' As he tried to pull back a little, he realised that her filigree earring had caught in his beard. He reached up to extricate himself.

'Ow.' Risala flinched. 'No, wait.' She deftly unfastened the earring and stepped away.

'Do you suppose my lord Zelin Raes will lend me a slave to trim my whiskers?' Kheda disentangled the delicate silver ornament and offered it back to her. 'I haven't worn them this long since I was younger than his eldest son.'

'Perhaps.' Instead of replacing her earring, Risala removed the other one. She held out her empty hand with a coquettish smile. 'We finally have some time to ourselves, my lord.'

Kheda noted the smile didn't reach her eyes as he stepped close again and slipped his hands around her slender waist. 'Where are the others?' he murmured as he bent to kiss her neck.

Risala pressed herself against him with every appearance of pleasure. 'I've seen Vel. There are two *zamorin* living here. They've welcomed him with every courtesy and all due privacy.'

Because they know better than anyone else how grievously their kind can be mutilated.

'Let's hope so.' Kheda stroked a wisp of Risala's newly washed hair away from her face. 'What about Sirince and Crisk?' he breathed as he kissed the corner of her mouth.

Let's hope neither of them slips and refers to Velindre as 'she'.

'I don't know. No one seems very interested in them. They're just barbarians.' There was nevertheless faint concern in Risala's murmured reply.

She twisted in Kheda's embrace to look at the bed still littered with the contents of his leather travel bag. 'Shall we make ourselves more comfortable, my lord?' she asked more loudly, openly suggestive as she shed her gossamer outer robe.

'Why not?' Kheda undid his belt, laying his dagger aside with a smile that verged on a leer for any watching hidden eyes.

Risala scooped up the vials and jars and shoved them back into the bag so quickly that Kheda worried a second time about spills staining the pristine white quilts. 'They went through my things as well,' she told him under cover of the rattle and clinking. 'They wanted to know about that sea-ivory dragon's tail you gave me.' Letting the bag slip down to the floor she slid onto the bed, opening her arms to him.

Kheda pressed close beside her, one hand resting on her hip. 'I didn't know you still carried that.' Lying on their sides, with their heads on the same pillow, no one more than a few paces away could have heard them with any clarity.

'You gave it to me.' Risala looked at him, unblinking. 'When you believed it was a talisman against the dragons.'

Kheda avoided that challenge by closing his eyes and kissing her.

I found the uncarved ivory washed up on a hostile shore and saw the shape of the dragon's tail in it. Carving it, I convinced myself it was a portent affirming my decision to go in search of lore to fight the magic of the wild men. Only now I know how very different a real dragon's tail looks.

He found a question to turn the conversation. 'Who do you mean by "they"?'

'Mian and Kauris Zelin.' Risala brushed a kiss against his lips. 'They wanted to know exactly where we had come from, as well as just how and when we had heard about the dragon here.'

Kheda raised himself on one elbow to look down at her. 'What did you tell them?'

'I played the witless concubine.' Risala's whisper was sharp with asperity. 'Too in thrall to my lord's commanding presence in my bed to betray his secrets. I said they must ask you.'

'I managed to avoid answering pretty well.' Kheda kissed her with an approving grin. 'So they turned to not-so-veiled threats, promising to ruin Chazen trade if I fail to deliver them from the dragon.'

Declaring myself may have won me the chance to challenge the dragon instead of being driven out of Zelin waters, leaving Risala and Velindre to whatever fate might befall them. But I've raised the stakes mightily by doing this. I've wagered Itrac's future, and that of our innocent daughters, without their knowledge or consent. Am I going to bring such grief on them as I did on my wives and children of Daish?

He found he was no longer smiling.

'They did their best to persuade me to stay here when you leave.' Risala looked up at him, her blue eyes opaque. 'Warning me that, talisman or no talisman, I would be going into mortal danger. That no epic poem I might make of the tale would be worth the risk.'

Kheda felt a cold qualm in his stomach at odds with the heat rising irresistibly in his blood at having Risala so close, so soft and compliant beneath him. 'That would make you a hostage against my success.'

'I don't think so.' Her gaze shifted over his shoulder, to stare at the glass-tiled ceiling. 'I think they're genuinely concerned for my safety.'

Kheda had been about to ask if she'd seen any shadow moving over the transparent patterns above them. The words died on his tongue. He stroked his hand up and down her hip. Rough skin on fingers callused by ropes and coarsened by wind and sun snagged on the fine silk of her gown. 'You can stay, if you want to.' He forced the words past the tightness in his throat. 'You know better than anyone how dangerous it will be.'

'You won't even look for the omens that might promise us success.' Her eyes flickered back to pierce him with antagonism. 'But how can I stay here? How could I live not knowing what had become of you, if you don't come back?'

She reached up to pull his head down, kissing him fiercely. Arching her back, she pressed her hips into his, prompting an answering surge of treacherous ardour in his loins.

You're more and more angry with me. Is this what I should be doing? We've had so few chances to make love. While I delight in your body, so close we're one flesh, it only serves to show me the gap widening between us. But if I turn away from you now, will that be the end of everything we might have?

Kheda couldn't have put the confusion of his thoughts into coherent speech if Risala had held her knife to his throat, so he yielded to her insistence. She shifted his hand to her breast and he felt her nipple harden beneath the sheer fabric. Risala pulled loose the ties that fastened his robe and ran her hand up his chest. His breathing quickened as he bent to kiss the soft skin just above her shift. He crooked a finger beneath the edge of the silk to see how far he could slide it down over the swell of her bosom.

A brisk double knock halted him. He looked up as the door to the corridor opened. It was the Zelin servant Dagil.

'Forgive the interruption, my lord.' Dagil gazed blandly towards the windows with practised discretion. 'My lord Zelin Raes and his ladies ask you to join them for some refreshment.'

'We will be honoured.' Kheda rolled over to sit on the edge of the bed and refasten the ties of his robe. He waited for a moment, his back turned to Dagil, until the most obvious evidence of what had been interrupted subsided.

Risala straightened her dress with a swift tug and shrugged into her gossamer robe. She spared Kheda a brief smile but her eyes were still impenetrable.

'Let's not keep our gracious hosts waiting.' Kheda stood up and did his best to pull the creases out of his clothing as he donned his belt and dagger.

Let's hope we find Velindre, Sirince and Crisk there, too. Will we get any chance to find out what they've been asked? Or what they have said?

CHAPTER NINE

The armoured slave knocked once, firmly, on the slatted double doors. Another swordsman opened to him, brows raised in faint surprise. Seeing who followed the slave who had knocked, the swordsman immediately stepped back, bowing low. 'My lady Laio.'

'My lord of Shek.' The woman entered, poised and graceful, and addressed herself to the warlord. He was sitting at the far end of the luxurious carpet that softened the polished and patterned wooden floor of this informal audience chamber.

'My lady wife.' As Shek Kul inclined his head, a fond smile softened the deep lines carved into his stern visage. His long, coarse hair had once been jet black but grey now lightened both his temples and his full beard. Though there was no sign that age had softened his powerful muscles, plainly visible beneath the fine tawny silk of his flowing tunic and the wide-legged trousers tied close at his ankles.

'Forgive the intrusion.' The warlord's lady addressed the domain's spokesmen sitting in obedient lines along either side of the carpet. She smiled winsomely. 'Tioq is still unwell, my lord. I had thought she would have recovered after a sound night's sleep.'

Considerably younger than her husband, she was visibly pregnant. One hand rested on her belly, discreetly swelling beneath the wide sash belting her sleeveless gown of fine blue cotton embroidered with green silk vines. Where Shek

Kul wore sturdy chains of silver around his neck and waist, his hands heavy with rings and bracelets, Laio Shek wore no jewellery beyond the silver combs holding her long, black hair off her face. The barest hint of colour touched her lips and deep-brown eyes. The bloom of impending motherhood lent a glow to her delicate tan complexion that needed no cosmetic enhancement.

'The health of your daughter—' The man in the centre of the row to the warlord's sword-hand cleared his throat. 'If you wish to set your mind at ease, my lord, we will gladly wait on your return.' Others murmured their agreement.

'You are most understanding.' Shek Kul rose to his feet as the men of the domain bowed as best they could from their seated positions. 'So, my lady wife, let's see if our beloved daughter recovers any faster for the promise of a vile-tasting glass of physic.' His smile gave the seated men permission to chuckle indulgently.

'If you think that's best.' Laio left the room, her faithful body slave close behind her.

Shek Kul nodded briefly to the swordsman guarding the door as he followed, his own personal attendant shadowing him. Outside the wide, wood-panelled hall, Shek Kul offered Laio his arm and they ascended the marble stairs set in the corner of the square hollow keep.

The warlord's slave went ahead, Laio Shek's following after. Both men wore their hair and beards cut short, not about to give an enemy anything to grab hold of in a close-quarters fight. Both wore hauberks of highly polished chain mail, their double-looped sword belts studded with brass ornaments. As well as two swords, each man carried two long daggers with serpentine blades. The pommels of Shek Kul's slave's weapons were golden hawks' heads, set with emerald eyes. Laio's slave's blades were tipped with iridescent moonstones, smooth and unblemished. He was half the age of the warlord's attendant, barely older than his mistress. But his eyes were alert and his face keen, the equal of Shek Kul's grey-bearded slave.

Reaching the floor above, both slaves set themselves to watch the stairwell and the long corridor. As his attendant nodded to confirm there was no one within earshot, Shek Kul halted. 'What is it?'

'I've had word from the Zelin domain, through the good offices of Lacil Senana.' Laio reached into a slim pocket hidden in her sash of silk vine leaves and handed Shek Kul a fine slip of paper. 'He's there, in Zelin.'

'The barbarian?' Shek Kul frowned as he peered at the cramped writing.

'No.' Laio shook her head, impatient. 'Daish Kheda.'

'Chazen Kheda now,' Shek Kul corrected her absently as he deciphered the script. 'Is the barbarian with him?'

'Not the one you mean, not Dev.' Now it was Laio's turn to frown. 'I think we can truly trust he is dead.'

'A fate richly deserved if half I suspected was true,' Shek Kul growled.

'Indeed.' Laio wiped sweat from her face, not only prompted by the cloying heat.

Her slave pushed open one of the louvred wooden shutters overlooking the palace's extensive grounds. It made no real difference. Even on the highest floors of this tall keep there was precious little breeze to stir the air.

Laio spared him a quick smile of gratitude before she continued. 'But there are barbarians with Daish Kheda — Chazen Kheda,' she corrected herself. 'A slave-trader and some attendant of his, and that *zamorin* scholar.'

Shek Kul looked at her, the crease between his brows deepening. 'The *zamorin* Risala fetched from the mainland, at that villain Dev's request?'

'The very same,' Laio confirmed. 'And Risala is there, too.'

'Is she?' Shek Kul ran a thoughtful hand over his magnificent beard. 'Just what are they doing in Zelin? Why are they in western waters at all, when we thought they were safely well away from us in the far south?'

'It seems Zelin is plagued by a dragon.' There was a slight tremor in Laio's voice as she pulled a second courier dove message from the discreet pocket in her sash and handed it over.

Startled, both armoured slaves stared at her. Laio shot them both a warning glare as Shek Kul deciphered the writing on the paper slip. Children's voices echoed in rooms down the corridor, penetrating the tense silence.

'Nec Clusa has no reason to lie,' Shek Kul breathed.

'No.' Laio watched him, tension in her face.

'Daish—' Shek Kul snapped irritated fingers. 'Chazen Kheda rid the southern domains of a dragon—'

'Two, if you credit some of the tales,' the warlord's body slave commented, still alert for anyone coming up or down the marble stairs.

'And now he turns up in Zelin waters, just as Zelin Raes finds himself plagued by such a beast.' Shek Kul's heavy black brows knotted above his formidable hooked nose.

Midnight tresses rippling down her back to her waist, Laio shook her head. 'Neither Chazen nor Daish has trading links with any of the western reaches, not even at a remove.' Perplexity mingled with annoyance in her words. 'Not that I have been able to discover, anyway.'

Shek Kul waved away the irrelevance. 'He can only be there to fight the beast.'

'Imagine the rewards Zelin Raes will shower upon him,' Shek Kul's slave murmured.

'I can reward him as richly.' The warlord glowered. 'So why hasn't he presented himself at my gates?'

'Perhaps he doesn't know how he could serve you?' Laio ventured.

Shek Kul looked at her, heavy brows raised sardonically. 'You think it's still a secret?' He gestured in the direction of the stairs and the floor below. 'You think that every man or woman of all those villages that have sent their spokesmen here to beg for my counsel have kept their mouths loyally shut? You don't think they've been begging for passage on any ship leaving our waters, voluble in their fear and dread?'

'We've heard of no great flight from our islands and villages, my lord.' Laio met the rising challenge in his words with a level gaze. 'Have we? Delai? Afik?'

'No, my lady,' Shek Kul's slave said firmly.

Laio's attendant echoed agreement. 'Your people have faith in you, my lord.'

'Thus far,' he growled. 'Perhaps.'

Laio continued resolutely. 'I can believe that word is slower to travel than we feared, my lord.'

Shek Kul nodded slowly. 'Our friends won't spread it beyond their immediate circle, for fear of worsening our situation—'

'While our enemies won't want anyone who might help us to know. Not before they have calculated how to turn this situation to their best advantage and our detriment.' Laio shuddered, vulnerability stripping away her poise. 'Not before the beast has laid waste to the domain.'

Shek Kul gathered her in his arms. 'If Risala is in Zelin, we have friends closer than Melciar Kir suspects.'

Laio rested her head on his broad chest for a moment. 'I wish Mahli were here.'

Shek Kul tightened his embrace. 'She'll be serving us best assuring her uncle of Kaasik that the Shek domain isn't in imminent danger of being destroyed by a dragon.'

'Is that what you're telling those spokesmen?' Laio Shek looked up, her tone mordant.

'What else can I tell them?' Shek Kul let slip a frustrated sigh. 'Thus far, the beast has kept itself to the craters of the fire mountain.'

'In so far as it has been seen lately,' the slave Delai volunteered. 'It seems to come and go, from our scouts' reports.'

'Perhaps it will go and not come back.' Laio's slave Afik spoke up hopefully.

'The omens suggest otherwise,' Shek Kul said sombrely, holding Laio close. 'So let's invite my lord Chazen Kheda to share whatever he knows of driving these vile creatures away and keeping them away.'

'I'll send word back through Lacil Senana.' Laio pulled herself free of Shek Kul's arms, her pretty face contemplating a new question. 'She'll want something significant in return for sending an unopened enciphered message onwards.'

Shek Kul's smile turned his stern face cruel. 'Tell her Gar Shek will return from her current trading trip to the unbroken lands to find herself divorced.'

'My lord, can we afford to break with my lord of Gaska just now?' Delai was openly alarmed. 'My lady Gar is his most beloved sister and he has long been friends with my lord of Senana—'

Shek Kul silenced the slave with a sideways cut of his hand. 'Do not presume to question me on this.'

Laio wasn't so easily intimidated. 'Gar has been loyal, my lord, and the children—'

'Is Tioq really still ailing or was that just an excuse?' Shek Kul turned to look down the corridor towards the rooms where the faint sounds of children playing had continued unperturbed.

Laio's immaculately plucked brows tightened briefly. 'She is perfectly well, my lord.'

'I'm glad to hear it. She had better appear at dinner tonight to prove it.' Shek Kul sighed again. 'There are those among the village spokesmen who will seize on any hint of sickness among us as an omen of dire things to come.'

'What will happen, my lord?' Laio bit her lip, unconsciously laying her hands protectively on her pregnant belly.

'The present omens can be interpreted in many and varied ways.' Shek Kul shook his head. 'As we have been discussing all morning.'

'Not all of the soothsayers foretell disaster, my lady,' Afik offered.

'True.' Shek Kul sounded sceptical nevertheless. 'Believe me, my beloved wife, as soon as I see some portent guiding me to a definitive reading, you will be the first to know. And now I had better return to our loyal spokesmen. We don't want to give them too long to discuss such weighty matters among themselves, or to wonder what really demanded my absence.'

'You can castigate me for fussing over a sick child.' Laio managed a wry smile. 'I must be oversensitive as this pregnancy begins to weigh upon me in the heat.'

'Those new to their responsibilities might just about believe that.' Shek Kul brushed a kiss on her glossy hair. 'The rest will soon have put them right. You cannot escape such a well-deserved reputation for astuteness so easily, my lady.'

'You flatter me, my lord.' Laio smiled with something of her usual pertness.

Shek Kul offered her his arm as they turned towards the stairs. 'While I'm calming whatever speculation is fermenting down there, you'll be sending word to Lacil Senana?'

'At once, my lord,' she confirmed.

As the two nobles walked down the stairs, the slaves fell into step behind them. Shek Kul paused on the floor below to kiss Laio's forehead. 'Don't tire yourself in this heat. As soon as you've sent your courier doves, I'd rather you went to rest instead of rejoining the children.'

'I'll see how I feel.' Laio shrugged, non-committal.

Shek Kul switched his gaze to Afik. 'You're responsible for your mistress's well-being.'

'I know that, my lord,' the slave assured him.

Shek Kul watched Laio and her attendant disappear down the stairwell. 'Do you think Chazen Kheda does know the secrets of driving out dragons?' he asked Delai, not turning his head.

'There are no dragons in the southern reaches.' The slave's certainty faltered a little. 'At least, none we've heard of recently.'

'Who knows what news the next flight of courier doves will bring?' Shek Kul mused. 'Perhaps Kheda will repay some of what he owes this domain by sharing his lore.' The warlord paused, shaking his head. 'If this beast plaguing Zelin isn't the death of him first. How often can a man test his destiny against such a foe and survive?'

'What will we do then, my lord?' ventured the patiently waiting body slave.

Shek Kul ran a heavily ringed hand through his thick hair, grimacing as grey strands caught briefly in the clawed setting of a diamond. 'Perhaps Risala will know something to help us, or this *zamorin*. We must make sure we know exactly where they go, if Chazen Kheda is lost.'

'I will see to it, my lord,' Delai promised.

CHAPTER TEN

What will I do if we can't get rid of the beast? Are we even in the right place? Velindre's not dared to scry for it.

'Are we certain the dragon is still somewhere close?' Kheda glanced at Zelin Raes, who was standing at his sword-hand.

'It is.' The warlord nodded with absolute certainty, diamonds glittering in the gold brow band of his helm. Gilded rings wove feathered patterns into the shifting chain-mail veil protecting his neck and throat. 'That last dispatch galley brought word culled from fishermen on all the local islands.'

Behind them, Zelin Raes's body slave Felash spoke up. 'We've had light triremes circling these waters since the beast first appeared. The creature's hiding there.'

The heavy trireme on whose stern platform they stood sped over sea gilded in the west by the sinking sun. The warlord stared at a solitary islet set like an emerald in the shining waters, his teeth audibly grinding. He was armoured with a magnificence that outshone all his men. A round steel plate set into the front of his chain-mail hauberk was decorated with a golden mirror bird, diamond chips marking out the stars of the constellation within the design.

'What will you do if we cannot rid your domain of this dragon?' Kheda asked quietly. 'We will do our best—'

'I shall make certain everyone from the barbarian coasts

to the open ocean in the far south knows that this failure is yours and yours alone.' The warlord looked back at him, unblinking. 'I shall challenge anyone who thinks I erred in trusting you.'

'Indeed.' Kheda looked out past the upcurved prow of the ship. Beyond the island ahead the empty waters spread wide to the horizon.

And beyond, presumably, to the unbroken lands far to the north.

Above, the evening sky was clear of cloud, faintly coloured with the haze of dust carried on the uppermost winds from beyond the setting sun. Kheda's back ached and his legs were stiff. The monotony of the long day spent standing at Zelin Raes's side had only been broken by occasional strolls along the side-decks and one brief chance to sit as a perfunctory meal was served at noon.

Though I'm sure any rower below decks would gladly swap his place for mine. We haven't slowed beyond running with only two ranks of oars through the heat of the day so the oarsmen could rest by thirds. Triremes are rowed like this in time of war. Well, only a dragon could devastate this domain more thoroughly than war.

Zelin Raes shifted beside Kheda. 'Your successes in driving dragons out of your own domain have been widely lauded by poets and scholars.'

You sound as if you want to convince yourself such tales must be true. Have barbarians truly heard of me and my battles with the dragons in Chazen? I had no idea my misbegotten fame had spread quite so far. What omens ever warned me of that?

His gaze slid to the prow platform. Risala was talking with apparent animation to the archers gathered there. That was where she had spent the whole of the day's interminable voyage. Kheda rubbed a hand over his bearded chin, feeling weary and stale.

Do you find it as difficult as I do to keep all our secrets hidden behind a smiling face, my love? You didn't come to me last night, when we were finally released a second time from the interminable hospitality of the Zelin wives. Did you lie awake as long as I did, wondering what this morning would bring? Were you as relieved and as full of dread, when dawn brought my lord of Zelin's invitation to join him on his ship and set a course for the dragon?

'If you fail—' Zelin Raes's hand strayed to the hilts of the twin swords at his hip. 'If there's some way of taking the creature unawares, perhaps we can hack it to pieces.'

Kheda shook his head. 'Poets have woven long songs around all the names of those who died in Chazen. They died fighting a dragon already wounded and near to death. Don't lead the boldest and best of Zelin's swordsmen into a futile slaughter, my lord.'

Who could justly condemn me for using magic to save so many lives?

'Then rid me of this beast.' Zelin Raes had a silken scarf twisted around his neck. He wiped sweat from his face with one end of it, careful in clumsy gauntlets. The steel plates on his sword-hand were engraved with the golden image and diamond stars of the Spear while the Hoe shone on the back of his off hand.

Much good such talisman signs will do if a dragon decides to eat you, my lord. I saw one of the beasts rip my warriors out of their armour as deftly as a man shelling a crab.

'I do not make any such rash promise.' Kheda met the Zelin warlord's challenge with a level reply. 'It may well be that I learn something new, something that requires me to retreat before attacking the creature a second time with better hope of success.'

'I've never yet been on a hunt where something unexpected didn't happen.' Zelin Raes reached up to fasten the chain-mail veil securely beneath his chin. He managed a fleeting smile before his expression turned deadly serious once again. 'Are you sure you don't want me to arm you more fully?' Beneath the hem of his hauberk the Zelin warlord wore stout leather leggings reinforced with steel and enclosing his feet. The nailed soles rasped on the solid wooden deck as he shifted his weight.

'No, thank you, my lord.' Kheda looked down at his own plain tunic and trousers of sturdy grey cotton, newly cut and sewn in the southern style by diligent seamstresses summoned by Kauris Zelin. 'We must move quietly and unseen if we are to succeed. You have been more than generous in providing me with these swords.' He rested his own hand on the hilts of the scabbarded swords thrust through his plain leather belt.

Not that I'll be stabbing this dragon through the eye if I can help it.

The trireme's shipmaster cleared his throat. He was a tall, long-limbed man wearing cropped trousers and a white silk robe hanging open over his muscular chest. 'My lord.' He had been standing with the steersman, as far forward as he could, to give Zelin Raes and this stranger as much privacy as was possible in the confined space. 'How much closer do you want us to go?'

'Kheda?' The warlord turned to him.

'This is close enough,' Kheda assured the rangy shipmaster. He stifled an absurd impulse to chuckle at the profound relief on the man's ebony face.

'Then this is where we will leave you.' Zelin Raes lifted one armoured hand.

The helmsman shouted down to the rowing master and the toiling oarsmen deftly slowed the speeding vessel. A horn screamed brassy commands from the prow platform and the armoured warriors lining the deck rails on either side looked back towards their lord.

Helmeted faces were indistinct behind metal face plates but each man's stance spoke of mingled apprehension and anticipation.

Why have you brought such a force into such danger, my lord of Zelin? Don't you believe I can do this? Are you prepared to raise arms against the beast yourself, despite all I can say to dissuade you?

Or have you brought so many men in hopes that one or two at least might escape, if the dragon does destroy this little fleet? To assure the noble ladies and people of Zelin that their lord died fighting for the domain?

Or do you want to be certain there are plenty of witnesses who can swear I took on this task of my own volition? That I was brought as close to the dragon's isle as was safely possible. That I was given no opportunity to flee and hide my shame and deceit with lies and excuses in some other domain.

Risala slipped down the ladder leading from the prow platform to the open gangway running between the ranks of rowers. An answering horn sounded from the stern platform of the light trireme following them. It was the *Reef Shark*. Kheda looked for Abari but still couldn't pick him out of the men standing beneath the curve of the stern. He wasn't among the men who had been deftly sailing the *Tacsille*. The little ship came sweeping this way and that across the sea to capture the capricious winds that both triremes could loftily ignore.

The heavy trireme slowed and stopped, triple-ranked oars barely shifting in the rolling swell. Kheda watched the *Tacsille* edging closer to the stern. The shipmaster scowled as the little ship's prow nosed perilously close to his steering oars. Crisk looked up from the seat by the *Tacsille*'s tiller. The red-headed barbarian waved, a nervous smile on his freckled face. He broke off to tug distractedly at the crossed fronts of his new brown robe.

Sirince stood stony-faced beside the brawny Zelin mariner currently manning the tiller. The wizard had also been favoured with new clothing in the local style: an ochre robe over dark-brown trousers.

Appropriate colours for a wizard attuned to the earth. Was that your choice or mere happenstance? What have you and Velindre been discussing? Have you mages come up with some plan that gives us more hope of success in driving away this dragon? We need to do better than last time. Has Crisk let slip anything to incriminate us all within earshot of some loyal Zelin man who speaks more of your Tormalin tongue than he's admitted to?

'Time to go.' Risala appeared at the top of the ladder coming up from the rowing deck. She was dressed much the same as Kheda.

'Indeed.' Kheda saw Velindre emerge from the hatch to the *Tacsille*'s hold, still in the unbleached cotton tunic and trousers of a *zamorin*, though she too had been provided with new clothes.

'My lord Kheda.' At Zelin Raes's nod, the shipmaster threw down a rope ladder fixed to the trireme's stern rail.

'My lord of Zelin.' Kheda bowed to the warlord. 'We'll take our leave, with grateful thanks for all your hospitality and assistance.'

'It will be as nothing if you can do this service for our domain.' Zelin Raes inclined his head. 'We look forward to seeing you soon, to reward you in fullest measure for your success.'

'Do you have a residence nearby, my lord?' Kheda asked as casually as if they had spent the day on nothing more than a pleasure voyage. 'Where you can rest and refresh yourself, and your rowers?' He watched Risala climb down the rope ladder.

All Zelin Raes's attention was on the isle where the dragon had last been seen. 'We will patrol these waters as long as the daylight lasts, to be certain no fishing vessel intrudes.'

To be certain we don't flee, or to try to learn just what our secret might be?

'Then I'll bid you farewell.' Kheda swung one leg over the rail and found the first rope rung with his questing toes. When he reached the bottom of the ladder, Sirince had reclaimed the tiller and the Zelin mariners were waiting eagerly to climb back up to the spurious haven of the warlord's vessel.

I shan't tell you how a dragon sank the Mist Dove *and slew nearly everyone on it. Dev saved me then, when I would have drowned without his magic. I don't think Sirince and Velindre could save all of you.*

The rowing master hidden behind the oarsmen shouted something unintelligible and the piper blew a shrill warning on his flute. The oarsmen of the *Reef Shark* raised their blades with a unanimous grunt of weary exertion.

Kheda watched the last of the Zelin men scramble aboard the heavy trireme before turning to the two wizards. 'I hope you have something in mind to deal effectively with the dragon this time.' He spoke unnecessarily quietly as the crash of the trireme's oars drowned out his words. Drops of windblown spray landed cold on his face. 'There was no one to see our failure before, but if we fail this time, our names will be vilified right round the compass of the Archipelago and back again.'

'I hope you don't need too much daylight.' Risala gestured towards the sinking sun. 'Otherwise we'll have to hide from the beast till morning.'

'Will it sniff us out in the dark?' Kheda couldn't restrain a shiver at the thought.

'We've time to do this before dark,' Velindre said calmly. 'For good or ill.'

The triremes sped away, leaving wakes of white foam nudging at the *Tacsille*. The little ship bobbed on the open water like a child's plaything.

'What are you going to do?' began Kheda.

'They gave me new clothes.' Crisk spoke up, faintly puzzled.

'They gave them to all of us,' Sirince reassured him.

'Where did you two get to yesterday?' Risala asked, a breath ahead of Kheda. 'How closely were you questioned?'

'We were comfortably accommodated in the slave quarters.' Sirince shrugged. 'A few of the northern-born slaves wanted to know if I had seen their kith or kin at any markets. Most were interested in any news from the domains beyond the Dawa Sea. None of my lord's personal attendants questioned us, and I don't think any of the wives sent anyone to spy on us.'

'I wouldn't be too certain of that.' Kheda spoke just before Risala.

'If they did, they won't have heard anything of interest. None of the household who spoke to us seemed to think that we two have anything to do with this business of the dragon beyond risking our necks and our boat for a fortune in gems.' Sirince smiled without humour. 'They think we're insane to do it, but we are barbarians and thus already touched by magic's madness.'

'Opal shines in the arc of foes and sinks into the sea. That's a water gem, so the beast must beware,' Crisk said solemnly. He smiled cheerfully at Kheda. 'Pearl returns to home and family where the Ruby counsels courage. Halcarion favours the bold and she's the moon maiden, so she'll be watching.'

No one could doubt that he isn't in his right wits.

'The *zamorin* slaves didn't doubt your status as one of their own?' Kheda nodded at Velindre.

'They were all consideration,' she said wryly. 'I repaid them with diligent interest in the endless records of Zelin portents and omens that they laid out for me in their lord's spectacular library.'

'Did you learn anything that might be of interest in Hadrumal?' Sirince asked with eager curiosity.

'They know more of wizards than most Archipelagans.' Velindre slid him a glance. 'They told me it's believed certain mages show a definite preference for magic with flame or storm. One of the proposed methods of defeating a mage is to throw warrior after warrior at him until he has exhausted all his magic and then someone can get close enough to cut his throat.'

Sirince winced. 'I wonder who they proved that theory on.'

'Did they make any note of which particular records you studied?' Risala wanted to know. 'Were they curious as to why you were looking at lore on wizards?'

'Not given we were discussing dragons, whose mastery of magic leaves the most powerful wizards lacking,' Velindre assured her.

'They wanted to do that to me,' Crisk burst out with sudden anger. 'To geld me—' His face twisted with ugly fear and grief. 'They beat me and burned me—' He clenched his fists, unfocused eyes fixed on some remembered outrage.

'Crisk, look at me,' Sirince instantly commanded. 'Look at me. It wasn't those men, not in that place. They're gone. We've left there. We're on the ship.'

'We're on the ship,' Crisk echoed. He looked around with sluggish recognition and his face grew calmer. 'Trimon brought me back to the ship.'

Kheda looked askance at the red-headed man and then at the balding wizard. 'We can't afford any distraction when we come up against the dragon—'

'What do you propose?' Sirince was still smiling at Crisk, who was now clutching his amulet, eyes vague, muttering to himself in his unknown tongue. 'Shall we shackle him in the hold or beat him senseless? He's suffered both, and worse treatment, in these reaches.'

'I propose we get a grip on this ship before some current carries us off to who knows where,' Velindre said briskly. 'Zelin Raes's men will certainly be wondering why we're drifting so purposelessly at the moment.'

'Where exactly are we sailing to?' Risala moved to the pulleys that adjusted the cant of the wide sail.

Kheda looked at the emerald island ahead. 'Have you any precise idea where the dragon is?'

'We think so.' Sirince sounded more confident than his words suggested. 'Crisk, why don't you go aloft and keep a lookout for us?'

'I can do that.' The red-headed man climbed the rigging with reckless speed and settled himself in the lofty perch.

'First we need to confirm the creature's location.' Velindre looked out beyond the prow. 'I can feel its presence in the water without scrying. I can lure it to us—'

'What are you going to do?' Kheda demanded. 'If the dragon's magic overwhelms you—'

'I don't intend to let that happen,' Velindre said crisply.

'You were all but lost when you and Naldeth tried to challenge those dragons on the wild men's island,' Risala countered from the other side of the tiller.

Velindre surprised Kheda with a disarming smile. 'That experience, along with every other encounter I have had with these creatures, has taught me the utter folly of trying to challenge their incredible strength with my own.'

'So what are you going to do?' Kheda asked yet again.

'First, we're going to sail round to the far side of that

island so no sharp-eyed lookout perched on some trireme's hastily raised mast can see what we're doing. Sirince, if I may.' Velindre took over the tiller and leaned into it.

The *Tacsille*'s sail bellied out, and at the top of the mast, Crisk began singing a jaunty song in a rasping, tuneless voice.

'You recall those rubies that came from the dragon's egg?' Sirince settled himself on the edge of the stern platform. 'How they overcame me when I first picked up Velindre's bag?'

'You're finally going to tell us why?' Kheda leaned against the rail.

'It's taken us some time to unravel that particular mystery.' Sirince looked up, a shadow darkening his faded blue eyes. 'All I knew that first time was that something vile had touched my affinity. Now, although I am an earth mage, and rubies are gems of elemental fire—'

'But Naldeth was a fire mage,' Risala protested. 'He's the one who gathered up the pieces when the egg shattered.'

The sail shivered as the wind veered and the great spar twisted slightly with a creak of rope and timber.

'Earth magic and fire magic are closely sympathetic,' Sirince told her.

'As I understand it, so are the magics of air and fire.' Kheda looked at Velindre, curious. 'Why aren't you sickened by them?'

The magewoman corrected their course before replying. 'I'm not really sure. I think there's still much to learn about the effects of exposure to a dragon's elemental aura on a mage's wizardry.'

'And the way earth magic is bound into any gem,' Sirince added. 'Now, you know Aldabreshin poets and wizardly scholars agree on some things, even if they'd cut out their tongues before they'd admit it.' He smiled briefly. 'One thing all the books of lore record is how loath dragons are to revisit a place where one of their kind has died.'

The *Tacsille* rocked as a rogue swell rose to break in a brief furl of foam just ahead of the prow. The solitary island was now approaching all too rapidly.

'We think a dragon's death corrupts the elements in that immediate area.' Velindre's expression was distant with contemplation. 'Which is essentially what Naldeth and I did with the nexus magic we worked, once we realised we couldn't fight those two dragons on the wild men's isle.'

'When you spoke of poisoning the well,' Kheda recalled.

'When you let loose a cataclysm that wrecked that whole island.' Risala stared at her, aghast. 'You can't be thinking of doing that here?'

'That's certainly not something Zelin Raes bargained for.' Kheda looked at the island growing ever larger ahead of them. 'But we undertook to rid this domain of the beast.' His voice shook with apprehension despite all his efforts to hide it.

'There shouldn't be anything like the same effect,' said Velindre testily. 'That western island is a place under-pinned by an unstable elemental congruence—'

'We won't be trying to work with a nexus of all four elements summoned by only two mages, however talented, or foolhardy,' Sirince added firmly. 'We won't be risking our lives and sanity by focusing magic through some monstrous gem forged through a dragon's desire to perpet-uate itself.' He shuddered. 'Who knows what tortured blend of element was bound up in that. I don't know how you dared touch it.'

Velindre didn't answer as the *Tacsille* sped on through waters paling from the dark blue of the deeps to the opaque green of shallows as the sea bed rose beneath the hull. The wind shifted and they could hear the crash of surf on the beach, a bright-yellow line between the white breakers and the many-textured greens of the dense vegetation ashore.

'Dev killed the nascent dragon that was growing inside the ruby egg.' A faint blush darkened the tan on Velindre's cheekbones as she finally spoke. 'That seems to have fixed some elemental corruption in the shards. We can use that against the dragon.'

'But even touching the bag that held the rubies sickened you.' Risala looked at Sirince, concerned.

'I was taken wholly unawares.' He smiled up at her. 'Now I know what I'm dealing with, I can manage the effect on my own affinity better. Besides, I'm hoping we won't need to use more than a few of the gem fragments.'

'So are you going to pelt the beast with the rubies?' Kheda demanded.

Velindre scowled at him. 'Since I doubt you'd understand if I explained it, why don't you just wait and see?'

The deck rocked violently beneath them and a current seized the ship. The sail flapped helplessly as the wind whirled around them, lashing them with spray.

Kheda saw they were being driven dangerously fast towards the vicious rocks ringing the island. 'Where are we going to make landfall? You can't be thinking of challenging the beast from the ship?'

He had to shout to make himself heard as the wind snatched his words away. He looked up to see where this squall had come from but there were no clouds in the sky. Then he saw Crisk, precariously exposed up on the masthead, pointing down to something beyond the *Tacsille*'s prow.

'It's here.' Velindre's quiet words defied the howling wind. 'Kheda, take the tiller. Keep us away from the rocks.'

She took one long-legged stride up onto the stern platform. Sirince disappeared through the hatch leading down to the hold.

As he grasped the wooden bar, Kheda saw the dragon's head broach the waters beside the little ship. The creature rolled over in a rush of green-laced foam to look more closely at them. Half as long again as the *Tacsille*, the dragon easily kept pace, wings folded flat to its long body and the thrashing of its mighty tail driving it through the water. Kheda realised with a calmness born of utter shock that its head alone was nearly twice as long as he was tall. The spark of white fire at the heart of its emerald eye glowed, then the dragon disappeared beneath the surface.

'Where did it go?' He looked wildly from side to side.

Crisk screeched something unintelligible from on high, gesturing frantically.

Risala stumbled across the rocking deck to join Kheda. He threw one arm around her, drawing her in close so he could hold on to the wooden bar with both hands once again. Together they leaned desperately on the tiller to keep the *Tacsille* from being wrecked on the island's shore.

'Velindre!' he yelled.

'Just keep the ship's course as steady as you can.' Quite composed, Sirince reappeared in the hatchway. He had the bag of ruby fragments in one hand, a faint red glow suffusing the leather.

'What are you going to do?' Risala twisted awkwardly to see Velindre coming down from the stern platform.

Kheda was watching the balding mage walk carefully forwards, holding the bag at arm's length. The elemental fire within glowed still brighter. Velindre followed him.

The dragon reappeared some way ahead of the prow, where the waves ran uninterrupted from the vastness of the open ocean towards the shore. It dived down, lashing at their hull with its thick, scaled tail.

Velindre raised a hand and a wall of water rose up to block the blow. Spray exploded in all directions, soaking everyone, even Crisk in the lookout's perch. The *Tacsille* stopped dead in the water, with a circle of flat calm spreading all around the hull.

Sirince wiped water out of his eyes before opening the neck of the bag of rubies, his face twisted with distaste.

The dragon erupted from the water amidships, mouth agape as it opened its blue-green wings. It sprang forward through the air, intent on Crisk who was frozen with terror at the top of the mast.

A swirl of mist threaded through with sapphire light spiralled up to hide the meagre barbarian from view. The dragon roared as it recoiled, a fearsome sound that struck Kheda with the force of a physical blow. It darted forward again, its terrifying maw opening wide. A spark of lightning flashed out from the cloud to strike one of the creature's jade fangs. The tooth cracked, emerald light running from its tip to lance deep into the dragon's jaw. The beast roared again, tossing its head to send droplets of muddy green blood flying. The pain in its cry struck answering agony in Kheda's head.

If anyone sees this, will they ever believe that all the magic is coming from the beast and not from any of us?

He could only hope the island was blocking this chaos from the view of Zelin Raes's triremes.

As the dragon threw its head back and fell through the air to plunge into the sea, Sirince held out one of the discoloured, misshapen rubies between finger and thumb. There was no fire within the gem, not even some sham struck from the cracks deep within it by the golden rays of the setting sun. The burly wizard twisted his head slightly, focusing all his attention on the fragment.

Velindre was intent on the water. The dragon re-appeared, springing up to land on the surface this time, extending its talons menacingly. Whiteness gathered all around its clawed feet, not foam but ice swiftly extending in all directions. The margins of the slabs coalescing around each of the dragon's feet met and flowed together.

Is she doing that or the beast?

As Kheda wondered, he saw the ice wasn't coming near the *Tacsille*.

The dragon roared and ripped a forefoot loose, sending shards flying to melt and vanish in the waters. It stamped, shattering the ice. Ducking down, it spat a lurid green haze with a furious hiss. Wherever the radiant breath touched the ice, it melted, leaving the magic hanging in the water, eerily slow to fade. Crowing with triumph once it had rid the sea of the ice, the dragon dived straight down into the deeps, a trail of phosphorescence curling behind it.

'As soon as you like, Sirince.' Velindre's voice was calm. 'I don't relish taunting the creature like this.'

Kheda looked up to see how Crisk was faring. The clouds around the masthead had gone and the simpleton crouched low in the lookout's barrel-like post. Both hands clinging to the rim, he was staring open-mouthed at the deck. Kheda looked back to the wizards.

'Bring it back.' Sirince let go of the ruby and it floated in the air. The older wizard held his hand beneath it, palm turned upwards. Amber light crackled around his outspread fingers, softly mimicking the sun setting to Kheda's other side. The yellow glow floated upwards to surround the dulled ruby. The gem darkened while Sirince's magic brightened to molten gold.

Kheda found the magelight too dazzling to look at. He closed his eyes, only to find the vivid circle burned into his mind's eye, the black blotch of the ruby like a pupil in the centre. Within the futile defence of his arms, he could feel Risala trembling with tension.

Are they going to sink us or will we be driven onto those savage rocks? If we end up in the water, will some magic save us or will we have to swim for it? Will the dragon still be there to eat us? Better to see whatever fate's coming upon us.

He opened his eyes.

The balding mage was still cherishing his magelight, now faded to soft amber. The ruby within was a dark smudge, slowly spreading. Dissipating like smoke, the blackness turned the magelight tawny. Light and dark striped the radiance like agate. The magic swelled and grew fainter, until the whole ship was washed with bands of sallow yellow and ashen grey. Sirince was standing in a solid sphere of ochre light, its edges hard against the wan magic hanging translucent all around.

Velindre raised a hand and drew a shaft of midnight blue down from some infinite height. Like Sirince, she was untouched by the pallid magelight draped around the ship. Sapphire radiance enveloped her, touched with aqua-marine at the edges. She didn't appear to notice, pointing her long-fingered hand to direct the cobalt magic down into the turbid green waters a few trireme lengths away.

The dragon shot upwards out of the ocean depths. Ignoring the *Tacsille* utterly, it launched itself at Velindre's magic, snapping and clawing at the midnight shaft. This sorcery seemed to have substance. The creature's talons sank deep into it, ripping out pieces that tumbled away, slow to fade in the evening light. Roaring with triumph, the dragon twisted in the air, lashing at this insupportable provocation with its muscular tail. The spiked tip bludgeoned the indigo darkness, leaving it ragged and torn. Velindre stood motionless, a tear sliding down one drawn cheek reflecting azure light. A bruise darkened on her hand.

Risala looked up at Kheda in wordless bemusement. He shrugged.

I have no answers.

Sirince folded his empty hands on his paunch, his face serene.

The sickly magic that had been hanging around the ship began drifting towards the dragon. Or so it seemed at first. Then Kheda realised the yellow magelight wasn't moving. Rather it was growing perceptibly brighter and cleaner as the greyness departed. As the clouded veils floated closer to the heedless dragon, a green light suffused the air all around the beast.

Where the magelight surrounding Velindre and Sirince extended barely beyond the reach of their arms, the radiance around the dragon reached as far as the *Tacsille*. Close to the beast the light was flawless emerald, purer than the most prized talisman gem that Kheda had ever seen. As it spread, it paled by infinitesimal degrees. Yet it was still strong enough to colour the setting sun where it interposed itself between the ship and the western horizon. He couldn't have explained the feeling, but Kheda was suddenly convinced that faint beyond seeing, the radiance reached all the way to the horizon.

The dragon didn't seem aware that it was bathed in its own magelight, or if it was, it didn't care. It was still ripping into Velindre's cobalt magic, shredding it with its lethal hind claws, great wings beating. Hissing with venomous triumph, its front talons grappled with the writhing sorcery. It didn't seem to realise this amorphous torment was constantly renewing itself, drawing elemental air down from above.

Kheda could see the greyness drifting towards the dragon like the first smoky hint of a distant forest fire. The gloom grew denser as it eddied in the magic-tinted air before swirling away once more to the edge of invisibility. Tendrils insinuated themselves into the dragon's aura. Cloudiness flowed inwards towards the beast, branching and spreading. Each new division into more insidious fingers prompted sparks of green light faint as fireflies. The dragon didn't notice, still consumed with fury as it fought to overcome Velindre's magic.

It's like those nets of golden fungus that spread unseen through the soil to poison a physic garden and blight the soil for years to come.

Kheda wanted to blink, to rub his eyes. He resisted, fearing that if he looked away, he wouldn't be able to see the pale workings of the magic again.

The green of the dragon's aura took on a sickly hue where the setting sunlight illuminated it. Slowly, the glaucous taint wrapped itself all around the beast. The dragon twitched a shoulder, as if some pinprick had slid beneath its armoured scales. It hissed and left off attacking the cobalt pillar with a cry of fury. Head lashing this way and that, it looked wildly around with burning eyes.

What if it attacks us now?

As Kheda stood paralysed, the dragon's fiery gaze swept over him, the ship and everyone aboard.

No, it's looking for something else. We're of no more account than flotsam on the waters.

The creature abandoned the lure of Velindre's midnight magic and dived down into the water. The greyness polluting its magelight followed inexorably. Appearing again in a surge of foam, the beast swam slowly around in a wide uneven circle. Lifting its muzzle, it uttered a sound unlike any Kheda had heard from a dragon. This was no ear-splitting challenge or agonised bellow of pain, nor yet the fierce roar of triumph that threatened to melt the bones of any creature within earshot. There was a wordless plea in the cry, along with a note of wretched uncertainty that reverberated through Kheda's chest. The dragon's call echoed back unanswered from the empty sea and the emerald isle.

It dived again. Kheda strained to follow the fading radiance of its aura through the ocean's depths until it disappeared utterly from view. Finally he blinked and found that the evening seemed brighter. A freshness on the breeze was coloured with the verdant scents of the island ahead.

'Where's it gone?' he wondered aloud.

'There are deep canyons in this sea bed,' Velindre said sombrely. 'It's gone looking for the bones of one of its own affinity, since there was no resonance from air, earth or fire when it called out into the elements. It's convinced a dragon died around here.'

'It wants to see the bones to be certain?' Risala shivered.

Velindre smiled without humour. 'It wants to claim the elemental emerald that made up the dead dragon's heart. Then it can make an egg of its own.'

'But there are no bones, no emeralds.' Now that Kheda didn't have to fight the tiller, he wrapped one arm tight around Risala.

Sirince took up the explanation. 'Which would mean that whatever slew this mythical dragon has already consumed heart and body alike, and that could only be another dragon.'

'Which would make it a dragon to be truly feared, and thus, fled from.' Velindre accompanied her words with a gesture that showed her hands were now mottled with excruciating bruises.

'You're sure?' Risala sought reassurance.

'No,' Sirince said briefly. 'It's an educated guess at best.'

'But the corruption of elements that goes with a dragon's death is now woven into that beast's aura,'

Velindre said sadly, 'which will only fade as the creature gets further and further away. Hopefully such sensations will deter it from ever returning here.' She heaved a sigh, heavy with regret.

'Once burned, twice shy.' Kheda nodded his understanding.

'Better that it leaves of its own volition, even if we have caused it pain,' Sirince said firmly. 'Would you like to discuss how certain members of the Council of Hadrumal might have tried dealing with it?'

Velindre grimaced. 'I don't even want to contemplate it.'

Wizards coming into the Archipelago, in numbers, uninvited and wielding their sorceries against dragon and Aldabreshi alike? That's certainly an appalling prospect.

Kheda tried to make out either of Zelin Raes's triremes amid the dusk now falling on the islands to the south and east. 'What do we do now?'

'Sail back to Zelin Raes, dusting off our hands and breezily telling him how simple it was?' There was a suspicion of hysteria in Risala's laughter.

'Hardly.' Sirince grimaced as he walked back to sit on the edge of the stern platform. 'I'm glad you thought that was so easy. I can't recall when I last worked such gruelling magic.'

Kheda saw the wizard's hands were shaking and the neck of his robe was darkened with sweat.

'I can.' Velindre wiped an obstinate tear from her gaunt cheek before joining Sirince on the makeshift bench. 'That left me so sorely drained I feared I'd burned out my own affinity.' She leaned her head back, closing her eyes.

'I don't know how we can explain their exhaustion to Zelin Raes or his ladies.' Risala looked at the two of them with concern.

'Will a good night's sleep put you to rights?' asked

Kheda. 'Ashore, if we can find safe landing on that island?'

'I'll be in your debt for some solid ground underfoot,' Sirince said fervently, his head hanging, 'after all we've done here, in the midst of elements antipathetic to my own.'

'Let's get ashore.' Risala hurried to the base of the mast and called upwards. 'Crisk! Can you see a break in the rocks? Can you see any place where we might land?'

Crisk leaned over the rim of the lookout post and pointed, nodding vigorously.

I suppose we can trust him. Halfwit or not, I don't imagine he wants to drown any more than we do.

Kheda kept his own sharp watch for any sudden white in the gloomy sea that might signify a rock ready to bite into the *Tacsille*'s hull. As it turned out, Crisk's urgent pointing directed them to a comparatively wide channel that ran up to a sharply shelving beach of golden sand. The red-headed barbarian slid down the mast as soon as the hull grated on the bottom and helped Risala set the anchors fore and aft.

She smiled briefly as she walked back to Kheda. 'Whatever else he lacks, he's had plenty of practice securing this ship on awkward shores.'

Kheda looked at the two wizards. Both were asleep, slumped in the boneless discomfort of true exhaustion. 'How deep's the water? I shall have to carry them ashore.'

She peered over the side. 'You can wade from here.'

Kheda caught Sirince's limp hands and bent to haul the inert mage across his shoulders like a fallen warrior retrieved from some battlefield.

'No!' Crisk's cry pierced the fast-deepening dusk as he ran down the deck to Kheda, grabbing at Sirince's dangling hand.

Kheda stepped backwards out of reach. 'No, Crisk,' he

said firmly. 'We don't want to wake him. I have to carry him ashore.'

Crisk stared back at him, jaw slack.

'It's all right,' Risala said more gently. 'He's tired. He needs to sleep. We have to get him ashore.'

Crisk looked at the island. 'Arrimelin wanders the woods,' he murmured.

'Does she, whoever she may be?' Kheda muttered to himself as he moved towards the *Tacsille*'s rail.

Climbing down the ladder of wood and rope with the mage's dead weight over his shoulders was a horribly awkward task. When he stood on the sandy bottom, the water reached to the middle of his chest. He tested every step he took towards the shore with exquisite caution.

If I drop him, he might drown before I could save him.

Making it to the beach without incident, Kheda laid Sirince down above the high-water mark as gently as he could. He stood upright, his back protesting. Crisk was splashing rapidly through the shallows, his eyes fixed on Sirince's motionless form.

'Can you make a fire?' Kheda asked as the barbarian dropped to his knees beside the mage. 'He needs to be warm.'

Crisk didn't answer, simply stroking Sirince's shoulder with a shaking hand.

Kheda shook his head mutely and began wading back to collect Velindre. Once on deck, as Risala helped him lift the snoring magewoman, he saw a bloom of fire back on the beach. 'So he can light a fire.'

'I wonder sometimes what else he can do,' Risala commented. 'And who he was, before he was reduced to this sorry state.'

'Indeed.'

As Kheda made the second back-breaking trip to the shore, Risala waded beside him. Arms raised high, she was carrying provisions from the generous supplies stowed aboard at Zelin Raes's order. As Kheda settled the magewoman on the sands, she satisfied herself that Crisk's fire wasn't about to go out. 'Can you find us plenty of firewood?' she invited with a smile. As Crisk nodded and vanished into the darkness, she looked up at Kheda. 'Do you think you had better go with him?'

He shrugged. 'There can't be much on an island this size.'

All the same, he went after the halfwit. With both moons at less than their quarter, Lesser waxing and Greater waning, the darkness under the spinefruit trees was almost complete.

'Crisk?' Kheda heard sudden rustling and hoarse breathing in the undergrowth down around the tree roots. Something snorted and rushed towards him, snapping twigs. With more instinct than finesse, he stepped sideways, drawing one of Zelin Raes's lethal swords to cut down into the attacking shadow. An outraged squeal told him he had struck a hook-toothed hog and he hacked at it a second time. The sharp twin toes of its frantically thrashing feet grazed his thigh as it died with a gurgle of pain and a sharp stench of blood. Kheda wiped sweat from his forehead.

That was absurdly easy.

'You killed it.' Crisk spoke softly in the darkness.

Kheda looked around, startled. 'Yes,' he said cautiously.

'We have fresh meat for dinner.' Crisk stepped forward. 'I'll help you carry it.'

Kheda watched, bemused, as the barbarian deftly cut a sapling from a lilla thicket. He thrust his dagger behind the dead hog's hamstrings and twisted the blade. Crossing its hoofs, he threaded the pole through the slits he had made.

You've carried the spoils of the hunt in a forest before. I wonder where and when that was?

They carried the dead hog to the beach between them. Kheda paused as they reached the sleeping wizards. Risala was sitting between them, feeding the hungry little fire. 'We don't know what else might be lurking in those trees. I'll gut this well down the beach.'

'Will you read any omens in the entrails?' Risala looked up, the firelight throwing shadows on her face. 'You don't think there's some significance in such a swift kill?'

'No,' Kheda said shortly. Tugging on the pole, he led Crisk away.

CHAPTER ELEVEN

When I was lord of Daish, I could consider myself the equal of Toc, Sarem or Aedis. Even if I acknowledged in my heart of hearts that Daish was a modest domain compared to theirs. Though Chazen was a paltry power even before wild men and dragons trampled it underfoot. But these western domains far outshine the likes of Redigal and even Ritsem. Neither Daish nor Chazen could boast one ship as splendid as this galley and Zelin Raes had the choice of a handful.

Kheda was irresistibly drawn to his feet as he surveyed the astonishing anchorage ahead. He stepped out of the shade of the gold-tasselled canopy of scarlet silk erected on the galley's main deck to get a better view.

'You will be most welcome in Galcan waters, my lord.' Zelin Raes stayed seated on his folding chair of golden velvet. He raised his sparkling goblet and his body slave Felash stepped forward to refill it from a ewer of crystal glass threaded with veins of gold and scarlet.

'I'd be honoured even to be allowed to drop anchor here.' Kheda's expression was openly admiring.

Even Ulla Safar with all the wealth and people of his mighty islands couldn't hope to rival this domain.

The Zelin mariners were busy furling the great sail hanging from the immense central mast. That left the massive ship relying on the smaller sails of the foremast up in the prow and the aft mast on the stern platform behind the warlord's silken tent. The shipmaster was up there conferring in low tones with his sailmaster. Down below, Kheda could hear the rowing master calling out muffled instructions as the oarsmen took on the responsibility for manoeuvring the great galley through the crowded waters.

Three to a bench, each with his own oar, his world the rowing deck and the holds below, sparing little thought for those sleeping in comfort on the accommodation deck above. What would have happened if I had succumbed to the temptations of that simple life? I thought more than once about letting everyone think Daish Kheda was truly dead and making a new life for myself as the humble rower I pretended to be, when I sought for the means to fight the wild men's magic.

Chazen, Daish and who knows what other domains would have been utterly laid waste by the wild men, their magic and the dragon that followed their scent. Just as Zelin and more besides would have suffered under that dragon Velindre and Sirince just dealt with, if I hadn't declared myself as warlord rather than a slave. So now I have to deal with the consequences of all our actions as best I can.

Zelin Raes glanced over his shoulder. 'Your barbarian friend's ship will be under my protection in this harbour. He has earned that much.'

Kheda could just see the tip of the *Tacsille*'s mast following close behind the great galley's stern. New scarlet pennants marked with bold black sigils flourished in the breeze.

'I hope the domain of my birth finds favour with you, my lord Kheda.' With her body slave Lec shadowing her, Mian Zelin emerged from the wide stair that led up from the galley's luxuriously appointed cabins. She wore a sleeveless close-fitted gown of scarlet silk brocaded with gold beneath a gauzy robe of soft yellow. Her hair was braided close to her head, woven with chains of gold studded with tiny rubies, and a wide collar of gold links and faceted rubies graced her elegant neck. Kheda noted a flintiness in her dark eyes, outlined with golden cosmetics. 'My brother's wives will be delighted to give you gifts to show all the domain's crafts to your lady wife on your return home.'

To offer craft and trade secrets in return for whatever arcane lore could save them from a dragon, should one appear in their own waters. Something you've been trying so desperately to win from me. While your lord and husband has us all sailing out of his waters the very day after we returned from driving off the dragon. Just in case I was right when I told him I feared misfortune still followed me?

He addressed himself to her first remark. 'Galcan's central trading beach is truly an awesome sight, my lady.'

The Zelin galley, the *Coral Fan*, passed between two solid towers built on bulbous headlands, each at the end of a long sandbar. Within, the waters opened out again into a bay so vast the far end couldn't yet be seen. Low islands sprawled on either side of channels so shallow that men were standing in water no deeper than their waists or chests. All were looking down intently, waiting to spear fish glittering in the silty murk.

There were truly astonishing numbers of people and boats. Each island had long been stripped of whatever frail scrub it had once harboured and the trampled sand was covered with gaily coloured awnings and booths of woven palm fronds. Every scrap of land was surrounded by ranks of galleys, great and small, swaying patiently at anchor. Flat ferryboats poled from ship to shore and slipped along the shallowest channels, each one loaded to the waterline with men and women, baskets, bundles and casks.

Beyond the water, a broad plain extended all around the rim of the vast bay. Shock-headed nut palms swayed above the high-water mark and Kheda could see verdant clumps of lilla and spinefruit trees further inland. Neat clusters of shallow-roofed huts were set amid the regular lines of diligently tended orchard and vegetable plots and muddy fields of saller grain.

Further still, shallow hills rippled up and down. Barely more than blurred green lumps, they hardly hindered the cooling breezes sweeping across the water to rattle idle sails and tug at visitors' pennants. Playful gusts brought a confusion of sounds from the throngs on the crowded islets along with an enticing medley of spices, dyes and food, cooked and uncooked. These odours aside, Kheda found both the air and the scent of the sea around the galley surprisingly clear, even if silt clouded the waters. This vast bay was plainly no stagnant sump.

This trading centre would hardly have survived if it were. Some pestilence would have come long since to wipe out half these visitors.

Seeing different pennants flying prominently on the largest islands in the bay, Kheda turned to Mian Zelin. 'Does each of the neighbouring domains have its own trade enclave here?'

She nodded. 'Galcan is at the heart of the western reaches. No other domain's sea lanes touch more than two or three of its neighbours, whereas Galcan ships can reach six domains swiftly and safely.' Her countless golden bracelets jingled as she pointed a beringed ebony finger. 'Since Zelin is at the north of the compass, you'll find our traders there. Follow the sun's course and you'll find Penik, Dawa, Bultai, Terze and Juduc, just as they lie around the compass.'

Kheda looked around. 'And everyone else?'

'They are welcome to whatever space they can find around the edge of the bay.' Zelin Raes smoothed the flapping silk of his robe, golden silk brocaded with red to complement his wife's. Heavy rings set with knobbly uncut rubies shone against his dark fingers.

'Galcan Sima's people must flourish providing food to all the traders who call here.' Kheda had already noted that the wide beaches were as crowded as the islands. Innumerable tents and flimsy shacks were crammed between the nut palms fringing the shore. 'Though I see my lord of Galcan doesn't allow anyone to build a permanent structure.'

'Thus no one forgets that their presence here is on his sufferance,' Mian said serenely.

'I'd have thought the heavy triremes governing access to the channel between those headlands would have made that clear.' Kheda looked past the *Coral Fan*'s prow and the burly vessels ahead to a light trireme circling in an apparently featureless stretch of water within the embrace of the sandbars. The brass sheathing the ram at its prow gleamed with dull menace. 'That vessel presumably guards the only navigable path through these shallows?'

'The whole trade of the western reaches crosses Galcan waters.' Zelin Raes commented wryly. 'It's a good thing this domain cannot claim a safe crossing out over the Dawa Sea to the rest of the Archipelago, otherwise my lord of Galcan would have a stranglehold on all of us.'

'You don't think my lords of Essa and Bultai like having their foot on all our necks?'

From Mian Zelin's tone, Kheda guessed this was an old bone of contention between husband and wife.

'As long as the rest of us can choose either over the other, neither can dictate wholly unreasonable terms.' The warlord waved an explanatory hand at Kheda. 'And all trade to the north through Essa has to pass through Matul waters. Passage to that domain is governed by sea lanes from Zelin and Penik. Essa Mol knows better than to challenge the rest of us by allying himself exclusively with Bultai Deir. Besides, our domains have agreed for endless ages that one of us will always sit as arbiter over any disputes between the rest. Such judgement is not to be denied.'

'My brother of Galcan has taken his turn more than any other lord, as the stars turn and the honour of being arbiter passes from one domain to the next with the new year.' Mian Zelin's pride was somewhat excessive given her marriage had shifted her allegiance to her new domain.

I don't understand the nuances of alliance in these waters, and to be frank, I don't feel any need to. Still, this is an interesting notion of theirs, to set one of them above all the others to keep the peace, but to share that responsibility equally. So they all know any injustice they perpetrate will rebound on them as soon as they are subject to someone else the following year. But I wonder how they would deal with someone like Ulla Safar?

Kheda smiled politely. 'It's always wise to aim for balance in dealing with one's neighbours.' He returned to his seat and Felash hastened to refill his faceted glass goblet with fresh lilla juice. 'Thank you.' Kheda sipped, careful not to let any drip onto his vermilion tunic or trousers. Kauris Zelin's seamstresses had once again garbed him in the southern manner, though now in their finest silks. He looked around for Risala but she was nowhere to be seen.

The galley's shipmaster called down from the stern platform. 'My lord of Galcan sends a light galley with an honour guard to take you ashore, my lord.'

'It will be my honour to make you known to Galcan Sima.' Zelin Raes handed his glass to his slave and rose to his feet. 'As some small part of the reward you have earned for cleansing my domain of that dragon.'

A substantial honour guard of Zelin swordsmen were drawing themselves up into crisp lines.

'We would gladly offer ten times the recompense you have accepted,' Mian Zelin added tightly, 'and make you a gift of a fitting ship for your voyage home.'

'You have been more than generous.' Kheda bowed low. 'To see your domain and the wider Archipelago free of the dragon's malice is sufficient reward.'

I've been saying that for the past five days of this interminable voyage. Such altruism is starting to ring a little hollow. What other warlord would fail to take full advantage if he possessed such priceless lore? Only I hold no such secrets. But I must continue with this deceit because the truth would still be the death of us all.

Kheda straightened up again, forcing himself not to look aft to the *Tacsille*. Zelin Raes moved away to confer briefly with Felash and the captain of the Zelin swordsmen. Mian's body slave Lec drew her aside to satisfy himself that her cosmetics were still perfection and not a hair had the temerity to escape her elaborate crown of braids.

'My lord Kheda.' Risala slipped through the side panel of the silken tent.

'Where have you been?' Kheda asked quietly, looking down to smooth his tunic.

'Keeping out of my lady Mian's way as much as possible,' Risala murmured.

'You're wearing a different perfume.' Kheda couldn't identify the precise spices in the warm, sensuous scent.

I'll wager they're the rarest and most prized.

'Another gift from my lady Mian.' Risala's wry comment was almost inaudible. 'She's determined to treat me as if I were your junior wife.'

The white silk of Risala's flowing gown was brocaded with vizail blossoms in vermilion precisely matching the shade of Kheda's tunic. Her dress was also expertly sewn in a southern style, with a close-fitted bodice and long, wide sleeves.

'I've told her time and again you're not even my acknowledged concubine,' he said with frustration.

'She's not listening.' Risala's full skirt rustled as she

twitched a recalcitrant fold. 'As well as enough perfumes and silks to sink a trireme, she's given me double-sealed letters for Itrac Chazen.'

'I wonder what those will say.' Kheda quelled an impulse to grimace.

Matters of trade are always a wife's province. What am I going to tell Itrac when she asks just what I did to earn Chazen the spectacular luxuries and overgenerous terms that Mian Zelin offers?

Mariners began hurrying to new tasks as the *Coral Fan* passed through the first scatter of islands thronged with traders. As the lumbering vessel emerged into the central expanse of the bay, wood and hemp creaked and the deck hummed beneath their feet as the rowers on the oar deck down below leaned into their task.

'They're keeping close behind.' Risala was discreetly monitoring the *Tacsille*.

'I'll make sure all eyes stay fixed on me.' Kheda smoothed his freshly trimmed beard and heavy gold chains around his wrist slid down his sleeve. 'So no idle suspicions turn to Velindre or Sirince.'

'I'll play my part.' Risala's tone was neutral as she fingered the intricate gold filigree necklace that graced her modest cleavage. The garnets among the coils were as red as rubies to an untutored eye. Her earrings were fine cascades of gold links brushing her shoulders. 'But the sooner we can leave, the better.'

'If you've been avoiding my lady Mian, you've presumably been mixing with the crew masters?' Kheda looked ahead to see land coming into view past the galley's prow. Another light trireme was on guard, archers on its bow platform vigilant. 'Do you know how far afield the ships here come from?'

'I'd barely said three words to the sailmaster before Lec found me. He made it clear his mistress would not want them talking to me.' Risala looked exasperatedly at Mian Zelin's body slave. 'If I'm to learn any news from the south I had better get ashore dressed in something less conspicuous.'

'My lord Chazen Kheda.' Zelin Raes turned from his shipmaster and beckoned to Kheda. 'And . . . Risala.' Everyone on deck noted his amusement as he omitted honouring her with any title. 'Fizai Galcan will have some excellently well-trained body slaves for trade. You can choose a new personal attendant while you're here.'

'You might like to reward your poet with a slave of her own as well.' Mian Zelin smiled indulgently while Lec and Felash allowed themselves just the hint of an indignant glare at Kheda.

Which would be as good as declaring you my wife. How would you react to that, my love?

'We'll see.' He offered Risala his arm. The talisman rubies in his rings were the equal of any that Zelin Raes was wearing.

She said nothing, simply threading her hand through his elbow.

The Galcan dispatch galley drew close to the side of the *Coral Fan*. In the centre of the deck a dutiful youth removed a section of the ship's rail and two brawny mariners waited with a railed wooden walkway. The rowers on the nearest side swept their pairs of blades upright with a precise flourish as their fellows on the far side deftly brought the vessel to within an oar's length of the great galley's lofty side. Ropes were slung back and forth and the wooden walkway was lowered to reach safely into the middle of the open craft.

'My lord Chazen Kheda.' Zelin Raes led the way, Mian Zelin on his arm.

Kheda and Risala followed carefully. The walkway was steep, though there were sturdy battens nailed across it.

He was grateful the waters inside this wide bay were so calm.

What would everyone make of that omen, if I fell into the water?

Lec and Felash followed, unconcerned by the precarious path, and the Zelin captain led a small detachment of warriors aboard. Galcan swordsmen on the stern platform of the light galley maintained aloof detachment, but Kheda saw them discreetly assessing these newcomers.

There will be wagers made around the warrior's practice ground tonight. And plenty of questions asked about this new lord from the south, and why he is travelling with no fit escort. What exactly did he do to drive out a dragon and return without so much as a scratch to show for it?

'Fizai Galcan, who is my lord's first wife, was born to Tabril.' Mian Zelin addressed herself to Risala as much as to Kheda as the four of them settled on a broad bench softened with azure cushions.

'Which makes her sister to your sister-wife Kauris Zelin?' Kheda drew Mian's attention firmly to himself. 'Of the same mother?'

'Of different, I believe.' Mian waved away the irrelevance with a jingle of bracelets. 'Perene was born to Kaive and my lord of Galcan is also newly married to Jasyl, who was daughter to my lord Dawa Trin.'

'I must remember to wish them long life and happiness.' Kheda smiled.

'Where will the *Coral Fan* anchor, my lord of Zelin?' Risala asked with humble politeness.

The warlord twisted in his seat and pointed. 'A small river enters the bay there. The Galcan dry-season residence is on the eastern bank and those ships permitted this close will anchor to the west.'

Will the Tacsille *anchor with her? How do I cross that river without every eye following me?*

'Galcan Sima's wives have made this one of their most comfortable homes.' Mian Zelin was talking to Risala as an equal again.

'I hope we don't inconvenience them,' she replied meekly.

Kheda could see a sprawl of wooden shingled roofs that might or might not signify the beginnings of a residence. 'Surely they must be making ready to leave for their rainy-season dwelling?' He allowed a frown of unease to cloud his own face. 'As Kauris Zelin is organising the removal of your whole household. Please don't make this a protracted visit on our account. We don't wish to inconvenience either domain.'

'Please don't concern yourself.' Zelin Raes smiled with broad satisfaction.

Because this visit isn't just about us. You're both here to show everyone in this busiest of anchorages that all is well with Zelin. Before the rains close the sea lanes, so all these traders will take word home that you two came here with your southern ally who was dressed in the finest garb and jewels you could offer him, with a concubine as good as his wife for the purposes of confirming the trade links now established.

Kheda made sure his expression was one of serene interest as the walkway was smoothly retrieved and they were rowed towards the shore.

While Kauris has stayed at home, along with all the domain's children, just to be certain this voyage could not be mistaken for any kind of flight from Zelin by the ruling family. Because the dragon is no more and the affairs of the Zelin domain are proceeding as happily and as profitably as ever.

The *Tacsille* swept past the dispatch galley on its way towards wooden piles driven into the shallows where a narrow river curled sluggishly into the great bay. Crisk was adjusting the ropes to the fore of the sail while Velindre managed the tiller. Sirince was busy with something beside her. The little ship rode low in the water, the hold now laden with chests of Zelin's fragile double-shelled pottery safely packed in saller straw, and bolts of fine flowing silks in the twin-coloured brocades that were the domain's prized craft. Mian and Kauris had personally selected costly perfumes and a silver gown with an overdress of a net of turquoise glass beads as their gift to Itrac Chazen. Zelin Raes had bestowed countless cuttings from his physic garden on Kheda and promised him the finest copies would be made of any book or scroll he might want from the domain's libraries.

At least that gave Velindre an excuse to hide herself away behind ranks of shelves with archivists who were probably too near-sighted ever to suspect she might be a woman rather than zamorin. I wonder what tomes of lore she ordered to be copied on my account. Will she wait for them to be delivered to Chazen and take them as her share of this payment? What will Sirince want by way of reward? Trade goods to buy freedom for more mainlander slaves? I wonder if Crisk understood exactly what I told him about keeping those plants dark and moist.

Risala stirred beside him. 'My lady Mian, how exactly are we to get ashore?'

Kheda saw the silty waters lapped an expanse of mudflats with no fixed jetty.

Offering no assistance to any invaders who might reach this far into the bay.

Mian pointed towards a group of waiting men. 'Galcan's servants know the secrets of this place.'

The light galley slowed and oarsmen at prow and stern thrust poles deep into the dark waters. The brawny men ashore lifted capacious canopied chairs onto their shoulders. All wading precisely in the same footsteps, they brought the litters out to the waiting galley.

There must be some solid path laid down beneath the

concealing mud. I wonder how often they shift it, to foil would-be invaders.

Zelin Raes smiled at Kheda. 'You'll find that whatever you've heard of Galcan hospitality is no exaggeration.'

He stepped up onto the rail of the galley and transferred himself easily into the first litter. Mian Zelin followed with nimble grace. Kheda drew a discreet breath and managed the move without incident, as did Risala. Somewhat to Kheda's surprise, Felash and Lec were also carried ashore.

Would that be a first warning that you'd fallen out of favour with Galcan Sima, if your body slave had to struggle ashore through this mud?

Kheda fought the urge to look down in case he unbalanced the litter and its supporters. He could see no hint of whatever secret signs must surely show the slaves where they could tread without sinking.

Once they reached solid ground, the visitors were carried to an open grassy sward by the burly men, their legs now coated with thick black mud. The servants slid the heavy poles from their muscular shoulders and lowered each litter to the ground within a half-circle of shaped and trimmed shrubs. Their thick green leaves were still glossy despite the dry season and the dust in the air. Richly dressed nobles were waiting to greet them.

'My lord Zelin Raes, you are most welcome, and Mian, it's ever a delight to see you.' The man who could only be Galcan Sima stepped forward. His hair was the palest grey of wood ash and wrinkles were deeply incised in his broad-featured, amiable face. His complexion was quite dark and mottled with spots that were darker still, some raised to roughen his cheeks above his close-trimmed white beard. Still tall and upright, his age was nevertheless plain in his bony hand, extended on a fleshless arm. Emerald and gold rings hung loose on his fingers. A jade

scarf swathed his wattled neck and he wore a silk robe
striped in subtle shades of green wrapped close around
his skinny body. Behind him, his personal slave was a
vigorous youth in plain black silk, watching everyone with
impartial suspicion.

'Sima, it's lovely to see you.' Mian embraced him with
every appearance of sincere affection.

*If you are his sister, my lady, I doubt you had the same
mother. What manner of man was the previous Galcan
warlord?*

Zelin Raes beckoned Kheda forward. 'My lord, may I
make known to you Chazen Kheda, now friend and ally
to Zelin. We owe him an incalculable debt.'

'My lord, I am honoured.' Kheda bowed low.

'The honour is mine.' Galcan Sima raised his voice
slightly so that all the assorted attendants on the shore
were left in no doubt. There was no tremor of age or infir-
mity in his words. 'All of us would have been imperilled
if a dragon had made its lair anywhere in these waters.'

'Mian, it's lovely to see you.' One of the women stepped
forward. A little older than the Zelin wives, she was notably
younger than her husband. Her long robe, striped in
indigo, jade and gold, was wrapped around her body in
the local style, though there was no indication she wore
anything beneath. The open front of the skirt parted as
she walked to reveal oiled legs adorned with heavy anklets
of silver set with lapis and moonstones. A wide green sash
decorated with plaques of figured silver was wound around
her waist and a gossamer scarf softened the robe's plunging
neckline to flatter a woman of her years.

'May I make known my first wife and joy of my waking
days, Fizai Galcan.' The warlord smiled fondly.

Fizai's diadem of silver wire threaded with sapphires
shimmered as she smiled pleasantly at Risala. 'And who
is our other guest?'

'This is my lord Kheda's companion.' Mian's gold-painted lips quirked with amusement.

'I am the least of Chazen's servants,' Risala said with as much firmness as was polite, sinking into a low curtsey.

'These are my beloved wives Perene and Jasyl, ever my delight,' Galcan Sima continued with affectionate pride.

Kheda composed a welcoming smile for the other two Galcan wives, one of whom was boldly displaying her alluring charms with a robe largely exposing both legs and breasts. Rather than being plainly sewn, the glossy striped satin was cut so that stylised waves rippled down every seam.

'We are all friends, then.' Galcan Sima clapped his hands together, his smile engaging. 'My lord Chazen Kheda, indulge an old man and let me show you my gardens. Fizai, take everyone else indoors for some refreshment.'

Kheda saw that this proposal took Zelin Raes and Mian both by surprise but neither could summon any reason to demur. Fizai Galcan was already walking towards the line of brushy green shrubs and the other Galcan wives slipped deftly either side of Mian and Risala to engage them both in brightly inconsequential conversation. The assembled servants melted discreetly away. Kheda saw Lec and Felash exchange a warily puzzled look but they were left with no choice but to follow their master and mistress.

You two have no idea why we've been so swiftly and rapidly separated. Nor have I. And I wonder what's become of Velindre and Sirince, and Crisk.

'My lord Kheda, what do you know of our islands?' Galcan Sima led him away from the buildings, his step swift and assured.

'Very little.' Kheda was happy to admit this truth.

'You know that our greatest wealth is spun by the humblest of creatures?' Galcan Sima shot Kheda a winning smile, his nut-brown eyes keen.

'By silkworms, yes.' Kheda wondered where this conversation might be leading, as their path wound between the glossy green shrubs. Well-tended pale-stemmed trees were planted between each cluster. Some still boasted sprays of delicate white blossom though most had gone beyond flowering to bear twisted black pods. These were breaking open to reveal pungent white fibres speckled with tiny black seeds.

A familiar scent teased Kheda. 'Are these crystal balsam trees, my lord?'

'They are.' Galcan Sima's eyes turned calculating. 'Do you want a cutting?'

'I don't believe they flourish in the southern Archipelago.' As they left the pungent trees behind, Kheda caught the faintest scent of some boggy ground unseen beyond the warlord's compound.

So this is another residence that doesn't rely on walls for defence. Any marsh still moist this far into the dry season must be formidable. Would we sink up to our necks if we tried to make a discreet departure? But how can we leave without causing offence or arousing suspicion when we're being treated with such honour?

'There are so many secrets in even successfully hatching the silkworms' eggs.' His brisk pace not slowing, Galcan Sima waved an airy hand. 'Each domain in these reaches prefers its own silkworm trees and cherishes the differences in the threads their precious cocoons yield.'

As they passed between the neatly trimmed bushes, Kheda saw a windowless building of light woven wood ahead of them. Armoured warriors guarded its door.

'Our silks are heavier and stronger than those of Matul, which they use to weave their gossamers,' Galcan Sima continued, 'while Essa weaves no cloth at all. But they know the secret of producing a silken filament strong enough to be used for fine nets for the smallest shrimp and fishes, or even for sewing up wounds. Did you know that?'

'Every domain has its crafts and the secrets that go with them,' Kheda said with careful neutrality.

'Sometimes such crafts and secrets are shared, between favoured friends and allies.' Galcan Sima's sideways glance was piercing.

Do you suspect that Zelin Raes has betrayed you all by telling me such lore, in return for saving his domain?

'I know no more of silk cultivation's secrets than I did when I first came into these reaches, my lord.' Kheda spared half an eye for the muscular slave dogging their steps. 'And that was nothing,' he added, to be certain he was understood.

'Would you like to know more?' As Galcan Sima's blunt question startled Kheda, the grey-haired warlord snapped his bony fingers.

The swordsmen guarding the unremarkable hut moved aside, one pushing open the light door. Galcan Sima went inside, and with the black-clad body slave on his heels, Kheda had to follow.

The loosely woven lattices of fine strips of wood allowed some dim light to penetrate the flimsy walls. The air was still and humid, pungent with a sharp animal odour. Wooden racks filled the building, each laden with trays covered with sprays of glossy green leaves. Shifting silk-worms as long as Kheda's smallest finger covered each tray, mindlessly gorging. The sound surprised him.

I could imagine the first rains had come, their soft showers rustling the palm thatch, if I didn't know what I was hearing.

'We have had honourable lords of other domains offer us wealth beyond counting in return for the lore concerning the curious moths that these little creatures will become.' Galcan Sima gazed around the gloomy hut. 'We have had their less scrupulous neighbours offer bribes and threats to our trusted servants in order to secure the eggs they lay. There is even outright theft, occasionally, from outlying villages where humble islanders do their best to raise a little silk for trade and their own adornment.' There was an ominous glint in his eye. 'Which is mostly a crime committed by barbarians. They don't get a chance to offend us twice.'

'I can vouch for the barbarians who travel with me, my lord.' As Kheda interrupted, he nonetheless swallowed a sudden qualm.

Apart from Crisk. Would he have the wit to steal silkworms?

'No attempts to steal our secrets has ever succeeded,' Galcan Sima continued conversationally. 'There are too many tricks and pitfalls for the untutored to hope to raise silkworms. Not even our own islanders understand the mysteries of successfully hatching their eggs.'

Kheda realised some response was expected of him. 'You are fortunate, my lord, you and your neighbours.'

'Would you like to share in that good fortune?' Galcan Sima looked directly at him, all geniality set aside.

'My lord?' Kheda returned his gaze, puzzled.

'Would you like to take the secrets of raising silk back to your southern domain?' Galcan Sima asked bluntly. 'Chazen's wealth, such as it is, rests upon the shifting sands of the pearl beds. You have had splendid harvests these past two years, so I am told, but there's nothing to say your waters won't be barren next year. There's rumour that the Daish domain has suffered just such a humiliation, for all that the young warlord's women have tried to disguise it.'

The young warlord and his women? You are speaking of my beloved son and my erstwhile wives.

Kheda tried to keep any hint of his anger from his words. 'Such matters are my wife Itrac Chazen's concern, my lord.'

Galcan Sima grunted as if he didn't quite believe Kheda. 'My wives have already sent your lady wife letters and gifts through every chain of friendship and acquaintance they have threaded through the Archipelago. Such things take time and I prefer not to waste it. I'm no longer a young man.'

He waved at the racks of gorging silkworms. 'The wealth of these reaches is built on these creatures because we can raise them year after year with near certainty. We feed the dead worms to our house fowl and the waste from these sheds goes to fatten the fish in our seas. Even if we suffer some outbreak of blight on one island, to plague the worms or the trees or even to corrupt the very silk of the cocoons, we can burn everything there to black ash and there will still be enough cloth to satisfy desires within and beyond our domains.

'Perhaps I have missed the signs that should have warned me against such complacency.' The aging warlord looked straight at Kheda, who noticed that the whites of the old man's eyes were yellowing. 'This dragon has come and some are saying it is a portent of how easily all this wealth of ours could be lost. Everyone has been waiting to see if the vile creature will burn each and every island of the Zelin domain. There has been much debate as to exactly what such an omen might mean. A few have even dared to speculate how our trade might benefit, if Zelin affairs were thrown into chaos, even for a little while.'

There was a scornful note in his words as he continued. 'Some are foolish enough to believe that the creature's arrival is merely a sign to be interpreted to set us on our best path. We believe otherwise – myself, my wives and my sons. We saw no reason to believe this creature would be satisfied with laying waste to Zelin. What was to stop it flying hither and yon, plundering each and every domain of these reaches? What would that mean for us? Even if we were not slain outright, we would see no more ships venturing here from the rest of the Archipelago. What then? We have more people in these islands than can be fed by the fish in these seas, or the ducks in our compounds, or the saller in our granaries. We cannot satisfy hungry islanders with handouts from storehouses full of silk or with empty glasses or ceramic bowls, no matter how fabulously coloured.' His voice rose on that anguished conclusion.

He paused and cleared his throat. 'What was to prevent such a disaster? It seems you are the answer to that, my lord Chazen Kheda. You have come out of nowhere in time of direst need and simply driven the creature away.'

The warlord folded his withered arms across his bony chest and looked steadily at Kheda, plainly inviting some response.

'I believe that these dragons pose a threat to us all,' Kheda said cautiously, 'which is why I am happy to use the lore that I have discovered in service of any domain facing such peril.'

Galcan Sima grunted again with more obvious scepticism. 'I see you're happy to take all the rewards that Zelin Raes's gratitude heaps upon you.'

'If you ask him, you'll find I haven't accepted a tenth of what he has offered me,' Kheda snapped back, provoked.

'Why is that? Is the creature gone for ever?' Galcan demanded abruptly before Kheda could answer his first question.

Kheda got a firm grip on his temper. 'I don't know,' he admitted warily. 'I believe so.'

'Who else knows of this lore?' Galcan took a step closer to Kheda.

'No one,' Kheda lied firmly.

'Then what happens if you are killed? What happens if this beast returns and you are nowhere to be found?' Galcan came closer still, his eyes searching Kheda's face. 'I must look to my own domain's future, my lord, you must understand that. So I ask you again, would you like to secure your own people's future? Would you like to return to your home with all the curious secrets of raising silkworms, with a supply of the moth's new-laid eggs and the tricks of hatching them, with saplings of their favourite fodder trees?' He swept a swollen-knuckled hand around to indicate the greedily oblivious silkworms. 'In return for this knowledge that has enabled you to rid your own domain and Zelin's of dragons. So I may save my people, should a dragon ever fly over these waters again. You claim that this learning is invaluable, my lord, but I find that ultimately men of goodwill can agree on the worth of just about everything.'

You clearly know that I told Zelin Raes this dragon lore was beyond price. Didn't your spies in his household tell you I refused to trade the lore to him? Do you think this offer will persuade me? You're not so far astray. In truth, if this lore were something I could hand over, I might well be tempted, for the sake of securing Chazen's future. What a gift that would be to take back to Itrac and our baby daughters. But I cannot, so I had better convince you of that before this turns ugly.

Kheda glanced at Galcan Sima's body slave. The warrior was a motionless shadow beside the only way out of the fetid shed.

'Is this an offer I am at liberty to decline, my lord?' There was an insulted edge to his words and he let his hand stray to the hilt of one of his scabbarded blades.

The warrior stiffened and looked past Kheda to his master.

'You may decline it, if you are a fool.' Galcan Sima was unrepentant. 'It is an offer I will not make a third time,' he promised ominously.

'Tell me, my lord – what would your neighbouring warlords think of this conversation?' Kheda opted for attack with words rather than swords. 'Do you hope they wouldn't retaliate when they learned you had given away the secrets that are the foundation of their wealth as well as your own? Do you think they wouldn't dare, for the sake of the dragon lore you now held over their heads?'

He took a pace forward, forcing Galcan Sima to step backwards. 'What of Chazen, my lord? You try to persuade me that you're offering me a boon here. I see a cunningly poisoned cup. You don't think that all the other lords of these western reaches wouldn't do all in their power to strangle any trade in silks and satins coming out of Chazen? They would call in every favour and debt owed to them, pulling on all the threads of trade and obligation that link the domains the length and breadth of the Archipelago. That's what I'd do, in their position. Wouldn't you? I know warlords who would go further, who would set out to stifle all dealings between Chazen and any other domain, no matter how trivial, to punish me for making such a bargain.'

Kheda paused and looked cynically around the dim interior of the flimsy building. 'Of course, that's assuming the silkworms would flourish in the southern reaches. As long as the lore you handed me was not lacking in some vital detail. That would be one way to protect yourself from the outrage of your neighbours and allies.'

'You are at liberty to decline my offer, my lord Chazen Kheda, but do not presume to insult me in my own residence,' Galcan Sima hissed. 'I currently hold the responsibilities of arbiter for the whole of the western reaches. I have made this offer for the sake of each and every domain.'

'My lord, I beg your pardon.' Kheda managed to sound contrite. 'These are difficult days. Facing the threat of a dragon makes desperate men of us all.'

Galcan Sima gazed at him, bemusement momentarily replacing the outrage in his eyes. 'What will the rest of us do, when you are eaten by some dragon? A man's luck when he chooses to face such an evil cannot last for ever.' Looking past Kheda, he snapped his fingers peremptorily at his slave. 'We shall return to my lady wives. They will be wondering where we have got to.'

'I shall be full of praise for your gardens, my lord,' Kheda said smoothly. 'We lost track of ourselves as we discussed their care and cultivation.'

Galcan Sima simply grunted as he pushed past with uncivil haste. All the same, Kheda saw a spark of relief in the old man's eyes.

Your allies would still disapprove most vehemently if they knew you had offered up the silkworms' secrets. Your wives could expect their trade to suffer, at least in the short term, to punish you for such temerity.

Kheda followed Galcan Sima and the warlord's silent slave brought up the rear. The Galcan warlord led them along different paths, past delightful pavilions whose russet wooden walls framed windows patterned with coloured glass depicting all manner of herbs and healing plants. Broad expanses of cropped grass were divided up with hedges. Some had variegated leaves while others boasted curious red foliage, dark as old blood. There were stands of aromatic plants, crystal balsam the most prominent, shedding drifts of pale speckled fluff that breezes swept into every sheltered corner. Arbours woven with roses were thick with thorns, their leaves brittle and dry and buds tight closed until the imminent rains prompted a glorious flowering.

They rounded a hedge and came upon a long wooden building of two storeys running from east to west. Each floor appeared wholly open to the outer air, offering one long room that ran the full width, entirely lacking walls or windows on its southern aspect. The ironwood pillars of the outer wall were furnished with shutters reaching from floor to ceiling that could be drawn closed if required, while free-standing screens waited ready to partition the interior. The upper level was evidently reached by two wide staircases, set to divide the whole into harmonious thirds.

'What do you think of my residence, my lord Kheda?' Galcan Sima asked, a sly glint in his eye.

Kheda was taken quite unawares. 'I've never seen a style of building like it,' he said honestly.

'I've long agreed with those philosophers who argue those domains of the greatest wealth should abstain from an excess of vulgar display,' Galcan Sima said, a trifle smugly.

'I've read their arguments,' Kheda mused. 'I see the wisdom in avoiding prompting dangerous envy in those who might prove ill-disposed.'

'I'm more concerned with avoiding the greedy eyes of those northern barbarians who anchor in my harbour and come sneaking around my dwellings.' Galcan Sima surprised him with sudden frankness. 'And of course, the white termites that thrive hereabouts mean few buildings last longer than a generation.' He slid a sideways look at Kheda as they reached shallow steps built into the stone foundation that underpinned the whole structure.

Kheda noted the uncomfortable appeal in the old man's eyes and laughed dutifully at the feeble pleasantry. As they walked up to polished golden floorboards, he realised that the rear half of the building accommodated a further selection of apartments, through irregularly spaced doors of solid black wood all opening off this one long room.

'My lord.' Fizai Galcan rose from her seat on a bank of plump black cushions with consummate grace. 'My lord Chazen Kheda.'

'My lady.' As Kheda bowed, a relaxed smile on his face, he saw Risala was ensconced between the Galcan domain's other wives.

The Zelin contingent sat opposite. Mian Zelin was sitting beside her lord, their slaves a few paces behind their cushions. Neither husband nor wife looked wholly at ease, their welcoming smiles failing to kindle any light in their dark eyes. Both slaves were as wooden-faced as the carvings decorating the yellow folding screens set to either side. These and embroidered hangings of dark-grey silk offered an illusion of privacy as the black-clad Galcan servants fussed with bowls of many-hued crystal glass holding some pungent, freshly crushed fruit that Kheda could not identify.

'You're just in time.' Fizai Galcan snapped her fingers and nodded to her slave. 'We were about to enjoy some mersa.'

'Excellent.' Galcan Sima settled himself where his wife had just been sitting. 'This is a delicacy of the region, my lord of Chazen.'

'My lord Kheda, please sit with us.' As Fizai sank gracefully down, tucking her legs beneath her, she gestured towards the third bank of black cushions where Risala was sitting between Perene and Jasyl.

Kheda managed an expression of polite interest as a servant woman approached with a tray of smoky crystal bowls heaped with vivid orange pulp. 'It smells . . . remarkable.'

It smells as if it's been buried under a log and left to rot for ten days.

Neither Galcan woman moved to allow Kheda to sit with Risala. Perene smiled at him. 'Mersa is highly prized in these regions, for conferring fertility on women.'

I was wondering how you ladies could sit decorously in such revealing gowns.

The cut of Perene Galcan's cross-wrapped gown of emerald-and-jade-striped silk was sufficiently generous to cover her folded legs to just above the knee, while the drape framed her cleavage with elegant folds.

'And matching vigour in our men.' Jasyl smiled invitingly and patted the cushions beside her smooth brown thigh.

I see that you're not concerned with such things, my lady.

Jasyl sat with her long legs outstretched, the skirts of her leaf-green and gold gown falling away to reveal a narrow clout of aquamarine-studded cloth of gold preserving her most intimate secrets. There was insufficient fabric in the dress for the fronts to cross over. Instead the sides met beneath a wide belt of that same aquamarine-studded cloth of gold. Jasyl's magnificent breasts were barely more than half-covered, the jut of her nipples plain beneath the edge of the fine cloth.

Kheda settled himself comfortably and treated Jasyl to a brisk fatherly smile.

You're not that much older than my eldest daughter even if you've got a more knowing look in your moist eyes than any of my wives have ever had.

He managed to exchange a swift glance with Risala and saw the same question in her eyes.

How soon are we going to be able to withdraw from this entertainment without causing offence?

CHAPTER TWELVE

Kheda smothered a yawn. He saw Risala shifting her weight on her cushions as discreetly as she could.

Is your delightful rump as numb as mine, my beloved? Are we to be allowed to rise now that my lord of Zelin has finally enlightened my lord of Galcan as to the current state of affairs in each and every domain that all his sisters and aunts have married into? Mian Zelin has already shared all the news from Kauris Zelin and every one of her connections.

'What of our other sisters, my lord,' Mian asked with eager anticipation. 'And their daughters?'

Kheda forced an expression of polite interest and resigned himself to more tedium.

Mian Zelin will doubtless have pertinent and lengthy comment to make on whatever Galcan Sima has to tell her. They haven't even begun to discuss what bearing the current state of the heavenly and earthly compasses might have on all these people and their plans. Possibly because that would lead us too perilously close to mentioning the dragon and its significance as an omen. In all this interminable conversation, that's the one thing no one seems to want to discuss.

As Galcan Sima embarked on a lengthy account of a recent visit to the domain by Dawa Trin, Kheda looked down and found his third bowl of mersa pulp was almost empty, despite the care he'd taken to eat it as slowly as possible. The taste, verging on the medicinal, wasn't actually unpleasant though the lingering scent had an increasingly sickly tang as the full heat of the day mounted outside.

The worst thing about it is the texture. How can some-thing be solid and slimy at the same time? I'd give a lot for another drink to wash the taste away. Are we going to be offered anything else to eat besides this and those insipid saller cakes?

'My lord?' Jasyl Galcan leaned against him to look into the crystal bowl. Her full breast pressed against his upper arm. 'More mersa?' She raised a hand to snap her fingers and an attentive servant stepped forward.

Your body would stir the blood in any man not blind or inclined to beardless lovers and you know it, my lady.

'No, thank you.' Kheda spread his hand over the top of his bowl and shot the servant a firm look.

'You say Narila Dawa was not with him?' Zelin Raes had interrupted Galcan Sima.

'Narila was born to Galcan.' Jasyl leaned confidingly close to Kheda. 'To one of my lord's sisters who chose not to wed out of the domain.'

Mian Zelin looked concerned. 'I have not heard from Narila in some while.'

'Is she newly married to my lord of Dawa?' Risala asked from Jasyl's other side.

'Quite recently.' Perene Galcan sat forward to claim Risala's attention. 'They were wed last year, when the Vizail Blossom shone in the arc of marriage. Now please, what can you tell me of Redigal Coron's wives? Is it true that he's also a lover of men?'

With Risala inexorably drawn into conversation with Perene, Jasyl shifted to fill Kheda's view. 'My lord of Galcan and I were married as the new-year stars came into alignment.' She draped a hand across her generous breasts, adorned with rings heavy with pale-blue gems of dazzling cut and clarity. 'As the heavenly Topaz crossed from the arc of fear and foe into that of life and self.'

'An auspicious start to your married life.' Kheda tried to make the platitude sound spontaneous.

'I hope so.' Jasyl shrugged in a sorely distracting fashion. 'I am most junior wife here, and my lord is an old fowl who no longer cocks his head at the hens. No matter how much mersa he eats.' She giggled frankly at Kheda. 'So I shall learn all that Fizai and Perene can teach me of managing craftsmen and conducting trade to best advantage, with both Archipelagans and barbarians. When the compass finally ceases turning for my beloved lord, I shall be well placed to take my talents to some other domain.'

In twenty years' time, you'll have worked your way through a handful of husbands and built a web of trade and obligation that will make you a power in your own right. Though you might do better if you learned to conceal your naked ambition and your luscious body.

Kheda kept his eyes firmly on Jasyl's face. 'Which of Galcan's crafts come under your purview?'

'You know that we possess the secret of silvering glass to make mirrors?' Jasyl sat up straighter, more genuinely animated and less mindful of her seductive poses. 'Have you seen the woven silks that our seamstresses adorn with tiny mirrors?'

'I don't believe so.' Kheda shook his head, brows raised in enquiry.

'I shall select some choice pieces as gifts for your lady wives.' Jasyl's evident pride was the most appealing facet of her personality apparent thus far. 'My women have worked wonders of late.'

'I have only one wife,' Kheda corrected her in fatherly fashion. 'My lady Itrac.'

'My lords.' An elderly balding servant with a full black gown trailing around his feet climbed stiffly to the top of the stone steps leading up to the long open room where they all still sat.

'Lacu?' Galcan Sima was surprised. 'What is it?'

'There is a visitor, my lord.' The old servant spread his hands helplessly. 'Here to see my lord Chazen Kheda.'

'There is?' Kheda recovered swiftly from his first unguarded response. 'Who is it?'

'Yes, Lacu, who is it?' Galcan Sima slid Kheda a speculative look.

The servant bowed obediently to his master before addressing Kheda. 'He says his name is Telouet.'

'Then he is certainly known to me.' Kheda wiped a hand over his beard. Out of the corner of his eye he saw Risala stiffen with surprise. 'A trusted member of the Daish household.'

How by all the stars above did Telouet know I was here? What does he want?

'What manner of vessel brought him here?' Mian Zelin idly wondered aloud.

Kheda saw her body slave Lec make a mental note to find the answer to that and more besides. He had his own questions.

Telouet should be serving my son. Has something happened to Sirket?

'It is a long voyage all the way from the southern domains.' Zelin Raes looked at Kheda, waiting for him to offer some explanation or contradiction. 'And a risky one to make with the rains due any day.'

'He is a bold and courageous warrior.' Kheda smiled to hide the raw apprehension twisting in his gut like a blade. 'Will you excuse me, my lords, while I see what has brought him here?'

'Let us—' Perene Galcan rose swiftly from her cushions.

'Shall we—' Mian Zelin was on her feet before her.

'Please, don't disturb yourselves, my ladies.' Kheda extended a swift hand to Risala and helped her up. 'You still have much news to share, I know. We will see what word has come from the south. Then, if you'll forgive us, we'll retire to rest through the remainder of the heat.'

That was a little brusque but within the bounds of accept-able politeness. Will either of you risk showing discourtesy in front of the other?

There was an instant of tension as everyone waited for Galcan Sima's reaction. Kheda couldn't see the warlord's face.

'As you wish.' The old man waved a wizened hand, unperturbed.

The aged servant relaxed visibly. 'Let me show you to your quarters, my lord. I will have your visitor brought to you.' He turned to make his way carefully down the stone steps.

Kheda followed with Risala slipping her hand through his arm. As she walked beside him with wifely poise, Kheda slowed his pace. They fell in step a few paces behind the elderly servant.

'Will you be sending some servant to invite Jasyl to our quarters tonight?' Risala murmured with amusement.

The old man turned down a path of irregular yellow stones set in the soft grass.

'Hardly.' Kheda was too tense to find anything funny in the situation. 'What did the wives want with you, while Galcan was trying to buy my secrets?' Though none of the bare-chested gardeners he could see were within earshot, he still kept his voice down to a whisper.

'To lure me into telling them whatever I know of your mysterious dragon lore,' Risala muttered caustically, 'under the guise of marvelling at Zelin's salvation and congratulating me.'

'Congratulating you?' Kheda was puzzled.

'For my boldness in drawing you into my bed.' It was difficult to tell who was the focus of Risala's ire. 'They are all eager to encourage my ambition. Perene Galcan offered to insist you acknowledge me as your concubine. Mian suggested I make a trade treaty with her, to anticipate my elevation to the rank of second wife.'

'If . . .' Kheda began, but couldn't think what to say.

They followed the elderly servant through a gap in a dense hedge thick with dead coppery leaves. It circled a smaller wooden house built on the same lines as Galcan Sima's residence. Here a single stair led to the upper storey, set to one side of the open-fronted room that made up the ground floor.

A man stood on the steps of the stone foundation. He was not quite as tall as Kheda, nor yet as old by a few years. His shoulders were appreciably broader, muscles displayed to full advantage by his sleeveless tunic of pale-blue cotton. Dark-green canthira leaves were embroidered around the neck and down the side seams of his loose trousers. With his full black beard and hair neatly trimmed, he appeared remarkably clean and well kempt for a man who'd just made such an arduous voyage. He also looked as prosperous as any placid merchant, with a heavy gold chain around his thick neck and shimmering bracelets of dog-tooth pearls pale against his warm brown skin. Though the most successful merchants left fighting to their subordinates. Someone, long past, had landed a blow on Telouet's face to leave his nose crooked.

I always thought your broad features stemmed from some western blood, Telouet. Now I see you in these waters, I think I was in error. Your blood is as mixed as mine.

A stout Galcan servant woman in a short black robe tied tight over a long skirt was hovering beside this unexpected newcomer. She hurried down the steps, wringing her hands. 'He insisted on being brought straight here, Lacu—'

'That's quite all right,' Kheda interjected.

The servant woman glared at him, black eyes bright. 'That's for my lord to say.'

'He surrendered his weapons?' The elderly steward Lacu looked suspiciously at Telouet even though it was plain the visitor's double-looped sword belt was empty of both blades.

Kheda noted the empty sheath where Telouet had even surrendered his belt dagger.

There's no hiding the fact that you are a formidable warrior. So who is guarding Sirket if you are here?

'These are our quarters?' Despite the blood pounding in his throat, Kheda shared a calmly enquiring glance between the old man and the woman.

'Indeed, my lord.' The woman recollected herself, shifting her shoulders like a plump duck settling her feathers. 'I am to see to your needs. I am Dacas.'

'Then I'm sure we won't lack any comfort.' Kheda found his most charming smile. 'Please bring some water, or fruit juice, whatever you have to hand to drink. It is a very hot day.'

'Something to eat would be welcome. Anything but mersa,' Risala said firmly.

'We generally eat lightly in the heat of the day, only fruit and saller cakes.' Dacas's response hovered between apology and rebuke. She looked Risala up and down with a calculating eye. 'My lord and his ladies dine after sunset.'

'When we will be honoured to join them,' Kheda cut in smoothly. 'In the meantime, we are thirsty, so please fetch us something to drink.' He turned to Lacu. 'Please give your lord our thanks for accommodating us in such elegant quarters.'

Kheda walked away from the two servants, drawing Risala firmly with him. Lacu and Dacas retreated down the haphazard path of yellow stones, their heads close together, their fleeting backward glances speculative.

Telouet would have come down the steps to meet them but Kheda waved him back. As they reached the wooden floor within the frame of the building, he looked warily around. 'Risala, my love, can you please make sure there are no curious ears to hand?'

'Of course.' She crossed to the closest of the two ebony panelled doors in the rear wall. Slipping through, she closed it behind her.

Kheda forced himself to wait for a moment before asking his most urgent question. 'Has something happened to Sirket?'

'My lord is alive and well.' Telouet stood braced like a swordsman ready for combat. 'A lot has happened in the domain. Two of your former wives have quit Daish.'

'What?' Kheda hadn't expected this news.

Telouet's beard jutted as he lifted his chin defiantly. 'My lady Janne has married Redigal Coron. My lady Rekha has married Ritsem Caid.'

'Why?' Kheda asked, startled.

'I couldn't say, my lord,' Telouet said stolidly.

'No, I don't suppose you can.' Kheda rubbed a hand over his beard as shock gave way to rapid assessment.

Rekha has always managed the domain's trade with consummate skill, but with the failure of the last two pearl harvests, Daish has had precious little to offer. Whereas the discovery of iron ores in the Ritsem isles has opened all manner of opportunities for that domain. Rekha would find that a tempting prospect, and she has always been close to Taisia Ritsem. Who is well advanced in pregnancy, if all has gone well since I last saw her. I can see how Ritsem Caid would want to relieve her of her duties by adding Rekha's formidable skills to those of his other wives. Rekha could well prefer to be even third wife in a domain enjoying such good fortune, rather than merely sister-mother to a young warlord whose fortunes are in apparent decline. His marriage must surely be expected soon, leaving her with no role at all.

'Is Sirket thinking of marrying?' he asked Telouet, frowning.

'My lord has shown no inclination to take a wife,' Telouet said dourly. He would have continued but Kheda held up a hand to silence him.

I thought I knew Janne's mind like my own but she was the one who drove me out of Daish. She was repelled by the deal she suspected I had made with some means of magic, even if that was only to save Daish from the wild men. Why has she quit Daish for Redigal? She's past any hope of childbearing. Besides, after begetting a safe quantity of children on his existing wives, Redigal Coron has openly acknowledged his nature as a lover of men. He shares his bed with his clean-shaven and openly adoring body slave. Who was instrumental in uncovering Ulla Safar's plots to kill Coron.

'Does my lord of Redigal still forswear his previous alliances with the Ulla domain?'

'He does.' Telouet nodded. 'And my lord of Ulla is beset by quantities of trouble at present—'

'Ulla Orhan?' Kheda guessed promptly.

'He's evaded his father's claws thus far,' Telouet said with grudging admiration. 'He is raising open rebellion on Avasir and his cause is being taken up in the outlying islands.'

'If he holds the northern third of the domain—' Kheda frowned in rapid calculation. 'If sufficient of Ulla's triremes declare for him, they'll be able to cut the sea lanes to Tule, Seik and Endit waters.'

Avasir is a sizeable island, thickly forested. Ulla Safar could find the lifeblood of even his vast armies draining away into the leaf litter, if all those islanders throw in their lot with Orhan.

'Does Dau Daish still favour marrying Orhan?' he asked sharply.

'She does, if he can take the domain from his father.' Telouet grimaced with patent disapproval. 'Her mother Janne is still promoting the match.'

'Is she?' Kheda chewed his lower lip.

Redigal lies to the south of Ulla and is the next largest domain in those reaches. If Viselis and Sarem follow Redigal's lead, Ulla Safar will be wholly without allies in this fight with his son. Is that what Janne is doing? Does our daughter know what she's doing?

'My lady Sain Daish remains in the domain.' Telouet's blunt reminder of his erstwhile third wife struck Kheda like a slap to the face.

He swallowed. 'How is she?'

She must regret the appallingly bad bargain she made in marrying me. But what of the domain? Sain cannot manage Daish's trade all on her own. She was a meek and uncertain maiden even when Daish offered peace and prosperity after the violence and infighting that drenched her home domain in blood.

'She is content, my lord.' Telouet's smile was fleeting. 'She has renounced all claims to status beyond that of mother to those Daish children not yet of the age of discretion.'

Kheda wondered if he imagined rebuke in Telouet's eyes.

My children. Clever, handsome Mesil, whom we raised so carefully to be his brother's loyal ally rather than any potential challenge to Sirket's rights as eldest son. Bold Efi and sweet Vida. Smiling Noi and happy little Mie. And Sain's son Yasi whom I've never even seen. I failed in my very first duty to him, to see him and his mother safely delivered from childbed. My children are the most innocent victims of all my manoeuvring and their mothers' scheming.

'There is more you should know, my lord.' Telouet said abruptly.

'What?' Kheda did his best to thrust aside fruitless regrets.

'I am no longer a slave to my lord Daish Sirket.' Telouet looked Kheda straight in the eye. 'My lord granted me freedom for my years of loyalty to the domain.'

Kheda was astonished. 'Who guards my son's back now?'

'A warrior I picked personally.' Telouet threw Kheda's challenge back at him. 'From body slaves that my lord's mothers traded their most valued talismans to obtain. His name is Zari and I'd back him against a heat-crazed jungle cat.'

'How old is he?' Kheda asked sharply.

'Younger than Sirket, just as you had always wished his attendant to be.' Telouet moderated his tone. 'He was taken into the Kithir household as an orphaned infant fifteen years ago. He was raised as a page for the noble wives of the domain. When their body slaves saw he had a deft hand and a good eye, they began training him with daggers and then with swords. He's young, but he's one of the best fighters I've tested myself against for many a year. Cautious, too,' the swordsman said approvingly.

I shall have to be content with that. I have no standing in my son's life.

Kheda addressed the more immediate puzzle of Telouet's arrival. 'If you are a free man, what brings you here?'

'Urgent need for you in the Daish domain—' Telouet turned, one hand going to his hip where his swords should have been as the second interior door opened.

It was Risala. 'There are servants hovering in the rooms on the other side of this corridor.' She jerked her head briefly backwards. 'Watch what you say and keep your voices down.' She smoothed a yellow silken tunic she had donned instead of her luxurious gown, her lithe legs clad once again in trousers.

'Where are you going?' Kheda guessed the answer before she gave it.

'To find Sirince.' She raised her eyebrows at Kheda. 'While my lords and ladies of Galcan and Zelin think I'm on my back and spreading my legs like a compliant concubine.'

'You're the poet—' Telouet frowned as he tried to remember exactly who she was.

'Risala,' Kheda supplied. 'Chief among my eyes and ears since I have been lord of Chazen.'

'I'm going before that Dacas woman comes back. She'll run off to tell her mistresses if she thinks I've slipped my leash.' Risala walked down the steps, looking warily around.

'Does she share your bed?' Telouet asked bluntly.

You spoke your mind as my slave but freedom has certainly changed you.

'She does.' Kheda watched her disappear beyond the clipped barrier of the varicoloured hedge. 'It's not widely known and I'll thank you to keep it so.'

Risala has always warned me she'll be useless as my confidential agent if she's known to be my concubine. What if the Galcan and Zelin wives spread their belief that she harbours ambitions to become my wife? Some warlords' ladies will condemn her and some applaud her. Everyone will be watching her to see what transpires. Will she stay with me on those terms?

He shied away from such thoughts. 'How did you find me?'

'Who's Sirince?' Telouet looked in the direction of the vast harbour where Risala was headed. 'I thought you were travelling with a *zamorin* scholar, the one who helped you find this dragon lore that's all the talk of this whole anchorage.'

'The *zamorin*'s ship was wrecked,' Kheda replied cautiously. 'Sirince is a barbarian trader who's been giving us the use of his vessel. Why have you come to find me? Daish Sirket is lord in his own right now.' He felt a pang of pain and pride. 'If anyone has the right to send for me, it's Itrac Chazen.'

'Itrac Chazen is fully occupied with the care of her twin daughters.' Telouet anticipated Kheda's next question. 'She is well and the babies thrive. My lord Sirket told me to set your mind at ease. As far as he knows, my lady Itrac still believes you are meditating in seclusion on Chazen's proscribed isle.' He turned an accusing scowl on Kheda. 'You never used to tell such lies, my lord, especially not to your wives.'

Unforeseen dangers have made a liar and worse of me, Telouet.

'You never used to be so bold when you were my slave.' Kheda forced mild anger into his words.

'I'm no longer a slave. Besides, you never expected me to be a mindless brute.' Telouet was unrepentant. 'You sought my counsel and trusted it.'

Could you ever trust me again if you learn all that I have done?

Kheda backtracked. 'How did you find me?'

'I was looking for that *zamorin* scholar, Vel.' Telouet's voice roughened with emotion. 'He was the last person to see you, or so I believed. You sailed with him when you fled so unexpectedly, when we were all gathered for Chazen's new-year celebrations. I reckoned if I could find him, I could bribe or beat some clue out of him as to where you were.'

'How did you find Vel— him?' Kheda cleared his throat.

'There are message-brokers the length and breadth of the Archipelago.' Telouet drew a deep breath through flared nostrils. 'I let them know they would be well rewarded for any word of the *zamorin*, or of your poet girl.'

'Why didn't you believe I was on the proscribed isle?' Kheda wondered aloud.

'I went and looked for you there,' Telouet said through clenched teeth.

'You did?' Once more, Kheda was astonished.

You believe with all your heart in talismans and portents, and in the sooth to be found in the heavenly compass. Yet you set foot on the most ill-omened piece of land in that whole domain. Where Chazen Saril's brute of a father imprisoned his brothers and then his remaining sons, gelded and blinded by his death-bed decree lest murdering them outright brought ill consequences for the domain. Where you and I first encountered the wild men's wizards. Where we saw our comrades in arms slaughtered by monsters wrought by their magical malice. You helped me set the fires that we foolishly believed would burn evil from that place.

'Why?' Kheda asked simply.

'A dragon overflew Daish, in the dark of the Greater Moon before this current one.' The fear in Telouet's eyes pierced Kheda.

You're afraid of the dragon. That's only wise. But are you also afraid of what you might learn? Of what exactly I might have done in my fight against the wild men and since, to defeat these creatures?

'A dragon overflew Daish?' Stricken with fear for his children there, Kheda grasped at a frail hint of hope. 'It hasn't landed? It hasn't laid waste to any islands?'

'Not when I left it hadn't,' Telouet said heavily. 'Nor when my lord last sent word. The latest news was waiting for me in Mahaf.'

'What were you doing there?' Kheda demanded.

'Looking for you.' Telouet shivered despite the hot sun. 'We had word there was a dragon in these reaches when the Greater Moon joined the Ruby in the heavenly arc for parents. Sirket judged that meant these reaches were an obvious place to look for the *zamorin*, if he was a scholar of such things.' He squared his formidable shoulders with a hint of defiance. 'Daish Sirket put his fastest dispatch galley at my disposal.'

Kheda wasn't concerned with any excessive courtesies bestowed on a mere freed slave. 'You made the voyage in what, twenty days? Your men must have been all but dead at their oars.'

'You underestimate the men of Daish,' Telouet said with stout pride. 'They would think their lives well spent if they save their families and villages.'

They grew to manhood trusting that I would guide and guard the domain, laying down my life if necessary. Now I'm supposedly lord of Chazen.

'So you've found me.' Kheda sat down on the top step, resting his head back against an ironwood pillar. 'What am I supposed to do?'

'You've proven yourself against these creatures once again.' Telouet looked a little happier. 'Without leading half a household of warriors to their deaths in a battle with the beast.'

Do I tell you the truth about that triumph or continue to lie to you?

'Don't ask me how, Telouet, I beg of you,' Kheda said tightly.

'All I want to know is can you do it again?' the warrior said bluntly. 'Can you rid Daish of this beast, or Redigal or Ritsem, wherever it may have laired?'

'I can try.' Kheda shot Telouet a contemplative look. 'I take it you brought plenty of courier doves ready to fly back to Daish? Have you made arrangements for news to be brought quickly to wherever you may be?'

I could get all the information I needed if Velindre could scry without fear of discovery. But that's going to be nigh on impossible with you at my shoulder.

Telouet smiled without humour. 'The domains we passed through were more than happy to offer their birds to relay news, in hopes that some means of defending themselves against a dragon might be their reward.'

Kheda frowned. 'How widely has word of this spread?'

'People have seen it from Sier to Jahal.' Telouet shook his head. 'It's overflown ten or more domains.'

'How many innocents has it slaughtered?' Kheda asked with growing dread.

'As far as we can tell, it hasn't killed whenever it's landed,' Telouet said cautiously. 'Though not every outlying island has been visited to make sure.'

Then it's not looking for food. Not yet, anyway.

'Where has it landed?' Kheda tried to think what might attract a dragon in southern waters. 'Near a fire mountain or some powerful tide race?'

They look for potent concentrations of the elements of air, earth, fire and water, according to Velindre. Or gems, to forge an egg and make a new dragon.

The plump woman, Dacas, appeared in the gap in the hedge. A dutiful maidservant in a modest black dress followed with a tray of polished wood laden with goblets of grey glass laced with white and a ewer to match.

Kheda rose to his feet as Dacas waddled towards the guest residence. 'What colour is it?'

'Some say blue, some say green.' Telouet looked anxiously at Kheda.

'Your drink, my lord.' Dacas folded her hands at her waist as the maidservant offered the two men their refreshment. 'Is my lady Risala resting upstairs?'

'She is not to be disturbed.' Kheda drank and found to his relief that the water was both clean and cool. A sprig of little yellow flowers on a stem thick with sodden silky grey leaves added a faintly sour flavour that cut through the cloying aftertaste of the mersa.

'How else may we serve you, my lord?' Dacas looked expectantly from Kheda to Telouet and back again.

'You can stay here.' Kheda handed her the glass goblet. 'We'll soon have need of more to drink. Come on, Telouet. It's been too long since I've tested my sword skills against a trained warrior.' He pulled one of the scabbarded blades that Zelin Raes had given him out of his belt and tossed it to the swordsman.

Telouet grinned readily. 'I'll be happy to help you raise a sweat, my lord.'

You recall the times you and I have won ourselves some privacy like this. Dacas can't leave without being impolite. So she can't go in search of Risala either.

Kheda led the way to the centre of the open sward between the residence and the hedge. It was still uncomfortably hot but some of the taller trees cast a modicum of shade.

Kheda drew his blade. 'We have to consider carefully how best to take our leave from here.'

'My dispatch galley's ready and waiting.' Telouet tossed the scarlet-lacquered scabbard to one side. He settled into a ready stance, taking a two-handed grip on the sword. The tip of his blade just crossed over that of Kheda's.

'Vel, the *zamorin*, will favour sticking with his friend's ship.' Kheda tapped Telouet's blade aside and twisted his wrists to launch a sideways thrust at the warrior's throat.

What will you make of Crisk?

'Besides—' he continued. The hilts of the two swords locked as Telouet stepped aside with a deft parry. 'It's already loaded with the gifts Zelin Raes is sending for Chazen.'

'My lady Itrac hardly needs any more treasures for her storehouses,' Telouet said a trifle sourly as he stepped back. 'Their pearl harvest exceeded even last year's, and there's been no sign of any dragon in Chazen skies.'

'They shun any place where one of their kind has died.' Kheda took a swift sidestep, forcing Telouet's blade down before rolling his own to threaten the back of the warrior's neck.

The swordsman circled to avoid the danger. 'You're out of practice, my lord,' he chided.

'Then school me,' Kheda challenged.

Then I won't have to talk to you and risk betraying myself to someone I used to trust like my own right hand.

'As you command, my lord.' There was a hint of mockery in Telouet's grin that Kheda couldn't recall ever seeing before.

He gave up trying to remember as Telouet launched an attack. Most guard-captains would have deemed it too risky on a practice ground with wooden swords, never mind with lively blades of shining steel. Kheda dodged and parried, retreating pace by grudging pace until he saw the narrowest of openings.

Shifting his own sword to a one-handed hold, he stepped inside the flashing arc of Telouet's blade. He seized the hilt of Telouet's sword, forcing his own hand between the warrior's. Stepping backwards, he ripped the hilt up, turning the blade inwards, threatening Telouet with disembowelling.

Telouet flung his hands wide in surrender as he took a long stride away. 'Not bad.'

Carefully Kheda tossed the sword back. 'Let's see if I can catch you out a second time.'

'Don't wager on it.' Telouet looked more cheerful than he had since he arrived.

They returned to slower patterns of thrust and parry, alternating with lightning-fast trials of speed and reaction. Sweat soon darkened Telouet's cotton tunic. Kheda's silken garb was clinging slickly to his limbs but he found his spirits rising. He set aside all the intricate cares and puzzles enmeshing him to focus on these simpler tests of strength and skill.

'My lord!' Risala's shout wrenched him back from this illusory peace.

Telouet cursed under his breath and pulled his blow just in time to save Kheda from a slice to his forearm.

'What is it?' Kheda sheathed his sword, breathing hard.

Risala ran onto the grassy sward. 'There's another dragon.' She was out of breath, sweat-sodden hair sticking to her forehead.

'I know.' He nodded grimly.

'My lord,' Telouet warned, retrieving his own scabbard from the shadow of the hedge.

Kheda saw Dacas and the maidservant hurrying towards them. 'That's what Telouet came to tell me.' He held out a hand to Risala. 'We'll sail south just as soon as we can.'

'No, Kheda.' Risala shook her head furiously. 'There's a dragon in Shek.'

'What?' Kheda stared back.

'It's laired in the crater of a dead fire mountain in the west of the domain.' Risala waved a hand vaguely over her shoulder. 'It's been plundering the whole island.'

'Did you know about this?' Kheda demanded of Telouet.

'No,' the warrior protested with genuine shock.

'A man found me with a message from Shek Kul.' Risala lowered her voice as the two Galcan servants approached. 'There's no talk of it around the anchorage, not yet, anyway.'

'I'll wager half Zelin Raes's gifts that Galcan Sima knows.' Kheda shut his mouth as the two women reached them. He and Telouet each took a goblet of the herb–flavoured water and drank deeply.

'My lady?' Dacas dipped an ungainly curtsey. 'We only have the two glasses—' The maidservant's quick eyes took in Risala's dishevelled appearance.

'Never mind.' Kheda took the smoky glass ewer and refilled his goblet for Risala. His serene smile hid the turmoil of his emotions. 'We had better all bathe before we are summoned to my lord of Galcan once again.'

'Is there sufficient water waiting in the bath chamber?'

Telouet's authoritative question prompted a flicker of perplexity on Dacas's plump face.

'There is,' she said with some affront.

'Then we shall bathe.' Kheda smiled with warm approval, offering Risala his arm.

Telouet thrust the sword he still held through his belt and fell into step two paces behind as they headed for their quarters.

Just as if you were still my most faithful slave and servant. When magic was no more than a distant dread blighting the unknown barbarians of the unbroken lands.

'What colour?' Kheda asked Risala in a low tone.

She understood what he was asking. 'Black.' She spared him a sideways glance of apprehension.

Tied to the element of earth.

'Sirince,' Kheda reminded her obliquely.

She wasn't to be comforted. 'Remember the last one?'

The last black dragon we encountered was very nearly the death of us all. We didn't kill it. Could this possibly be the same beast?

Kheda shivered as they walked up the stone steps and

into the shade of the open front of the dwelling. 'Where do we bathe?' he asked Risala quietly.

'Upstairs.' She led the way.

'I take it there is everything my lord will require?' Telouet turned on the two women who were following close behind him. 'Has all his baggage been safely brought ashore?'

'Indeed.' Dacas was sufficiently off balance to be more conciliatory than offended.

'Then you may be about your duties.' Telouet nodded briskly. 'How do I summon you if my lord wants anything further?'

Kheda looked back as he and Risala reached the bottom of the staircase.

'Ring for the girl.' Dacas pointed at a silver bell hung on a bracket by one of the interior doors.

'It will be my honour to serve.' The maidservant sank into a hasty curtsey.

Telouet set his goblet back on her tray. 'That will be all for now.'

The girl disappeared through the door and Dacas waddled away down the stone steps to hurry across the grass towards the gap in the hedge.

Telouet looked up to Kheda and Risala, who had halted halfway up the stairs. 'We had better hurry if we're all to be calm and collected when some curious Galcan wife turns up.'

'The old maid is bound to carry whatever tale she thinks she has to tell.' Kheda hurried upstairs, Risala two steps ahead of him.

Telouet came after them.

'Through here?' Kheda went past the wide bed draped with translucent gossamer curtains that occupied the centre of this upper floor. The walls were panelled with fragrant pale wood and screens cunningly wrought of coloured glass could be pulled across to close the open front. Two doors were set in the opposite wall to match the ones below.

'This one.' Risala pushed at the closest. 'The other leads to an inside stair and rooms for your personal servants. That's where they've stowed your travel chests.'

'I'll find dry clothes, my lord.' Telouet headed for the other door.

Kheda followed Risala into an airy room panelled with pale-grained wood varnished with golden lacquer. A table topped with white marble held bowls and bottles of soaps and unguents. A second table set against the far wall bore sturdy ceramic jugs resting in wide basins and a stack of cotton towels. Two circular baths of dark wood bound with brass stood between them, already half-full.

'Galcan Sima was ready to trade me every secret of rearing silkworms in return for lore on driving off dragons.' Kheda stripped off his sweaty tunic. 'He must know what's afoot in Shek. That's why he was so desperate.'

'Shek Kul is desperate.' Risala didn't move.

'He knows the secret of that powder that stifles magic.' Kheda tested the water in the closest bath with a careful hand.

'What good is that going to do him?' Risala asked, scathing.

'There are dragons in the south.' Kheda stripped off rings and necklaces and tossed them down on the white marble table. 'Where I have left all my children and all those islanders I've taken responsibility for, past and present.'

'I have not wholly abandoned my loyalties to the Shek domain,' Risala retorted.

'We have to talk to Vel—' Kheda cut the magewoman's name short in case of listening ears. 'And to Sirince. First we have to get safely out of these reaches—'

'If Galcan Sima knows what's afoot, he'll expect you to go to Shek. You're the only warlord who knows the secrets of driving away dragons or killing them if need be.' Risala moved to intercept Kheda as he picked up a shallow bowl of creamy soap. 'You'll be disgraced if you don't, you and Itrac and Daish Sirket as well, if you turn your back on Shek for his sake. Galcan Sima will tell everyone, to pay you back for refusing his offer.'

'And if our secrets are discovered?' he challenged her with a meaning only the two of them could perceive. 'The more places we go, the greater the risks.'

'You have to help Shek Kul,' Risala insisted with clipped anger. 'You owe him a mighty debt, Kheda. You'd never have defeated those wild men and their wizards without . . . without that concoction of herbs and rare earths to defeat their magic—' She stopped, her lips pressed tight together. 'You have to repay him.'

Kheda heard her unspoken words.

We'd never have defeated those wild mages without Dev's magic. It was Shek Kul who first suspected Dev was a wizard though he couldn't prove it. There are those among the warlords of the central and northern domains who'd condemn Shek Kul for even allowing Dev to live once he first suspected him. While we in the south would have been condemned to die under the wild men's magic, even before the first dragon came, without Dev's sorceries. I owe Shek Kul a mighty debt for daring to send me in search of Dev. But if there's a dragon in the south . . .

'We'll talk to Vel and Sirince.' Kheda gripped the shallow bowl of soap. 'As to where we go first, we'll see—'

'We'll see what?' Risala burst out. 'We'll see what the omens say, in the heavenly arcs or in the earthly compass? You don't believe they will show you anything any more, so don't try to deceive me! You'll see what Velindre has to say? Or some other barbarian? You let her talk you into sailing into the west for lack of any other conviction to guide you and look where that got us!' She choked on her fury.

Kheda wanted to tell her to keep her voice down but found he couldn't speak, he was so utterly taken aback.

'You have to make this choice, Kheda.' She shook her head slowly, her eyes never leaving his. 'You had better make the right choice, if you look for any future with me in it. I helped you first because my lord of Shek ordered it. I stayed with you because that's what I thought the omens approved. Then I followed you because I loved you, even when you turned your back on Aldabreshin lore time and again for barbarian . . . for barbarian learning. I've stayed with you, even though I've felt more and more lost and every step seems to take us further astray and you won't look for any guidance in the stars or anywhere else—' She ran out of words.

'I know you've been angry with me—' Kheda took a step towards her.

'I know you owe Shek Kul a debt.' She took a pace backwards, her raised hands warding him off. Kheda saw that she had a fine slip of paper folded beneath her silver emerald-set cipher ring. 'You had better repay it.'

She pushed past him and caught up a ewer from the side table. Heavy and unwieldy, it slopped water onto the floorboards as she strode towards the inner door. Pushing it open with her hip, she revealed Telouet outside.

He stepped aside to let Risala pass before turning to Kheda. 'There's no one else upstairs.' He entered the room, a fresh set of clothes for Kheda over one arm. 'But wooden walls and floors are thinner than stone.'

'I never said I wouldn't go to Shek.' Kheda stared into the bath. 'Just that it's risky.'

'Do you owe Shek Kul sufficient debt that he's entitled

to call on you to repay it this way, no matter what the risk?'
Telouet's words were weighted with more than that
question.

'Yes.' Kheda poured the soap into the bath and stepped
out of his sweat-stained trousers. 'And she's right about
more than that.' He got into the cool water and sluiced
his face.

'I can't look for omens to guide me, Telouet,' he said
abruptly. 'I've lost all faith in such things. There were no
signs that Chazen was about to be laid waste by the wild
men. I don't believe those readings in the stars that Janne
Daish used to justify poisoning Chazen Saril. We knew
him to be an amiable weakling but that shouldn't have
cost him his life. I cannot believe any conjunction of
earthly or heavenly compass could ever have made him
equal to that challenge. How could such things show him
how to face magic and brutality overrunning his people
and slaughtering his family? These past few years, I've
made decisions after racking my brains over signs and
portents and I've made ones that fly in the face of all
custom and belief. There's been no difference in the
outcomes, not beyond blind chance. Not that I have seen.'

He sighed and slid down to let the water close over his
face. All sound was muffled, locking him inside his own
head with his turbulent thoughts. He sat up again, water
running down his chest.

Telouet threw him a washcloth before stripping off and
getting into the other bath.

'Have you really found barbarian lore to be a better
guide?' he asked at length.

*I don't want to lie to you but I cannot tell you the whole
truth.*

'No.' Kheda took a moment to wring out the washcloth and began scrubbing at his shoulders. 'But I have
learned that there are barbarians with as fine a sense of

honour as any Aldabreshi. There are those among them
who can argue as cogently as any of our philosophers.
They have scholars who treat our beliefs and histories
with more courtesy than we might show them and theirs.'

'They have this lore that we find we need so badly,'
Telouet said grudgingly, 'if this powder that Shek Kul
knows of isn't going to work against dragon magic.'

'It worked against the wild men's mages.' Kheda
continued washing himself. 'But no, I don't imagine it
would work against a dragon.'

'So we're going home by way of the Shek domain,'
Telouet said briskly. He finished washing and stood up.

'You don't have to run that risk.' Kheda got carefully
out of his bath. 'Go home and assure Sirket that I'll join
him as soon as I can.'

'I came all this way to find you.' Telouet tossed Kheda
a towel and began drying himself. 'We'll go home together
or not at all. You've got no one to watch your back but
your poet girl, some *zamorin* scholar and a barbarian trader.
I'm a free man now, so you can't gainsay me, my lord.'

'I wouldn't dare to try.' Kheda contemplated the fibrous
scars on Telouet's shoulder as the warrior rubbed his chest.

*Legacy of the time you saved my life when Ulla Safar
would have had me killed. I thought the omens demanded it
when I left you behind, injured and unconscious, to wake and
grieve when you believed the deceit that I was dead.*

He crossed to the fresh clothing Telouet had set out
for him: rich garments of scarlet silk brocaded with brilliant blue. He dressed slowly and carefully.

*Are you staying with me now to protect me, Telouet, or
because you will never trust me again? Do you think I would
abandon Sirket? All the warlords and their ladies between
here and Chazen will soon be learning I have apparently
abandoned Itrac, to come to these western reaches. There's no
keeping that a secret now. How can I go back and face her?*

But all other considerations aside, I owe Shek Kul a mighty debt. If I renege on that, I will lose Risala for certain. If I haven't already done so. So what choice do I have? If I have nothing else to guide me, no omens or portents, if I cannot be true to anyone else, I can at least be true to myself.

CHAPTER THIRTEEN

The heavy-set youth wiped grime and sweat from his face with an already filthy kerchief. He tucked it back through the studded leather belt cinching his plain chain-mail hauberk tight to his hips. Hot and wearisome as the armour was, it provided invaluable protection against the piercing thorns and lacerating vines of this dense jungle. And against any murderous arrows or treacherous swords that might surprise him from outside his tight-knit band of followers. Or from within.

He waited, watching a small group of men toiling along the narrow path snaking up the steep mountainside. The warriors around him stood ready, naked blades in every hand, beneath the shelter of the few meagre spinefruit trees that had found a foothold on this precipitous slope. Most were older than the warlord, though generally only by a few years. There was nothing in their dress to distinguish them from each other, nor the warlord from the rest. None wore any visible adornment and their armour was smeared with soil to stifle any chance of reflected sunlight betraying them. Though that was unlikely, given the overcast sky. With the rains so close, the humidity was brutal. The only concession the men had made to the punishing heat was taking off their helmets, dropping them at their feet. Every face showed the strain of long days in the forest with inadequate food or water, and nights without comforts to grant sufficient rest for recovering from the rigours of this life.

Dirt darkened the creases in the foremost man's brow as he squinted to see who was approaching, pushing through thickets of half-grown sard-berry bushes tangled around lilla fruit saplings.

'It's Inais, my lord,' he announced with visible relief, 'with Dechel and his men.'

The burly young warlord sheathed his sword and held out a hand. A formidable swordsman who topped him by head and shoulders immediately set a leather-bound brass water flask in it.

'We must find a spring soon, my lord,' he said firmly.

The younger man nodded as he unscrewed the cap. Shaking the flask to determine how much water remained, he drank half with careful restraint before handing it back. 'Don't go thirsty yourself, Nami,' he warned.

'No, my lord.' The looming warrior swallowed what remained in a few gulps.

The rest of the men shared what water they had and some scraps of stale saller-grain bread spotted with mould. No one spoke.

'The rains should come any day now, shouldn't they?' one man said finally.

No one answered.

The contingent of newcomers eventually reached them.

'My lord Ulla Orhan.' A clean-shaven man markedly less soiled than the rest pushed his way forward and bowed low.

'What news of my father, Inais?' the youth demanded without preamble.

The man looked around at the grim-faced warriors. Unarmed and unarmoured, he looked ill-suited to such company, his hands soft and his midriff plump. He was more than twice the age of most of them, grey threaded through the wiry brown hair at his temples. 'He is still in Derasulla, my lord,' he rasped, winded from the punishing climb.

'How did you get away unseen?' Ulla Orhan asked tautly.

'There are those among your father's guard who are willing to look the other way if anyone tries to leave the fortress,' Inais assured him. 'And those who take little or no notice of *zamorin* at the best of times.'

'An oversight I have learned better of.' Orhan shifted his stance and felt the sweaty leather squelch inside his nail-studded footwear. He wriggled toes unaccustomed to such confinement. 'So what can you tell us?'

All the men looked expectantly at the *zamorin*, both those who had waited with the young Ulla warlord and those who had arrived with him.

Inais drew a deep breath, pressing one hand to his chest. 'He claims to be watching the skies and reading the omens as he prepares to launch a decisive strike against you.'

The warriors surrounding Ulla Orhan stirred. Some silently sneered their disdain, though others looked openly apprehensive.

'Has he gathered sufficient swordsmen to launch an attack on us?' Orhan asked calmly. 'Or ships?'

'He has summoned levies from all the fortresses he still commands around the domain,' replied Inais, 'but they are slow to respond, as are the triremes. It seems too many messages are going astray. Ulla Safar is refusing to use message birds as he believes you have renegade hawk-handlers working for you. He insists on using warriors from his personal guard as couriers.'

One of the soiled, weary men barked with sardonic laughter. 'Which will just make it easier for us to slit their throats.'

'You'd raise your dagger against a man you trained with?' someone unseen growled. 'Or one who taught you how to keep yourself alive in battle?'

Ulla Orhan silenced them both with an upraised hand and a frown that knitted the thick black brows above his astute eyes. 'What do Safar's guard-captains make of that?'

'They're not pleased,' Inais said frankly, 'but they are too afraid to gainsay your father. And they are eyeing each other with growing suspicion as they wait for him to declare one of them paramount commander to lead this attack.'

'Could we provoke open strife among them?' the man who had led the newcomers úp the mountain suggested.

'Perhaps, when they're out of my father's reach,' Orhan said briefly. 'What else, Inais?'

'He is already suspicious of them himself,' the plump man said with careful satisfaction. 'He has executed Guard Captain Kuer. No one is quite sure why. And a dead concubine was found floating in the river two days ago. She had been beaten and strangled.'

The warriors stirred again with murmurs of angry frustration.

'My father continues to take out his disappointments on those unable to resist him,' Orhan commented with contempt.

'Who was she?' Nami asked hoarsely.

'We cannot tell.' Inais's mild eyes were shadowed with sorrow. 'She was too badly disfigured, even before the river lizards had mauled her corpse.'

Nami turned away with a wordless groan of anguish.

'Can't you tell who's missing from among his women?' Orhan asked with barely concealed distress.

Inais shook his head. 'Several are missing, already fled, or so we believe. My—' He swallowed. 'Ulla Safar beat his first wife with his own hands, telling her to school the rest of the women in proper loyalty. Since then she has had her own guards barring every door to all the women's apartments.'

'I don't suppose there's any chance Mirrel Ulla will die of her beating?' Orhan's face tightened with loathing. 'What of Chay?'

'She is busy sending letters to all her sisters and to all those daughters of Ulla that she and your father have been so keen to see marrying out of the domain these past few years. As yet she has received few replies, and none of any substance beyond the blandest greetings and evasions.' The faintest of smiles lightened Inais's plump countenance. 'She is determined to prevent Mirrel or anyone other than Safar communicating with anyone beyond Ulla waters. It is her hawk-handlers who are bringing down so many of the courier doves.'

Orhan allowed himself a brief laugh. 'I wonder if we could find a way to let my father know that.'

'I have been waiting for just such an opportunity, my lord,' Inais assured him.

Orhan shook his head. 'Don't put yourself at risk. Safar could just as easily have your head as hers, simply for telling him such news.'

Inais bowed his head in acquiescence. 'As you command, my lord.'

'What of my sisters?' Vulnerability flickered across Orhan's intent expression.

'I have made sure only slaves and servants I can trust attend them,' Inais assured him. 'Tewi Ulla is held in close seclusion with all the younger girls, by Chay Ulla's command. She won't risk any possibility of losing hold of her. But beyond that, both Chay and Mirrel ignore Tewi, as does Ulla Safar.'

'There are guards who will lay down their lives to protect them,' the warrior Dechel interjected, 'fighting against their own comrades if need be. I made sure of that before I fled the fortress.'

'Let's hope it doesn't come to that,' Orhan said grimly.

'What is our next move, my lord?' Dechel asked hopefully.

'That depends on when the rains come.' Ulla Orhan looked upwards at the sultry sky. 'And what I might see in the stars tonight. These are strange days. The Opal that is talisman of hope should come out of the darkness into the arc where we look for omens for all that we value, in hopes of prosperity. The Sapphire is there, as it has been for so long, so we may hope for clarity of vision, and truth. But the stars of the Hoe shine there at present, so we can take that as a firm promise of hard labour to come. There are no other conjunctions in the sky. And the Topaz has crossed beyond the western point of the compass while the Emerald has risen in the east. There are truly uncertain times.'

Each man stood quite still, hanging on the young warlord's every word. The silence in the forest was broken only by the insouciant twitterings of unseen birds and occasional nameless rustlings some distance away.

'The Amethyst has slipped into the arc of foes.' Orhan spoke more briskly, looking around. 'So we should look for new ideas, both among ourselves and among those who oppose us. The stars of the Yora Hawk with it remind us to be ever vigilant. I will keep close watch on the arc of travel on my own account, where the Diamond shines as talisman for warlords, along with the Horned Fish, for new beginnings.'

'My lord.' Inais spoke up. 'Concerning warlords and travel—'

'What is it?' Orhan was more surprised than irritated by the interruption.

'My lord.' Inais laced his smooth brown fingers together, knuckles paling as he tightened them. 'There is still some trade being done on the domain's outer beaches. I have heard things from the servants that Chay Ulla thinks are still loyal to her, whom she still sends out to gather news from the message-brokers who are still happy to take her gems.' The *zamorin* fell silent, looking down at his hands.

'What have you heard?' Orhan prompted after a moment.

'Daish Sirket has given his body slave Telouet his freedom.' Inais raised his head to look anxiously at Ulla Orhan. 'He made him a gift of a light galley, a dispatch boat. Telouet immediately set the ship on a course to the north and west.'

'Where is he going?' Orhan looked utterly baffled. 'Why would Sirket want rid of such a loyal man?'

'I believe he is still loyal, even more so now he is free. I think he has sailed for the western reaches,' Inais quavered. 'Where there is word of dragons.'

'What?' Orhan stared at the *zamorin*, astonished.

A murmur of disbelief ran through the men who'd been with him in the forest.

'It's true, my lord. Word has come from north and west.' Dechel spoke up amid the men surrounding the *zamorin*. 'Men coming to the trading beaches from domains to the south speak of such beasts closer to hand as well. A dragon has overflown those reaches.'

'When?' Ulla Orhan demanded furiously. 'How long have I been kept ignorant of this? Why didn't you send word immediately?'

'The beast was first seen just after the last full of the Lesser Moon, but word was slow to travel the domains, my lord.' Inais hunched his shoulders as if he expected a blow. 'No one could believe it. I dared not tell you until I heard more, from truly reliable sources. Then I had to wait for a chance to leave the fortress without being seen.'

'It's my fault that he has taken so long to reach you, my lord,' Dechel added humbly. 'I had to be certain we weren't followed. We dare not risk betraying you, my lord, not even by accident.'

Visibly restraining his temper, Ulla Orhan looked up at the secretive grey clouds. 'No dragon has been seen in Ulla skies.' His words hovered midway between question and declaration.

'No, my lord.' Inais spoke half a breath ahead of Dechel's stout agreement.

'It has flown over the domains all around us but it has not landed anywhere, my lord, nor attacked any ships,' the swordsman added. 'We would have brought you word of that at once, whatever the risks to ourselves.'

All the warriors who had arrived with them nodded confirmation.

Orhan raised his hand and the murmur of disquiet among his own swordsmen stilled. 'What does my father make of this?'

'He makes much of it, my lord.' Inais's face twisted with dislike. 'He claims that it is a sign that his foes will soon be defeated, because the dragon's shadow has passed over all those who either oppose him or merely refuse to support him, while Ulla skies remain free of its taint in token of the rightness of his rule.'

'Its shadow has not passed over us,' Orhan said instantly, challenge in his eyes. 'The Ruby that is talisman for strength rides with the Mirror Bird whose stars turn aside magic. Both are in the arc of the heavens where one looks for signs for home and family. We need not fear for our loved ones. It is for their future that we have taken up arms against Ulla Safar. The Pearl that is talisman against dragons and their evil rides in the arc of the compass where children may seek omens. I am my father's son, foul tyrant though he may be. My blood is bound to this domain and there is nothing he can do to change that. I will claim this omen for myself and not for him.'

'There is more, my lord.' Inais hesitated. 'The only other domain that the dragon has not ventured towards is Chazen.'

'The Pearl is both talisman against dragons and token of all that domain's hopes,' Orhan said thoughtfully. 'Even if it has been beleaguered by misfortune in these past few years.'

'Chazen men slew a dragon.' The strapping slave Nami was openly envious. 'They have prospered ever since.'

'Chazen Kheda led them to that victory,' mused Orhan. 'Telouet that was slave to Daish Sirket was formerly slave to Chazen Kheda.'

'Before—' Inais swallowed.

'Before he was grievously injured in my lord Kheda's service,' Orhan said steadily, 'when my vile father sought to have Kheda killed, betraying every law and custom of hospitality. When my cowardly sire so arrogantly refused to contemplate joining with my lords of Daish, Redigal and Coron in fighting against the wild men who were even then laying waste to Chazen.' He glowered, quite unaware how much that strengthened his resemblance to his despised parent. 'Countless portents have convinced me Ulla Safar's actions that day set insidious and persistent evil in motion. Perhaps even that first dragon—' He shook his head. 'Whereas Chazen fortunes began improving as soon as Kheda that was Daish took hold of that masterless domain. What do we know of Chazen Kheda, Inais? Has he emerged from this strange seclusion of his?'

'Not yet, my lord.' Inais plainly had no news. 'But my lady Itrac Chazen remains serene. She thrives, as do her infant daughters. The domain prospers and their pearl harvest exceeds even last year's largesse from the seas. No shadow falls on them.'

'The Daish domain thrived under Kheda's rule, as Chazen has done since he won it back from evil magics.'

Orhan smiled wryly. 'Daish Sirket has also proved himself a worthy lord, despite his youth.'

'You will do the same for all of Ulla, my lord,' Nami assured him.

'I will do so or die in the attempt,' Orhan said, utterly serious. 'And if I win through, I will bring Daish blood to help restore the Ulla domain, if Dau Daish will consent to be my wife.' He frowned in thought. 'But we have a great deal to do before I can hope for that day.'

Everyone stood still, intent on the brawny young man.

'My lord Kheda, when of Daish, drew many other domains together to fight the wild men who had overrun Chazen,' Orhan said slowly. 'He even turned the evil of my father's assault on him to some good, when he travelled in secrecy to the north to find the lore that drove the invaders out. I don't doubt my father would have sent someone after him to stab him in the back if he hadn't feigned death.' He shook his head with contempt. 'He discovered the means to set one dragon against another, if half the tales we hear are true. My lords of Redigal and Ritsem and all the domains beyond will be looking to him for counsel if a dragon's shadow has touched their isles. Perhaps the distant lords of the western reaches have done the same,' he mused. 'Perhaps he was hidden aboard this galley with his former faithful slave.'

'That is possible,' Inais agreed hesitantly.

'Bring me any word you hear of Chazen Kheda,' Orhan commanded with brisk decision. 'Find out all you can. Without putting yourself at risk,' he added hastily. 'Are you quite sure you can return to the fortress without arousing suspicion?'

The *zamorin* nodded. 'I believe so, my lord.' He gripped the dagger at his belt with a well-manicured hand as one of the warriors behind Nami opened his mouth. 'And if I am suspected, my lord, I will die before I betray you.

If I cannot raise a son of my own blood for Ulla's future, I can spend my life in service of the domain.'

'I have no doubt of your loyalty,' Orhan said with utter conviction. 'Forgive me if I seemed to say otherwise.'

'My lord.' Nami looked up at the sky, frowning. 'We should be moving if we're to reach safety before night-fall.'

Dechel looked back down the mountainside. 'I don't believe we were followed, my lord, but we'll hold the path behind you, just in case.'

Orhan nodded. 'You two had better get back to serving my esteemed father before you're missed.'

The warrior bowed his acquiescence. 'I have ten more good men to leave with you, my lord.' He grinned ferociously as he straightened up. 'Twenty more have fled Derasulla to their home villages to persuade their fathers and brothers to rise up for you when we bring the fight to Safar.'

Orhan's smile lifted the weariness from his solid face. 'Let's look for the omens that tell us when that day will be.'

CHAPTER FOURTEEN

How soon will we get there? The question Sirket would plague me with as we sailed from one Daish residence to another. He'd ask time and again, more often than any of my other children, apart from Efi. Because Sirket wanted to arrive as soon as he could, to see everything in its place and his life set in order again. While Efi wanted the voyage to last for as long as possible, to see new things and meet new people, even when she was barely old enough to talk to them. We always encouraged that in her, her mothers and me. It's a positive trait for a girl born to spread her wings by marrying out of her domain. But that was long ago and far away and there are more immediate challenges to contemplate.

Kheda decided against asking Velindre up on the stern platform for an update on their course or likely arrival time. He was sitting on the bench behind the steersman's position for want of anything better to do. Their course was set fair and the sail securely rigged. He looked for Risala instead. She was sitting up in the prow of the *Tacsille* with Crisk. The red-headed barbarian had been teaching her some complicated strategy game that the barbarians played among themselves.

We're going home as far as you're concerned, my beloved. In fact, you are home. We've been in Shek waters since last night.

He looked around. They had left the outer islands of the domain behind when they had set sail just after dawn. The morning's passage had taken them through a scattering of islets, some little more than reefs, others large enough to sustain a few trees and here and there a fishing village. But they had seen no skiffs out on the water or drawn up on the sombre sands. Now there was nothing beyond the *Tacsille*'s prow but slate-blue sea, ridges rising and falling.

'If the weather was clearer, we'd see the largest island of the domain almost directly ahead.' Velindre looked down at her route record. 'We've made good time.'

'Are the winds from the south always this steady?' Sirince was at the tiller.

'You can thank the arrival of the rains for that.' Kheda looked up at roiling clouds pale overhead. Noon had come and gone with the clouds refusing to allow the sun to burn through, and the air was heavy and humid. He contemplated the darker grey blurring the southern horizon, presaging stormy squalls.

We've had six days of rains thus far, so that probably means the first storms struck Chazen ten or so days ago. Itrac should have left in good time to travel to the rainy-season residence. Are both babies strong enough to throw off any lung fevers brought on by the dampness in the air?

'When do you think we'll get today's first soaking?' Sirince hunched his shoulders as if he already felt the first drops.

Kheda grinned despite himself. 'The rains will fall when they will. Just get used to being wet and enjoy it.'

'I suppose I'll have to.' Sirince looked unconvinced. He tugged at the neck of his old brown robe where sweat darkened the faded cloth. 'At least it's washed all that dust out of the air.'

'We left the worst of that behind when we crossed out of the western reaches,' Kheda commented. 'Though I would have expected the air to feel fresher now the season's turned.'

Velindre spoke up above his head. 'The cooler winds you're used to in the south at this season are slowed by their passage this far through the Archipelago.'

Kheda answered her with a shrug, his attention returning to Risala and Crisk. The mainlander was hunched in his shabby overlarge clothes once again. Risala had set aside her newly acquired finery as soon as they were out of Galcan waters and currently wore her old grey cotton tunic and trousers. Both were intent on shifting small pieces of carved wood across the leather game board spread out between them. Some were representations of crude trees, painted green; some were roughly carved birds daubed with various colours. All were battered and faded.

'Why does playing that game calm Crisk, Sirince?' Kheda wondered.

'I really don't know,' Sirince admitted. 'Perhaps it reminds him of home. The White Raven game originated among the forest dwellers of the mainland. They're mostly red-haired and fair-skinned like Crisk.'

Kheda frowned. 'Is this another one of his gods, this white bird?'

'It's a myth.' Sirince shook his head. 'Did he tell you the tale?'

'He's barely spoken since we left Galcan.' Kheda moved to stand beside the wizard. 'Precious little of what he has said makes any sense.'

'He does seem more agitated of late.' Concern knotted Sirince's greying brows. 'But the myth is simple enough. The raven, a black forest bird, was seeking wisdom. He couldn't find it in this world, even though it was right under his nose, or rather his beak, according to variations on the tale. So he flew through the rainbow to the Otherworld, where he found wisdom. But when he flew back, the rainbow stripped all the colour from his feathers. Which left him unable to share his newfound knowledge, because all the other birds mobbed him, not recognising him.'

Time was when I would have called such a tale an omen. Is that what Risala thinks? I need no barbarian fantasy to tell me my fellow warlords would do worse than peck at me, and still refuse the knowledge of magic and dragons that I could offer.

'That's the basis of the game,' Sirince continued. 'The white raven must use the cover of the trees to reach sanctuary without being driven from the forest by other birds—'

'Is this Otherworld where Trimon and these other gods that Crisk prays to are supposed to live?' Kheda found the notion bizarre.

'Trimon is the god of travellers and so passes freely between this world and the other,' Sirince said solemnly, 'mostly in the guise of a stranger. Sometimes he reveals himself, sometimes not. He guides those who are lost, either to the Otherworld or to some sanctuary in this one.' He slid a sideways grin at the warlord. 'No, I don't believe in Trimon or any of the archaic and inconsistent gods of forest, plain or mountain whose shrines dot the mainland, whose greedy or deluded priests offer unverifiable succour to the credulous.' He chuckled. 'We in Hadrumal focus on the logical, the tangible and provable.'

This from a man who can tell me whether a rock I pick up on a beach was blown out of a fire mountain or laid down in the depths of the sea without even having to hold it.

Kheda couldn't speak those thoughts aloud, mindful of Telouet busy somewhere in the hold below. 'What is this Otherworld supposed to be like?'

'Much like this one.' Sirince shrugged. 'With a door between the two guarded by a humourless deity called Saedrin who permits the spirits of the virtuous dead to pass through and be born anew, all innocent and unknowing. Otherwise he keeps them in some demon-filled darkness until they've made sufficient reparation for their misdeeds.'

'I can see why someone like Crisk would cling to hope of a god like Trimon, and the promise of a better life in the Otherworld.' Velindre's tone was neutral.

Kheda twisted around to look up at her. 'You don't think he'd be better off looking to his more immediate future in this world?'

'Spoken like a true Rationalist,' approved Sirince.

'What's one of those?' Kheda queried.

'A man who has seen the wisdom of rejecting the empty consolations of religion.' Velindre was plainly quoting someone, faint mockery in her words. 'Who relies upon rational philosophies derived from the study of the world as it exists.'

'Rationalists study the natural world all around them, as well as mathematics and disciplines like alchemy.' Sirince smiled with wry amusement. 'They admire Aldabreshin intellectual rigour in detailing and recording the behaviours of birds and beasts and the circuits of the stars. Aldabreshin treatises are eagerly sought. Though Archipelagan belief in portent and omen is derided as the ultimate irrationality. Natural philosophers find that particular paradox most vexing.'

'While those who deal in Artifice—' Velindre broke off as Telouet threw open the hatch.

'Can you take the tiller for a while?' Sirince didn't wait for Kheda to answer before retreating to the stern platform to join Velindre.

'Was it something I said?' Telouet scowled as he wiped at the sweat glistening on his forehead. 'Or do I need to wash more thoroughly?'

'Don't mainlanders generally keep their own company?'

Kheda tried for a shrug of unconcern. 'And *zamorin* are always inclined to reserve.'

'Those two are friendly enough.' Telouet looked towards the prow where Risala and Crisk were still intent on their game. He let slip a faint hiss of frustration. 'Who's winning?'

'I'm not sure.' Kheda allowed himself a smile.

'Don't you want to make a wager on it?' Telouet asked with unconvincing casualness.

'I'll make a wager but I won't read any omen in the outcome. I told you, I've lost all faith in such things.' Kheda saw the ex-slave's expression was coloured by something else. 'You want to try your hand at that game, don't you?'

'How can you have an equal contest between such uneven sides?' Telouet sighed with frustration. 'I've asked as gently as I can but the halfwit just runs away from me.'

'His name is Crisk,' Kheda said mildly. 'He seems afraid of his own shadow some days. He's had a hard life.'

'Hanyad would never talk about his servitude to a northern warlord,' Telouet said darkly.

'No,' Kheda agreed, though he rarely recalled Sain Daish's taciturn body slave saying much of anything.

'I'm starting to understand why.' Telouet shook his head slowly. 'Have you seen the scars on the halfwit's back, and his belly, when he washes himself or his clothes? These are strange domains, my lord.'

'Where they treat their slaves far worse than we do in the south, while they show their sons far greater mercy,' Kheda commented frankly. 'I've been surprised to find out just how much I don't know about the Archipelago.'

'We know there's a dragon hereabouts.' Telouet looked apprehensively ahead. 'What do you suppose it's been doing while we've been travelling?'

'I don't know,' Kheda admitted. 'But surely we'd have heard if it were wreaking havoc. Or seen those fleeing in panic.'

'Do we have sufficient talisman gems to sate it?' Telouet asked anxiously. 'Like you did in Chazen?'

'I believe so.' Kheda feigned confidence.

We'll buy some peace for Shek islanders with Zelin's gifts if we need to. Though we won't feed the beast sufficient means to forge some offspring of its own. The only gems we really need are those ruby shards from the shattered egg. It's a shame we can't just use those to poison some cache of jewels, as if we were laying a trap for a maneating jungle cat. But Velindre doubts the beast would go near them. Sirince isn't so certain but he definitely agrees that they must get close to the beast to wrap it in a magical deceit to drive it away for good. How are we to convince Shek Kul to let us go in search of the creature, just the few of us? How am I going to stop Telouet seeing something that arouses his suspicions?

Up on the stern platform, he could hear the magewoman in low-voiced conversation with Sirince. They were speaking their mainland tongue, too swift and colloquial for him to understand.

Is that to keep secrets from Telouet or from me?

Telouet broke the silence that had fallen. 'I should bring the courier doves up for some fresh air. We don't want them to sicken.'

Kheda nodded. 'As you think best.'

'We can't afford to lose any of them.' Telouet scowled. 'When should I next send word to Sirket?'

'When we know exactly what's afoot in Shek Kul's domain.' Kheda stared beyond the ship's prow.

Is that shape in the haze ahead land or wishful thinking?

'My galley should reach Daish in a few days,' Telouet said after another moment of silence. 'As soon as Sirket's read the letters it carries, he'll be anxious for the latest news.'

'As will Itrac Chazen, when he sends the ship on to her.' Kheda felt the thrum of the ship's passage through the waters in the wooden tiller. 'I wonder what she'll make of all those silks and ceramics and glasswares.'

'She'd trade them all for word that you're safe, and offer double their worth to have you back home again.' Telouet hesitated and plainly changed his mind about what he was going to say. 'I thought the rains would freshen the air.'

'We're a long way north of the winds and currents we're used to.' Kheda looked ahead again.

Those shapes in the haze are surely too fixed to be merely cloud.

'My lord.' Telouet pointed suddenly. 'A trireme.'

Risala said something to Crisk. The red-headed man immediately swept up all the game pieces. He pulled at a drawstring threaded through the edge of the leather that made up the playing surface, turning it into a scarred and dirty bag. Kheda could see Risala trying to reassure him, one firm hand on his forearm. Crisk wouldn't be calmed, shaking his head vehemently. Once he was quite sure he had recovered every last carved tree and bird, he ran down the deck.

'The moons are sinking either side of the empty arc of friendship.' Halting by the hatch, Crisk looked straight at Kheda. 'The Spear shines all alone and the Ruby set against it warns of heated passions and jealousy.'

He disappeared to hide himself in the hold as Risala walked more slowly towards the tiller.

'Who was winning?' Telouet asked with a friendly smile.

'He was,' Risala answered. 'He's no fool, even if he's so seldom in his right mind.'

'Do you recognise that ship?' Velindre called down from the stern.

'I hope we find a warmer welcome than we did in Zelin.' The tightness in Sirince's words belied his attempt at a jest. 'I don't have a pennant for these waters.'

As the trireme emerged more clearly from the haze, it proved to be a lightly built vessel rather than a heavy warship carrying a full complement of swordsmen.

'Shek Kul's word has seen us safe this far.' Risala nevertheless betrayed a degree of apprehension as she twisted the silver cipher ring with its bulbous emerald around her finger. 'I sent word on ahead of us from every trading beach and treaty isle.'

Eight domains in nineteen days. All unknown to me but their warlords were all too soon made well aware that I was passing through their waters, and doubtless soon discovered my destination. There really is no escaping my past or my birth. That's what the sages always say, pointing to the ineluctable turns of the heavenly and earthly compasses. But what of my future? Am I ever to escape this entanglement with magic and dragons?

The trireme swept towards them, scorning the contrary wind. Disciplined oars dug up gouts of white foam from the clouded sea, leaving a swirling furrow of a wake. No brassy horn echoed through the moist air to demand their surrender. The trireme drew closer and closer, until they could all clearly see the archers poised on the bow platform, arrows ready.

I don't think I ever appreciated what traders must fear meeting such challenges up and down the sea lanes.

Kheda gripped the tiller bar as the trireme heeled deftly around to match her course to the *Tacsille*'s. The surge of the sea set the smaller boat rocking uneasily. He saw an armoured man high up on the trireme, deep in conversation with the shipmaster.

Sirince came down to join Kheda on the main deck. 'What do they want us—'

He gasped, startled, as an arrow buried its head in the squat housing sheltering the ladder to the hold. A length of green cloth was bound tightly around the shaft.

Risala went immediately to retrieve it, unsheathing her belt knife to slice through the knotted leather thong. 'Here's your pennant, Sirince.' She shook out a long blade of silk marked with an intricate black design.

'Let's fly it.' He took it and hurried to run it up the signal flagstaff.

'Can you put a name to the ship, Risala?' Telouet was watching the trireme closely, hands on his hips, bearded chin thrust forward.

She was intent on a letter that had come wrapped inside the pennant. 'We're to sail for a trading anchorage on Lastu. It's not far.'

'That's the main island of the domain,' Velindre said instantly, 'where the fire mountain is.'

'It's where the dragon is.' Risala deciphered the next line, lips moving slightly.

Kheda saw Telouet's hand slide instinctively to his sword hilt.

'This trireme, the *Cinnabar*, will lead the way.' Risala looked up, startled. 'Shek Kul will meet us there.'

'Is the Shek rainy-season residence close?' Kheda asked.

'No.' She looked down at the letter as if it held secrets she hadn't fathomed. 'That's well out to the east of the domain.'

'The warlord is taking the battle to the beast.' Telouet approved.

'And we are here to help him,' Kheda said resolutely.

How difficult is it going to be to pay my debts to Shek Kul without betraying us all to so many curious eyes?

'What if we lose them in these mists?' Velindre was

watching the trireme ease ahead of the *Tacsille*. 'How are we to know where to go?'

'Here's your course.' Risala took the first step up to the stern platform, holding out a leaf of reed paper.

'Your lord seems to trust us.' Velindre studied the page intently. 'Any shipmaster would be deep in another's debt for this.'

'There's land ahead.' Sirince pointed forward.

'And I know these waters, once I see some landmarks.' Risala looked out to the prow, a thoughtful line creasing her forehead.

The opacity in the haze resolved into an angular promontory of coarse grey stone, capped with a tangle of greenery. Behind the headland, a steep hillside was densely wooded with tall trees wound around with sluggish skeins of vapour. They couldn't see the crest of the ridgeline nor any break in the trees as the mists grew more dense towards the heart of the island. As the land slid past, soft waves breaking on the rocky shore, the scene barely seemed to change. If it weren't for the *Tacsille*'s white wake disappearing behind them, Kheda could have believed they were hardly moving. The trireme forged on ahead, keeping a constant distance between the two vessels.

Some while later, he tasted sulphur on the air. 'Is the fire mountain close to this trading beach?' As Risala nodded, he looked at the two wizards. 'I think it's smoking.'

'Sirince?' Velindre looked up from sewing the new sheet of paper securely between two pages of her precious route record. Her hands still showed the bruises she'd suffered working her magic against the last dragon. 'Can you tell if it's likely to erupt soon?'

'It's difficult to know out here on the water.' The older mage looked thoughtful. 'I'll have a better idea once we're on solid ground.'

'So the sooner we get there, the better.' Velindre scanned the vista ahead. 'Sirince, be ready to shift our course as soon as I give you your bearings. Risala, can you let me know as soon as you recognise anything ashore?'

Have I brought you home only to lose you? But wouldn't that be better, for you at least? How can I look to a future with you if I can't rid myself of these ties to magic and dragons?

As he surrendered the tiller to the balding wizard, Kheda found dread suddenly threatened to overwhelm him.

Telouet caught the warlord's elbow. 'Let's get the message birds up on deck before the air gets too foul. We'll want them ready to fly.'

'Indeed.' Kheda drew a resolute breath and tasted the sour hint of ash once again.

The tightness in his throat didn't lessen as he followed Telouet down into the hold. Blankets hung from ropes to divide the interior, ostensibly to ensure Velindre the privacy customarily accorded to *zamorin*. Crisk was huddled in a corner, clutching the bag containing his game pieces. His eyes were screwed tight shut as he muttered in thickly accented, incomprehensible Tormalin.

Kheda joined Telouet in carefully fetching the white wood cages housing the courier doves. Up on deck, they set them gently down in the prow, checked every bird for signs of distress and removed any soiled straw. While Telouet made sure each had fresh water, Kheda fetched a small sack of gritty saller grain gleaned at the tail end of some isle's harvest. The dove closest cooed with interest, black eyes sparkling.

'We want them hungry to fly their fastest,' Telouet warned.

'We don't want them so hungry that they stray to go foraging.' Kheda let a judicious portion trickle back from the palm of his hand into the sack. As he let the remaining grain fall from his hand into the cage, the bright-eyed dove immediately began pecking it up.

'This is the start of the anchorage,' Risala said suddenly.

Ahead, Kheda saw they had reached a wide stretch of sea between the steep hill of the island to their west and a chain of rocky islands on their eastward flank. These rose abruptly from the sea, their sides sheer for twice the height of a ship's mast before the grey rock broke into clefts and uneven steps. Plants and birds disputed every foothold; vivid red wings and golden crests fluttered among the green shades of vegetation. White basket flowers prompted by the rains rambled in unpruned ecstasy. Those that had bloomed first were already turning red and pink.

'Some of these ships have come a long way,' Sirince commented. 'Those pennants mark domains reaching all the way up to Jagai.'

A surprising number of vessels were anchored beneath each grey cliff and outcrop. Local fishing skiffs were weaving slowly between them, their bare-chested crews deft with ropes and tightly rigged sails. As the *Tacsille* passed by, one slid up alongside a fat-bellied galley whose three ranks of oars were all drawn up to idle above the water. A man on the skiff held up a vivid orange crab, its long legs waving and its vicious claws prudently lashed with twine. As someone shouted down from the galley's rail, he gestured to a basket piled high with more of the same.

'That galley over there's from the mainland,' Sirince said with interest.

Kheda looked and saw a strangely built ship, longer and straighter sided than the Aldabreshin vessels with only a single bank of densely clustered oars. It wasn't the only one. 'I'd have thought they'd have sailed for home as word of this dragon spread.'

'They don't look too happy to be here.' Risala was troubled.

Kheda had noted the unfriendly stares directed at the *Tacsille*.

'Perhaps Shek Kul can explain their presence.' Velindre was searching for any sign of a landing on the main island's rocky shore.

'I think that's one answer to the question.' Telouet was looking at a gap opening up between two sheer pillars of grey rock rising out of breakers marking lethal reefs. The heavy triremes patrolling the waters slid away into the haze only to be replaced by more of the same.

'The Shek domain has a substantial fleet,' Kheda remarked.

'Might at sea is life and death to these domains,' Risala said tersely. 'There, Vel.'

A smoothly irresistible current drew the *Tacsille* outwards as the long slope of the shore ended in a knife-edge of grey rock thrusting out into the sluggish foam. Sirince corrected their course, rounding the promontory to find a broad bay beyond. Coarse dark sand could scarcely be seen beneath a substantial encampment. Tents and huts of green wood had been recently erected and roughly thatched with palm fronds now turning brown. The forest beyond showed deep scars where hacking blades had sought both firewood and building materials.

'That's no trading encampment.' As Telouet spoke, a detachment of warriors left a long, low tent of heavy dun cloth to draw up a line of steel above the desultory surf.

'Shek Kul's keeping watch on this dragon in person.' Kheda nodded towards a tent taller than most and separated from the rest by a broad circle of open ground. Peaked roofs indicated multiple rooms within and embroidery splashed colour across green panels rich with the sheen of satin. He tugged at the hem of his creased cream tunic. The plainest of those that the Galcan wives had insisted he accept, at least it was silk, with a tracery of gold glass beadwork around the neck. Though he had set aside all jewellery but Shek Kul's ring.

'Where are we supposed to anchor?' Velindre scanned the shoreline.

'Over there.' Telouet pointed to a green-clad man pushing between the Shek warriors to shout and beckon. Two bare-chested youths dragged a shallow rowing boat down the beach and shoved it into the meek waves.

Sirince leaned on the tiller and the *Tacsille* turned gracefully into the shore. Kheda followed Risala forward and they hauled anchors from the lockers beneath the prow rail. At the first touch of the keel on the unseen sand, he heaved the heavy iron over the side and helped Risala do the same. Splashes from the stern followed in the next breath. The ship shifted for a moment until the curved flukes bit into the sea bed and held firm.

Where's Telouet gone?

As Kheda wondered, walking back to the tiller, the warrior emerged from below decks, his twin swords grasped in one strong hand.

The rowing boat was already within hailing distance. 'You are welcome to Shek Kul's domain, my lord Chazen Kheda.' The man in the green tunic stood in the bow of the shallow vessel.

'We are honoured to be his guests,' Telouet replied, swiftly doubling his sword belt around his hips.

'My lord will greet you ashore.' At the man's nod, the two youths drove the little boat up beside the *Tacsille*.

'He's not wasting any time,' Sirince murmured.

'He hasn't time to waste.' Risala bit off stifled anger.

'He'll have a revolt on his hands soon if he's keeping this many ships penned up.' Telouet looked back down the long anchorage. 'Never mind any danger from the dragon.'

Velindre silenced him with an impatient hand. 'Who's going ashore and who's staying aboard?'

'My lord awaits your presence,' the man in the green tunic called up more insistently from below.

'My lord will be with you in a moment.' Finding a rope ladder to sling over the rail, Telouet looked to Kheda.

We had better have a wizard with us, to make most sense of whatever news they have of this dragon. Velindre has had more practice in passing unremarked in the Archipelago than Sirince and it makes more sense to take a scholar ashore than some barbarian slave-trader.

'You should come with us.' He looked at the mage-woman, hoping she could read in his eyes what he couldn't say in Telouet's hearing.

'We'll stay aboard, me and Crisk,' Sirince said firmly. 'It's my ship, after all.'

'Indeed.' Kheda moved to the rail and swung himself over.

Risala followed close behind and Velindre barely waited for the two of them to set foot in the stern of the rowing boat before she climbed swiftly down. Telouet followed, careful of his swords.

The man in the green tunic looked at Risala, faint puzzlement wrinkling his forehead.

'Hello, Mevri.' She smiled at him.

His answering grin widened with recognition. 'Onori's girl! Where have you been?'

'You'd be amazed.' Risala's apparently light-hearted reply couldn't hide her tenseness.

'I imagine so.' Mevri looked at Kheda with barely disguised curiosity. 'Have you come to help us, my lord?'

'If we can,' Kheda answered levelly.

He couldn't tell if Mevri was satisfied or not. Telouet

met the man's glance with a practised lack of expression that nevertheless held a challenge. Mevri looked away as the rowing boat swung around for the beach. Kheda reached out a hand to take Risala's but she didn't seem to see it. Her blue eyes were searching Shek Kul's encampment as she knotted her fingers in her lap. Velindre too was focusing all her attention ashore.

The line of armoured warriors parted as the rowing boat grounded in the shallows and the nearest swordsmen came to drag the vessel clear of the surf.

Kheda waved them away. 'I can stand to get my feet wet.'

He waited for the waves to retreat, judging his moment carefully. Even so, the hems of his cream trousers were caught by the rushing waters before he reached the high-water mark. Grey sand clung to the damp cloth in unsightly smudges.

So much for arriving with the customary dignity of a warlord ruling a wealthy and respected domain. Well, what will Shek Kul make of my retinue?

Kheda squared his shoulders, his face amiable and composed as he walked up the beach. He refused to hurry, despite Mevri's urgent beckoning.

'My lord Shek Kul awaits you.'

Telouet slipped naturally into the bodyguard's role, two paces behind on his off-hand side. Kheda noted the Shek swordsmen's eyes slide past him to assess this newcomer. Anyone with swords was a potential threat to their own lord. They passed through the encampment and reached the open area around the extensive tent.

I can only assume Risala and Velindre are following. It would hardly befit my dignity to look round.

All the same, he managed a glance behind Telouet when they reached the entrance to Shek Kul's temporary dwelling. Two unwelcome realisations struck Kheda in rapid succession. Firstly, Risala was absolutely nowhere to be seen. Secondly, out on the water, a light galley had drawn up beside the *Tacsille* and several unknown figures were on the deck beside Sirince.

'My lord.' Mevri threw back the wide flap that served as a door, a sweep of his other hand indicating Kheda should enter the tent. Armoured guards instantly rose from benches set against the silk-hung walls of the antechamber.

'My lord Chazen Kheda.' A burly, copper-complexioned man with close-cropped grey hair and beard took a pace forward. He wore ornate brass-inlaid vambraces and a sleeveless hauberk of fine mail rings over an arming jacket of plain green leather. As he bowed with every apparent courtesy, Kheda noted a flash of amusement in the man's eyes.

Have you told these others that you were once my jailer? That you had me humbled before you, homeless, nameless, indigent and hungry? That you were kind enough to offer me soap and water so I could cleanse myself of my own filth before you brought me before Shek Kul's judgement? Or was that only so I wouldn't offend your lord's nose?

'Good day to you, Delai.' Kheda smiled graciously. 'I hope I find you well.'

The slave straightened up, a faint smile on his face. 'As well as can be expected, my lord, with a dragon lurking in the heights of a fire mountain that's smoking worse than a hearth with the wind in the wrong quarter.'

A shiver of metal and leather ran through the assembled swordsmen.

'I have come to offer what counsel I may, as your lord Shek Kul faces this crisis.' Kheda noted fine red veins threaded through the whites of Delai's eyes, from weariness and doubtless from the stinging of ash in the air.

'He'll be glad to see you,' Delai said frankly. 'There are no other lords who've slain a dragon, nor yet driven one off.'

So failure will mean all accusing eyes turn on me before they condemn Shek Kul. Is that why you are so ready to acknowledge your master's weakness?

Kheda let nothing of this show on his face as Delai drew back the curtain shielding the inner room of the tent. Thick carpets worked with patterns of interlaced leaves were laid over woven saller-straw matting hiding the sand. Tall chests of black wood bound with dark iron stood on either side. The lid of one revealed layers of little drawers within and a central hollow packed tight with tooled-leather books. To the rear of this sanctum, hangings of smoky gossamer half-hid a canopied bed where some maid's hand hadn't yet been permitted to straighten pillows and quilts.

'My lord Chazen Kheda.' Massive in his armour, Shek Kul rose from a sturdy cross-framed stool of ebony inlaid with pale golden wood. 'You are most welcome. I am most grateful that you chose to hurry here by the speediest means, forgoing all the usual comforts of your rank.'

That's for the benefit of any of his warriors unimpressed by my meagre retinue and modest ship.

'We of Chazen recall what it is like to have such an unwelcome visitor.' Kheda bowed low. 'I only hope I can be of service to you, my lord.'

Anyone outside this room, or indeed this tent, should have heard that. I'm offering no guarantees.

'I have every confidence in you.' The warlord's voice was rich and resonant as he extended a hand to clasp Kheda's forearm. Faceted emeralds adorned the heavy bracers drawing the Shek warlord's mail sleeves tight around his muscular wrists. 'Even here, we've heard how Chazen has prospered since you rid your domain of the evils of magic and dragons. You've been blessed with twin daughters. Such omens cannot be doubted.'

We're plainly speaking for the benefit of more than these soldiers. I wonder how far any lurking servants will carry our words. How far can Shek Kul trust his people?

'Chazen's good fortune is my constant solace. You're looking well, my lord,' Kheda observed briskly.

Which is no lie, though you've certainly lost weight since I was last standing before you. And there is markedly more grey in the midnight of your hair and beard. But only a fool would think you were sinking into any kind of decline.

'I am very well, thank you.' Shek Kul hooked his thumbs into a wide black leather belt buckled tight to spread the load of his chain hauberk over his hips as well as his broad shoulders. The steel plates inset to protect breast and stomach were etched with intricate black designs of cassia bark quills tied with some thorny vine that Kheda didn't recognise and framed by sprays of myrtle.

Cassia, which survives flood and any amount of destruction wrought by storm and whirlwind. A man can hack it down to nothing and still it will regrow. Thorns, for defence, whatever else that particular vine might signify. Myrtle for victory, long life and future fertility. Do you truly believe these tokens will protect you, my lord?

'I trust your lady wives are well, my lord?' Kheda smiled as if they had no more weighty matters in hand than the exchange of such customary courtesies.

'My wives, and my growing children, they all thrive.' Shek Kul nodded with patent satisfaction.

The weight of his present burdens didn't appear to trouble Shek Kul. There was no shadow of recent illness around his eyes, so it was presumably recent events that had pared any softness of peaceful living from his face, leaving his hooked nose more prominent than before. To Kheda's eyes, he had the air of a watchful hawk.

A hawk wise and guileful enough to live into a grizzled old age.

Shek Kul turned his attention to Telouet. 'I had heard you were travelling without any bodyguard, my lord of Chazen.'

Kheda inclined his head towards his erstwhile slave. 'Telouet was my attendant when I was of Daish. Since my removal to Chazen, Daish Sirket rewarded his years of loyalty by giving him his freedom.'

'I serve my lord of Daish by bringing my lord of Chazen news from the southern reaches.' Telouet bowed respectfully. 'I offer whatever assistance I may until my lord of Daish summons me home.'

'As long as you remember that a man trying to keep one foot on each of two boats all too often ends up falling in the water,' Shek Kul commented thoughtfully.

The warlord's emerald-banded black helm was currently set aside on a leathern stand. The gleam of lacquered steel behind the apertures in the face plate gave an uncanny impression of watchful eyes. Once Shek Kul donned that, and the heavy gauntlets set beside it, with his leather leggings reinforced with more chain mail and footwear wrought of overlapping bands of steel, he would be encased in armour from head to toe.

Which will melt like wax if this dragon breathes its magical fire upon him.

'Are you intending to lead your men in a direct assault against this beast, my lord?' Kheda asked bluntly. 'If so, may I advise against it, at least until we have had a chance to take its measure?'

'Who precisely is "we"?' Shek Kul looked pointedly at Velindre, standing still and silent by the open curtain.

'This is Vel.' Kheda beckoned her forward with an easy smile. 'A scholar who has learned much lore of dragons, from both Archipelagan and barbarian sources.'

'Of which domain?' A frown creased Shek Kul's fore-head.

'Of none,' Velindre replied, unintimidated. 'By my own choice. Since I can offer nothing to the future of any domain, I choose not to make any claim. I need nothing that I cannot earn from day to day with my skills and lore.'

'You're of barbarian stock. I hear the echoes in your words.' The Shek warlord's eyes cut sharply to Kheda. 'Like Dev.'

Like Dev. Whom you sent me to find, because you suspected he was a mage but dared not act against him for fear of being accused of consorting with sorcery yourself. What would you do if I told you Velindre is a wizard? What if I told you she is nevertheless your only hope of driving off this dragon?

'Vel is nothing like Dev,' Kheda said firmly. 'He was a scoundrel and a deceiver.'

'May I ask, what manner of dragon has come here?' Velindre began.

In the same instant, Telouet spoke up. 'My lord, I'm surprised to see this anchorage so full of ships—'

'I've gathered the bulk of my fleet and my warriors here.' Shek Kul's penetrating stare lingered on Velindre before he addressed Telouet. 'As for the rest—' He broke off. 'Forgive me, I am remiss in my duties as your host. Please, let us take some refreshment.'

Kheda turned to see Delai indicating that a line of cotton-clad servants should enter the tent's antechamber. They brought low folding stools, platters of food, ewers and goblets, wide trays and the trestles to support them. Once everything was arranged to his satisfaction, Shek Kul's body slave nodded and the servants withdrew. The warriors in the antechamber also left, to form an armoured ring some twenty paces beyond the tent.

Does this mean we can talk more freely?

'Thank you.' Kheda accepted a goblet of lilla juice from Delai. He managed to sip it without letting slip any sign of his dislike of the fruit.

'I concentrated my ships and forces here in case the beast leaves the fire crater to ravage the island,' Shek Kul continued, as if there had been no interruption. 'If it does, we will kill it or die in the attempt. For the present they keep all these other vessels in check.'

'Why are they here?' Kheda asked.

'Because certain of my neighbouring lords are keen to take advantage of my present situation,' Shek Kul said with suppressed wrath. 'Barbarians who trade here with scant scruple at the best of times are doing the same. They claim no one dare trade with this domain while the dragon is here, so they have been seizing Shek ships and cargos found in their waters or ports. This is supposedly to balance their ledgers, since every vessel they have here is sure to be destroyed by the beast.' Contempt outstripped the irritation in his voice. 'So I am making sure that none of those vessels can slip away to reach safe harbour without proper note being made of the fact.'

'You don't think that keeping such a quantity of men and ships all in one place might tempt the dragon?' Kheda ventured.

'I don't know. You're the one with all the lore of dragons at your scholar's fingertips.' Shek Kul's expression hardened as he reached for a bowl of fruit set at his elbow. 'If that does prove to be the case, I'd rather see the beast gorge on those trying to cheat my domain than have it devastate my loyal islanders' villages and crops. But let us look to a better outcome than that.' His slow smile was fierce. 'When we have defeated the beast, they can all sail away, so there will be no shortage of witnesses to our success. They can inform everyone of the renewed vigour of the Shek domain, now proven strong enough to defeat even the evil of a dragon's presence.'

Kheda nodded reluctant acknowledgement. 'You've deployed sufficient ships and swordsmen to protect your rainy-season residence?'

'Enough to give the illusion of a guard. My wives and children aren't there, though none beyond my immediate household know it.' Shek Kul stripped red berries from a stem, his teeth bared. 'I want them well clear of any malice that my enemies might connive at, never mind far beyond the reach of this dragon.' He paused, chewing, favouring Kheda with a trenchant look. 'Mahli Shek is presently the guest of Kaasik Rai. That is the domain of her birth and she was there when the beast fell on us, so it seemed best for her to remain. She is managing what remains of the Shek domain's trade, thanks to the good graces of his wives. Even those who aren't seeking to cheat us outright are calling in all the debts they can lay claim to. Laio Shek, Gar and the children—' He shrugged and tossed the naked berry stem back into the bowl of fruit. 'They are safe.'

You're not about to tell us where. You don't even trust your immediate household with that knowledge.

Kheda reached for a tray of nut and saller grain sweetmeats sticky with scented honey.

'No, try one of those.' Shek Kul directed him to an unpromising tray of pale morsels speckled with dark flecks.

Politely, Kheda took one. Even before he put it in his mouth, the luscious aroma astonished him. The taste was warm and sensuous, sweet yet not cloying, with an undercurrent of fruity astringency.

'The black straw spice.' Shek Kul smiled at Kheda's startled expression. 'I'll wager you don't use it in such quantities in the southern reaches.'

Kheda swallowed, savouring the lingering exquisiteness. 'We seldom see it at all, my lord.'

'Save my domain and you'll see it by the barrel load,' Shek Kul promised. 'If you don't, or if you cannot drive off this beast within ten days or so, none of the islanders that tend the vines will see a harvest this year.' He shook his head, grim-faced. 'This is the richest forest in my whole domain for the spice, and these vines grow thicker and more fruitful in Shek than in any other domain.'

'Exactly when did this dragon arrive, my lord?' Velindre sat composedly on her stool, cradling a beaten-brass goblet in her long-fingered hands. 'Before or after the fire mountain began smoking?'

'Just after.' Shek Kul frowned at the recollection rather than at her. 'The islanders were already retreating from the closest villages, so none of my people were lost to the dragon, none that we know of at least. Since then—' He scowled. 'Most have fled to the lesser isles of the domain, where there is barely sufficient food for them all. Spices may be vital for our trade but if we don't rid ourselves of this beast before the harvests, half the domain will go hungry even before the rains end. Fruits that should be gathered at this season are rotting on the trees and vines. Forest hogs are digging up vegetable plots while village geese and ducks take flight with their wild brethren. We will need to bargain for surplus harvests across whatever remain of our trading links when this is all over.'

For the first time Kheda heard a distracted note in the warlord's words and glimpsed the full weight of the older man's years shadowing his eyes.

You are much the age my father would have been, had he lived.

'Can you tell me what colour the creature is?' Velindre asked calmly. 'And how big?'

'It looks like shale.' Delai spoke up, his voice harsh with the effort of controlling his emotions. 'Black in shadow, then grey where the light strikes it. It's the length of a heavy trireme, near enough, and it's a big beast, heavier set than a whip lizard. You've seen those?'

Velindre nodded. 'Did you see its claws?' Her fingers flexed as if they sought paper and pen. 'Its underbelly, or its teeth?'

'It has talons like quartz.' Delai looked to Shek Kul for guidance. He continued at the warlord's nod. 'Its belly scales are pale, too. We didn't see its teeth.' He couldn't restrain a shiver of loathing.

'Where did you see it?' Velindre didn't seem to notice his revulsion. 'What was it doing?'

'What were *you* doing?' Telouet couldn't help asking.

Delai shot him a challenging look. 'I was doing my lord's bidding. We've been scouting the rim of the fire crater daily, to be sure it hasn't slipped away from us.' He looked back to Velindre, quite mystified. 'All it has done thus far is bathe in the molten rock. How can it do that and not be burned?'

'Does this help you?' Shek Kul asked curtly.

'All information has its uses.' Velindre glanced briefly at Kheda.

He saw his own thoughts reflected in her hazel eyes. At least, he hoped he did.

It doesn't sound like the black dragon that we fought on that western isle. That's good news, as that beast was the most wily of all those we encountered.

'Can you rid us of the creature?' Shek Kul wanted to know. 'Without setting it loose to devastate my domain?'

'We will do all we can,' Kheda promised simply. 'I owe you no less. You sent me in search of Dev, and the lore he brought to the southern domains enabled us to drive off the wild men and the dragon that followed them.'

'Vel's learning was key to ridding the Zelin domain of the dragon that recently landed there.' Telouet offered encouragement in all innocence.

Shek Kul turned a forbidding scowl on the supposed *zamorin*. 'Did you learn your lore in the same places as Dev?' the warlord asked suspiciously.

'We must have consulted some of the same books,' Velindre replied calmly, 'but my studies have gone far beyond whatever he might have known. We have recently returned from the island in the far western ocean where the dragons and the wild men both originally dwelt.' She nodded at Kheda to make it plain she was including him in this.

'What?' This news distracted Shek Kul from whatever misgivings he harboured. He looked to Kheda for explanation.

Kheda cleared his throat. 'Dragons may be creatures of vile magic but the wild men that assaulted the southern reaches were flesh and blood. Their wizards were mortal, too, as we proved once we were able to stifle their magic with that blend of herbs and rare earths that you provided us with. Those long-ago warlords whose records you found, my lord, they had truly discovered a means to banish barbarian wizards from their islands. Those attackers, the savages, we knew they had to live somewhere before they came to our shores.' He shrugged. 'Vel spent several seasons sailing the western edge of the Archipelago, searching out any lore hinting at what might lie beyond the furthest fishing grounds.'

'Why?' Shek Kul glanced at the magewoman.

'Too many questions remained, even after the wild men and the dragons were dead,' she said simply. 'I wanted answers.'

'Always reason enough for a scholar,' Shek Kul grunted. 'Once attacked, it's always wise to know where your enemy has come from.' Kheda swiftly reclaimed the warlord's attention. 'There was scant evidence, but what little Vel found encouraged us to believe there was some unknown land beyond the western horizon.'

'You sent a trireme?' Shek Kul queried.

Kheda shook his head. 'No, my lord. We set sail, just the two of us and two companions.'

'You must have seen powerful omens to warrant such a decision.' Shek Kul leaned forward, his expression intent.

'We knew it would be a long voyage.' Kheda hoped evading that question wouldn't anger the warlord. 'A small ship well stocked with food and water could take us further out into the ocean than a trireme and still give us some hope of returning if all we found was empty water.'

'Such a ship would also be more likely to escape notice, if we reached a hostile shore,' Velindre added composedly. 'Cunning had already proved more effective against all these foes than force of arms alone.'

'Cunning, yes, that's one word for it.' Shek Kul contemplated her for a moment before looking at Kheda. 'So what did you find?'

'A vast isle.' Out of the corner of his eye Kheda saw Telouet was as avid as the warlord to know more. 'Parched and desolate and much of it ravaged by convulsions of land and sea. We believe those upheavals were what sent the wild men and those dragons that came to Chazen in search of a new home.'

'Looking to take land and livelihood by brute force and savagery from those who already held it,' Telouet growled. 'Whatever their misfortunes, they deserve no pity from us, my lord.'

'There were still men living there.' Distasteful recollection twisted Kheda's face. 'Living like beasts in caves and thorn thickets, preyed upon by monstrous birds and vile lizards. Their only defence was the wizards, who ruled as the worst of tyrants, abusing whomever they chose. The wretches could not hope to challenge their magic. I found I could pity them.'

'The wisest philosophers say the innocent victims of magic aren't to be condemned,' Velindre added swiftly.

'Not according to some of my neighbouring lords,' Shek Kul said bitterly. 'Do you suspect that these wild wizards still look to attack the Archipelago?' he asked.

'I don't believe so.' Kheda chose his words with exquisite care. 'Not for the present. We showed the wretched savages that their mages died as easily as any other man, once the dragons that were the source of their magic flew away—'

'And you had already learned how to harry the beasts into flight,' Shek Kul interrupted. 'For which we must all be grateful.' He nodded to Delai, who summoned the soft-footed servants with a loud double clap.

Kheda sat calmly as the food and drink they had barely touched were deftly removed. He noted Telouet was still frowning.

Plenty of questions remain unanswered as far as you are concerned, my faithful companion. Too many questions.

Velindre drained her goblet and handed it to a servant, her expression bland. Delai bent close to Shek Kul as the warlord spoke briefly in low tones, one hand raised to shield his lips.

You're not about to ask for any more details as to how we made such a voyage and returned from an ocean where countless ships have vanished. Nor indeed how we can put a dragon to flight without ending up in its belly. You have to suspect magic is involved, my lord, but you are beset with enemies on all sides, not merely the evil of this dragon. As long as you have no direct knowledge of wizardry's involvement, you believe you can hold yourself aloof from its taint. I wish you more success in that than I have had, my lord, with all my heart.

'As you command, my lord.' Delai strode out of the tent.

The warlord fixed Kheda with a piercing gaze. 'I can provide you with guides up to the fire crater where the dragon is lurking. I see no virtue in delay, unless you have some pressing needs that must be addressed first.'

Kheda looked at Velindre. 'There will be aspects of the creature's nature that you'll want to check in your books of lore, won't there?'

I hope I'm not making myself too obvious. But at the very least we must retrieve the ruby shards. And Sirince, come to that, if the creature is attuned to the elemental earth. But I want to know what's happened to Risala before I risk my life against another dragon.

Shek Kul looked at Velindre. 'Well?'

'I will need to return to our ship for a little while.' She rose gracefully from her seat. 'But I see no reason for any great delay.'

'Then we'll see you taken aboard at once.' Shek Kul promptly clapped his callused hands.

Telouet got to his feet and bowed respectfully to Shek Kul. 'May I ask that your man Delai be spared while my lord and the scholar prepare themselves, to tell me everything he knows about the paths and craters of the mountain, my lord?'

'Of course.' The rest of Shek Kul's reply was lost in a sudden commotion of angry voices outside the tent. The warlord sprang to his feet and tore the curtains aside with an audible rip of cloth as he left the tent.

CHAPTER FIFTEEN

Kheda followed the warlord, Velindre and Telouet close behind. They emerged from the tent to see Shek Kul's slave Delai break through the circle of armoured men who had been safeguarding their conversation.

'We found this vermin skulking around the latrine pits again—'

The warlord raised a hand to silence the grey-bearded warrior. Unintelligible shouting echoed across the beach, rising to a shriek cut short by a leather-clad hand's brutal slap.

Kheda saw turmoil down among the tents as the breach in the Shek warriors' line widened. Three swordsmen approached, two of them dragging an undernourished man between them. They threw him down on his face before Shek Kul.

'You may silence me—' As he tried to rise to his hands and knees, one of the swordsmen planted a leather-shod foot on his bony shoulder and forced him down again. Raising himself more cautiously on one elbow, the man spat sand, pawing at his untrimmed, unkempt beard with filthy fingers. 'You cannot deny the heavenly compass. The stars have spoken!'

As the other swordsmen shouted the prisoner down, indignant and derisive, one of the warriors bent to seize the collar of the man's stained and faded tunic. The rotten cloth ripped as he hauled the captive upwards.

'You shut your mouth!' He lent weight to his words

with a backhanded blow that left the ragged man's nose
bleeding. Some of the warriors who had been on guard
took a pace towards him, their own hands half-raised.

'What is it you believe you have seen in the stars –'
the whole beach fell silent at Shek Kul's words '– that's
so important you must harass my men when all they want
to do is take a piss or ease their bowels?' The warlord's
voice was cold with contempt.

The warriors who had dragged the man forward
promptly stepped back. Those swordsmen who had been
so eager to join in beating him retreated hastily. Through
gaps in the palisade of armoured men, Kheda saw servants
and slaves standing motionless, clutching baskets or quilts,
firewood and water jars. Delai drew back to his lord and
master's side, scowling.

The prisoner had fallen forward, face pressed into the
sand, knees drawn up beneath his body. His ribs and spine
were plainly visible through the tight-drawn cloth of his
filthy tunic. Bony arms wrapped close around his head,
he panted like a cornered animal. After a tense moment,
he looked up, slowly lowering his arms. Fresh blood soaked
sluggishly into the stains on his ripped sleeves from where
matted hair had been torn from his scalp. One of his
captors discarded a tangled tuft caught in the steel plates
of his gauntlets, his face twisted with distaste.

'Your rule is doomed, my lord of Shek!' The man's
dark eyes glittered with gleeful mania. 'As the stars of the
Winged Snake rise above the Diamond that is talisman
for warlords, so this black and evil dragon rises high to
overwhelm the final days of your dominion. The heavenly Opal is there—' Still crouching on his knees, the
ragged man whirled abruptly around. His shrill words
reached beyond the silent warriors to the immobile household. 'Gem of ill omen according to many, so frail and
capricious, demanding such anxious care lest it crack or

flake.' His wild eyes were rimmed with white above a ragged beard that largely obscured his gaunt features. 'The moon fades and wanes, whenever it can be seen through these ominous clouds that shroud the skies. Prepare yourself for the death of all your ambitions, Shek Kul. Look for the long-expected reward for your shame and dishonour.' He addressed the warriors surrounding him rather than the warlord, his voice dying away in a malevolent hiss.

'Yours is the only death foretold here.' Furious, Delai's blade slid from its scabbard, watered steel bright in the muted sunlight.

'All in good time.' Shek Kul's tone fell somewhere between mockery and disdain. 'Tell me, my importunate friend, what else do you see in the skies that should concern me?'

The captive sat back on his heels and stared undaunted at the warlord. 'You should heed what's hidden beneath the horizon, lord of Shek.' He spread his crooked fingers wide, long yellow nails like dirty claws. 'Amethyst for inspiration is sunk in the west, so one might look in vain for hope. The Sailfish for life and expectation languishes in the darkness with it. The Bowl that should nourish and nurture is lost beneath the eastern horizon, where the Ruby fills it with blood and fire for your children.' He swept his hand around towards the fire-mountain's slopes. 'The Bowl has become a crater filled with molten destruction waiting to engulf us all!'

Kheda saw the man's eyes narrow, calculating, as he looked swiftly around.

To see what impact he's having on these men. What manner of soothsayer lurks around latrines? One who wants to be sure of encountering everyone at least once a day.

Kheda stood still, arms folded across his chest, making sure his own face was wholly impassive. Out of the corner of his eye, he could see Telouet and Velindre both standing just as motionless and expressionless.

Unperturbed, Shek Kul waited until the seer betrayed the first signs of discomfiture at the resolute lack of response from those encircling him. 'Anything else?' he queried derisively.

As he sank down to huddle on the dark sand, the sooth-sayer's eyes slid to Kheda. 'You look to Chazen Kheda for help but the Pearl that is talisman for that domain rests in the arc of foes. Its last shard sinks into darkness this very night, plain for all to see,' he warned with sly malice. 'It dies among the stars of the Yora Hawk, fabled bird that is ever predator. This lord of Chazen does not come to help you but to pick what he can from the ruined bones of your rule.'

Shek Kul turned with a courteous smile. 'What do you think of this, my lord of Chazen?'

I think it's a good thing I no longer believe in such omens. I think we will all be in serious trouble if people are persuaded by these interpretations.

'I think I would pay little heed to any soothsayer so lacking in honesty that he would prophesy on my beaches without first seeking my permission. Or one who came before me half-starved and so vilely dirty.' Kheda allowed a faint smile to curl his lip, echoing Shek Kul's contempt. 'This man's recent predictions don't seem to have been rewarded with food or clean clothing from those grateful and prospering under his guidance. I'd say the latrine pits are the right place for his prophecies.'

Emboldened by Kheda's words, the assembled warriors jeered their agreement. There were some nods of assent among the slaves and servants clustered over by the lesser tents.

'Would you like to hear my reading of the heavens?' Shek Kul's voice stilled the derision spreading across the sands. 'Test my understanding of their turning patterns through these next few days.'

The seer flinched, though Shek Kul hadn't made the slightest move to strike him. 'You may silence my voice but you cannot deny the declaration of the skies above you!'

Shek Kul stared down unblinking at the filthy man. 'I have no intention of stilling your voice,' he said enigmatically.

Bemused, the soothsayer looked back up at the warlord, ashen with mounting apprehension.

Shek Kul looked at his swordsmen with a sly smile of his own before briskly addressing Kheda. 'My lord of Chazen, pearl and opal have both been long held as talismans against dragons. Did you find this borne out as you so successfully battled the beasts?'

'The beasts shunned such gems, my lord, despite their greed for other jewels.' Kheda sought to match the other warlord's relaxed demeanour.

Which isn't exactly an answer, but it's as close as I will go without forswearing myself.

'So pearl and opal both repel dragons, not merely in lore but in proven fact,' the Shek warlord continued in a conversational tone, walking around the soothsayer in a wide circle. Irresistibly, his gaze claimed the attention of every one of his swordsmen. Servants and slaves beyond drifted closer, straining to hear his words.

'But both moons are currently sinking to their dark. Should we see this as ill omen? No, because that darkness means both will return in a matter of days to rise to a double full moon, a most beneficent portent. Opal and Pearl alike will shine to bathe our domain in a blended light that is wholly inimical to such beasts. Why am I so confident? Because Chazen Kheda is here and the Pearl has ever been the sign of that domain.' The Shek warlord turned to gesture towards the three newcomers, inclining his head courteously.

'He comes here as our ally, his good faith proven by the Pearl traversing the arc of friendship as it followed his voyage through our domain. He arrives here as mortal enemy to this dragon, that warning is plain as the heavenly compass moves the Pearl into the arc of foes on the very day he reaches this isle. The Opal tells us the same and more, passing through honour's compass as it has looked down on his voyage. Tomorrow it moves into the arc of friendship, where the stars of the Spear shine bright in earnest of the battle to be raised against our common adversary.' Shek Kul lifted a fist as if he brandished an unseen weapon, his words loud enough to carry across the whole width of the beach.

As his warriors cheered their agreement, the household beyond echoing them, the clamour turned heads all across the waters of the anchorage.

Shek Kul smiled fiercely and lowered his clenched hand. 'One whole third of the heavenly compass will be in harmonious alignment tomorrow. The moons ride close together. Opal for harmony shines with the stars of the Spear for battle in defence of our own. Pearl for Chazen and for integrity gleams with the Yora Hawk for strength and alertness. On one side, Diamond that is talisman for warlords shines in the arc of honour and ambition. On the other, Topaz that is talisman against fear and Amethyst to turn aside anger and impatience both rest in the arc of life, where the Sailfish turns our thoughts to freedom and new beginnings.' His resonant voice was confident as he turned to Kheda once again. 'Do you agree, my lord?'

Can a man as wise as you truly believe such things, my lord? Or are you simply turning your formidable intelligence to telling these people what they need to hear? You're not answering the soothsayer's dire predictions point for point around the compass.

'Your reading of the skies is both shrewd and thoroughly reasoned.' Kheda bowed low. 'I am awed equally by the breadth of your learning and your astute focus.'

'You'll be ready to face the beast tomorrow, when the heavens are in such propitious alignment?' Shek Kul's question allowed no possibility of denial.

Kheda nodded with absolute certainty. 'At first light.'

Shek Kul bowed. 'Then we will let you prepare yourselves in seclusion aboard your vessel. Send word if there is anything you require. All of Shek is conscious of the debt that we will owe you.'

The warlord gestured and the assembled swordsmen parted to show a rowing boat waiting for Kheda and his companions at the water's edge.

I didn't see anyone summon that.

'I'd say that's our dismissal, my lord,' Telouet murmured at his shoulder.

'What do we do with this vermin, my lord?' Delai went to stand over the soothsayer cowering in the sand. The man was now glancing furtively from side to side.

'Flog him,' the warlord called back curtly as he returned to his tent. 'Perhaps that will teach him to kneel and ask permission before daring to spread his doleful ignorance in any other domain.'

'Fetch rope and spars and find me a whip.' As the nearest warriors hurried to do his bidding, Delai wound his fist in the seer's long, tangled locks and dragged him to his feet. Pressing his face close to the soothsayer's, the slave's words were barely audible as Kheda passed by. 'I can keep you alive for days, you filth, and make every breath of them a torment. Or you can be free in death before sundown, if you tell me who sent you here.'

Kheda's stride towards the shore didn't hesitate, his expression of serene resolution not wavering.

'What was that all about?' Telouet wondered as they left the warriors busy lashing together a crude scaffold for the soothsayer's punishment.

'Perhaps Risala can explain,' Kheda said grimly. Sudden desperation gripping him, he searched the bustle of activity among the tents and shelters for any glimpse of her.

'There's Sirince.' Velindre betrayed surprise and some unease.

'Where?' As Kheda asked, he saw the balding wizard.

Sirince pushed past some hapless maidservant with scant apology, anxiety plain on his face. 'Have you seen Crisk?' he asked breathlessly.

'No,' Kheda responded sharply. 'Where did he go?'

'I don't know.' Sirince looked helplessly around. 'We came ashore—'

'You said you were going to stay on the boat,' Velindre snapped.

'We saw that light galley alongside the *Tacsille*,' Telouet commented. 'What did they want?'

'To offer us fresh food and water.' Sirince managed a sardonic smile. 'To make a swift but quite thorough search of the boat. I wasn't about to stop them, even if I could have. They were Shek Kul's men, after all, and there was nothing untoward for them to find.' He waved a distracted hand. 'But that started Crisk fretting and muttering worse than ever. He was talking of his gods and that was arousing concern, if not suspicion. Are these waters always so hostile to mainlanders?'

'I don't know.' Kheda was frustrated with his own ignorance.

'Ask Risala,' said Velindre tersely.

Kheda followed her gaze to see Risala threading her way through the bustle.

Telouet concentrated on the problem at hand. 'If the halfwit was so troubled, why did you bring him ashore?'

'To see if new faces might distract him.' Sirince looked helplessly at Kheda.

You know that excuse rings hollow with untruth. But we can hardly tell Telouet you had to set foot on shore to read the tremors deep within the earth with your magic.

'What's done is done.' Kheda overrode Telouet's next question with one of his own. 'What happened, exactly?'

'We were looking at the fire mountain. I was talking to one of Shek Kul's stewards.' Sirince gestured along the shore. 'Some ragged seer began abusing Shek Kul, foretelling all manner of doom. The household cooks were shouting him down and then swordsmen came and took the troublemaker away. Everyone fell silent to hear Shek Kul. By the time everything had quietened down, Crisk had vanished.'

Risala reached them in time to hear the wizard's last words. 'Crisk?'

'I've lost him.'

A scream tore through Sirince's distressed reply.

Kheda flinched as the second crack of a whip ripped another screech from the soothsayer. They saw the man sprawled against a wooden frame, arms and legs spread and bound tight at wrist and ankle. The back of his ragged tunic hung awry, already torn to rags by the cruel leather lash. Blood trickled from deep scores in the brown skin beneath. Delai walked up to the man's side, neatly coiling up the long whip in his hands. He leaned close to say something to the pinioned prisoner. The man shook his head in vehement denial before turning his face away, the only movement left to him. Delai pursed his lips and walked away in a leisurely fashion until he had room to wield the whip once again.

'What's that going to achieve?' Velindre wondered with remote curiosity.

Telouet grimaced. 'Is unsanctioned prophecy such a crime hereabouts?'

'I'll tell you when we're back on the boat.' Risala was stiff with tension.

Rapid snaps of the whip were drawing rising shrieks of agony from the soothsayer.

'If Crisk sees that happening, he'll run until he runs out of land.' Anguish deepened the lines on Sirince's face.

'They're wondering what's keeping us.' Kheda indicated the rowing boat waiting for them at the water's edge.

'Come on.' Risala began walking.

Kheda followed, Telouet at his heels. After a moment, Velindre did the same, leaving Sirince with no choice but to follow. As they all clambered into the rowing boat, Telouet's stern look stifled the oarsmen's protest that the vessel was overburdened. As the Shek islanders toiled over their sweeps, Kheda scanned the *Tacsille* for any sign that someone was aboard.

Could Crisk have got himself back to the boat on his own?

But there was no sign of movement on deck. As soon as they reached the boat, Telouet seized the dangling rope ladder and climbed swiftly aboard. By the time Kheda had thanked the Shek rowers with something approaching appropriate courtesy, Risala, Velindre and Sirince were all up on the deck.

As Kheda climbed over the rail, Telouet returned from a rapid search of the hold.

'He's not here.'

'Where could he have gone?' Sirince was asking himself more than anyone else, staring at the dense forest ashore.

Velindre moved to interrupt his gaze. 'I appreciate you're concerned, Sirince, but we have a dragon to deal with here. Thanks to that soothsayer, we're committed to tackling it at first light tomorrow.'

'What?' Sirince looked at Kheda.

'I'll explain later.' The warlord looked at Risala. 'What can you tell us about that soothsayer? Why is he being flogged?'

'To find out whose service he's truly in,' she answered grimly. 'This domain has been plagued with false seers since long before the dragon landed. It's a favourite ploy of Shek Kul's enemies, especially Danak Nyl and Melciar Kir.'

'What do they hope to gain by it?' Kheda asked, apprehensive.

'To undermine these people's faith in their lord.' Risala spread her hands. 'To lessen Shek Kul's standing among the lesser lords of these reaches. To make them fear they've made a dangerous error in allying with him.'

'That seer accused him of some shame or dishonour.' Telouet winced as the merciless crack of the whip cut through the noises that had arisen ashore.

Risala sighed. 'That goes back to the death of Kaeska, who was Shek Kul's first wife for many years. She was born Danak and it was a match of expediency. Love never followed. The stars turned and Danak Mir was killed. Shek Kul no longer needed to secure his borders by safeguarding Kaeska's status and allowing her to favour Danak in all her trades. Her greatest tragedy was that she had proved barren. Worse, she was unwilling to adopt a child to secure the Shek succession.' Risala shook her head, torn between pity and exasperation.

'Once Shek Kul and Mahli Shek begot a child between them, Kaeska became desperate. Mahli was his second wife but she'd be raised above Kaeska as soon as the child was born, and Shek was paying every attention to his lesser wives, so they could soon expect to be pregnant. At best

Kaeska faced a life as fourth wife. So she allowed herself to be seduced into suborning sorcery.'

'What?' Telouet was revolted.

'I don't defend her.' Risala's protest wasn't wholly convincing. 'But I'd rather believe she was seeking a child of her own through the magic, not intending to kill Mahli and her baby, which is what she was accused of.'

'What difference does that make?' Telouet brushed aside such a plea. 'She paid the penalty?'

'She was pressed to death,' Risala confirmed unhappily. 'Every hand in the domain added rocks to the pile stifling the life out of her.'

Telouet nodded with grim satisfaction before new perplexity furrowed his brow. 'If Shek Kul acted so promptly and properly, why does this soothsayer talk of ill fortune rewarding dishonour?'

'There was some suspicion there were others involved.' Risala glanced ashore, though Kheda couldn't tell what she was looking at. 'Most crucially a barbarian slave. He was the one who first accused Kaeska. And he provided proof by fighting an attendant of hers, who betrayed them both by fleeing by means of magic. There were plenty who said the slave was as mired in magic as both of them; that it was the only way he could have known what was going on. Others said the barbarian was simply a tool of his mistress, Laio Shek, and he was lying at her bidding, to have Kaeska murdered. Regardless, people have seen ill omens as proof that the domain is still stained with the magic Kaeska brought here. Others have argued over ill fortunes proving Kaeska was unjustly condemned. Many say the slave should have been executed regardless, for complicity or for lying.'

'Those saying so the loudest are from the Danak domain?' Kheda queried.

Risala nodded. 'But Shek Kul simply banished the

barbarian. He said there was no proof he was anything but an innocent caught up in events. There were omens warning against spilling his blood.'

Sirince laughed without humour. 'In these reaches merely being a mainlander can see you accused of any crime from the theft of village ducks to the sinking and looting of a galley lost at sea.'

Risala shot him a minatory look. 'These people have good reason to look askance at mainlanders.'

'How so?' asked Velindre, irritated.

'The wealth of these reaches is based on many trades, but spices are the most lucrative.' Risala contemplated the forest beyond the shoreline encampment. 'Mainlanders have long been eager to steal the spice plants, to grow them for themselves.'

'Gullible investors lose carefully hoarded gold every year, when they believe smooth-talking merchants,' Velindre commented scornfully, 'swearing they have a foolproof plan to manage such a miracle and return everyone's outlay a thousand times over.'

'Honest merchants hand over metals and mainland wares in all good faith to Aldabreshi who deceive them with worthless shoots and sprouts,' Sirince retorted, 'which either die in northern soils or turn out not to be the plant that was promised.'

'Well, some mainlanders have decided to cut out all these middle men of late,' Risala said, exasperated, 'both the honest and the corrupt. They've taken to landing wherever they think they can anchor unseen to search for the trees and vines bearing the various spices. They are ruining what they seek in their ignorance and arrogance. Black straws must ripen on the vine for two full turns of the Ruby around the heavens. Mainlanders harvest them green and useless. Archipelagans know which trees and vines belong to each family. Mainlanders think any unfenced plant is there for the taking. Islanders who stumble across gangs of these barbarians are threatened and robbed, and then beaten for good measure, until they confess where the finest spices are to be found, or explain how to tell good from bad.'

'What's Shek Kul doing about such outrages?' Kheda asked sharply.

'Granting his people licence to administer their own justice to anyone they catch plundering. Trying to find proof that Danak is sheltering and encouraging the worst of these mainlanders,' Risala answered caustically. 'While he spends his nights looking for omens to give the lie to the seers who claim all this misfortune is plaguing the domain as a result of his misguided rule.' She slid Kheda a look heavy with meaning. 'There's rumour the mainlanders are using magic to hide and raid and to assail Shek islanders with disease and accident. There are even some who claim that's what's brought the dragon here.'

'I can't believe—' Sirince recollected himself and coughed to cover his abrupt silence.

'So Crisk is loose on a shore where the local islanders are strung taut with fear over this dragon and inclined to hostility to any mainlanders.' Velindre looked grim. 'When suspicion that he has the remotest association with magic could see him strung up from the nearest tree.'

'Do people in these reaches know anything more of mainlander religion than we do in the south?' Kheda frowned. 'Could his babbling to his gods be taken for some attempt at sorcery?'

'He won't be able to explain himself, not when he is in fear of his life,' Sirince said unhappily.

'What else might he say?' Velindre wondered grimly.

'We have to find him.' Kheda looked at Telouet. 'Will

you go ashore and look? If there's such hostility to main-landers—' He waved a hand at Sirince and Velindre. 'And I can hardly go looking for some errant slave.'

Fettered once again by my rank.

'As you command, my lord.' Telouet didn't look too pleased at being set this task.

'I'll come with you.' Risala moved to the ship's rail and waved at a lad idly sculling between the anchored ships looking hopefully for some passenger.

'Are you sure?' Kheda didn't know what to make of this.

Risala glanced over her shoulder. 'We want to find out all we can about this dragon. Knowing the mood ashore could prove critical, too.' She looked back to beckon the lad in the rowing boat again. 'No one knows I'm here with my lord Chazen Kheda. They'll tell me things they won't tell you.'

'Is that why you slipped away so fast when we first went ashore?' Kheda asked as the rowing boat nudged up against the *Tacsille*.

Risala didn't answer. Kheda couldn't tell if she had heard him or not as she climbed deftly down to the lad's boat. Telouet followed, stern-faced.

Velindre watched the warrior's departure with discreet satisfaction. 'We can try scrying now he's out of the way.'

'That had occurred to me,' Kheda admitted.

'You can try.' Sirince ground his teeth in frustration. 'I'm cursed useless stuck out here on this water.'

Velindre had no time for his irritation. 'Let's go below. We don't want some curious watchman on some mast-head wondering what we're up to.'

'Did you get any feel for the precise state of that fire mountain while you were ashore?' Kheda asked Sirince as he followed the mage down the ladder. 'Is it about to erupt?'

*What do we do if it does? We can't use your magic to avert
the cataclysm, can we? Could you even do such a thing?*

The air was still and heavy below decks, though the
blankets slung from the ropes had been pulled down or
pushed aside, presumably by Telouet as he searched the
hold for Crisk.

'There's no sign that it's about to erupt in the immediate future,' Sirince said succinctly. 'Something is
drawing elemental power from the rifts deep within the
earth hereabouts. I can only think it's the dragon.'

'What do you think it's doing?' Velindre looked up
from searching through bottles of oil packed in a straw-
filled coffer. She pulled out one with a sprig of herb twisted
inside.

'I can't begin to guess.' Sirince cracked his knuckles
absently. 'Not until I get closer to the beast.'

'We're here to drive it away,' Kheda reminded them
both sternly. 'Then our debts to Shek Kul will be settled
and we can all leave.'

'To chase the next dragon out of Daish,' Velindre
commented with a half-smile.

'Not without Crisk,' Sirince said mutinously.

Without Risala?

Kheda shied away from that painful thought and
watched Velindre dip a cup of water from a lidded barrel.
'Can you see him?'

'Give me a moment.' She held out the battered tin cup.
'Hold this.' As he took the cup, she uncorked the bottle of
oil and Kheda smelt the faint odour of rosemary. Velindre
carefully let a drop fall onto the surface of the water where
it spread a rainbow radiance, barely visible. 'I'm not trying
this for long,' she warned as she took the cup. 'Certainly
not long enough to risk alerting the dragon to our presence.'

'We just need a glimpse of Crisk.' Kheda looked in
vain for any image forming within the tin circle.

Velindre frowned. 'That's odd—'

The boat rocked beneath them. A low rumble penetrated the wooden hull and over in their racked cages the courier doves fluttered and chirruped.

'Stars above!' Velindre dropped the cup, startled.

Kheda stepped back hastily only to find he wasn't splashed.

The cup tumbled slowly, gouts of oily water slipping from it as viscous as molten wax. The drops didn't hit the floor, shrinking instead until they vanished into nothingness. The dents in the cup deepened still further, the metal pressing in on itself. Crumpled as if it had been crushed by a massive hand, a twisted disc of discoloured tin landed on the planks.

'The dragon?' Velindre looked askance at Sirince.

The older wizard wasn't looking at her, focused instead on something beyond the solid wooden wall of the hold. 'The elemental focus of the earth—' He broke off and scrambled back up the ladder.

Kheda bit down on frustrated questions as he followed, Velindre pressing close behind him.

They emerged onto the deck to see grey-white smoke issuing from some hidden height among the trees. Countless birds screeched and fluttered. On the beach, tents flapped and quivered with no breath of wind to provoke them. Shek Kul's household stood on the sands in frightened knots, watching the smoke spreading across the featureless haze of cloud above their heads. A flurry of white-crested ripples ran out from the shoreline, setting every boat in the anchorage rocking before vanishing as suddenly as they had appeared. Startled cries and belligerent demands for explanations rang out across the anchorage. The air hung hot and heavy all around, tainted with mingled scents that reminded Kheda of a swordsmith's workshop.

'It's going to be very, very difficult indeed to work any magic that's not immediately overwhelmed and sucked into whatever that dragon is focusing upon,' Sirince said thoughtfully.

'It's working with earth and with fire?' Velindre peered at the rising ashy plume. 'Which are unfortunately wholly inimical to air and to water. I'm not sure how much use I'm going to be to you.'

Sirince surprised Kheda with a grin. 'Fire can't burn without air, and water percolates through the deepest recesses of earth. You're not telling me you cannot find a way into a beast's instinctive magic? Didn't you fancy yourself as Cloud Mistress before you were caught up in Dev's escapades?'

She looked quizzically at him. 'Don't underestimate these creatures.'

'I don't believe I'm underestimating you.' There was challenge as well as encouragement in the wizard's eye.

Velindre looked at Kheda, her expression sober. 'This is going to take some serious thought. Warn us as soon as you see Telouet and Risala coming back. Your man had better not overhear us.'

'You can talk in your own tongue, can't you? You have until first light.' Kheda turned to watch the frozen panic ashore begin to dissipate.

Slaves and servants returned to their tasks, slowly at first, then with more purpose once it was plain that neither burning ash, nor molten rock, nor indeed a ravening dragon were about to erupt from the fiery crater up on the mountain's summit. The mariners on ships close at hand descended from rigging and rails where they had sprung to get a better view of whatever transpired ashore. Seeing one man carrying cages of courier doves up on deck, Kheda belatedly went down below to check on the ones Telouet had brought.

He'd flay my hide with his tongue if I let any harm come to them.

Fortunately all Kheda had to do was soothe a few ruffled feathers. At the other end of the hold, Velindre and Sirince were already deep in intense conversation. Books were laid carefully open on blankets spread all around them and both mages sat with reed paper and ink to hand. Pens hovered in their hands before striking down, swift as a bird's beak, only for second thoughts to see the page screwed up and discarded.

I can't help them. I can't even delude myself that I could make myself useful by seeking out omens and portents.

Kheda went back up on deck. Some little while later, a heavy trireme and a more lightly built one escorted a shallowly laden galley with a double row of oars into the sound between the main island and the outlying isles. As the galley sullenly anchored under the watchful gaze of the heavy trireme's archers, the lighter warship swept across to a galley with three tall decks and thick masts permanently stepped to catch whatever winds might help push such a weight through the waters. The trireme's shipmaster summoned the galley's master and their angry exchange echoed around. Kheda heard enough to learn that the light galley had recovered from the shock of the tremors under her hull fast enough to make a hopeful dash for freedom.

Which is not going to be permitted. Shek Kul's mariners and warriors are wholly loyal to their lord. So I wouldn't wager much on our chances of slipping away from here if we fail to rid the domain of this dragon.

He resisted the temptation to go below and listen to whatever debate Velindre and Sirince might be having.

Even supposing I could understand their mainlander speech, I couldn't hope to comprehend the intricacies of what wizards could be planning. I don't want to. I just want to have them

*drive off this beast so we can sail to scare off whatever dragon
is tormenting the southern reaches. Then I can go home. But
where is home? I thought it was Chazen now, but every time
I look at Telouet, I think of all I have left behind me. I was
born to Daish. I never thought I would live anywhere else.
And how long will it be before news of some other dragon
drags me away again, to lie and deceive for the sake of saving
innocent lives?*

*Shek was Risala's home before she ever knew me and found
herself snared in my affairs. Is she going to decide it's time
to return here and leave me and this treacherous coil of magic
behind?*

Kheda brooded fruitlessly as the afternoon drifted sluggishly past. A sharp burst of rain washed away the
remnants of the ashy cloud that the mountain had coughed
up, then the skies cleared for a time until dark overcast
from the east began spreading across the clear blue. The
sun edged slowly towards the west and the approach of
evening touched the clouds with spurious gold. The mountain basked in the softening sunlight, tree-clad flanks
peaceful. Far in the distance, the summit was visible for
the first time: a steely slope cut short at a ragged rim.
Wisps of steam drifted up to be lost in the vastness of the
sky.

A steady procession of delegations came to Shek Kul's
encampment from the various anchored boats. Eventually
it slowed and ultimately ceased. Fires were lit and the
warlord's cooks and maidservants bustled about, feeding
successive detachments of swordsmen and archers.

Half-expecting a couple of rowing boats to bring them
some share of Shek Kul's bounty, Kheda braced himself,
ready to warn Velindre and Sirince. No such boat came.
Kheda wasn't sorry. His stomach was knotted too tight
to contemplate eating.

Besides, it's not as if I have anyone to play the part of an obedient servant fetching and carrying my food for me, as befits my dignity as a mighty warlord and slayer of dragons.

At long last, as the dusk gathered beneath the trees was sliding across the beach, he saw a rowing boat heading for the *Tacsille*. Even in the gloom he couldn't have mistaken Risala's outline, or Telouet's. He called down into the hold. 'They're on their way back.'

'Have they got him?' Sirince's face appeared, pale in the darkness.

'No.' Kheda shook his head with regret.

Sirince turned away, cursing in his Tormalin tongue.

Velindre took the older wizard's place at the bottom of the ladder. 'We think we can work around whatever the dragon is doing to achieve something of the same effect that we used against the water dragon,' she said heavily. 'If we're going to stand any chance, we need to be fully rested. So I'm going to sleep.'

'What about Sirince?' Kheda asked, concerned. 'Will he be able to rest if he's fretting about Crisk?'

Velindre shrugged. 'I've told him any excessive weariness is likely to be the death of him if he's facing down a dragon of his own affinity.'

That should convince him to sleep soundly.

Kheda kept such sarcasm to himself. 'I'll wish you a good night.' He looked up as Telouet hailed the ship from the rowing boat. 'You found no sign of Crisk?' he called.

'None.' The swordsman climbed rapidly up the rope ladder and stepped away to give Risala room to board the ship.

'Which is good news in some sense.' She brushed sweaty hair out of her eyes. 'At least no one's seized him for some barbarian mage.'

'Unless they've just cut his throat and dumped the body in a cesspit,' Telouet growled.

'No one would do that without Shek Kul's nod.' Risala

shook her head. 'Though it was nigh on impossible to hold anyone's attention long enough to ask if they'd seen him. All the talk is of Shek Kul's rebuttal of that sooth-sayer.'

'And speculation as to just what your secret might be, my lord of Chazen,' Telouet remarked, 'that enables you to drive dragons away.'

You don't think I know you'll be wondering that, too? How long until you ask me outright? What do I do then?

Kheda was glad he hadn't yet lit any lamp that might cast light on his face and show Telouet something he didn't want the warrior to see. 'Did you give that rower some reward?' He moved to the rail, acutely aware how little largesse he had to repay the slightest service.

'He said that you freeing the Shek domain from the dragon's shadow was reward enough.' Risala stood beside him, watching as the youth rowed away to be lost in the dimness.

Telouet cleared his throat. 'You're expected to do them this service at first light, my lord. So, if you'll permit me, I'll get some rest.'

'Of course.' Kheda looked out over the waters. 'Vel and Sirince are already trying to sleep.'

'I'll try not to disturb them,' said Telouet dourly.

Kheda looked up as the swordsman went below. There would have been no moons to be seen even if the clouds hadn't drawn a dark pall over most of the stars. He didn't bother assessing which aspects of which constellations were obscured or revealed. Rather, he looked inland. The fire mountain's crater threw a sullen red glow up to reflect back from the opaque billows above. As Kheda watched, a dark shadow of movement among the burning rim of broken rocks shifted across the cloud.

Did you see that, my lord of Shek? What kind of omen would you call it?

He shivered as his gaze slid down to the warlord's encampment on the beach. Lights within lit the tents now isolated by the night. They looked like coloured lanterns strung in trees, ridiculously small and frail against the featureless darkness. Twinkling lamps bobbing on the ships now falling silent all along the anchorage seemed even more paltry and pathetic.

'Vel and Sirince think they can do this.' As he heard the doubt in his own words, Kheda wished he hadn't spoken.

Risala wasn't listening. 'I met a friend of my mother.' There was a catch in her voice.

Kheda was ashamed to find it took him a moment's struggle to recall anything about Risala's family.

Your mother was a seamstress, much favoured by Kaeska when she was first wife of Shek. Your father was a faithful underling in Shek Kul's residence guard, now pensioned off to enjoy the tithes of a peaceful hill village.

'Do your parents live anywhere near here?' he asked with concern.

Risala shook her head. 'They live on the far side of the domain.' She sighed, looking into the darkness. 'Where they tell their friends and neighbours how proud they are of their daughter, who has made such a name for herself as a poet, travelling the length and breadth of the Archipelago. A poet who has already enjoyed the patronage of two great lords, of Shek and of Chazen.' She fell silent, biting her lip.

'You should be welcomed home with honour and delight.' Kheda looked down at his hands, fingers interlaced, the pressure painful. 'The services you've done Shek Kul certainly merit considerable reward. I would send you pearls every year from Chazen's harvest by way of thanks for all you've done for us.'

'Do you want me to go?' Risala asked distantly.

'No.' The breath caught in Kheda's chest, blood pulsing in his throat.

'They'd be proud of me. I'd share whatever fortune you or my lord of Shek bestowed on me.' Risala stared out towards the shore, unseeing. 'My mother and my father's sisters could trade pearls to great advantage. My father could see his nephews freed from working the land to join my lord's warriors or to sail with merchants travelling between the Shek islands and even beyond.'

She leaned her elbows on the rail and cupped her pointed chin in her hands. 'Everyone would want to hear my stories of distant domains, and every place I have seen on my journeys. They'd want to know about the people I've met, from lowest to highest. My mother would want every last detail of the dresses and jewels I've seen adorning the noble wives of Chazen and Daish and anywhere else. My father would want to hear whatever I could tell him of their warriors.'

Even in the dim light, Kheda could see tears shining in her eyes.

'How long do you suppose it would be before they heard how I had been flattered and courted in the western reaches as if I were your acknowledged wife? How do I explain why I've turned my back on such status and privilege? How soon would I have to start lying to them about other things? Because I cannot tell them where I have been and what I have done. How soon before they started doubting what little truth I was telling them? Of all people, they would be the first to hear the evasions in my voice and wonder at the gaps in my stories. They know me too well. How could I agree with them, when talk around the village fires turned to the undoubted evils of magic and the endless iniquities of irredeemable mainlanders? Because now I know there's as much good and bad among the barbarians as there is among any Aldabreshi. I've even come to accept there's no evil in magic beyond the uses it's put to.'

Tears spilled down her cheeks, though she wasn't yet weeping outright. She looked up at the blankly uninformative sky.

'How could I return to living my life according to whatever omens might be read by the village spokesman and sanctioned by Shek Kul when so much has happened to confound what I truly believed were portents? I believed the omens approved me loving you, that they meant I wasn't betraying Shek Kul's trust. Then you abandoned all faith in such things and I didn't know where that left me. Now I see honest men and charlatans read the self-same things in the earthly and heavenly compasses and interpret them quite differently to suit themselves. Am I as much a fool as Crisk, to trust in such things? And what about these barbarian gods of his? I don't understand how he can believe in them so absolutely, and yet the mainland is full of people who do.' She scrubbed at her cheeks with the back of one hand. 'No,' she said desolately. 'I can't go home.'

Wordlessly, Kheda wrapped her in a close embrace. She stiffened, resisting for a moment, then yielding. As she buried her face in the hollow of his neck, he felt hot tears against his skin and her narrow shoulders shook.

Is this how you'll stay with me? Because you believe you have nowhere else to go? I thought I could cope with you being angry with me, because at least I believed you still loved me despite it. Can I hope that such despair won't turn to resentment and ultimately to hatred? I must hope. I must find a better future for you. For us both. Together.

He held her until he felt her silent weeping slow and finally cease.

She lifted her face, drawing a wavering breath. 'We should get some sleep.'

'We should.' He kissed her damp and clammy fore-head. An echo of childhood consolation that his father had been wont to offer sounded in his memory. 'Who knows what tomorrow may bring.'

'We know it's going to bring us a dragon.' Risala pulled away and went down the ladder.

Everyone else was already asleep. Discarding her grubby clothes, Risala wrapped herself in a light quilt and lay down on a spread of blankets. Kheda did the same, lying close beside her. She didn't edge away. Later, in the absolute dark and quiet of the deepest night, he felt her sleeping body press up against him.

At least you still seek some comfort from me in your dreams.

He stared up into the featureless blackness.

What will first light show us all?

CHAPTER SIXTEEN

Voices floated up the spiral of the observatory tower's stair. Daish Sirket stiffened.

'My lord and brother will wish to see me. I am not accustomed to discussing the business of the domain with anyone but him.'

As he looked up, a reluctant grin lifted some of the weary tension from Sirket's face.

Footsteps grew louder on tiled treads, a second set following close on the heels of the first. A tall figure emerged from the opening in the floor.

'My lord, your brother my lord Mesil is here.' Sirket's personal slave Zari was a dark outline against the golden light issuing from a lantern following him. The youthful warrior's tone was unflustered.

'Have you read the portents to your satisfaction?' Mesil sounded less sure of himself than he had when challenging the slave. Lifting his lamp, his other hand was ready to open it and snuff the flame. He was both shorter and less broad across the shoulders than the muscular warrior, though they were much of an age.

'I have,' Sirket said shortly.

'What did you see?' Mesil walked forward and set the lantern on the pedestal in the middle of the square table that Sirket was leaning over. Deep lines carved into the pale wood were stained with coloured inks to mark out the circles and arcs of the heavenly and earthly compasses, together with the sweeping paths of the jewels that traversed the

night skies. The angular shapes of greater and lesser constellations processed in their degrees, each quadrant marked
into the three equal arcs within it. The recurrences of those
rare and wandering stars that might appear only once or
twice in a lifetime were indicated in the corners of the table
that abutted the relevant quarter of the compass.

'Clouds.' Sirket picked up a disc of silver set with a
circle of white opal. Iridescent flecks in the gem danced
in the lamplight as he returned it to a shelf on the central
pedestal. Other jewelled tokens glowed darkly in the
shadows.

'That's hardly unusual at this time of year,' Mesil said
cautiously.

'Indeed.' Sirket stepped back and looked down. Books
were lined up on the shelves set beneath each side of the
tabletop, making a solid block set precisely in the centre
of the square room. Gold embossing shone on some, soft
bindings still bright with dye. Others were so worn that
black leather had faded to creased grey, once bold scarlet
reduced to muted pink. 'Our grandfather Daish Reik
amassed considerable records of portents involving clouds.
There's considerable evidence that they can be a harbinger
of far more than the rains bringing a fertile growing
season.'

Sirket looked to the north. The upper half of each wall
was faced with wide panes of glass, exactly aligned with
the sides of the table. Thus the circle carved on the table
was just as perfectly centred in the wider circle of the
whole tower. Outside the room, a sturdy railing ringed
the circular balcony where the warlords of Daish had read
the skies and the land for countless generations.

There was nothing to see in the present darkness. The
lantern in the middle of the room made black mirrors
out of the windows, confining the reflections of the three
individuals to the room.

Sirket and Mesil were none too alike, their features both favouring their respective mothers. Sirket was taller and darker skinned, with closely curling black hair and beard neatly trimmed. Dedicated practice with sword and bow had built formidable muscle on a frame that had left the awkwardness of youth behind. Mesil was still caught between boyhood and his full growth, though it was already probable he would retain a longer limbed, more wiry build than his brother. Yet as they looked at each other, they could not doubt that they were brothers. Mesil had inherited Kheda's coarser brown hair, which he had tamed into long ringlets with scented oil. The barest hint of whiskers shadowed his firm jaw. Sirket gazed back at him with eyes as vividly green as their father's, set above sharply defined cheekbones. Both were dressed in crisp cottons, Sirket in red, Mesil in orange.

'Clouds can be harbingers of momentous portents,' Sirket said slowly. He twisted a braided rope of pearls around one wrist. 'I think we must see the moons both fading so closely together as significant. It's a rare occurrence in itself. I believe the omens we will see by the light of the new moons will be of vital importance for the domain.'

Mesil bit his full lower lip, looking younger than he would have wished. 'Do you think we might see some news from Telouet?'

Sirket glanced involuntarily towards the north again. 'He should be in Shek waters by now.'

'He still has courier doves, as long as they haven't sickened or been lost in the storms.' Mesil ran a fingernail along a groove carved in the tabletop. Lamplight slid over the obsidian in his golden ring. 'Do you suppose our father will send any word?'

'If Chazen Kheda has word to send, doubtless he will contact his wife Itrac Chazen,' Sirket said repressively.

'Not if he has no courier doves reared in that domain,' Mesil said stubbornly.

'He has,' Sirket retorted. 'Telouet has, I mean. I told him to take some of those Itrac last sent to us.' He unbent a little. 'Itrac Chazen is most certainly a friend to Daish, so hopefully she will share whatever she might learn.'

'You could always give her sound reason to share all her news with us,' Mesil suggested hesitantly. 'My lady mother Rekha said—'

'Neither of our lady mothers has any say in Daish affairs, not since their departure from these waters.' Sirket's precise words barely repressed his anger. 'By their own choice, which, as you doubtless recall, they didn't see fit to discuss with either of us.'

'No.' Mesil concentrated on picking something out from beneath a blunt fingernail.

Sirket rubbed a hand over his beard. 'You were saying something to Zari about having business pertaining to the domain to discuss?' he continued with resolute calm. 'Has the dragon landed again? Has it attacked some village? Are there many dead?'

'No, it's nothing like that. Not this time.' Mesil looked up, his expression still apprehensive. 'Dau has had a most trusted courier bring her word from Ulla Orhan.'

'What does he have to tell her?' Sirket enquired with some urgency.

'She said the only thing she has to share with us is his news that the Ulla domain remains untouched by the dragon,' Mesil said unhappily. 'Which Ulla Safar is proclaiming far and wide as vindication of his rule and condemnation of Orhan's insurrection.'

'Orhan can't know everything that's happening across the whole domain.' Sirket shook his head in instinctive denial. 'Not when he's hiding in the hills, watching every shadow in case someone still loyal to Safar betrays him.

Is Dau sure her courier can be trusted? Any link in the chain between them might have been twisted into betrayal by Ulla Safar's brutality. He could be using their letters to deceive them both.'

'Dau is certain of her couriers, and of Orhan,' Mesil said stoutly. 'Don't you think Ulla Safar would have been wading in blood up to his knees by now if he had any hint of a trail leading to Orhan? His latest edict said every man, woman and child would be executed in any village proven to have sheltered or even fed Orhan or any of his rebels.'

'My lord.' The slave Zari held out a callused palm. 'Sword-Captain Serno had just brought this from the courier dove loft with his own hands when my lord Mesil arrived. I was about to bring it up to you.'

A cleft deepened between Sirket's brows as he took the small silver cylinder from the young swordsman. He unscrewed the two halves and teased out the paper, fine as onion skin. Mesil and Zari waited, anxious, as the warlord bent over the table to hold the minute writing close to the lantern. Sirket scowled still more intently as he deciphered the message.

'It would appear that Orhan is right about this much at least,' he finally said heavily. 'That the dragon is sparing Ulla territory.'

'You're certain?' queried Mesil.

'This is from a *zamorin* slave called Inais.' Sirket bent forward to open the lamp. Touching the fine slip of paper to the flame, he made sure it was well alight before he dropped it into a shallow silver cup haphazard on the table top. 'He's a trusted member of Ulla Safar's household in the inner circles of the fortress at Derasulla.' The paper burned down to an unenlightening twist of pale ash, dissolving in the dregs of lilla fruit juice.

Mesil watched wide-eyed. 'You honour me with your confidence, my lord.'

'You are my heir.' Sirket looked around the observatory. 'You have always been raised to be my supporter and counsellor. It's time you were involved in the innermost councils of this domain. You should spend more time with Serno and the other guard-captains, to learn everything they can teach you of warfare and strategy.'

'Our father always said my education was to be limited to healing and the law,' Mesil protested.

'Our father is not here,' snapped Sirket. He looked away and drew a steadying breath. 'So much has changed, Mesil. You must remember, if anything happens to me, the lordship of Daish will fall to you.'

'You'll be getting an heir of your own blood soon enough.' Mesil looked alarmed. 'My mother—'

'My lords.' Unobserved, the slave Zari had moved to a low cupboard set beneath a window. He returned with a silver tray bearing a ewer of citrus-scented water and two shallow cups. Setting it on one corner of the table, he poured refreshment for both Sirket and Mesil.

'Our lady mothers can suggest all the fine matches and alliances they can devise.' Sirket managed a crooked smile to soften his words. 'Do you think any warlord's daughter with her wits about her would entertain my proposals?' He sipped at his drink. 'While a dragon is loose in these islands, plundering wherever it chooses?'

'I think Ritsem Caid's daughters would, or Redigal Coron's,' Mesil said with feeling. 'Or those of Endit Fel or Aedis Harl. They'd be willing to wager they'd be safer with the son of a dragon slayer than where they are at the moment.'

Sirket winced. 'I wish the beast would fly away from Daish but I hate to think of it landing anywhere in any of those domains a second time.'

'There will be omens to be read wherever it flies,' Mesil said unhappily. 'Do you suppose it might head south?'

'I hope not,' Sirket breathed fervently. 'No,' he continued, his voice strengthening. 'I don't believe it will. The blood of two dragons has been spilled over that domain. All the lore our father gathered from the northern reaches says that will protect Chazen. Even the barbarians agree that the beasts shun places where their own have died. That must be what's defending Itrac and her infant daughters.'

'So what's protecting Ulla Safar?' Mesil wondered bitterly. He looked down into his cup and set it on the table, its contents untasted.

'I don't know,' Sirket admitted in frustration. He looked at the opaque blackness of the north-facing window once again. 'I'm not about to start looking for a wife who can give me an heir, Mesil, but I think it is time we began looking for a suitable body slave for you. I shall write to our allies of Redigal and Ritsem to see if they have any likely prospects in their households or warrior contingents. Dau can try her hand at making the trade.' He grimaced. 'Let's hope Daish doesn't lose out too badly on the exchange.'

'Dau may not yet be the equal of our lady mother Rekha, but she's no fool when it comes to bargaining,' Mesil protested. 'But what's the hurry? That can all wait until Telouet gets back. You know he'll want to test the paces of every slave we look at.'

'We've no idea how long it might be before Telouet comes back.' Sirket nodded to his own attendant. 'Zari, tell Sword-Captain Serno that I want him to command the most skilled craftsmen in the household guard's workshops to make my lord Mesil a coat of nailed leather. He should be properly armoured as befits the heir of the domain.'

'Sirket, what are you planning?' Mesil demanded with sudden anxiety.

'Dragon's blood shed in a domain is said to protect it.'
Sirket set his jaw. 'Our father slew a dragon in Chazen.
Why shouldn't I slay one in Daish to defend our people?
To relieve our allies of the fear that blights their lives?'

'Father slew one that was already half-dead thanks to
another beast biting lumps out of it,' Mesil cried. 'And
the creature he fought still managed to kill countless
Chazen warriors despite being too crippled to fly!'

'Then we will only ask for volunteers to join me on
such a quest.' Sirket looked sternly at Zari. 'We will only
take men without children or wives who would otherwise
be left to grieve for them.'

'You can't mean to do this?' Mesil was aghast. 'You
can't anyway,' he said with rough satisfaction. 'You don't
even know where the beast is.'

'We know it will lair for some days once it lands again.'
The faintest of tremors underlaid Sirket's resolute words.
'While it gorges on the carrion in the remains of whatever hapless village it has chosen to trample into ruin.
That's what it's done in Redigal and Aedis. How many
more people can Daish stand to lose, Mesil? How much
of the harvest and trade goods?'

'How will you stop it just flying off again as soon as it
sees you coming?' Mesil challenged belligerently.

'I've already asked that,' Zari broke in. 'More than
once.' His scowl made it plain he didn't like any part of
the young warlord's plan.

'You're here to do my bidding,' Sirket reminded the
slave curtly.

'And to safeguard you, life and limb, my lord.' Zari lifted
his bearded chin defiantly. 'Which means asking every hard
question I can think of, to make sure you think through all
the aspects of any action you might intend. Telouet said
he'd beat me bloody with his own fists if he came back to
find I hadn't made you think better of some folly.'

'I imagine enough nets could entangle it.' Sirket glared at them both. 'They used nets in Chazen.'

'On a dragon that was already broken-backed, if half the tales are true,' Mesil reiterated angrily.

'I have to do something.' Sirket slammed his cup down on the table top, heedless of the water spilled across the engraved compass. 'How long will our people trust in me, if I stay hiding safe within these residence walls while they are out there dying the vilest deaths? A warlord is supposed to lead his warriors against every enemy that threatens the domain.'

'Against enemies he has some hope of defeating.' Mesil stared at his brother, incredulous. 'You can't be this stupid, Sirket!'

'What else would you have me do?' Sirket clenched his fists, fingernails scraping across the pale wood. 'Or not do? Chazen Saril fled before the wild men that invaded his domain. He refused to fight. His people would never have taken him back, even if he'd lived to beg their forgiveness on bended knee.' He leaned forward, resting on his hands, and stared at Mesil, vivid green eyes unblinking. 'Our father Kheda had to lead the battle within Chazen's borders, against all law and custom. Our lady mother Janne put them both to the test for that, and wagered her own life lest she was fated to die, condemned by her own presumption. She served them both white mussels gathered after a red tide and ate some herself. That's the true tale of how Chazen Saril died, Mesil, and my mother Janne said he proved himself a snivelling coward to the last.'

'I didn't know.' His mouth slack with horror, Mesil's response was barely a whisper.

'But you're right about one thing.' The passion died in Sirket's eyes. 'We don't know where the dragon is, not at the moment anyway. And I'm not about to lead any attack on it until we've seen the omens in the light of the two new moons.'

'Both new moons,' Mesil insisted, a treacherous break in his voice. 'You must wait until they have both risen, one after the other. The whole compass of the heavens will be different once the Vizail Blossom clears the eastern horizon.' He ran his empty hands over the table as if he wanted to slide bejewelled tokens across the lines that divided the circle. 'You mustn't do anything without reading every conjunction.'

'It's four days till the new Lesser Moon,' mused Zari. 'Four more after that till the Greater Moon returns. We may well have heard from Telouet by then.'

'I wish we could get word back to him as quickly,' Mesil muttered.

'We've no courier doves raised in any domain they might be visiting.' Sirket shook his head stubbornly. 'Not closer than Tule, and we've no idea how long it might be before they make landfall there.'

'Telouet could talk you out of this folly.' Now Mesil was visibly upset. 'Or our father could.'

Sirket stood up straight, folding his muscular arms across his chest. The golden chain around his neck twitched with the pulse of blood in his throat. 'The only way Telouet could change my mind would be by telling me how Chazen Kheda plans to drive off this dragon that's plaguing Shek. And telling me how to do the same.'

CHAPTER SEVENTEEN

On waking, Kheda was slightly surprised that he had slept. Then he realised he couldn't feel the pressure of Risala's sleeping body. Sitting up showed him he was quite alone in the *Tacsille*'s hold. The hatch to the deck was open, letting in light and voices. Kheda rummaged for sturdy cotton trousers and a plain tunic, together with nailed sandals.

Clothes for hunting this most abnormal prey.

He ignored the splendid swords that Zelin Raes and Galcan Sima had given him, picking up instead the hacking blade he had carried in his guise of slave. Black grime was deeply ingrained in the wooden handle while stains and notches marred the blunt-ended steel. Kheda didn't care. After gulping a few handfuls of water from the lidded barrel by the stern bulkhead, he hurried up the ladder. As he wiped the sleep from his eyes with his wet hand, he was reassured to see the sun wasn't yet visible above the forested island. The grey waters were motionless in the breathless stillness between night and day.

'There's still no sign of Crisk.' Sirince's face was drawn, shadows of weariness under his eyes.

'There's been no upheaval ashore.' Velindre spoke with a distinct air of repeating herself. 'We can at least hope he hasn't got himself into any trouble.'

Risala and Telouet both looked at Kheda with the stiff expressions of unwilling witnesses to a quarrel. Like Kheda

and both wizards, they were dressed in plain cottons to
foil forest thorns. Telouet, Risala and Velindre all wore
Aldabreshin sandals laced high over their feet and tying
the hems of their trousers tight around their ankles. Sirince
stood incongruous in heavy mainlander boots, high tops
currently turned down just below his knee. He had
retrieved a hacking blade of his own from somewhere and
weighed it in his hands with the air of a man who knew
how to handle it.

Kheda gestured towards the shore. 'I believe we're
expected.'

While few lamps shone in the ships anchored in the
strait, the tents of Shek Kul's encampment glowed and
flickered. Dark shadows passed to and fro with distinct
purpose. A few armoured figures were standing on the
sand, the shimmer of dawn light on polished steel slowly
strengthening.

'What are we going to do about Crisk?' Sirince
demanded obstinately. 'We can't just abandon him.'

Kheda nodded. 'Telouet and Risala must continue
looking for him while we climb the mountain in search
of the dragon.'

That prompted immediate protest from them both.

'My lord, you need my sword at your back!'

'Whatever I said, I'm not about to—'

'I need the two of you to stay safe for Daish's sake,
and Chazen's.' Kheda silenced them both with this uncompromising bluntness. 'This isn't a battle we will win
through strength of arms. Five of us are no more likely
to prevail than three if things go wrong. Three of us are
less likely to be seen as we try to sneak up on the beast.
If we three are lost in this struggle to free Shek Kul's
domain, you two will have to head south to see if the
dragon there can be driven off somehow.' He managed a
mirthless smile. 'My father Daish Reik was acclaimed as

one of the wisest men of his generation. He always said to plan for the worst while hoping for the best.'

'A valid sentiment, if hardly original,' Sirince remarked grudgingly.

'How are the two of us supposed to defeat a dragon in Daish?' Telouet was gripping his sword hilt so tightly the bones of his knuckles showed pale through his skin. 'Without you and this scholar's lore?'

'Vel, do you have those rubies with you?' Kheda looked at the magewoman.

She narrowed hazel eyes at him, irritated. 'I do.'

Kheda switched his gaze back to Telouet. 'You've forgone asking me just what we plan to do, my friend. Well, now you need to know. You heard how we cached gems last year to draw the plundering dragon away from Chazen villages?'

Telouet nodded reluctantly. 'My lady Janne's eyes and ears told her as much.'

'One of the things we discovered about dragons is they find certain gems repellent.' Kheda held out a commanding hand to Velindre.

She reached reluctantly into the tooled leather sack she had slung on a braided cord over one angular shoulder. 'Which knowledge will be worthless if anyone besides ourselves hears of it.' She weighed a substantial wash-leather bag in one hand, of the kind mainlanders were wont to carry their coin in.

'It's that simple?' Telouet looked dubious.

'No,' Velindre retorted, her nail-bitten fingers clutching the bag of gems tightly. 'You don't—'

Kheda spoke loudly over her. 'If we're lost, Daish's only hope will be you two seeding some cache of jewels with a share of these tainted rubies and hoping that will drive the dragon away.'

'Not that we have any intention of being lost.' Sirince

spoke with a modicum of his usual vigour. 'And there's something to be said for not carrying all our eggs in one basket.' He fixed Velindre with a cryptic look.

Her eyes narrowed, this time in contemplation. 'Indeed.' Turning her attention to the pouch, she began teasing undone the knots in the leather thong holding it closed.

Risala had turned away, her face unreadable. 'They're sending a boat,' she said suddenly. She pointed to the shore where several of Shek Kul's attendants were carrying oars down to the water's edge.

'Or they're bringing Crisk back to us.' Sirince took a hopeful step towards the rail, peering into the half-light.

Velindre had the leather bag open now and looked commandingly at Telouet. 'You had better fetch something to keep these secure in.'

'I suppose my swords wouldn't be too much use against dragon hide.' The warrior moved unwillingly towards the ladder. 'Will you have any kind of chance if the beast sees you first?'

'We can look after ourselves,' Velindre assured him, all her attention fixed on sorting through the cracked and darkened gems.

As Telouet disappeared down into the hold, Kheda drew Risala aside.

Her blue eyes were slatey in the dawn. 'She said there wasn't one chance in a hundred that using the gems like poisoned bait—'

'I know what she said.' Kheda laid a gentle finger on her lips. 'But one chance in a hundred of driving a dragon out of Daish with these gems is better than none. And I want you away from this mountain in case we fail Shek Kul. I don't want you sharing any blame.' He lowered his voice still further. 'Or stained with any guilt if our friends' true nature is somehow revealed. You don't deserve that.

I know all this has thrown your life into disarray, and it's my fault for the most part.'

Risala would have protested but Kheda shook his head, silencing her with a caress to her cheek. 'I want to make amends, for everything. I can start by being sure you can leave here uncondemned if the worst should happen to me. You must claim all that you're owed from Itrac, and make a new life as best you can.' He broke away as Telouet reappeared on deck carrying a leather belt with a nail-studded pouch attached to it.

'So, Sirince, have you any idea where Crisk might be hiding himself?' the swordsman asked with exasperation that had little to do with the missing halfwit.

Frustration twisted the mage's face. 'He'll shun armoured men, and any trader or ship that looks like a slaver. He does like music—' He fell silent, shaking his head.

'That's something,' Telouet said grudgingly.

Velindre caught the warrior's attention with a peremptory snap of her fingers. 'These rubies should be sufficient for your purposes, if worst comes to worst.' She held out a handful of jewels.

Telouet opened the belt-pouch to receive them, his eyes wide. 'What happened to damage them like this?'

'I honestly can't tell you,' Velindre said dryly.

'My lord Shek Kul bids you breakfast with him,' a voice called up from the rowing boat now drawing near.

Kheda stepped to the rail and smiled politely. 'Our compliments to your master, but we would rather start on the climb up the fire mountain while the dawn cool still lingers.'

He glanced at the rest of them on the deck, his words low enough to avoid carrying any offence to the rowers. 'I don't know about anyone else but I'd choke if I tried to eat anything, and that's hardly the sort of omen we want to start the day with.'

Velindre nodded. 'I've bread and fruit and dried meat if we're hungry later.' She patted the leather sack before she slung it across her back once again.

'Shek Kul can set a feast for us all –' Telouet buckled on the leather belt with a vicious tug at its tail and a fierce scowl '– when you've returned in triumph.'

I've just realised: you've quite given up prompting me to read the omens. Don't you want to know how this day is supposedly fated to turn out?

Kheda noticed Velindre and Sirince were both looking expectantly at him, and not for any portents he might be claiming. 'Let's be on our way,' he said curtly. 'Who knows, we may even catch the beast napping.'

Whatever the outcome of this day, it'll be governed by their skills, not the turns of any stars above us.

'Don't count on that,' Sirince muttered as he descended to the rowing boat.

Velindre followed and Kheda sent Risala after the magewoman with a gentle push. Telouet would have stepped after her but Kheda held him back with a swift hand.

'My lord?' The swordsman looked at him warily.

'If we don't return, see that Risala travels safely to the south,' Kheda said quickly. 'She was the chief of my eyes and ears while I was in Chazen. Make sure that Itrac knows she is to be rewarded fittingly for all the service she's done me and the domain.'

Telouet studied the warlord's face, his own expression taut. 'She's more than that to you, isn't she?'

'She's the one woman I've ever honestly loved,' Kheda admitted.

'Then you'd better be sure you come back down that mountain to tell her.' Telouet took a step towards the *Tacsille*'s rail. 'But if you don't, yes, my lord, I will look after her.'

That's something salvaged, if everything else goes wrong today.

Kheda held on to that meagre comfort as the rowing boat took them to the beach. Shek Kul's household turned expectant faces towards the sound of the oars. Kheda returned their gazes with a self-assured smile.

I might feel a little more certain if either of you two wizards showed some confidence.

Oblivious to his silent sarcasm, Velindre and Sirince sat isolated, deep in their own thoughts, their eyes distant. The rowers pulled at their oars, barely raising a ripple on the smooth surface of the sea.

'There's Shek Kul's body slave.' Telouet pointed out Delai foremost among the troop of warriors ready to greet them.

The boat grounded on the sand. This time the uncapped wavelets were barely sufficient to slide over Kheda's sandalled feet.

Delai gestured towards Shek Kul's extensive tent. 'My lord bids you breakfast—'

Kheda sought his most charming smile. 'Our compliments to your master, but we would rather start the climb before the sun rises too far. Can you set us on the right track?'

How will you deflect the accusations of your neighbours if we fail in this, Shek Kul? Will you be utterly discredited if I am exposed as dealing with wizards to defeat these creatures?

Delai didn't seem too surprised by Kheda's apparent eagerness to get going. 'We'll do more than just show you the path. I'm to be your guide, my lord.'

'This isn't a battle that will be won with swords.' Telouet fixed Shek Kul's slave with a stern look. 'I'm going looking for that strayed barbarian I told you about last night.'

'There's been no sign of him.' Delai wasn't wasting time on that irrelevance. 'If you're ready to go, my lord Kheda, it's this way.'

The Shek swordsmen parted to allow him through, leaving Kheda, Sirince and Velindre with little option but to follow. Telouet stayed behind, Risala at his side.

As he followed Delai, Kheda was startled to see that the soothsayer who had so offended Shek Kul was still clinging to life. Hanging from the scaffold of lashed spars, the white bone of his ribs showed pale amid the gory wreck of flesh and bloody rags on his back. None of Shek's men spared the wretch so much as a glance.

Kheda lengthened his pace to draw level with Delai's shoulder. 'Have you learned anything from him?'

Delai shot him a challenging look. 'Only that the sooner this dragon flies and lifts the shadow of magic from this domain, the better for us all.'

'One hardly needs to be a soothsayer to know that,' Sirince muttered under his breath.

Kheda looked back once when they reached the fringe of forest where the underbrush and lesser trees had been cut away to feed the fires of Shek Kul's encampment. Ironwoods soared upwards, lifting leafy branches high out of reach, their buttressed roots defiant. Spinefruit trees clawed at the rising ground with their sprawling roots, spared for the sake of the harvest swelling on their twisted limbs.

Delai veered off to follow a narrow path between immature tandra trees. 'Keep your head down,' he advised with a half-smile.

Kheda looked up to see red-and-white-winged crookbeaks rousing from their roosts to bicker, gaping and fluttering. White splats hit the ground and muttered curses towards the rear told him some warrior had been anointed by the quarrelsome birds.

'How far are you intending to take us?' He rested his hand on the hilt of his hacking blade. 'This will be done with stealth, if it's done at all. We can't risk your men startling the beast.'

'We'll go far enough to see you on the right path with no chance of going astray.' Delai picked up the pace, despite the increasing steepness of the path and the shadows persisting amid the trees. Vines hung thick all around and Kheda noticed a fleshy green creeper he didn't recognise. These were heavy with ribbed buds, some splitting to reveal waxy yellow petals within. They turned around a dense brake of afital grass and startled a youth sitting at the base of a lilla tree swathed with these strange vines.

'What are you doing here?' The lad rose, gripping the sturdy hacking blade that had been resting across his knees.

'My lord Shek Kul's bidding,' Delai said repressively. 'You tend to your vine flowers.'

The boy's eyes slid past him and Kheda to fix on Sirince. 'What does that barbarian want?'

'None of your spices,' the mage replied mildly.

'There's been trouble.' The lad scowled at Delai. 'With so many barbarian ships held in the anchorage.'

'Imeco!' Delai called back to one of the men bringing up the rear. 'Find out what he means and identify the ships involved.' He pushed on without speaking further.

The boy watched them pass, his suspicious gaze lingering on Sirince.

Are these warriors here to protect Shek Kul's spice forest from us, or to guard us from the local islanders who've grown to detest all mainlanders?

Kheda let Delai get some way ahead, curbing his pace until Sirince caught up with him. 'What manner of spice grows on that vine?'

'Black straws.' The wizard wiped sweat from his balding

head. 'In the flowering season, the blooms wither and die within the day unless they're visited by bees, or more likely, that lad proves handy with a tuft of afital grass.' He grinned at Kheda. 'They think we don't know that particular secret to ensure the flower sets its fruit, back on the mainland.'

'How do you know?' Kheda asked, curious.

The wizard slid him a sideways look before continuing in the Tormalin tongue, his words swift and low so as not to be overheard. 'Risala's right about mainlanders being perpetually eager to grow their own spice plants, especially ones as valuable as black straw vines. I've seen plenty of pots of blighted seedlings and withered cuttings. All too often they're not even the right plant, just something akin that's never going to produce a spice. Fake or not, all of them die; most sooner than later from some blight or rot. The few that grow well enough never flower or set seed, despite all the best plants-men can do for them. I've often been asked what property in Archipelagan soils keeps these plants healthy.' He smiled ruefully. 'It was such a puzzle that I finally came to see for myself. Once I began travelling, I saw the plight of wretches like Crisk.'

As the wizard shrugged, Delai stopped to look back suspiciously at the two of them.

Kheda met the slave's gaze calmly. 'How much further?'

'Quite some way.' Delai turned to continue up the path.

The forest grew thicker all around, with tassel-berry bushes and rustlenut saplings running riot. The sun strengthened overhead, drawing thick skeins of mist from the saturated leaf litter. The air was thick with the scents of decay, threaded through with hints of spices and, sharper, the lingering musk of some unseen animal. The path narrowed to a trail worn by forest deer and hook-toothed hogs. As the trees closed in around them, tangles of striol vine threw out hopeful tendrils to threaten them with vicious thorns. Kheda drew his hacking blade and found he could cut through the corded stems like saller straw. The blotched steel had been honed to a razor's edge.

As is customary for any weapon or knife that comes within Telouet's reach.

Behind, he heard efficient slicing as Sirince discovered his blade had been similarly sharpened. They pressed on. Making sure he could always see Delai's mailed back forging steadily on ahead, Kheda glanced back down the path from time to time. He noted the Shek swordsmen gradually falling away. Some reappeared to run up the path past the wizards and himself, to speak privately to Delai. Once the slave's responses had been relayed, others slipped down side trails. Several failed to return from forays to the storm-swollen streams washing away the soil to carve shallow gullies in the dark rocks.

Eventually the last of the mists burned away as the sun came and went through breaks in the clouds. Lilla trees and sard-berry bushes grew more sparse and stunted, leaving stands of afital grass and red cane increasingly unchallenged. Only two warriors were still toiling along in Velindre's footprints. The magewoman caught Kheda's eye as she paused to drink from her water flask. She grimaced as she tugged her sweaty cotton tunic away from her chest.

'This is where we leave you.' Delai halted at the last of the lilla trees.

'So I see.' Kheda accepted the water flask from Velindre and drank deep to quench his own thirst.

Immediately ahead, the red canes and afital mingled with purple-tinted ferns and low, rambling plants with a thick pelt silvering their grey-green leaves. Beyond, a barren brown scar cut across the dense growth. Just a few ferns had claimed rain-carved fissures, with tentative fire-creeper or tufts of the silver-haired plants venturing out from their shelter. Rising beyond, a broken landscape of black and grey divided land from sky. A wide, shallow cone broke the skyline, wisps of steam issuing sluggishly from its ragged edge.

Despite the water he'd just drunk, Kheda felt the sulphurous air drying his throat. 'The dragon's in there?'

'No one's seen it leave, or seen it anywhere else.' Delai wasn't trying for levity, his grizzled jaw set with tension.

'Then let us see what we can do to repay our debts to your lord Shek Kul.' Kheda bowed to him with plain dismissal.

'Don't you want me to wait for you?' Delai's hand drifted towards his sword hilts.

'No.' Kheda shook his head firmly. 'There's nothing you can do to help us.'

'If we fail, there'll be nothing you can do to help us, either,' Velindre added sardonically.

'We'll be able to find our own way back,' Sirince assured the slave.

Delai looked at the wizard for a long moment.

Are you wondering what business I have bringing some aging barbarian mariner and slaver three-quarters of the way up this mountain to see a dragon? This lore we're pretending to have is supposed to be the province of warlords and scholars.

Kheda looked up at the sky. 'The sooner we do this, the sooner we can return to celebrate with my lord Shek Kul.'

'Then I'll bid you farewell, my lord.' Delai bowed low. 'And wish you good luck.'

'Until later.' Kheda bowed in return, feigning complete confidence.

'Follow me.' Sirince sheathed his hacking blade, cracking his knuckles as he pushed on through the ferns.

Looking warily from side to side, Velindre followed him, her long-fingered hands outspread.

Kheda drew a deep breath, regretting it as the sulphur-tainted air burned his throat, and went after her. As Velindre carefully matched her nailed steps to Sirince's blunt-toed boot prints in the barren expanse of scorched earth and ash, Kheda did the same. The black and grey rock was rumpled like cloth yet hard and unyielding. Awkward angles strained Kheda's ankles at every second or third step. He was glad of the sturdy lacing of his sandals.

Sirince hurried towards the jagged rim of rock far up ahead. Pausing, he stooped and plucked a handful of cinders from the ground. He grinned at the two of them. 'You'll be glad to know there's no great likelihood of this mountain burning us up just yet. The fires within are quite calm.'

That was scant reassurance as Kheda toiled up the seemingly endless slope, feeling horribly exposed.

No dragon could fail to see us if it flew over now.

They finally reached the summit and Kheda forced himself forward to stand with the mage and Velindre on the precarious rim of the crater. He looked down into a vast bowl of frozen rock of every shade from darkest black to palest silver. Ominous reds and deceptively cheerful yellows broke the monotony, lurking in pits or threading seams through the crackled surface.

'So where's the dragon?' He did his best not to cough in the sour air.

'Somewhere over there.' Sirince pointed to the other side of the daunting expanse. A small cone had thrust itself upwards through black ash riven with red scars. It was coughing up gobs of fiery golden rock with petulant irregularity. 'Now, if there should be a sudden flow of molten rock, it'll most likely go that way.' The wizard pointed to a collapse in the far wall of the great crater bowl. 'So we should be safe enough coming from this direction.'

'Until the dragon sees us,' Kheda objected. 'We'll stand out like lizards on an empty beach.'

'That's why I'm here,' Velindre said curtly. 'Kheda, hold this.' She tossed him the wash-leather pouch of broken and blighted rubies.

'Which is why you're here.' Sirince made it sound obvious. 'Neither of us will prevail against this concatenation of elements with the tainted magic in those gems weighing on our working.'

'Won't magic draw the dragon to us?' Kheda held on tight to the leather bag.

Will the dragon spare me, if it attacks these wizards daring to work magic on its very threshold? Will it be repelled by the gems?

'Not just at present.' Velindre cupped her hands tight to her chest and stared fiercely into the emptiness she cradled.

'Wait,' Kheda said sharply. 'We should go beyond the crest, in case Delai or his men are watching from some cane-brake.'

Velindre looked up, her eyes taking a moment to focus on him. 'Very well.'

They clambered over the ragged rim and down the inner slope of the crater, until the broken rock rose behind their heads.

Velindre cupped her hands together again. After a few moments, faint sapphire radiance began to gather.

'Careful.' Kheda couldn't help himself.

'Trust me, Kheda, I've spent days on end devising the best ways to work the elements without those beasts noticing.' The magelight in her hands swelled to flow over her long fingers. As it swept up her arms, her hands faded from sight. The tide of blue haze ran down her body and towards her shoulders and face, completely wiping her from sight.

'What about us?' As Kheda wondered, a tendril of misty blue magic slid across the dark-grey rocks to wind itself around Sirince's thick-soled boot. A second finger touched his other foot and the wizard began to disappear from the ground up.

'Just stand still,' Velindre's disembodied voice instructed Kheda.

He held himself motionless as a tongue of faint azure licked at his toes, insinuating itself beneath the leather and laces. His skin crawled with anticipation until he realised he could feel no touch of the magic. As his feet turned transparent, he could see the fractured edges of the grey rock beneath where he stood. At the same time he could feel them digging into his leather soles.

There's no way I can ever claim to be untainted by magic.

Shutting his eyes as his gorge rose, a new concern assailed him. 'How can we do this if we can't see each other?'

'Open your eyes, Kheda,' Velindre ordered with cool amusement.

Reluctantly, he obeyed. 'Oh.'

'As you so astutely observe, being unable to see each other would add an unnecessary complication.' Sirince grinned at him.

At least, Kheda thought the wizard was smiling. Sirince looked like a blue-tinted shadow cast against the dark rock behind him, oddly flat.

'What if we're stupefied by these vapours?' Blood pulsed painfully in Kheda's head, his chest aching as if the sulphurous fumes were wrapping tight bands around his ribs.

'I can cleanse most of the air we're breathing, but these aren't easy workings,' Velindre said tightly. 'We should hurry up before I let something slip and that dragon does come looking for us.'

'Of course.' Sirince hastily led the way. Slipping, the wizard started brief cascades of cinder and ash every few steps.

Kheda looked anxiously at the splattered cone thrusting up on the far side of the bowl. Fresh golden splashes faded slowly to bloody red on its flanks, but there was no sign of any dragon.

He was nauseous by the time they finally reached the floor of the crater. Sharing discomfort freely with his stomach, his eyes protested whenever he looked at either shimmering and insubstantial mage. Even with the benefit of Velindre's magic, the foul, sour smell was still brutal down in the great bowl and the full strength of the sun fell on them, while the rocks beneath their feet breathed out still more heat.

Why does this morning have to be the first without cloud since the start of the rains? Blind ill luck, I suppose.

'Stay close behind me.' Sirince struck out across a silver-grey flow of molten rock long cooled into wrinkled contortions.

Kheda followed Velindre as she traced the older wizard's path. Amid the slicks of smoother rock, rough clumps like slag from iron-smelting were piled high on each other. The sun struck mysterious green lights from scattered nuggets of spongy rock and nests of golden tendrils sprouted from fissures. Most were shattered into splinters where unseen forces had flung destructive cinders into their midst. Silver light danced across a spread of rock with a surface patterned like glassy scales.

That black dragon attuned to the earth of that western isle could hide itself by blending its very substance into the rocks.

Fear stalked behind Kheda, Velindre a dusky shadow ahead. He could feel the knife-like edges of glassy rock cutting deep scores into the leather soles of his sandals.

How soon before I feel my feet sliced open?

'Wait.' Ahead, Sirince stopped, staring intently as a crevice belched out searing-hot steam. The shade that was Velindre rippled, distorted where burning moisture suddenly vented at her feet. She gasped and stumbled backwards onto a stretch of scaly silver rock. Still substantial if invisible, her foot broke though the surface. The scales crumbled to grey dust as her leg sank to the knee.

She fell forward onto her hands, gasping. 'I'm stuck.'

'Careful,' Sirince warned as Kheda moved warily towards her. 'Put your foot on the seams between those flows. And there. Yes, that's right.'

Kheda did exactly as the wizard indicated, testing every step before trusting his weight to it. Velindre waited, all her attention focused on something.

Let's hope she's maintaining her magic.

Reaching Velindre safely, Kheda held out a hand. She reached for him with her flimsy-looking fingers. Closing his eyes helped, as he felt her firm flesh grip his own. He pulled her free of the tenacious crumbling rock and bent to try to see if her leg was injured.

'Never mind that,' she snapped. 'Sirince, are we close enough to begin this working? The sooner we're out of this death trap, the happier I'll be.'

Sirince gazed around the vast bowl before narrowing his eyes thoughtfully at the spattered cone. 'Velindre, were you on hand when that red dragon was actually forging its egg from those rubies down in Chazen?'

'No,' the magewoman said sharply. 'Why do you ask?'

'Because that dragon's gathered an unholy quantity of amber in that lair.' He was intrigued. 'It's drawing the elemental power of the earth into it.'

'It's making an egg for itself?' Kheda wouldn't have believed it possible to feel chilled in such a furnace atmosphere.

Sirince's translucent face contorted as another gust of

heated gas passed behind him. 'I'd say we can either drive off this dragon or disrupt whatever spell is forging that egg. I don't believe we can do both.'

Velindre looked quite horrified. Then she shook herself, visibly gathering her wits. 'The earth dragon is the more immediate threat.' Ripples ran down her shadowy form. 'We came here to get rid of it. Then we can work out how to deal with an egg.'

'Dev was able to smother the spark of life within that ensorcelled ruby.' Sirince nodded.

'Which was the death of him,' Kheda forcefully reminded both mages.

Velindre winced, pain clear to see on her shadowy face. 'Perhaps the Council of Hadrumal will be able to nullify the elemental weave without losing themselves in the magic.' Her voice strengthened. 'Regardless, a newly hatched dragon must be less dangerous than one in its prime. Who knows, perhaps an egg won't even hatch if it's deprived of its parent.'

'I wouldn't wager much on that,' Kheda commented, 'but I agree that we must be rid of the black dragon first. Then you two can take the egg far away and deal with it as you see fit.'

If it does hatch, it can hatch a long way away. Would that mean the creature it births has no business flying back here?

'I wonder what we can learn from the magic that's making it.' Sirince's eyes brightened unnervingly at that prospect.

'Let's be rid of the dragon first.' Velindre limped heavily into the dubious shelter of a hollow extrusion where a bubble of molten rock had swelled up and burst. 'A judicious blending of fire and air should draw it out.'

She gestured towards the cone that was still spitting golden globs high into the air and a swirl of wind gathered ash from the floor of the vast crater. As the spiral thickened, it gathered up loose cinders and fragments of spongy pitted rock that rattled angrily against each other. Dirty purple light flickered deep within the magic as the narrow whirlwind danced towards the hidden dragon's lair. Wherever its questing tip touched lightly down, gouts of fiery gas burst upwards to leave shallow pockmarks scarring the rock. Scattered dust was instantly sucked into the claw-like vortex.

'The rubies, if you please, Kheda.' Sirince was standing calmly beside Velindre.

With a shock, the warlord realised that both mages were quite solid to his eye. As he held out the open leather bag, he saw his own hands had returned to normality, along with the rest of him.

It must know we're here by now. Let's hope they can give it more to think about than eating us alive.

Sirince scooped out a handful of the gems. He clutched the ruby slivers so tight that Kheda wondered how the mage wasn't cutting his hand to ribbons. But no blood oozed between his gnarled fingers, merely dull golden light. The magic shimmered and spread. Sirince opened his hand and the rubies on his outstretched palm darkened and disintegrated to thread their malicious tendrils through the magelight. The striped ochre cloud began drifting slowly away, faithfully following the dancing whirlwind that Velindre was now guiding towards the distant cone.

Red haze floated upwards from the cracks in the crater floor. The banded cloud slowed. As red haze flowed into it, the darker strands drawn from the corrupted rubies glowed ominous crimson. Confused eddies twisted through the golden magelight, which took on an odd orange hue. As the cloud hesitated, there was no sign of a dragon emerging from the small cone.

'That's tiresome,' Sirince observed tartly.

'What is?' Kheda's unguarded question went unanswered.

'I don't believe it's tempted by my little charade.' Velindre drove the whirlwind on with fluid twists of her long hands.

The ground shivered beneath their feet. Kheda clamped his hands tight around the bag of spoiled rubies as he staggered. Velindre fell to her knees with an oath and the whirlwind exploded into a rain of dust and cinders. Triumphant scarlet brightened and bled through Sirince's cloud of discoloured magelight. He snatched his hand back, trying to brush black dust from his palm. Kheda saw his callused skin was pitted like cloth struck by a shower of sparks.

The crater floor shuddered again and the small cone in the distance began melting away, the rock that formed it turning from dull grey to sullen red. Brightening through shifting shades of gold and yellow, the molten stone flowed away in white-hot streams. As the walls of the cone sank down to a token rampart, the dragon was revealed. Motionless, it was looking straight at them.

It was easily the biggest dragon Kheda had ever seen, not merely in length but in sheer physical presence. Where water dragons were sinuous, this beast was uncompromisingly solid. Where dragons born of air were long-legged and lithe, the creature before them was deep-chested, braced on massive limbs. Where fire dragons stood tall and proud, necks arched like preening birds, this one made no such arrogant show. Its sheer size was sufficient to terrify any opponent.

Amid the misshapen gouts of molten rock, its outline was sharp as crystal. As it lashed its thick tail slowly to and fro, trails of volcanic glass spun away to cool and fall and shatter on the crater floor. Every black scale on its basalt flanks was outlined by the radiance rising from the glowing pool of molten rock it stood in. It snapped erect the crest of obsidian spines around the back of its wide-muzzled head, each one as sharply faceted as crystal. At first glance its eyes looked wholly black, lit only by a point of white flame. Then Kheda saw that myriad iridescent flecks gave its unblinking gaze the sheen of the darkest opals.

'Why isn't it attacking us?' he wondered aloud.

'It doesn't want to leave that,' Sirince murmured.

White light cast up by the molten rock was reflected back from the scales of the dragon's belly, pale as quartz. Its claws were clouded crystal, resting easily on the surface of the liquid stone despite its great size. Secure between the fanned talons of its forefeet, an amber egg nestled in a shallow depression.

'Is it alive?' Kheda rubbed at his eyes, dazzled by the burning rock.

'The egg?' Sirince narrowed his eyes, chewing on his bottom lip. 'I'm not sure.'

'What now?' Velindre struggled to her feet.

'What can you do?' As Kheda looked from Sirince to the magewoman, he saw deep wounds torn in her calf muscle where her leg had plunged through the crust of cooled rock. Blood had soaked her shredded trouser leg.

'You two get out of here.' Sirince plucked the bag of tainted rubies from Kheda's hand.

'No,' Velindre protested.

'There's nothing more you can do.' Sirince began walking towards the dragon.

'What can you—' As Kheda reached for the wizard's shoulder, a sheet of flame shot upwards from the ground, filling the space between them. Kheda snatched his hand back, only to realise there had been no damaging heat in the fire.

'Go back,' warned Sirince.

As Kheda was about to protest, he saw that the white-hot rock pooled around the dragon had suddenly begun flowing towards them, faster than a man could run. He felt the first furnace breath of a scalding wind coming faster still, sweeping up cinders and dust into a roiling billow. The shining black dragon opened its mouth to reveal glittering teeth, sharp as diamonds. It roared and the deadly burning vapours accelerated towards them. Satisfied, the dragon ducked its massive head and licked tenderly at its egg with a tongue as pale as milk.

'Quickly.' Velindre reached for him, nearly falling as her injured leg failed her.

He slid his shoulder under her arm to hold her upright. 'What now?' he bellowed over deafening rumbling deep beneath their feet. Steam was rising out of fissures widening on all sides.

'We save ourselves.' The magewoman's voice cracked as she shouted back.

'What about Sirince?' Kheda yelled.

He saw the old wizard walking calmly across the shaking floor of the crater. Sirince stepped onto a flow of cooled rock which instantly melted beneath his sturdy boots. He strode on, unconcerned by the little flames licking around his heels. A crevice zigzagging through the crackled surface towards him spat fire. The mage brushed the burning drops aside like inconsequential rain. Digging his hand into the bag of tainted gems he'd taken from Kheda, he threw a handful out across the surface of the crater. Each one exploded into scintillating motes of dust. As far as Kheda could tell, the older man was intent on the living amber that the creature was cherishing.

Is every dragon's egg going to be the death of a wizard?

The dragon roared with a violence that struck Kheda like a blow to the head and cold mist enveloped him. The fog hissed and crackled with sapphire light as the leading edge of the burning vapours slammed into Velindre's magic. Within, the air was fresh as rain, marvellously cooling and invigorating after the stifling heat and gases of the crater.

'Backwards.' She dug her fingers into Kheda's shoulder. 'We have to go backwards.'

'I'm certainly not going forward,' he yelled back.

He supported the magewoman as best he could, matching his steps to her uneven stride. Veils of cold mist swirled around them, moisture soaking their clothes. Beyond the whiteness Kheda heard venomous hissing rise and fade as the scalding wind swirled around them and passed on. Nuggets of bubbling stone fell out of the cloud, some still steaming, bouncing off his head and shoulders to vanish in the vapours.

'Wait!' Velindre sank down to force him to an abrupt halt.

An infinitesimal fracture in the grey rock beneath their feet darkened to a thick black score running away in both directions. It widened to a hand's breadth with an ear-splitting crack before doubling its width again and again in successive breaths.

Kheda wrapped an arm around Velindre's waist and she knotted her hands around his shoulders.

'Over it!' His nailed sandals skidded on the slick stone as he attempted the jump. Velindre's weight pulled at his back and arms, excruciating, threatening them both with disaster.

Stumbling as they landed, Velindre yelped with pain. Kheda looked back to see red light boiling up from the depths of the fissure. He hauled the magewoman forwards. A crimson surge flecked with ashy grey and threaded with burning gold boiled up from a cleft ahead of them. Velindre warded it off with a swift flow of magic-laden mist. The sorcery slowed the leading edge of the rock, dulling it to sullen grey. The molten rock behind was only held back for a few moments before it bulged, welled up and spilled over this temporary obstacle.

'This way.' One arm still around his shoulders Velindre's weight pulled Kheda off at a tangent.

Quickening its pace, the molten flow pursued them relentlessly. Sliding around obstacles to come at them from new angles, it slowed only to melt the heaps of piled slag to add to its ominous bulk.

Kheda held Velindre tight around her waist, threading a path across what looked like the most solid patches of rock. The cracks of the crater breaking up sounded in every direction and the cloud protecting them blushed with the reflections of new fires on all sides.

Does Sirince have any idea what he's doing?

They struggled on and finally reached the sloping wall of the crater. Digging his feet into the slippery scree of ash and cinder, Kheda hauled Velindre upwards step by agonising step until they reached the broken rim. They tumbled headlong over it. Velindre lay on her back, panting. She waved a limp hand and the cloud that had saved them evaporated. Kheda raised himself on hands and knees to crawl back to the rim of the crater.

He could see no trace of the path Sirince had so painstakingly picked out. The twisted layers of newly molten rock recently cooled over more ancient flows had all vanished. The whole crater was melting into a mosaic of golden fissures. Black fragments initially slow to melt were now shrinking fast. Fires erupted from the seething cauldron, throwing out skeins of flames and sending searing sprays of liquid rock high into the sky. The heat was incredible. Kheda could feel the skin on his face tightening as he watched. He couldn't tear himself away.

Sirince stood alone on a solid black pillar of rock that was still defying the fiery chaos. The dragon faced him, shifting its stance, intent on defending its egg. Liquid rock swirled and spat beneath its crystal-clawed feet. As it bellowed, crimson fire laced with white circled around the burning golden hollow.

Kheda rubbed his eyes, parched by the heat thrown up from the crater. Sirince's hands were empty as he drew rhythmic circles in the lethal air.

'He's used all those rubies.' Velindre had dragged herself up to crouch beside him.

'Will it be enough?' asked Kheda breathlessly.

'Let's hope so,' Velindre said fervently.

Kheda barely heard her as he noticed two things. Firstly, that the crimson magic around the dragon was swirling at exactly the same rate as the circles Sirince was drawing in the air. Secondly, that the molten rock surging up from the depths of the fire mountain to fill the crater was rising fast.

'Sirince is going to be swamped,' he said with alarm.

'Only if the dragon's sanctuary is, too.' Velindre watched intently.

The circling red fires were rising into a menacing rampart around the creature, buoyed up on the rising tide of liquid stone. The clean gold circle within was shrinking. Where it had been twice as broad as the dragon was long, the crimson rim now threatened the lashing spike at the tip of its tail. The creature roared with fury, swinging its head to and fro, breathing out pale clouds. Where its breath touched the crimson radiance, the hostile magic faltered. But as soon as the dragon's attention was turned elsewhere, the magelight brightened and sped up once more. With every revolution, the scarlet snare drew a little tighter around the embattled black creature.

'Is it going to die for its egg's sake?' Velindre's voice was raw with anguish.

The dragon answered her with a scream of utter despair. It sprang, unfurling blunt wings with membranes mottled like grey marble. The red tide of magical fire spiralled inwards to close over the amber egg. The dragon heaved itself upwards with laborious strokes of its wings. As soon as it had gained enough height, it plunged down again, attacking Sirince with its murderous talons extended. Mouth agape, it roared its hatred at him. The pillar where he stood exploded under its assault, collapsing into rubble that dissolved instantly into the fires. Molten rock surged up, reaching for the dragon with greedy claws. It barely escaped as it struggled upwards once again. Now it did fly away, over the far edge of the crater, its laments making the air tremble.

As the beast vanished from sight, the ground beside Kheda shook. Dusty ash flowed away down the outer slope of the crater to leave a hollow deepening between him and Velindre. He rolled away, alarmed, even though there was no fire or heat rising up to threaten them. A hand emerged, coated with what looked like clinker from a metalsmith's hearth. The fingers flexed and the unnatural carapace cracked away, revealing gnarled joints and a palm dotted with fine black holes.

'Sirince?' Kheda knelt to dig with his bare hands.

Velindre joined him. 'What did you do?' she demanded as soon as they had uncovered the older wizard's face.

He shook his head, eyes and mouth tight closed as the ash ran away. When he was free to his waist, Kheda stooped to catch him under his arms. Sirince kicked and struggled for a foothold as Kheda heaved him up.

'What did you do?' Velindre repeated.

Sirince wiped the flaking coating carefully away from his eyes. 'I turned the elemental confluence it was binding into the egg into the fires of the mountain instead.' He didn't sound any too pleased.

'Will that drive it off for good?' Kheda gazed into the empty sky. 'Or will it go rampaging through the Shek domain, to repay you for the loss of its egg?'

'They don't think like that.' Sirince sat down heavily. 'It'll just want to get as far away from here as it can, as swiftly as possible. It poured part of its very substance into that egg. The pain will be excruciating.'

'The egg is lost?' Velindre frowned as she hugged her injured leg to her. 'Not dead?'

'Not dead, though I don't believe it's viable without the dragon to tend it.' Sirince looked at Velindre, haggard and filthy. 'I must ask your forgiveness for an arrogant old man, madam mage. I didn't fully appreciate everything you have been telling me. We cannot kill these creatures without losing some part of our own souls.'

'Nor without seeing something of our own possible fate,' Velindre said cryptically.

'But you can drive them off.' Kheda looked from her to the older wizard and back again. 'Don't forget we have another beast in the south to deal with.'

'If you can give us a few days to catch our breath,' Velindre snapped.

'The first thing we had better do is give Shek Kul the good news.' Sirince managed a bitter smile. 'Hopefully his pleasure at that will balance everyone's dismay when they learn this fire mountain is about to overflow.'

'Oh.' Kheda looked into the crater to see that the level of the molten rock was still rising steadily.

'Let's get out of here.' Sirince struggled wearily to his feet. 'I don't think I could stop a pebble rolling down a molehill at the moment.' He began stumbling down the slope.

Wordlessly, Kheda held out a hand to Velindre. The magewoman slung her arm across his shoulders once again and the two of them followed Sirince in an ungainly embrace.

CHAPTER EIGHTEEN

Rumbling pursued them down the mountain. Kheda looked up to see the previously clear skies being rapidly obscured by louring clouds.

Is that smoke from the volcano or a sudden rain squall sweeping in?

Fat drops of water answered him, throwing up splashes of ash that left the barren soil pocked and marred the ferns with scabrous splashes.

A few paces ahead, Sirince looked over his shoulder, not at the two of them but beyond, back towards the crater.

'Can you see the fires overtopping the rocks yet?' Kheda cringed at the thought of trying to outrun such a torrent, encumbered as he was with Velindre.

'What?' The wizard looked momentarily confused. 'No, no. Besides, the breaches in the crater wall will guide the flow well away from here.' He turned to hurry towards the inadequate shelter of the sparse trees.

You're angry about something. Angry with yourself. What's gone wrong?

The tang of fresh rain mingled oddly with the rank fumes pervading the air. Kheda's chest ached as if he'd suffered a lung fever as he half-carried Velindre to a stunted lilla tree.

'Let me see your leg.' He forced her to accept the support of a low branch, wiping his face. As he did so, he discovered each drop of rain was bringing down ash from the skies. One sweep of his hand left his forehead gritty and sore.

Kneeling to pull aside the blood-soaked cloth of her torn trousers, Kheda discovered the magewoman's injury wasn't as bad as he had feared. Sharp shattered rocks had ripped deep scores into Velindre's calf muscle, but dark clotted blood was keeping out the muck and dust. It was the ugly sprain to her ankle that was giving her the most pain.

'I shall have to cleanse these cuts thoroughly when we get back to the *Tacsille*,' he warned all the same. 'If there's dirt beneath those scabs, the leg will fester.' He pulled his tunic over his head and used his belt knife to slice the sturdy cotton twill into broad lengths. 'I'll bind this ankle tight. Sirince, can you cut her some kind of prop?'

'My lord!' Telouet's bellow startled all three of them.

Kheda looked down the mountainside, trying in vain to pick out the swordsman among the cane-brakes and grasses tossing in the wind as the rainstorm worsened.

'Did he follow us?' Sirince shouted angrily. 'What has he seen?'

'I don't know.' Kheda concentrated on tying firm support around Velindre's rapidly swelling ankle.

'My lord.' Telouet hurried up the slope, one drawn sword clotted with damp smears of greenery.

'What is it?' As Kheda stood to greet the warrior, he saw Risala coming up behind.

Surely she must have kept him from seeing anything incriminating?

Risala paused to catch her breath in the cruel atmosphere and her eyes found his. For the first time in a long time, she smiled at Kheda. He held out his hand to her.

'What are you doing here?' Sirince gripped his hacking blade. 'You were supposed to be looking for Crisk!'

Kheda dragged his attention back to Telouet. 'Did you find any word of him?'

'Several people had stumbled over him gibbering about the dragon.' Telouet barely spared Sirince a glance, addressing himself to Kheda. 'As best they could tell, he was getting up the courage to come and see it. That's the last anyone had seen, so we came to look.'

'Why would he do that?' Kheda looked at Sirince, nonplussed.

The wizard hesitated. 'I have no idea.'

Risala reached them, holding her side as she caught her breath. 'Delai showed us the path you'd taken.'

'We've seen no sign of Crisk.' Kheda shook his head regretfully. 'You've had a hard climb for nothing. It's too dangerous for you to search any further.'

'I can look,' Sirince instantly countered.

'No, you can't.' Velindre glared at Sirince and he subsided with a sullen scowl.

'How've you fared?' Telouet glanced at Velindre's bloodstained leg before gazing uphill to the crater's edge. Trepidation showed plainly on his broad features as he saw the smoke and sparks issuing from the mountain's hollow summit. The rain coming down still more heavily had no hope of quenching it.

'Where's the dragon?' Risala asked.

'Flown.' Pain twisted Sirince's face. 'For good.'

Telouet frowned at the older wizard, perplexed.

'Can you help Vel?' Kheda drew his hacking blade as Telouet helped the magewoman up from her seat on the low branch to balance on her one sound foot. 'I'll find something for a crutch.'

Sirince suddenly grabbed at the warrior's leather belt. 'You're still carrying those rubies?'

Taken unawares and encumbered by Velindre, Telouet couldn't stop the older wizard unbuckling the tooled strap. 'What do you think—'

'Get down the mountain, all of you.' Sirince ripped the

belt away from Telouet. Clutching the pouch tightly, he began running back uphill with a startling turn of speed.

But we need those gems—

After an instant of frozen surprise, Kheda set off after the wizard. 'Wait!'

Several paces later he realised Telouet wasn't following and wasted a precious moment to look back. Velindre was hindering the warrior with a suspiciously convenient collapse. Then he realised Risala had stepped into the swordsman's path as well.

Because whatever Sirince is up to might condemn us all.

He looked uphill to see the wizard slowing as his heavy boots sank into the sodden ashy soil. Chest heaving in the tainted air, Kheda forced himself to run as fast as he could. The drenching rain soaked his trousers, sodden cloth clinging to his thighs. Treacherous ashy clods slid away beneath his feet. He was still several paces behind Sirince as the wizard reached the crater's rim.

'What are you doing?' He grabbed at the wizard's shoulder, but the older man twisted out of his reach.

'What . . . needs . . . to be . . . done.' Sirince's breath rasped in his chest. Stooping, his free hand groped for the ground. The merciless edges of slick and broken rocks lacerated his fingertips.

'We need those gems—'

As Kheda lunged for him, Sirince hurled the studded leather pouch high over the broken wall of the crater. A scarlet tongue instantly shot upwards from the lake of fire to curl around the little bag. Molten rock exploded outwards in a shower of sparks. Both men cowered away, hiding their faces in their arms.

Burns stung Kheda's back and shoulders like angry hornets. Ignoring the pain, he seized the wizard and dragged him around. Choked with incoherent rage, he punched Sirince full in the face. The mage couldn't fall far with the warlord's hand twisted in the shoulder of his tunic. Kheda hauled him up, drawing his clenched fist back for a second blow. As he did so, some vestige of calm reason cut through his insensate anger.

I've just punched a wizard who can walk unscathed through the burning depths of a fire mountain. Is he going to turn me to stone where I stand?

He let his fist fall and settled instead for shaking Sirince like a hound with a captured cane rat. 'What did you do that for?' he bellowed over the roars of the turbulent crater just beyond the broken rim. 'We needed those rubies for Daish!'

'The gems we had were only enough to drive off that dragon.' Sirince made no attempt to fight back. He dabbed at the blood oozing from a split in his lip. 'I couldn't leave the egg.' Tears stood in his faded eyes.

'But you said it wouldn't have hatched.' Conflicting emotions clawed at Kheda.

'It wouldn't have died.' The pain in Sirince's voice had nothing to do with the bruises swelling his jaw. 'It could have suffered in the depths of that mountain for an endless age. I had to give it a clean death.'

Kheda shook the old man brutally once again. 'How do we drive off the dragon that's plaguing the southern reaches without those rubies?' he demanded wrathfully.

'I don't know.' Recovering something of his composure, Sirince struck Kheda's hand from his shoulder. 'I'll have to think of something!'

'Yes, you will.' Kheda raised his fist and the wizard flinched. The warlord felt the pain of his own bruised knuckles for the first time. 'We came here to pay my debts to Shek Kul, wizard. Now you owe me for this, mage, me and mine. I trusted you and this is how you repay me?' Not trusting himself, he turned and stalked away down the mountain. He didn't look back to see if Sirince was following.

Telouet was waiting, his sword roughly cleansed and his weight balanced ready to fight. 'What was that all about?'

Kheda was still trembling with anger. 'Never mind.'

Velindre was standing with Risala supporting her on one side. Kheda pushed past with a wordless growl of disgust. As he struck the magewoman with a glance of searing accusation, she had the grace to blush, colour vivid on her angular cheekbones.

Kheda curbed an ungenerous urge to pull Risala out from under Velindre's shoulder and vented his feelings instead by hacking at a hapless sapling until he had cut a crude staff. Flinging it at the magewoman, he stalked off down the mountain. The bruising rain hammered down on the tender skin of his back and shoulders. He ignored the pain. It was nothing compared to the anger burning within him.

They had reached the thicker stands of trees when Risala appeared at his side, now swinging Sirince's hacking blade in her slim hands. Swapping the blade to her off hand, she reached for Kheda, sliding her fingers in between his.

'They can scry for Crisk now the dragon's gone,' she reminded him, her low tone barely rising above the thrum of the rain.

Kheda glanced back lest Telouet was close enough to overhear. He need not have worried. Slim as Velindre was, she was tall and thus a not inconsiderable burden now she could barely manage to put her injured foot to the ground. Sirince trailed after the two of them. His tunic was pulled askew as he had wadded up the end of his sleeve to press a pad of sodden cloth against his battered face.

Shame stung Kheda worse than the pinprick burns still throbbing across his shoulders. 'I shouldn't have hit him.

He's an old man. Even if—' Despair threatened to overwhelm him.

'We'll find a way.' Risala's fingers tightened on his hand. 'You'll find a way.'

Kheda looked helplessly at her. 'How can you be so sure?'

Don't tell me you've seen some omen. I couldn't bear it.

'Because you always have so far. I've been talking to Telouet,' she added cryptically.

As if that explains everything. How does it explain this warmth in your blue eyes where I've become so accustomed to seeing coolness?

Unable to contemplate this riddle, Kheda turned back to the path. But he kept hold of Risala's hand.

The rain was falling now with all the careless extravagance of the season. It swept through the forest in glistening curtains, too thick to see through. The trees had no hope of sheltering anyone. Berry bushes cowered beneath the onslaught, once-bright flowers dulled and fruits bruised. The path was a slick torrent of dead litter, washing all around their feet. Noise on the leaves all around drowned out any ominous rumblings from the heights behind them.

Water oozed through Kheda's beard and hair. As the sodden laces stretched, his nailed sandals grew slack, his feet slipping within them. The fiery crater seemed a distant memory as the ceaseless flow of rain chilled him further and further. The only heat he could feel was in the stinging burns on his shoulders. He blinked and winced as gritty water trickled through his eyebrows and insinuated itself into his eyes, harsh and blurring his vision. He sheathed his hacking blade awkwardly so he could rub away the worst. He wasn't about to let go of Risala's hand. Her presence at his side gradually coaxed a knot of warmth deep within him as they made their way down towards the shore.

Once they reached the lower levels of the forest where the spice vines were to be found, Kheda caught sight of movement ahead. As he and Risala rounded the next twist of the path, men appeared, their armour as leaden grey as the waters in the strait now visible through the gaps in the trees.

'My lord of Chazen!' Delai was shouting to make himself heard through the downpour. 'What news?'

Kheda forced a triumphant bellow. 'The dragon has flown!'

There was nothing feigned in the elated response that burst from the Shek warriors. Several immediately broke away to run back down towards the shore.

Delai hurried up the path, a wide grin lifting ten years from his grizzled face. 'Come and be honoured by my lord of Shek.'

'It is my honour to serve him,' Kheda said smoothly.

Risala slipped her arm around his waist and walked entwined with him along the last stretch of more level path that ran through the forest fringes already plundered for firewood. Thankfully the rain began to slacken as they approached the open beach and Shek Kul's encampment. Delai was walking behind them, two paces to Kheda's open side. Other swordsmen hurried past to help Velindre, Telouet and Sirince.

'No, that's fine. We're fine.' Telouet was having none of it.

Kheda turned to see his warrior firmly warding off two Shek swordsmen who were offering to carry the mage-woman on a seat made from their linked hands. Risala looked up at Kheda, offering a shrug of incomprehension to equal his own. They waited together to allow Telouet and Velindre a chance to catch up. Telouet showed no sign of weariness, his broad face impassive. Velindre by contrast was grey with pain, her face drawn, her sodden

cotton clothes stained with ash and spattered with muck
from the forest.

Not that I look much better, bare-chested like some beggar.

Kheda forced himself to wait a few moments longer,
to let Sirince catch them up. Soaking wet, his sparse hair
slick around his bald pate, the older wizard was a sorry
sight. The vicious bruise on his cheek where Kheda had
hit him had already bled across his wrinkled face to blacken
his eye.

'My lord of Chazen!'

As the path underfoot turned from the dark moistness
of forest soil to the gritty black sand of the shore, Shek
Kul hailed them from an awning erected in front of his
great tent. Wearing his formidable armour, the warlord
stayed prudently beneath the shelter even though the rain
was now tailing off. The slaves and servants of his household paid no heed to their finery getting wet as they
emerged from the other tents. Eager anticipation warred
with anguished apprehension on their faces.

Beyond, the decks of the ships forced to anchor in the
wide strait were thronged with their crews. Smaller boats
began hurrying towards the shore, oars ripping into the
murky waters. The hum of expectation grew loud as Kheda
and Risala approached the warlord's tent. Kheda noted
dread and disbelief still threading through the low-voiced
conversations.

*These people want to believe in their lord but they've heard
too many naysayers spreading doubt and despondency.*

'You return in triumph?' Shek Kul raised his face plate
and removed his helmet. 'Am I truly relieved of my duty
to lead the men of Shek against the beast?'

'The beast is gone, never to return,' proclaimed Kheda
with ringing certainty. He disengaged himself from Risala
and bowed low. 'We are honoured that we might present
such a gift to you, my lord.'

Shek Kul walked out from beneath the oiled silk awning. The last few drops of rain pattered down to glisten like jewels caught in the links of his chain mail. 'This is no small gift, my lord of Chazen.' His resonant voice echoed across the sopping sands. 'You of all people know how much blood would have been shed if we had been forced to fight the dragon ourselves.'

'Which is why I have sought out all the lore of the northern lords of old.' Kheda pitched his words with similar volume and clarity, for the benefit of their avid audience. 'I would not see any domain forced to pay the price in men's lives that was demanded of Chazen.'

That is most emphatically no lie, my lord.

'Then let the auspices of this day mark the beginning of an alliance between our proud domains.' Shek Kul swept a broad hand around, inviting the crowd now gathered on the beach to assent to his declaration. 'An association that will be admired the length and breadth of the Archipelago.'

'That will be condemned!' The tight press of bodies ringing the warlord's tent convulsed as a gang of mariners forced their way through. With broad shoulders muscled by years at the oar, they hefted cudgels cut from broken spars as well as brandishing a wide assortment of daggers. Shek islanders hurriedly retreated as the mariners spread out to form a formidable circle, looking around for any challenge. A knot of strong men stood shoulder to shoulder at its core.

As Delai's warriors ran up to form rapid ranks between Shek Kul and this unexpected threat, the man who had first spoken out stepped forward. 'The fire mountain over-flows, my lord,' he shouted with scant courtesy. 'What manner of good omen is that? The spice forests will burn. Villages will lose their huts and their gardens when we already face a hungry season—'

'Silence!' Shek Kul took a pace forward and gestured

to Delai. The slave looked grim as he indicated that the Shek warriors should open up a gap in their armoured line. Shek Kul studied the speaker, though he didn't go any closer. 'Who are you, to dare interrupt me?' he demanded with barely controlled anger. 'Who are you to claim such concern for the Shek harvest? You are no shipmaster guiding any galley of mine.'

Taking Risala's hand and moving so his bare-chested body shielded her, Kheda retreated a few discreet steps closer to Telouet.

Are we on our own if these men decide we're a threat? Or an easier target? My lord of Shek's wearing the finest armour in this domain. I haven't even got a tunic.

'We are of Danak, my lord,' the mariner answered boldly. 'We came to ask why you have so cruelly abused an honest soothsayer who sought passage on our ship.' He thrust out a hand towards the flogged man still hanging limp and motionless on the frame of spars.

Kheda could see no sign of life lingering in the tormented seer.

Surely he must be dead. He couldn't have withstood the shock of that rainstorm after such a savage beating.

'We have found his prophecies most enlightening.' The Danak mariner was addressing the multitude on the beach as much as Shek Kul. More and more rowing boats were ferrying the curious from the anchored vessels. There were even a few pale mainland faces, some eager to see what was going on, others more obviously keen to know if they could finally leave.

'He warned us not to enter these waters.' The Danak mariner hung his head with apparent sorrow. 'He said the taint of magic polluting this domain would be the death of him. But once we had been snared by the Shek triremes, we had no way to leave!' His anguished face appealed to the crowd not to blame him.

'That soothsayer brought punishment down on himself with his falsehoods.' Delai stepped forward to challenge the mariner's claims.

'The taint of magic has flown from this domain.' Shek Kul waved away his slave's anger with a casual hand and an unexpectedly broad smile. 'The very land itself has rejected such contamination. The dragon could not gain so much as a foothold beyond the fire mountain's crater and now it has fled in defeat. These fires that are born of Shek are the ultimate purification, flowing to burn away whatever miasma might have drifted to stain the earth around the heights.' He sighed with regret. 'There will be some cost in burned trees, that is true, but no victory is ever won without sacrifice. And we have the omens of this sudden rainstorm to reassure us.' He smiled confidently once again. 'The fires will be slowed and cooled by the wet forest before they can leave the heights.'

Shek servants and loyal islanders among the crowed cheered loudly. A few even began walking away, gestures making it plain they felt nothing more needed to be said.

'This domain is still cursed with sorcery.' The Danak mariner planted his feet solidly on the sand, callused hands insolently braced on his hips. 'I'm not speaking of magic born of that dragon. I speak of far more despicable crimes.'

His words were a signal. The ring of men backing him opened and the heavy-set sailors inside strode forward. They dragged a limp figure between them and flung him forward onto the dark sand.

Risala stiffened beside Kheda. 'Crisk,' she breathed.

Kheda instantly shot a forbidding glare over his shoulder, to freeze Sirince in his place. The wizard had already taken half a step forward, only to find Telouet had moved instantly to bar his way. Velindre had paled even more beneath her tan.

'What is this?' Shek Kul demanded, outraged. 'Do you dare usurp my authority?'

Crisk's red hair was clotted with gore and his face was deathly white beneath his freckles. The back of his over-large tunic was torn to reveal fresh bruises and bloody scores amid the scars of his old injuries. His trousers were foully stained where he'd lost control of bowels and bladder. Bloody sand crusted his feet, too thick for Kheda to see what torments had been inflicted there.

'This is proof of vile deception practised on you all.' Unafraid, the Danak mariner circled around to claim the attention of everyone on the beach. 'This man's confession will prove that Shek Kul has lied to you. That Chazen Kheda has lied—'

His words were drowned out by outraged shouting from Shek islanders and, louder still, from the domain's swordsmen. The line of warriors defending Shek Kul flexed and swayed as several men took an involuntary step towards this man offering such insult to their lord. They recollected themselves at Delai's ferocious bellow and hastily withdrew.

'My lord!' Telouet's full-throated yell cut through the hubbub. Even the Danak mariner was startled into silence. 'May I be heard?' Telouet walked quickly forward. With her arm caught over the warrior's shoulder and unable to put her wounded foot to the ground, Velindre was helpless. She was half-carried, half-dragged along at his side.

Shek Kul's beard jutted. 'You may speak.'

'You have been deceived, my lord.' Telouet's voice was thick with emotion. 'But I will not have it said that my lord Chazen Kheda has been a party to this.'

Oh, my friend, you don't know what you're doing. You're going to be the death of us all.

Kheda felt Risala trembling. He didn't dare look around

to see Sirince's reaction. Any movement would have instantly drawn everyone's unwelcome attention.

Shek Kul's gaze didn't even flicker in their direction. The Danak mariner tried to say something but Shek Kul spoke mercilessly over him, his words ringing out across the sand. 'What is this deception you speak of?'

'This is no *zamorin* scholar.' Telouet suddenly withdrew his arm from Velindre's waist and seized her instead by the back of the neck, forcing her head up. 'My lord has been grotesquely misled by calculated falsehood.'

He kicked away her crude staff. With her injured foot, the difficulty of remaining upright made it impossible for Velindre to struggle against his merciless grip. Their gazes locked as he drew the Daish dagger from his belt. Her mouth opened a fraction. Telouet narrowed his eyes, a sneer curling his lip.

'See for yourself, my lord of Shek, my lord of Chazen.' Releasing Velindre's neck, Telouet seized the front of her tunic instead and sliced the fabric clean down to the hem with his razor-sharp blade. He ripped the ruined garment away, leaving her nakedness exposed. She swayed and might have fallen, but Telouet caught her bare upper arm. Stepping close, he hooked the tip of his knife under the knot tied in the drawstring of her loose cotton trousers. A swift jerk sliced through the cord and the garment sagged.

'See for yourself.' Telouet sheathed his dagger with a slithering rasp of metal. 'This is no *zamorin*. This is a barbarian woman!'

The stunned silence on the beach was broken by gasps and a few muffled sniggers. Kheda's hand itched to slap the smirks from those avid faces closest to him.

Velindre lifted her chin defiantly as a ferocious blush stained her tanned cheeks and neck. The colour spread to skin untouched by the Archipelagan sun, almost to the

creamy swell of her modest breasts. No fuller than those
of an unwed girl, they were still unmistakably breasts,
even on a woman so plainly well past the first bloom of
youth. The curve of her hips was similarly unassuming,
but stripped naked, her buttocks were wholly feminine.
Most unarguable, there was no scarred ruin where a castration knife had done its work but rather a mature woman's
cleft roundness, dusted with hair as golden as that on her
head.

'Chazen Kheda?' Shek Kul was utterly astounded.

'My lord.' Kheda hoped his shock at this turn of events
would be taken for equal astonishment. 'We have always
given him – her – every privacy due to a *zamorin*—'

'This is no woman!' The Danak mariner recovered
himself only for his words to be drowned out by derision
from all.

'This plainly *is* a woman.' His words instantly silencing
the crowd, Shek Kul walked slowly forwards. 'And just
as plainly a barbarian one at that. What is your purpose
here?' he hissed venomously.

'I am a scholar.' Velindre's voice quavered as the
warlord halted before her, standing so close that his
armoured chest threatened her rosy nipples, tight with
cold or fear. She tried to reach down to catch up the
waist of her trousers but Telouet tightened his grip on
her arm with a warning shake and she gave up the
attempt.

'I wished to travel the Archipelago to learn more of
Aldabreshin wisdom.' Her voice strengthened. 'Lords and
scholars throughout the domains have studied the movements of the stars, the natures and behaviours of birds
and beasts and plants for countless generations.
Aldabreshin herb lore can cure ailments that leave mainland apothecaries shaking their heads and wringing their
hands. The elegance of Archipelagan mathematics far

outstrips the tortuous calculation of mainland scholars—'
She fell silent at the commanding sweep of Shek Kul's
hand.

'I could believe you are some kind of scholar,' he said
with sour amusement. 'You have that facility for ready
rhetoric. I plainly didn't make myself clear so I'll ask you
again,' he continued menacingly. 'What is your purpose
in travelling to my domain cloaked in this deceit?'

'This was the only way I could travel safely.' The blush
of humiliation was fading from Velindre's cheek to be
replaced with a red hint of anger. 'This charade ensured
me privacy and courtesy. Could I have escaped enslave-
ment or rape if I had sought passage through the
Archipelago as a solitary mainlander woman?'

'You insult Aldabreshin manhood,' growled Shek Kul.

'Forgive me, but I do not.' Velindre didn't sound
contrite. 'I'm speaking of those mainland merchants who
sail south to trade with the domains. Even those who
aren't outright pirates would have soon taken advantage
of me. I knew as much before I set out on my voyage.
Since then I have heard time and again of the wicked
abuse they routinely inflict upon Aldabreshin women of
the most northern domains,' she added bitterly. 'I
wouldn't presume to insult Aldabreshin manhood when
all I have been offered on countless trading beaches has
been courtesy and kindness. Not while my own countrymen can be no more trustworthy than heat-crazed
hounds.'

Shek Kul nodded thoughtfully as an undercurrent of
reluctant agreement ran around the crowd. 'That at least
is something we can agree on.' He studied her nude body
with insolent curiosity before glancing at his soldiers with
an infinitesimal shrug of bewilderment. 'How long have
you practised this deceit?'

'I have sailed the length and breadth of the Archipelago

for more than a full year, my lord.' Velindre looked straight ahead, her gaze fixed somewhere in the depths of the forest. 'I can list the domains I have visited, if you wish to assure yourself I have never caused any offence.'

'And no one ever guessed.' Shek Kul shook his head, incredulous. He looked penetratingly at Telouet. 'How did *you* come to suspect her?'

Telouet bowed respectfully. 'I have just carried her down that mountain, my lord. My hands can tell the difference between a hart and a hind, whatever my eyes might be telling me.' A ribald note in his answer prompted a ripple of salacious laughter in the crowd.

Shek Kul smiled despite himself before turning to Kheda, quite bemused once more. 'Did you truly have no idea?'

'I was more concerned with looking at books of lore.' Kheda spread his hands helplessly. 'Not at the scholar who brought them to me.'

'My lord.' Velindre pulled against Telouet's hold to reclaim Shek Kul's full attention. 'Have I actually committed any crime? I have lied, and for that I'll ask your forgiveness, and that of my lord Chazen Kheda. But have I broken any law as set down by your decree, or that of any other warlord? I swear to you that I haven't taken anything that I haven't earned by fairly sharing my knowledge, just like any other scholar who travels the domains. I have traded mainland lore for all Aldabreshin learning I've been so generously granted—'

'Mainland lore?' The Danak mariner shook off one of his men who would have pulled him back. 'Mainland magic, that's what you have dealt in! This woman—' He nearly choked on the word. 'This milk-skinned barbarian bitch – she's a wizard. That's what this scum told us.' He punctuated his words with vicious kicks to Crisk's belly as the halfwit lay sprawled and motionless on the sand. The red-headed unfortunate barely stirred.

Kheda felt Risala's fingers dig deep into the muscle of his forearm as each kick struck home.

Is the poor wretch mortally hurt? He could be bleeding inside, his liver split or a broken rib lacerating a lung. Might that not be for the best? What exactly did he tell them under such excruciating duress? We're not out of this by any means, even if Shek Kul is inclined to believe Velindre's explanations. Telouet, what did you think you were doing by revealing her so?

'A wizard?' Velindre's voice rose above the buzz of confusion permeating the crowd. Scorn sharpened her tone to caustic, distinctly female contempt. 'You think I am a wizard?' She couldn't shake off Telouet's hold but she planted her free hand on her waist, tilting her hip in a movement that emphasized her woman's form.

'You're a barbarian,' the Danak mariner spat. 'Magic's in your blood.'

'What *do* you know of mainland magic, woman?' Shek Kul barked, abruptly hostile once again.

Velindre ducked her head, her bony shoulders hunching. 'I know mainland wizards are reputed to be arrogant and self-absorbed, my lord. I have heard they are too wrapped up in their own mysteries to concern themselves with much else. I don't believe any have ever shown an inclination to learn much of the Archipelago since magic is so reviled here.'

She glanced around towards the Danak mariner. 'From all I've heard, I doubt one would ever find himself stripped naked for all to see on an Archipelagan trading beach.' Her voice shook and a single tear escaped one hazel eye, still hard as agate. 'Don't you think I would have found a better way to travel the Archipelago if I had all the powers the tales ascribe to wizards? Don't you think I would have simply walked across the waters and passed though the domains as invisible as the breeze? Or transformed myself into a man? Or some creature? Or moved from place to place as fast as the blink of an eye? That's what they say wizards can do, back on the mainland.' She surprised everyone with a harsh, humourless laugh. 'That and far more, though precious few can ever say that they've seen such things with their own eyes.'

'See how readily the bitch admits to knowing such things!' The Danak mariner raised his hands, inviting the crowd to agree with him.

The warlord abandoned Velindre and strode rapidly across the sand towards him. 'I see yet again how readily you men of Danak are to raise the accusation of magic against Shek.'

Delai hurried after Shek Kul but the warlord swept a hand backwards to warn the slave to keep his distance. The mariner stood his ground, though he did glance over his shoulder, only to see his supporters had retreated a handful of paces and more.

'You men of Danak have made far too free with your accusations for far too long,' Shek Kul said with cold menace. 'This domain has been touched by magic. I have never denied it. That magic, that sorcerer, was brought here by Kaeska, who was once my wife. Everyone knows that. Every hand was lifted against her when she was pressed to death for such a heinous crime,' he growled. 'Do you deny that she was punished justly and swiftly?'

He held the mariner's gaze for a long, silent moment. The man swallowed hard and didn't speak.

'You, barbarian woman, you claim to be a scholar.' Shek Kul's head snapped around towards Velindre. 'What have you learned of Aldabreshin philosophy concerning magic's taint?'

'To suborn sorcery is to be irrevocably contaminated,'

Velindre replied steadily. 'The wisest lords and philosophers are united on that. Just as they are agreed that the
innocent victims of such sorcery and those merely
witnesses to such a crime are not to be condemned.'

'Even a barbarian knows as much.' Shek Kul fixed his
dark gaze on the Danak mariner. 'Yet you men of Danak
continue to claim that the whole Shek domain is tainted,
doubtless at Danak Nyl's behest. What authority does he
claim for defying the collected wisdom of warlords and
sages amassed over so many turns of the heavenly
compass?'

Shek Kul shook his head before he continued with
mock anxiety, 'Tell me, man of Danak, so wise in such
things, how does your own domain escape this all-
encompassing stain? Kaeska was born of Danak, sister to
Danak Mir, and to Danak Sarb who slit his own brother's
throat and died so soon afterwards of his own wounds
that their blood mingled in the sands. Kaeska's sister Erazi
had married into Melciar but she was swift enough to put
forward her second son to become your present lord Danak
Nyl. Thus the blood that flowed in Kaeska's veins still
flows in his.'

A murmur of agreement ran around the crowd. Shek
Kul looked away from the mariner towards his people.
'Not a drop of Kaeska's blood was spilled on Shek soil
when we killed her for her crimes, and we conducted every
purification afterwards. I expelled the barbarian who
proved her guilt, lest he had some unknown association
with magic that had enabled him to smell out the sorcery.
What rites has Danak Nyl ever performed to excise magic's
evil from his domain?' he demanded suddenly of the
accusing mariner. 'Kaeska spent long seasons in your
domain before her treachery was discovered. If all who
had dealings with her are to be condemned, how many in
Danak are to be spared?'

The sailor had no reply for this. The crowd jostled and jeered and echoed Shek Kul's questions. Folding his arms across his chest with a rasp of leather on metal, the warlord fixed his gaze on the mariner.

'I won't kill you for your insolence. You can be my envoy to Danak Nyl. Ask him for the answers you cannot give me. Delai!' Shek Kul summoned his slave with a jerk of his head. 'Make sure these men get safely to their ship and are escorted to the edge of Danak waters by our triremes. Let all my shipmasters know, and indeed, tell every vessel currently anchored here, that no ship from Danak will be welcome in Shek waters until I have my answers from Danak Nyl.'

Shek Kul frowned in thought for a moment. 'In fact, I don't think we had better risk allowing any ship, from whatever domain, to pass into Shek waters if they have been trading in Danak. Not until we can be sure Danak Nyl isn't correct in his craven beliefs.' Scorn dripped from his words, raising an appreciative laugh from the crowd.

'As you command, my lord.' As Delai stepped forward, a detachment of Shek warriors broke from their ranks to swiftly encircle the Danak sailors, forcing them away towards the water. As the crowd parted to let them pass, men and women began to drift away. Heads close, they debated this unexpected turn of events.

'What's Danak got to offer that's valuable enough to forgo trade with Shek?' one islander wondered behind Kheda.

'The *zamorin* they deal in?' Her companion didn't sound convinced. 'Do you suppose many of those are barbarian spies like this one?'

Kheda was watching Velindre as discreetly as he could. She glanced at Telouet, her lips moving briefly. He slackened his hold on her arm sufficiently to let her bend and pull up her trousers.

'Don't think that I am finished with you.' Everyone froze as Shek Kul stalked back towards the half-naked woman. 'You may not have committed a crime – I don't believe there is any edict in the Shek domain against such a pretence – but this is most assuredly a grave affront to all custom and decency among the Aldabreshi.' He scowled at her. 'No lord would see the need to make a law against such a thing because no Archipelagan man or woman would contemplate it. I hate to think what perversion of omen and portent you have set in motion with your foolishness. Innocents may yet suffer because of your ignorance of our ways, however learned you think you have become.'

'I most humbly beg your pardon, my lord.' Velindre sounded genuinely contrite this time, looking down at her feet. As she did so, she deftly knotted the cut drawstring to secure her trousers around her slim waist.

'You had better seek forgiveness of Chazen Kheda.' Shek Kul shook his head, plainly still angry. 'But you are a barbarian and ignorance is to be expected, if not excused. You have been revealed for what you are, for all to see. I will not punish you further. Not least because you have had some hand in finding the lore Chazen Kheda has used to drive a dragon from this domain.'

Velindre glanced up, apparently about to speak. Shek Kul held up a hand to forbid her.

'I banish you, not merely from my waters but from the whole Archipelago. There isn't a warlord who will gainsay me.' He looked around for Delai. 'Make sure this word spreads as far and as fast as courier doves can take it.'

'Yes, my lord.' Delai bowed low.

'One of my triremes will take you north and set you ashore in a port of your choosing.' Shek Kul shook his head again with lingering disbelief. 'You will not be so foolish again, woman. Your life will be forfeit if you set foot in the Archipelago, do you understand that?'

'I do, my lord.' Velindre ducked her head submissively.

'I want your oath on it,' said Shek Kul implacably, 'by whatever you hold most sacred, that you will never return to any Aldabreshin domain.'

Velindre folded her arms beneath her bare breasts. 'I swear by the memory of Otrick Cloud Master,' she said, unblinking as she met the warlord's gaze, 'that I will never return to any Aldabreshin domain.'

Kheda felt a chill of disappointment undercut by guilty relief.

She's forsworn herself. A mage's only binding oath is by the element they are attuned to.

'That must be one of their heathen gods,' someone standing behind him observed to a friend.

Shek Kul grunted with satisfaction. 'Delai, have her on a fast trireme by the next tide.'

'May I at least collect my possessions?' Velindre asked quickly. 'All fairly won or traded for, my lord.'

Shek Kul considered this for a moment before acquiescing with a curt nod. 'Delai, find her something fitting to wear on the voyage. Burn every *zamorin* garment she possesses.'

'Yes, my lord,' the slave promised fervently.

Shek Kul turned to Kheda with a smile, only to be distracted by the body of Crisk still prone on the sand. 'Who is this?'

'He's a simpleton in the service of the shipmaster we took passage with to get here, my lord.' Kheda walked forward rapidly, shaking his head with a sadness he didn't have to pretend. 'I don't know what those villains from Danak thought they had forced him to say but it wouldn't have been any kind of truth. He has been so brutalised by slavers and cruel masters that his wits are utterly addled.'

'It's not only barbarians who dishonour themselves by

inflicting cruelties on the helpless.' Shek Kul looked down at the motionless body. 'What do you want done with him?'

Is there anything to be done for him? I have to try. I owe Sirince that much. Besides, he might still betray us, all unwitting, if he opens his mouth to some unknown nurse. If he ever opens his eyes again.

'By your leave, we'll take him back to our ship.' Kheda hesitated.

Risala spoke up beside him. 'If he wakes up among strangers – if he wakes at all – he'll panic, my lord.'

'As you wish.' Shek Kul dismissed the matter. 'Now, my lord, before we were so rudely interrupted, I was about to invite you to join me to celebrate this momentous day.' He smiled with genuine pleasure, teeth white against his beard. 'After all, you didn't join me for breakfast. Now we have an alliance to negotiate and I must reward you in full measure for driving off that dragon.'

Kheda was surprised to realise he was utterly famished. 'I will be honoured to join you, my lord.' Behind Shek Kul's shoulder he noticed Velindre making her way painfully across the sands on her sound foot and her makeshift staff. Telouet had stripped off his own tunic, giving it to the magewoman to cover her nakedness. Delai was walking along beside her, offering no hint of assistance.

As Telouet drew up discreetly at his shoulder, Kheda gestured ruefully at his own bare chest. 'Please permit me to dress myself and my attendants in more fitting garb, my lord.'

Shek Kul laughed. 'I don't think we'll take offence, but as you prefer, my lord.' He bowed low and Kheda did the same.

As the warlords parted, the lingering crowd finally accepted that the spectacle was over and began to disperse.

Telouet scooped up Crisk with a grunt. 'Even lighter than he looks, my lord.'

Sirince came up to join them. 'Is he dead?' he asked tensely.

Kheda felt for the beat of the wretched man's heart. 'No.' He was surprised. 'He must be tougher than he looks.' He looked at Sirince. 'I will do all I can for him.'

'I know,' the older wizard replied. 'I am in your debt, my lord of Chazen.'

Kheda held his gaze. 'Yes, you are.'

'You.' Risala snapped her fingers at a Shek swordsman. 'Summon a boat for my lord.'

The warrior bowed low. 'As you command.'

Kheda saw Velindre was being ushered towards a shallow ferryboat by Delai. 'Let's all get back to the *Tacsille*.'

In the event, they went in two boats, Telouet still carrying Crisk in the first, Sirince hovering at his side. Risala and Kheda went in the second. He was desperate to talk to her.

But I can't ask why you seem to have softened towards me. Not with this young oarsman sitting there with his ears wide open for any gossip to add to the speculation around the cookfires today.

He settled for sliding an arm around her shoulders. Risala didn't pull away. All too soon they were drawing alongside the *Tacsille*.

Kheda helped Sirince and Telouet manhandle Crisk's limp body aboard. 'Fetch the physic chest Galcan Sima gave me, please, Risala.' He knelt on the deck beside the poor mistreated man. 'Sirince, we need water and rags. Let's clean him up and see what the damage is.'

The hollow bump of a rowing boat against the hull announced Velindre's arrival. Telouet went to help her aboard. 'No, don't worry,' Kheda heard him assure Delai.

'I'll see she's ready for your man before the tide turns. With nothing she's not owed,' he added firmly.

Kheda drew his belt knife and began cutting Crisk's bloodstained clothes from him. Sirince brought him a bucket filled from their fresh-water barrels, soft scraps of cotton clutched in his hand. Risala set the physic chest down beside him. Telouet lowered Velindre down to sit on the deck.

'How is he?' she asked faintly.

'Badly beaten.' Kheda soaked a rag and wiped cautiously at the blood clotted thickly in Crisk's red hair. He found a deep gash in the little man's scalp but was encouraged to feel the skull beneath still firm and unyielding. Checking behind his ears for any ominous sign of blood gathering beneath the skin, Kheda grimaced. Crisk's amulet had been torn away, the leather thong gouging a deep score into his tender neck.

'His ribs seem intact.' Risala was running gentle hands over the barbarian's skinny chest.

'Let's hope his innards are, too.' Kheda winced at the bruising mottling Crisk's shrunken belly but his probing fingers found nothing too alarming.

'What did those bastards do to his feet?' Telouet carefully sluiced water to wash away the worst of the blood-soaked sand.

'I would say they beat his soles with a thin cane,' Kheda said distantly. 'It's a torture Ulla Safar is known to favour, for getting information out of captives. I'm told most men will say anything you want them to after a few hours. Those that don't die from the agony of it.' He grimaced at the pulpy cuts crisscrossing the bottom of Crisk's feet.

'Will he live?' Sirince asked hollowly.

'I think so.' Kheda sat back on his heels. 'At least, his body should heal. I can't speak for his mind.'

'I can clean and salve his wounds, my lord.' Telouet

opened the physic chest. 'You have to negotiate a treaty with Shek Kul.' He glanced up at Risala. 'You ought to go, too.'

She nodded. 'We should take you to play my lord's attendant for good measure. Sirince can watch Crisk.'

'True enough,' Kheda said reluctantly. 'All right, Telouet, clean him up while I find something respectable to wear. I can mix a draught to keep him sleeping, to help him heal.'

Velindre grimaced as she shifted her swollen ankle. 'Can someone help me down the ladder? I have to pack for my journey north.'

'Let me.' Kheda looked up from the vials of potent tinctures and much more besides that Galcan Sima and Zelin Raes had pressed on him. 'And I'll rebind that ankle before you go anywhere.'

He helped Velindre up onto her sound foot and with Risala's assistance they made their way below to the hold.

'I can give you a gown.' Risala began searching through her own baggage.

Kheda lowered Velindre down onto a heap of blankets and began carefully stripping away the crude bandage he'd wound around her ankle earlier. 'Please don't think too badly of Telouet,' he began stiffly.

'I'm hardly going to do that when he's just saved my life.' Velindre sounded amused. 'And given me the tunic off his back.'

Kheda looked up, open-mouthed. 'He knew you were going to be accused?'

'He asked for my pardon for what he was about to do.' As Velindre chewed at a thumbnail, Kheda saw a slight tremor in her hand. 'He told me to keep my wits about me and I might just get off that beach alive.'

Risala stood, her yellow dress in one hand. 'Does he know what you are?'

'I'm not about to ask him outright,' Velindre said frankly, 'but I'd say he suspects.'

Kheda concentrated on rebandaging Velindre's swollen and discoloured ankle. 'I don't suppose you can avoid being taken all the way to the mainland by Shek Kul's ship. We must sail south as soon as we can. When will we see you there? Where will you meet us?'

'I'm not coming south.' Velindre crawled on her hands and knees towards her own collection of blankets and baggage.

'What?' Kheda was appalled. 'There's a dragon——'

'Shek Kul asked for my oath and I gave it.' Velindre refused to look at him as she began sorting quickly through her possessions. 'Besides, we have no more tainted rubies.'

'What am I supposed to do?' Kheda demanded. 'What of Daish or whatever other domain the creature's plaguing?'

'See what Sirince can think of.' Velindre tightened a strap around a pile of books. 'Today's given him a whole new insight into this business of dragons,' she commented with grim satisfaction.

'Sirince?' Kheda ran a despairing hand over his gritty damp hair.

'His learning is sound.' Velindre paused, looking upwards lest they were overheard. 'No one suspects him, apart from Telouet, possibly. I can't be seen in the south with you, Kheda, not without dishonouring you and Shek Kul. Word of all this will spread like wildfire.'

'She's right about that.' Risala dropped the saffron dress beside Velindre and returned to her own chest of clothing.

Velindre stripped off Telouet's tunic and wriggled her way out of her grubby trousers. 'There's no Archipelagan lore on dragons that I haven't turned up already.' Her voice was muffled as she pulled Risala's gown over her head. 'But there might just be something somewhere in a mainland library that could still be of use. Keep Sirince with you and I can bespeak him.'

'I suppose so,' Kheda said unwillingly. 'But you can make a simulacrum of a dragon—'

'No, Kheda.' Velindre shook her head with utter finality. 'I won't do that again. I've told you. Nor will I teach Sirince the trick of it.'

'Do you want to wear the cream tunic or the crimson one?' Risala nudged Kheda, garments hung over either arm.

'The lightest, given the burns on my back.' He heaved a sigh of frustration.

Can Sirince truly help us in Daish? Will he want to, after I hit him like that?

As he took the crimson tunic Risala held out, she startled him by letting the unwanted garment slide to the floor. She reached up to clasp his face and kissed him, long and lingering.

He cocked his head on one side when she released him. 'What's changed?'

'I talked to Telouet.' She shrugged as if that should answer everything. Turning away, she stripped and dipped a clean rag in a barrel of fresh water, wiping the dust and grit from her soft skin. As she tossed Kheda the cloth so he could do the same, she rapidly swapped her stained cottons for a form-fitting shift in finest scarlet silk. Glass beads rattled as she fastened a latticed over-dress in the western fashion behind her neck. She bent to take earrings and a handful of jewelled combs from a small coffer.

Velindre cleared her throat. 'I don't know precisely when the next tide is but I had better not keep Shek Kul's trireme waiting.'

'No.' Still confused, though cleaner, Kheda donned

embroidered satin before helping Velindre back up the ladder to the deck.

Telouet and Sirince had made a good job of tending Crisk's wounds and the injured man was now laid on a blanket in the shelter of the stern platform. Telouet was deftly salving the worst of the gashes on his feet. Crisk stirred feebly, his eyes tight closed, faint whimpers escaping him.

'Sirince, please can you help bring Velindre's bags and books up on deck?' As the wizard went mutely to comply, Kheda knelt beside Telouet. 'Is he showing any signs of coming to his senses?'

'Not really.' Telouet looked dubious.

'I'll mix a draught to keep him subdued. He'll heal better for it.' Kheda opened the physic chest. 'I gather you've been talking to Risala today.' He glanced up to see her standing beside Velindre at the hatch, directing Sirince in the gloom below.

'Learning something of what you've been up to since I last saw you.' Telouet wiped his hands on a cotton scrap and sat back on his heels to study Velindre. The mage-woman looked remarkably feminine in Risala's yellow gown, even if it barely reached her calves and the bandage around her ankle struck an incongruous note. 'Though I'll wager there's more to know.'

'Do you want to know?' Kheda asked cautiously.

'No,' Telouet said firmly. 'As long as I don't know, as long as I'm only guessing—' He broke off and stood up. 'I'm going to send a courier bird to my lord Daish Sirket. We should be heading south as soon as Shek Kul grants us leave to depart.'

CHAPTER NINETEEN

'Thank you, my dear, and a good day's trading to you.'
Ari smiled at the girl who had just filled his brass cup
with velvet-berry juice. He handed her a slim silver ring.

Slipping it on a finger, she held out her hand to admire
the effect. 'Come back whenever you get thirsty.'

Ari smiled again, moving on, sipping at his drink and
taming the billows of his dark-green robe with his free
hand. He was only one of countless men and women slowly
circling the vast expanse of patterned brick paving. All
around the edges, merchants had set up booths offering
an astonishing range of finished wares and unworked materials. Away to either side, the lines and squares made up
by the traders' tents were taking on an air of permanence.
The local islanders seemed to be conducting as much business there as the visitors were doing in the broad marketplace. Water-sellers were sitting at each junction while
orderly midden pits had been dug at each outer corner.
All this activity was supervised by armoured men
patrolling a broad, high wall that ran away to enclose a
substantial area. A tall, solidly built keep was just visible
some way within.

'Ari!' A man hailed him, sitting beneath a sailcloth
awning sagging under the weight of earlier rains.

The bead-trader raised his cup in acknowledgement.
Despite his bulk, he threaded his way deftly through the
crowd to reach the man sooner than might have been
expected.

'Voru.' Ari smiled expectantly. 'It's good to see you. How's trade?' He sipped at his juice. 'Not too many people scared away by the news from Shek, I see.'

'No,' the merchant agreed. 'But after all, my lord Beloc Unel has been taking the omens daily, from the very gates of the residence.' He gestured towards the formidable entrance in the tall wall, a forbidding fortification in its own right. 'He's invited every soothsayer who's come here to sit out the rains to join him and debate his interpretations,' Voru continued. 'They've all agreed this domain is safe from the dragon.'

'How fortunate for everyone.' Ari grinned into his cup. 'There would be empty holds and storehouses all round the central domains if this gathering had to be abandoned. Never mind the empty hands and bellies in Beloc.'

'My lord of Beloc has been proved right.' Voru looked slightly affronted. 'You do know the beast has flown from Shek?'

Ari simply looked at him, raising his shapely black brows in question.

'Of course you do.' Voru shook his head at his own folly in even thinking otherwise.

'I don't know everything,' Ari said pointedly. 'Do you have anything for me?'

'What you see before you.' Voru swept a hand over the small boxes and coffers set out on the trestle table in front of him. They ranged from choice caskets of gold and silver set with shining chips of gemstone to boxes of soft silkstone inlaid with slips of coloured rock. Still more humble, perfectly jointed wooden coffers had been expertly carved or merely polished to bring out the natural beauty of the wood.

Ari pursed his full lips. 'You don't have anything else?'

Voru pretended thought for a moment. 'Do you

remember those boxes I bought from Mahaf? I still have a couple of those.'

'Let me see.' Ari's response was a trifle curt for a would-be purchaser.

Voru reached underneath his trestle table and produced a glossy box of most unusual design. The unknown artist had shaped the piece with flowing lines and rounded corners to follow the natural curves and quirks of the wood. Where most of Voru's wares were simply hinged or had fitted lids, this box was opened by removing a long peg slid into a hole driven from top to bottom. Once that was withdrawn, the lid lifted to reveal a complex of trays hiding deeper compartments.

'A fine piece.' Ari didn't spend any great time studying it. He pulled a heavy gold ring set with an amethyst off his thumb and handed it over. 'Thank you.'

He tucked the curious box into the crook of his arm and covered it with a fold of his green mantle. Showing no further interest in any of the merchants, he hurried away from the vast marketplace.

'I fetched the basket.' Hasu was lying on his back outside their round black tent pitched on the very edge of the sprawling encampment. They had an excellent view of the track leading up from the distant harbour. 'I'm sure my lord of Beloc's esteemed forefathers could have built their residence a few hundred paces closer to the shore.' The youth had swapped his exquisite grooming for a rougher-hewn look and plainer clothes that nevertheless still flattered his masculine allure. He gestured vaguely towards the distant perimeter wall. 'Could that all be washed away by even the fiercest rains?'

Ari threw the tent's front flap up onto the roof and dragged a cushion forward with one foot. 'I have a message box from Etaish.'

Hasu sat up immediately. 'What does he say?'

Courier doves cooed inquisitively in the shadows as Ari sat.

'Give me a moment.' He removed the peg that held the lid secure and took out all the little trays within.

Hasu got to his feet and looked warily around in case anyone was taking an undue interest.

The rotund man reached deep into the empty box, his plump fingers nimble. There was a soft click and the bottom panel that had apparently been seamlessly fitted came away in his hand. A sheet of finest paper was folded tight in the thinnest of hollows hidden there.

'Put that back together.' Ari unfolded the message, frowning over its cipher.

Hasu sat down beside him, fingers deft as he reassembled the box. 'What does he say?'

Ari ignored him, intent on the cramped black writing covering the translucent page. Finally, he nodded, catching his lower lip between his white teeth.

'Well?' Hasu set the remade box down, edgy with frustration.

'We have a new client,' Ari said slowly.

'Why all this secrecy?' Hasu stared at the paper Ari held, as if he could read its secrets for himself. 'Who's the client?'

'Etaish doesn't say.' Ari's eyes ran over the fine script again.

'Your own brother doesn't trust you?' Hasu was insulted.

'My own brother doesn't know,' Ari said thoughtfully.

'Then how are we to keep this client informed?' Hasu looked perplexed. 'How are we to be certain we'll be suitably rewarded?' he added with rather more concern.

'Etaish says we've already been handsomely paid in mainlander metals.' Ari gazed around the extensive encampment. 'So the first thing you are to find out is who'll be interested in taking those off our hands.'

'There's scant interest in barbarian goods at present,' Hasu said dubiously. 'Too many people are muttering about the taint of magic.'

'Remind them that metal melts and fire is the ultimate purification,' Ari retorted. 'Don't worry too much about making the best deal. While you're talking to people, find out all you can about what's been happening in Shek.'

'What is there to learn?' Hasu protested. 'Chazen Kheda drove the dragon out with his closely guarded lore. The *zamorin* scholar helping him was revealed as a barbarian woman.' He broke off to chuckle. 'She was lucky to escape with her life.' He shrugged, serious once again. 'Everyone's talking about it. Why should we reward anyone for passing on common gossip?'

'We want to know what's not common gossip.' Ari leaned back to reach into the recesses of the tent. Sitting forward again, he snapped a spark-maker at the frail paper. It caught light instantly, burning unnaturally fast with pungent smoke tinged purple.

'We want to know every version of what happened, most particularly from those who were actually there.' Ari tilted the page to be certain it was utterly consumed by the flame. 'We want to learn all the shades of opinion among the Shek islanders. What their lord and his ladies are telling them, and what they think of that. We want to know exactly what happened to those Danak mariners who tried to accuse Shek Kul of suborning sorcery. We're particularly interested in finding out just where that soothsayer the Danak men were sheltering had been beforehand. It can't hurt to know Kaasik Rai's attitude either,' he mused. 'As well as all that, we want to know exactly where Chazen Kheda has gone.'

'He's sailing for his own domain,' Hasu objected. 'Everyone knows that.'

'Do they?' Ari fixed him with a sardonic eye. 'That's

what they *think* they know. We want to be certain, and to find out every treaty isle and trading beach he stops at.' He crushed the ashes of the message into black dust beneath the heel of his hand. 'Just as we want to know every landfall made by the Shek trireme taking that barbarian scholar-woman north.'

'He doesn't want much, does he?' Hasu shook his head in disbelief.

'Etaish says it'll be worth our while.' Ari gazed northwards, a crease between his brows. 'When was he last wrong?'

'Assuming we can learn something worth his while, which doves are we sending to him?' Hasu glanced into the tent's dim interior. 'Is he still in Donta, or did he get back to Asyl for the rains?'

Ari shook his head this time. 'We're not sending word to him. We're to sail north to Ikadi's rainy-season market. We'll meet a merchant who'll give us courier birds to fly straight to our client. And we're to be there when the Amethyst slips into the arc of wealth,' he said pointedly, 'so we had better not waste any time finding out everything we can for this client.'

'If we're going north to Ikadi, is this merchant coming south to meet us?' Hasu wondered curiously. 'Who's to the north of there who could be interested in such things?'

'If we're being paid in barbarian metals, it could be Jagai or Nahik.' Ari twisted his fingers through his lush beard as he contemplated the puzzle. 'They both have significant trade with the unbroken lands.'

'Dangerous trade at the best of times.' Hasu looked uncertain. 'Never mind when there's mighty ill will swirling around. What about all these rumours of mainlander magic drawing the dragon to Shek? Then there's the outrage over this *zamorin*-woman's deceptions. Is this really something we want to get involved in?'

'We're not involved.' Ari waved such concerns away. 'We're just gathering and trading information. Besides, there's nothing to say any northern lord is the client. Just because we're going to Ikadi to collect these birds, there's no saying where they'll fly to.'

'True enough.' Hasu sucked his teeth in an unattractive fashion. 'So who else could it be?'

'It could be any one of half the warlords between here and the southern reaches,' Ari told him firmly, 'all of whom want to know exactly what Chazen Kheda is doing. Someone's decided it's worth their while to make sure they get word ahead of the rest. Don't waste your time trying to guess who we're dealing with. Put all your efforts into finding out everything you can, so we wring all possible profit out of this.'

'We're to be in Ikadi when the Amethyst passes into the arc of wealth.' Hasu looked up at the clouded sky. 'Let's hope that's an omen.'

'Do you think I'd consider this, even for Etaish's sake, if the portents weren't good?' Ari asked seriously. 'The Greater Moon's at dark, so there's plainly some mystery. But it's rising tomorrow in the arc of wealth, along with the Pearl already waxing there.'

'Pearl for Chazen.' Hasu nodded. 'Everyone's looking for omens on that score.'

'Pearl for intuition, same as the Sapphire, and that's in the same arc. Never forget the Sapphire, even if it's so faint and slow to move,' Ari advised. 'With the Sailfish stars rising there for good luck, especially favourable for voyaging when they shine with either moon.'

'True enough.' Hasu looked visibly happier.

Ari gave the youth's shoulder a shove. 'Go and use your charms on anyone who might have something useful to tell.' He got to his feet. 'While I set the word running around the merchants with the best eyes and ears.' He paused to look into the tent. 'It'll be interesting to see how many birds this unknown client sends us,' he commented, 'how many copies of the message we're told to send, and in what cipher.'

'I take it we'll mark whatever direction they first fly in?' Hasu cocked his head on one side.

'For the sake of any omen.' Ari smiled. 'And anything else useful that might tell us.'

CHAPTER TWENTY

'How long are you intending to wait?' A broad-shouldered shadow fell across the deck in front of Velindre. 'The day's half-over.'

'Are you trying to get rid of me, Shipmaster Suis?' Straight-backed by the stern ladder, Velindre refused to yield to the tremor running up and down her spine.

'You've been no trouble as a passenger but you've been confined below decks for fifteen days. I'd have thought you'd want to get ashore.' Suis replied equably. The shipmaster rarely had to raise his voice; a head taller than Velindre, he topped everyone on the vessel. 'For myself, wind and wave wait on no one's pleasure and I wouldn't be surprised if there's a storm brewing.' He glanced up at the pale overcast blanketing the sky. 'We want to be on our way back south as soon as possible.'

'To see how your master fares?' Velindre lifted a sardonic eyebrow. 'You don't think his enemies will be retreating in confusion now that the dragon has fled?'

'Shek Kul's enemies connived against him long before the dragon came.' Suis looked straight at Velindre, something she'd noted he did very seldom. 'I want to see how my lord fares now he's decided to challenge their lies outright.'

The mariner surprised her with a frank grin that relieved the severity of his appearance. Youthful apprenticeship at an oar had built an impressive physique and he wore his hair and beard close-shaved to a solid shadow

of bristle, black against his coppery skin. His smile
vanished as quickly as it had appeared as he looked out
over the broad quay.

'The dragon's departure finally gave him a long-sought
opportunity to defy their sly whispers. Whatever part you
played in that, my lady, you have my gratitude. But you
should be away from this enclave,' he continued, his voice
studiedly neutral, 'before news of events in the Shek
domain spreads, together with word of your presence on
this ship. There will be some who will take grave offence
at your disguising yourself as you did, all the more because
you went undetected for so long.'

Breezes welcome in the heavy humidity flirted with the
hem of Velindre's orange gown. Whoever had hurriedly
fulfilled Shek Kul's command to supply her with women's
clothing had plundered the wardrobe of someone equal
to her in height but far more generously built. The loosely
draped bodice was only secured at her shoulders with a
pair of silver brooches, leaving her neck and arms quite
bare. With nothing approaching a shift to wear beneath
it, Velindre had tied a wide blue sash tight around her
waist, drawing the slippery fabric close to preserve whatever might be left of her modesty.

Smoothing the rebellious silk of her full skirt, she looked
down the long sweep of the harbour. She gritted her teeth
against another treacherous shiver of apprehension.

Local rulers had long seen the sense of accommodating
Archipelagan merchants. Great stone foundations had
been driven deep into the muddy margin where the River
Rel's broad delta finally yielded to the open sea. The wide
circle of the harbour wall offered a welcoming embrace
to fat-bellied galleys and lean and menacing triremes alike.

On the far side of the wide dock, tall warehouses stood
shoulder to shoulder, wide doors tight locked or standing
open to reveal the shadowy promise of treasures within.

Knots of armed men stood at every entrance, scrutinising everyone passing by. Modestly dressed merchants hurried to and fro, ignoring such guards and yielding instantly whenever a warlord's lady robed in bright silks and laden with jewellery crossed their paths. The Aldabreshin women rarely spared these lesser traders the briefest of glances. Intent on their own purposes, their painted faces were unreadable. Easily identified by their shining armour and plethora of ready weapons, their personal body slaves assessed everyone who came within arm's reach, offering a warning scowl to all and sundry. Other elegantly dressed and bejewelled women and bearded men looked down from the wide windows that cast light into the upper levels of each building. Those warlords who deigned to spend their nights on the mainland did so in customary opulence.

Despite the warm, humid day, Velindre felt a chill as she recalled something Risala had told her when they had first met, on this very dockside. The Relshazri would hardly risk losing access to Aldabreshin gems and hardwoods and all the vast range of the domains' fabled craftsmanship. Not for the sake of defending one wizard woman who'd been so foolish as to risk travelling in the Archipelago. Not when everyone knew the penalties exacted for crimes of magic.

She looked at her way off the trireme. A solid stair of weathered wood was planted firmly on the pale stone of the quayside and fastened to the ship's stern. Thick ropes held the vessel quite secure, even when swells ran around the confines of the wide harbour wall. The upcurved prow might nod and strain, as if the ship sought to free itself, but the wooden stern stair never shifted its footing.

Looking beyond the stair, she contemplated the countless Aldabreshi she would have to pass before she left this Archipelagan foothold on the mainland. Even the urchins diligently sweeping the solidly built dock looked

Aldabreshin, along with most of those sturdier men unloading boats or shifting cargoes. The only true main-land pallor belonged to the gangs of slaves hauling long, low pallets along iron rails set into the cobbles to ease their labours. Harnessed with braided ropes buckled to broad belts, the four closest at hand strained to shift a load of bolts of cloth tight sewn into protective canvas coverings. Half a dozen other slaves dragged anonymous crates and barrels containing whatever mainland luxu-ries had caught the acquisitive eye of some warlord's ladies. Armed and armoured, the domain's swordsmen strolled alongside the toiling unfortunates. Three were holding small iron-bound coffers, their companions on either side walking with their hands ostentatiously resting on their sword hilts.

Shipmaster Suis was looking at the pennant flying above the galley the slaves were making for. 'That's my lord Penik Dila's ship,' he warned. 'He's married wives born to Dawa, Kaive, Tabril and Bultai. They're all here, and they'll be trading news and gossip along with their patterned silks and glass beads. Everyone in the western reaches will be clamouring for news of Chazen Kheda's actions against the dragon that landed in Shek. The tale of his *zamorin* scholar revealed as no such thing will already be spreading far and wide.'

'For the entertainment of those who have nothing better to do with their time.' Try as she might, Velindre couldn't suppress a blush.

Suis wasn't to be deterred. 'You would be well advised to leave us as soon as you can.'

Sounds of movement prompted Velindre to turn her head. 'I see you're keen to hurry me along,' she said caus-tically.

The oarsmen who'd been ordered to bring up her belongings looked uncertainly at the shipmaster.

'Take everything down to the dock,' he ordered implacably.

Velindre watched the rowers manhandle a substantial chest down the steep wooden stair. 'Please convey my apologies to your men,' she said with mock courtesy. 'The rewards that Shek Kul felt obliged to bestow on me are inconveniently unwieldy.'

'You're sure you want to take all those books?' Suis gestured at two other men, one carrying a stack of books secured with a complex weave of leather straps and brass rings. 'Haven't you read them all twice through on this voyage?'

'Three times, some of them,' Velindre said tartly. 'It's not as if I had much else to do.'

'My lady, are you ready?' A third man halted by the ladder. He carried the battered leather sack that had held all her possessions during her travels in one hand, her neatly tied roll of quilts tucked under his other arm.

'You're lending me some assistance to carry all this?' Velindre was surprised.

Suis shook his head. 'My lord Shek Kul cannot afford to be seen to do any more than return you to your homeland.' The faintest regret touched his dispassionate words.

'This is very far from being my home,' Velindre muttered unguardedly.

Suis frowned. 'This is where you asked to be taken.'

Velindre recovered herself. 'It doesn't concern you.'

'If this isn't your home, where will you go?' The shipmaster's unease was more marked.

'I have friends here,' Velindre assured him with a pretence of confidence that she hoped was convincing.

'You should be able to find a porter easily enough.' Suis scanned the dockside, his face stern. 'Make sure we see who it is. Be certain that he knows he's been seen.'

'Thank you.' Velindre drew a resolute breath. 'For all your courtesies on this voyage.'

Suis bowed briefly. 'I've been most interested to learn what you've had to tell me of the unbroken lands beyond the few harbours I know on this shore. That's been fair exchange for your passage.'

'You are, most naturally, welcome.' Velindre replied to Suis's bow with one of her own.

Suis folded muscular arms across his broad chest. 'I should remind you that the moons are a day from their double full. Both are presently within the Vizail Blossom, and shine with the heavenly Emerald in the arc of marriage. Such a conjunction is considered highly favourable for women.'

'Thank you, but I am not married,' Velindre said dryly.

'The heavenly arc covers far more than that, as I'm sure you know full well.' Suis nodded with discreet satisfaction. 'I'll take it as an omen that you'll fare well enough.' He turned to stride back along the trireme. On the side-deck, the rowing master instantly claimed his attention.

Plucking up her long skirts to be certain she wouldn't trip, Velindre walked swiftly down the steps to the dock. Passing by the oarsmen waiting with the chest and her other possessions, she felt the stones under her naked soles. The sudden strangeness of finding herself barefoot in this mainland city momentarily halted her in her tracks. Shaking her head, she forced herself on, striding over to tap a broom-wielding urchin on one shoulder.

'Find me someone to carry that chest and the rest through to the high road for me and I'll make it worth your while,' she said brusquely, tapping a pouch of finely wrought chain mail that she was wearing on a belt of heavy silver links.

The child gaped for a moment before scampering off. He returned almost immediately with two heavily built men of patently mixed blood wearing coarse cotton tunics and trousers.

'I want everything carried beyond the docks until I can find a carriage for hire.' She took the initiative before any of the three could open their mouths. 'Don't think about leading me astray or robbing me. You will live to regret it.'

The child looked startled at the suggestion, while the two men regarded her more warily. One ducked his close-cropped head. 'Yes, my lady.' His accent was an ugly blend of the mainland lilt and the sibilance of the northernmost Aldabreshin domains.

'Thank you.' Velindre managed a tight smile for the child and snapped open the steel clasp securing the mail purse. Delving inside, she caught a slim ring between her long fingers. It proved to be a copper band enamelled with delicate pink flowers on a lustrous green ground. She pressed it into the child's open palm.

He grinned up at her. 'Thank you, my lady.' To her surprise, his accent was pure Relshazri, for all his Archipelagan colouring and features.

'Which way, my lady?' the crop-headed docker asked with an obsequious bob.

'Over there.' Velindre nodded to a narrow street offering a way off the dock.

An Aldabreshin noblewoman in a flame-coloured gown paused to stare openly. Despite superficial similarities in their dress, the contrasts between the two of them were striking. The warlord's lady's dark neck was adorned with a lattice of twisted silver wire trembling with garnets and citrines, and silver chains studded with amethyst bound her profusion of lustrous black hair into a towering confection. Vivid cosmetics outlined her full lips and dark, seductive eyes. Ten or more women within easy view were dressed with similar elegance. There was no one within sight with hair as golden as Velindre's, nor any woman with her arms and neck so bare of jewellery, her face so wholly unpainted. Behind the noblewoman, her body slave was no more circumspect in his curiosity.

'This way.' Velindre blandly avoided the woman's gaze and began walking towards the narrow street. The two men opted to carry her chest between them, catching up the books and everything else in their free hands. Silk swished around her ankles and clung to her thighs and she twitched the hampering fabric aside more than once. The inconveniences of the dress hadn't become apparent when the greatest distance she could walk was the length of the trireme's side-decks and back again.

The street rapidly narrowed to an alley overshadowed by the windowless sides of the warehouses. The high buildings channelled a breeze to stir the heavy airlessness and Velindre spread one hand wide to let it run through her fingers. For the first time since setting foot on Suis's trireme, she was tempted to twine the elemental power around her. But between one step and the next she realised that she couldn't risk using any magic. It would be easy enough to vanish from this alley and return in an instant to Hadrumal, but these men and the child would go running back to the quayside with the tale. That would assuredly condemn Suis and Shek Kul to grave suspicion or worse.

Besides, she wasn't sure she wanted to go back to Hadrumal. Certainly not just yet. There were precious few people there she would call friends. Unfortunately, there were fewer still that she could even claim as acquaintances in Relshaz. And the mainland had none of the Archipelago's fine tradition of unquestioning hospitality towards unknown travellers.

'Which way, my lady?' The crop-headed docker let his end of the heavy chest fall to the ground with a thud as a lane cut across their path.

Velindre pointed in the direction she hoped would lead to the major roads circling the seaward quarter of the city. She had visited Relshaz before, even if she didn't know the city as well as others on the mainland. 'Over there.'

The men heaved up the chest with a grunt of exertion. Velindre strode on ahead. As they crossed a second lane, they left the warehouses keeping Aldabreshin goods safe behind barred and guarded doors. Relshazri merchants' yards opened up on either side, where all the wares of the mainland rested after their long passage through countless hands and endless leagues. Doors and gateways were busy with men and women buying and selling, for their personal use and for their own trade with the Aldabreshi.

Velindre stiffened as a column of bruised and filthy men passed by, manacled to a heavy length of chain. Bored-looking Relshazri walked beside them, one idly flicking his cruel whip at garbage in the gutters to amuse himself. Fresh weals on the slaves' naked backs showed the lashes were put to frequent use.

The road divided at a broad pool crowded with the shallow punts that carried bales and crates through the convoluted network of channels made by the spreading river. The barges that ferried the goods down the rolling flood of the Rel were too big to be permitted in the city proper. On the next corner, mules whickered in a stable yard, relieved of burdens they had carried, nose to tail, along all the lesser byways and highroads that linked these traders with like-minded men across the vast breadth of the mainland.

A laden dray rumbled over the cobbles, blocking their way. Velindre felt something soft and sticky yield under her bare foot. She looked down to see some nameless filth oozing between her toes. There were no diligent street-sweepers hereabouts.

'You'll get a carriage here.' The crop-headed docker

dumped his end of the chest with an air of finality and laid her leather-bound books on top. 'We go no further.'

His companion nodded firm agreement as he set her bag and quilts carefully on the chest. His inarticulate garble to his companion revealed that some merciless hand had long since cut out his tongue.

'Very well.' Velindre tried to dismiss that unpleasant sight as well as the foul sensations underfoot. She reached into the chain purse at her waist and pulled out a triple-stranded necklace of glass and enamel beads. 'This is sufficient reward?'

'If you've got no coin.' The crop-headed docker snatched it out of her hand.

Velindre saw her books were about to fall off the chest and caught at the strap just in time to keep them out of the muck. She watched the two men jog away towards the shadowy alleys running down to the quay. They didn't look back. She snapped the top of her chain-mail purse closed, resting her hand on the lumpy contents.

Turning slowly around, she realised she was attracting just as much attention here as she had done on the dockside. Her colouring was not quite so remarkable, as few Archipelagans mixed with the mainlanders, but her Aldabreshin dress shone like a flame at twilight. There was a tavern on the opposite corner to the mule stable, the doors to the taproom open wide in the heat. A knot of men in rough breeches and boots lounged on benches outside, their sweaty shirts open to the waist. Tankards of ale in hand, they were looking at her. Several heads drew close together in speculative conversation.

She made a rapid decision. As an open, empty cart rattled past, she raised a hand. The carter either didn't see her or chose not to. Narrowing her eyes, Velindre fixed her gaze on a hireling coach that had just deposited a prosperous-looking merchant outside a low-roofed building with heavily barred windows. The coachman whipped up his bay horse, the weary creature's harness rimmed with sweat. As the vehicle approached, Velindre wound a gentle hobble of invisible magic around the horse's legs. She tightened the weave, careful not to trip the animal. It slowed and whinnied in confusion, halting just beside her.

'Take me to the house of Mellitha Esterlin.' Velindre snapped commanding fingers at the coachman. He was staring at his horse, perplexed as the animal nuzzled at its forelegs.

He looked up at her with a baffled frown before speaking slowly and loudly. 'Beg pardon, mistress, but I don't speak the foreign.' Velindre scowled and repeated her request in icily precise Tormalin.

'Mellitha Esterlin?' The coachman tried surreptitiously to flick the tip of his whip around the horse's rump. 'I don't know the lady.'

Still hampered by the magic, the animal shook its head and whickered, annoyed.

'Take me to the temple square and ask directions from there.' Velindre put an end to any further discussion with a flick of her fingers. The heavy chest rose on a cloud of vivid magelight and slid onto the luggage rack at the rear of the coach. Velindre's look at the coachman dared him to make any further objection.

'As you like, mistress.' The coachman wiped his sweating forehead with a shirtsleeve. 'If I can get this cursed horse moving.' He made no move to climb down from his seat to help her with the rest of her belongings.

Velindre let the magic around the animal's hooves unravel as she opened the coach door and heaved the books, her bag and the roll of bedding inside. Startled to find itself free, the animal sprang forward as Velindre scrambled inside. She stumbled sideways and fell onto the shabby leather seats. She found herself trembling, hoping that no one who knew she'd arrived on Suis's ship had glimpsed that petulant display of magic. Or anyone who knew her from Hadrumal.

The coach rapidly left the vicinity of the docks and trading houses for the flourishing streets of shops and markets crisscrossing the heart of the city. Velindre let the noise and bustle slide unseen past the unglazed windows. Tension stiffened her spine so thoroughly that she felt every jolt and jar of the cobbles and ruts of the roads. Surely Mellitha would offer her at least some temporary accommodation. If not, what would she do next? She couldn't even relax when the smoother thrum of the wheels announced they had reached the vast expanse of flagstones paving the square in front of the great temple.

The coach slowed and she heard the coachman hail some acquaintance. 'Where's Mellitha Esterlin live?'

'You don't know that?' The acquaintance laughed. 'You've not been paying your taxes lately. You want to head for the eastern ferry road—'

As this unseen authority gave the coachman detailed directions, Velindre leaned forward to look out of the windows. On one hand, a fountain threw shimmering spray high into the air. Its wide bowl was barely visible behind the people sitting all around the broad stone rim. Some were dipping their hands in the water to quench their thirst, others merely resting their weary feet. Looking down, Velindre wrung a splash of clean water out of the sultry air to wash the gutter's vileness off her own tanned and callused toes.

Opposite, the city's vast temple stood on a broad pedestal ringed with steps. Its white marble walls gleamed despite the cloud still subduing the sunshine. Beggars and supplicants, hawkers and priests were continuously moving between the soaring main doors that opened into the cavernous interior where the main altars lay, and the lesser entrances to chapels and transepts added with rigid symmetry to the original building.

Velindre was surprised to realise that the edifice she'd always considered one of the most substantial and impressive on the mainland wouldn't seem in any way remarkable to an Archipelagan who'd seen Matul Saib's palaces. Or indeed, when compared to many of the warlords' residences she'd encountered.

The coach lurched as they passed from the smooth flags of the temple square to the unevenly worn cobbles of a quieter quarter. Carefully tended trees reached over garden walls to cast welcome shade on the paved sidewalks. The houses were freshly whitewashed, with pots of flowers bright behind wrought-iron balcony railings. Those few people walking on the streets were unhurried: dutiful servants following well-dressed matrons or shepherding lively children.

Despite the calm, Velindre found herself growing still more tense. The coach drew to a halt alongside a high wall of seamless masonry broken only by a solid double gate topped with stubby steel spikes. The coachman banged on the roof with the butt of his whip, evidently not about to get down to announce her arrival. Drawing a deep breath, Velindre reached through the window to twist the handle and opened the door. Despite her flowing gown, she managed to step down with reasonable decorum and walked up to knock a curt double-tap on the green-painted wood.

Her heart pounded even as she schooled her expression to calm authority. What would she do if the lady of the house were not at home? Mellitha Esterlin was a tax-gatherer, as the coachman had learned from his better-informed friend. More than that, she was deeply involved in the affairs of the magistracies that kept Relshaz trade free from interruption and inconvenience. There was no saying where she might be, if she wasn't here.

A porter's small door opened in one half of the gate and a smooth-faced lackey in a mossy livery looked out. 'May I help you?'

Velindre folded her hands at her waist, her shoulders back and her spine straight. 'Is your mistress at home?'

'She is.' The lackey inclined his head with the suggestion of a bow. 'Whom shall I say is calling?'

'Velindre Ychane.' She ran her tongue over dry lips. 'Would you be so kind as to pay the coachman for me? I've been travelling and find myself short of funds.'

'Of course, madam.' The lackey bowed as if such a request was entirely unremarkable. 'Please step inside.' As Velindre did so, he summoned a less formally uniformed lad with a brisk wave. 'Take this lady to the mistress, Rab.' He bowed again to Velindre before stepping through to negotiate with the coachman who was sitting open-mouthed up on his seat.

'This way, madam.'

Velindre followed the boy across a spotless courtyard that yielded to a velvet lawn where artfully planted fruit trees complemented a sparkling fountain. A flight of shallow steps ran up to the freshly varnished door precisely set in the front face of a stone-built house. The building had been designed with all the geometric rigour of the most fashionable rationalist architecture. The lad's knock was answered by another immaculately liveried servant.

'Madam, good day to you.' He ushered Velindre inside with a welcoming smile and no hint of surprise. 'This way, if you please.'

Velindre followed the man through an airy hall and into a long salon where tall windows stood open to admit whatever breeze might relieve the oppressive summer heat. For the present, the fine muslin curtains hung still and limp, no breath of air to stir them. Velindre's bare feet whispered on the polished blocks of wood making up the patterned floor as the lackey's buckled shoes rapped smartly ahead of her. Watered silk hangings of Aldabreshin manufacture decorated the walls while side tables bore a varied yet harmonious collection of statuary and ceramics drawn from every mainland realm. Velindre noted styles from Penar in the furthest west of distant Solura set beside the most expensive wares to be found in Tormalin, Dalasor or Gidesta. Roses filled bowls in styles she recalled seeing on her travels all up the eastward coast to the great trading centre of Inglis.

'Madam.' The lackey bowed low. 'I present Mistress Velindre Ychane.'

Mellitha was sitting at a delicate rosewood table thickly spread with papers and parchments. An ebony and silver writing slope was pushed slightly to one side as she examined a ledger. Setting her pen carefully down across a crystal and silver inkwell, she studied Velindre with amiable amusement. 'That's an interesting choice of gown, my dear. It's certainly striking and that colour is flattering on you, but I don't know that such a daring cut will catch on with our leading hostesses. I certainly couldn't wear it,' she added frankly. 'Not without frightening coach horses.'

'I gather I'm expected?' Velindre couldn't help the acerbic note in her question.

'I told you last time you were in Relshaz.' Mellitha's smile prompted a dimple in one damask cheek. 'I'm always at home to you.'

'I owe you for a carriage fee from the dockside,' Velindre said stiffly. 'Sirince pressed his store of readily tradable trinkets on me for my voyage but I didn't have time to turn anything into coin. I had to call on your porter to pay.'

'We can settle up in good time.' Mellitha waved that away. 'How is Sirince?'

'He was well enough when I last saw him. I take it he's bespoken you since then?' As Velindre's nostrils flared, her wizard senses caught a blend of fragrances in the air that owed to more than the perfume of Mellitha's exquisite roses. 'You've been scrying for me?' She glanced towards a sideboard where a shallow silver bowl half-concealed vials of essential oils.

'I've plenty of sources of information besides Sirince. Though he and I have known each other for many years.' Mellitha's good humour was undiminished. 'He and I have long had interests in common.' A hint of steel entered her tone. 'As I believe I also told you the last time you were in this city, there are plenty of things to occupy wizards who prefer to live their lives beyond the narrow-minded confines of Hadrumal.'

'Have you spoken to Rafrid? Or to Troanna?' Velindre stopped short, her composure treacherously threatening to desert her. The translucent curtains stirred in a sudden breeze. 'Does all of Hadrumal know about my recent banishment from the Archipelago?' She managed a thin-lipped smile. 'I hate to think what my erstwhile colleagues in Hadrumal will make of that story. I suppose they're all scandalised by the tale of my masquerade as a *zamorin*?'

'I suppose you've spent most of your voyage fretting over such nonsense.' Mellitha rose from her elegant chair and walked to a generously upholstered settle. 'Don't worry. I saw no need to bespeak the Cloud Master just at present and our esteemed Flood Mistress and I haven't been on speaking terms for years.'

Where Velindre was tall and slender, Mellitha was no more than average height and as plump as the goose-feather cushions she sat upon. The years had been kinder to her than to Sirince, frosting her thick chestnut hair with silver that enhanced rather than detracted from her considerable charm. The same was true of the fine wrinkles that deepened around her eyes with every ready smile.

Velindre stayed where she was. 'You'll have told Planir. I imagine I can expect his censure before the Council for venturing into the Archipelago?'

'I don't know why you should think that, dear.' Mellitha arched precisely plucked brows. 'Planir has never issued any edict forbidding travel into the islands.'

'He does his best to discourage any mage's curiosity about the Aldabreshi,' Velindre retorted.

'So he does, if he thinks it'll get them killed.' Mellitha smoothed the fine muslin of her beautifully cut aquamarine gown. 'But he won't be sorry that you've insisted on going your own way, you and Dev before you, and Sirince besides. The last thing he wants to establish is any kind of precedent that an Archmage's wishes should be binding on anyone. He won't be Archmage for ever and he knows it. How do you imagine we'd manage if someone like Kalion succeeded him and everyone was used to doing exactly as they were told? But I do find Hadrumal's politics tedious. It's one of the reasons I left.' She patted the grey brocade cushions beside her. 'Sit down, my dear. What can I do to help you? Beyond finding a dressmaker to turn that glorious silk into a gown that'll have every wizard in the Council picking their jaws up off their chests.'

Velindre hesitated, fighting an unwelcome impulse to tears of relief and release. She cleared her throat. 'I'm surprised to find you haven't already had a new wardrobe sewn for me.'

'That would have been presumptuous.' Mellitha cocked her head to one side, dark eyes bright as a bird's. 'I've no doubt you can manage your own affairs without me. That said, I will be pleased to help, and personally, I'm delighted you chose to call on me.'

'What did Sirince tell you?' Finally yielding, Velindre walked over to join Mellitha on the settle.

'He said you'd spent this last year learning an astonishing amount about Aldabreshin courtesies and customs.' Mellitha rang a silver bell waiting ready to hand on a marble-topped side table. 'Few other wizards would have had the audacity to do so in such a disguise.'

'It was forced upon me to begin with.' Faint anger towards Risala stirred in the back of Velindre's mind and then faded. 'But it doubtless saved my life. Now I find I'm thoroughly unaccustomed to wearing skirts,' she added wryly.

'How did you grow accustomed to being so alone for so long?' Mellitha slid a glance at her. 'I know you've always been a solitary mage but that's not quite the same thing.'

'I had people with me for the most part.' Velindre gazed out of the windows. 'Today, I've felt more completely a stranger in Relshaz than I ever did in the Archipelago.'

'That'll pass, dear.' Mellitha patted the younger woman's thigh, briskly comforting. 'And whenever you choose to go back to Hadrumal, the mages there will have far more interesting things to ask you about than your choice of wardrobe. You've added more to proven lore on dragons than any mage since Azazir. Unlike him, you've done so without losing your wits.' She raised a hand, straightening one finger for every point she was making. 'You've gained the trust of an Aldabreshin warlord, something no mage has ever done. You've sailed with this warlord to discover a land in the western ocean that no one even suspected was there. You've driven two dragons out of the Archipelago, even if none of these other

Aldabreshi warlords know that it's you they owe their
safety to.'

'They wouldn't have been facing dragons in the first
place if we hadn't thrown that western island into confusion,' Velindre said tersely.

Mellitha waved her words away. 'Finally, Sirince tells
me you were in mortal danger of being accused of sorcery.
You didn't flinch, not even when one of your companions had no choice but to reveal you to all and sundry as
a woman rather than *zamorin*, in the most brutal fashion
imaginable. Which was doubtless a deeply unpleasant
experience, but at least preferable to being skinned alive,'
she commented with robust practicality.

'Indeed.' Velindre managed to match the older woman's
dry tone. 'I've decided not to hold it against the man.'
She rubbed her bare arms, feeling gooseflesh rising in the
breeze.

Mellitha glanced towards the windows where the
curtains were stirring as thickening clouds dimmed
the daylight. 'I've had some dealings with Aldabreshi
who've subsequently learned I'm a mage.' She smiled as
the door opened and the lackey who'd conducted Velindre
through the house appeared with a tray. Two cut-glass
goblets with gold twisted through their stems stood on
either side of a tall silver-mounted wine jug engraved
with vine leaves.

'One of them spat at me in the street,' Mellitha
continued with distaste, 'but I didn't hold it against him.
Not after I'd had him summoned before the magistrates
and he'd paid his fines for such gross incivility. I've met
wizards who are quite as ignorant and closed-minded.
Another of the reasons I choose not to live in Hadrumal.
Thank you, Darden.'

'I've met Aldabreshi of good character, of bad, and
plenty in between.' Velindre accepted a glass of sweetly

scented yellow wine from the servant. 'In that respect, the Archipelago's no different from the mainland.'

'The mainland isn't currently plagued with dragons.' Mellitha studied Velindre as she drank from her own glass. 'Where we mages would at least be free to act against them openly. Do you see any prospect of the beasts flying north?'

'Not if the ones we've driven out thus far haven't already arrived.' The unaccustomed warmth of alcohol spread through the coolness of the wine on Velindre's tongue.

Mellitha shook her head. 'There's been no news of anything like that.' Outside, the darkening clouds flashed briefly to violet as a storm far out over the Gulf of Lescar announced its arrival. 'I believe such news would spread like lightning,' she added with a pert smile.

'There would be plenty of wizards arrogant enough to believe they could drive the dragons off with the sheer force of their elemental proficiency.' Velindre took another drink. 'Who'd soon learn the error of their ways, believe me. I wonder if they'd show the courage of the Archipelagans? There are Aldabreshi warlords ready to challenge the beasts without any hope of magic, to fight them with only the faintest expectation that their weapons could even pierce the creatures' hides. Their warriors are willing to follow them without regard for their own fate, in hopes that their lives will buy those of their women and children, the weak and infirm.'

'Then they certainly are nothing like wizards,' Mellitha said dryly. 'Most of them, anyway.'

'They convince themselves with their omens and portents that such bravery will be rewarded.' Velindre was struck by an abrupt realisation. 'How strange. I've spent so long alert for such things. Now I've no more need to track the paths of the stars and planets and moons.' She felt oddly bereft. 'That's not to say they're fools,' she added fiercely. 'I've met rulers and scholars who could hold their own against the wisest on the mainland.'

'I have a library of Aldabreshin tomes that prove your point.' Mellitha nodded amiably. 'And I imagine making note of such things must have helped you gauge the likely mood and attitudes of the people you were dealing with.'

The clouds flung rain down to rattle against the open windows and the curtains lashed at the casements. Darden, the lackey, who had retreated to stand patiently by the door, moved to close them.

'No, leave it.' Mellitha waved a hand and green mage-light swept through the air to deny the rain entry.

Distant thunder rumbled as the storm came down with sudden ferocity. The breeze blithely entering where the rain was forbidden filled the room with welcome fresh-ness. Velindre felt the storm's vigour thrill through the air, as intoxicating to her wizardly senses as the wine on her empty stomach. She drained her glass.

'Have you thought what you're going to do?' Mellitha asked, tone deceptively mild, brown eyes intent. 'Once we've seen to your wardrobe and so on. With everything you've learned, you could certainly challenge Rafrid's authority as Cloud Master. Or would you like to work with me on a few projects I have in hand? Before Sirince sailed off to help you, he and I were devising a plan to seriously inconvenience the corsairs who lurk in the Nahik domain. I've laid the groundwork with the magistrates here, and in a few other cities, so we're nearly ready to act.'

Velindre held out her glass and the obedient Darden hastened to refill it. She was surprised to find it difficult to recall her burning outrage when she had been passed over for the title of Cloud Mistress. Not even a sulking ember remained.

'I'm not about to return to Hadrumal to play selfish games and leave the Archipelago to its fate,' she told Mellitha abruptly. 'Not when I share the responsibility for stirring up those dragons that are threatening them all. There has to be more to learn, some better solution to all these puzzles.' Lightning flashed across the sky again, brighter, its energy suffusing the elemental air. 'I want to know what's become of Sirince and the others,' she said with strengthening determination as she looked over to the sideboard where Mellitha's scrying bowl rested. 'I've no idea what's happened to them since I was shipped off here.'

'We can try looking for them now,' the older wizard woman agreed obligingly.

'They were heading almost due south, so they'll have had the rainy-season winds to contend with.' Velindre couldn't stay sitting down. 'But Shek Kul will surely have granted them a fast trireme.' She walked over to the window, calculating rapidly as she scanned the pages of her lost route record in her mind's eye. 'They should have reached Endit waters by now, or even Ritsem Caid's domain.'

'Then that's where I'll scry.' Mellitha nodded to her servant, who promptly fetched a little table and set it in front of her. 'But Sirince has warned me never to bespeak him myself, in case that reveals him to be a wizard.'

'That would be the death of him,' Velindre agreed, the thought sobering. As the servant went to fetch the scrying bowl and the tray of perfume vials, another unwelcome recollection dampened Velindre's eagerness. 'I'm not sure this is a good idea. We don't know where this dragon is in the south. Didn't Sirince warn you that these creatures can inveigle themselves into a scrying? If we're looking for him and there's a dragon close by, attuned to air or water—'

'He did warn me.' Mellitha poured water into the silver bowl from a glass ewer Darden offered her. 'But you should know that I didn't challenge Troanna for the office of Flood Mistress because I chose not to, not because I doubted my skills. If I had set myself against her, she'd have been hard put to best me.' The magewoman was quite matter of fact.

Velindre shook her head. 'A dragon's different—'

'Don't worry that I'm about to suffer the same humbling as Sirince.' Mellitha unstoppered a vial of rainbow-hued glass. 'He was quite determined to make sure that I fully understood that everything I thought I knew about dragons didn't tell half the story.' She let a single drop of potent attar fall into the water.

'Be careful.' Half-eager, half-reluctant, Velindre walked over from the open window.

'I haven't lived this long and this well by being careless.' Mellitha spread her richly beringed fingers around the outer surface of the bowl. The spreading oil glowed green with the piercing clarity of an emerald held up to the sun. Thunder crashed closer as dark clouds swirled over the surface of the water. Mellitha frowned. 'There is certainly something interfering with the spell.'

'It's such a long way, and with the rains at their height—' Velindre broke off as the image cleared to show a pale sandy beach beneath an overcast sky. Only there was no ship on the shore. Instead a dragon lazed in the roiling surf, its scales as green as the new leaves sprouting on the bushes tangled along the high-water mark.

'It's the distance.' Mellitha clicked her tongue with irritation. 'Its magic's stronger than mine over so many leagues. It draws my spell like a lodestone draws a compass needle.' She passed her plump hand over the water and the vision of the dragon disappeared under a new swirl of cloud.

'Did it feel you scrying on it?' asked Velindre apprehensively. 'Will it be wary of some wizard in the vicinity?'

'No.' Mellitha sounded quite confident. 'Ah, now—' She caught her breath as the scrying cleared a second time.

Now the dragon was a fleeting outline of cobalt blue glimpsed between scudding clouds.

Mellitha shook her head regretfully. 'I might be able to work my way around one of them. I can't see how to evade them both.' Her tone made it plain this wasn't open to debate.

Velindre wasn't interested in arguing with her. 'There are two dragons in the south?' She stared at the bowl even though Mellitha had swept away the second image. 'When they've no tainted gems left at all.' She looked up. 'Did Sirince tell you about the rubies?'

'He did.' Mellitha nodded, a faint smile teasing the corner of her mouth. 'When he was explaining just how overwhelming the impact of a dragon's elemental essence can be. He says he really doesn't know what came over him.'

Velindre saw nothing to smile about. 'What are they going to do?'

'That's up to them.' Mellitha sat back, settling herself amid the cushions. 'We have to decide what we're going to do.' She waved to Darden and he promptly removed the scrying apparatus.

'If Sirince has no rubies to use against the beasts, we have to find them some alternatives.' Velindre rose to her feet and walked over to the window once more. Lightning crackled across the clouds. 'We have to go over everything we think we know about dragons, search out every scrap of lore lurking in Hadrumal, or in the university libraries in Vanam and Col. Then we must think of anywhere else that might be hiding some clue.'

CHAPTER TWENTY-ONE

'This isn't exactly the homecoming I envisaged when I last left Daish.' Kheda fought an urge to smooth the red silk of his gold-embroidered tunic again.

Though I don't know what I envisaged when I left Shek. Twenty-one days ago. How can this voyage have dragged so interminably yet passed with such speed?

'Didn't you believe you would be coming back?' Telouet folded his arms across his broad chest, heedless of the strain on the seams of his own plain blue silk tunic. He wore no swords, merely the dagger at his belt whose design declared his allegiance to Daish.

Kheda felt the unwelcome weight of a Chazen dagger on his own hip and clenched his fist against an impulse to toss it into the sea.

Telouet doubtless thought he was doing me a favour by finding one for me, but I don't want to wear it here. Yet I cannot discard it without dishonouring Itrac. She doesn't deserve that.

'I'd seen no omens to suggest I wouldn't return.' He answered the swordsman's question with merciless honesty. 'Which is another reason why I've given up trusting in such things.'

That silenced Telouet. He stood on the stern platform of the Shek fast trireme, frowning.

Kheda kept his expression blandly unreadable, seemingly unaware of the four Daish triremes that had followed every twist and turn of their wake since they'd reached these waters.

If they can be spared to follow us, does that mean the dragon isn't an immediate concern?

He looked past the upcurved prow as the watchful towers of the domain's rainy-season residence came into view.

Some vigilant sentry will have run to alert his lord as soon as we were spotted on the far horizon. What portents will Sirket have read in the earthly and heavenly compasses to guide him through this meeting? How do I tell him I no longer pay heed to such things without seeming to insult him and his interpretations?

The rowers drove them inexorably towards the shore. The trireme passed beneath a tall headland to slow in a natural harbour of rocky hollows interspersed with a few brief stretches of sand. A gentle slope stretched away inland, with low houses scattered amid vegetable plots and stands of diligently tended fruit trees. All were well above the reach of the most violent storm-summoned tides and prudently set back from the stream that rippled down the long incline. It was currently frothing exuberantly in full rainy-season spate.

A broad path wound between these humble dwellings before crossing a shallow bridge. Twisting seawards, the track climbed the steeper slope of the inner face of the headland. The path came to a halt at a tall gate of iron-bound and studded black wood. This was the only apparent opening in the forbidding stone wall that enclosed the broad expanse on top of the steep cliffs. Tall towers looked down on the harbour and away over the seas to the north.

Ancient warlords advise against going to war in the rainy season but that doesn't stop their rash descendants trying it. It didn't stop Ulla Safar's father attacking mine.

Kheda looked at the fortifications on the inner face of

the headland. Enclosed walkways would protect Daish archers hurrying to rain lethal arrows on attackers. Swordsmen would run down precipitous covered stairs to meet foes at the water's edge with deadly steel.

It's surprising how many people fail to notice that those walkways and stairs have no apparent link to the fortress up above. How soon will Sirket have a son to come running one day to ask him where the entrances to the tunnels are? Because there must be tunnels. How long will Sirket make his son wait before trusting him with such secrets?

Or will Sirket's sons be more inclined to complain that the residence is too exposed to the rainy season's storms? My father Daish Reik never bothered to answer such petulance from any of my brothers. He expected us to work out for ourselves that the bulk of this island shelters us from the worst of the weather while the embrace of the headland makes this the safest northern harbour in the domain.

How old was I when I first suspected that those of my brothers who couldn't naturally see such things were fated never to rule this domain? How will Sirket make such choices among his sons? Guided by meaningless omens born of wishful thinking?

'My lord.' Telouet's warning put such unhelpful thoughts to flight.

The trireme pulled up alongside a rock outcrop with steps long since shaped by hammer and chisel to accommodate the rise and fall of the tide. Several of the men and women working on the natural jetty ran inland across a narrow causeway built of massive stones. Their shouts were snatched away, twisted into uselessness by the gusting winds. Doors further up the slope opened as people came out to stand and stare, a few still holding tools or cooking pots ready for washing after the noon meal. Some began drifting down the curving path towards the harbour.

Kheda watched Shek mariners throwing ropes to the

Daish men waiting to secure the ship. 'You had better tell Sirince we've arrived.'

'He knows.' Telouet nodded towards the ladder leading up from the trireme's rowing deck.

The balding wizard climbed slowly up, deep creases of concern in his face emphasising his years. The lingering remnants of bruising around the eye that Kheda's furious punch had blacked were almost equalled by the stain of tiredness beneath the other.

A weary wizard can be less help than no wizard at all. But what can he do, now we've no rubies? Dare we have him scry for the beast? And have the creature sense him, and come here to kill him? What good will that do Sirket?

'Did you get any rest last night?' Kheda asked.

'A little.' Sirince shook his head. 'I don't know how you can sleep so soundly out on an open deck.'

'Practice.' Kheda shrugged.

'Do you think we can get ashore without too much commotion?' Sirince frowned at the knots of men and women waiting some distance from the shoreline. 'I want to settle Crisk somewhere quiet as soon as possible.'

'I'm not sure what the people of Daish will make of my return,' Kheda said honestly. 'Telouet?'

The swordsman nodded. 'I'll take Risala and Crisk straight to Yalea.'

'Yalea?' It took Kheda a moment to put a face to the name. He recalled an amiable woman, plump and always standing behind her superiors. 'Will she—?'

'She's been managing the residence's women since Janne and Rekha left,' Telouet explained, exasperated. 'A lot of slaves were given their freedom and quite a few servants chose to return to their villages.'

How many other familiar faces will I meet in new roles? Or find missing altogether?

Kheda didn't have time to dwell on such questions as

Risala appeared. Like Sirince, she wore the green cotton garb that had been among Shek Kul's many gifts.

Dressed as befits my servants. At least that should help Sirince go more readily unnoticed. Is Risala happy to abandon the silks forced on her by the Galcan wives' assumptions? She's been warmer to me ever since we left the Shek domain but I've had little enough chance to speak to her, let alone share anything more with her. Crisk won't let her out of his sight.

'You want to get off the ship, don't you?' Standing on the ladder, she turned, holding on with one hand. She stretched out the other, coaxing Crisk to follow. 'Sirince is waiting.'

The mage stepped forward, resolutely replacing his anxious frown with an encouraging smile. 'Let's go ashore, shall we?'

Telouet retreated as far as he was able given the confines of the stern platform. As Crisk emerged from the cramped cabin beneath the planking, those rowers closest to the ladder sat quite motionless. The trireme's archers and sail crew had already withdrawn to the crowded stowage space beneath the bow platform.

No one wants to risk Crisk flying into another frenzy. What manner of omen for our arrival would that be?

Risala stepped up onto the stern platform and the red-headed barbarian climbed gingerly after her. He wore a threadbare and faded tunic of Risala's.

We certainly won't chance trying to persuade him into new clothes again. And Risala will have to stay with him, for everyone's peace of mind.

As Crisk took every slow step with painful caution, Kheda winced. Raising his hand to shield his mouth, he whispered urgently to Telouet, 'The soles of his feet may have healed but the skin will be so sensitive that the smoothest path will feel like sharp gravel.'

'Could we get him to wear sandals?' Telouet wondered dubiously under his breath.

Crisk heard them. He froze at the top of the ladder and sank back down, whimpering faintly.

'No, it's all right.' Risala set her hand over his. 'It's only Kheda. You know he won't hurt you.'

'Let's get ashore,' Sirince invited again. 'It'll be safe. Trimon protects all travellers.'

Crisk shot the wizard a wary look, sharp with the distrust he'd shown everyone when he'd first woken from his stupor. Where he had looked thin and undernourished before, now he looked starved to the point of collapse, cheeks gaunt and eyes sunk in dark hollows.

Would he have been better off if he'd never woken? Will he ever speak, to reproach me for salving his wounds and keeping him sleeping while his head healed? Or has some injury inside his head that I can't tend left him mute like this?

Kheda stood quite still, along with everyone else.

'Let's find you a nice quiet room all for yourself.' Risala was holding Crisk's hand quite firmly, so he couldn't retreat down the ladder. Making an unhappy noise deep in his throat, the barbarian began climbing upward.

'I'll find Yalea.' Telouet swung himself over the rail to take the stone steps two at a time. Once on the jetty, he grabbed a lad by the shoulder, speaking urgently to him. The youth ran off towards the residence, pushing through people now thronging the path. A murmur of voices was swelling, notes of confusion and speculation rising. Then the crowd parted and a small detachment of armoured men appeared. Crisk whimpered and sank to his knees. Pressing his face to the planking, he wrapped his arms around his head.

Kheda made a swift decision. 'I'll go first and see if I can thin out this welcome. Wait until Telouet comes back for you.'

He disembarked, then hesitated. Standing on the close-fitted stones of the causeway, he found everything familiar and yet so strange. He knew every crevice in the rocks, every curve of the path ahead. He remembered the varying pitches of the shingled roofs, yet newly painted shutters caught his eye among the weathered wood. As the contingent of Daish swordsmen approached, Kheda recognised faces, names flickering through his memory. But there were too many he didn't recall.

How many here believe that I have betrayed them, that all my loyalty is now to Chazen? How can I ever explain the choices I made to them?

The warriors separated to form a line either side of him. They began walking and Kheda followed. He saw the leading swordsman brusquely brush aside a man keen to detain him with questions.

I'm not exactly a prisoner, but this is hardly the escort for an honoured guest.

He walked along the beaten earth of the path with measured steps. Between the armoured warriors he saw some of the islanders smile, as welcoming as they had always been, though more than one hurriedly looked away when they realised what they had done. Others hesitated, their confusion plain. Plenty were openly wary, glancing over towards the main gate of the residence.

A few clutched sprays of flowers or handfuls of herbs, habit prompting such offerings for a newly returned lord or lady. But no one knew whether they should strew the aromatics in his path or not. A girl clutching a perfect logen bloom stepped back, hanging her head. Kheda walked on, his half-smile betraying no sign that he had even seen her.

Sirket hasn't come down to the harbour here to meet me. What should I read into that? He managed to offer me all such courtesies owed to a neighbouring warlord the last time we met.

His expression determinedly amiable despite the apprehension burning in his throat, he walked steadily up the incline towards the residence. The silk of his tunic was sticking to his back.

Let's hope everyone accepts it's the heat and humidity that's making me sweat so.

The swordsmen on either side marched with an unfaltering rhythm. Kheda fixed his eyes on the forbidding ebony gate, looking for Telouet. His taut senses strained backwards and forwards: trying to hear any unwelcome commotion erupting around Crisk down in the anchorage, alert for any uncertain reception awaiting him ahead.

The sentry door in the main gate opened. Telouet stepped through as Kheda reached the high wall's shadow falling across the path. Kheda would have spoken to the warrior but the great double gates swung open, releasing a flurry of voices. In the next breath the noise died utterly.

'I'll see to Crisk and the others.' Telouet's rapid stride didn't falter as he passed by.

Kheda forced himself to keep walking with the same even pace. More expectant swordsmen were standing in an armoured crescent spanning the gateway. Their captain gazed at him, his face quite unreadable.

What do you make of my return, Serno? I left you without warning or explanation. What will you make of whatever tale Telouet chooses to tell you of my travels?

Two young men stood within the protective embrace of the arc of warriors, dressed alike in azure silks. Sapphire-studded gold chains adorned neck, wrist, waist and ankle. A youth whose rich weaponry and crystal-ornamented helm proclaimed his status as a warlord's personal slave stood one pace behind the pair of them. Beneath the shadow of his helmet, his eyes glittered as he studied Kheda.

You must be Zari. It seems Telouet chose you well.

Composing a courteous smile, Kheda bowed low. The movement hid the deep breath he drew to steady his nerves. 'My lord Daish Sirket.'

'My lord Chazen Kheda.' There was the merest stumble in Sirket's reply.

You look weary to the bone, my son, and anxious, as if you expect me to catch you in some mischief. Mesil looks much the same. How he's grown.

Kheda bowed again, this time to the youth standing stiff-backed beside Sirket, to hide the anguish piercing him. 'Mesil, honoured heir to Daish, I am very glad to see you.'

Mesil took a pace forward. 'And I to see you, my—' He recollected himself, thrusting his hands roughly through his braided chain belt. 'My lord.'

'My father!' A slight figure in a saffron silk dress twisted her way between two mail-clad warriors and ran straight past Sirket, taking him quite unawares.

'Efi, be careful.' Kheda stepped forward to catch her before she slipped in her haste. She flung herself into his arms. Before he realised what he was doing, he had picked her up, hugging her close.

You've grown, too, my little one. You're certainly heavier.

'Where did you go? Why didn't you come home?' Efi's rebukes were stifled as she buried her face in his neck.

He felt her hot tears on his skin and had to hide his own pain in her tousled black hair. 'I'm so sorry, my little one,' he whispered for her ears alone.

'Efi!' Sirket rubbed at his beard. 'Come here.' There was a crack of anger in his voice.

She ignored him. 'I wanted you to come home,' she complained fiercely to Kheda. Her arms tightened still further. 'And you didn't!'

Shifting her weight to one hip as he'd done so often before, Kheda walked forward, unable to do anything to wipe away the tears filling his eyes. 'May I see them all, Sirket?'

Sirket stood motionless for a moment. Then he nodded, a single brief jerk of his head. 'They're with Dau, in what was my mother Janne's audience chamber.'

'Efi.' Mesil tried to insinuate his fingers between her skinny brown arm and Kheda's silk-clad shoulder. 'You were supposed to wait.'

'Dau says she isn't going to see him.' Even muffled, Efi's voice was shrill with anger. 'She says none of us will be allowed to. I want to!'

Mesil muttered something inaudible as he continued to try to disengage Efi's limpet-like hold.

'Mesil, it's all right.' Kheda caught the boy's eye as he looked up, startled. 'I'll carry her.' He looked at Sirket. 'We have matters of grave importance for your domain to discuss, my lord. Is this dragon anywhere close at hand?'

Sirket shook his head reluctantly. 'It was last seen in the reefs north and west of the isle of Nagel five days ago. We've had no reports of it since.'

'I'm here to offer whatever help I may.' Kheda looked into his son's eyes, unblinking. 'May I see the younger children of Daish, my lord, before we consider our choices?'

'If that's the price of your cooperation. I'll be in the observatory.' Sirket turned abruptly around and stalked away.

No, that's not what I meant.

Kheda watched the line of Daish swordsmen part to let their lord and Zari through. The warriors wavered, uncertain.

'Go about your duties.' Mesil's angry gesture was more suited to shooing geese than dismissing an honour guard.

'My lord.' Their captain promptly slapped his metal-plated gauntlet on his mailed breast and the swordsmen melted wordlessly away.

'Efi, get down,' Mesil pleaded, vulnerability showing through cracks in his composure.

'No.' Her determination resounded in Kheda's ear.

He tried to placate Mesil once again. 'It's all right.'

And if I'm holding her, I can't hug you, my son.

Otherwise he would have been overwhelmed by his urge to embrace the troubled youth.

'No, it isn't,' Mesil said with barely repressed ire. 'How's she going to feel when you leave again?'

'He's not going to leave again.' Efi's grip tightened so violently that Kheda was half-strangled.

Oh, my little one, I wish I could promise you that, you and all your brothers and sisters. But I can't. What am I going to do?

Mesil abruptly decided to abandon this conversation. He strode on ahead, long legs covering the ground rapidly. Kheda was struck again by just how much taller the boy had grown in the two years he'd been absent. And his back was aching from the unaccustomed burden of Efi, who had most assuredly got a good deal bigger. He shifted her round to his front, lacing his hands together beneath her rump to support her.

They crossed the open space between the outer wall and the first circle of narrow-windowed buildings that housed the warlord's warriors and those servants who were trained and ready to take up arms should danger threaten. There were precious few people to be seen.

So most of the household has decided discretion is the better part of valour. I can't blame them.

Kheda followed Mesil between two buildings crowned with matching watchtowers. Beyond, the severe countenance of the residence softened. A lush and colourful garden spread out before them, revelling in the profligacy of the rains. Dark-leaved casturi shrubs bloomed gold and orange, seizing their chance before the water retreated into the rocks beyond their deepest roots. Stands of redlance and honey-cane tossed shocks of exuberant new growth. Milkpod and shihaya-nut trees clustered where the rise and fall of the headland offered soil deep enough for their tenacious taproots. The only signs of life were glory-birds and palm finches hopping insouciantly from perch to perch in a shining white-wood aviary in the middle of the garden. Grey-barred quail diligently scratched amid the leaf litter beneath them.

Mesil headed for one of the battlemented towers set four-square amid the curving paths of the garden. The lowest level of the tower was half above ground, half below, solid walls blind. At head height to those outside, wide windows on the next level were open to the ready breezes, muslin drapes softening their touch on whoever might be within.

Kheda followed Mesil up the pedestal of steps to the great double doors. A solitary figure, a full-bodied woman of implacable calmness, waited in the marble-floored hall that ran straight through the heart of the building.

You're still here? I thought you were one of Rekha's most devoted attendants.

'I take it this is who you're looking for, Kekri.' Kheda unknotted his fingers from beneath Efi's plump bottom and raised his hands behind his head to take her wrists. She did her best to hold on with her legs but as he eased her arms gently apart, she had to yield. Dropping to the ground, she instantly slipped her arm around Kheda's waist and pressed tight against him. As she looked mutinously at the slave woman, her mouth curved ominously downward.

'She's not to be punished,' Kheda said firmly as he gently detached her and pushed her towards the slave woman.

But I no longer have any authority to order such things. How easy it is to forget.

Kekri made no answer, simply bowing as she took Efi's hand in a firm hold. The little girl made no effort to pull away. Biting her lip, she stared down at the lozenges and triangles patterning the floor with smoky grey and blue-veined white marble.

'Dau's in here.' Mesil walked down the hall to a polished door of slate-coloured wood inlaid with pale slips of nacre.

Kheda lifted his chin, squared his shoulders and entered.

Over by the far wall, which was painted to deceive the eye with an impression of marble pillars to match the floor, Dau was reclining on a day bed upholstered with turquoise brocade. Apparently intent on the reed papers in one hand, she shoved at the white cushions beneath her elbow. If she wasn't going to look at Kheda, the youthful body slave close at hand showed no such reluctance. He stared, unblinking, unfriendly, muscular in his sleeveless cream tunic.

Lemir. Rekha chose you to adore Dau, to serve her every need and indulge her every whim. She didn't choose you for your ability to disguise your feelings.

Kheda let his gaze fall to the thick carpet of leaf green embroidered with swirling skeins of red nerial vines and yellow fire-creeper. Comical crookbeaks, black and gold, amiable loals mottled brown and engaging blue-striped lizards were woven into the design. This bright jollity sat oddly with the serene decoration of the rest of the room: tall alabaster vases set back against the walls and white-wood tables inlaid with rosewood and ebony. Kheda recognised the carpet. It had graced his children's nursery since Efi's birth.

Efi and Kekri had followed him into the room. Released from the slave woman's hold, she ran forward to join her smaller sisters on the rug. 'See. I told you he would come.' There was triumph as well as challenge in her tone as she set her hands on her narrow hips and glared at Dau.

The three little girls playing with an array of brightly

coloured wooden animals looked up. The eldest barely spared Kheda a glance before concentrating once more on the progress of a carved matia along a tufted frond.

'Vida!' Efi tried to snatch the wooden creature away.

You're older now than Efi was when I left you all. You were always her faithful shadow. But you're not following her lead today.

'Let her be, Efi.' Kheda switched his attention to the smaller girls and realised with a shock that he had confused the two of them. The shyly smiling child just leaving babyhood behind wasn't Noi. It was Mie, a babe barely able to toddle the last time he had seen her. Noi was almost as tall as Vida had been. Lustrous eyes huge and solemn, with a resemblance to Dau that he'd never anticipated, she looked at him curiously, sucking her fingers.

You don't recognise me. Nor does Mie. Neither of you have the slightest idea who I am.

Kheda ducked his head. He felt unutterably weary.

'Noi, it's our father.' Efi's insistence teetered on the edge of tears.

Paper rustled as Dau handed her sheaf of documents to Lemir. 'Chazen Kheda.'

Her greeting all clipped civility, she swung her legs down to sit upright on the day bed. The movement showed the lithe elegance of her thighs as the crimson silk of her side-slit skirt parted. She smoothed the fabric closed and crossed her ankles demurely. Such an air of modesty was at odds with the plunging neckline of her bodice; silver brooches at shoulder and cleavage further drew the eye to the satin swell of her breasts. She wore no other jewellery and Lemir's careful hand had applied the barest touch of cosmetics.

You're daringly dressed to welcome an honoured guest. Is this to show me you are quite grown up and have no interest in my return? Do your mothers know you wear gowns like that?

Kheda met Dau's cold stare with an unblinking gaze of his own.

After a breathless moment, she looked down at the younger children. 'Efi, if you can't behave, I shall send you upstairs.'

'Oh, be quiet, Dau.' Mesil scowled at her and walked over to kneel on the carpet. He drew nervous giggles from the little girls as he made a wooden forest hog prance along and knock over a spotted deer.

Involving yourself in their games is one way to stay out of our conversation. You never did like confrontation, Mesil. Whereas Dau never willingly backs down from a challenge. No wonder she and Efi are striking sparks off each other.

'Dau.' Kheda commanded her attention with firm authority. 'I left this domain in the manner I did because I believed that was the only course open to me when grave danger threatened. I knew I was risking my life to do it. I know you've all suffered——'

'Did you suffer?' Dau's warm brown eyes smouldered. 'You have a new home, a new domain, a willing new wife who has borne you two beautiful new daughters. Did you ever spare us a thought——' She choked on her fury, pressing her eyes tight shut against tears.

'I'm sorry, Dau.' Kheda twisted his fingers behind his back. The physical pain distracted him from the anguish in his heart, enabling him to continue. 'I was looking outward, at my duty to the islanders, at all the wider considerations of this domain. I followed what I took to be omens——'

'Because if he hadn't, Daish would have been lost to the wild men just like Chazen,' Mesil broke in fiercely. He set the hog dancing madly with a cinnamon crane. Mie chuckled.

'Would the dragons have come to plague us?' Dau snapped at him with the readiness of a much-repeated argument. 'Orhan says——'

'Orhan says—' Mesil mocked her. 'Try using your own wits, Dau.'

Kheda saw Efi's little mouth was pursed with an ugly effort not to cry. Beside her Vida gazed fixedly down at the toys now motionless in Mesil's hands, her shoulders hunched in miserable uncertainty. The littlest girls simply looked bemused.

My lack of dominion here can be cursed. I'm not having this.

'Kekri.' Kheda snapped his fingers at the slave woman. 'Take all the younger children upstairs. No—' He raised a hand to silence Efi's wail of protest. 'I'll come up and see you, I promise. But there are matters I must discuss with Dau and Mesil.'

At least he detected some faint approval in Kekri's broad face. She clapped her hands and the younger girls all rose at the familiar command, even little Mie, holding tight to Vida's hand. Efi trailed behind, looking backwards as the slave woman led them from the room, her face beseeching.

Kheda watched the door close behind her. 'We shouldn't argue in front of them.'

'We're just supposed to behave as if nothing has happened?' Dau had had time to rally herself. 'As if you've come back from some voyage around the domain to counsel village spokesmen, to advise their healers and judge their disputes?' she wondered sarcastically.

'I'd like you to accept that I am truly sorry for what is done.' Kheda managed to hide the effort it took not to react to her bitterness. 'Which cannot be undone. Will you accept that I'm here to do all I can to help now?'

'What makes you think we need your help?' Dau challenged. As soon as she spoke, her face betrayed her realisation that she sounded petulant and foolish.

Mesil pounced mercilessly. 'You're going to rid us of this dragon, are you? Or is Orhan going to come out of hiding and slay it with one stroke of his sword?'

'You're just jealous.' Dau rounded on him. 'Because when I am first wife of Ulla, you'll still be here as Sirket's spare bowstring.'

'Enough!' Kheda's anger rang back from the bare walls and marble floor. 'Didn't I teach you better than this? Didn't your mothers?'

What were Janne and Rekha thinking, to leave all the children like this? Even the eldest are still so young, with so much to learn about life.

He bit down on his anger as such questions couldn't possibly improve this situation. Mesil shot a fulminating glance at Dau before concentrating on gathering up all the carved animals. She stared unseeing off to one side, her neck and back stiff with outraged emotion. Lemir laid a consoling hand discreetly on her shoulder and she pressed her cheek against it.

Are you building Ulla Orhan into an ideal husband in your hopes and imagination? All this courtship has been done by letter and latterly by secret messenger, so what can you truly know of his character? Because you believe he offers you a way out of this domain, so that you can leave this pain behind? Don't you know that you'll simply carry that grief and resentment with you unless you choose to lay it down before you go? How else do you think I was able to make a life with Itrac?

A knock on the door broke into the tense silence. Before anyone could answer, the door was opened by a tall, heavy-set northerner with grizzled hair and a leathery complexion creased by years of relentless sun.

He really is enormous.

'Hanyad.' Kheda cleared his throat. 'Come in.'

'My lord.' Filling the doorway, the man bowed. There

was no trace of a mainland accent left in his words. 'My lady Sain Daish.' Emotionless, Hanyad stepped to one side.

'My lady.' Kheda realised he was staring and bowed.

My lady wife that was.

'Kheda.' Sain Daish walked slowly into the room. 'I thought you should meet your youngest son. This is Yasi.'

She was wearing a russet gown of simple cut, her sole ornament a string of amber beads above the modest neckline. Paradoxically she looked more composed and commanding than she had ever done adorned with all the paint and finery expected of even a minor wife.

You never expected to be even the most minor wife of any significant lord. Then your brother's ambition secured the domain and made a valuable marriage bargain out of you.

'You're looking well.' Kheda managed a smile. 'Both of you.'

The little boy Sain cherished on one slender hip was of an age to walk but still clung like a little loal to his mother. He had her coppery skin and the lustrous straight black hair that Sain wore in a braid as thick as her wrist. Though Kheda realised with a shock that the toddler's eyes were as green as his own. The child looked back at Kheda with lively curiosity. Then his gaze switched to Mesil, who was still sitting on the carpet, and his chubby little face broke into a gleeful smile. 'Play!'

'Good boy.' Sain lowered the wriggling child to the floor, bending to tug down the creamy cotton tunic rucked up around his breech clout. Yasi ran to the carpet and plumped down on his knees, snatching the carved beasts out of the box where Mesil had just stowed them.

The youth grinned despite himself. 'Find me a jungle cat, Yasi. A black one.'

Kheda watched the two of them. 'Does he know I'm his father?' he asked Sain quietly.

'He doesn't know, or not know.' She walked towards

the day bed where Dau still sat, tense with upset. 'There'll be time enough to tell him when he's old enough to understand.'

She sat down beside Dau. The girl's taut expression softened a little, as if she now had an ally. They might have been taken for sisters, albeit ones of half-blood who didn't really favour their common parent. Sain wasn't more than a handful of years older than Dau. Always slender, she had quite recovered her figure after Yasi's birth and looked as much a maiden as Dau beside her.

Though you do have that serenity that comes to so many women with motherhood. Once the initial shock has worn off.

'Thank you for staying with the younger children,' Kheda said stiffly. 'Since their other mothers saw fit to leave them in Daish.'

Those words sounded harsher than he had intended.

Sain looked up at him, her gaze steady. 'I stayed for the children and for Janne and Rekha's sake, too, to defend Daish in my own way while they did what they felt they must.'

'Sain Daish has ensured that the fields are tilled, the fruit trees pruned and the vegetable plots tended all across the domain.' Dau's words challenged him to suspect otherwise. 'All the ducks and geese and housefowl are bred wisely and well.'

'I have no doubt about that,' Kheda tried to assure them both.

Are we going to do nothing but argue, Dau?

'Janne and Rekha left to protect Daish as best they could with their own skills.' Sain spoke with an assertiveness Kheda couldn't recall hearing from her before. 'Redigal Coron is the strongest and most influential warlord to hand now that Ulla Safar is weakened by fighting against his own son. She may only be his fifth wife, but Janne makes sure his decisions favour Daish interests wherever possible, and at very worst, do us no harm. Ritsem Caid's newfound wealth in iron and ores has vastly expanded that domain's network of trading connections. Rekha is ideally placed to see to it that Daish gains as a result wherever possible—'

'While everyone else's wife thinks that Daish's current parlous deficits are due to my lack of experience in trade,' Dau broke in unhappily. 'They tell each other that's why I'm reluctant to enter into any negotiations.'

'Your brave daughter endures such spiteful whispers for the sake of Daish.' Sain reached out and wrapped her delicate hand around Dau's. 'We all fight for Sirket in different ways.'

Kheda felt a cold chill. 'Are the pearl reefs still barren?'

'They are.' Dau shot him an accusing glare.

Is that something else you blame me for? Would you listen if I asked you to consider the futility of imagining mindless molluscs are in any position to pass judgement on Sirket's rule?

'Who knows what next year will bring?' Sain tightened her hand around Dau's. 'As for doubting your acumen, they'll soon learn differently when you're mistress of the Ulla domain's trade.'

Kheda saw how Sain's touch comforted the girl. He longed to put his own arms around his daughter and hold her tight, heedless of her newly adult poise and perilous beauty.

There was a time when I could make everything right with her world. When my mere presence could make her as happy as young Yasi chuckling there as he plays with Mesil, without a care to shadow the sun. No longer. Now you are making your own choices; ones that will irrevocably change the course of your life, my daughter, and I've scant chance of influencing you one way or the other. Because I left you behind when I went in search of a way to save you.

'You'll be mistress of Ulla trade just as long as Ulla Orhan proves he's worthy of you,' he said curtly.

When I've held his hand in mine and looked deep into his eyes to know he's worthy of you, and crushed his knuckles, if need be, to make sure he knows how much he will suffer if he ever wrongs you.

'Indeed, my lord.' Lemir spoke up for the first time, nodding firm approval at Kheda's words.

Over by the door, Sain's slave Hanyad chuckled his agreement. 'He'll be getting the best of that bargain so he'll have to earn it.'

'I do want to marry him.' Dau looked down at her hands, a tremor in her voice.

'He's not looking to marry you for your bargaining skills,' Mesil muttered.

'Don't be coarse, Mesil.' Sain patted Dau's hand. 'If it's meant to be so, he'll prove himself for you.' She looked up at Kheda. 'We do have more immediate concerns. What do you propose to do about this dragon?'

For a moment, Kheda couldn't answer.

I never had to prove myself to you to win your hand. That deal was struck between me and your brutally ambitious brother. You're quite indifferent to me. I've been gone from here longer than you and I were married and you've no interest in having me back as any kind of husband. All you want is to know how I'm planning to save all that you truly care about: your son, these other children that you have come to love and your peaceful home.

'Kheda?' Sain looked at him, unblinking.

'I'm going to talk to Sirket,' he said abruptly. 'Whatever we do will depend on the latest news.'

He smiled as reassuringly as he could at Mesil who was sitting on the carpet, his face anxious. Little Yasi blithely set out lines of little animals only to knock them tumbling into each other, giggling mischievously.

As Kheda walked towards the door, Hanyad stepped aside with a perfunctory inclination of his head. A thought struck Kheda and he paused, one hand on the door. 'There's a slave, Crisk, or rather a former slave, arrived with us. He's with Telouet, or at least, Telouet will know where he's being housed. If you can do anything to help him—'

'My lord?' Hanyad looked bemused.

Kheda realised he wasn't explaining matters very clearly. 'He'd been badly mistreated before he came into the hands of the northern trader who's accompanying me—' An unforeseen concern momentarily froze the breath in his throat.

Will Hanyad have had any experiences in his former life that might lead him to suspect Sirince is a mage? I've no notion who or what he was before he arrived here as merely one more of Sain's possessions. Telouet might be looking the other way but Hanyad's loyalties are most definitely to his mistress.

'Never mind.' He passed through the door and let it fall closed behind him.

CHAPTER TWENTY-TWO

Familiarity took Kheda's feet down the path to the tower crowned by the observatory, oblivious to the colourful gardens. All he could see was the indifference in Sain's face and the hurt in Dau's. Mesil's bickering with his sister, outlet for the confusion tormenting the youth, rang in his ears.

'Kheda?' Risala was hurrying towards him. Whatever she saw in his face prompted a frown of concern.

'I'm on my way to see Sirket in the observatory.' He managed a thin smile. 'Though I'm still certain all those sages insisting a man can never stand under the same stars twice are correct.'

'Has a great deal changed here?' Risala wondered.

Of course. You've never been here. How could I have forgotten that?

'My youngest children don't recognise me.' Kheda couldn't help a sigh. 'Of the older ones that do remember me, some want me to stay, others want me to go, and some simply don't know what they want.' He grimaced as treacherous tears stung his eyes. 'Whatever I do will affect Itrac and my daughters of Chazen. All my choices cause pain to those I cherish. I cannot imagine how I'm ever going to make you happy.'

'You can no more go home than I can.' Risala surprised him by sliding her arms around his waist and holding him close. 'Now you know how I felt when we went back to Shek.'

'I thought I did.' Kheda wrapped his arms around her. 'Now I realise I had barely half a notion of your pain.'

Risala's next words surprised him. 'Your eldest son loves you. Sirket has just insisted on speaking with me. He warned me I'd answer to him if I brought you grief. He told me he wants you to find happiness with someone who will truly cherish you.'

'What?' Kheda clasped Risala's shoulders and would have drawn her back so he could search her face. She resisted, her cheek pressed against his chest. Kheda yielded and embraced her instead. 'Risala, what changed between us there? Why did you stop being so angry with me?'

'Telouet told me to.' Risala's voice was muffled. 'Or rather, he said I should be honest with us both and leave you for good before I brought you any more pain. He said it wasn't fair to blame you for all the things that terrified me. Until he said that, I hadn't realised that's what I was doing. He said he knew what that felt like. Then he told me about your life here, what manner of ruler you'd been, and what kind of father you were to your children.' She reached up to the shark's tooth necklace she still wore. 'He told me to remember why you'd given me this, and the sea-ivory dragon's tail. That you carved that when you'd given up everything in hope of saving your people. I'm sorry, Kheda. I've been so unfair to you.'

'There's nothing to forgive,' he insisted, bemusement giving way to wondering relief. 'You would never have been caught up in all this if it hadn't been for me. I'm the one who should be asking your forgiveness.'

'You had precious little choice, once the wild men came. If you hadn't done what you did, more domains than Daish would have been lost.' She looked up at him. 'When Telouet was telling me how you ruled here, I remembered how dedicated you were to ruling Chazen fairly. You were always doing your best for the people, and for Itrac, even though you were never born to that domain and you only wed her to save her from the first warlord to land his triremes on her beaches.'

She hid her face in his chest again. 'I remembered all the reasons why I'd fallen in love with you. Telouet told me I should leave if I didn't love you any more. Why else would I stay? So I had to admit that even when I was still so angry with you, I couldn't bear the idea of being without you. And Telouet asked if I'd chosen to sail to the western isle with you freely or done so because you ordered me. I did make up my own mind about that. So I really couldn't keep blaming you when it was my own choices that had nearly got me killed.'

'We made the choice to sail with Velindre together.' Kheda held her tight. 'I wish we never had, given how things have turned out. But I'll stop blaming myself if you can do the same.'

'I'll try.' Risala sighed and fell silent for a moment before pulling away. 'I came to tell you about Crisk.'

Kheda released her. 'He's let you out of his sight at least, without screaming like a hog having its throat cut.'

'He seems quite calm for the moment. I think it helps that it's so difficult to tell slaves from islanders here.' Risala looked uncertain.

Kheda frowned. 'There is one barbarian slave here – Sain's attendant Hanyad. I began to tell him about Crisk, thought he might help him—'

She was unconvinced. 'Someone Crisk trusts had better be there when they meet. Telouet's girl Yalea has found him a quiet room in the servants' quarters.' Risala's pointing finger wavered for a moment before she was certain of her bearings. 'Though I'd be happier if he would say something, even if it was just his confused stories or barbarian prayers.'

'Yalea is Telouet's girl? In what sense?' Kheda frowned.

Risala looked at him, faintly exasperated. 'In the sense that she loves him and he loves her, now he's free to do so.'

Did he say that? What did he mean?

Kheda rubbed a hand over his beard. 'How are the Daish household treating you?'

'With every courtesy.' Risala looked surprised at the question.

'No.' Kheda shook his head, irritated with himself. 'I meant, are they treating you as my servant or—'

'No one seems quite sure what to make of me.' Risala looked away, avoiding Kheda's gaze. 'I imagine some suspect I'm your eyes and ears. The rest probably assume I'm your concubine.'

'We will find a way to be together.' Kheda cupped her face in his hand and gently forced her to look at him. 'But you needn't be my concubine or my wife or anything that doesn't please you.'

'That may not be so easy. You're still Chazen's warlord after all.' Her smile was a little strained. 'But given all the burdens you have to bear, the least I can do is suffer silken gowns and jewels, if that's what it takes to be with you.' She twisted her head to kiss his hand before continuing briskly, 'But we have a dragon to deal with before we can address such trivial concerns.'

'I'm going to see what news Sirket has.' Kheda looked up at the observatory. 'Where's Sirince? What do the household make of him?'

'He's just a barbarian servant as far as anyone is concerned,' Risala assured him.

'He's with Crisk?' Kheda assumed.

'No.' Risala shook her head with slow unease. 'That's the other thing I wanted to tell you. He was saying there was something strange here, something troubling. He was pacing up and down, and that was unsettling Crisk, so he went off to try to find whatever it was.'

Kheda looked warily around the garden. 'Was it something to do with—?' He couldn't bring himself to say the word aloud.

Magic. The secret at the heart of all the explanations I could give my children for my absence. The one thing I can never tell them lest I see fear or loathing or condemnation kill whatever love they might still have for me.

Risala was similarly satisfying herself there was no one within earshot. 'He said something was "brushing against his affinity".'

'He's wandering around the residence on his own?' Apprehension chilled Kheda. 'We had better find him.'

Risala shook her head. 'You were on your way to see Sirket. Don't forget why we came here.'

'The dragon.' All the same, Kheda was frustrated.

'Find out what Sirket knows.' Risala gestured towards the tower capped with the observatory. 'Once the beast is dealt with, we can all choose where we go from here.' She broke away from him to head down a different path. 'I'll be with Crisk.'

Kheda nearly called out to tell her to send Telouet to find Sirince. Then he thought better of it.

What if Sirince does something to betray his wizardry? Would Telouet's loyalty to me hold fast in the face of such proof right here in the heart of the Daish domain? And I have no right to see Telouet condemned by such a thing.

'My lord?' a hesitant voice ventured behind him.

Kheda turned to see a youthful gardener whom he quite failed to recognise.

How many of the household have come and gone since I departed?

'Can I help you, my lord?' The lad clutched nervously at a pair of pruning shears.

Kheda shook his head. 'No, thank you.'

I don't think anyone can help me. They all expect me to help Daish, though. And I have no idea how I'm going to do that.

He took the path that led inexorably to the tower with its lofty observatory.

I certainly don't imagine I'll find any answers in the earthly or heavenly compasses.

Nevertheless he walked up the steps to the double doors of the tower and climbed the relentless flights of stairs to the uppermost level. The whisper of feet on tiles disappeared ahead of him as the Daish servants continued to efface themselves.

'My lord.' Sirket's slave Zari was waiting at the bottom of the steps leading to the observatory itself.

He bowed with all due deference but Kheda saw that same searching gleam in the youth's dark eyes.

He yielded to the irritation this sparked in him. 'Are you going to announce me or should I simply go up?' As soon as he heard the curt sarcasm in his voice, he regretted it.

I'm behaving no better than Mesil, picking an easy fight because I can't think how to address what's really bothering me.

Zari proved equal to the challenge. He took the stairs first, his voice ringing back from the windows as they reached the observatory. 'My lord Daish Sirket, my lord *Chazen* Kheda—' he said with emphasis '—begs an audience.'

'Thank you.' Kheda was perversely gratified to see that his mild reply surprised Zari.

Sirket was leaning over the age-old square table where the circles of the earthly and heavenly compasses were engraved. He looked up, quite oblivious to the tensions wound around the men. 'There are two of them.'

Kheda was momentarily stunned. 'Two dragons?'

'One blue and one green.' Sirket brushed a scatter of curling courier dove messages away from an intricate intersection of arcs. 'I've finally confirmed it.' He didn't sound thrilled with this success.

'Where are they?' demanded Kheda.

'The green dragon has been seen in the Redigal domain, among the islands on either side of the deep channel to the north of the island of Ocal.' Sirket traced bearings across the compass with both his forefingers: just north of west on one hand; precisely at the midpoint between north and east on the other. 'The blue one is in the southernmost islands of Ritsem.'

'So neither threatens Daish just at present.' Kheda was relieved to learn that much.

Sirket's hand strayed above the jewelled roundel betokening the Ruby. 'The Mirror Bird's tail reflects magic away from the innocent, and those are the stars in the arc of children, along with the Ruby for talisman against fire. Is that what protects us?' He glanced up at Kheda, strain making him look much older than his years. 'The Pearl for Daish is in the arc of travel and learning, where the Net speaks of sustaining care, of subduing evil and magic. Pearl and Opal bracket the zenith and both are talisman against dragons. The Opal stands for harmony besides, and the Diamond rises on its western hand, symbol for warlords in the arc of friendship. Both must surely be set against the Winged Snake, because those stars will shift into the arc of foes within days. Don't you agree?'

You look at me so trusting that I've brought the answers to all of your problems. When I can no more supply them than I could console Dau for all her anguish.

Kheda couldn't bring himself to destroy the boy's hopes, nor yet to lie outright to his face. 'I don't believe the warlords who first read the heavens would have expected us to look for guidance in the stars under such unforeseen circumstances.'

Sirket looked puzzled but still trusting. 'Because the arcs that led the dragons here are empty of any heavenly jewels?' He looked down at the table where he'd traced those same bearings scant moments before. 'You mean we should look to the earthly compass for omens?' He shook his head, bemused. 'I've seen all manner of omens to explain why no beast has overflown Chazen, my father, but nothing to explain why Ulla should be spared. Not when every indicator in the skies above or below the horizon speaks so plainly of Ulla Safar's dishonour and depravity.' Hatred thickened his voice.

'You don't think Ulla Orhan deserves to be spared?' Kheda couldn't help himself. 'If you're prepared to let your sister marry him?'

'You think I can dissuade Dau when she's set her heart on something?' Sirket shot back. He looked down at the table again and traced a new bearing to the north-west, towards the unseen Ulla domain. 'Besides, Ulla Orhan has got to secure his domain before he can think about looking to secure any bride. And the rest of us have got to free our domains from these cursed dragons before anyone will be prepared to wed into Daish, Ritsem or Redigal.'

'That's true enough.' Kheda felt hollow inside.

Just as he feared, Sirket looked up at him again with keen expectation. 'What does your lore tell us, Father? How are we to defeat these beasts?' The young warlord's voice wavered. 'We're all ready to take up our swords and spears against them, just as you did in Chazen. We've been waiting for the clearest omens.'

Kheda was horrified. 'No, you mustn't.'

The hope in Sirket's face faded into confusion. 'Then what are we going to do?'

I don't know. But I'll try killing one beast after another with my bare hands before I let you throw your life away. You won't die trying to equal my glorious achievement when it was no such thing.

Kheda couldn't meet his son's eyes. He looked down at the table instead and his gaze fastened on the scatter of paper slips. 'We will see what we can learn from the earthly compass.'

Only not in the way you think.

His voice strengthened. 'Before we do anything, we have to gather every record of every place either of these dragons has been seen or suspected.'

We won't learn anything from omens or portents but we might discover just what has attracted the beasts here. There might be something that will give Sirince an idea of how we might drive them away.

Thinking about the wizard brought one of the concerns he'd managed to set aside back to the forefront of Kheda's mind.

Where is Sirince?

'Let me know when you have all the sightings of the beasts collated, my lord.' He bowed courteously.

Sirket's brow creased with disappointment. 'We're not going to draw up the record together?'

'Forgive me, but I have other calls on my time.' Kheda steeled himself to walk out of the room and down the stairs.

By the time this is done, am I going to have disappointed all my children so thoroughly that they'll be glad to see me leave again?

His rapid departure from the observatory took some of the servants tending the luxurious rooms of the tower unawares. Kheda ignored them as he descended the three storeys and went out into the garden. A few curious faces were now daring to venture out to catch a discreet glimpse of him. He paid no more heed to them than to the nodding stands of grasses.

Where is Sirince? Will there be anything here he can find to use against the dragons?

He headed for the tower Risala had pointed out to him. It had been Rekha Daish's stronghold.

If Janne or Rekha were still here, I'd wonder what message or rebuke was woven into this decision to house me and my paltry retinue here. But I don't imagine Sain had anything else in mind beyond the practicalities.

Kheda took the wide steps up to the main double doors two at a time. As he reached the threshold, he froze. He could hear children's laughter inside.

Efi's laughter. And one of the littlest ones.

He crossed the corridor in a few rapid paces and pushed the door to Rekha's old audience chamber wide. 'What is going on here?' he demanded sternly.

Efi jumped up, startled. 'My father.' Flushed, with her tousled hair escaping its silver combs, she was kneeling with Mie in the midst of a prodigious heap of cushions piled on the dais on the far side of the room.

No, it's not Mie. It's Noi!

As Kheda corrected himself angrily, the cushions erupted to reveal Crisk. Noi stumbled backwards, giggling. Quick as thought, Crisk reached out to save her from stepping unawares off the dais to a painful fall onto the hard marble floor.

Kheda took a pace forward before he managed to halt his blind impulse to drag the barbarian bodily away from his little girls.

Because I don't know if I could restrain him in a frenzy without Telouet's help and I can't risk my children being injured in such a fracas.

'Come away, Efi, and you too, Noi.' He did his best to keep his voice calm.

Crisk gently set little Noi on her feet. She sank down onto a cushion and hugged her knees. Crisk rose to his feet, dishevelled and sweaty, watching Kheda warily.

'We wanted to see you. We came to find you.' Efi's pointed chin quivered despite her best efforts. 'You weren't here and he wanted to play,' she burst out defiantly, a tear finally escaping one bright eye.

Crisk's face crumpled and Kheda took another pace forward before he realised what he was doing.

'Don't worry. He's not going to hurt them.'

Sirince's words startled Kheda almost as much as his own arrival had surprised Efi. He saw the older man sitting unnoticed in one of the many curtained niches that lined the walls of the wide chamber. It was the only niche that hadn't been completely stripped of its cushions.

'What—' Kheda couldn't decide whether he was relieved to find the wizard here or furious that the old man had allowed his children to romp with such a chancy playmate. Though now he saw Crisk's concern was all for Efi, his distress mirroring her own. The barbarian had taken the little girl's hand and was stroking it, making shushing noises. She giggled despite herself and tugged her hand away. The barbarian smiled cheerfully, making no effort to keep hold of her.

'What's he doing here?' Kheda demanded tersely. 'Where's Risala?'

'Gone to find Telouet. To find out something.' Sirince shook his head, contemplative. 'There's a puzzle here.'

Kheda walked reluctantly towards the mage, still keeping an alert eye on Crisk. The barbarian lifted up a cushion and hid his face behind it. Efi giggled as he peeped out at her, first over the top, then around the side. Noi's delight rose to an ear-splitting squeal.

Sirince winced. 'Why are little girls always so shrill?'

Kheda paused as he bent to pull up a cushion for himself. 'You have children?'

Why did I never think to ask that before? The man must have had a life before he came to the Archipelago.

'Several. They live with their mothers.' Sirince's dismissive tone was at odds with his regretful expression. 'Men such as myself aren't apt to make the best of fathers. You know what it's like when other responsibilities take up so much of your time.'

Don't have the impertinence to pity me, barbarian.

He sat down beside Sirince, all his attention still fixed on Crisk. 'What's puzzling you?'

Sirince's eyes grew vague and unfocused. 'What's kept in the lowest level of the tower at the north-western corner of this inner ward?'

Kheda saw Crisk toss aside his cushion and begin a gentle clapping game with Efi. 'That's the treasury.' He spared Sirince a warning look. 'We don't assume every barbarian to reach these waters is a thief, not like the northern domains, but you had better not be found trying to get in there. What are you looking for, anyway?' Faint hope struggled to find a way through the cares ensnaring him. 'Could we lure the beasts away with gems, as we did in Chazen?'

Sirince shot him a mordant glance. 'To buy them off until they forge an egg and create a new life that we'd just have to kill as well?'

Kheda curbed ready anger stemming from all his frustrations. 'Then what are you thinking?'

'That all depends on what's in that treasury.' Sirince shivered like a man caught in an unexpected breeze. 'There's something very strange in there.'

'Strange? How?' Kheda hesitated.

Is there any possibility we'll be overheard condemning ourselves out of our own mouths? Not unless there's been some

*major rebuilding done here. There are none of the hidden
passages concealing greedy ears that Ulla Safar relies on.
Rekha saw no need for more than the touching trust people
show when a thin curtain of silk offers an illusion of privacy.*

'Strange and wrong,' Sirince said austerely.

'Does it threaten my children?' Kheda demanded.

'No.' Sirince was quite certain. He shivered again. 'But
it grates on my nerves like a sour tone in a musician's
melody.'

The door opened and Risala entered. Efi and Noi
paused briefly in their game to smile winningly at her.
Crisk smiled almost as cheerfully, patiently waiting for
the little girls.

Risala grinned briefly before hurrying to join Sirince
and Kheda. The mage had only managed to retain two
cushions so Kheda shifted to offer her a share of his.

'You said the strangeness was strongest at the southern
corner of the tower?' She sat down, her voice low.

Sirince sat forward, half-eager, half-apprehensive.
'Yes.'

Risala looked at Kheda. 'That's where they sequestered
the gems that Chazen traded for pots and pans and cloth
and everything else that the domain needed to make good
the devastation wrought by the wild men and the first
dragon.'

'Sequestered?' That made no sense to Kheda. 'Why?'

'Because Janne Daish wasn't certain there might not
be some miasma of ill luck surrounding them,' Risala said
with careful neutrality.

He tried not to be distracted by the warmth of her
pressed close against his arm. 'How did you find this out?'

'I asked Telouet.' Risala made that sound obvious.

'He didn't wonder at such a question?' Kheda asked
uneasily.

Risala wasn't bothered. 'He knows we had those fractured rubies that drove the dragon out of Shek. Once I found out the treasury was in the base of that tower, I asked if he knew where all the gems had come from, in case there might be something we could use against the dragon.'

'But why would gems from Chazen—' Sirince wondered.

'Dev.' Abrupt realisation shocked Kheda. 'Janne was right to be suspicious.'

'What do you mean?' Sirince asked, frustrated.

Risala knew what Kheda was talking about. 'They're the gems from the cave where Dev died.'

The warlord tasted sour bile. 'I told Itrac to keep them separate, to use them in trade with Ulla Safar. If there was any ill luck to be had, I favoured sharing it with him.'

Itrac plainly favoured sharing just a little with Daish. She didn't enjoy being humiliated by Janne and Rekha. They didn't spare her, never mind that they had formerly been my wives.

'Janne Daish always had the best informed network of eyes and ears,' Risala observed wryly. 'She must have suspected something.'

'I don't imagine she knows that ill luck's the last thing those gems have brought Daish.' Sirince chuckled.

'What do you mean?' Kheda hardly dared hope, lest he be disappointed.

'If those gems were in the cave when Dev died, when he killed the nascent dragon . . .' Sirince leaned forward, his words barely more than a whisper. 'Even if they weren't part of the egg, they'll resonate in elemental sympathy with that death. With both those deaths.'

'Like the ruby fragments,' Risala breathed.

Kheda felt light-headed. 'Can you use those gems in the way Velindre showed you?'

'No.' Sirince shook his head.

'Why not?' Risala demanded heatedly, her words shockingly loud.

'The resonance just isn't strong enough.' Regret deepened Sirince's wrinkles. 'But it's been strong enough to keep the beasts from landing anywhere close. It will probably be sufficient to save your son's treasury if one of those dragons gets an itch to propagate itself.'

Kheda barely registered that reassurance. 'We handed Ulla Safar the means to ward off dragons without even realising it,' he said bitterly.

'What do you mean?' Sirince looked from Kheda to Risala for an explanation.

'Itrac traded with Ulla Safar's wives for a great many things to rebuild the Chazen residences.' Kheda shook his head. 'Consoling herself that she was repaying them with the misfortune in those gems. I was happy to let her do it. If the Ulla wives saw us as a fertile trading partner to be mercilessly milked, I hoped they might just find a way to dissuade Safar from concocting some revenge for me escaping his plot to kill me.'

'So now we know why no dragons have set foot in Ulla territory.' Risala was sickened.

'That's a very big domain.' Sirince pursed speculative lips. 'Just how many of those gems do you suppose Ulla Safar has?'

'But you said they couldn't be used like the ruby fragments.' Obstinate hope nevertheless taunted Kheda.

'The quantity we have here couldn't.' New vigour brightened the wizard's faded eyes. 'But enough of them? It would be worth trying.'

'Would those still in Chazen combined with those held by Daish be enough?' wondered Risala.

'No.' It was Kheda who answered her. 'If those gems and these are protecting the two domains, we're not removing them. That's some recompense to my children for all they've suffered, even if they don't realise it.' He raised a hand to silence the others as he thought fast and furiously. 'We'll take what we want from Ulla Safar,' he concluded ominously. 'And settle a few old accounts at the same time.'

My father always said to think any action through before taking it, because the stars always follow the heavenly compass back to the same point, bringing the consequences round, too. Safar can learn that he'd have been well advised to do the same.

CHAPTER TWENTY-THREE

The knock on the door sounded shockingly loud. Velindre froze. Sunlight lanced through the tall, narrow windows of the silent tower room to strike the brass handles on the cupboards set on either side of the fireplace. The hearth was swept quite bare for the summer. A high-backed leather chair and an empty side table stood disregarded by the fireplace, the mantel shelf above barren of any personal touch. On the opposite wall, books were neatly shelved from floor to ceiling, their regular ranks only broken by parchments and scrolls stacked in orderly piles.

'Velindre? I know you're in there,' a voice said petulantly. 'Don't think I'll just go away if you don't answer.'

Stifling a sigh, the magewoman put down the book she'd been leafing through and went to unlock the heavy oak door.

'Ely.' Velindre stood on the threshold, not quite barring entry but plainly indicating she was occupied.

Her visitor wasn't about to take the hint. Slender and petite, she slipped deftly past Velindre. The gauzy wrap draped over her elbows fluttered as she fanned herself with a delicate hand. 'Don't you find this heat oppressive? At least it's cooler indoors.' Her bright chestnut eyes rapidly assessed the open books spread all over the table and the rest piled on the floor still closed. 'I had no idea you were back in Hadrumal, and for a handful of days now. I'd have thought you'd have sent word before I heard it from one of the laundry maid's gossip.' There was an edge of rebuke beneath her light-hearted chatter.

'I don't intend staying long,' Velindre said neutrally, closing the door reluctantly.

'You have to eat. Come to dinner with me and Galen this evening,' Ely invited generously. 'Just the three of us in the pupil-master's parlour. Unless you're already engaged to dine with your father, or your mother, perhaps?'

'My parents have as little interest in seeing me as I have in seeing them.' Velindre shrugged. 'If they want to know how I'm faring they can scry for me.'

'Did the maids take it on themselves to pack away all your paintings and anything else they found inconvenient to dust?' Ely's gaze lingered on two chests undisturbed and out of the way beneath the windows. 'Or perhaps the Cloud Master sent word that these rooms might be required for some other mage?'

'I neither know nor care,' Velindre said briskly. 'I'm sorry, Ely. I can't help you fuel rumour for or against the hall servants or Rafrid or anyone else. What else can I do for you?'

'I just thought I'd come and say hello.' Satisfied she had taken in every detail of the room, Ely's gaze turned to Velindre herself, half-incredulous, half-avid. 'Rumour had it you'd gone off to study with that madman Azazir, despite the Archmage's decree that he should be shunned. Then other people were saying you had set sail for the Archipelago.' Unbidden, she lifted a pile of books from one of the upright chairs beside the table and sat down. The full skirts of her low-cut sleeveless gown of emerald linen flowed around her neat ankles and soft calfskin shoes.

'I've done both,' Velindre replied steadily. 'I'm hardly the first wizard to make either journey.'

'You're one of very few who hasn't rapidly reappeared in a cloud of dust.' Ely's artless admiration invited explanation. 'How did you avoid translocating yourself away from some mob of savages' skinning knives?'

'Because I took care not to offend local beliefs,' Velindre lied without a qualm.

'Why did you cut your hair?' Ely's fine-boned hand strayed unconsciously to her own immaculate coiffure. Her long black tresses were piled high to accentuate delicate prettiness now enhanced with skilful cosmetics rather than the bloom of youth.

'On account of the heat.' Velindre reached down to take the books that Ely still clasped on her lap.

The other magewoman held on to them just long enough to read the faded titles stamped into the creased leather spines. 'You're reading Otrick's diaries? You *are* looking to bring some new discovery before the Council? Something about dragons? That's why you've come back?'

'Why would you think that?' Velindre set the small volumes down beside the inkstand pushed to one side of the table. Quills and knife lay ready in the tray below the glass well freshly filled with dark ink.

Ely shrugged one pale shoulder, setting her delicately wrought beryl and silver necklace shimmering. 'There's all manner of discussion and debate about dragons in all the halls and libraries.'

'Saying what, precisely?' Velindre moved a sheaf of parchments from the other upright chair and sat down. She smoothed her blue muslin dress, higher necked and more severe in cut than Ely's. 'I imagine you're still the first with any gossip.'

'You were always glad enough to hear my news when you were cherishing ambitions to be Cloud Mistress,' the petite magewoman commented, sardonic.

'Times change,' Velindre said tersely.

'And people,' Ely observed speculatively. 'Or so they say.'

Velindre refused the challenge. 'What's the chatter about dragons in the halls and libraries?'

'Beyond wondering why you've plundered every shelf for any book that has half a line written on the beasts?' Ely asked with a spurious air of innocence.

'Just tell me what you know.' Velindre folded her arms and leaned back against the unyielding wooden chair. 'Don't you want to be the first to know exactly what I've been doing? Isn't that a fair trade?'

'You never used to bargain like a merchant.' Ely coloured slightly, twisting the silken fringe of her sage-green wrap around one finger. 'But if we're reduced to the level of the market square, rumour has it there are dragons flying across the Archipelago. Is that true?'

'It is,' Velindre said grimly. 'And you can take it from me that nothing you've ever read conveys half the truth about the elemental power of a dragon's aura. Or accurately details the impact it has upon a mage's affinity.'

'That's the new knowledge you'll be using to challenge Rafrid?' Ely leaned forward, keen-eyed.

Velindre shook her head. 'I've no intention of starting any dispute over his office.'

Ely shook her own head in patent disbelief. 'Why else would you come back? You can tell me,' she persisted. 'You could be so useful to Galen if you can claim the rank of Cloud Mistress. He'll certainly be useful to you, before you challenge Rafrid openly, and afterwards.'

'You accuse me of trading like a merchant. Does Galen honestly think he stands any chance of becoming Stone Master?' Velindre didn't hide her scepticism.

Ely studied her for a long moment. 'You never used to be so dismissive of his ambitions.' There was more curiosity than indignation in her words. 'Have you really given up any thought of challenging Rafrid?'

'Ely, the petty rivalries of this place hold absolutely no interest for me now.' Velindre surprised herself and her visitor with a genuine smile. 'Rafrid's welcome to the Cloud Mastery. I wish him every joy in managing the instruction of half-baked apprentices and quarrelsome pupils.' Her voice took on a taunting edge. 'If you really want to see Galen as Stone Master, enjoying whatever power you think you'll wield as his wife or betrothed, you should persuade him to leave Hadrumal for a while. I've learned more travelling the Archipelago for a year and a half than I did in the previous ten years in Hadrumal's libraries.'

'Hadrumal's libraries are a lot less perilous than even mainland roads.' Ely folded her arms, pulling her wrap tight around her shoulders. 'Only the deluded or desperate would venture into the Archipelago. What could southern savages who won't even countenance magic teach us?'

'The dangers of arrogance and closed-mindedness?' Velindre shot back. 'The benefits of not focusing so narrowly on some imagined future that one loses sight of what's at hand to be learned?'

'You've certainly learned to prevaricate like one of their philosophers,' Ely remarked coldly. 'The fact that *you* were prepared to take insane risks and somehow managed to survive doesn't recommend such a course of action to the rest of us.' She glanced around the unlived-in room, her face accusing. 'So you're not proposing to share this dragon lore with any of us?'

'I shall share what every Element Master needs to know, so they can warn off their more foolish pupils who might be tempted to try tasting a dragon's power for themselves,' Velindre said grimly as she rose to her feet. 'Beyond that, these dragons pose a grave threat to the Aldabreshi and I'm searching for some way to help remove them. So if you'll excuse me—'

'You strive to save savages who'd thank you for your magic by cutting your throat?' Ely stayed stubbornly seated. 'If you have new lore on the elemental natures of dragons, you should be sharing it all, from every confirmed discovery to the least supposition. A mage's highest responsibility is to the greater good of wizardry,' she said sententiously.

'Then I'm plainly unsuited to the rank of Cloud Mistress and it's to the good of all wizardry that I now realise it.' Velindre walked to the door and opened it. 'At the moment, I see my principal responsibility as helping to save as many Aldabreshin savages as I can. Even if they would see me dead before they showed any gratitude. So, if you'll excuse me, I have a great deal of reading to do.'

'Perhaps you'll need this.' The saturnine man who was sitting unnoticed on the stone spiral stair outside the dark door proffered a slim book. The covers were battered and the pages dog-eared and torn.

'Who are you?' Velindre stared at him, nonplussed. 'Do you make a habit of listening at doors?'

'One can hear voices without hearing the details of a discussion.' Unhurried, he rose to his feet and bowed to her in a courtly style. 'I was brought up to believe it's impolite to interrupt someone else's conversation.' His mainland accent and his Tormalin clothes were as untypical of Hadrumal as his manners.

'Who is it?' Curiosity spurred Ely to her feet and halfway to the door.

'He has yet to introduce himself,' Velindre said dryly as she took the book the man was holding out. Standing upright, he proved to be half a head taller than she was.

'My name is Lasul.' He bowed to Ely. 'Newly arrived from Relshaz.'

'You're a mage.' Ely's sharp eyes took in every detail of his polished dark leather boots, buff broadcloth breeches and the full-skirted grey coat most fashionably cut from fine and costly wool woven light enough for summer wear. 'One of those who proved unsuited to life here in Hadrumal?' There was the slightest hint of disdain in her question.

'One who has preferred to see what opportunities may be found elsewhere.' Lasul smiled placidly. 'One who has found them pleasantly profitable.' His smile widened as his steely grey eyes challenged Ely, crow's-feet deepening at their corners. Where Ely was a year or so older than Velindre, he could have been anything up to a handful of years her senior.

'You've come from Relshaz?' Velindre claimed his attention. 'Do you know Mellitha Esterlin?'

He turned to her. 'I'm to present you with her compliments along with that book.'

'What is it?' Ely craned her head to look for some indication on the anonymous brown binding.

Velindre glanced briefly at the spine. 'Nothing of consequence. But do come in, master mage. Tell me how Mellitha is.'

She stepped away from the door and Lasul followed, leaving Ely wrong-footed on the threshold. Velindre resumed her seat on one side of the book-laden table. Lasul promptly took the other chair.

'I imagine I'll see you later.' Velindre spared Ely a farewell nod. She opened the battered brown book and perused the first page. 'Give my regards to Galen.'

'Good day to you, madam mage,' Lasul chimed in politely.

Ely spared him the briefest suggestion of a curtsey.

'Till later, Velindre. Don't forget you're to dine with us.' Her smile sweet, she departed, apparently intent on settling the drape of her gauzy green wrap.

'Would you care to shut the door?' Velindre raised a golden eyebrow at this second uninvited guest of the day. 'Or do you think that risks finding some other curious ear pressed against it?'

'That depends on the wizard.' Lasul pursed his lips judiciously. 'A mage with an air affinity such as yourself can eavesdrop from any distance. Both water and fire can be blended with shifting breezes. Even a mage attuned to earth could probably make something out from anywhere else in this building, if he wove his consciousness into the stones.'

'What's your element?' Velindre asked bluntly.

'Water,' Lasul answered readily as he left his seat to close the oaken door with a solid clunk. 'As your friend will rapidly discover. I take it she has gone to find out whatever she can about me?'

'What will Flood Mistress Troanna say about you? Ely will go straight to her,' Velindre warned.

'There are many reasons why I prefer to live away from Hadrumal. The incessant nosiness into everyone else's business comes high on the list.' Lasul walked over to the tall window and looked out across the roofs and quadrangles of the close-knit buildings. 'But Troanna hasn't seen me in nearly twenty years since I spent the summer seasons as her pupil. She won't have much to tell beyond the fact that my hair was wholly black in those days.' Though his brows were still darkly emphatic, the silver at his temples was spreading inexorably through the rest of his close-cropped, slightly receding hair.

'You live in Relshaz?' Velindre turned a stained page in the battered book and frowned at the crabbed and blurred script. 'Is that how you know Mellitha?'

'We have our element in common.' Lasul leaned back against the stone sill. 'And other interests. She told you about her plan to frustrate the corsairs who have been raiding the coasts of Caladhria and Ensaimin. I'm here to find some mages willing to settle in the towns between Col and Pinerin, to keep a weather eye out for their ships.'

'Does Planir know?' Velindre queried tartly.

Lasul smiled with a shake of his head. 'You really don't know Planir that well, do you?'

'And you do?' she retorted.

'I know he's always happy to see mages travel to learn more of the lands and people outside Hadrumal's confines,' Lasul assured her. 'He never held Otrick back, did he?'

Velindre looked down at the book again. 'So you share Mellitha's fascination with the twisted theories and dangerous obsessions of Azazir T'Aleonne?' She shut the creased tome with a snap and held it up accusingly. 'Do you have any idea where she got this? I thought all his journals were long since lost or destroyed by the Council.'

'You misunderstand me.' Lasul's smile hinted at unforeseen charm. 'Mellitha said you'd want to see the book, but I'm the one who found it. I brought it to her, which she found more than a little exasperating, given you'd just left after thirty days and more of scouring the shelves of antiquarian book dealers.'

'Where did you get it?' Velindre wasn't about to be distracted.

Lasul crossed his long legs at the ankle and folded his arms. 'I found a village in the wilds of Gidesta where Azazir had spent some time many years ago. He was inclined to abandon his possessions whenever he became fascinated by a new idea. I bought a chest of his discards from an alewife.'

'In Gidesta?' Velindre stared at Lasul, unblinking. 'Did you go and see him?' she demanded harshly. 'Didn't Mellitha warn you he's deranged? He's utterly in thrall to his element. He'll force you to a communion that could be the death of you.' She couldn't go on. The terrifying memories of her own dealings with the insane wizard assailed her.

'Mellitha warned me.' Lasul's grey eyes met hers. 'But he's gone.'

'Gone?' Velindre shook her head in denial. 'Where? How? Have you told the Council? They only spared his life as long as he stayed away from everyone.'

'He's gone nowhere as such.' Lasul's face tightened with sorrow tainted with revulsion. 'You told Mellitha he had discovered how to transform himself into a semblance of water? I think he finally let himself dissolve wholly into the lake.'

'How—' Velindre's throat closed on her questions as she recalled the barren waste of scoured rock that the old wizard had wrought in the remote valley he had claimed. She drew a resolute breath. 'What's become of the lake?'

'It's still there, crystal clear.' Lasul looked out of the window, unseeing. 'His elemental affinity is spread through every drop of water, every breath of mist, for countless leagues all around.'

Velindre shivered convulsively at the memory of Azazir's brutal assault on her own affinity. 'He said that self-restraint was merely self-doubt.' Her fingers were aching and she looked down to see she was holding the battered journal so tightly that her fingernails were flushed with blood.

'His affinity is there but there's no intellect, no thought or reason.' Lasul swallowed hard. 'He's been overwhelmed, diluted, subsumed. All those hostile spells he'd hedged the paths and tracks with are withering and plants are sprouting on the valley sides. The streams he'd twisted to run back uphill have returned to their natural courses.'

'So Azazir has finally fallen victim to his own arrogance,' Velindre said curtly. She forced herself to set the book aside on the table. 'As so many wiser mages predicted. I hope you will take that as a warning, to curb whatever ambition drove you to try finding him.'

'Perhaps,' Lasul answered obliquely. 'Or perhaps he was seduced into such folly by the auras of the dragons that he summoned there.'

'Possibly.' Velindre folded her hands in her lap.

'Whenever wizards have written about dragons, here in Hadrumal or elsewhere, they circumscribe every hint and theory with dire warnings. According to Hadrumal's records, the only mages in living memory who knew how to summon dragons were Otrick and Azazir. Otrick's been dead these past few years and I find Azazir most assuredly lost.' Lasul turned back to look at her. 'Now there are dragons loose in the Archipelago, and Mellitha tells me that you've encountered them.'

'Did she tell you that the first mage who became involved in this business died a truly horrible death?' Velindre challenged. 'That he became intoxicated with the elemental power that the beast had drawn to itself, until he was consumed by his own fires?'

'Dev?' Lasul nodded briefly. 'But Mellitha said he sacrificed himself to save you, and some Archipelagans.'

'Mellitha is mistaken,' Velindre said crisply. 'Dev was not a man inclined to any self-sacrifice. If his death saved the rest of us, that was a wholly unforeseen consequence. His destruction resulted from his overconfidence in his ability to control such a focus of power. As would seem to have happened to Azazir.'

'But you've encountered these dragons and you've lived to tell the tale,' Lasul countered swiftly. 'You travelled to learn something of Azazir's insights before he died and it's common knowledge that you were Otrick's lover for many years—'

Velindre cut him short. 'Why do you want to know about dragons?'

'Because Sirince is my father,' Lasul responded without hesitation. 'I don't want to see him lost like Azazir or Dev or anyone else.'

'Your father?' Astonished, Velindre sought for some more pertinent question.

'In name at least, and intermittently in practice.' Lasul walked back to the table. 'He made sure I was apprenticed in Hadrumal once it became apparent I was mageborn. He also made very sure that I knew there's a wide and varied world beyond these halls and showed me that a wizard can live out there as easily as here.' He glanced around the whitewashed, book-lined stone walls with no great affection. 'For which I am very grateful.'

'He introduced you to Mellitha,' Velindre guessed.

'No, as it happens,' Lasul replied more equably. 'That was my mother's doing.'

Velindre saw the obvious explanation. 'Her affinity was with water – your mother's.'

'No.' Lasul grinned. 'My mother was no mage. She's an artist, as is Mellitha's eldest son. They've been friends for years.'

'Oh.' Once again, Velindre was left wondering what to say.

'My father met my mother when he was exploring the way that the different hues for oil paints are made from crushed and burned and otherwise alchemically abused earths and ores,' Lasul explained lightly. He was evidently used to answering that particular question. His expression grew more serious. 'Mellitha has helped him in recent years with his efforts to restore those enslaved in the Archipelago to their families.'

Velindre nodded her understanding. 'So here you are as a dutiful son.' She heard an edge she didn't intend in her voice and regretted it.

'Mages may not make the best of parents.' Lasul looked steadily at her. 'My mother, on the other hand, has always taught me that family ties are not a matter for barter, payment, accounting or repayment.'

Velindre glanced at Azazir's tattered and faded journal. 'The potential peril to Sirince is your whole reason for being curious about dragons?'

'First and last, pretty much,' Lasul said easily. 'I am curious on my own account, up to a point, but I've seen for myself what obsession has made of Azazir. And I feel no pressing obligation to make any startling discovery about dragons or anything else that will add to the sum of proven wizardry, for the greater good of Hadrumal or anywhere else. I live very happily without bothering with such things.'

Velindre narrowed her eyes at him. 'You were listening at the door, when Ely was being so pompous.'

'I never said I wasn't.' Lasul was unrepentant. 'You were right to tell her she should get out and see the world beyond Hadrumal's halls. Are you planning on telling her that dress would be far better suited to a hopeful maiden than a magewoman expecting her equals to respect her?'

'She wouldn't listen if I did. Don't think I haven't tried,' Velindre said dryly. 'So what are you looking for from me?'

'First and foremost, can you scry for Sirince for me?' Lasul managed a wry smile. 'I'm sure few water mages of Hadrumal would humble themselves to ask such a thing of a wizard attuned to the air, but you've spent more time with my father than I have for quite some years.' He twisted an antique gold ring on one callused finger. 'The fires of their first passion have long since died, but my mother still thinks warmly of him. So I scry for him now and again, to let her know how he's faring.' He shook his head ruefully. 'We've become used to him risking his hide in the Archipelago but these latest ventures of his have caused us some concern. Now I can't see him at all. He's either too far away or something has happened to him.'

Velindre frowned. 'You've been scrying into the Archipelago? Where you know there are dragons? Haven't you found your magic entangled in their auras?'

'If you're asking whether my scrying was twisted to a dragon's own purposes, yes.' Lasul grimaced at the recollection. 'Which sent me running to Mellitha like a startled apprentice. That's when she suggested I try to find Azazir. That was before you returned to Relshaz, obviously.'

Velindre looked at the book on the table. 'Have you learned anything from his journal?'

'I think so,' Lasul replied cautiously. 'Mellitha and I both read it and compared our conclusions. We think the mainland is safe enough from the beasts as long as there are plenty of wizards settled in the towns and cities. If the dragons truly see mages as akin to their own kind, they'll only fly north to challenge us when there is no empty territory left for them to claim in the Archipelago.'

'Which is scarcely good news for the Aldabreshi,' Velindre said grimly.

'I believe I have worse.' Lasul looked sombre. 'As long as there are so few dragons in the islands, their main interest will be in propagating their own kind rather than fighting among themselves. Azazir said something about jewels—'

'They gather them and forge a new life within an egg of elemental gemstone. Dev was killing just such an egg when he died.' Velindre rose to her feet. 'Sirince has gone to look for some way to drive the beasts out of the southern domains. The means we had to drive the dragons out has all been used up. I came here looking for some new stratagem.'

'Mellitha told me.' Lasul watched as the magewoman knelt by the tightly strapped chests set beneath the window. 'Have you found one?'

'Not yet.' Velindre unbuckled the leather strap securing the first chest. 'Azazir is lost and Otrick is dead.' She picked out a flute made from a slim hollow bone and smiled with reluctant reminiscence before setting it aside. As she lifted out a bundle of parchments and papers, several slid from her grasp to scatter across the floor: a study of a gull alert on a harbour bollard, sketches of Hadrumal's high road in chalk and in ink, a small oil painting of a cliff-top pine tree warped by incessant winds against a stormy sky.

Lasul came over to bend down and gather them up. 'You're an artist yourself,' he complimented Velindre.

'Such frivolity is hardly a constructive use of a talented mage's time.' She took them out of his hand and set them face down. 'According to both of my parents.' Reaching into the chest she found a broad silver dish. 'Let's see if we can find your errant father.'

'Can you evade the dragon's magic?' Lasul offered her his hand as she stood up. 'I don't want to draw the beast's attention to him.'

'Mellitha and I discussed some ways around the difficulties.' Velindre set the bowl on the table. 'At very least I'll know if the creature's mind's eye is turning towards me so we can break the spell before it ensnares us.' She looked at Lasul, her head inclined to one side. 'I haven't yet bothered asking the hall maids to see to my wash stand, so you had better summon up some water.'

'If you'd be so good as to open a window.' Lasul sketched a bow before passing his hands over the shallow dish.

Velindre went to open one of the tall iron-framed casements. A warm breeze flowed into the stillness of the room, carrying a scent of sun-kissed stone and the fragrance of the coarse hay spread to dry in the tussocky meadows beyond the walls of the wizards' city. A torrent of birdsong rose from the exuberant creeper that cloaked the windows of the rooms below with dense purple-tinted leaves.

'That's better.' Lasul swiftly wound his hands around each other to wring glittering drops of water from the empty air.

The room filled with salty freshness drawn from the verdant salt marshes away beyond the outlying houses where Hadrumal's ordinary folk lived.

Velindre returned to the table, new confidence buoying her up.

'Even if we can scry him out, don't expect to bespeak him,' she warned Lasul nevertheless. 'His life will be forfeit if anyone but the warlord Kheda ever sees him having dealings with what can only be magic.'

'You'll have to tell me the whole tale of your dealings with these Aldabreshi.' Lasul looked down into the turquoise light now swirling around to cloud the water with magic. 'Would you care to dine with me?'

Velindre sat down and clasped the sloping sides of the bowl. 'If I can work the scrying high enough above the ground, any dragon not directly attuned to the air may well not notice, to begin with at least.'

The circling radiance ringed the water with vivid mage-light. In the centre of the bowl, fluffy white clouds mimicked a reflection of the summer day outside the window. Velindre eased her wizardry through the distant vapour, nudging swathes of white aside. Far below, a mountainside materialised, remote and rocky, the lower slopes densely covered with countless shades of green.

'Is this the warlord Kheda's domain?' Lasul looked over Velindre's shoulder.

She refused to be distracted by the orris scenting his linen shirt and the faint musk of sweat beneath it. 'I don't think so.' The magic shivered and blurred like a rain-streaked window pane.

'Is it the dragon?' Lasul gripped the back of her chair.

'No.' Velindre took one hand away from the bowl and spread her fingers to wind a skein of pure blue magelight out of the teasing breeze. The radiance pulsed as the threads drifted out of the window to float upwards, thinning and vanishing. Velindre sat motionless. Lasul stood still and intent behind her. 'There's no dragon anywhere near them,' she said at length.

Snapping the threads of this secondary magic with a flick of her wrist, she returned both her hand and her full attention to the scrying bowl. The vision cleared and steadied and skimmed over the treetops. The magic took them close enough to distinguish between the mighty ironwoods, spinefruits and lilla trees. Dark scores indicated paths worn by men and beasts through the tangled forest.

She shook her head, bemused. 'This is the Ulla domain.'

Velindre's vision swooped down through the canopy of leaves to show them a handful of men standing in a close knot in a misshapen clearing. A massive tree had recently fallen, roots clawing at a raw scar in the rich dark earth. Sirince was readily identifiable by his balding head.

'That's Kheda, standing in the centre, and his slave, Telouet, or rather his former slave.'

'Who are those other two?' Lasul bent to try to make out more detail.

'I don't know.' Velindre frowned.

'What about all those others?' Lasul studied the substantial number of men gathered around the outer edge of the glade.

'Their weapons are grimy and their armour's mismatched,' Velindre said slowly. 'If I had to guess, I'd say that's some force backing Ulla Orhan's rebellion against his father.'

'Does this rebellion have anything to do with the dragons?' Lasul asked, frustrated.

'Not directly,' Velindre said absently. 'But why would Kheda and Sirince be there, if there wasn't something to be gained to use against the beasts?'

Lasul stared down into the bowl where the tiny figures were still deep in conversation. 'I might have a better chance of making some useful suggestion if I knew who these people were and something of their business.'

'We definitely daren't bespeak Sirince if he's in the midst of an Aldabreshin revolt.' Velindre withdrew her hands from the bowl and flexed her fingers as the vision dissolved. 'We'll just have to scry as often as we can, in hopes that we see some clue.' She glanced up at Lasul. 'Mellitha and I have been discussing possibilities for two or more mages blending their spells into a scrying over such a long distance, especially when there's the need to avoid brushing against a dragon's aura. Would you be willing to try such a working with me?'

'Of course.' He smiled at her with the charm she'd noted from his first words to her. 'I'm the one who's been telling Mellitha about the mages outside Tormalin who've been exploring the potential of cooperative magic.'

'Is that so?' Velindre looked back at the empty bowl. 'You'll have to tell me all you know. Wizardly abilities to work with more than one element seem to be one of the few advantages we have over the astonishing power that stems from the purity of a dragon's affinity.'

'Then tell me all you know,' Lasul invited as he went to sit on the other side of the table.

CHAPTER TWENTY-FOUR

Ulla Orhan seems certain he can do this. I hope his confidence isn't misplaced. If it is, it means more than our deaths. There'll be no one left to drive off the dragons.

Kheda made sure there was no misgiving in his face as he followed the younger warlord along the narrow game trail. Flourishing thickets of tandra trees pressed in on both sides, shedding glistening drops of rain whenever an arm or shoulder brushed their leaves. Ulla Orhan's warriors made their way cautiously along the valley side. Straying too high risked being seen on the crest of the rising land. Wandering down into underbrush thinned by the local farmers' constant plundering for firewood risked catching the eye of some early riser.

Gilded clouds drifted overhead, pale stretches of blue strengthening in hue. Though pale mists still dulled the lofty crowns of the ironwood trees, the colours of the forest were beginning to emerge as the grey of early dawn yielded to the true light of day. Underfoot, sharp scents cut through the rich darkness of churned-up leaf mould. Fire-creeper leaves were crushed by nailed sandals and hacked nerial vines bled red sticky sap slow to clot in the damp air. The Ulla rebels pressed on, their tunics already damp with apprehensive sweat despite the lingering cool left by the passing night.

Kheda had his own concerns to torment him.

If the worst happens, will Sirket do as I ordered? He's had ten days to brood over this plan, which he didn't like in the first place. Will he obey me and abandon Daish for the sanctuary of Chazen? Will he add those gems touched by Dev's death to those protecting Itrac, to at least secure that domain for all my children? Will Risala be able to persuade him? Will she be able to talk Sain or Rekha or Janne into convincing him? Are they even receiving her? Surely they'll be sufficiently curious about what I'm doing here to give her a hearing when she arrives asking for audience.

Would Sirket see such a retreat as too shameful? Will he still waste his life leading some futile attack as he planned to before I came? What manner of life could my children hope for, if dragons take hold of Daish and Ritsem and Redigal? Leaving Ulla and its present lord quite untouched.

The men ahead of him slowed as whistles mimicked glory-bird calls. An unseen crookbeak squawked an indignant retort while scarlet-headed waxbeaks heedlessly trilled their own morning greetings, bouncing from twig to twig.

Ulla Orhan must know better than anyone how fiercely Safar will resist. Yet he shows no hesitation, no fear of his father. Perhaps the lad will make a worthy husband for Dau. If he lives to win her hand. If I win through to assert myself as her father once again. Custom be cursed; I won't be denied a voice in an alliance as important as this. Or in the marriages of any of my children.

The long, drawn-out column slowed piecemeal to come to a final standstill. Silent and alert, the motley force's rearguard clustered around them.

'Finally.' Grimacing, Sirince twisted his shoulders beneath his dirty chain-mail hauberk.

Telouet grinned. 'You're finding that armour a little wearisome?'

'Better weary than gutted.' Sirince managed a faint smile as he mopped his brow with the rag he had tied around his head. With a notched and rusted sword and grime darkening his skin, he didn't look out of place among Ulla Orhan's army.

None of us look anything special. Sirket was careful to kit us out with the meanest armour and oldest blades that his sword-captains keep to disgrace any Daish warrior on punishment duty.

Kheda tried to make out the edge of the forest. 'There's a perilous expanse of farmed land still ahead.'

'We'll cross vegetable plots and saller fields fast enough,' Telouet said dismissively.

Ahead, Kheda saw stained and ragged scouts slip through the ring of armoured men guarding Ulla Orhan to report on what they had seen. The young warlord nodded and gave new instructions. He cut off some objection with an emphatic sweep of one hand, a frown ominously increasing his resemblance to his odious father. The scout bowed in instant submission and retreated to vanish into the trees.

'The lad's grown into quite a leader,' Telouet observed quietly.

He's lost the fat of soft living and abandoned the lifelong pretence of foolishness that led so many of us to dismiss him. What does his father think, now his son's true mettle has been revealed?

'He mustn't underestimate Safar, or his most senior captains,' Kheda said severely. 'My lord of Ulla has long shown a knack for finding men as vicious as himself, and for securing their loyalty by indulging their depravities.'

Orhan came back along the path, his faithful slave Nami two paces behind him, as ever. 'There are still some among my men who would prefer to take on Derasulla directly,' Orhan said frankly.

'You must convince them that would be throwing their lives away needlessly.' Kheda looked severe. 'If you want the fortress delivered into your hands, you have to trust me.'

'I do.' Orhan lifted his chin. 'Once I have the fortress, I have the domain. You will win my eternal gratitude, my lord.'

For Daish or for Chazen?

'Make sure your men understand their role in this fight.' Kheda stared back, uncompromising. 'If they do not draw Safar's forces right out beyond the walls, we won't be able to do this.'

'Have we truly got this close without anyone being seen?' Telouet chipped in.

'We were seen last night, so the sentries say.' Orhan was unconcerned. 'But my scouts assure me none of the locals dwelling hereabouts have run to warn the fortress. I take it as an omen.' He nodded, grimly satisfied. 'Even in my father's heartland, the people of Ulla reject his rule.'

'We had to rest overnight,' Telouet said grudgingly. 'We couldn't sustain a battle without sleep.'

'We still have to carry the day,' Kheda said sternly, 'otherwise Safar will slaughter every man, woman and child in this valley, whether they could have raised any alarm or not.'

'We will prevail,' Orhan assured him with an unexpected smile. 'The Winged Snake writhes in the arc of foes where the Diamond and the Pearl shine as our twin talismans. The only other star above the horizon is the Emerald that is talisman for youth. It foretells a fertile future in the arc of marriage where the Bowl promises rewards for all. My father's rule is done.'

'Not yet it isn't.' Kheda refused to be drawn into such optimism.

'Then let's see his fortress taken and his power brought so low that all may openly despise him.' Orhan took his helmet from Nami and set it firmly on his head. A ferocious whisper ran through his men: of steel leaving scabbards and the rattle and chink as sword belts were unbuckled and drawn tighter around hauberks.

'My lord.' A ragged runner came pelting along the path, breathless and bright-eyed. 'Our first detachments advance on the outlying settlements. Courier doves are flying towards the river.'

'So our foes know we're here as well as our friends.' Orhan fastened the fine chain veil hanging from his helmet's brow band beneath his bearded chin. He bowed low to Kheda. 'My lord of Chazen, I look forward to welcoming you to my domain's finest dining chamber after today's exertions.'

Kheda bowed in reply. 'Until this evening, my lord of Ulla.'

'We will restore the glory of the Ulla domain, for the sake of all who dwell here,' Orhan shouted, drawing his sword. 'Show no mercy. Remember that any man with a shred of decency has quit the residence guard to join us, or at very least fled to safeguard his home. Those who have chosen to stay with Ulla Safar must now pay for the privileges and pleasures they've bought with so much misery.'

The men cheered heartily as he strode forward, Nami at his shoulder. The warlord slid the face plate of his helm down the nasal bar, twisting the clasp that secured it, and his slave followed suit.

Kheda moved to the shelter of a stubborn spinefruit tree as the swordsmen of the rearguard hurried past. Telouet and Sirince joined him.

'I'm no tactician, Kheda, but surely an army holding a fortress will stay safe within its walls?' Sirince took care not to be overheard by any of the Ulla men. 'They could hold such a place against twenty times their number.'

'In the normal run of affairs.' Kheda nodded. 'But Ulla

Safar must know his rule hangs by a thread now that so many have joined Orhan's rebellion. If his son can mount even a token siege of Derasulla, thousands could flock to his banner and turn a flimsy blockade into a strangling grip. If Ulla Safar is penned up inside his own walls, the rest of the domain will be free to declare allegiance to Orhan. Safar's forces will desert him. Those forced into his service will take their earliest opportunity to flee. Those whose loyalty has been bought with licence for plunder and rapine will soon decide there's no future on a losing side.'

'Vermin are the first to flee a sinking ship. My lord, we don't want to be left too exposed,' Telouet warned as the last warriors passed by.

'We'll tag along with the tail end.' Kheda suited his actions to his words. 'Besides, Sirince, you're assuming Ulla Safar will assess this situation with cold logic. Orhan has been a festering thorn in his side for over a year. If the lad can claim the support of even half the domain, Redigal Coron and Ritsem Caid will proclaim their support for this new regime. So Safar will make every effort to defeat the boy now that he's come within reach. He won't only want to scatter these rebels. He'll want to capture Orhan. He'll send his finest troops out of the fortress to hunt him, on pain of death if they fail.'

'Hoping Orhan's punishment and death will serve as a fearsome deterrent to anyone else challenging the fat snake's rule,' grunted Telouet.

'What happens if Orhan's men rout for real?' As they walked on behind the Ulla forces, the older man still sounded unconvinced. 'Safar's troops have a formidable reputation—'

'Orhan only needs to draw them out. If he cannot lead his forces back to the attack—' Kheda fell silent and shook his head. 'It doesn't really matter in the wider scheme of things. Not as long as you can do your part.'

'It'll matter to Dau,' Telouet commented under his breath. 'There's more to making a future here than just ridding these reaches of dragons, my lord.'

'Let's hope we live to see it.' Kheda picked up the pace 'At least Risala will be safe,' he said involuntarily. 'She can sail away in the *Reteul* if we fail here.'

'Yalea can't,' Telouet growled.

Kheda put a hand on the warrior's shoulder. 'I'm sorry. I know everyone's fate is equally important.' He yielded to curiosity. 'How long has she been special to you?'

'Since my lord Sirket freed me.' Telouet fixed Kheda with a challenging look. 'I've looked fondly on her for the last few years but I couldn't say anything while I lived at your command.'

'I wouldn't have objected.' Kheda was quite taken aback.

'When I might have died in your service? When you had first call on my every waking moment? Don't misunderstand me, my lord, I was honoured to serve you—'

As Telouet broke off, Kheda was pierced by the disillusion in the man's eyes.

Honoured until I betrayed you, first by letting you think I was dead, now by consorting with wizards, or so you suspect.

'How could I make any declaration when I had nothing to offer her?' Telouet shook his head to forbid any further conversation and strode away.

The wide valley opened up before them. On the middle slopes, clawthorns already much harvested for kindling were still sprouting defiant new shoots. Striol vines laced treacherous snares between the stumps and Orhan's men were hacking at them with their swords. The first cohorts were already pushing through stands of sard-berry bushes and lilla trees, more valuable for their fruit than for firewood. Ahead, the regular squares of vegetable gardens made a patchwork of reckal beets and shirrel and sawhearts swelled with the rains. Farmers' huts in twos and threes were set back from the broad swathes of saller fields flooded with the mighty river's bounty. The waters threaded glistening ribbons amid the feathery tufts nourished by the rich silt carried down from higher ground.

'This way, my lord.' Telouet slid past Kheda to take a lesser path branching off from the well-trodden route the rest were following.

This was a more direct route to the river. It curved towards them before twisting away once more in a shining arc fringed with green. Clouded waters raced for the sea, braided by turbulent currents. Tree branches and other detritus swept down from the forests inland were discarded in eddies of dead water. The only thing defying the mighty flood was the fortress of Derasulla.

It was an implacable obstacle. An island that had once lain in the waters' embrace had been wholly consumed by the fortress. Unbroken ramparts of red stone rose from the water, rising sheer to lofty battlements. Towers at every angle kept watch upstream and down, on both banks, and each turret spied on its neighbours for good measure. Unseen behind that first wall, Kheda knew there lay a wide moat, kept constantly replenished by the river's flow. Anyone trying to cross it would be at the mercy of archers loosing their arrows from every vantage point on the second wall behind those outer defences. More turrets measured its long passage around the hidden island. Surmounting that would merely bring attackers up against a third wall, to perish in the killing ground before it.

Kheda recalled Safar's frequent boast that there wasn't an open expanse anywhere on Derasulla where a man could stand and not be at the mercy of his household's deadly archers.

Within that innermost circle, the roofs of Ulla Safar's

lofty citadel could just be made out amid the lingering mists. Fortified towers rose among the audience halls and private accommodations to keep watch over all the outer defences. The Daish rainy-season residence would look paltry beside such a dwelling. The largest fortification Chazen could claim could be tucked within the walls and mislaid.

Kheda turned his attention to the progress of Orhan's troops. He tried to pick out the young warlord but all he could find was a cluster marked by tighter discipline and superior armour.

Deserters from Safar's own household warriors. Presumably Orhan's somewhere among them. Let's hope none are still secretly loyal to Safar.

'Kheda.' Sirince pointed as the first skirmishers reached a cluster of mud-brick, palm-thatched huts.

Men were pouring from the buildings. These were no startled islanders but armoured warriors, their swords and hauberks gleaming in the first sunlight. Steel clashed with shouts of challenge and defiance. Within a few breaths, shrieks of pain mingled with screams of dying hatred.

'A wise lord prepares for every eventuality.' Telouet's words sounded like a curse.

A handful of Orhan's men broke and ran.

'Are they starting to fall back already?' Sirince wondered.

'They have to make a fight of it,' Telouet said through gritted teeth, 'to make the main garrison venture out.'

'We have to cross the river.' Kheda continued down the haphazard track. It ended at a solitary hut, mute and shuttered in the early morning. Beyond, a walkway of planks was raised up on posts driven in crossed and lashed pairs into the earthen banks dividing the waterlogged saller fields.

'There'll be a rope stretched across the river and looped

back.' Telouet indicated the posts marking a matching walkway on the far side. 'With a boat attached.'

Kheda drew his sword. 'Sirince, stay behind us.'

Telouet hurried on through exuberant berry bushes and sprawling yellow vines swelling with warty green melons.

Ahead a shutter shifted to betray some watcher within the hut.

'I knew they wouldn't have left a river crossing unguarded.' Telouet sounded almost relieved.

'Let's hope they haven't cut the rope.' Kheda's words were lost as the door crashed open and a handful of men rushed out towards them.

Telouet charged forward, yelling obscenities. Silent, dry-mouthed, Kheda followed. In a few paces his sword smashed aside the first blade seeking his throat. He instantly saw these were no reluctant islanders, weapons forced into their hands for fear of Ulla Safar's displeasure and his men's reprisals. They wielded their swords with the fluid familiarity of trained warriors.

The man who'd attacked him hacked at him a second time. Unhesitating, Kheda rolled his wrists around to twist the tip of his sword as he evaded the blow. Reaching through the man's guard, his blade sliced deep into the meat of his enemy's forearm. The warrior flinched but renewed his attack. Kheda stepped deftly around the murderous down-stroke to rip a cut across the back of the man's neck. A chain veil saved the Ulla warrior from beheading but the blow forced him to stumble. Kheda brought his knee up. The Ulla warrior hadn't slid down the face guard of his helm and the metal plates reinforcing Kheda's leather leggings smashed into his lips and cheek. The man recoiled, half-falling, half-staggering, his helm ripped askew. Kheda slashed his bloodied sword at the man's bared throat and he fell dead before Kheda drew his third breath of the fight.

As the second Ulla warrior charging towards him faltered at the death of his ally, Kheda assessed their wider situation. Telouet had already downed two but a double handful had poured out of the hut. Trampling the ripe melons, the Ulla warriors spread out to surround Kheda and Telouet, and to circle around to attack Sirince. Each man lifted his feet high to avoid the tangled vines, their exaggerated gait almost comical.

Kheda wasn't amused. 'Telouet,' he shouted. 'We have to kill them all before someone sees the skirmish and sends reinforcements.'

A snarling Ulla swordsman ran at him, shining blade levelled at Kheda's gut. With his humble hauberk lacking metal plates to turn aside the bruising impact, Kheda twisted sideways. Avoiding a blow hard enough to rupture stomach or bowel robbed his own counterstroke of its full force. Though the man was dangerously overextended, Kheda's sword merely rasped ineffectively over the steel links on his shoulder. The Ulla warrior whirled around, renewing his attack. Kheda stepped sideways, saving himself with a deft parry.

As he took a step backwards, still defending, movement beyond his attacker caught the warlord's eye. Sirince was about to be caught between two Ulla warriors. The wizard held his hands wide, sword wavering feebly in one, his dagger in the other. The northerner's age was as painfully apparent as his utter lack of fighting skills.

Thinking his prey was fatally distracted, the man facing Kheda launched a lightning-fast attack. Kheda moved faster still to get inside the arc of the blow spiralling towards his unprotected head. Slashing at his enemy's sword-arm with his own blade, Kheda clawed at the man's eyes with his dagger. The man recoiled, all his concentration on the dagger. Kheda gave him no chance to realise his error before he smashed the pommel of his deftly reversed sword into his nose. The Ulla warrior fell back, blinded by pain and choking on blood. Kheda thrust his sword up under the hem of his foe's chain mail to rip into the sinews behind his knee. The man collapsed and Kheda used his chest as a stepping stone to go to Sirince's aid.

He was still too far away. The Ulla swordsmen attacked the wizard. One man's blade landed squarely in the angle of Sirince's neck and shoulder. The other struck a blow to cleave the mage's dagger hand from his wrist. Both blades rang with the outrage of tempered steel meeting unyielding stone. No blood spurted; there was no obscene tearing of flesh or shattering of bone. The wizard stood quite unharmed, not even knocked off balance. As the warriors gaped, Sirince slashed back at them, awkward and ungainly. The shocked warriors failed to block his blows like the greenest of novices, but the tip of the mage's sword merely scraped a shallow slice across one man's cheek. His dagger barely managed a scratch on the back of the other one's hand.

Kheda lunged forward, desperate to attack before the men recollected themselves and hacked the wizard to quivering pieces. Then he saw blood. The scratch on the closest man's hand spread and deepened. The skin gaped to reveal ivory bones streaked with scarlet. Then the tendons ruptured and the bones fell apart. Shockingly vivid, heart's blood gushed as if the wrist had been severed with an axe. The man fell forward, his dying breath spent on screaming with uncomprehending horror.

In the moment it took Kheda to take a second stride, an obscene void blossomed in the second man's face. In the blink of an eye, the scratch Sirince had inflicted

transformed into a monstrous wound. The warlord saw
the man's teeth and tongue and the pale arc of his cheek-
bone stripped of flesh. For a stomach-churning moment,
an unprotected eye rolled wildly in its socket. Then the
spreading gash ruptured blood vessels in the man's brain
and a merciful flood of scarlet veiled the ghastliness.

'Kheda!'

As Telouet shouted his warning, the warlord caught
movement in the corner of his eye. Meeting a blow slashing
round at head height with a solid riposte of his own, he
saw unearthly blackness flow down the length of his blade.
As Kheda couldn't help but flinch, the strike lost its full
force and the darkly glistening steel barely grazed the
man's armoured forearm. All the same, the chain mail
splintered like woven cane and the man's elbow was laid
open. The joint was utterly shattered, as if a butcher had
taken a cleaver to it.

*Now they all have to die. Not just so we can cross the
river. So there are no witnesses to this vile magic. But what
about Telouet?*

Chilled, Kheda saw the same ominous shadows sliding
like oil down Telouet's sword. A brush of Telouet's
weapon left a wound in his foe's throat like the swipe of
a jungle cat's claws. Gritting his teeth so hard his jaw
ached, Kheda fought on, slaughtering the Ulla warriors
by inflicting the merest injury.

The last man fell and Kheda paused, panting. The air
was sour with the smell of blood, ordure and smashed
melons. He saw Telouet's gaze slide past him to fasten
on Sirince.

'We have to cross the river.' Sirince pushed past
Telouet, intent on the walkway leading to the tethered
boat. As he passed by the swordsman, never thinking he
was in peril, Kheda saw Telouet raise his weapon. There
was nothing the warlord could do to stop his erstwhile

slave landing a killing blow on the unprotected back of the wizard's neck.

Only it won't kill him, will it? He's made himself impervious to such things.

Telouet didn't make the stroke. His arm fell back to hang nerveless by his side. Sheathing his sword with a ferocious thrust, ugly passion twisted his face as he turned to Kheda. 'Come on, then.'

They ran for the posts marking the ferry, the raised walkway shaking beneath their pounding feet. Reaching the river, they saw the long rope joined in a circle threaded through pulleys on either bank. Tied securely into the loop, a flat-bottomed boat had been dragged askew downstream as the river rushed for the sea. Telouet began hauling it in and Kheda went to help. It took all their strength to reclaim the ferry from the relentless flood.

Sirince kept watch on both sides of the river, his sword hanging at his side. The mage paid no heed to smoking drops of shadow falling from the blade to leave hissing pock marks in the mud. 'Is that where we're heading for? That black outcrop?'

Kheda nodded, his shoulders aching. 'How's Orhan's battle going?'

Sirince peered downstream. 'Well enough, I think.'

'Get in, my lord.' Telouet dug his nail-shod feet into the soft bank as he steadied the recalcitrant ferry.

Kheda stepped warily onto the flimsy planking.

Sirince followed. 'Do you want me to—'

'No!' said Kheda forcefully. 'Save your . . . strength.'

Telouet scowled ferociously as he stepped aboard and began to haul on the rope to ferry them across.

As Kheda helped, he looked downstream. Confused and indistinct commotion rang around the broad valley. There was no way to make out the ebb and flow of the fighting. He looked instead at the fortress, hoping to see some sign that Ulla Safar's formidable garrison was being drawn out. It was no good; they were too far away.

Fighting the ceaseless drag of the surging waters, Kheda was breathless with effort by the time he and Telouet had pulled the flat ferry into the sluggish shallows on the far side of the river. A bevy of ducks peaceably dabbling among the weeds scattered with noisy quacking that they had no hope of silencing.

'Do we cut the rope?' Sirince had his dagger ready. 'To stop anyone following us?'

'No.' Telouet glared at him. 'The islanders farming this valley are going to suffer enough.'

All three of them looked around. There was no one to be seen on this bank thus far.

'Come on.' Kheda forced himself into a run along the rattling walkway that led to solid ground. He fixed his gaze on the black crag ahead. The raw, angular rock was a brutal intrusion into the softly flowing greens of the gentle valley. Mist dissolved into shining damp on its sheer facets, unmarred by any audacious mosses. Scant vegetation crowned it, the merest suggestion of greenery amid the sprawling tangle of branches that was a silver eagle's nest.

What omens will Orhan claim if the great birds startle into flight? Will Safar concoct some spurious justification for his victory from their soaring?

As they left the saller fields behind, the crag loomed ever more ominous ahead. Kheda's heart pounding, he hurried on, the black-veined leaves of reckal beets snatching at his ankles. At first he felt he was never getting closer to the outcrop. Then he would glance back and see that the river had retreated by another substantial measure. As soon as he looked to the fore again, the great rock seemed closer.

Cultivation ceased well short of the black crag's shadow.

There were no footprints to indicate anyone came here to draw water from the pool at the base of the rock. It boiled with foam beneath the cataract erupting from a shadowy crevice high above. Overflowing, the water spread out across a wide marshy margin of drowned grass and sodden seedlings. The ceaseless tumbling crash of the waterfall overwhelmed cheerful birdsong close at hand and the distant cacophony of battle. Insistent, demanding, the noise isolated all who came close. The never-ending, ever-changing spectacle of the cascade drew the eye remorselessly, fascinating as the spray wove endless variations of broken rainbows in the mist.

Sirince was gazing at the black crag, brow creased with curiosity. Telouet scanned ahead and behind for any sign of movement. Kheda passed him, heedless of dampness squelching through his sandals. He was looking at the topless tower standing just to the south of the great outcrop. Pale as mist, it was surrounded by a white stone wall. The lofty platform was bounded by four pillars marking the cardinal points of both heavenly and earthly compasses.

'A tower of silence?' Sirince turned his attention to it. 'You're quite sure we won't find anyone here?'

'The Ulla islanders only approach the crag and the waterfall to deliberately seek an omen, or to draw water when the dry season reduces the river to a poisonous sump.' Kheda walked towards the white wall. 'Only a warlord may open this gate, when the domain's most honoured dead are brought to be laid here.'

'Forgive my ignorance. No one in the northern domains is prepared to discuss such things with a barbarian,' Sirince explained politely.

'Thus all the deceaseds' virtues may be spread as widely as possible.' Telouet glowered at him. 'As the stars turn, the breezes blow and their bodies are consumed by insects, birds and decay. The only other time anyone enters the enclosure is when a warlord's wife lies down on the bare earth to dream beneath the dry bones that are token of the threads of blood and birth woven around her life. These threads bind her to all who have died and those yet to be born to rule the domain.'

'Ulla Safar pays scant heed to any proper observances and I don't imagine his wives are allowed out of the fortress.' Kheda steeled himself to lay a hand on the bronze latch green with verdigris.

And I'm here with a wizard whose evil sorceries have just butchered a troop of warriors. It's a good thing I don't fear the consequences of profaning such a sanctuary.

The ebony gate wasn't locked. He went through.

Telouet shoved Sirince roughly after him, immediately turning to push the gate closed, leaving just a crack for him to keep watch on the valley outside.

Sirince looked around at the few wind-seeded plants, the feathers and fragments of rotten cloth blown into the angle between wall and earth. He gazed up at the unrailed stair spiralling around the tower's solid core and the sun struck translucence from the compass pillars high up above. 'What stone is it made from?'

He broke off as a man appeared from behind the pale tower, wearing the unbleached cotton garments of a *zamorin* slave.

Kheda stepped forward, weapons sheathed and his hands outstretched. 'Inais.'

'My lord.' The newcomer smiled crookedly, tension in his dark eyes. 'Still of Chazen? Or of Daish once again?'

'That hardly matters.' Kheda shook his head. 'Not until we've seen this through.'

The *zamorin* nodded with determination at odds with his plump, ineffectual appearance. 'Let's get you inside the fortress.'

Sirince looked from the warlord to the slave, perplexity knotting his brows. Where Kheda was lean and muscular, Inais was portly, his hands soft. His face was clean-shaven and faintly imprecise, jowls blurring his chin where Kheda's beard enhanced the masculine firmness of nose and jawline. But there was more similarity between them than merely their wiry brown hair, touched with grey at their temples.

'You're—' The mage hesitated. 'Related?'

'Brothers,' Kheda said with forbidding terseness.

'Until Daish Reik's death decreed otherwise.' Inais corrected him courteously enough, though he looked askance at Sirince for asking such a question. 'I've been content to serve Daish as a pair of eyes and ears noting all Ulla Safar's conniving and treachery.'

'He's an ignorant barbarian,' Telouet growled, still looking intently through the crack as he held the gate ajar.

Sirince bowed low to Inais. 'I apologise if I have offended you.'

'It's of no consequence.' The *zamorin* waved his words away with a gesture remarkably like one of Kheda's. 'Shall we go?'

'There's nothing to be gained by delay.' Kheda drew his sword. 'Telouet?'

'There's no one in sight.' The swordsman eased the gate open and slipped through, his back pressed against the white wall.

Kheda went next, Inais close behind. Sirince brought up the rear, leaving the tower enclosure with a last reluctant brush of his palm over the pale masonry.

Telouet was hurrying for the concealment of the closest sprawl of burgeoning vegetation. 'Which path?'

'That one.' Inais slipped past Kheda.

'The sooner we get there the better.' The swordsman broke into a slow run.

'The worse for Ulla Safar,' Inais muttered with grim satisfaction as he loped after him.

Kheda followed, checking back now and again to make sure Sirince wasn't being left too far behind. Staunch, the wizard picked up his pace every time Kheda looked at him. All the same, the gap between them grew gradually wider and wider. Ahead, Inais's tunic clung to his back, sodden with sweat, and Kheda could hear the rotund *zamorin* puffing laboriously.

'Telouet, slow down.' He tried to pitch his voice to carry without being overly loud.

The swordsman made no reply but did drop his pace to a brisk walk. Their path veered away from the water-logged saller fields, rising to follow the low contour of the valley side. As before, the great fortress seemed unattainable as long as Kheda kept his eyes fixed on it. Then if he dropped his gaze to the path ahead or to some lilla thicket or farmer's hovel that might hide attackers, he looked back up to find the forbidding fortifications closer.

The clusters of huts grew larger and more frequent, many with their storm shutters hastily battened. There was still no sign of any inhabitants. Kheda wondered if the Ulla farmers had barred their windows and doors before fleeing into the uncertain sanctuary of the forest. Or were they still inside, cowering in the gloom and begging their baffled children to keep as mute as mice?

What concatenation of spurious omens or stars' conjunctions are they clinging to, in hopes of coming safely through this?

When they slowed to climb a swelling knoll, Kheda had a chance to see the fighting on the far side of the river. Scattered skirmishes were spread all over the flat land. Larger contingents of men were making a stand or launching some assault on an obdurate foe. Broken handfuls fled headlong or pursued unseen prey with murderous intent. The fickle breeze carried unintelligible fragments of hoarse voices and the brutal clash of weapons before snatching the sounds away, half-heard.

Whose men are whose? All of them are of Ulla. Can Orhan truly reclaim this domain if his revolt has launched brother against brother?

He broke into a jog-trot to catch up with Inais. 'Do you think they've drawn the troops out of the fortress?'

The *zamorin* stopped to squint across the river. Telouet halted, looking back over his shoulder. Forcing himself into a run, Sirince finally caught up with them, his breathing hoarse.

'I'd say the main elements of the garrison have been dispatched,' Inais said eventually. 'I can't be sure. I don't imagine Ulla Safar will release his reserves without good reason.'

'We'd better be alert in case we trip over them inside.' Telouet gestured at the fortress now looming ominously close. 'How are we going to get in?'

'How do we get out again?' mused Sirince.

'There are secret passages woven through every level.' Inais reached inside his tunic for a bundle of reed paper. Moist with sweat, the ink lines were blurred but still legible. 'I thought a plan would be quicker than trying to explain them.'

Kheda studied the precise drawing. 'This would have meant your death if you'd been discovered.' His hand shook and the paper fluttered in the breeze.

Inais rubbed a hand over his close-cropped hair. 'I've been living on borrowed time since Daish Reik's decree offered me the choice of a quick death or a long life cut off from my own blood and future.' His voice wavered. 'But now there's a chance that collateral blood to my own can join with Orhan and build a better future for the honest people of Ulla. I felt that was worth wagering against my own fate,' he concluded doggedly.

He's lived in the heart of this domain for more than half his life, so if he believes there are honest men worth saving in Ulla, I must believe him. If I won't look for futile omens to sanction Dau's marriage to Orhan, I can at least heed the words of such a man, zamorin *or not. Daish Reik didn't raise fools for sons, even if he couldn't see past the fate that custom demanded for them.*

Kheda cleared his throat. 'So how do we get in?'

Inais surprised him by pointing to a mean and solitary hut set in the midst of small, misshapen saller fields. 'There's a tunnel running right under the river bed. It comes out there.'

'It must be guarded.' Telouet scowled.

Inais nodded. 'At this end, by a man loyal to Orhan. At least, that's who I left there.'

Telouet gripped his sword menacingly. 'Let's see if he's still there.'

'Don't slip off the banks into the saller fields,' Inais warned. 'There are stakes and pits hidden under the water.'

Kheda was glad of the warning. The banks between the waterlogged fields were sufficiently narrow and steep that it might have seemed more sensible to wade through the green tufts instead. He looked warily from side to side with what attention he could spare from keeping his footing. Haze rose from the water to shimmer across his vision. This wasn't mist drawn up from the waters by the heat of the day but something more akin to the deceptive reflections struck up from barren rocks by the full force of the brutal dry-season sun. He looked back over his shoulder at Sirince.

More magic.

'I take it we don't want to be seen,' the mage said quietly.

Kheda made no answer.

Telouet's already seen proof he's a mage, so no more damage can be done there. Will Inais notice anything? What can he do if he does?

Kheda focused his attention on the meagre hut ahead. He saw movement.

'Who's that?' Telouet demanded.

'A friend,' Inais said with relief as a single swordsman stepped out of the doorway. 'Gyran.'

The slave retreated into the hut, holding the door open and beckoning urgently. Entering, Kheda saw that the shabby building was a temporary storage for newly cut saller. The last dry stalks of the previous crop were tangled in the boughs of clawthorn strewn thickly across the floor to raise the harvest above the damp earth as well as discouraging curious lizards and greedy rodents. The viciously spiny branches also concealed a narrow shaft lined with the same red stone of which the formidable walls of Derasulla were constructed.

Gyran pushed the door closed and stood with his back to it. Kheda gripped his sword, ready for treachery as Inais peered down into the tunnel.

'Has anyone else come through?' the *zamorin* asked.

'No.' Gyran shook his head, his drawn blade unbloodied.

'Did anyone see you come this way?' Inais didn't wait for an answer but began climbing down the rusted rungs fixed into the masonry.

'Safar's been sending runners out since we first got word of Orhan's forces reaching the valley,' Gyran said dismissively. 'Anyone who misses me will assume I'm with them.'

'Sending runners where?' Telouet asked instantly.

'Hurry up.' Inais had already disappeared into the darkness and his voice resounded strangely up from the shaft.

'Let's get into the fortress before there's some lull in the battle and Safar's bullies start taking notice of who's where again.' Kheda indicated Telouet should precede him, before moving to go ahead of Sirince.

Grim-faced, the warrior sheathed his blades and began climbing down. Kheda followed, testing the rusty iron rungs cautiously with his feet before trusting them with his full weight. Deciding the corrosion was merely a surface patina, he moved more rapidly. Beneath him, he heard Telouet muttering a choice selection of oaths. Despite everything, he grinned in the darkness. Then his own sword hilt caught on a rung, forcing the weapon back to catch awkwardly in the narrow angles of the shaft. As he paused to adjust his scabbards, Sirince's questing foot nearly kicked him in the side of the head.

'Careful,' he protested.

'Sorry.' Sirince peered down, a formless darkness against a receding square of daylight.

As Kheda looked up, the wizard vanished. Gyran had blocked the light entirely with his body. The darkness was made absolute as the Ulla warrior dragged some covering over the shaft with a grating noise that set Kheda's teeth on edge.

He counted seven beats of his heart and climbed down seven more rungs before a spark flared beneath him. Telouet jumped down to land with a squelch beside Inais. The *zamorin* was touching the first torch he'd lit to a second ironwood spar tipped with plaited saller straw soaked in tandra seed oil. The flames burned clear and golden, virtually without smoke. Kheda looked as far as the light penetrated down the tunnel. The walls were made of stones mortared closely together, rising to form a low arched roof. Flagstones underfoot were lost beneath a layer of sodden silt and the air was unpleasantly moist.

Kheda noted straw and rag packed into a worrying number of crevices in the masonry. 'How much water seeps in here?'

'Ulla Safar makes sure it's always kept passable.' Inais led the way confidently. 'It's his last rat-run out of Derasulla in case of disaster.'

'Let's hope Orhan doesn't win a quick victory, then,' Telouet quipped. 'We don't want to meet the fat snake coming the other way.'

'Could he be trapped in the fortress if someone brought this tunnel down?' Sirince ran a speculative hand over the ancient stonework. 'Or are there other routes beneath the river?'

'I don't know.' Inais looked dubiously at the older man. 'Ulla Safar never trusts any one individual with all his secrets.'

'We want this tunnel left just as it is until we've got in and out again,' Telouet said harshly.

'Quite so,' Kheda agreed mildly. 'Besides, I don't see Ulla Safar managing the climb up that shaft any too easily.'

Telouet acknowledged that sally with a curt laugh. 'Not without men at the top rigging a block and tackle.'

They went on in silence, the sloping surface underfoot treacherous. Kheda found it difficult to judge exactly when they stopped descending and proceeded on the level. In the very depths, the dampness trickling down the walls gathered into shallow puddles and the warm air grew unpleasantly thick with a smell of mould. The torchlight cowered and flickered, reflected back from the glistening stones. Unbidden, they drew closer together and picked up their pace. No one slowed, not even when they reached a more emphatic upward slope than the one they had descended. Finally, the questing torchlight picked out an iron ladder, counterpart to the one they had climbed down.

'Where do we come out in the fortress?' Kheda asked.

'In a remote and little-used cellar,' Inais assured him as he quenched his flame.

'Let me go first.' Gyran doused his own torch and Kheda heard him begin to climb deftly up the rungs.

Not waiting to be asked or ordered, Telouet followed close behind. Inais went next, his breathing harsh in the absolute darkness as he hauled himself laboriously upwards. Following him, Kheda bumped his head against Inais's heels once and then a second time in his haste. Below, he could hear Sirince climbing at a more measured pace, the nails of his sandals scraping on the metal rungs. Gyran flung open a trap door overhead with an echoing crash.

A harsh voice challenged, 'Who goes there?'

'Burai?' Inais's call overrode the steely swish of Telouet drawing a dagger. 'It's me, with friends of the Ulla domain.'

'Which means no friend to Safar.' The unknown voice hovered halfway between a declaration and a question.

Telouet resheathed his dagger with a click. 'We fight for Ulla Orhan.'

As Kheda followed the others up into a cramped room lit by a single candle, the warrior waiting bowed briefly. 'Then you're welcome.' He broke off to look more closely at Kheda. 'My lord of Chazen?'

I've visited this fortress too many times. A great many people could recognise me. Will that become a problem?

Then he noticed what might have been a roll of discarded sacking kicked into one corner. Only the sickly-sweet smell of blood overlaid the noisome reek of voided bowels polluting the already close atmosphere in the small room. 'Who's that?' he demanded.

'One of Safar's men,' the warrior Burai said without remorse. 'He had come to make sure the tunnel was passable.'

'Is Safar thinking of running already?' Inais was startled.

'No matter.' Kheda shook his head. 'Do you have any news of the fighting in the valley?'

As Gyran moved to watch the door leading into the corridor, Burai looked from Kheda to Inais, his bearded face anxious. 'The last I heard, Orhan's forces had overrun the watchtower downstream on the western bank.'

'That wasn't in the plan,' Telouet objected under his breath.

'Presumably the opportunity presented itself.' Kheda frowned, picturing the massive towers set on either side of the great river. More importantly, he contemplated the gigantic chain strung between them to bar passage to virtually all ships. 'That gives Orhan some control over who goes upstream or down.'

'Which would improve his chances of effectively besieging the fortress,' Inais said thoughtfully. 'Or at very least make everyone think he has a better chance.'

'Which could well bring more men rallying to his cause,' agreed Kheda.

The lad made the right choice. Ulla Safar can't sit tight within his walls and risk losing control of the river defences.

'Ulla Safar has sent a sizeable force from the fortress garrison to retake the western tower, and more warriors to prevent Orhan's men from attacking the one on the eastern bank.' Burai's distress deepened. 'He threatens to kill the families of any man who retreats. He says any captain who fails in his duty will be flayed alive. He's already had two men beheaded today, saying they were about to betray Ulla to Orhan by killing him.'

'Where is he?' Kheda demanded.

'Where are his women?' Fear chased anger across Gyran's face.

'He keeps moving around.' Burai shook his head. 'And

he says he will cut the throats of Orhan's sisters himself if anyone loyal to him sets foot in the fortress. He has the girls locked up with Mirrel Ulla and my lady Chay,' he continued with open trepidation, 'who have said they will have their body slaves strangle any lesser wife or concubine who shows the slightest hint of disloyalty to their beloved husband.'

Inais looked at Kheda, his plump face taut with dread. 'He will kill them all, even if he knows he's defeated.' He corrected himself. '*Especially* if he thinks Derasulla is lost. Ulla Safar will leave the corridors running with blood for Orhan before he tries to escape.'

Burai wasn't finished. 'Chay and Mirrel have their own plan in case the fortress falls. They've rounded up every slave or servant they suspect of attachment to any deserter from the household warriors. They'll use their lives to buy their way out.'

'After killing the wives and lovers of the men they know are close to Orhan, to make it clear they're in earnest,' Gyran spat. 'They have Nami's girl in there?'

Burai nodded bleakly.

'Could you find enough men loyal to Orhan to rescue these women?' Kheda asked Inais. 'And get them out of the fortress?'

'Possibly.' The *zamorin* looked at Kheda, the candle-light casting dour shadows on his face. 'You asked Orhan to get you inside, so you could deliver the fortress to him without seeing his army slaughtered in a frontal assault. Are you going to share your plan with us now?'

'No.' Kheda smiled swiftly to take the sting out of his refusal. 'Because I don't want you to know in case you're captured. You have to trust me.'

Inais managed a twisted grin. 'I always have thus far.'

'Then do your best to see that Orhan's victory doesn't turn to ashes in his mouth.' Kheda looked from Inais to

Gyran and Burai and finally to Telouet. 'Help them save the domain's innocent daughters and women who've suffered long enough under Safar's vileness.'

'My lord,' Telouet protested.

Kheda drew his sword. 'Sirince and I can do what is necessary.' He held Telouet's gaze with his own. 'You can serve Daish far more honourably this way.'

Telouet shot Sirince a fulminating glance. 'You trust this . . .' He struggled for a moment, his hand straying to his sword hilt. 'Barbarian?' he spat.

'I do,' Kheda said steadily.

What is he going to do? He was willing to look the other way when he only suspected Velindre was a wizard. But now there's no room for doubt as far as Sirince is concerned. And his magic has been all that the philosophers and warlords of old condemn: an unanswerable means to absolute, dishonourable victory through the slaughter of the helpless. I don't think Telouet could stand to see what else I am contemplating now.

'Where will we meet you?' Telouet stayed stubbornly still.

'At the water gate,' Kheda said swiftly, 'so we can open it for Orhan's troops once everything else needful has been done. For you, that means rescuing the women from Mirrel and Chay. Take them there. And if I don't live through this, go back to Yalea, Telouet, and live the life of a free man. I owe you so much more, but that's all I can give you now.'

Inais looked uneasily between them. 'Whatever we're doing, we had better do it quickly.' He gestured at the corpse lying on the floor. 'Before he's missed, for a start.'

'This way.' Burai drew his own sword and flung the door to the corridor wide open.

CHAPTER TWENTY-FIVE

Kheda lost count of the turnings they took as the gloomy corridors of damp stone gave way to walls of whitewashed brick. Passing beneath narrow skylights stretching up to the day above, they climbed one stair after another, some short, some long, and one a spiral twisting up through the thickness of a massive wall. Inais doubled back on himself more than once, not through error but with definite intent, cutting down one short flight of steps, then back up another. Several times they heard voices and the *zamorin* pressed an urgent finger to his lips to demand their silence.

I found this place confusing enough when I was here at Ulla Safar's invitation, with his lackeys on hand to escort me. Will any of us find our way back out again, or down to the water gate, even with Inais's maps?

They left a plain stair for more elegant corridors and Kheda recognised familiar surroundings. This tasteful labyrinth was at the very heart of the fortress. Graceful arches opened into sumptuous apartments for guests of every rank and shallow stairs led up and down to audience rooms and dining halls and council chambers. Painted tiles were bright with interlaced patterns of canthira leaves and logen vines. The walls were clad with marble, the stone's natural veining blended by the domain's most skilful craftsmen.

Kheda's nailed sandals slipped on the floor, scraping noisily. He paused to remove them, ripping at the laces. 'Let's not be heard coming.'

The others hastily did the same. Laces knotted and sandals slung around their necks, they went on. The tiles were cool underfoot.

Where any two passages crossed or met, sprightly fountains played in wide basins. Fed from hidden cisterns, they were filled to overflowing by the profligate rains. Streams ran away to spread cool freshness throughout the fortress, down narrow channels purposely set in the angles between wall and floor. The soft chuckle of the flowing water was the only sound besides their hurrying footsteps.

'Where have all the slaves and servants gone?' Telouet's whispered question was still shockingly loud. 'This fortress was always like an ant hill whenever we visited, eyes and ears everywhere.'

'They're manning the outer rings of the fortifications,' Burai said tersely, 'willingly or at the lick of a whip.'

'Ulla Safar's hold on power must be more tenuous than we thought if his people defy him by fleeing or hiding.' Telouet gripped his sword tighter, ready for any unexpected encounter.

Kheda grunted. 'Let's not forget a snake's at its most dangerous when it's penned but not yet pinned.'

Inais led them around a right-hand turn and a left-hand corner. They passed through a six-sided lobby roofed with flame-tree blossoms worked in painted glass. Coloured sunlight spilled across the white-tiled floor.

A flicker of movement down one of the passages caught Kheda's eye. By the time he had taken a proper look, whoever it was had vanished.

'Whoever that was may try to win some favour by betraying us,' Gyran said with consternation.

'They'll have to find some guard or chamberlain to tell first,' growled Burai.

Inais had other concerns. 'If we're to try rescuing the

women that Mirrel's holding, we part company here.' He halted and looked at Kheda.

Belatedly, Kheda recognised the hallway's lustrous tiles of jessamine and vizail blossoms. The passage led to Mirrel Ulla's private apartments, and beyond to those of Safar's second wife Chay. On the level below, isolated by guarded stairs and doors, the lesser wives and concubines of the domain were kept in perilous luxury, waiting to submit to the Ulla warlord's whims, or those of any guest he offered them to.

I never thought I'd be grateful for Safar's taunting, as he mocked me for declining to rape some dead-eyed girl he'd snatched from her village and family. But I can find my way from here to his observatory, or to his library, or even his own bedchamber. I wonder where he'll be lurking?

He cleared his throat. 'Do what you can but don't run any foolish risks. We don't know how many warriors Chay and Mirrel will have with them, never mind their own brutes of body slaves.'

'Till later, Kheda.' Inais didn't falter as he led Telouet, Gyran and Burai around a sharp corner.

Kheda watched the three swordsmen follow the *zamorin*.

'Let's go.' Sirince was bright-eyed, not with anticipation but more like a man running a fever.

'Safar has far more than one treasury,' Kheda said slowly. 'Can you be sure you'll find the right one?'

'I can sense the gems.' The wizard hurried off, his stride rapidly lengthening.

Kheda made haste to follow, drawn sword ready. 'The treasury's bound to be guarded,' he warned Sirince. He looked down at his blade, the steel smeared with blood but free of the unearthly black taint of the wizard's sorcery.

Do I want his magic turning my every stroke into a lethal blow once again? We can't afford to lose any fight between here and our objective. But using such sorcery on men, however misguided their allegiance, is truly foul.

The mage suddenly bent down to set his hand flat on the floor. Taken unawares, Kheda nearly tripped over him.

'You said this place was riddled with secret passages.' Straightening up, Sirince smiled with satisfaction. 'There's one under here that leads straight to the treasury we want, unless I miss my guess.'

'What if you do—' Kheda nearly lost his balance as the coloured tiles melted beneath his feet and the solid stone underlying them turned soft and yielding as quicksand. Sinking, he fought against panic as the magically transformed floor rose steadily, inexorably, past his thighs, around his waist and up his chest. He struggled for breath, the pressure around his ribs far more constricting than any water, dense as clay. Instinctively, he lifted his arms to try to keep his sword free.

'Just relax,' Sirince reproved him.

Kheda didn't dare open his mouth to respond as the cloying tide reached his chin and flowed up over his face. As he screwed his eyes tight shut, he felt empty air around his bare feet. Far more sluggishly than he could have wished, the void reclaimed him from the glutinous grip of the transmuted rock and tile. As his upraised hands and sword finally came free, he fell, a shorter distance than he had expected, to land in an ungainly crouch.

'This way.' Sirince waited, one hand raised with a mist of golden magelight swirling around his fingers.

Kheda rose, brushing himself down until he realised that passing through the floor had left no trace on his hauberk. Though his sword was as clean as if Telouet had been scouring it with sand and oil and rag.

You can do all this as naturally as breathing, master mage. You've been holding back thus far, haven't you? What else can you do? What else will you do, without reference to me or anyone else?

Sirince hurried away. His pale magelight reflected back from whitewashed brick, little different from the lower reaches of the fortress. Other tunnels joined their path. More could be presumed behind narrow barred doors. Every so often, blind curtained alcoves jutted off to one hand or the other.

Where Ulla Safar's spies can sit and listen to everything that's being said on the other side of the wall.

'Can you tell where these passages go?' Kheda asked. 'Or what rooms we're behind?'

'I could but it's not necessary.' Sirince was utterly intent on his quest.

A few twists and turns later, the wizard halted by an unremarkable curtain of coarsely spun hemp, no different from countless others they had passed. 'This is it.'

Kheda drew the curtain aside with a swift tug. A heavily reinforced door with an uncompromisingly solid lock faced them. He glanced at Sirince. 'Can you tell if there's anyone in there?'

Laying the hand that wasn't wreathed in magelight flat on the wall, the mage closed his eyes for a moment. 'No, no one.'

'That's something to be grateful for,' Kheda said grimly. 'Can you get us in there?'

'Of course.' Sirince's mischievous smile lifted years from his face. 'No doors are barred to wizards with an earth affinity.' He touched the plate of the lock with a delicate forefinger.

Kheda heard the tumblers obediently roll and click. 'Let me go first.'

There was no one in the treasure chamber. If there had been, they would have been horribly startled unless they knew the secrets of the hidden passages. The inner surface

of the door was covered with a thin layer of stone crafted
to blend seamlessly with the wall on either side.

Kheda held the door for a moment rather than let it
swing closed. 'You can find whatever hidden mechanism
opens this thing?'

'Naturally.' Sirince kicked the door shut.

The vaulted room was still and silent, lit only by
daylight falling down shafts concealed in the thickness
of the fortress's walls. Kheda stood in the pool of light
beneath one and squinted upwards. Any thief bold
enough to climb the inner fortress's roofs and try cutting
through the thick glass and the costly steel bars beneath
it would still find the way too narrow for even the
smallest child to pass. He turned his attention to the
room itself.

Leather-covered and nail-studded, mute coffers were
ranked on wide stone shelves between sturdy pillars. They
ranged from massive iron-bound chests with curved lids
rising higher than Kheda's knee to strongboxes that a
sturdy slave might carry on a trading voyage or a diplo-
matic visit. Delicate caskets were carefully stowed on the
highest shelves, protected from the hard stone by cloths
spread beneath them. Wrought of silver, ivory and fragrant
woods, some were carved or embossed, others inlaid with
coloured stones and nacre iridescent in Sirince's magelight. In the middle of the room open baskets were massed,
piled high with cloth-wrapped bundles. Here and there a
gleam of precious metal escaped its shroud.

Kheda shifted a rag with the tip of his sword to reveal
a golden plate with a rim of embossed triremes. 'Where
are the gems from the cave where Dev died?'

'Over here.' Sirince was prowling along the far wall.
'Ulla Safar wasn't concerned with any taint of ill luck.'
He gestured at a row of squat chests and the first lid flew
up, then the second, third and fourth. 'They're all mixed

in together.' Countless pouches of fine fabric were packed tight within each one.

'Can you draw out the tainted gems?' Kheda asked.

'We certainly can't carry all that lot away with us.' Sirince looked around the room. 'What do you intend putting them in?'

'This will do.' Kheda upended a basket of tightly woven saller straw, sending a noisy cascade of brass goblets skittering over the polished stone floor.

'As you wish.' Sirince rubbed his hands together and the magelight he had been summoning faded.

Kheda blinked as the room darkened, the colourless pools of daylight on the floor growing paradoxically brighter. A fiery spark shot across the gloom, then another. A blue glint followed, like a splinter of a cloudless sky, then a flurry of green fragments, brilliant as a glory-bird's breast feathers. Rubies, sapphires and emeralds burst through the fine cloth of the bags that had contained them and darted across the room. They fell into the basket at Kheda's feet, pattering like a fall of hail on the wide leaves of a pitral plant. Diamonds sped through the air to join them, sparkling with all the colours of the rainbow.

A heavy hand banged on the outer door of the room. 'Who's in there?' an angry voice wanted to know.

Sirince looked at Kheda and the rain of jewels into the basket ceased. Splinters of radiance swirled uncertainly in the centre of the treasure chamber.

Kheda shook his head, warning the wizard to silence.

The door shook again, the metal ring of the handle rattling wrathfully.

Another voice joined the first. 'The key.'

The rattle of a belt chain dashed Kheda's hopes that someone might have to go and find it. 'Get behind the door,' he ordered Sirince.

The mage didn't move. 'Don't fret,' he said calmly.

Before Kheda could protest, a key squealed in the lock and the door was flung open. Two men burst into the treasure chamber, each with twin swords ready. A third hung back on the threshold.

Sirince swept his hand around. The rigid tiles of the corridor floor reared up beneath the third man's feet like a breaking wave, knocking him sprawling into the room. The door slammed behind him.

Snatching his dagger out of its sheath, Kheda took a pace to meet the first two. Both men spread out to flank him, intent on his death. He took a half-step back as the one on his off hand twitched the tip of his leading sword upwards. It was only a feint. The second man launched a lightning-fast attack, one blade scything in after the other.

Neither blow landed. The man froze in mid-stroke, like some child surprised in mischief. The one whose gambit had tempted Kheda coughed with surprise as his body betrayed him. He stood there, mouth half-open, only his eyes moving frantically from side to side, rimmed with white. The third man lay sprawled on the floor, unable to ease his awkwardly angled arms and legs.

Kheda's gorge rose at the thought of being rendered so helpless. 'What have you done to them?' Painfully swallowing his nausea, he swiftly ripped the swords out of each man's nerveless grasp.

'Don't worry.' Sirince frowned at the door and wound a skein of amber magic around the handle.

'What now?' Kheda hesitated over what to do with the confiscated swords. He dumped them in the basket along with the jewels.

'Let's not risk any more interruptions,' Sirince said wryly.

The bindings and hinges of the outer door glowed as if the iron was fresh from the forge. Metal spread out over the dark wood. There was no smell of burning as Kheda half-expected, merely a soft crackling noise. The flowing iron didn't stop at the edge of the door but flattened itself out further, crossing jambs and lintel to sink ragged claws deep into the ruddy stone. More questing fingers thrust down into the floor.

The wizard's glance summoned a second coil of mage-light to illuminate the hidden entrance to the secret tunnels. It flared and faded and now Kheda found it quite impossible to pick out the infinitesimally darker line that had marked the door in the pattern of the masonry.

Footsteps sounded in the corridor outside. 'Anjae!' a demanding voice shouted.

One of the men held in place by Sirince's spell managed a faint mewling sound. Kheda saw death dull the man's eyes. He realised with a chill that the others had already died.

'How did you kill them?' he asked Sirince with hollow distaste.

'More swiftly and more mercifully than you would have done with a sword,' the older man said calmly. 'Now we finish what we came here to do.' The mage nodded towards the open ranks of chests and the rain of jewels resumed. Falling thrice as thick, gemstones bounced off the weapons shoved in the basket.

'Anjae? Are you in there?'

They'd seen us. They'd seen a wizard indisputably wielding magic. They felt it wrapped around them. They would have denounced us. I would have slain them without a second thought if we'd met them in the corridors. Orhan said no one who's chosen allegiance to Ulla Safar can be called inno-cent.

Kheda winced as mailed fists pounded on the outside of the door. 'How are we going to get out of here?'

'I can translocate us wherever you want to go.' Sirince was unconcerned.

The torrent of magelit stones finally began to thin as something more solid than a fist crashed into the planks hidden behind the skin of metal that Sirince had spread over the door.

'Can you send us to different places?' Kheda asked tensely.

'Yes.' Sirince's eyes narrowed speculatively.

Voices outside broke into confused debate.

'What about these jewels?' Kheda looked down into the glittering basket. 'Do we have enough to defend Daish and Chazen?'

'And many more domains besides, I would say.' Sirince was in no doubt about that.

Kheda frowned in urgent thought, trying to ignore the redoubled hammering on the door. 'Do the stones have to be all gathered together like this?'

Sirince looked at him with growing curiosity. 'Why do you ask?'

'Caches of gems gathered together in Daish or Chazen could be stolen just as easily as we've stolen these.' Kheda rubbed a sweating hand over his beard. 'Word will surely get out that it's these gems that protect Daish and Chazen against the dragons, which will put a dreadful strain on even our closest ties with the likes of Redigal and Ritsem. Could you scatter them across all the southern domains? Single stones could be hidden in the soil, in the streams and under tree roots.' He looked up at the wizard. 'Would their influence still be powerful enough to ward off the dragons if you did that? We have to do more than simply drive these beasts from place to place. I've been wondering how to achieve that ever since we left Shek.'

A new rhythmic stroke began assaulting the door.

'You didn't think to ask me?' The mage waved a hand. 'Though I grant we've had scant opportunity for such conversation. You know, spreading the gems like that might well work even better than bringing them all together.' Sirince scowled at Kheda. 'But what about the Ulla domain? Are you going to leave it vulnerable or do you want it protected for your daughter's sake?'

'Protect it.' Kheda licked dry lips. 'As long as you can bring the two dragons in these reaches here first.'

'Why would I want to do that?' Sirince asked dubiously.

'To destroy this fortress.' Kheda managed a twisted smile. 'Then you must leave. As long as you never set foot in these reaches again, there can be no proof that the calamity was anything other than an unprompted attack by the beasts. Let Ulla Safar talk his way out of that omen.'

'Where am I to go?' Startled and somewhat hurt, Sirince's protest was overwhelmed by the blows of some kind of battering ram in the corridor.

'Wherever you wish.' Kheda took a breath as the attack on the door reverberated around the room. 'I don't want to seem ungrateful, but you must realise you'll be safer that way. Telouet has seen you use your magic against men just like himself. That's not the same as suspecting you and Velindre were working some sorcery against the dragons. I don't think you should risk your life on the chance that he will stay silent. I'd hate to see you killed for corrupting omens and portents and the natural order but I don't think I could save you.'

I won't condemn magic like my forefathers, not when it's saved my loved ones from the brute power of dragons. But I can see very good reason to bar such powers from the Archipelago, now I've seen you open and close doors and locked chests as you see fit, and murder helpless men with casual sorcery. No warlord could risk his enemies having such resources.

'I could go back to Hadrumal for a rest.' Sirince managed a resigned half-smile. 'I'll certainly need it.'

Kheda winced as men outside the door shouted encouragement to those wielding the ram. 'Can you bring the dragons here?'

'What then?' Sirince demanded. 'Orhan brought you here in good faith,' he warned Kheda. 'Are you going to betray him by demolishing his fortress?'

It's a good thing you do have some sense of honour to counter all that you could do with your magic if you chose to.

Kheda surprised the wizard with a grin. 'If the dragons break down the walls, Orhan's men can enter unopposed.'

'To be eaten by the dragons?' Sirince protested. 'I thought we were just going to open the gates.'

'I want the beasts to attack the fortress only to find something to drive them away.' Kheda's head pounded in parallel with the thundering on the door. 'Can you contrive that outcome?'

Outside, a new voice arrived and began bellowing questions, merely winning a confusion of shouted replies.

Where have all these men come from, if everyone was sent to defend the outer ramparts? Has Orhan been defeated?

'I believe I could,' Sirince said eventually. 'What then?'

'You leave by means of your magic.' Kheda calmly sheathed his sword and picked out the best of those dumped in the basket of gems. 'And send me back to the corner where we left the others.' He thrust the second sword through his doubled belt.

'What are you going to do?' Sirince's alarm rose over the renewed cacophony outside.

'I have a score to settle with Ulla Safar.' Kheda's expression challenged him to object. 'Whether or not Orhan wins the battle, this domain should be freed from his malice.'

'Have you been planning this all along?' Sirince narrowed his eyes at the warlord.

'Not really, but I don't know why it took me so long to realise this is what must happen.' Kheda managed a sardonic smile. 'Sirket will doubtless see predestined inevitability, if I can ever confess the whole story to him. I'd never have gone in search of magic to save Daish from the wild wizards if Ulla Safar hadn't refused to help and then tried to kill me. That's what gave me the chance to head north unnoticed. Now this whole course of events has brought me back here. I can put an end to so much mayhem if I cut the fat snake's throat.'

'As you see fit, my lord,' Sirince said with a hint of scepticism. He rubbed his hands briskly together. 'Well, there's plenty here to tempt dragons.'

'What—' Kheda's question was lost as brilliant light erupted all around the room.

Coffers sprang open, tumbling over to scatter necklaces and rings and talisman stones all across the cloth-covered shelves. Strengthening sparks glowed at the heart of every faceted gem and cabochon: emerald and ruby, sapphire and amber, and brightest of all, diamonds. The strongboxes below them burst, hinges and corners giving way to disgorge jewelled daggers and belt buckles, bracelets and anklets. The very heaviest chests down on the floor warped, split sides still stubbornly keeping their contents hidden though they were helpless to prevent beams of enchanted radiance from escaping.

The strands of light wove in and around each other: crystal clarity and fire red as heart's blood, the cold blue of a clear dawn, molten gold and the green of sunlight striking into the depths of the sea. Threads of similar hue plaited together, before unravelling to drift and eddy in dazzling confusion.

Kheda's eyes ached and his stomach churned. Sirince

by contrast looked quite content. The spectrum of mage-light swirled around him and the stones beneath his feet glowed with an unearthly radiance. As the glow touched the dead men still standing, they toppled over to lie across their companion, all three still rigid as bone.

'How soon?' Kheda's shout echoed around the room, unnecessarily loud as startled silence fell in the corridor outside. Shouts of shock and alarm were followed by the sounds of running feet scattering, fading into the distance.

'Every jewel on this island will be resonating to its element,' Sirince said with satisfaction. 'That will bring the dragons soon enough.'

'What then?' Kheda stood up.

'Then they will rip this place apart to claim these gems.' Sirince glanced around the room. 'There won't be much of this palace left,' he warned.

'It's been a symbol of all that's cruel and brutal during Safar's rule,' Kheda said obdurately. 'Let its ruin remind Ulla Orhan never to follow his father's practices. He can make a new start by building a new residence.'

A new sound sent shivers through the stone of the fortress and the swirling patterns of light.

'They're here.' Kheda looked up as a shadow far above blotted out one of the shafts of daylight still feebly trying to make its presence felt in the room. A new fear struck him. 'What if they just fight each other?'

'They won't do that, not when there are gems to be had,' Sirince assured him.

Kheda was shocked to see that the fingers of magelight were no longer merely coiling around the wizard. He blinked and was certain of it. The elemental colours were sliding through Sirince's body, oddly refracted. The wizard's eyes glittered like crystal.

'Dev died because he was overwhelmed by dragon magic.' Kheda took a step forward, reaching out instinctively. He snatched his hand back as a rainbow barrier snapped upwards from the floor.

'Let me enjoy it while I can.' Sirince closed his eyes, his expression disconcertingly lustful. 'The dragons will put an end to it soon enough.' He waved a vague hand at the basket of gems he had plucked out of Safar's hoard.

Kheda looked and was nearly overwhelmed by an urge to vomit. A vile brew of darkly lit jewels seethed like a boiling pot. The white of old bone vacillated with the aching blues and sickly greens of fading bruises and the threatening red of clotted blood broke through the suppurating yellow of a scabbed and festering wound. The swords he had left in the basket were discoloured and rusting.

'As soon as one of the dragons touches that, a spell of corruption will shoot through them like lightning striking a tall tree.' The mage's blithe smile was at curious odds with his ominous prediction. 'The scars they'll carry will keep them far away from here for even a dragon's long life.'

Kheda ducked instinctively as darkness swooped over the skylights. A distant crash of masonry was lost beneath a dragon's defiant screech. 'Are you sure you can get yourself away from here?'

'With dragon auras to draw on?' Sirince nodded dreamily, his eyes still closed. 'I could reach Hadrumal in a single step and still have the power to challenge the Archmage.' His eyes snapped open and Kheda saw that the crystalline glitter had fled, restoring the humanity to his gaze. 'Make sure you look after Crisk. If I can't come back to the Archipelago, I can at least write letters. As soon as I'm settled, I'll send word. If you're not prepared to give him a home, send him to me.'

'Of course.' The red-headed unfortunate's fate was the last thing on Kheda's mind. Still, he was hugely relieved that Sirince had remembered the barbarian.

Is that the crucial difference between you and Dev?

The whole building shook beneath the massive weight of a dragon landing somewhere close by. Its bellow deafened them. Footsteps massive beyond imagining paced overhead.

Kheda gripped his sword. 'I have to catch Ulla Safar before he flees.'

White light enveloped him before he had finished speaking. As he closed his mouth on a startled yelp, the magic vanished to leave him dazzled by brilliant reflections from a marble-clad passage. He was at the corner of the corridor where Telouet, Inais and the Ulla swordsmen had left them.

CHAPTER TWENTY-SIX

The crashes of devastation as the dragons wrought all the destruction they saw fit were mercifully distant. Kheda hurried around the corner, counting doors beneath his breath, searching his memories of unwilling visits to this fortress in former days.

That's Mirrel's audience chamber for greeting merchants from lesser domains, and her sitting room for entertaining visiting wives. That's her hall for summoning her tile-makers, and the one where she berates the spokesmen from the villages in the depths of the forest who cut sandalwood for her. There's her private dining chamber.

The doors were all ajar, no sound or hint of movement within. Kheda kicked each one fully open nevertheless, swiftly making certain no one lurked inside to pursue him all unawares. Turning the next corner, he stopped dead.

An armoured man lay sprawled on his belly across the floor, dark blood pooling around his unseen face. A gory footprint crushed the pretty yellow flowers of the tiles and a scarlet smear showed where the man's killer had kicked away his fallen sword.

Kheda hooked a foot under the man's midriff and rolled him over, not without difficulty. His head lolled at an impossible angle, almost completely severed. A sword stroke had laid open the man's throat to the spine. His features were obscured with stickily clotting blood so it was a moment before Kheda could be certain the corpse was neither Gyran nor Burai, nor Inais or Telouet. He breathed a sigh of relief before apprehension returned, redoubled.

There was at least one warrior still loyal to the Ulla wives. Are there others, and where are the women now? No. I left that task to Inais and Telouet. It's my responsibility to see that Ulla Safar answers for his offences.

He reached a stairwell and hurried down, one sword drawn ready, his other hand running along the marble balustrade. The ruination of the fortress echoed behind him. More blood was pooled on these steps and splattered up the pale walls, though there were no more fallen bodies. He reached the floor below and a slender woman ran out of a side room.

She fell prostrate at his feet, full skirts bunched up in disarray around her shapely legs. 'Save me!' She scrambled up to grasp his knees before she even looked to see who he was. Recognising him, she gasped. 'Kheda?'

'Mirrel.' He laid his naked blade on her shoulder, bright edge threatening her ebony neck. 'Where's Safar?'

'Save me.' Too panicked to hear his question, she stared up at him, matted black locks tumbling around her shoulders. 'Do what you want, just don't kill me.' She tugged at the low neckline of her tightly fitted bodice, tearing the silk to bare her generous breasts in a gruesome parody of seduction.

Kheda noted unattractive hollows where her ribs and breastbone were plainly visible beneath her dark skin. He took in the sweat stains and frayed embroidery marring the silver gown and saw that desperation and deprivation had carved deep lines in her face long before the chaos of this day.

'So you have indeed been punished for failing to give Safar a son to replace Orhan,' he said with cruel satisfaction. 'How did it feel to suffer the brutalities you were happy to see him inflict on other women?'

'Save me,' Mirrel wailed, and tried to bury her face in his thighs.

Taken unawares, Kheda was slow to move his sword and the razor edge drew a fine thread of scarlet below her ear. She recoiled, whimpering.

'Where's Safar?' he demanded again. 'Don't you want to see him dead?'

A second set of footsteps sounded on the stair below them.

'You!' Chay Ulla rounded the turn and gaped at Kheda.

Her hair was in wild disarray, her wide eyes bloodshot. Always handsome rather than beautiful, starvation and Safar's punishments had left her haggard. She gripped a dagger, her forearm and hand red with blood. Her single coarse garment was crudely made from a doubled length of orange cotton seamed up each side. Mere openings were left for her arms instead of sleeves and an unhemmed hole had been roughly cut in the fold for a neckline. Flapping around her naked feet, the fraying hem was stiff with blood, while lines of spattered drops crisscrossed her body.

'She'll kill me!' Mirrel scrambled around Kheda with surprising alacrity, frantic to put him between her and her sister-wife.

'We should have poisoned you when we had the chance,' Chay spat, advancing up the stairs. 'And that slave of yours. Who is he to steal Ulla Safar's wives and concubines?'

'I told my slave to lay down his sword.' Mirrel clasped Kheda's shoulders, her frenzied breath hot on the back of his neck. 'I said we surrendered to Daish. I won't hold your men to account for his death.'

'Where's Safar?' Kheda shook her off and retreated upwards a step, to be quite certain he was out of Chay's reach. A head taller than Mirrel, her long limbs were solidly built.

'He'll die before he's taken.' Chay's maddened gaze fastened on Mirrel, her empty hand clenching and unclenching. 'As will she. As all the women should have.' Her voice rose in outrage.

'You always were the most like-minded of Ulla Safar's wives, an eager partner in his perversions, aroused by his cruelty.' Kheda thrust his sword forward and down to stop her advancing any closer.

She kept coming, not looking away from Mirrel until the sharp tip of Kheda's blade penetrated the coarse cotton between her breasts. She looked down, almost puzzled.

'Are you wondering if I could kill a woman instead of a warrior?' Kheda asked menacingly. 'Until this moment, I'd have said not, but now, for you, I'm not so sure. Tell me where Safar is, Chay.'

'I will never betray my beloved lord.' Her eyes glittered with madness.

'Then you tell me where he is, Mirrel,' Kheda said harshly, not looking back over his shoulder. 'Or I'll let her have you.'

'There's a hidden chamber behind his audience hall,' she babbled in panic. 'The one with the ironwood panelling.'

'You'll die for that, you traitoress,' breathed Chay.

'The door's hidden between the pillars capped with water oxen,' Mirrel panted. 'The latch is concealed in the striol leaves.'

'Run, Chay,' Kheda advised her. 'Safar's rule is over. You want to be far from here before Orhan calls you to answer for all you've done in your husband's name.'

'Orhan will never rule here.' An ugly sneer twisted her gaunt face. 'Every omen forbids it.'

Whatever else she might have said was lost beneath a crashing cascade of masonry somewhere unnervingly close. Mirrel shrieked and flung herself at Kheda's armoured back. His foot slipped on marble slick with blood and he stumbled down a handful of steps. Chay screamed as his ungoverned sword gashed her flaccid breast. Reeling back, she fled down the steps. Kheda barely saved himself from falling headlong, fighting off Mirrel's hysterical embrace.

Chay returned, her dagger raised high. Skirting around Kheda, she wound her free hand in Mirrel's hair, hauling her off the warlord. Mirrel's terrified screams echoed off the marble walls louder than the roaring of the dragons high up above.

Before Kheda could do anything, Chay had Mirrel caught in front of her own body, brutal grip still tight in her hair. Wrapping her other arm around Mirrel's waist in an obscene embrace, she pressed the dagger point into the smaller woman's midriff. Mirrel screwed tearless eyes tight shut, dry sobs of dread racking her. Her gaze fixed on Kheda, Chay drove the dagger into Mirrel's belly with a vicious grunt.

'Your life was forfeit before you took hers.' He raised his sword as Mirrel sagged forward, her dead weight doubled over Chay's arm.

Chay tore her hand free at the cost of losing her dagger, throwing Mirrel's helpless body at Kheda. As he stepped aside, Chay flung herself on him. He fell backwards, betrayed once again by blood on the floor. Chay landed on top of him, her bare legs straddling his thighs. Her ragged and broken nails clawed at his face and her spittle stung his eyes as she screamed obscenities. Blood from the wound to her breast was rank in his nostrils.

Kheda abandoned his sword to seize her wrists, ripping her arms out wide. She hung above him, writhing, as his arms burned with the effort of supporting her weight. Suddenly bending his elbows, he forced his head up from the floor to smash his forehead into the bridge of her nose. Stunned, she went limp, and Kheda drew his feet up flat to the floor, ready to throw her off with his hips. Then the weight bearing down on him doubled, knocking the breath out of him.

It was Mirrel. He could see her ashen face over Chay's shoulder. Kheda fought his way free of the two of them to see that the smaller woman had forced herself to her feet and wrenched the dagger out of her own entrails. Spending her last breath in taking her final revenge, she had driven the blade hilt-deep beneath Chay's angular shoulder blade.

Both mortally wounded, neither woman was quite dead. Chay screamed with agony and outrage, flailing fruitlessly, trying to reach behind her own back. Mirrel dragged herself away, the front of her soiled gown soaked in blood and darker matter from her torn stomach. She slumped to the floor, hiding her head in her arms, moaning in mindless agony.

As Kheda retrieved his sword to put her out of her misery, Chay's screams were drowned in the blood bubbling in her lungs. Kneeling, he found Mirrel was dead without need of his merciful sword. When he looked over at Chay, he saw her lying still and glassy-eyed, no breath stirring the scarlet foam around her gaping mouth.

Shaken, Kheda got to his feet. A deafening crash sounded up above and fragments of marble flew down the stairs followed by a choking cloud. He hurried away, leaving the dead women to their shroud of dust.

Is this folly? Safar could be anywhere. How could Mirrel be certain where he is, if she's been running from Chay? But how can Orhan be certain of his rule unless the fat snake's body is displayed for all to see?

Another catastrophic collapse somewhere close made the walls and floor tremble. One dragon's triumphant bellow was capped with another's challenge. Kheda found a wide corridor and ran in what he hoped was the right direction.

Can we hope that Safar has already died, crushed beneath the ruin the beasts are making of this place? We can hope. But I must see if he's still hiding in this bolt hole Mirrel betrayed. If he is, perhaps I can make certain of him.

Kheda stepped over more armoured bodies showing evidence of deft swordplay. He ignored them, concentrating on keeping his bearings amid the maze of passageways.

Suddenly, both dragons halted their rampage and howled with eldritch agony. Purple-tainted radiance like a reflection of lightning shivered through the air, bringing tears to Kheda's eyes. Violent scalding winds blasted through the halls, sending him staggering. Everything looked distorted and insubstantial. Kheda fell to his knees, reaching for the reassuring solidity of the floor. It trembled beneath him, seeming to slide away from his fingertips. This was worse than fever madness. The dragons roared again and the air was torn by giant wings flapping with frantic haste.

They're gone. Was Sirince still there, waiting until the last moment, waiting for the creatures to break through the vault over his head? Did he save himself or succumb like Dev?

Chilled by the realisation that he might never know, and worse, the certainty that there was absolutely nothing he could do to influence either outcome, Kheda forced himself to his feet. Stomach churning and head swimming, he began running once again.

We have to be certain that Safar is dead. If the dragons are gone and he has survived, Orhan will never be able to rest easy.

The disorientation from Sirince's vile magic faded more swiftly than he had feared. He ignored stairs that would take him to the hallways leading to the outer fortifications.

All the same, he nearly missed the short corridor he had been seeking. Then he recognised the blunt carvings on the double doors of solemn black wood.

The audience hall.

He pushed at the heavy doors, half-expecting them to be locked. They yielded, pivoting silently on well-oiled hinges. Kheda drew both the swords he carried and entered, taut with caution.

Open to Daish Kheda, son of Daish Reik, reader of portents, giver of laws, healer and protector of all his domain encompasses. No, better not to announce myself in the formal manner.

There was no one to meet him, living or dead. The vast room was quite empty and silent. Long windows revealed that the hall had been built in the outermost circle of the citadel's highest tier. As he advanced over the sumptuous carpet, Kheda could see the roofs of the outer fortress and the crenellations of the successive walls. The river was hidden from view, but beyond the emptiness where it lay he could see the farmland of the valley and the denser green of the forest beyond. Overhead, gathering clouds presaged another rainy-season storm.

Approaching the windows, he could hear noises. Looking out, he saw the lower, outer ramparts were thick with people, shoving and jostling with fraught shouts and desperate pleas. Even though the dragons were gone, everyone was still fleeing.

There's no way Safar could escape through that chaos. Perhaps he is still here.

Another horrendous crash drowned out the distant hubbub and Kheda looked up at the roof. It was supported by sturdy pillars of ironwood covered with vines of burnished gold leaf and reaching up through two storeys of the citadel. As he watched, dust drifted down from the hammer beams to dull their splendour. There was an ominous splintering sound.

Whatever damage those dragons did has weakened this whole fortress.

Kheda quickly turned his attention to less terrifying beasts carved into the hammer beams, brilliantly painted to stand out against the dark ceiling. Jungle cats crouched as if ready to leap across the room and devour the hook-toothed hogs that bristled angrily opposite. Loals with their man-like hands and dog-like faces gathered to chatter defiance at them all. Water oxen chewed placidly on trailing strands of water pepper, too big and dangerous to be prey for anything but a hunting party armed to the teeth.

Wincing at another sharp crack from the ceiling, Kheda examined the panel between the pillars crowned with oxen.

How do I get in? Where's a wizard when you need one? Could I lure him out? Ah, what was it Mirrel said?

Kheda studied the striol vines carved into the dark panelling, no gilding to make them stand out. He looked more closely as a blurred smear caught his eye. Touching it, he felt stickiness. Bringing his fingers to his nose, he smelled blood. He pressed the leaf and then gripped it between finger and thumb, twisting it this way and that. As the panel gave way he heard a growl on the other side.

'Who's there?'

'It's me.'

Kheda stepped through to see Safar sitting on the edge of a woven cane day bed. A low cherrywood table was set to one side. Several small coffers stood open on it, haphazard between a brass ewer, a goblet and a plate of melon rinds. A lamp stand burned with three still flames to supplement daylight filtering through a narrow window. He noted a decorative lattice of stonework disguising it on the outer face of the wall.

'Daish Kheda. Forgive me – Chazen Kheda. What can I do for you?' The Ulla warlord sat with his feet planted wide, his vast belly hanging between his thighs. His hands rested on his knees. One fat fist gripped a bloodied sword and the scent of death hung in the motionless air.

Kheda looked at the two dead swordsmen sprawled on the midnight-blue carpet amid the pattern of horned fish and mirror birds.

'Mirrel sent her household steward Udea to kill me,' Safar said conversationally. 'My boy Ruki only proved capable of laying down his life as a good body slave should. Fortunately Udea was as ignorant as everyone else of the sword practice I have always kept up.'

'I'll bear that in mind.' Kheda watched closely for any sign that Safar was about to spring at him. 'Though I'll wager I'll still be faster on my feet than you, you slug. You're even fatter than you were at the turn of the year.'

'And how is your dear wife?' Safar smiled nastily. 'Oh, but you seem to have abandoned her. You do make quite a habit of that, don't you? No wonder your wives of Daish have taken themselves off to better men. I'm only surprised they didn't do so long ago.'

'Your wives are dead.' Kheda matched the Ulla warlord's relaxed tone. 'Chay gutted Mirrel. But Mirrel didn't die before she'd killed Chay herself with her own knife.'

Kheda wasn't sure in the uncertain light but he thought Safar paled. His skin was unhealthily muddy, glistening with sweat, and his jowls sagged beneath his full black beard.

Then the Ulla warlord smiled with malicious approval. 'Sisters to the end.'

Kheda noted muscle still corded Safar's bracelet-laden forearms even if his many gold rings bit deep into his swollen fingers.

'So, my lord of . . . now, where is it these days?' Pig-like behind folds of fat, Safar's eyes were unusually pale for a man of such dark complexion. 'Of Chazen? Has that pretty young wife of yours thrown you out, now that she's been made to look such a fool? You were supposed to be in medi-tative retreat, not voyaging round distant reaches with some concubine you've not even had the decency to acknowledge. Or are you of Daish once again? Are you finally throwing that wastrel of a son of yours to the sharks? Not even his mothers stayed to try to salvage the domain's fortunes.'

'I was wondering if I had the right to kill you,' Kheda said easily. 'I thought I might leave that honour to your son.' He nodded towards the narrow window. 'He'll be here soon enough.'

'One traitor joining forces with another.' Safar shook his head sorrowfully. 'Hardly unexpected.'

'But I think the sooner these reaches are rid of your vileness, the better,' Kheda continued, as if the fat man hadn't spoken.

Safar pursued his own thoughts. 'Orhan will never prosper in his rule. The omens make that plain.' He fixed Kheda with a malicious smirk. 'Your daughter will rue the day she marries him, if he lives so long.'

'The omens?' Kheda jerked his head towards the calamitous sounds overhead. 'You don't think dragons tearing your fortress apart is an omen that your day is done?'

Safar's eyes rolled upwards for a moment, sallow and discoloured. 'I'm still here, and by the sounds of it those dragons have gone away.'

Kheda opened his mouth in instinctive denial, before shutting it. 'It doesn't matter, Safar. I have every right to kill you. You tried to slaughter me and mine—'

'After you had brought the taint of magic here, fleeing from those wild men who were ransacking Chazen,'

Safar retorted swiftly. 'I was merely cleansing my domain.'

'You don't believe that and neither do I.' Kheda held his swords ready and took up a fighting stance. 'Are you going to at least fight for your life or shall I cut you down where you sit?'

'Will you let me die by my own hand?' Safar tossed his sword down onto the carpet. 'You're no killer, Kheda. Not in cold blood.'

'You're too kind, my lord.' Kheda acknowledged the supposed courtesy with a brief nod, never taking his eyes off Safar. 'Go ahead. Have you a dagger to cut your throat or would you like to borrow mine? Perhaps you'd like to fall on your sword?'

'You don't think I've prepared for this day?' Safar grunted as he fumbled in the folds of fat at his waist. He threw his dagger down to land beside his sword. 'Whatever the omens promised me?' He spread empty hands wide in apparent surrender and nodded towards the side table. 'I have poison in that ivory box.'

'Poison?' Kheda hadn't expected that. 'But of course. You would want to secure that last hollow victory, wouldn't you? To deny anyone else the glory of killing you. To fuel rumours that you were slain by treachery to poison Orhan's inheritance.'

'You don't want my blood staining your destiny, do you?' Safar's hand strayed towards the table.

'Go on, then.' Kheda watched unblinking as Safar picked up the small creamy box.

The warlord grunted as he sat up straight. Sighing, he opened the lid with a soft click. He held a wide-necked vial of blue glass up to Kheda. 'Leaf-snake venom.'

'That should put an end to your cares.' Kheda stood alert as Safar slowly unscrewed the silver cap and raised the vial to his fleshy lips.

At the last moment, Safar's pale eyes flashed to Kheda's face. He flung the contents of the vial forwards, springing up from the day bed with a gargantuan effort. Kheda didn't stand still to fall victim to the acid. It splashed across the floor, burning an acrid scar into the opulent carpet. Safar stooped to retrieve his discarded sword, surprisingly deft for a man of his size. But he was fatally hampered by his grotesque stomach.

As his swollen fingers reached for the hilt, Kheda had already stepped around behind him. He kicked Safar in the side, just below his ribs. The Ulla warlord fell to his knees, back arching to lift his quivering chins. Kheda swept his sword around in a fluid arc, beheading Safar in a single stroke. The warlord's gross body wavered for a moment, blood spurting from his severed neck. Collapsing forward, the tide of blood flowed to mingle with the smoking acid still etching the floorboards.

Kheda coughed at the foul atmosphere and ripped a silken drape from the day bed. Quickly, he retrieved Safar's head from a dusty corner. The golden chains the warlord had worn woven through his hair and beard rattled as he swathed the gory trophy.

Orhan deserves more proof than my word. Now I just have to take it to him.

Kheda ran from the hidden room, leaving the door open behind him. The ironwood audience hall was still empty. As he reached the outer corridor, he paused to take stock of the ongoing destruction. It sounded as if the whole far side of the fortress was collapsing.

Where the entrance to that tunnel beneath the river is. Better to try for the water gate. Will Telouet be fool enough to still be waiting for me there?

Kheda ran down the passage that he hoped led in the right direction. Steps took him down one level to a long empty hall opening ahead of him. A second stair descended to another marble-paved thoroughfare. The next flight he found would have taken him down to a level lit with guttering lamps rather than daylight. He turned away, not wanting to go too deep into the bowels of the island. The deserted corridor twisted and turned and finally gave onto a sweeping hallway. A barred and studded door was set between two iron-latticed windows opening onto a wide walled terrace. Sheathing his sword, still clutching the silk-wrapped bundle that was Safar's head, Kheda wrenched the bar aside one-handed and hauled the door open.

He had come further than he intended. Looking down, he found he was on the parapet crowning the second of Derasulla's three rings of fortification. In more peaceful times, canopied rowing boats ferried honoured passengers along the channel below. Now the water between the outer wall and this one was dotted with what might have been bodies or merely bundles discarded by the citadel's fleeing inhabitants. Walking slowly along, he saw a few solitary stragglers down in the courtyards on the inner side, hurrying towards their only hope of escape. Ahead, he heard shouts raucous enough to rise above the violence of the destruction. Glancing over his shoulder, Kheda saw clouds of dust exploding with every new cataclysm on the far side of the fortress.

Finally he drew close to the landing stage that was the sole link between the inner and outermost walls. On one side were the arches in the outer wall that led to the dock on the far side, where galleys coming up or down the river unloaded distinguished guests or more prosaic cargoes for the fortress's store rooms. On the island side were the barred doors that led to the lofty hall offering heavily guarded access to the heart of the fortress. Kheda found a spiral stair leading down from a watchtower. In the courtyard below, he fought his way through the crowds, kicking and shoving mercilessly with his feet and elbows.

The doors to the entrance hall stood wide open, within and without. Those who might have defended it were struggling along with slaves and servants who had fled the dank cellars and mean halls of the lower levels. Everyone was fighting to reach the fishing skiffs and rowing boats that were braving the bucking waters of the swollen river. The noise was deafening, the crush suffocating.

Kheda forced his way forward until he reached the perilous edge of the outer dock. He grabbed the shoulder of an islander trying desperately to prevent too many passengers from swamping his boat.

'Do you know where Ulla Orhan is?' he bellowed.

The man looked blankly at him, then pointed downstream towards one of the massive watchtowers flanking the swirling flood. Kheda didn't catch whatever the islander said but that was sufficient.

'Take me to him.' Straining his throat, he put every measure of authority he had ever claimed into his voice.

The man just stared at him, overwhelmed by the events of the day.

'Take me to your new lord Ulla Orhan.' Kheda ripped a fold of silk aside and thrust Safar's dead face at him.

Previously unnoticed at his shoulder, a woman screamed with piercing shrillness as she saw the grisly trophy. Kheda winced, his ears ringing. The man sprang into action, shouting at those already in his boat and waving away those pressing close to try to board. The Ulla islanders were already retreating, out of respect or from abject fear, and Kheda soon found himself isolated on the crowded dock. He stepped carefully into the boat with a curt nod and the frozen-faced islander grabbed his oars. No one else tried to jump aboard as they pulled away.

Kheda turned his back on the fortress. Ahead, the turbid waters foamed as the great chain was hauled up from the river bed by the immense windlasses in the lowest levels of the squat watchtowers. Crowds thronged around their walls while armoured men crowded the sprawling battlements. Kheda couldn't pick out individual faces and gave up trying. He sat on the central thwart of the rowing boat and closed his eyes, letting his chin hang down to his chest. Nausea lurked at the back of his throat and a headache tightened behind his eyes. The stench of blood and acid-burned carpet still lingered in his nostrils. His fingers were numb, one hand clinging to his sword, the other holding, unwilling, untiring, the bundle that contained Safar's head.

He did his best to ignore the voices screeching across the water, trying to listen instead to the susurrus of the river beneath the hull, to breathe in the freshness of the breeze now rising around him. Drops of rain began to fall, soft and cleansing. Eyes still closed, he turned his face upwards to welcome them. Frail peace hovered almost within reach.

'Kheda!'

The boat jolted him painfully as it struck the river bank. He opened his eyes to see Telouet standing over him.

'I was keeping watch on all the boats. I thought it must be you.' The warrior glowered down at him. 'Where is he?'

'He's dead.' Kheda held up the bloodstained silk bundle. 'Orhan is unopposed lord of Ulla.'

'That's not who I meant.' Grim-faced, Telouet didn't reach out either to take the bundle or to help Kheda step ashore.

He rose cautiously to his feet, the boat shifting beneath him. 'Sirince is gone.'

'For good?' Grudging, Telouet offered him a hand.

Kheda grasped it and jumped for solid ground. 'You rescued Safar's women before Chay could kill them?'

Telouet gripped his hand tight, increasing the pressure. 'Is he gone for good?'

Kheda looked the swordsman in the eye. 'Yes.'

'Don't ever bring his kind here again,' Telouet growled through gritted teeth.

'I won't.' Kheda looked upwards, blinking, the strengthening rain stinging his cheeks.

Not as long as Archipelagan skies stay empty of dragons, anyway.

CHAPTER TWENTY-SEVEN

'Have you ever been this far north?' Hasu wrenched at the silver sash securing his black silk robe as he retied it.

A passer-by hurrying along the shoreline slowed to stare at him. The man was plainly a barbarian, clean-shaven and wearing a loose linen shirt and knee breeches, though he had discarded his stockings and boots for bare legs and a battered pair of Aldabreshin sandals.

Hasu halted to challenge the man with an unblinking stare, hooking his thumbs into his sash and squaring his shoulders. 'Is he *zamorin* or a lover of men?'

'Quite probably neither. They seldom wear beards and if they do, it means nothing.' Ari smiled politely at the barbarian and bowed just a fraction, his generous ochre robe billowing around his bulk. 'I have been here once before and I was here long enough to learn that no one will thank you for starting a fight. Our client can't reward us if you've got us driven back out to sea by my lord of Jagai's swordsmen.'

Hasu let his gaze slide past the barbarian, folding his arms instead. 'We've more important business than teaching these people some manners,' he allowed.

Catching Hasu's elbow to force him onward as the mainlander strolled away, Ari wasn't finished. 'And my brothers will all get in line behind Etaish to beat some sense into you if you foul this up.'

'This client is worth so much?' Hasu shook his arm free with a scowl.

'Yes,' Ari said simply.

'So where is he?' Hasu looked around the bay, chewing on his lower lip. 'Do you know his ship?'

The waters were crowded with both barbarian merchantmen with their steep sides and curiously rigged sails and Aldabreshin vessels ranging from the lightest dispatch boats to the greatest three-masted galleys.

'He's paying enough for us to wait on his convenience.' Ari was more interested in the view inland. 'There are plenty of opportunities for us to pursue while we're here.'

He studied the range of open-fronted buildings where merchants were opening up secure storerooms. Some were already setting out their wares in shaded comfort beneath brightly painted wooden canopies. Others were rigging the more customary awnings, casting envious glances at their more fortunate fellows. Neatly dug footings and stacks of pale stone blocks fresh from some quarry showed that the lord of Jagai was keen to accommodate them all in like fashion as soon as possible. There were a few customers around, mostly barbarians taking advantage of the morning cool.

Hasu looked along the coastline, frowning at the solidly built stone jetties newly thrust out into the sparkling seas. 'Doesn't Jagai Kalu worry about being invaded as he builds such easy access to his shores?'

'Perhaps he's relying on his new mainlander friends to come to his aid if he's attacked.' Ari pursed his lips. 'Anyway, who would invade? Nahik Jarir certainly isn't going to give the mainlanders any more reason to condemn him and shun his sea lanes. His trade is crippled as it is.'

'Will he be able to drive the corsairs out of his islands?' Hasu plainly doubted that.

Ari shrugged again. 'He's every incentive to try his utmost, if Relshaz and Col won't allow ships using his sea lanes to anchor until he puts an end to their raids on the mainland.'

'There are other barbarian ports,' Hasu said with the suggestion of a sneer.

'None so large or welcoming,' Ari retorted. 'Besides, the word is that the lesser anchorages are starting to impose the same conditions.'

'But how do they know which ships have sailed where, and who's had dealings with the corsairs?' Hasu wondered, frustrated.

'They're mainlanders.' Ari succumbed to a shiver of disquiet. 'They have all manner of resources we wouldn't contemplate using.'

'You mean magic,' Hasu said bluntly. 'Aren't we running grave risks of its taint by dealing with this new client? The Opal's in the arc of death, you do know that?'

'We don't know that this client is necessarily a barbarian,' Ari said evasively. 'Besides, the Opal's waning and the Pearl is waxing, in the arc of family where the Hoe promises reward for diligent labour. The Ruby and the Mirror Bird are both safeguards against magic and they're both in the arc of health. We should be safe enough.' All the same, he fingered the long necklace of jet beads sliding across his chest. His other hand continued to rest protectively on a sturdy leather pouch hanging from the belt cinching his generous waist.

Hasu looked at the carved round of satinstone pale green against his dark, muscular wrist. 'We should still cleanse all our talismans as soon as we leave these waters, with water, smoke and sunlight.'

'It couldn't hurt,' Ari allowed.

'Excuse me.' An Aldabreshi strolling with a companion beneath the nut palms planted to shade the paved walkway approached them. He was a tall man with a coppery hue to his hair that suggested some mainlander blood in his line. 'Are you the master of the *Scarlet Jewel*?'

'I am.' Ari swept a florid bow.

The man slid an engraved copper ring from one callused finger. His clothing and bearing made it plain he was a mariner. 'I believe you have news for me.'

'Who's your friend?' Hasu was looking insolently at the second man. Though his hair was black enough to be Aldabreshin, where it wasn't touched with grey, his pale skin and eyes as well as his dress made it plain he was a mainlander.

'Mind your manners.' Ari looked up from setting the mariner's copper ring next to one he had taken off his own finger. He rotated the two and the engravings aligned to make a new pattern. 'Your name, master?'

'Lento.' The mariner looked expectantly at Ari.

'Then you are well met.' Ari bowed again.

'I said, who's your friend?' Hasu was looking the barbarian up and down with disdain.

The man smiled back with genial incomprehension.

'No one to concern you,' Lento said briefly. 'He doesn't speak our tongue, so we can talk freely.'

'You can keep your mouth shut, Hasu, if you can't be polite.' Ari shot the younger man a warning look as he unbuckled the secure pouch on his hip. 'As for what we have to say, Master Lento, I'll let my writings speak for me.' He took out a tight roll of fine paper dotted with intricate wax seals. 'Oh, and I have those books that you were asking for – the mathematical discourse and the herbal from Barbak. Do you have the metallurgical treatise you promised in return?'

'I do, two copies.' Lento turned the sealed roll of paper this way and that. 'This is a full report?'

'As full as we could make it,' Ari said apologetically. 'All my brothers and I have gathered every report, every rumour, just as we were bidden. But with the Ulla domain so far in the south . . .' He shook his head sorrowfully. 'The birds can only do so much. If we don't have them where we need them, they can't carry news. By the time we've sent a boat to take them there, events have all too often moved on—'

'I'm sure you have done your best,' Lento assured him, 'and that will be better than the efforts of any ten other message-brokers all put together.'

'You are too kind.' Ari bowed. 'Though correct, naturally. I take it you have suitable recompense for all our time and trouble in gathering this news?'

'I do.' Lento grinned. 'Mainlander steel and bronze, thrice as much as we delivered to your brother Daride.'

'Already worked or fresh from the furnace?' Hasu asked instantly.

'Virgin ingots.' Lento's smile broadened. 'And for your personal trade, I've a sizeable chest of amber beads and feldspar, together with a good quantity of this.' He reached into the neck of his tunic and pulled out a silver chain. A pendant hung from it, braided silver wire framing a polished disc of pale-grey stone veined with wavering blue and purple lines.

'What is that?' Ari asked, mystified.

Lento slipped the chain over his head and offered it to Ari. 'A rare stone from the furthest barbarian north, where the rivers are rimmed with ice all year round.'

'That's impossible,' scoffed Hasu.

'Don't show yourself up for a fool, boy. All manner of things may be possible that you've no knowledge of.' Ari examined the stone with an expert eye. 'What is this talisman for? What are its healing properties?'

'No one knows.' Lento shrugged. 'The barbarians know nothing of such matters, do they?'

'Are all your pieces crafted and polished?' Ari looked still closer at the patterns in the disc.

'By no means,' Lento assured him.

'Then I can think of several soothsayers and philosophers who will be fascinated to see such a stone, raw and worked.' Ari reluctantly held out his hand to return the pendant jewel.

'That's yours.' Lento glanced at his barbarian companion as the man shifted his feet and cleared his throat.

'Are you sure he can't understand us?' Ari asked casually.

'Perfectly.' Lento nodded at the banded stone dangling from Ari's fingers. 'When you show that to those philosophers and seers, get as much lore on dragons from them as you can. That will be sufficient recompense.'

'The dragons have flown.' Hasu gestured at the tightly rolled and sealed paper Lento still held.

'There's nothing to say they can't fly back again,' Ari said frankly.

'We know.' Lento tucked the dispatch into his tunic.

The barbarian surprised them all by speaking in the strange clipped tongue of the mainland. Lento replied with careful precision.

'Do you want predictions?' Ari queried. 'Whichever omens the seers agree will warn us of their return?'

'If you hear any.' Lento didn't sound too concerned. 'But it's old lore, old tales, poems and the like that we're seeking,' he said, more insistent.

'Who's "we"?' Hasu couldn't help himself.

'The people who are paying you handsomely for your services.' Lento's voice took on a warning note. 'Who will reward you still more richly for delivering this.' He snapped his fingers at the barbarian beside him.

The dark-haired man looked bemused for an instant, then reached into the leather pouch hanging from a strap over his shoulder. He took out a brass scroll case, the caps at both ends secured with crimped lead seals.

Lento took it and held it out to Ari. As the rotund man reached for it, the mariner raised it higher. 'You're to take this to Chazen Kheda himself. You're to deliver it in person, into his hands and no other. Do we have your word on that?'

'Naturally.' As Hasu bristled, indignant, Ari smiled placidly. 'What oath would you like me to swear?'

Lento handed over the scroll case. 'Your word alone is all the guarantee we need.' He bowed low with respect. The barbarian beside him was caught unawares, so it was a moment later before he made a creditable attempt at doing the same.

Ari studied the scroll case in much the same way as Lento had examined the sealed roll of paper. 'Do you know where I will find Chazen Kheda?'

Lento made a vague face. 'He'll be in the southern reaches, I assume.'

'Not necessarily,' Ari said dryly. 'My lord of Chazen seems to have been struck with a bad case of wanderlust. How urgent is this?'

Lento considered this. 'It's urgent enough that the sooner it reaches him the better. But the crucial thing is that it finds him, however long it takes. You are the man with all the information, after all. I'm sure you can locate him.'

'Oh, we will,' Hasu informed him. 'His name is still on every tongue on every trading beach and treaty isle.'

'Indeed.' Lento said something to his barbarian companion in the mainlander speech before bowing to Ari with an air of finality. 'Now, if you'll excuse me, I have other business to attend to. My ship's the *Diamond Serpent*. Call on me whenever suits you best to take on your cargo.'

'At sunset, then.' Ari bowed as the two strangers walked briskly away.

'What were they talking about?' Hasu asked under his breath.

'The mainlander wanted to get over to the slave-traders before the day grows too hot,' Ari told him absently. He examined the sealed scroll case one last time before buckling it securely within his belt-pouch.

'These clients had better be paying us handsomely,' Hasu muttered, 'if we're to travel the whole length of the Archipelago at their behest. The rains are barely half-done. We'll be heading into some filthy weather.'

'We'll find ample trading opportunities along the way, especially if foul weather pens us in the more profitable trading anchorages.' Ari smiled contentedly. 'Learn to look for the positive omens, lad. Now, let's see if we can learn which domains will be most eager for mainland steel and bronze before we plot our course south. And if you can't keep yourself in check when we're talking to barbarians round here, you can go back and sit on the ship. And you'll have to oil your hand and console yourself for the lack of a willing woman because I won't let you come ashore again.'

CHAPTER TWENTY-EIGHT

Finally, I return to what is supposedly my home. But I don't think I will ever come to Chazen without feeling like a visitor. I felt more at home back there in Daish, even with Sirket as undisputed warlord. This was Chazen Saril's home, where his children were born. Where they and his wives died before him, leaving him so disabled with grief. None of them deserved their fates.

A wall of steep mountains faced Kheda as he turned the little ship he was sailing single-handed on a southerly tack. Black against the pale-grey clouds, bare pinnacles and precipices of crumbling stone thrust upwards through dense forest woven into an impenetrable tangle by coiling vines. Kheda shivered.

I could almost imagine that ridge line was the spine of a dragon hidden within the rocks by means of its mastery over the earth, just waiting its chance to come forth, like the black beast on that western isle.

No. The dragons are gone. There's been no word of a sighting from any domain and flocks of courier doves have been flying in all directions these past fifteen days.

His gaze slid downwards. The mountains divided to embrace an isolated expanse, no paths or passes scrambling over the heights. Obdurate walls of rock on either side ended in pitted and broken headlands falling into dark-green water that boiled with foam. Man-made fortifications ensured that any gap in these natural ramparts and any path along the beach was blocked.

The only access to this warlord's residence must be from the sea.

Anyone sailing close to the steeply shelving shore uninvited was as doomed to disappointment as anyone trying to come over the high ground. A formidable embankment ran between the headlands, topped with a thick wall of pale-grey stone. Angled bastions thrust catapults forward to assault any hostile ships. Enemy warriors would be assailed by Chazen archers, raining arrows onto every grain of coarse sand from the oblique faces of the ramparts.

Will these defences suffice once again now that the dragons are gone? As long as the wild wizards who burned Chazen Saril's catapults to ash and twisted metal don't return. Has everything I've done since I last left here, all the lies and betrayals, has all that ensured brave men and honest men need never face such iniquitous attack again?

Swordsmen patrolled, ceaselessly pacing. Archers stood motionless, ever watchful, on the tops of the towers rising at regular intervals along the wall. Kheda noted that the wide wooden gate set into a central deep recess stood open nonetheless.

It would seem everyone here is confident. Chazen offers a general welcome.

Kheda counted fast triremes from the Daish and Ritsem domains, from Redigal, Aedis and Sarem, even from Viselis, distant Toc and, still further away, Tule.

There are galleys as well. Merchants are the first to vanish from the sea lanes if there's any hint of peril. I'll be happy to read a positive omen in the trade that has sprung up again so fast. That's no fancy woven from stars and wishes.

An unexpected gust of wind curled around the eastward headland to tug roughly at the little ship's triangular sail. Kheda hastily looped a rope over the steering oar and hurried forward to adjust the angle of the spar. Ceaseless vigilance on this last stretch of his journey had left his eyes stinging with weariness and the merciless salt-laden winds. His shoulders ached.

I've braved the rainy-season weather to come here. What storm lies ahead of me ashore?

A brassy warning announced the arrival of a fast trireme, its bronze-sheathed ram ploughing through the waters. Wreaths of foam curled away from the prow only to be beaten into submission by the triple ranks of oars.

Kheda spilled the wind from the sail and returned to the tiller to let the little ship idle. The trireme swept up to bar his way to shore, expertly slowing with a crash of dripping blades.

'You're showing no pennant,' a burly man by the upcurved stern timbers rebuked him, his sleeveless purple mantle thrown over workaday cotton trousers.

'Why should I have to, Hesi?' Kheda waved a cheery hand. 'How long have you been shipmaster of the *Brittle Crab*? I thought your heart belonged to the *Yellow Serpent*.'

'My lord?' The shipmaster leaned perilously outwards from the unrailed platform. 'My lady Itrac said to expect you but we were beginning to think you were lost.'

'When you were the one who taught me every back channel through these islands?' Kheda shook his head in apparent amusement. 'Didn't you make allowance for storms at this season?'

'We were expecting you in a Daish trireme, not some island trader's cockleshell.' Hesi frowned down from his vantage point. 'Do I know this ship, my lord?'

Kheda contemplated denial.

That would be foolish. As soon as he recollects where he's seen it, Hesi will wonder why I'm lying to him.

'It's the *Reteul*,' Kheda called up. 'The poet girl Risala used to sail the islands in it.'

'Ah.' Hesi looked thoughtful as he stepped back from

the lofty stern platform. 'Then we'll see you ashore, my lord, and in proper fashion,' he added severely.

The mariners of the *Brittle Crab*'s sail crew were already slinging rope ladders from the side decks and jumping lithely down to the little ship.

'My lord.' A competent-looking youth strode towards Kheda, reaching out to take the steering oar. Two others addressed themselves to the sail.

He halted the boy with a forbidding frown. 'You are not to touch anything in the hold, do you understand me? No one is to come aboard once you have anchored, no one at all.'

'As you command, my lord,' the youth assured him fervently.

'Very good.' Kheda waited as the *Brittle Crab* deftly shifted before making the less perilous climb to the trireme's stern platform.

He braced himself for questions from Hesi but none were forthcoming. The shipmaster concentrated on directing the helmsman through the dense gathering of vessels. Round-bellied, triple-decked galleys wallowed lazily as light galleys with their single tier of oarsmen, sat three to a bench, passed between them. Every vessel was watched by an outer ring of lean and menacing light triremes drawn from many domains. The heavier warships of Chazen surveyed these warlike visitors, even more daunting with their greater width and the warriors lining their rails. Plenty of faces turned to the *Brittle Crab*.

How many of these people will recognise me at this distance? I'm hardly dressed in a warlord's finery.

'Go close inshore so no one need ferry me,' he said. 'I don't mind getting my feet wet.'

'As you command, my lord.' Hesi called down brief instructions to the rowing master and then, unbidden, sent a man running to the bow platform. The trireme's signalman lifted his brass horn and sounded a clarion call. Warriors pacing the battlements of the shore defences halted to stare out to sea while the patient archers stirred into immediate action.

So everyone is going to know I'm back. And Itrac, as soon as a runner reaches her.

Biting down on his irritation, Kheda tried to follow the *Reteul*'s progress through the crowded waters. To his frustration he lost sight of the little ship as the *Brittle Crab* wheeled stern-on to the beach. As rowers appeared to slide the wooden stern ladders down into the surf, an honour guard hastily convened as swordsmen from the outer wall came running out of the recessed gate.

'Thank you, Hesi.' Kheda made certain his expression gave no hint of the exasperation and apprehension fighting for the upper hand within him. Climbing down, he acknowledged the warriors' captain with a courteous nod. That immediately set the men marching briskly over the white sand.

Islanders and visitors coming and going through the single entrance to the residence's outer precincts promptly withdrew as Kheda and this armoured entourage approached. The outer gate was merely the first of the defences guarding this vulnerability in the solidly built wall. Portcullises were hidden in the vault overhead, in the middle and at either end. All showed their teeth, ready to divide the tunnel. Thus caged, any attackers would soon perish beneath whatever the warriors overhead rained down on them through the hidden apertures.

The only other way out of here is through a secret tunnel that I've never actually had occasion to explore. Dev reckoned he knew its secrets, but Dev's dead.

There were countless curious faces inside the three-sided compound formed by the shoreline rampart and the uneven walls of sheer rock to either side. Kheda fixed his

attention on the residence directly ahead. The outer wall
was built of the pale, gritty rock that formed the spine of
this island. Angular towers were banded with darker stone.
There was something different, though. Kheda had
covered nearly a quarter of the grassy expanse between
the walls before he realised what it was: the recent rains
had finally obliterated the smoke stains left by the magical
fires of the invading wild men.

*There will be plenty taking that as a positive omen. Let's
hope they are not brutally disabused.*

He acknowledged the salutes of warriors standing on
the wall-walk before catching the eye of the captain of the
shore guards. 'You may leave me here and return to your
duties.'

As the warriors retreated, exchanging unreadable
glances, Kheda entered the inner compound. The gate-
house was easily the equal of the one in the beach defences.
Beyond, a water garden was spread out, its casual grace
offering a striking contrast to the dour fortifications.
Natural springs were channelled into crisscrossing streams
to enclose arbours brilliant with flowers. Pools foamed as
artful spouts threw sparkling arcs of water, setting azure
lily leaves ashiver. Tiny fish, white and silver, shimmered
in the green darkness between the swollen boles of
flagflowers. Cocky songbirds with plumage bright enough
to rival the blossoms serenaded anyone taking their ease
in these delightful surroundings.

*Anyone trying to attack by running through these shal-
lows rather than sticking to the narrow and capricious paths
would soon discover the spikes and hollows set to trip them.
What pitfalls should I be wary of?*

The innermost fortifications rose ahead. A solid wall
of banded stone enclosed the warlord's residence, entered
through a colonnaded forebuilding. Suppliants awaiting
his pleasure would be accommodated on shady benches,

or could admire the rose garden in the hollow heart of the square. Warriors atop the towers at each corner would keep an eye on them. But for the moment, there was no one there. Kheda walked swiftly over the blue and brown tiles towards the double doors at the far end. Swordsmen bowed instantly and opened the entrance to him.

Kheda passed through an ante-room and slowed as he reached the first of the gardens diligently tended in the courtyards that divided the various suites of rooms accommodating the warlord, his wives, their children and, when necessary, a multitude of guests.

Chazen Saril's physic garden. His legacy. He was no warrior, no great thinker or even an overly astute lawgiver, but that was no matter in such a minor domain. He loved his gardens and he married for love, wooing women who shared his delight in nurturing and cherishing his roses and these waxflowers and pitral plants and countless other specimens culled from the length and breadth of the Archipelago.

A young man cleared his throat and stepped out of the shadow of a broad pillar. 'My lord, you are very welcome.'

'Jevin.' Kheda favoured Itrac Chazen's body slave with a smile. 'Where is my lady wife?'

'This way.' Jevin's answering smile was quickly cut short. He didn't turn towards the inner courtyards where the warlord's wives were wont to hold their audiences. Instead he led Kheda through the successive reception rooms culminating in the domain's greatest hall.

What is my lady wife doing here, in the warlord's seat of power?

Jevin opened the door for him and Kheda stepped through.

The warlord's audience hall was stark white and empty in contrast to the ante-rooms' painted bowers mimicking the gardens and their luxurious cushions and elegant side tables. Anyone admitted to the warlord's presence stood on plain white tiles to await their ruler's pleasure. The only colour to ease the eye came from the stained-glass windows of the lofty clerestory. On a sunny day, bright colours dappled the floor, shifting and blending. With the overcast of the rainy season, there were only confused hints and shadows.

Itrac sat on the gilded cross-framed chair set beneath the white silken canopy draped from a bronze-sheathed beam fixed high in the far wall. Magenta skirts flowed around her, the bodice of her gown tightly fitted and high-necked. Wearing a triple-stranded choker and bracelets of pink pearls together with a long necklace of plaited gold and a profusion of gem-studded rings, Itrac sat bolt upright, slender and composed. Only her hands betrayed disquiet, tightly folded in her lap.

'My lady wife.' Kheda walked calmly to stand before her and bowed low. 'I trust you are well.'

'I am.' Itrac's painted face was an elegant mask of coral lips and gold-dusted eyes. 'And you?'

'I'm tired.' Kheda yawned and rubbed at grittiness in one eye. 'But yes, I am well.'

'You've been away a long time, my lord.' There was a slight edge to Itrac's statement.

'I have,' Kheda acknowledged. 'And as you know, I haven't been sitting in island seclusion meditating on my rule over this domain.' He smiled ruefully at Itrac and sat down on the hard tiles.

You evidently want to have the upper hand in this meeting, my lady. Besides, I'm too tired to stand up.

'Your gifts and letters from the western reaches were certainly unexpected.' Itrac looked more intrigued than cross. 'Though remarkably uninformative.'

'My apologies.' Kheda shook his head. 'It's a simple enough tale. The northern *zamorin* scholar who came here at the turn of the new year had found tales of a land far out in the western ocean, where savages and dragons lived. We went to find it,' he said with a shrug. 'We found it and we nearly died for it, but we discovered some answers to the puzzles of these past few years.'

'Will the wild men come again?' Itrac interrupted tensely, abrupt pallor beneath her cosmetics.

'No,' said Kheda firmly.

Not as long as Velindre keeps her word, and I believe she will.

'Dragons flew throughout the Archipelago.' Itrac didn't exactly sound as if she doubted him but her reservations were obvious.

'We found the means to drive them away on that distant isle.' Kheda decided that wasn't precisely a lie. 'Which we used to good effect in the western reaches and to repay our debts to my lord Shek Kul, by ridding him of a dragon.'

'As your letters said. But what of the southern domains?' Itrac looked over his head to Jevin. 'Please bring my lord a cushion and fetch us some refreshment.'

As the door closed behind the slave, Itrac continued. 'What of this northern scholar, the one that was friend to Dev? Are we still to be reliant on such lore?' Her lips thinned as she pressed them tight together.

You want Jevin out of the room in case I let slip that there has indeed been magic used to rid us of magical peril?

'We have no more need of any barbarians.' Kheda chose his words carefully. 'The Chazen domain has always been safe from dragons, thanks to the deaths of the first two to come here. Now northern lore tells me we can protect ourselves and all our allies if we scatter the gems that the beasts hoarded before they died.'

'Scatter them?' Itrac evidently disliked that idea.

'Throughout all the islands, as widely as possible, and in secret,' Kheda said firmly, 'so that no one can hoard them and withhold such protection from anyone else.'

'So that's why you attacked Ulla Safar.' Itrac stared at him with rueful comprehension. 'Not because of his transgressions against you, but because I had traded away so many of those jewels.'

Why did I ever make the mistake of thinking you were any kind of fool, just because you chose to marry Chazen Saril?

'You weren't to know,' Kheda said firmly.

'So you killed him.' Itrac glanced involuntarily towards the distant anchorage. 'And Mirrel and Chay, according to some.'

'His vile wives killed each other and richly deserved their fate,' Kheda said forcefully. 'We rescued the rest of Safar's women and the domain's remaining daughters, when Chay would have cut all their throats.' He saw a faint tremor in Itrac's coral lips and forced himself to a wry smile. 'Haven't these last few years taught us that all domains must work more closely together? I have much to tell my lords of Ritsem and Redigal of the various ways other warlords in other reaches cooperate. But Ulla Safar refused to help Chazen when the wild men first came, before we even dreamed we would be facing dragons. He would never have shared those gems to protect any other domain.'

'There are those who say you killed him to secure your own advantage,' Itrac said neutrally, 'through marrying your daughter of Daish to Ulla Orhan. I gather we are all to be invited to the wedding.'

'I've no ambitions to rule the Ulla domain through Dau.' Kheda looked down to see his own fingers laced tight. 'But I have decided I won't stand apart from my children's lives any longer. Not any of my children. I want to be able to offer Sirket my guidance, to mediate between him and Mesil when necessary. I want to see all my daughters of Daish wisely educated and happily married, as well as being the best and most loving father I can to Olkai and Sekni of Chazen.'

'So you have been meditating on the future.' The tip of Itrac's tongue flickered over her lips, and for all her finery, she looked very young. 'As have I.'

'You have something of importance to the domain to tell me, my lady wife?' Kheda encouraged her with a grin.

She smiled down at him with sudden sweetness. 'I was expecting this to be far more difficult.'

'Is that why you got rid of Jevin?' Kheda cocked his head towards the door.

Itrac took a breath. 'Here without you, with our daughters, I've been thinking about the past and the future. I've been remembering life before all these cataclysms, with Olkai and Sekni who were my sister-wives, and with Chazen Saril.' Her smile turned sadder. 'I dreamt of them, beneath the tower of silence where we laid Olkai's bones.'

'Go on,' Kheda prompted.

'I married Saril out of love.' Itrac ran a gold-varnished fingernail along the tightly strung pearls of one bracelet. 'I married you out of fear. I was afraid of what might happen to me, to the domain, if I had no one to protect me.'

'You were right to be wary,' Kheda said gently, 'with a monster like Ulla Safar to the north and no other warlord hereabouts ready to risk defying him.'

'You did.' Itrac looked at him. 'Don't think I'm not grateful, Kheda, I am. I will always be grateful to you for our daughters' birth. Never think I regret our marriage and all the good that has come of it.'

'But?' Kheda raised his brows.

'But the heavenly compass has turned and we live under different stars.' Itrac took a deep breath and forced herself to look him in the eye. 'I don't love you, Kheda. I respect you. I am fond of you. I owe you more than I can say.

You have been a true friend, to me, to Chazen and to the memory of those who died here. But I don't love you and I have been thinking of our daughters' future. With you away, I have had to rule in your place. I've decided I should continue to do so. Consider the stars, Kheda, on your return. The Amethyst is in the arc of parenthood where the Hoe signifies the labours we must undertake. It stands beside the Pearl, in the arc for omens for children, and next to that, the Ruby and the Mirror Bird shine together, both speaking of our duty. The Diamond stands directly opposite the Ruby and the Opal in the arc of honour opposes the Amethyst.'

She was speaking so rapidly he had no chance to interrupt. 'You were not born to Chazen, Kheda. You were born to Daish and you've said yourself that you cannot cut your blood ties to that domain. Olkai is born to Chazen and she will rule when she comes of the age of discretion. I want her to grow up seeing that a woman can rule. I don't want her to learn that marriage is an accommodation forced by circumstance and fear of the alternatives, however well you and I might be able to get along together. I don't want her or Sekni to feel they must settle for second best, when I have known true love—' She broke off and frowned at him, perplexed. 'What are you smiling at?'

Kheda rubbed a hand over his unruly beard now sorely in need of a trim. His grin widened. 'I was wondering what Janne will think, when she learns I've been thrown out of my domain by my wife a second time.'

'Kheda!' Itrac was startled into a laugh. 'But it's not like that.' She looked distressed. 'Though I can understand something of Janne's reasoning now that I am a mother myself. I truly believe she was thinking first and foremost of her children—'

'Forgive me, I was teasing you and that wasn't kind,'

Kheda broke in. 'This is nothing like the situation between Janne and me.'

She looked at him uncertainly. 'Then how do you see our future?'

'I don't regret anything I have done, believe me,' he said firmly, 'but everything's been done with an eye to the immediate situation and the short term. It's time to take the long view, for ourselves and our children, for all my children. I want to see this domain secure and I think you're right. In the longer term, Chazen will be best served by Olkai learning from the example of a ruling mother. When the time comes I'll teach her what she must look for in a commander of her swordsmen. In the meantime, I will continue to watch over the domain's warriors – with your permission, of course.'

'Gladly,' Itrac said with obvious relief. 'But—' She faltered.

'I see my responsibilities lying beyond these islands now.' Kheda smiled. 'I plan on bringing some drastic new ideas to our neighbouring lords.'

'You've seen this in the stars?' Itrac looked at him, her enticing mouth half-open. 'That I was going to tell you I didn't want you back?'

'No.' Kheda shook his head. 'That's another reason why I cannot return here as warlord. I still cannot trust what I read in the heavenly or earthly compasses, Itrac. You will have to find someone else to make predictions for the domain.'

The door to the audience hall opened and Jevin looked cautiously in. Itrac waved him away with an abrupt gesture.

'There's something else. I haven't given up all hope of finding love for myself again, Kheda.' Her coppery complexion was sufficiently fair that Kheda saw a furious blush rise beneath the gold cosmetics dusting her cheekbones. 'I would be happy for you to find it, too, to show

Olkai and Sekni the joys of a true meeting of minds.' She cleared her throat. 'Jevin tells me you came back in the boat that the poet girl used to sail, the girl who was the chief of your eyes and ears around the domain.'

'Risala? I don't know what the future holds for the two of us, but I hope we can make a life together.' Now it was Kheda's turn to avoid Itrac's gaze. He continued with brisk determination to turn the subject. 'The reason I brought her boat here was to sail to the island where I first encountered the wild men's magic. I wasn't lying when I told you that's where I was going, in the first instance at least. I promised you I'd bring Chazen Saril's remains back to lie with honour on the tower of silence. I've done as I said I would. All that was good in him should be carried on the winds to be shared with his entire domain. His bones are in a chest in the ship's hold.'

Taken aback by this revelation, tears welled in Itrac's eyes. 'Thank you.'

'I should have done him that honour long since.' Kheda got up, trying not to grimace at the stiffness in his legs and back. He held out his hand. 'Come, show me our daughters. I can't imagine how much they've grown.'

Itrac rose gracefully, wiping away a stray teardrop with a careful finger. 'You'll be amazed,' she said with tremulous pride.

'Jevin!' Kheda called. As the slave opened the far door, clearly apprehensive, Kheda grinned. 'We're going to the nursery.'

'It's all right.' Itrac rid herself of another tear, smiling reassurance.

'My lady.' Jevin satisfied himself that she was truly all right and his gaze shifted to Kheda. 'My lord.'

Kheda offered his arm to Itrac. 'My lord of where? We shall have to think about any title I claim after this.'

'Indeed.' She tucked her hand through his elbow and

he laid rough, weathered fingers over her immaculately varnished nails.

Jevin slipped into his place two paces behind Itrac as they left the room. They passed through halls and chambers whose lush decoration seemed all the richer after the echoing emptiness of the audience chamber. Kheda didn't register if any changes had been made while he was away. Soon they passed through louvred doors of dark wood into a secluded garden where countless perfumes mingled in peaceful harmony.

'Those cuttings you sent all the way from the western reaches have mostly survived.' Itrac looked around. Augury doves blinked back at her from an aviary.

Kheda only had eyes for the two baby girls playing with their attendants on a scarlet carpet spread over a lawn of pale, fragrant grasses. Olkai was sitting up, chubby legs splayed, safe between the outstretched legs of her nurse. The girl looked on indulgently as the baby played with a cunning knot of interlaced rings. The pale wood was damp and dinted with the marks of determined little teeth.

Sekni was chuckling with delight as the second maid, plainly sister to the first, set her down onto her back. The little girl instantly rolled herself back onto her front, lifting herself up on her sturdy arms. Her plump feet scrabbled at the carpet, not quite finding sufficient purchase to get her knees under her. Smiling, twin teeth already showing in her upper and lower gums, Sekni pushed herself backwards towards the edge of the carpet.

Kheda walked forward and stooped swiftly to pick her up. The baby's indignant protest faded as Kheda turned her around, cradling her in his arms. She smiled engagingly, bright eyes lively. Kheda smiled back before glancing at Olkai. She was regarding him with amiable curiosity, gnawing on one ring of her toy. Sekni reclaimed

Kheda's attention by tugging at his beard with a crow of delight. Wincing as he unwound her fingers, he looked up to see Itrac laughing.

'If I'm no longer warlord, of Daish or of Chazen, I don't regret it,' he told her simply. 'I've rid these reaches of the most dreadful threats, and if that's been at the cost of my own power, it's a price I'm willing to pay. This is my future – these little girls and all my children. What's done is done.'

I just have to make certain of what's to come without a warlord's power to call on.

CHAPTER TWENTY-NINE

Another ship, another shore, a dozen days since I made landfall in Chazen. Another gathering of friends and allies who may well harbour the most dire suspicions of me. Will this be the last time I have to explain myself? Will the one face I want to see above any other be here?

Kheda stood on the prow platform as the *Brittle Crab* cut a white furrow across the wide bay.

At least I won't ever have to see Ulla Safar's face again.

Caught unawares by that casual thought, Kheda stifled revulsion as his mind's eye recalled the gruesome relic he'd bestowed on Orhan.

'I wonder why Ulla Orhan has chosen to bring us here.' Hesi the shipmaster came walking along the unrailed side-deck. 'Safar scorned this place as the least of his domain's main islands and wholly unworthy of a warlord's residence.'

'I imagine all will become clear.' Kheda glanced back to see that the *Brittle Crab* had rapidly outpaced the *White Waxflower*. 'Let's circle to let my lady Itrac's galley catch up with us.'

'As you wish, my lord.' Hesi bowed briefly, noting every ship in the anchorage. 'Ulla Orhan has certainly invited plenty of people to bear witness to his marriage and his first formal declarations as warlord. It looks as if we're the last to arrive.' The delays imposed upon him plainly chafed his pride.

'I shall make sure everyone knows it was my choice to

make a leisurely voyage,' Kheda assured him, 'so no one else's shipmasters may impugn your skills.'

'I serve at my lord's pleasure,' Hesi protested unconvincingly.

Kheda saw him exchange a glance with the rowing master looking up from the open aisle down between the ranks of toiling rowers.

'I imagine all these other crews will have as many questions about the changes in Chazen as they do about this new regime in Ulla,' he warned.

'No histories relate a warlord removing himself from the domain's main residences to leave his wife in possession.' Hesi still sounded as if he couldn't quite believe it himself.

'Not to amicably set about having a modest dwelling built at her gates instead of setting out to raise an army to retake his usurped domain.' Kheda grinned. 'Make sure everyone knows that's what I'm doing, and that is all I'm doing. That this is no feint or deceit. I've truly set aside all claim on Chazen. I have no plans to return to claim Daish either.'

'As you say, my lord,' Hesi agreed in a strangled tone.

As the *Brittle Crab* wheeled around to let the *White Waxflower* and the *Green Turtle* draw close, Kheda surveyed the anchorage curving all around them. Wide white beaches cupped waters at peace in the evening calm. The route record open and unregarded in Hesi's hand showed the whole island was bent in a rough half-circle. Bathed in the soft golden light of the sinking sun, the land rose to gentle hills dotted with humble palm-thatched huts and patterned with cultivation. In the far distance, darker green clumps were strung out like dull beads on an unseen thread, suggesting some remnants of uncut forest.

Hesi nodded at the prodigious array of luxurious galleys

anchored in generous berths of golden stone built into the shoreline. 'Whichever lord of Ulla built this place wasn't worried about giving his enemies easy access for invasion.'

'Let's hope this new lord of Ulla is going to be on such good terms with his neighbours.' Kheda narrowed his eyes as he studied the tongue of higher land that thrust forward from the half-circle of hills. It ended in a blunt plateau looking down on the wide waters of the great bay. Whoever had built the anchorage had naturally chosen that vantage point for his residence. Tall, wide halls ringed with imposing colonnades stood four-square to the earthly compass, facing each other across open courts adorned with fountains. Smaller pavilions were set to either side, with lines of clipped trees marking out gardens and avenues linking them. All was plain to see, with no rampart raised around the plateau's rocky boundary.

Hesi was looking too, now he was satisfied he'd identified every ship. 'How can a warlord feel secure in such a place?' he wondered aloud.

'I saw residences without walls in the western reaches,' Kheda observed. 'And it's a viciously steep climb up any of those faces. I'll wager discreet work with chisels and hammers soon put paid to any easy footholds when this place was built. My new lord of Ulla's choice of residence isn't quite as undefended as it might appear.'

'Let's hope Dau Daish thinks so,' Hesi muttered.

'Let's hope she relishes the chance to turn Ulla's trade to securing everything she needs to return the residence to its former glory.' As the *Brittle Crab* drew closer to shore, Kheda saw this place wasn't quite as awe-inspiring as first impressions suggested. The roofs of the halls looking down from the forward edge of the plateau were blotched where tiles had slipped or broken. Stains marred the stonework of the platforms they stood on. Gaps like broken teeth showed where some accident had felled pillars in the colonnade of a lengthy building at the midpoint. The trees leading away to a pavilion just visible on the corner looked leafless and moribund even after the copious bounty of the rainy season.

'You're not the only one setting new construction in hand, my lord.' Hesi pointed at wooden poles piled up along the edge of the plateau and the skeleton of some scaffolding rising around the broad hall with the fallen pillar.

'It's a time for new beginnings all round, my friend.' Kheda watched as down on the dockside a gang of men sweating in dusty tunics hauled on ropes to swing a derrick to and fro. A wide barge had nearly been relieved of its cargo of newly dressed stone blocks.

The other two Chazen vessels drew level with them and a peremptory signal horn demanded Hesi's attention as a dispatch galley cut swiftly across their path. The harbour steward aboard waved brisk signals with flags snapping in the breeze. The *Brittle Crab*'s helmsman obediently leaned into his steering oars to turn the trireme towards the dock they were allocated.

'Take the berth on the inland side,' Hesi directed him. 'Leave the central one for the *White Waxflower* and the *Green Turtle* can anchor on the far side.'

Kheda was busy surveying the other ships.

Where is Sirket? I don't see any Daish ships yet. Will Sain have come with him? What will Risala have to tell me? Will she have managed to get passage here?

He soon spotted the great galleys that had carried his former wives to the new marriages they had chosen for themselves.

The Crystal Oyster *and the* Rainbow Moth. *So Janne and Rekha are both here. Are they going to make trouble? Or is Dau right to insist they were only ever striving for the greater good of Daish?*

The *Brittle Crab*'s stern nudged up against fenders of woven saller straw, each one packed tight with more seed pod fluff than an entire tandra tree's crop could supply. Ulla men poised on the dockside sprang into action. They snatched up ropes flung down from the trireme and had the vessel securely moored before Kheda had walked back down the length of the ship.

'My compliments to your crew, and my thanks.' Kheda inclined his head to Hesi. 'I shall go ashore to await my lady Itrac.'

Wooden stairs were already set firmly against stone ridges built into the dockside. Kheda made a careful descent. He looked up from taking the final step to find a clean-shaven figure awaiting him, plump and placid in unbleached cottons of impeccable cut.

Kheda stood still for a moment, then embraced the *zamorin*. The Ulla dockers and those Chazen rowers already coming ashore from the trireme all halted, astonished.

'Inais.' Kheda stepped back to hold him at arm's length. 'My brother.' He pitched his voice to carry quite deliberately.

'My . . . lord.' Inais was as startled at the rest. 'Of—'

'Just Kheda,' he interrupted firmly. 'Neither of Chazen nor Daish.'

'Yet in so many senses still of both, and most assuredly our trusted friend.' Itrac arrived, Jevin two paces behind her.

Inais took refuge in a low bow. A few bystanders did the same but more simply stood and gaped. Kheda could hear strangled whispers from men and women in the rearmost ranks of the crowd.

Inais straightened up and cleared his throat. 'My lord, do we await your slave?'

'No.' Kheda shook his head with casual unconcern. 'I have no personal slave these days.'

That set even more startled speculation buzzing through the onlookers.

'Then, my lord Kheda, my lady Itrac Chazen,' Inais continued with commendable composure, 'you are both most welcome to the residence of my lord Ulla Orhan. He bids you join in the celebrations of his wedding to Dau Daish.'

'I trust that his marriage to my daughter——' Kheda broke off with a sudden grin '——and she is your niece, of course, will be long, happy and blessed with many sons and daughters.'

Itrac waved a graceful hand back towards her great galley. 'My lady Dau's newest sisters are asleep, I fear. The nursemaids will bring them ashore presently.'

Kheda saw the curiosity burning bright in Inais's eyes before the *zamorin* turned around to lead the way off the dock. 'This way, my lord, my lady.'

They soon reached the long shadows cast by the neat row of storehouses set back from the lapping waters. Kheda could see the news of this remarkable arrival was spreading out along the arc of the harbour in visible ripples. Men and women hurried to find friends to confide in, to tug at the sleeves of acquaintances and astonish them.

'Your luggage, my lord?' Inais glanced at Kheda.

The warlord was walking beside him as if they were both escorting Itrac. 'On my lady Itrac Chazen's galley. Together with a few servants to see to my needs.'

'That's as well,' Inais commented sardonically. 'I don't think ours would be much use to you. They'll be paralysed with uncertainty.'

'We'll have to see if our neighbouring warlords hide their confusion any better,' Kheda said with relish.

Behind them, serene and gracious, Itrac smothered a laugh. Inais rubbed a hand over his greying hair and said nothing further as they made their way along the shoreline.

'Itrac, there's the *Scorpion*.' Kheda was relieved to recognise Daish's finest trireme.

'And that proud galley must surely belong to Sain Daish?' She raised her voice in a question for Inais.

The *zamorin* nodded. 'My lady Dau Daish asked that her lady mother bring all the younger children of the domain to share in her joy.'

'That's good of her,' Itrac said warmly. 'They can all meet little Olkai and Sekni.'

Kheda couldn't manage to say anything.

Does that mean Dau's forgiven me, even just a little? Or just that Efi and Mie made such a fuss about seeing their birth mothers again that Sain and Dau gave up the struggle to persuade them to stay at home?

'My lady Dau will be relieved that you're finally here.' Inais turned a corner into a paved walkway between the two long arcs of the harbour buildings. 'If you had missed the last tide, you'd have missed the wedding.'

'There was no danger of that,' Kheda assured him.

But we've managed to escape being cornered with questions before the ceremonies. So I can tell all our friends and allies what I want them to know on my own terms.

The walkway led them up a gentle slope, running between parallel lines of artfully trained shade trees. Birds were twittering amiably among the dusky branches.

'You've left your lady wife scant time to bathe and change out of her travel clothes. I take it you'll be honouring the gathering with suitable dress?' Inais looked disapprovingly at Kheda's own unpretentious green cotton tunic and trousers, ornamented with a simple pattern of embroidered leaves.

'There's time enough,' Itrac said calmly. In any case, her gown of iridescent black silk was pristine and the opalescent cosmetics enhancing her eyes and lips were flawlessly applied. Her unbound black hair was

immaculately dressed with ropes of pearls, while gold filigree ornaments dangled from her bracelets and necklaces
of nacre beads.

Kheda looked up at the spreading boughs and thick
glossy leaves overhead. 'These trees look better than those
scrubby specimens up on top.'

'All the water lies down here.' Inais accepted the change
of subject with the smooth grace of a well-trained servant.
He pointed ahead to a spring emerging from the base of
the plateau, confined in a broad basin edged with scal-
loped stones.

'The residence must have deep wells.' Kheda studied
the precipitous rock face ahead. 'Surely an Ulla warlord
wouldn't have built here without a reliable source of water?
Or perhaps that's why this place was abandoned?'

'There are unfailing wells,' Inais confirmed, 'and vast
cisterns carved deep into the rock. Long ago, there were
great screws of bronze turned through some contrivance
of fire and water to raise still more water up to the top
from springs such as this one. There are various mechan-
isms set around the edge of the plateau to lift food and
baggage and more besides. One works by balancing the
load going up with another coming down and everything
moves at a tremendous speed. But until the domain's arti-
sans can restore such wonders, everything must be carried
the long way round.' He pointed to a line of porters
heading for a track of beaten earth. They balanced loads
between them on poles and swinging in panniers from
wooden yokes across their shoulders.

'How long's the walk?' Jevin asked from his place
behind Itrac. His armour gleamed and crystal ornaments
in his brow band and belt glittered in the setting sun.

'Ulla Orhan doesn't ask honoured guests to make such
a trek.' Grinning, Inais pointed to an unremarkable
building beside the wellhead.

Kheda heard the rhythmic turning of oiled wood within it and saw a many-stranded cable of strong hemp stretching up the flattened rock face between fine wooden runners. He followed it up to a framework on the edge of the plateau where it threaded through a complex of pulleys and ran back down again. 'What's in there?' he asked suspiciously.

'A quick way up,' Inais said, offhand.

A slave opened the door to the low building and bowed. Kheda passed inside to find there was no back wall but rather a railed wooden platform at the edge of the floorboards. It was attached to the ropes coming down from the pulleys at the top of the rock face. Set to one side to get the benefit of shade and any breeze, a great treadmill waited to turn a vast wooden drum around which the thick cable would be wound. Two muscular slaves stood inside it, mute and submissive.

'We stand on here.' Inais lifted the bar that governed access to the wooden platform.

'Do we?' Kheda went first, doing his best to hide his misgivings. Itrac and Jevin followed.

As he joined them, lowering the bar, Inais nodded to the overseer by the treadmill and he gave the men inside a curt order.

Kheda couldn't help grabbing for the rail as the platform shifted under his feet. Then he realised he had seized the loose bar that Inais had lifted and hastily shifted his grip to a more solid one. Itrac was holding unobtrusively onto Jevin's arm, while the young warrior's other hand was clamped vice-like to the rear rail.

'I'm assured it's all quite safe.' Inais didn't bother hiding his amusement as they rose slowly and steadily up the cliff face. 'Ulla Orhan's most experienced shipmasters examined every detail of the rigging and every piece of the mechanism. Then they renewed all the ropes and sent whole troops of rowers and swordsmen up and down before they allowed him to risk his neck.'

'They'd hardly want to risk the instability that would follow his death,' Kheda said ungraciously. He held tighter to the rail and looked out over the sea. Anything was better than looking down.

'He's won more loyalty than that.' Inais glanced upwards to gauge their progress.

'What stops us coming down without anything to save us if a rope breaks or a spar slips?' Kheda forced himself not to sink towards the platform, no matter how much his knees wanted to bend. Then a startling absurdity occurred to him.

I have been shifted from place to place by wizards' magic. Unearthly sorcery has saved me from death by dragons and drowning and catastrophic upheavals of the earth beneath me. Now I am as craven as a child in the face of an unexpected mechanism carrying me up a cliff face. While Itrac looks entirely composed.

Taking a determined breath, he looked to either side. There were grooves carved into the rock at regular intervals and old stains of rust where iron posts had been driven deep into the stone. 'I see some other device has been ripped out of there. Was Ulla Safar responsible for such destruction?'

'His father was eager to melt down the metals for armour and swords,' Inais said with contempt. 'He was the one who abandoned this place.'

'Who built it?' Itrac asked as more of the buildings on top of the plateau came into view.

'Safar's great-grandfather began it,' Inais answered. 'Ulla Sabir. He was a great believer in openness.'

'Was he?' Kheda made a mental note of the name. 'I wonder if Ulla Orhan will let me read any writings this forefather of his left behind.'

'If any survived the ruination of the library at Derasulla,' Inais murmured guiltily.

Kheda refused to yield to such regrets. 'So Ulla Orhan has chosen to rebuild here?'

'He has,' Inais confirmed with approval. 'Though this was always the dry-season residence of the domain,' he added, 'until Ulla Safar's father made so many enemies that he decided it wasn't sufficiently defensible. He built Derasulla for the rains and another fortress on the north-ernmost isle for the dry season. It was Ulla Safar who decided he would live year-round in Derasulla. Between them they stripped this place of most things worth having.' His voice was dark with disapproval.

Kheda saw what the *zamorin* meant as they finally drew level with the upper surface of the plateau. At least one building showed the blackening of fire and another bore scars where carved stone panels had been ripped piecemeal from the masonry beneath. The fountain that Kheda could see in a gap between the two buildings was dry, with great cracks running through its shallow basin.

Inais looked to the west where the sun was gilding the sky, already half-hidden behind the rolling hills. 'My lord Ulla Orhan has asked that all our honoured guests join him for a brief welcome at sunset, before we celebrate his marriage.'

'Now?' Kheda's grip tightened on the rail as the plat-form jarred to a halt against a wooden spar.

'If you would be so kind,' Inais said firmly. 'We had expected you would be here sooner.'

'I was always going to have to explain myself sooner or later.' Kheda shrugged. 'Lead the way.'

Itrac shot him a reproving look. 'We are naturally at my lord Orhan's disposal.'

Inais squared his shoulders and strode towards the

central concourse. Kheda saw slaves or servants in clean,
dust-free clothes turn aside from whatever errand they
had been running to hurry in new directions. Elsewhere
craftsmen in grimy cottons continued with their tasks,
apparently oblivious. Stonework was scoured with harsh
brushes or washed down with handfuls of sopping rag.
Scaffolds were raised and up on one roof a gang of men
were busy pegging new tiles on bare battens.

Itrac discreetly plucked up the skirts of her gown to
keep her hems from picking up grime. 'Ulla Orhan wants
his visitors to see this renewal going on as long as the
daylight lasts,' she observed quietly.

'He wants us to see the reality rather than some pretence
of wealth and serenity.' Kheda followed Inais towards the
largest of the vast square halls in the centre of the plateau.
'This should be an interesting meeting.'

Fewer depredations were obvious here, probably
because this building's decoration of glazed tiles couldn't
have been stripped off without shattering them. Where
the other halls were set on pedestals with steps all around
to give access to doors on all sides, this building had only
one entrance and the sides of its foundation platform were
sheer. At the front, sloping walkways rose up from either
corner to meet in a wide dais in front of the massive twin
doors in the centre. The outer face of the double ramp
was decorated with detailed reliefs. Countless men and
women were seemingly climbing the slope, the closest life-
sized. As Kheda drew near, he saw that the long-dead
artists had depicted various styles of dagger and dress to
represent many domains, near and far. The colours of the
tiles were a little faded but the overall effect was still most
impressive.

They followed Inais up the sloping walkway and
Kheda smelled fresh paint. Canthira leaves on the heavy
ebony doors gleamed with fresh gold leaf and carved

wooden loals on either side were bright with new colour. The doors opened before them to reveal a vast hall, recently refurbished. Tall pillars marked off wide aisles on either side. Each column was crowned with carvings of perched eagles, their wings spread wide as they craned their necks beneath the ceiling to stare down on the gathering below. Each bird's wings were banded with bronze and gold feathers, eyes of jet and talons of nacre catching the evening light streaming through windows set high under the eaves. Jungle cats coiled around the bases of each pillar, life-sized and lifelike, carved from black stone polished to a sheen like bronze. Where shadows gathered in the side aisles, lamp stands with bases fashioned like seated hounds banished them. The walls were decorated with more tiled reliefs of life-sized visitors carrying prized examples of craftsmanship or natural bounty.

All these silent figures motionless on the walls were smiling happily. The living men and women standing in front of them looked at Kheda stony-faced, with open reservation or frank curiosity. There were more warlords and their ladies gathered here than he could ever recall seeing in one place. He met their gazes with blank amiability while Itrac smiled, perfectly tranquil.

There was no seat of honour built anywhere in the hall, nor any carpet and cushions where the lord of this residence might take his ease as he received his waiting guests in precisely calculated succession. Ulla Orhan stood over towards the far side, his back to Kheda, in conversation with a white-haired warlord. Daish Sirket stood close by, listening intently.

'That's Seik Lanis,' Jevin murmured discreetly to Itrac.

Ulla's neighbour to the immediate north and an ally of Ritsem.

Some instinct alerted Sirket to his father's gaze. He looked back, faint hope in his eyes.

Have you talked to Risala? Where is she?

Kheda caught sight of Ritsem Caid standing just beyond earshot of Ulla Orhan's conversation with the Seik warlord. His wives were gathered around him, in matching gowns of scarlet shot with gold. Slender and beautiful, richly bedecked with rubies like the rest, Rekha looked straight at Kheda, faint challenge in her eyes. Pretty in gold silk and pink pearls, Sain Daish turned to see what she was doing and reclaimed her attention with a nudge and a swift question.

So where is Janne?

Kheda picked Redigal Coron out of the crowd. He was one of the tallest of the southern warlords. Janne stood beside him, showing none of the humility expected of a fourth wife. Her brilliant blue gown was side-slit and low-cut to display her elegant legs and generous bosom to best advantage, while a wide belt of silk brocade defined her waist in defiance of age and childbearing. Indigo dye turned the grey in her hair into an artful reflection of her lapis lazuli jewellery.

No longer playing the dowager, now that you're Redigal's wife instead of Sirket's mother. Well, Moni doesn't seem to mind and she's perfectly capable of asserting her rights.

Moni Redigal wore a gown of sumptuous amethyst silk, gems to match studding her tightly curled russet hair and the profusion of silver gleaming around her throat and wrists. She was smiling, her arm slipped through her husband's. Redigal Coron looked more relaxed than Kheda could ever recall seeing him, turning to favour his body slave Prai with a loving glance. The youth smiled back with open affection.

You must be happy to know Ulla Safar is dead, my lord of Redigal, after he tried to turn your household to plotting against you.

All the same, Kheda felt a pang and wondered if Inais suffered the same.

Did you know our brother Refai was hidden among the ranks of the Redigal zamorin? He was as assiduous as you in serving Daish, until the deceits of the rest drove Coron to sink the boat that carried all his zamorin counsellors, innocent and guilty alike. Is that one more death I can lay to Ulla Safar's account? But Safar is dead. We're here to look to the future.

'My lord Kheda, and my lady Itrac Chazen.' Ulla Orhan turned around and held out his hands to them both in welcome.

Kheda noted the gathering mark such an unusual form of address. 'My lord of Ulla. My apologies for our tardy arrival.' He bowed to Orhan.

Orhan waved his words away. 'You're here now. It's of no consequence.'

A stir ran through the room. The assembled nobility couldn't indulge in the whispers of the dockside but they were just as intrigued as any humble islanders.

The young Ulla warlord turned around in a slow circle. 'Now we are all gathered here, I beg your indulgence before we begin the celebrations of my wedding. I want there to be no misunderstandings left unresolved before I turn my efforts from the restoration of this domain to restoring Ulla's wider reputation in these reaches. Before I embark on my married life.'

He paused. Absolute stillness hung in the vast hall. A few of the women looked on indulgently as the young man smiled shyly. Orhan's next blunt words shattered the silence.

'As we look to the future, we cannot ignore the past. My father of cursed memory delighted in causing and exploiting division. He would lie and connive, for advantage or merely for the delight of it. He flourished as a result. He abused his power and he abused the people of this domain, when it was his duty to govern them with wise laws, to ensure their healers protected them from the perils of injury and disease while his warriors defended them from outside malevolence. He abrogated his responsibilities as reader of omens, and when the vilest threat of magic appeared on our southern horizon, in a savage invasion and later with the shadow of dragons' wings, he did nothing.'

Orhan shook his head. 'No, he did worse than nothing. He watched and waited, looking for any way to win some advantage from the deaths and misery of countless innocent islanders across other domains, when he might have used the strength and resources of this domain in the battles fought by Chazen and Daish. When Redigal and Ritsem and Aedis all offered alliance and spent the precious blood of their warriors in defence of another lord's islands, he sat tight behind the walls of Derasulla and plotted how best to exploit his neighbours' distraction. I take it there is no one who will deny it was my right and my duty to save the Ulla domain from such a man. Does anyone cite any portent that argues against me?'

Warlords on all sides hastened to shake their heads and a supportive murmur spread among the women.

Orhan raised a hand to silence it. 'Such selfishness has not always been the Ulla way. This residence was built by Ulla Sabir, who saw this domain as a meeting place. With so many of the safest sea lanes passing through our islands, he saw it as his duty to facilitate trade and communication. You can see for yourselves how these halls were once all decorated with the riches that he won from such generosity. I have read the omens as the stars have turned above Ulla and I swear to you all that his is the example I will follow. I will leave the river to wash away the fallen walls of Derasulla. That foul fortress was condemned in the clearest way by the dragons that destroyed it. I will live here, without walls.

I swear to you that all my deeds and dealings will be laid open for all to see.'

As he drew breath, the murmur of approval grew loud, most of those present assuming he had finished his remarkable declaration. Orhan shook his head with a wry smile as he surprised the gathering by speaking further.

'I could not have won through against my father's malice without the courage of Kheda, sometime warlord of Daish and of Chazen. Just as you have all speculated long and with good reason over the recent events in Ulla, I know we have all wondered at the strange turns of fate that have thrown his life into new and unexpected paths. Like me, he wishes to make his new situation plain to you all.'

He turned to Kheda and bowed low.

As we agreed with Ulla Safar's severed head set between us. Now, like you, I'll leave plenty of things unexplained behind a façade of candour wrought from carefully calculated truths, admissions and omissions. And I hope my eccentricity will be a mere footnote to the upheavals in this domain.

Kheda bowed with equal courtesy. 'My thanks, my lord of Ulla.' Back straight and head held high, he surveyed the gathering, unblinking. 'My lords and ladies, my friends, my allies, I killed Ulla Safar. I do not deny it. Believe me when I tell you I lay no claim to this domain as a consequence, neither to its resources nor its favours now or in the future. I am not interested in any privileges that I could demand in recompense for such a victory. I am not interested in bringing any new threat to the stability of this region. We have all suffered enough uncertainty thanks to Ulla Safar of cursed memory.'

He turned to bow to Itrac and then to acknowledge Sirket with an outstretched hand.

'No child of mine nor no child of theirs will ever claim such rights. Daish Sirket rules in his own right and Itrac

Chazen rules until Olkai Chazen grows to discretion and maturity. I will govern my lady of Chazen's warriors and oversee her fighting ships, but our marriage is at an end now that the shadow of ruinous magic is lifted from the domain. You will honour her as the widow of Chazen Saril, no longer as my wife.'

He could see mingled relief and perplexity on faces all around. Hiding a smile, he continued. 'I married Itrac Chazen because magic and dragons had come to plague these reaches and that was the only way I could see to save innocents from death and destruction. I killed Ulla Safar because, all-unknowing, he held the means of driving out the dragons that had come to plague these reaches. The gems that these beasts hoarded had been coloured with the death of the dragons first seen in Chazen. Such jewels are now repellent to the creatures.' Kheda looked around, unsmiling. 'Does anyone here doubt that if Ulla Safar had known this, he would have extorted every possible payment and submission from every domain he could reach?'

He startled them all with a wide grin. 'I preferred to see these talismans scattered as widely as possible, my lords. I don't ever want to see a dragon's shadow fall on a single barren reef anywhere in the Archipelago. I have mingled them with the treasuries of Ulla, Daish and Chazen. I couldn't pick the stones out now even if I wanted to. No one can. I encourage you to take up Ulla Orhan's offer of this place as a centre of trade and exchange.' He waved an airy hand around the hall and towards the wider concourse beyond. 'As merchants spread these gems, all unwitting, ever wider, the safer we all shall be.'

And if that trade does spread such gems to add to the ones Sirince scattered, so much the better. Let this be the last lie I tell to hide a mage's involvement in Aldabreshin affairs.

While that revelation left most of his audience astonished, he could see questions rapidly forming on some lips.

'How do I know this?' He barely paused before supplying his own answer. 'Because I went in search of the means to challenge the dangers of magic and these dragons. You all know that I found it among the knowledge of these beasts hoarded by the barbarians of the unbroken lands far to the north.' Kheda spread his hands. 'Did you know there are barbarians who hold our scholarship in the highest regard, our knowledge of mathematics and the stars' compass, our lore of birds and beasts and all our philosophies? I wouldn't have believed such a thing had I not seen it for myself.'

He shook his head, dismissive. 'That's by the way. What's far more important is how much more I learned from the distant reaches of the Archipelago on my voyages. The warlords of the westernmost domains make agreements among themselves to curb any of their number inclined to abuse their position and power. They have found ways to raise all sons born to their wives without risking dissent that could destroy their chosen heirs and tear their domains apart. Yet there is much we can teach them, and other domains besides, especially with regard to the fair treatment of slaves.'

He paused, nodding thoughtfully. 'I found the answers I sought on my travels, my lords and ladies, and we are now rid of the dragons. But I found many new questions. Now that circumstance has left me with no domain to rule over, I intend to travel as widely as possible until I find answers. I will share whatever lore I find, have no fear. We have suffered too much from the habits of concealment propagated by men like Ulla Safar. Let us all repudiate such secrecy and selfishness, following the example of Ulla Orhan.'

He took half a breath to look around, his eagerness

persuasive. The mention of some new solution to the perennially fraught questions of inheritance had certainly caught everyone's attention. He risked the briefest of glances at Janne and Rekha.

Are you going to keep whatever suspicions you may have to yourselves? Has Risala managed to convince you there's nothing to be gained by accusing me of links with wizards? Dev's dead, Velindre's gone and Sirince was barely here long enough for anyone to remember him. If I have no domain, I have no power and I cannot be a threat to our children's future.

He wasn't sure, but he thought he could see some hint of acquiescence if not approval in both women's faces.

The silence in the room took on an uncertain quality as the assembled warlords and their ladies waited to see if Kheda had finished his startling speech.

Ulla Orhan broke it with a confident smile. 'My friends, the sun has set. The evening stars bring us a new day. Let us all go outside and see what omens may be read in the heavens for this new beginning marked by my marriage.'

He led the way and the gathering followed him slowly. Kheda could hear whispered discussions in all directions. He couldn't make out the words but the tone was hopeful, if puzzled, rather than sour with any antagonism. He allowed himself to feel a little less tense.

Outside, Ulla Orhan moved to the far side of the wide dais between the long sloping ramps. Everyone else spread out and gasps of surprise diverted the gathering from the unexpected declarations they had just heard.

The empty expanse at the centre of the wide plateau was now filled with bowers of brilliant flowers, woven in garlands around swiftly erected trellises. Trees grown in wooden tubs shimmered as oil lamps of coloured glass twinkled in their branches. Illuminated by larger lamp stands, embroidered screens offered protection from importunate breezes. Servants waited discreetly at outer edges of the overlapping pools of light and an impressive gathering of musicians sat motionless beneath awnings stretched either side of a tent of white silk. The first tantalising scents of what promised to be a fabulous feast drifted through the evening air.

Kheda looked round for Inais, to congratulate the Ulla household on achieving such a remarkable surprise, but he couldn't see the *zamorin*.

Movement inside the white silk tent silenced the wonder on everyone's lips. An armoured warrior drew every eye as he appeared and held the doorflap aside.

Lemir. And Dau.

Kheda caught his breath as she emerged from the tent.

She wore a simple dress of plain white silk that left her coppery arms bare, with a plain high neck and a straight skirt. Her hair was plaited into a single braid and her face was bare of cosmetics. Her youthful beauty needed no adornment. She wore a single necklace of talisman diamonds that outshone every other woman's jewels. Walking forward, she raised her face to look up at Orhan and Kheda saw the uncomplicated happiness shining in her dark eyes.

My daughter. And Janne's. Who always knew when to leave every other woman's splendour in the shade by dressing with magnificent simplicity. She is her mother's daughter.

'My lords.' Orhan's voice trembled for the first time. 'Will you do me the honour of reading the omens in the heavenly compass for me and my bride?'

You're no coward. Anyone wishing you ill could blight this whole day with some spiteful prediction.

Redigal Coron instantly stepped forward and pointed a commanding hand into the darkening eastern sky. 'The Emerald is in the arc of marriage for the first time in your lifetime, my lord. It is talisman for heroism, which you have plainly shown. It is talisman for peace and new beginnings, which you are determined to promote. This very night, the stars of the Mirror Bird that is emblem of wisdom and defence against magic rise with it. I see this wedding as a blessed new beginning for this domain and for you and your new wife.'

I wonder how much Janne prompted you to that conclusion? No, that's unfair of me.

Kheda rebuked himself, acknowledging the sincerity in Coron's ringing tones.

Seik Lanis surprised him by being the next to step forward.

'The Amethyst that is talisman for clarity of vision and wards against anger shines in the arc where we look for omens of parenthood and family.' The older warlord spoke with dry composure. 'None can deny you have seen your father's example for the evil it was. The stars of the Sailfish shine bright in expectation that your own marriage will be happy and fertile as you cherish such honesty.'

Ritsem Caid cleared his throat. 'The Ruby that is talisman to strengthen love and courage shines amid the stars of the Canthira Tree that regrows after fire and any amount of destruction. Both jewel and constellation are to be found in the heavenly arc of health. I see nothing but good in your future arising from the dead ashes of all that is finished with here.'

Viselis Ils nodded agreement as he raised his hand. 'Diamond that is talisman for warlords and warns us against all corruption joins the Topaz that moves from arc to arc with each new year, showing us vital clues for the paths we must follow. Look to them both, my lord, as they mark your wedding in the arc where we seek the omens for our own lives. The Winged Snake is there, that brings all things into the light and offers cures for many ills.'

Cryptic, my lord of Viselis, but honestly meant advice, which is generous given the trials your domain faced thanks to Ulla Safar's endless plotting.

Daish Sirket stepped forward and Kheda froze. 'The Vizail Blossom that blooms in the night, most potent talisman for all women, shines in the arc of travel. The Pearl that is talisman for Daish shines there, too, waning as she passes from that domain to this.' He looked up at the half-circle of the Lesser Moon and smiled, though tears glistened in his eyes. 'I rejoice that my sister's journey to her new life begins under such auspicious stars.'

Kheda swallowed a lump in his throat, his eyes prickling as Endit Fel waddled forward to raise a hand.

'The Sapphire that reminds us of the value of communication and truth is in the arc of wealth, my lords. The stars of the Spear that is symbol of all a man's striving in defence of his own shine with it. Though it is dark at the moment, we will soon see the first crescent of the Opal waxing there, too, gem for harmony.' He looked around, commanding despite his short stature. 'This is an omen we should all mark, my lords, not merely Ulla Orhan.'

So you certainly see the advantages to your trade from cooperating with Orhan instead of spending all your energies working around Safar's malice.

Alert as he was for any other warlord offering an opinion, Kheda was startled as a hand laced slim fingers through his own.

'You won't be saying anything, I take it.' Risala had slipped unnoticed through the crowd to his side.

'No,' he breathed as he kissed the top of her head. There were no more warlords coming forward. Down in the open space below, Kheda could see Ulla servants setting out a wide silver bowl and virgin candles for ceromancy on a white-draped table. A charcoal brazier burned golden and smokeless, a brass plate and talisman jewels on the table waiting to be set upon it and every movement of the stones marked. A deer calf lay curled in a basket, forelegs and hind firmly bound, its eyes hooded to keep it calm. A bright knife reflected a faint glimmer of moonlight.

'I thank you, my lords. We will gather here when the stars of the Mirror Bird rise, to bear witness as my wife and I make our promises to each other and take the omens for our future together.' His voice thick with emotion, Orhan turned to descend the far walkway.

Everyone else began filtering down either side.

'I won't dishonour their marriage by pretending to see something I cannot be certain of,' Kheda said softly. 'I tell anyone who asks I still can't find any certainty in prophecy.'

Risala nodded rueful acceptance. 'That should help satisfy anyone still wondering why you've declared your-self no longer a ruling lord.'

Kheda lowered his voice still further. 'What did Janne say when you told her what I intended? Did you manage to talk to Rekha before the news came from Derasulla?'

Risala nodded. 'Janne reserved her final judgement until she saw you had escaped the destruction of Derasulla,' she murmured. 'She takes that as an omen. Rekha was more inclined to read significance into you finally killing Safar and repaying all his crimes against Daish. They're both happy enough for you to do what-ever you want, now you've made it plain you're not going to challenge Sirket or threaten Dau's happiness.'

'So I'm free to travel where I want, to love who I want.' He grinned at her. 'Where shall we go?'

'First you need to speak to a man called Ari,' Risala whispered as she moved him firmly to one side so that the other warlords and their ladies could pass them by. 'He has a letter for you in a lead-sealed scroll case. He says it was given to him by a trader in the far north, a man who was travelling with a barbarian who was interested in the slave markets.'

'Sirince?' Kheda asked with sudden hope.

Risala shook her head reluctantly. 'Not going by this Ari's description. He won't give the letter to me or anyone else. It's for your hands only.'

Kheda rubbed a hand over his beard. 'Where is this Ari?'

'In the anchorage.' Risala nodded vaguely towards the shore.

'I've no time to get down there again tonight, not and make ready for the wedding celebrations and the feast.' Kheda shook his head. 'Whatever it is, it can wait till the morning. I'm here to celebrate my daughter's wedding.'

CHAPTER THIRTY

The unbroken lands. How can these people call them anything else? How do their rulers know where one man's domain ends and another's begins?

Kheda stood on the promontory, a prudent distance from the cliffs given the gusting wind. Ahead, the grey billows of the white-capped ocean rolled in to break in an unceasing roar, unseen down on the rocky shore far below. He looked slowly from west to east. Solid ground stretched away as far as he could see. As he turned full circle, the expanse of wood and pasture finally disappeared into indistinct haze some truly prodigious distance inland.

Three days and we barely travelled half a finger's length on that map Risala showed me. When the whole parchment was as long and as wide as my arm and only showed a coast on two edges. And I never realised anywhere not on the top of the highest mountain could be so cold.

He shivered despite the warm, long-sleeved jerkin he wore over a thick cotton tunic and a sturdy undergarment. Mainlander trousers of confining heavy cloth were belted securely around his hips.

All woven from sheep wool. Which are those dirty white things we kept seeing by the track side. Like a goat, only hairier. No wonder they need to keep so many of them if they all have to live through such cold seasons. Still, these socks of theirs are a pleasant discovery.

He wriggled chilled toes inside the knitted fabric that did at least soften the unforgiving leather of the boots.

'It's all so different from the city.' Risala came up and slipped her arm through his. 'Relshaz is strange, but you don't see so much of the sky. You don't realise just how far the land goes.'

'How are you feeling?' Kheda hugged her arm close, relieved to see her colour was improved.

'Better,' she said cautiously. 'But how do you feel about walking back to Relshaz?'

'I could be convinced, even in this mainlander footwear,' he said with feeling. 'How do these people survive a journey of any great distance in those peculiar conveyances?' He glowered at the coach that had bounced and shaken them all along the broad track that scarred the green hills of this curious coastline.

'I suppose they get used to it.' Risala didn't sound convinced. 'Like sailing through storms. Didn't your belly betray you the first few times?'

'Perhaps we'd have fared better if we weren't eating such strange food.' Kheda watched Velindre, deep in conversation with the man tending the two horses that had pulled the carriage.

Familiar and yet not, now the sun's tan on her skin has faded back to barbarian pallor.

Risala snuggled into his side. 'I could get a taste for this mutton of theirs.'

'I don't think the beasts would survive an Aldabreshin dry season.' Kheda extricated his arm to put it around her shoulders, oddly soft and bulky in her sheep's wool garment.

Velindre concluded her conversation with the coachman and walked over towards them. The mainlander began winding scarves around his horses' eyes. They stood still and patient, merely shifting their weight occasionally.

'I still can't get used to such a big animal being so placid,' Risala remarked.

'Nor me,' Kheda agreed. 'And I still can't get used to seeing Velindre in a mainlander gown and overmantle. She looks more woman than I might have imagined now her hair has grown longer.'

'Why do you suppose she's still carrying that?' Risala wondered.

The one discordant note in the magewoman's barbarian garb was the battered Aldabreshin leather bag she carried slung over one shoulder. 'Now we can make some progress,' she said cheerfully.

'I'm sorry we had to stop so often,' Kheda said stiffly.

'What?' Velindre looked puzzled for a moment, then shook her head. 'Don't worry. You're not the first to get coach sick and you won't be the last. I was warning him to stand by the horses' heads. It's midday, near enough.' She brushed at a golden tendril teasing her eyes. Her hair had grown nearly to her shoulders but was not quite long enough to be braided in any of the styles Kheda had seen on mainland women.

He looked up and saw the sun hovering at zenith behind the fine layer of smoky cloud. 'Now will you explain why we're here?'

'Is that important?' Risala pointed to a weatherworn pillar of masonry on the other side of the track. The niche facing the sea was empty but for a bird's abandoned nest. 'The coachman said there used to be a shrine to Trimon here.'

'You'll understand all in good time,' Velindre told them both with quiet satisfaction.

Kheda did his best to curb impatience that had been growing since their arrival on this deserted headland had put an end to the misery of their journey. 'The coachman said this day marks the turn of your year, when the sun reaches solstice. Is that—?'

'Oh!' Risala stiffened, startled.

A grey-haired figure stepped out of a flash of brilliant white light.

'Sirince, thank you for coming.' Velindre smiled.

'And good day to you, my lord, my lady.' The older wizard swept off a broad-brimmed hat with a mottled green feather thrust in the band as he favoured them all with an extravagant bow. He wore the mainlander clothes that Kheda found so irksome with enviable aplomb. 'Where are the others, my lady mage?'

'They should be here presently.' Velindre regarded him with some amusement. 'You've found some profitable business in Toremal, I see?'

'Indeed.' Sirince looked at Kheda, his eyes keen. 'How was your voyage here? It's been, what, a hundred days since you celebrated your daughter's wedding? What have you been doing with yourself?'

'Making visits that have proved both useful and informative,' Kheda replied with satisfaction. 'We've renewed and extended ties from south to north, and I'm happy to say Shek Kul's hold on his domain and that region is as strong as ever.'

'Stronger,' Risala commented firmly.

'And I had some debts to settle in Ikadi,' Kheda added. 'With a galley master called Godine.'

'How is Crisk?' Sirince held himself braced for the reply.

'He's well,' Kheda assured the mage with genuine pleasure. 'He lives with the Daish household. There's a barbarian slave there, Hanyad, who keeps an eye out for his interests and plays that game of the birds and forest with him.' He grinned. 'So does Telouet. Crisk finally agreed to teach him.'

'I'm glad of it,' Sirince said with profound relief. 'That he's happy, I mean, though I'm sure Telouet's pleased to play White Raven with him.'

'He will be once he can beat him consistently.' Kheda chuckled. 'Telouet wasn't expecting Crisk to be such a strategist.'

'How is Telouet?' The wizard looked quizzically at Kheda. 'Does he spit if my name's mentioned? Has he forgiven you?'

Kheda hesitated before replying as honestly as he could. 'We don't discuss such things. We don't mention you. Telouet serves Sirket as a free swordsman. He's made it quite clear he's no plans ever to do anything else, not even for me.'

'We offered to bring Crisk with us.' Risala was concerned that Sirince know this. 'But he said he had found his place and would stay. He read all manner of justification in the stars and in his tales of Trimon.'

'He speaks of such things again?' Manifestly relieved, Sirince managed a wry smile. 'It's all nonsense, of course, but it was one of the few things he had to console him. When he's lost so much—' The wizard's voice hoarsened with emotion. He broke off and rummaged in a pocket. 'When you go back, take him this, and remember me to him.'

He handed Kheda a shining copper amulet on an untarnished chain. The owl embossed on its surface was perfect in every detail of every feather.

'I'll be glad to,' Kheda said honestly. 'And he'll be glad to have it. He does think of you. At least, he mentions you when he's reading the stars or telling his tales.'

Risala spoke up again. 'He's a great favourite with all the children. He plays music for them and sings them songs. He can get a tune out of any instrument, even if he's never seen it before.'

'He can?' Sirince was intrigued.

A second bright light interrupted them, with another coming before the first had faded, like a double flash of lightning. The horses stamped their hard feet on the muddy turf with a jingle of leather and buckles.

'You're late,' Sirince chided the new arrivals. 'Couldn't drag yourself away from the midwinter festivities in Hadrumal?'

'Forgive me, father, I'm mortified.' The taller of the two men didn't sound in the least concerned.

Kheda barely registered this unknown younger man's resemblance to Sirince. He was staring at the other wizard. 'Naldeth?' For a moment he had failed to recognise him, dressed in mainlander clothes.

'Velindre didn't tell you to expect me?' The young mage walked forward with a rocking gait. A smile widened on his unremarkable, amiable face.

'How are you?' Risala couldn't help looking down at the wooden post that served Naldeth in place of one leg. His own flesh and bone ended at mid-thigh, his trouser tied tight around the stump.

'I'm well.' Naldeth held out one hand and Kheda shook it in what he had learned was mainlander custom.

'The wild men?' Pleased as he was to see the young mage, Kheda felt a cold frisson of alarm. 'What of their magic?'

'I've left a trusted friend behind to keep an eye on them while I'm away, a mage called Shiv,' Naldeth said, confident. 'And Eiz knows to alert him to the first signs of anyone coming into a painted man's power.'

'I'm sorry.' Kheda didn't understand.

'Forgive me, I forget who knows what these days.' Naldeth waved an apologetic hand. 'Eiz is the old woman, the one who helped us find that cave?' As Kheda nodded his comprehension, he continued to explain. 'And painted men, and women – that's what they call their own wizards.'

'You've learned their language?' Risala was impressed.

'Enough to make myself understood.' Naldeth shrugged.

'Thanks to aetheric magic?' guessed Sirince.

'To a certain extent,' Naldeth admitted.

Kheda wasn't interested in such things. 'Have any of the dragons we've driven out of the Archipelago returned to the island?'

'No.' Naldeth was absolutely certain. 'And without their aura to draw on, I think it will be a long time before anyone with an elemental affinity surfaces among the wild tribes.'

Risala was looking at the other man, the one who was apparently Sirince's son. 'Do you have something you wish to ask?'

Kheda wasn't too happy with the way the man was staring at the two of them. 'Would someone do the honour of introducing us?' he said in formal Aldabreshin fashion. He was amused to see the man's self-possession falter. Evidently he didn't understand the Archipelagan tongue.

'This is my son Lasul.' Sirince spoke up with a father's mix of pride and exasperation.

Kheda switched to the mainlander tongue. 'Then you are well met.'

'Forgive my curiosity.' The man, much of an age with Velindre, bowed low. 'I haven't seen many people of your complexion.'

'We have been turning heads since we left Relshaz.' Kheda had been finding such curiosity intrusive. He was used to being the focus of attention as a warlord but this was different. 'I can understand that we must be as unusual a sight here as you would be in Daish or Chazen.'

'Kheda, Velindre tells me you've given up all formal power in Chazen, and in Daish,' Naldeth said with eager curiosity. 'What are you going to do now?'

'I'm going to travel the length and breadth of the Archipelago.' Kheda looked around at the strange landscape again. 'And, it would seem, journey on the mainland, too. I'm going to bring new ideas to the southern reaches, on the nature of power, and on warfare and ship-building and swordsmithing and whatever else I come across. I want to search out old healing lore whose bene-fits have been lost. I want to see such things traded as readily as spices and silk.'

'You've set aside all your rank to do it?' Naldeth was bemused. 'That's truly an adequate trade?'

'You don't think there's plenty of power to be had in being the man who commands such knowledge and chooses where it's spent?' Kheda held the younger wizard's gaze. 'You don't think I can have far more influence if I travel through tens of domains, with ready access to curious warlords and their ladies, who cannot conceive I am any kind of threat since I have no army at my back?'

'Perhaps.' Naldeth was still nonplussed. 'And you're going along with him, are you?' He raised his brows at Risala. 'No more slipping in and out of side doors and leaving his bed before dawn so the maidservants don't gossip?'

'Now I can be his lover without any of the burdens of a warlord's wife or acknowledged concubine.' She smiled contentedly. 'I've always liked to travel and to make sense of what I see.'

'What do your noble neighbours make of this new life of yours?' Sirince asked thoughtfully.

'They are happy to tell themselves I have no power as they understand it.' Kheda grinned. 'Though I have reclaimed my *zamorin* brothers to travel and trade along with me.'

'So now every warlord suspects you know secrets of their households that they might prefer you didn't,' Risala added pertly.

Kheda spread his hands in mock innocence. 'I've merely done so to make a stand against the spying and secrecy that has bred so much mistrust.'

'Well, I'm glad for you, Kheda.' Somewhat impatient, Sirince attracted Velindre's attention with a brisk hand. 'Now we're all here, perhaps you'd like to explain just why you needed us all.'

'Indeed.' She opened her leather bag and reached inside to draw out a small casket of plain rock crystal.

'What's—'

Before Naldeth could ask, Kheda had the answer, Risala echoing him within half a breath.

'Dev's ashes.'

'Dev's ashes,' Velindre confirmed. 'Which you were good enough to give me to take back to any who valued him in Hadrumal.'

Sirince snorted with scepticism. 'Did you find anyone?'

'Planir knew Dev's uses.' Velindre shot the older mage a hard look. 'And the Archmage has given us, myself and Lasul, permission to use this final remnant of Dev's magic in service of the Archipelago. If you agree, Kheda.'

'What do you want to do?' Kheda was at a loss.

'We were scrying for Sirince, Lasul and I, when you risked your necks joining Orhan's rebellion. We saw you heading into Derasulla.' Velindre's angular cheekbones coloured. 'We were quite ready to use our magic to snatch you out of there, if you seemed to be about to get yourselves killed.'

Lasul anticipated Sirince's ferocious frown of objection. 'We were in Hadrumal, so if the dragons had come for us, we reckoned there were sufficient mages to drive them off.'

'Then we saw you scattering those gems from the treasury,' continued Velindre.

'It took us quite some while to work out just what you were doing,' Lasul said with feeling.

'I don't know whose idea it was but it was a good one.' Velindre looked from Kheda to Sirince. 'There's a taint spread throughout the southern reaches now that will certainly send any dragon in search of a purer elemental focus elsewhere.' She looked down at the crystal casket in her hands. 'But that still leaves the rest of the Archipelago unprotected. Unless we spread Dev's ashes on the winds and tides.' She looked at Kheda, unexpectedly beseeching. 'You've used magic to drive out magic that threatened you and yours. I know there are many who would say any hint of magic is a grave contamination, but—'

'No.' Kheda cut her short. 'I mean, no, I won't forbid such a thing out of fear of imagined evil. I've come to understand that wizards are no different from other men or women—' He corrected himself with a rueful smile. 'Well, obviously you *are* different, but not in terms of being any more or less honest or immoral.'

'Can you truly do that?' Risala was looking at the crystal casket with frank disbelief. 'Defend the whole Archipelago from dragons with a few handfuls of dust?'

'A little of Dev always did go a long way.' Sirince's sarcasm was muted.

'If we combine in a nexus magic.' Velindre looked at him and then to Naldeth. 'We have a responsibility here. It was our magic that set those dragons flying into the Archipelago.'

'We have been working out how to do this very carefully indeed,' Lasul assured them. 'You will only have to follow our lead.'

'Which is why you needed the two of us.' Naldeth nodded with understanding. 'Wind and tide is air and water, but for nexus magic you'll need fire and earth woven into the spell.' He grinned at Sirince.

'I assume Archmage Planir wants it all kept in the family, so to speak.' Sirince cracked his knuckles.

'So to speak.' Velindre exchanged a lightning-fast smile with Lasul.

He cleared his throat as he glanced at Sirince. 'You should expect Velindre's father to bespeak you soon. He's given us his blessing, though not with any good grace.'

So I'm not the only one who's found freedom to love?

'Kheda?' Risala looked at him, plainly still harbouring reservations.

'I don't believe any touch of magic can alter omens,' he said slowly. 'Sirket and Orhan are still reading guidance for Itrac in portents brought from islands where the wild men wrought the vilest wizardry, where dead dragons have rotted into the very soil. They are all content that the earthly compass still reads true.'

'Indeed.' Risala looked happier.

'Surely the most important thing is to save any other domain from all the upheavals that dragons would bring in their wake if they ever came again,' Kheda went on fervently. 'Every other domain, whether allied to us or not, ruled by some deserving warlord or not. No island's people should suffer such destruction ever again.'

'No, they shouldn't.' Risala nodded with more certainty.

'So you're happy for us to do this?' Velindre asked again.

'I am,' Kheda said, unhesitating.

'Then how do we work this?' Naldeth asked eagerly.

'Very carefully,' Velindre said repressively. She bent to set the casket down on the ground at her feet and looked at Kheda as she straightened up. 'You might like to step away.'

'Of course.' He nearly tripped over Risala's booted feet

as the two of them hastily retreated more than twenty paces.

'Ready?' Velindre looked at Lasul standing opposite her on the other side of the casket before glancing to Sirince and Naldeth on either side.

What an oddly assorted quartet.

Kheda braced himself as Velindre stretched out her hand and a faint blue glow sparked in the depths of the ash-filled crystal.

Risala huddled close inside his arm. 'Is it going to shatter?' she wondered apprehensively.

Nothing so dramatic happened. The sapphire brightness grew stronger as Lasul reached out to touch his fingertips to Velindre's, emerald mist swirling around his hand. The magelight overflowed and began curling round and around the crystal casket, its colour shifting to vivid turquoise.

Naldeth nodded with incomprehensible understanding and began snapping his fingers to flick crimson sparks at the swelling, swirling magelight. Unearthly fire flared and the sparks coalesced into a spinning circle, painfully bright against the cold grey day.

Kheda momentarily closed his eyes and could still see the vivid ring drawn against the inside of his eyelids. He opened his eyes and saw Naldeth throwing still more sparks into the magic. Fiery circles were now carving brilliant trails all around the blue-green globe of magic enveloping the casket.

'Don't let it get away from you.' Sirince's voice was startlingly loud.

Kheda was surprised to realise there was no sound to the magic, merely the distant rush of surf on the unseen shore, the rustling of breezes in the scrub alongside the track and the horses shifting in their harness.

That humble mainlander who tends them sees nothing remarkable in this?

He glanced over at the coachman and was obscurely pleased to see the man's mouth hanging open in awe.

Sirince bent down with a grunt and his knees clicked audibly. He spread out his palms like a man warming his hands at a fire and a new amber glow appeared in the midst of the misty turquoise magic.

'Whatever he's doing, he's doing it to the crystal itself,' Kheda murmured to Risala.

Sirince stood up slowly, stiffly, and the ball of mage-light rose with him, wound all around with Naldeth's sparks of ruby fire. All four mages took a step backwards and the swirling sphere floated upwards past their heads, beyond their reach.

Kheda watched it rise, further and further, relieved to see it do so. The magic was growing ever brighter, the colours still painfully vivid. He could feel Risala stiff with trepidation beside him.

Then the colours began to fade. But the brightness didn't lessen. The magelight became a white luminosity, a star defying the daylight. It passed through the very highest layer of cloud, still so bright that it could clearly be seen. Then it winked out.

Kheda blinked and rubbed his eyes. Looking up, he saw filaments of light shifting through all the colours of the rainbow as they streamed away to the south, towards the Archipelago. He looked again and all the radiance was gone.

'That,' said Sirince with profound satisfaction, 'was very well done indeed. My compliments, Master Naldeth, and to you, Velindre.' He favoured his son with a brief nod. 'I'm impressed, Lasul. You can rise to the occasion.'

The tall wizard wasn't listening. He was folding Velindre in an embrace she was gladly returning.

'So that's it?' Risala said at Kheda's side.

'It would seem so.' He bent to kiss her.

'We should find somewhere to celebrate.' Sirince walked towards them, rubbing his hands.

'There's a decent inn in Markyate.' Naldeth followed him with his rolling gait.

'That'll do,' Sirince approved.

Kheda realised this meant another trip in the coach and steeled himself. 'Where did you go when you fled Derasulla, Sirince?'

'Relshaz.' Sirince sounded as if that should have been obvious. 'Make sure you spend some time there, Kheda. Then travel more widely while you're here. You should certainly see Toremal. A real live Aldabreshin warlord in the city will give their guilds and merchants something to think about.' He laughed. 'I said I'd teach you to ride a horse, didn't I?'

'You did.' Kheda looked out to the south, past Velindre and Lasul, who were now walking towards the cliffs, arms linked.

The cold waters stretched out to the horizon, to be lost where the sea merged with the grey of the clouds. He could see no trace of the magic. He could see no hint of the northernmost Aldabreshin islands that he now knew for a certainty lay no more days' sail away than the city of Relshaz was in that vile coach.

Strange as this land is, the same seas lap the shores of the Archipelago. My home lies that way, no matter how far to the south. Now it is safe, or as safe as I can make it. Safe thanks to an alliance with Ulla Orhan that I never imagined I would make. Safe thanks to wizards and magic, something I never conceived I would ever have dealings with.

I have done what I set out to do, in utter ignorance of all it would cost me and the changes it would make in so many lives. Nothing ever foretold any of this future for me. No one ever predicted I would make such journeys, face such perils, suffer such loss and find rewards that I didn't even seek.

'So where do we go from here?' Risala asked softly.

'Home, eventually.' Kheda held her close. 'The stars will turn and even if they have no bearing on anything beneath them, life will bring many changes for Sirket and Dau and all my children and all those we're bound to, one way and another.'

But who knows what I might find on the journey?